The Old Town Horror:

Murder and Theft in America's Most Historic Locale

A Novel

COPYRIGHT PAGE

Names: Moser, Edward P., author.
Title: The old town horror : murder and theft in America's most historic locale / Edward P. Moser.
Other titles: Murder and theft in America's most historic locale
Description: Seattle, Washington : Kindle Direct Publishing, 2023. | Summary: "A historic Border South town suffering from a pandemic is shaken by racially charged slayings and high-profile robberies during turmoil over alleged police misconduct and the removal of Civil War memorials."— Provided by author.
Identifiers: ISBN 9798390045213
Imprint: Independently published

Subjects: Fiction —Mystery. | Fiction—Crime. | Fiction —Thriller. | Fiction—History. | Alexandria, Virginia—Travel. | Fiction —Romance. | History —United States. | Politics —United States.

Also by Edward P. Moser

The Lost History of the Capitol: The Hidden and Tumultuous Saga of Congress and the Capitol Building

The White House's Unruly Neighborhood: Crime, Scandal and Intrigue in the History of Lafayette Square

The Two-Term Jinx!: Why Most Presidents Stumble in Their Second Terms, and How Some Succeed: Volume 1, George Washington– Theodore Roosevelt

Foundering Fathers: What Jefferson, Franklin, and Abigail Adams Saw in Modern D.C.! Second Edition

A to Z of America

Armchair Reader: World War II (contributing author)

The Politically Correct Guide to the Bible

The Politically Correct Guide to American History

Thanks for the Inspiration

Anthony Beevor, Dan Brown, James Cameron, Raymond Chandler, Willkie Collins, Michael Crichton, Franklin W. Dixon, Arthur Conan Doyle, Umberto Eco, Vince Flynn, Frederick Forsyth, Dashiell Hammett, Alfred Hitchcock, Stieg Larsson, Robert Ludlum, Heather Mac Donald, Walter Mosley, Andy Ngo, Anthony Pitch, Edgar Allan Poe, Monsignor Thomas J. Shelley, Rick Steves, Tom Wolfe.

Preface

Major events in American history have often produced compelling literature. One thinks of the novels of Dos Passos and Hemingway after the First World War, Steinbeck during the Great Depression, James Jones and Gore Vidal after the Second World War, and the many popular novels, from *The Red Badge of Courage* to *Cold Mountain* & *Gods and Generals*, in the long, continuing wake of the Civil War. So it seems odd that few authors have written notable novels about the tumultuous events of recent years.

Namely the virus lockdowns & restrictions, disputes over historic statues and other artefacts, riots in various cities, cultural clashes over sex and ethnicity, a surge of crime in many localities, among other contentious matters. This book telescopes some of that turmoil into fictional events occurring in an actual town, a town that has a great many historic locales, locales that figure in the plot of the book. It imagines how riotous and other illicit behaviors might have played out in that municipality, which fortunately was in fact spared any serious disorder.

Although reflecting the events of the day, this fictional work is in its essence a thriller. It may in fact be considered six books in one. A combination adventure tale, murder mystery, travelogue & tour book, treasure hunt, and romance, as well as social commentary. In the spirit of Rabelais, it throws much into the steaming pot. May the reader savor the resulting cuisine.

Acknowledgements

Alexandria, Virginia boasts many institutions that can aid a writer, or any interested person, who is intrigued by the city's incomparable history, and exciting present. These include, but are no way limited, to:

Alexandria Colonial Tours, Alexandria National Cemetery, The Athenaeum, The Basilica of St. Mary, Carlyle House History Park, Christ Church, Contrabands and Freedmen Cemetery, Gadsby's Tavern and Museum, George Washington Masonic Temple, Ivy Hill Cemetery, Kate Waller Barrett Branch Library, Lafayette Square Tours of Scandal, Assassination and Intrigue, Lee-Fendall House, The Lyceum, Manumission Tour Company, Murray-Dick-Fawcett House, Old Presbyterian Meeting House.org, Principle Gallery, R.E. Lee Camp Hall Museum, St. Mary's Basilica, St. Paul's Episcopal Church, Stabler-Leadbetter Apothecary Museum, Torpedo Factory Art Center, Wilkes St. Cemetery Complex, Richard Wright.

A Note About Fictional Aspects

This is a work of fiction; it is purely the product of the author's imagination. All of the contemporary events and illicit or lawless actions depicted in this book are fictional, as are all the contemporary characters. Any resemblances or similarities to specific, contemporary events or persons in Alexandria, Virginia or elsewhere are entirely coincidental. The public speeches and statements described are fictitious, as are the events in which such remarks are made.

Some long-standing institutions and public offices are mentioned; however, the characters and events involving them are completely imaginary. The contemporary crimes that are described in and around them are utterly fictitious.

Almost all of the distant, historical events discussed in the book actually happened, and are based on various historical sources. Most of the book's locales and buildings, many of them several centuries old, are actual. Yet the contemporary events described at and in such actual locales and edifices are purely fictional. Most of the removals of historic artefacts mentioned in the book have actually occurred.

For the purpose of the story line, some recent, nation-wide events, which took place over some months or years and in many cities, have been refashioned, placed in a single town, and condensed into a period of weeks.

The opinions expressed in the text are those of the book's characters, and should not be confused with those of the author or any living person.

Quotations Page

"The angel of death has been abroad throughout the land." – John Bright

"We are adrift here in a sea of blood." – Robert E. Lee

"He that says he is in the light, and yet hates his brother, is yet in the darkness." – 1 John 2:9-17

"The world could use more harmony." – Anonymous

Table of Contents

The Old Town Horror

Chapter 1 – Assault at the Waterfront Dig

A restless, sleepless Ted Sifter decided on one of his favorite things: a walk around historic Old Town, the site of his flagship tours. He never tired, day or night, of tramping its centuries-old streets and alleys, in the steps of famous persons who trod before him, often discovering a previously undiscovered house or historical marker.

Early that morn, the lanky, bespectacled historian soon found himself at an Alexandria, Virginia "history sweet spot". It was one of the handful of Colonial Era intersections where, at all corners, notable incidents had occurred, or famous personalities had dwelled.

This square was the best-known sweet spot, featured on tourist brochures and websites world-wide. From where Prince Street crossed with Lee Street, it dropped down the cobblestoned road to the Potomac River waterfront. Dubbed Captains Row, from the several dozen brick townhomes, dating from Washington's time, that lined either side. Some of the homes with three stories had "widow's walks" on the roofs, where the wives of ship captains looked longingly down the Potomac for the hoped-for return of spouses from transoceanic voyages, some never to return home from shipwreck or piracy.

Behind the 43-year-old Sifter, on the crossing's northwest corner, was the stately Athenaeum, fronted by thick Greek Doric columns. It resembled Arlington House, the former residence of Robert E. Lee, who'd been raised in the town, which had long been a centerpiece of Arlington National Cemetery, located in the town immediately north of Alexandria.

Civil War tales and other lore suffused the Athenaeum. It was one of the three rich merchant banks in Old Town during its glory days after its 1749 founding, by Washington's older brother, Lawrence, as a grand merchant city. It was one of the ten busiest ports in America, rivaling Boston, Savannah, and Baltimore, sending tobacco, corn, and timber around the world, and taking in glass, china, and rum. The future General Lee, while still a Federal Army officer, had kept his savings at the corner bank. Its pro-Confederate owner, when the war came, had hid its deposits from the Yankee occupiers of the town, then returned them to depositors when the war quelled. The Athenaeum was now a fine art gallery. Across Prince St. still looms the massive Hooe townhouse. That day, its giant arched roof seemed ready to jump off into the overcast skies above. It had been the home of Alexandria's first mayor, Robert Hooe, who worked with Washington himself on the town's governance. He was also one of several Alexandrians who acted as privateers—pirates—during the American Revolution. Hooe is pronounced "Who" —and on his tours Ted Sifter would jokingly ask his guests, "What was the name of Alexandria's original mayor?" "Who!" they'd laughingly reply. He'd then ask for the name of the man who, in 1776 in fact, invented the steam engine. "What!" As in James *Watt*, was the response. And what was the name of the plantation in Maryland where Frederick Douglass grew up? The Wye plantation, pronounced Why, was the correct reply. Then, what was the name of the pair of British brothers, a ranking general and admiral, that Washington defeated in the Revolution? "Howes!" was the shouted response. Enunciated as, "How".

"And that," Sifter would conclude, "is the particle-of-speech history of early America!"

Across Lee St. from the Hooe mansion is a far more modest, and also extant, wood-frame home, of Philip Marsteller, an officer in Washington's army. Marsteller means a provisioner or quartermaster in German, a marshaller of goods, and Philip Marsteller, descended from a line of German quartermasters, was a key supply officer for Washington. He also was a pallbearer at the General's funeral.

Halfway down the cobblestoned street, Sifter liked to ask who laid down the rocks for the quaint-looking path. Some guests guessed slaves; others figured it was indentured servants. The correct answer may be Germans—not immigrants to America, but captured Hessian mercenaries, hired by King George to fight the American rebels. These prisoners of war were let out of a rancid waterfront prison and set to work filling in the town's dirt roads with ballast stones from the ships of the bustling harbor.

Sifter would close out this history sweet spot with the tale of Captain John Harper, another supplier of Washington's forces who settled in Alexandria at the time of the Revolution. The prolific Harper had at least 23 children with at least two different wives. His progeny was so large it was hard to keep track, as some records indicate he had three wives, and as many as 29 children. One wife alone, Sarah, bore him 13 children. One can imagine what she died from. Several of the Harpers became prominent local officials. They had plenty of relatives to vote for them.

Captain Harper had so many progeny, Sifter would announce, that it has he—and not George Washington—who was the "true father of his country!"

Ted stepped carefully down the cobbled stones, careful not to turn an ankle, his balky knees aching slightly. He got on the sidewalk to save his joints some discomfort. He grimaced a bit, reflecting on how he once had been literally able to walk all day, but now had to limit himself to one or two hours at a time. He passed a much-restored, brightly painted townhouse that stood on a parcel of land that Washington had bought as an investment. The front door opened, and its elderly, masked owner took a step down the stoop to the sidewalk—then jumped back up back on seeing the maskless Sifter. Her eyes glared angrily as she went back inside and slammed the door.

At the start of the pandemic, Sifter had perused articles showing that one didn't get the virus from walking past someone outside, or from exercising outdoors. He'd also examined science reports that the fabric in cloth masks were far too porous to block the tiny viruses. And that dirt, bacteria, mucus, and viruses would collect in the cloth. And, that one's general immunity suffered from lack of exposure to fresh air.

So he only wore a mask when required, as in a store, or to protect the elderly or those with preconditions. His reticence had triggered angry looks or heated remarks more than once. But he loved nature, exulted in sports and exercise, and felt like he was choking when putting on a face covering. Also, wearing a mask during his walking tours would be almost impossible, as he found it not only hard to breath, but difficult to be heard by his guests. Moreover, his tours lasted as long as three hours, an exceedingly long time to wear a face covering. He billed himself, given the events' length, and energetic expositions, as "the Bruce Springsteen of travel events".

And so, at the start of a tour, he'd tell his guests that, "I find it hard to wear a mask, as I have to talk for a long time. But I urge everyone to protect themselves as he or she sees fit…and I promise not to sneeze on anyone!" Almost all the guests, who were almost all masked, gladly went along. In fact, most were overjoyed, after being in lockdown for

weeks, or away from the offices or from their friends and family
members, to finally have something fun to do.

After each tour, indeed after any exercise since the viral outbreak
began, Ted washed his mouth, throat, and nostrils out with Listerine or
salty water. A believer in natural preventives, which to his
disappointment the public health and political authorities ignored, he'd
start every morning off with toasted garlic on bread or bagel, and a fruit
juice containing anti-viral substances like blueberries or chunks of
apple. And his constant exercise, he felt, afforded him plenty of
Vitamin D-providing sunlight, another natural anti-infective. On this
and other matters, it seemed the pandemic had only strengthened his
strong, anti-authority streak.

Shrugging off the scared woman's reaction, he took solace in the warm,
late-spring weather. Perhaps, with the arrival of summer heat, the
pandemic would peter out.

He walked along the red-brick sidewalk to where Prince St. leveled off
onto Union St., its asphalt moist from that morning's rain. "Union" St.,
not for the triumphant federal Union after the Civil War—the Border
South town wouldn't have made such a name change—but for the
looser confederation of the thirteen States after the Revolution. Times
had changed much since then. The town was at the time debating
whether to toss the name of Lee St., given it was named after Robert E.
The crossing is a normally favorite place for engagement pictures, with
professional photographers snapping the image of ecstatic couples
against the evocative backdrop of Captains Row. But with the early
hour, and the panic the virus had caused, the streets of Old Town were
empty.

Out of habit, Sifter crossed Union toward the waterfront one block
away. He often started his tours at Waterfront Park, near the historic

Torpedo Factory of the world wars, and the near the sites of several tragedies in Alexandria, and American, history. Including two antebellum incidents: the explosion of the *USS Princeton*, and the failed slave escape aboard the *Pearl* schooner.

At the edge of the park, Ted had begun to think over those long-ago events, when he felt a buzz in his pocket.

The text was from Harmony, up early for work for what was becoming the region's largest employer, Amazon, after Jeff Bezos had decided to build its East Coast headquarters just north of town. Like her friend Sifter a voracious consumer of news, she had noticed on her news feed a story certain to intrigue Ted.

"A violent crime," she texted, "at the ship excavation!"

Both she and Ted had previously visited the site, just four blocks from Captains Row. Construction gangs laying the foundation for the new Pineapple Offering Hotel on the riverfront had unearthed the remains of an ocean-going ship from the 1780s. In a town with so many layers of history, it was common for men wielding excavators and pickaxes to come upon artefacts from the Colonial and Revolutionary Eras, or even Native-American times. In fact, for a major building project like the hotel, city ordinances required construction teams to work with town archaeologists to preserve valuable artefacts they uncovered.

Ted immediately changed direction, forgoing Waterfront Park and striding south down Union.

"I should be there in minutes," he texted back.

"I'm in the area. I'll meet you there!" replied Harmony Jain. Despite her usually calm façade, she was in fact as restless as he.

Ted rushed past the old brick warehouses, now restaurants and boutiques, that dated from the early 1800s. At one shop he stole a glance at a blackened archway, a lingering sign of the catastrophic fires that had once ravaged the waterfront businesses. Before stone dwellings, sprinkler systems, and a modern fire department banished that threat. The walls of many old townhouses had brightly colored wooden plaques depicting a horse-drawn fire engine. Owners had displayed them in the days of private fire departments, as proof they'd paid their private fire insurance. If they hadn't, and a fire broke out, the firemen would let the house burn to the ground. Fortunately, Philadelphia's Ben Franklin and Richmond, Virginia's John Marshall, among others, introduced the revolutionary notion of a public fire department, that would put out anyone's fire, no matter what.

On Ted's right were ancient, restored townhouses, as well as new condominiums made to look they were from long ago. All had the plain brick look from the era of the early federal government. When Americans presented themselves as sturdy, sober citizens of a republic, not the showy, spoiled acolytes of a king. One townhome spoiled the effect with a splash of modernity: its large open garage contained several flashy,1960s sports cars. Their genial owner was, as usual, cleaning up from the party he'd hosted the night before.

To Ted's left was the Hotel Orinoco, a boutique hostelry a block back from the newly renovated waterfront on the south side of town. Beyond it was a very popular restaurant, the Starboard, that just been opened on the riverfront. It had replaced some of the old docks that had been rotting there for decades.

Ted sped past the hotel, paused to stretch his knees, then hurried on. The excavation site for the town's next hotel came into view. It was a big dig, stretching 150 yards down Union St., and another 75 yards in toward the Potomac. And a deep dig, extending down 35 yards. Ted was surprised to see no water at its bottom, as the river level couldn't be that much below Union St. In fact, at the founding of the city in

1749 the future Union St., built on landfill, had been below the river line.

On the site's southern end, the excavation sloped up toward Wolfe St., named for a British hero of the French and Indian War. Scattered about the riverside site were Bobcat excavators and construction workers. The men were almost all Latinos, wearing hard hats, muddy work boots, blue overalls, and bright yellow vests, and stoically waiting to begin anew the day's labors.

To the astonishment of the construction gangs, and to the delight of the town's archaeology department, some of the workmen had weeks before uncovered a ship from the time of the American Revolution. From examining archival records, a lead archeologist found it had belonged to a privateer, or pirate deputized to attack British ships. He was named Jonathan Swift, and later became a wealthy Alexandria merchant. He happened to have the same name as the famous author of *Gulliver's Travels*.

Its keel and a part of its superstructure had survived over 240 years of decay. Curved planks like the tusks of woolly mammoths stuck out from the hull. Oxygenation, and the pressure of piles of mud, dirt, and filth that had layered on top of it, had worn away or destroyed much of the vessel. But not enough to make out its broad outline.

Ted had been down to the site several times since its discovery, and had eagerly read about it online. But what caught his eye, along with the sight of Harmony, was the gaggle of cops and paramedics on hand, along with the police cars and an ambulance. And the yellow crime-scene tape that cops were stringing around a prone figure and a bulky container near the remnants of the ship. A breeze blew in from the river, making the scene seem colder and even grimmer than it might have.

The thirtysomething Harmony met Ted some 40 feet from the police. "What took you so long?" she smiled.

Before answering he took in the lithe, Eurasian beauty, a mix of East Indian, Dutch, and Japanese. Embarrassed about his knees, especially in front of someone as athletic as she, he replied, "I got here as fast as I could."

They gazed at the crime scene.

"Who's the man on the ground?" Ted asked.

"The night watchman," answered Harmony.

Ted, Alexandria's unofficial historian, immediately thought of the night watchman murdered 180 years before at the town's Old Cotton Mill. A look of apprehension seized him. "Is he dead?"

"No," said Harmony, suddenly saddened, "but he got quite the knock on the head."

The walked slowly over to the crime scene, and stopped a few feet from the police and EMS workers. Given the early hour, perhaps, and with their attention focused on the stricken man on the ground, no one paid them much attention. Ted noticed one of the policemen, Detective Dmitri Yiannis "John" Greco, a short, husky, and plain-spoken man. Ted had provided the middle-aged Greco with insights into the town's history which the detective had found useful in solving several criminal cases. They briefly made eye contact. Ted nodded in recognition, and Greco, his yellow Shantung straw hat in hand, stepped over to the hunk of rusted metal between the watchman and the ship.

Ted and Harmony took a few steps in his direction, and stopped at the police tape. The watchman, a West African immigrant of about 30, was flat on his back, but conscious. The EMS workers had placed a stretcher next to him. A bandage covered a gash on the left side of his head. In a thick accent which reminded Ted of the Caribbean, he moaned something about not knowing who had attacked him.

Ted looked over at Greco, who was bending over the hulk of metal, poking at its insides, his Greek Orthodox cross faintly visible on his neck. His left hand held what appeared to be a dirty piece of paper, which he slipped into a plastic evidence bag.

Ted had a wise-ass habit of blurting out what was on his mind, and he called out to the detective:

"Is that the treasure chest?"

Greek shot Ted back a hard yet knowing look, which seemed to say, 'How did you figure that out?' Ted wondered if it could indeed be a chest of some sort, that had held valuables or personal possessions of Jonathan Swift. Ted liked to refer to him as "J. Swift" to differentiate him from the great satirist.

Then out of the corner of his right eye he saw movement. It was Harmony, scampering around the ground, on all fours, like a bloodhound, before quickly standing up and stepping on what looked like a dirty piece of paper. Her foot kept a riverside breeze from blowing it away from the site. She picked the paper up, looked it over briefly, then bootlegged it over to Ted.

She pressed against him, placed it in his right hand, and breathed, "Don't grip it too hard. It's fragile. And we might get away from here before examining it."

Ted briefly thought he should hand it over the detective, but Harmony's curiosity and sense of adventure, and his own, won out.

His mind fixed on the purpose of the paper, Ted stepped onto Union St., without looking. A vanity BWM raced toward him, driven by an oblivious, retired government lawyer. The observant Harmon tucked Ted hard on his T-shirt; he stepped quickly back onto the curb. As

Harmony's look of fear and exasperation faded, they crossed over
Union and headed up Wolfe St., and its steep incline of Colonial Era
townhouses and gardens cut out of riverside bluffs. They went a quarter
of the way up the slope to be sure they were out of sight.

They huddled together, hip on hip, and examined the parchment. Its
dimensions were roughly those of an 8-1/2 by 11-inch loose-leaf paper,
but much thicker, with several of its left and upper sections torn away,
and splotches obscuring other parts. Vertical and horizontal lines ran up
and down it, with words, some decipherable, others blurred, alongside
them. The lettering had an 18th-century elegance to it.

The purpose of the parchment was unclear. Its reverse side seemed to
have sketches of buildings, but its drawing and inscriptions were more
faded, harder to make out.

"Let's try another angle," stated Ted, who turned the front side of the
paper 90 degrees. It was still a puzzle to the two onlookers. He rotated
the paper another 90 degrees, and its purpose clicked inside his head.
He'd often looked over maps of the town from near the time of its
founding in Crescent Bay, just north of today's Founder's Park, and
during its rapid growth by landfill into the Potomac. He told Harmony
the parchment was the faded portion of such a map.

"A treasure map?" she asked, half-jokingly.

"Unlikely," he replied.

Any affluent Alexandrian of the time, including Swift, he thought,
might have found such a map handy for getting around, and for locating
the homes and enterprises of fellow businessmen. Still, the chart was
not a typical town map of the time, showing just the grid pattern of Old
Town's streets and their names. It was more akin, as far as could be
discerned, to a contemporary illustrated map of a tourist town.

Along with the streets, the vintage illustration depicted some of the town's early,

Federal Era highlights. At the bottom-right corner, near the southern outskirts of the time, was the Bank of the Old Dominion. Named when Virginia was the largest and richest state, stretching from the Chesapeake to the Ohio Valley. Truly a dominion. The structure was one of the three main merchant banks of the wildly successful riverport. The bank building still exists, at Ted's sweet spot, as the Athenaeum. To its north and east, Ted and Harmony could make out a zig-zag line that marked the hundreds of yards of the old waterfront, before further landfill moved it further east into the Potomac. In the far north of the diagram was a discernible curve of land, the sheltered, crescent-shaped bay that held the original wharves. Unfortunately, much of the area of the map north of it had been torn away.

Indeed, many of the lines marking main thoroughfares—King, Prince, Duke, and Queen Streets—were very faded. However, south of where Duke should have been was a little square with a cross inside it.

"This must have marked the Old Presbyterian Meeting House," noted Ted. "The church of the Scotch-Irish founders of the town." Its massive interior and ancient graveyard, which resembled the North Church of Puritan Boston, had been built in 1774, just as the American Revolution was erupting.

Near the map's left-center was a recognizable image of the town's Market Square. "The oldest, continuously operated farmers market in the nation," as brochures pitched it to tourists. A smudged image of a building to its immediate north had to indicate City Hall, Ted knew. It is still one of Old Town's prime sights. Its spire, designed by Benjamin Latrobe, the architect of the U.S. Capitol Building, still soars beside it.

To the right or east of City Hall the map markings were very worn, except for an image of a mansion across North Fairfax St. Ted bent over the chart, his blue eyes glistening below his temple of graying hair. He knew this spot very well.

"This was one of the town's history 'sweet spots', really the sweetest of all," he explained to Harmony, sounding like a tour guide, or a college professor. "The intersection just to the north and east of City Hall and Market Square may be," he went on, with little exaggeration, "the most historic crossing in America."

Straining their eyes, they strove to make out that portion of the chart. They discerned the faint trace of the east-west street, Cameron, and a bit of scrawled imagery that likely marked prominent buildings near its intersection with N. Fairfax St.

Clockwise, at the northeast corner of Cameron and N. Fairfax, at 1 o'clock, was the old John Wise tavern. It is still there, as a private home. President-elect George Washington had stopped at the public house on his way to the first inauguration, in the temporary capital of New York City. Ted smiled at recalling that event.

Though Washington was then perhaps the richest man in the United States, he was short of cash. This was embarrassing, as there was yet no Treasury Department, no new federal government at all, to fund the inaugural. So the first President-elect borrowed money from Mr. Wise to put on his own inauguration. Wags say that was the start of federal deficit spending.

Across the street today is a plaque marking the occasion of a Christmas Eve banquet honoring Gen. Washington for his triumphant conclusion of the Revolution, which was marked by his resigning his military commission in Annapolis, Maryland the day before. In a sign of how much politicos then liked to imbibe, in an era when downing liquor was often healthier than drinking untreated well or river water, the future President took part in 13 toasts of Madeira, one for each newly independent state. The event presaged a drunken party four years later in Philadelphia that celebrated the imminent ratification of the U.S. Constitution. Washington and his 54 fellow guests downed 54 bottles of Madeira, 60 bottles of Bordeaux, and 57 bottles and jugs of whiskey, punch, and ale. The price of the bacchanal, in today's dollars, was $20,000.

Three homes north of the old Wise Tavern is a three-story, white-painted townhome that had been one of the first schools for women in the nation. Its endower, the Thompson family of Georgetown, had been, like its relatives the George Mason family, visionary in providing education for both sexes.

At 11 o'clock on the map was a smudge that indicated something across North Royal St. from Wise's business. Ted stared at it, and figured it might mark the red-brick townhouse, now a private home, of Charles Lee. Lee, a member of the Old Dominion's most prominent family, had been Washington's private attorney. He was canny enough to site his home, and his law office, right across from City Hall, and its myriad of political connections. However, he was not the hardest worker. When President Washington brought him up to the temporary federal capital of Philadelphia to serve as his second Attorney General, he assured Lee the workload would be light. Light enough to keep his private practice by City Hall. People worried less about apparent conflicts of interest then.

Not long before Lee's residing there, the house was a tavern, run by a Mr. Duvall. It was just yards from the Wise Tavern, and City Hall: the politicos of the time definitely liked their liquor, as they often do today. In his tours, Ted pointed out Duvall was an ancestor of the famous actor Robert Duvall. In a strange historical coincidence, Robert Duvall played, in the movie *Gods and Generals*, General Robert E. Lee. Gen. Lee was in fact the nephew of Washington's Attorney General. Reflecting on this, Ted laughed out loud. "What's funny?" queried Harmony.

"Part of this intersection has the Duvall Tavern," he explained, "and on a bench in front of it is a statue, of a man in long hair and colonial garb sitting down. Tourists pose for pictures with him. The figure is George Washington." Ted laughed again. "Except it's a ridiculous statue. Because, while Washington six-foot, two- or three- inches, and very muscular, the statue is of a scrawny fellow about five feet tall."

"Washington the runt?" asked Harmony.

"Either the sculptor got the dimensions of his subject wrong," continued Ted, "or they ran out of funds for the project, forcing the artist to shrink the Founding Father's dimensions. To that of a Founding Teen." They smiled and continued to examine their find.

Across Cameron St., at eight o'clock on the intersection of the map, was a vague image of the corner meeting hall attached to City Hall. This site had a profound impact, Ted realized, on America's founding documents. There in 1774, George Mason wrote part of his Virginia Declarations, a litany of laments against King George III that Mason's colleague Jefferson incorporated into his Declaration of Independence. And after the Revolution, Mason may have met there with Samuel Chase, of Annapolis. The two regional leaders hashed out a kind of free trade agreement between Virginia and Maryland. It tossed out the restrictions on Potomac River trade between the two newly independent states. They discussed clearing away the onerous taxes and regulations the 13 colonies-turned-states had thrown up, hamstringing commerce. The talks were fruitful enough to lead to the 1786 Annapolis

Convention of five states. Which led the following year to the Constitutional Convention in Philadelphia, of all the states. And a free trade zone, and much else, under the U.S. Constitution, for all the original colonies, and every state that followed.

Rarely if ever has one place, this City Hall meeting room, given birth to writings of so much import.

But down N. Fairfax, at 7 o'clock, Ted recalled grimly, as he looked down the map, was a remnant of a bloody blot on the society of old Virginia. On the exterior wall of the City Hall offices there still exists a marker titled, Police House. It indicates the police station and jail that was inside City Hall back in 1897. That year, it was the scene of an atrocity. Against a black man, 19-year-old Joseph McCoy, who'd been accused of sexual assault of a white girl, of 9 or 10 years old, and her two younger sisters. He was arrested without warrant and placed in a cell of the jail. World of the alleged incident spread around town, and a crowd of over 400 people formed. The mob broke into the jail, and rushed to the cell, only to find the accused man had evidently escaped. In fact, the terrified McCoy had pulled himself up to the cell's rafters, and out of sight. The crowd was about to leave in frustration when one of its members spotted a shoe of the prisoner dangling down. The outraged vigilantes rushed in, and dragged the man outside, beating him bloody. They then hauled him down one block east on Cameron to Lee St. As hundreds watched, some in the mob hoisted him up on a lamp post, and hanged him. Someone took an ax to his head; others ripped his body with bullets.

Harmony watched Ted's countenance change from keen interest to gloom as he thought of this. She had noticed a similar expression come over him whenever he reflected on the carnage of the Civil War. Then he returned to his normal expression, as he ran his finger across the dim

28

outline of N. Fairfax St. A small, square-like figure, at four o'clock, surely represented a place where there was a cornucopia of history. Though usually less grisly, and sometimes uplifting. Namely the grand Carlyle House, of the Scottish immigrant and businessman John Carlyle, a co-founder of Alexandria. His two-story Georgian mansion dripped Civil War lore, and even French and Indian War legends. Finished just four years after the town's founding, the manse earned an early military pedigree. It was there that British General Edward Braddock, with a young colonial officer named Washington looking on, planned a disastrous expedition into western Pennsylvania against the French and their American Indian allies. It touched off the mighty conflict for control of the North American continent. During the Civil War, as the mansion-turned-hotel was owned by a Southern sympathizer, the Union Army turned it into a hospital, as depicted in the PBS series *Mercy Street,* a drama based on actual events there.

Ted and Harmony stared, and stared, at the Carlyle mansion marks. There was lettering around it, but it was frustratingly blurred, or erased entirely by the ravages of time.

Finally, Ted pointed at two o'clock, at the southeast corner of Cameron and North Fairfax. "There's a place to keep a fortune indeed," he remarked, as he looked warily back down toward the harbor excavation, and kept his voice low. A small square marked a building, which also is still there. Namely, the towering hulk of the former Bank of Alexandria. The merchant city's richest bank, and founded by William Herbert, the personal banker for President Washington, who needed a depository for his and Martha's vast fortune.

Herbert started up a dynasty of town bankers. Indeed, the town's best-known bank is still Burke & Herbert, begun in 1852 through a partnership between William Herbert's great-grandson, Arthur Herbert,

Jr., and John Woolfolk Burke. Both would be prominent Southern advocates in the Civil War. And Burke's descendants went on to found towns and libraries in the region.

The Bank of Alexandria, a soaring, Federal Era structure, with a roofed colonnade and a two-story rear wing, would have been, it seems, a natural acquisition by the contemporary Burke & Herbert bank. It had transformed several colonial townhomes into modern financial spaces. Indeed, it has a branch office as well as a headquarters just down N. Fairfax. But a financier was acquiring it and, Ted noted to Harmony sadly, "would turn it into a mammoth private home." In fact, the grounds of the site were now a messy mix of excavations, construction machines, and building materials. "Oh well," Ted shrugged, "better to renovate it, while saving much of the original, than to destroy it altogether."

He and Harmony looked over the rest of the map. Several blocks west of the Bank of Alexandria and City Hall was a marking of two short, intersecting lines. The left edge of one line was missing, but it was clear the symbol represented a Christian cross. Ted pointed at it, saying, "That has to be Christ Church." Its graveyard holds many Revolutionary War and Civil War figures, including William Herbert, and even has a mound of Confederate dead. Along with banks, the map seemed to give churches and cemeteries special prominence.

The chart didn't show the countryside to Old Town's north, south, and west. Or if it had, those former farming regions had been torn away. Ted looked in vain at its bottom for a racetrack, behind today's Greene Funeral Home, where Washington had watched the jockeys of the time rush around a quarter-mile track. It's said the famed soldier had repaired with friends to the clubhouse, on the site of today's funeral parlor, for cigars and whiskey.

But it was hardly all fun and games back then. While most jockeys today weigh under 120 pounds, riders back then were brawny. When a jockey tried to pass another, he'd likely lash out with fist and whip. Racing was more akin to *Ben Hur* than Churchill Downs. It reflected a violent, frontier society, as Americans, British, Native-Americans, French, and Spanish battled for control of a continent.

Washington might then have walked over to S. Washington St. for more drinks and smokes at a plusher gentleman's club, now the George Washington Club Condos. This stands across from another funeral parlor, Demaine, still in business after a two-centuries run, as the commerce of death is eternal.

"South Alexandria is missing from the map," Ted pointed out. "For instance, today's Freedmen's Cemetery," a graveyard for former slaves who'd fled to Alexandria during The War Between the States. "Alas," he sighed, "that part of town was then deep country, so the map maker didn't think it important."

Harmony looked over the top of the map. "No Cotton Mill either," she noted. Ted examined the series of blank blotches and ragged edges there. "The Cotton Mill wouldn't be on the map," he replied. "The chart dates from the late 1700s, and the Mill wasn't built until the 1840s." Constructed two blocks up Washington St. from the still-extant homes where Robert E. Lee had grown up. It was a remarkable symbol of the town's Antebellum, as it processed the raw cotton shipped up from the slave plantations of southern Virginia, or the Deep South states.

Also missing was Shuter's Hill, the sprawling prominence at the western end of King St., now graced by the soaring granite pile of the George Washington Masonic Temple. Jefferson and James Madison had examined the hill as a possible pedestal on which to place the planned Capitol Building, before that got built eight miles up the Potomac. Shuter's Hill hosted a Union Army encampment long before welcoming the masonic creation. But it was too far outside of town to make it onto their map of the compact village of the late 1700s.

The two looked at each other. "Why don't you put the chart into your purse?" Ted suggested. "And into a safe place at your apartment. I bet we'll be looking it over a lot more." Their minds swirling with possibilities, the two friends walked up the incline of Wolfe St., away from the crime scene, the map their personal secret for now.

Chapter 2 – Escape from the Terrorist Prison

For a town that had been around 270 years, Alexandria's Detention Center was quite new. And it presented a startling contrast to its predecessor.

The prison in Old Town that had existed for the bulk of its history had been built in the mid-1820s and, remarkably, endured as the city jail until 1987. It was small and stately looking, more like the home of a successful merchant than a jail. Partly because its designer was one of the best. Namely, Charles Bulfinch, the architect of Boston's 1798 State House, and the rebuilder of the U.S. Capitol Building after its immolation by British troops during the War of 1812. Bustling Alexandria was wealthy enough to afford the very best architects, even for its prisons.

Bulfinch's building was a vast improvement over the original town jails, which were smaller and squalid. One was on Market Square, which allowed magistrates to take those convicted at the nearby courthouse directly to prison. The other was a vermin-infested place, little more than a shack, on the waterfront. It's said that German-speaking mercenaries hired by the Brits during the American Revolution, the Hessians, of Hesse, Germany, were sequestered there. And were thankful to be let out of the dank holding pen for work duty. The Bulfinch prison is now a private home with attached condominiums. Still, the high wall on its corner at Princess St. and N. St. Asaph St. hints at a grim past that held within many a felon, Confederate spy, or escaped slave. The façade hides a yard that was the site of the gallows. It's said to be haunted: the spirits of rebels and the enslaved, once enemies, now together for eternity.

A prominent ghost may be young Benjamin Thomas, whom a mob seized in 1899 after accusations the African-American teen had tried to assault a white girl. A replay of the 1897 outrage followed. The unhinged crowd, perhaps up to 2,000 in number, surrounded the place, baying for blood. The callow mayor, George L. Simpson, urged the throng to go home, pledging to lynch the prisoner himself if a court didn't assemble the next day to try him. Ignoring the plea, dozens of men pushed their way into the jail past two dozen police and deputized citizens. They grabbed the terrified Thomas, who jailers had hidden in the cellar, and hauled him outside. As the 16-year-old cried out for his mother, they beat him with sticks and iron rods, and tore off his clothes. They dragged him down cobblestoned streets a half mile to the corner of St. Asaph and King Streets, and then down to King and Fairfax, at the southeast corner of City Hall square. They fired a fusillade of bullets, a fatal one striking his heart, and strung him up on a lamppost just down from the Quaker-owned Stabler-Leadbetter pharmacy. Ghouls then took from the corpse "souvenirs": pieces of cloth and bits of bullets.

Mayor Simpson responded by arresting blacks who'd striven to protect Thomas, while never charging any in the mob. Thomas' broken body was embalmed at the Demaine funeral home; he was buried at the Penny Hill graveyard of the Wilkes St. cemetery complex on the town's outskirts. His stricken mother had to wait three weeks before a memorial service was held for him at upper Duke St.'s Shiloh Church, across from an old slave jail and a former hospital for black Civil War soldiers. The only good news relating to the atrocity: it was the last racial lynching to take place in Old Town, and perhaps Virginia generally.

Like the rest of the Washington metropolitan region, Alexandria seemed to leave the grisly part of its history behind in the 20th century. The city exploded in extent and in population with the Second World War, the construction of the Capital Beltway ring road in the early 1960s, and the region's Metro underground, which had a King St. station by 1983. But as its population rose with transplants from other parts of the U.S., and immigrants, both legal and illegal, from throughout the world, the number of prison inmates rose too. By the 1980s, the 19th-century town jail was outdated and crammed. In 1987, the new Detention Center opened on the town's southern fringe.

It had none of the elegant look of the structure brought about by the Capitol Building's renovator. A far more typical prison, it had the aspect of a grim fortress. Able to hold 350 inmates, the main building is eight squat stories of Virginia red clay brick, attached to a smaller administrative building. It stands on desolate land in what's always been beyond the border of Old Town, on an isolated locale next to an exit of the Capital Beltway, beyond the damp Bottoms land where slaves and freemen of color dwelled. It is just five hundred yards southwest of the Wilkes St. cemeteries.

To prevent escapes, the prison windows are narrow slits, like the apertures of a castle. The south side of the jail faces the Interstate, whose high, concrete sound barriers make scaling them onerous. Any inmate seeking to escape also has to get past the razor wire of the interior fences, and the nine-foot-high metal barricades of the outer perimeter.

Security is extra-tight because, along with holding local and state convicts, notorious federal prisoners are detained there, often during trial before transfer to maximum-security prisons in other states. In fact, the Detention Center has held perhaps the two worst traitors in American history, worse than Benedict Arnold.

There was Aldrich Ames, the CIA official who in the 1980s and 1990s gave his KGB handler Victor Cherkashin the personnel records of some 100 American agents and contacts working behind the Iron Curtain. The Soviet Union's security service "harshly interrogated" those Ames unmasked. The aftermath often was a bullet to the head: ten or more contacts were executed at Moscow's grim Lubyanka Prison. The Center has also detained Robert Hanssen, the FBI counter-intelligence manager, and Soviet mole, who like Ames turned over top-secret documents and betrayed Soviet officials working on behalf of America. Captives from the "War on Terror" have also been confined there, sometimes while undergoing high-profile trials at Alexandria's fortress-like U.S. District Court a mile away. For instance, the "American Taliban", John Walker Lindh, the U.S. citizen who before and after September 11th fought with the Taliban in Afghanistan. And Chelsea Manning, a U.S. Army soldier who, while known as Bradley Manning before hormone replacement procedures, gave Wikileaks hundreds of thousands of classified documents on the Afghan and Iraqi wars. Also the "Beltway snipers", John Allen Muhammad, a Nation of Islam member, and his young "protegee", John Lee Malvo, who went on a rampage of seemingly random shootings in the Washington region in the year after September 11th, killing 10 persons and badly injuring three.

Ted had conversed with people who, mirroring the panic of the time, had run from their cars to filling stations and back, while watching out

for the white van from which those killers were wrongly rumored to
operate.

In the realm of Islamic terrorism, the most famous inmate, before his
transfer to a "Supermax" prison in Colorado, was Zacarias Moussaoui,
a possible backup hijacker for the 9-11 plot.

Then there was, germane to this tale, 44-year-old Abdullah Hamaas,
originally from Pakistan, who'd trained as a teenager at an al Qaeda
training camp near Tora Bora, Afghanistan. In the late 1990s, Abdullah
settled in Alexandria, overstayed his visa, and kept a low profile. He
attended a Saudi-financed Wahabi mosque in suburban Falls Church,
Virginia, formerly known mostly for its James Wren-designed English
Episcopal country church, thus the town's name. At the mosque,
Abdullah crossed paths with several participants in the 9-11 plot.

In mid-2002, perhaps acting on his own, or with several collaborators
who were never apprehended, he put together a scheme to blow up a
portion of the Woodrow Wilson Bridge that links Alexandria to
Maryland. The Bridge, first built in 1961, and later replaced by 2008, is
a vital part of Interstate 95, the main north-south highway on the East
Coast. Damage to it would devastate the economy of "Great Satan",
Abdullah reasoned.

His outlandish plan was to don frogman gear and, during a night when
the tidewater river was neither at ebb nor at full tide, but neutral, swim
to the span's supporting, underwater archways. And attach bombs
timed to detonate at the peak of rush hour. He brightened at the
prospect of killing hundreds of commuters while sending scores of cars
and trucks crashing into the river, while inflicting long-term, structural
damage to the bridge. Given the array of massive, steel-supported
concrete struts that hold up the bridge, his plan seemed impractical. But
he spent many hours studying the use of PE-4 explosives, of which he

acquired a modest stockpile, through contacts with British soldiers of Islamicist outlook stationed in the capital region.

Abdullah Hamaas made himself into a strong swimmer through long hours of practice at "long course", 50-meter facilities at, ironically, the Woodrow Wilson high school in D.C., as well as the East Potomac pool on Hains Point, near the Jefferson Memorial. To grow accustomed to open-water swims, which are daunting compared to indoor pool swimming, he'd drive out to Sandy Point Park near Annapolis, Maryland. In the late afternoon hours, he'd slip on a black wetsuit, strap a bag jammed with Play-Doh onto his strong shoulders, and swim out to the Chesapeake Bay Bridge. With the constant roar of traffic overhead, he accustomed himself to swimming under the trusses of a great span, and practiced slabbing material that mimicked C-4-style explosive onto the Bridge's supports.

He also attended scuba classes at T.C. Williams High School just west of Old Town. During the pandemic, that school would undergo a name change controversy, as Williams had been an influential educator during the days of school segregation. In a dinner after one such class, and in the aftermath of 9-11, Abdullah had raised suspicions with the swim instructor, Greg Dennis, when he asked about the best techniques for staying stationary, above water and under water, in the river currents near the Bridge. It was an odd comment, made soon after another remark of Abdullah's expressing joy at the death of a Navy SEAL in the early days of the Afghanistan war. Dennis contacted the Alexandria police. Soon after, a young cop, named John Greco, took part a sting operation that transferred inert PE-4 explosives to Abdullah, for use in his planned attack.

As he never put his plan into action, Abdullah might have gotten off with a light sentence. But during his arrest, in a desperate attempt to flee, he knifed to death a local cop. After a trial at the U.S. District Court, in which the presiding judge had him shackled and gagged due to a violent outburst before the jury, he was convicted of second-degree murder, and sentenced to life.

The two decades that passed changed Abdullah in some ways, but not in others. He learned discipline and a measure of patience, even as a desire for revenge grew. Abdullah had made it his mission to not be ground down by imprisonment, but to make it to the outside world someday, to strike a tremendous blow for jihad.

During his jail stay, inmates marveled at his attention to fitness. He haunted the prison gym, becoming a fixture in its weightlifting room. Noticing how the young prisoners admired well-defined abdominals, he knocked out 500 sit-ups a day on the prayer mats of his 12-foot-by-six-foot cell, despite concern such a focus might be a sin of pride. A few tried nicknaming him "Abs Abdullah", but the ugly frown such remarks elicited quieted the jibes. He did calisthenics next to his Koran and a symbolic homage to Allah propped up against the slit window opposite his cell door. He punished his six-foot-frame until he was in far better cardio and muscular condition than when he was a young man training for the Wilson Bridge attack.

The rack on the shelf opposite his cot that reached up to an eight-foot ceiling was filled with books, magazines, and religious tracts that one of his wives, a social studies teacher residing in nearby Loudon County, Virginia, had sent him. He would smile at the leniency of America toward its detainees, so different from his native Islamabad. Such leniency, such weakness, as he saw it, begged to be attacked. Meantime he took special solace in growing indications the U.S. military would withdraw from Afghanistan. He knew the Taliban's leaders were confident they would soon be at the head of that country again.

Given his religiosity, and notoriety in fighting Great Satan, Abdullah had over the years been made an organizer and prayer leader of the Islamicist inmates, and a preparer of Halal meals in the cafeteria. His group skirmished with other gangs, comprised of "white power" skinheads, or a black, "Gangsta Rip Rappers" group. While telling his adherents not to look for fights, he urged them to get in top condition if fights were to come. And through his punishing physical regimen, he set a personal example.

While mentoring these brawlers in self-defense, Abdullah took pains to stay out of the melees himself. He was determined to avoid getting hurt, or killed, in a pointless encounter. He was convinced Allah held a special, future mission for him. Further, he didn't want to lose the perk of the video sessions with spouses the prison was considering for inmates during the pandemic.

Some of the prison authorities, strong believers in rehabilitation, were happy to see the inmates spending their time online, or reading and studying, or working out. Along with enabling progress for many toward eventual release, in the short run such hobbies meant fewer brawls and generally more compliant behavior.

Abdullah had been spending more time with his favorite wife Miriyam via his sturdy HP Envy laptop. They conversed and sent Koranic prayers to each other; the prison's IT worker charged with intermittently vetting his messages found nothing amiss. However, the bored computer wonk was ignorant of any languages other than English and Java, and certainly did not know Arabic. So, in using an online translator tool, he missed the meaning of the short phrases at the start of each prayer the duo sent each other. The phrases employed a substitution cipher that swapped the characters by a fixed sequence. At

Miriam's insistence, the messages were kept quite brief, to attract less attention, even if it did take four weeks to transmit her information. Which detailed the plans for Abdullah's escape.

On his end, Abdullah blackmailed the guard in charge of security at the prison cafeteria. The man, Ron Limon, of black and Latin descent, projected a public image of an irresistible Don Juan. However, wielding the power of coercion, he forced some of the male inmates into having sex with him, either in their prison cells or at his office. Learning of this, Abdullah persuaded one of the victims to videorecord such an encounter. The device was a cell phone Abdullah had acquired from an obese inmate in return for unlimited desserts at the cafeteria. After making copies of the video, which included oral and anal sex, Abdullah arranged for a meeting with the guard by intimating he wished to have a sexual encounter. In Limon's office, he drew on interrogation techniques he's gleaned from Taliban officers charged with obtaining intel from captives in Afghanistan. He employed a carrot and a stick. The carrot was the implicit threat to release the video to the guard's superiors, which would result in his dismissal, trial, and incarceration as a prisoner himself, with unimaginable sex degradations performed on him. The carrot was a bribe of cash that Miriam had smuggled in during a pre-pandemic conjugal visit.

Meantime, that wife worked with elements of Al I-Sahn Ketha, a northern Virginia Wahhabi mosque her husband had attended before his arrest. After years of laying fallow, its terrorist cell had sprung up again. A prime operative was 26-year-old Ahmed Muhannad, a hefty, seemingly laid-back man whose placid façade hid a bulldog loyalty to any hero of jihad. Along with an active role at the mosque, Ahmed drove a lorry that supplied Halal food to the Detention Center.

Along with Miriam and the mosque's building maintenance head, Ahmed concocted a plot to free Abdullah. A key component was the driver's seat in Ahmed's truck. Whenever he arrived at or departed the prison, guards carefully checked for contraband in the crates and food bins in the back of the lorry. But they made a less meticulous check of the cab, which contained no storage containers. Usually, a guard would just look into the glove compartment, checking for weapons, with just a cursory glance at the padded driver's seat and the equally plush, well-padded "shotgun" seat. They had gotten to know Ahmed pretty well, and rarely searched him for weapons.

The head of the mosque's maintenance, a handy craftsman from Aleppo, Syria, crafted a facsimile of the passenger's seat that contained a hollow bottom and a thick, hollowed-out recliner. A man of Abdullah's size could just about fit inside it. When the craftsman's work was complete, and the seat installed, Miriam and her husband exchanged coded messages that spelled out the date and time of the escape.

At exactly 5:54 p.m. of the appointed day, Ahmed drove his truck up to the barbed-wired entrance of the prison. He was sweating profusely through his cloth mask; he feared his nervousness would give away the plot. But as expected, two guards familiar with Ahmed from his work in supplying the jail were at the checkpoint. They robotically gazed up through the flaps of the back of the truck. Without even checking the driver's cabin, they waved Ahmed inside.

Relieved, he motored the short distance to the seven-story, chockablock brick prison, its light-red brick walls rising up against gray clouds. Ahmed drove around the back to the loading dock of the prison cafeteria.

Having taken that short route countless times, he knew he would arrive at the dock at 6 p.m., give or take a minute. The time chosen was deliberate, as Guard Shift 1, after 12 hours of tedious work, would be replaced by Guard Shift 2, at exactly 6 p.m. It was anticipated the guards would be preoccupied with their own coming and going. Abdullah had informed the other mosque plotters via Miriam that the incoming guards were usually sleepy-headed, and the outgoing ones always tired and bored.

At 6:01 p.m., Ahmed backed the truck up to the dock. At precisely that moment, the steel loading gate opened, and out stepped the muscular figure of Abdullah, along with two inmate helpers, as well as Limon, the guard Abdullah had blackmailed and bribed. All wore masks, which were strictly mandated for handling edibles, especially so given the pandemic. Ahmed and Abdullah exchanged quick glances: the latter impassively; the former nervously, hoping the others wouldn't notice. Abdullah knew Limon had temporarily disconnected the video feed from the loading dock.

The two helpers, Jamaal and Jackson, wearing their one-piece, pajama-like garments, with "Inmate" or "Alexandria Prisoner" stamped on the back, stepped into the truck's rear. They slowly unloaded crates of food, placing them on the dock. Abdullah had personally chosen them for the work that day—he knew they would accept without question any order from him. Ahmed, his pulse racing, stayed in the truck, its motor running. Limon stepped down to the truck and, instead of watching over the delivery, watched for any guard that might be approaching the dock. When Jamaal and Jackson finished unloading the last batch of crates, Abdullah told them, "Bring the load into the cafeteria kitchen. I'll join up with you in a bit." They nodded and, arms full, walked away.

Abdullah stepped down to the vehicle and went up to Limon. The guard bent over and, as arranged, the prisoner hit him hard, but not viciously, on the side of the head. Limon was stunned, but conscious as he eased himself down to the concrete floor. Abdullah gave him several hard kicks to the thighs, enough to leave bruises. He bent over, and scratched Limon on the cheek. Enough to leave scratch marks, but not enough to hurt him badly. This would bolster the guard's cover story that the prisoner had overcome him. Abdullah felt like spitting on the crooked guard for good measure, but restrained himself.

Abdullah stepped off the loading dock as Ahmed came around to the passenger side. He pulled aside the bottom of the seat and unzipped the recliner. Abdullah hesitated, then pulled off his mask and drew in a deep breath. In a few seconds, he had crammed himself inside, and Ahmed had zipped up and pushed back the seat.

Ahmed pulled away, forcing himself to drive slowly and breath slowly, and steered back to the entrance gate. Very nervous now, he felt behind his mask like he was choking. One of the guards made just a perfunctory check of the truck cabin. But Ahmed felt his stomach churn as another guard, who had just arrived on scene, appeared outside the window of the passenger seat. He drew his mask down to his neck, and mouthed at Ahmed stiffly: "Unlock the door."

Ahmed didn't recognize this guard. He was a new hire, and thus his behavior unpredictable. His heart nearly exploding, Ahmed's head felt dizzy. He pressed the unlock button to the door. The guard, instead of reaching over to open the glove compartment, as the monitors normally did, got into the cabin and, leaning the top of his left leg on the front of the seat, adjusted his gun holster.

In the days leading up to the escape attempt, Ahmed hadn't been able to decide whether he should surrender or try to flee if discovered. Now, expecting the worst, he found himself in terrified indecision. Sweat broke out on his forehead; he imagined visible streams of perspiration pouring down toward his dark-brown eyes. He even imagined he heard Abdullah's breathing from inside the seat. The guard looked at Ahmed fixedly, suspiciously Ahmed thought, as his right hand reached toward the glove compartment, and his left hand patted his pistol holster, with his left leg perched inches from the hidden passenger.

In his concealed place, Abdullah felt like he'd been buried in a landslide. The seat's plastic and cotton inner lining pushed upon his eyelids, and rubbed against and tickled his nose. The muscles of his thighs ached from being scrunched up toward his knees. Figuring Ahmed would quickly drive away from the gate, he had held his breath, while staying utterly still. Then he heard the guard's order, listened to him enter the driver's cabin, and felt the weight of his leg press upon the car seat.

His lungs began to burn. He had to take a chance of breathing. He let air out through his mouth, thought he heard the exhalation whistle, and then breathed out and in through his nose, which seemed quieter, though his nostrils were squished together. The cotton fabric made his nose tingle all the more. He clenched his teeth tight, and stifled the impulse to sneeze.

It was becoming unbearable to hold his position. He heard the guard open the glove compartment. He feared the guard suspected, or knew. He breathed again, ever so slightly, but the sound of it seemed louder. Luckily for him and Ahmed, the guard's loud shuffling through the car manuals, inspection papers, and bric-a-brac in the glove compartment overcame any other sounds.

The guard looked over at Ahmed and said, "You're sweating—what's the matter?" Alarmed at this, Ahmed responded without thinking: "I assure you, I don't have the Covid!" Then thinking fast, he added: "Maybe I do. If I keep feeling the symptoms, I'll get tested."

The guard took on a worried look. An elderly aunt of his with diabetes had been hospitalized the previous month after a negative, then positive, test for the virus. Hands now trembling, he tried to shut the glove compartment, failed, and quickly got out of the passenger side. He stepped away from the truck, and waved Ahmed on.

The driver, now somewhat less nervous, reached over to close the door, and drove the truck through the prison gate. Beneath him, Abdullah exhaled deeply, relieving the pain in his lungs. Still, as other guards were likely near the exit, he stayed silent, and tried to endure the terrible ache in his muscles and the wretched tingle in his nose.

From the gate, Ahmed took a preplanned route. He followed the flat landscape of Mill Road, named for the old mill powered by the Cameron Run stream. Named after the Earl of Cameron, or Lord Fairfax, the largest landowner in colonial times in what became Fairfax County. Pulling his mask down, and glancing anxiously at the rearview mirror, Ahmed turned onto busy Eisenhower Avenue, then went onto a deserted side street. It faced a broad expanse which for generations had held the Roundhouse, a circular, plank-covered railway track where the trains of Alexandria, a rail center since the 1850s, had swirled about, then shunted off into different directions.

In the early evening, the few shops in the adjacent mini mall not closed from the virus had shut down for the day. Ahmed spoke toward the seat on his side. "Now I can get you out," he told Abdullah. "Just one moment, Sayyid." He sidled the truck to a curb, then jogged over to the passenger side, and tugged at the chair's long zipper. It was stuck. He heard a choked voice from within, and saw the surface of the upholstery move back and forth as Abdullah pushed out his arms and

46

legs. "Be still, Abdullah!" he cried. The passenger obeyed. The zipper line became less wrinkled, and bit by bit Ahmed unzipped it. Finally he pulled a gasping Abdullah up and out of the chair and out of the truck. The terrorist was red-faced, sweat-soaked, dirty. He sucked in air, coughed it out, and brushed himself off. He stretched out his arms, and stood tippytoe to stretch out his hamstrings. He stared at Ahmed with a look mixing angst and relief. Moments later he looked elated. They clasped each other's hands and, grinning, recited a brief Quranic prayer of thanks. They finished the votive, and nervously looked about. There was no one around, and no sound of alarms or police sirens. Limon was supposed to pretend to be unconscious, thus delaying reports of the escape. It seemed the ploy was working.

Abdullah stretched again, easing cramps in his thighs, then entered the truck again and fell into the passenger's seat. The two exchanged more greetings and congratulations in Arabic. Ahmed asked, "Is it all right to speak in English? I'm much more comfortable with that tongue now." Abdullah was disappointed in hearing this, but replied, "That is all right. I spoke both languages in prison, and before." He paused to cough up some dirt and dust. "And, and I need my American accent to be good, I suspect, for any, any of my future missions here."

They had to move fast, to reach their destination before the prisoner's absence was found out. Just a hundred yards to the east, just out of sight, was the old bottomlands, now the African-American Heritage Memorial Park. Another hundred yards further east was the Alexandria National Cemetery, where Union soldiers, white and "colored" alike, lay at rest, at the fringe of the old graveyards of the town's "gentry churches" of wealthy, often pro-Confederate Protestants.

Ahmed got back onto Eisenhower Ave., and turned into John Carlyle St., named for the town's co-founder, and drove past the massive concrete-and-brick complex of the Patent and Trade Office. Most of the lights in its buildings were out. Almost all its employees, like almost every office worker during the plague, were working remotely. Abdullah blinked at the array of federal buildings, which represented a regime he had vowed to destroy. The patent and copyright offices, it seemed to him, symbolized the many technological changes which had devastated the kind of traditional society and culture he had sworn to defend. Ahmed and Abdullah veered right onto Dulany St., named after one of the founding families of the Tidewater region. Then left onto the broad boulevard of Duke St., one of the old colonial thoroughfares that had retained its name from the time of King George.

Ahmed, his expression cloaked by his loosely fitting cloth mask, looked at Abdullah, who was unmasked, and suggested sheepishly, "Do you think you should wear a face covering, Sahib?" Abdullah seemed startled. "I mean," Ahmed continued, "we've heard the virus spreads very fast through prisons. I-, I'm a little afraid of getting it from you." Abdullah had been enjoying the air of freedom. But he accepted an extra mask from the driver and slipped the blue-colored covering on. He noted, "Even with this, I can breathe much better now than when stuffed inside that accursed seat." He thought of the damage the pandemic and its lockdowns were doing to America, and he smiled behind the cloth.

They passed a Whole Foods store on their left, and on the right a renovated, two-story house, an Alexandria classic, with stately brick walls, rooftop dormers, and matching chimneys high atop. It was now the offices of a very busy area real estate firm, due to plunging interest rates brought on by the pandemic, and the construction of Amazon's East Coast headquarters in the adjacent town of Arlington. But though the exterior gleamed spanking-new, the building was very old.

Before the Civil War it housed the notorious Bruin and Hill firm of slave traders. A few blocks down Duke was another former slave pen, now a museum, of the even more notorious Franklin and Armfield slavers. They sold thousands of human beings in the decades years before the war, then marched or sailed them, "sold down the river", for resale at the New Orleans slave market. Period photos exist of Union soldiers posing triumphantly before the shuttered slave emporia. Unknowing of this, Ahmed steered toward the nearby metro station. He knew the route well from his deliveries. Even so, he doubled-checked the directions by switching on the robotic voice of the GPS. Imprisoned for 20 years, Abdullah had never heard a car's computerized voice directions, and he listened with fascination to the female voice. "This seems useful, but irritating," he told Ahmed. "That is, having a woman tell a man what to do."

They turned into a short, slanted street named Diagonal Road. The byway had been constructed in the 1800s to shunt cattle off of King St., where the animals had snarled that main street's traffic. The two jihadis turned left onto another, even shorter street, Daingerfield Road. Some residents, and more tourists, thought it was named for the comedian Rodney Dangerfield. Naming a street after a modern comic was unlikely in a sedate town awash in a historic past. In fact he Daingerfields—spelled with an "i"—were a family that helped construct, in the pre-railroad days, two nearby canals, one of them under the leadership of Washington.

Abdullah looked about through the car's one-way windows, which the mosque's maintenance chief had installed to foil prying eyes. He was ecstatic at being outside a jail, able to see and experience the outside world. But his mood darkened as they drove up toward a tiny, shaded park, where Daingerfield cuts into King St. His deep-brown eyes widened at the sight of 15 people, mostly youths, but some elderly, some of them musicians, and all banging on drums and bongos or blocks of wood in loud and more-or-less rhythmic patterns. Ahmed noticed Abdullah's surprise.

"It's a 'drum circle'," he told him. "They gather here frequently." Ahmed laughed. "They think they can tap 'into the power of the Universe' with such performances. The 'Cosmic Spirit'." His lips looking narrow and hard, Abdullah felt disgust at the stark paganism of the performers. He felt grateful for his creed's ban on many forms of artistic expression, and their mockery of the Creator of all things. "It is beyond doubt," he told Ahmed, "that any culture producing such naked blasphemy is destined to fall." Ahmed, surprised at his passenger's vehemence, stopped smiling, and contemplated his companion's evident wisdom. Perhaps, he thought, his own work amidst the infidels had made him too accustomed to their errant ways.

They motored onto King St. and under a train overpass next to an Amtrak depot. In front of the commuter rail station is an 18-foot-high pillar of polished granite, capped by a large stone cross. Abdullah winced at the Christian symbology.

"I've stopped by here before," noted Ahmed, a bit hard to hear behind his mask. "It's a war memorial, for the First World War."

"When the Zionists," replied Abdullah, "began to seep into Palestine. And the imperialist French and British asserted control of Islamic lands."

Ahmed replied, "I've read its explanatory sign. It actually wasn't put up until 1942, during the Second World War."

"Another major step in the creation of the Zionist State," answered Abdullah, who had a large, if selective, knowledge of history. "When Hitler failed to completely attain his Final Solution," his voice sounded

50

a disappointed, "and many of the remnants of the Jews moved to
Palestine, displacing the Muslims from their sacred soil."

Abdullah reached a hand to the car stereo, but was unfamiliar with the
digital controls. It seemed futuristic compared to the car radios he had
known before prison. Ahmed turned it on, and on Abdullah's command
found a news station. An official from the CDC was instructing people
to keep at least six feet of distance between them. Ahmed looked at
Abdullah and laughed, "I guess that's impossible for us right now."

Abdullah smiled faintly under his mask and had the driver scan other
news stations. One was talking about whether the Washington
Nationals baseball team would play that season, another about the
economic downturn brought on by the plague. "This is good," said
Abdullah, "no news about the prison break. My absence has not been
discovered yet."

Ahmed considered that and said, "If they did discover it, they may not
broadcast it everywhere, like after the September 11 attacks."
Hesitating, afraid to offend Abdullah's vanity, he stated, "They may not
see it as that big a story. Everything has been pushed aside by the news
of the pandemic."

Abdullah snorted through his mask. "I think it is the biggest story, and I
would interrupt all the other news." He fell quiet, then continued
sternly, "And before I'm through, I'll make the headlines again."

They drove along the steep hill of upper King St., which flanks the 333-
foot-high George Washington Masonic Temple. In the 1920s, after the
Great War, Alexandria had an outpouring of patriotism. It built the War
Memorial. It also added its own Tomb of the Unknown Soldier—of the
American Revolutionary War—at its Old Presbyterian Meeting House.
And, with 10 years of labor, it created the Masonic Temple.

Abdullah was astonished at the size of the pagan infidels' Temple, and the extent of its terraced, well-trimmed lawns. As someone who despised America, he had a special animus toward a place named after Washington, the founder of Great Satan's military, which went on to occupy so many holy lands. And a particular disdain for the Masons. "For centuries," he told his driver, "That secret, conspiratorial society of non-believers and Zionist pigs has plotted to bring down the institutions of the devout." Ahmed, who respected Abdullah's knowledge of the outside world, listened hard as he drove up the incline. "At first, the Masons undermined the Christians, which was good, one devil against the other. But now they attack the followers of the Prophet." Ahmed heard this with some surprise, as he rarely saw anyone but tourists enter the Masonic Temple, and knew no one who knew anyone who was a member. A local resident had once told him the membership among the Masons had plummeted, as no young people were joining. 'It must truly be a conspiratorial organization,' he concluded. 'One that really knows how to keep its ways secret.'

The duo entered a plateau of the long hill. They went by Janney's Lane, which led several miles west to Quaker Lane. That was apt, as the Janneys were one of Alexandria's Quaker merchant families who, in the years before the Civil War, pushed for abolition. The family's most prominent member, John Janney, was a lapsed Quaker who ran both of Virginia's 1861 secession conferences, which convened to decide whether to leave the Union. Though he'd become an Episcopalian, John Janney had Quaker-like ideas on war, believing the looming conflict would a catastrophe. He urged continued Union, but his pleas were overridden. Catastrophe ensued.

To their left, bordering preserved woodlands, was a public recreation center with a large indoor pool, and next to it a historic school, T.C.

Williams High. In 1971, as sketched in the Denzel Washington film *Remember the Titans*, its integrated football team triumphed for a town that not long before had enforced the Jim Crow laws. Abdullah's attention, however, was arrested by a clutch of religious institutions nearby.

They passed an evangelical, Disciples of Christ church whose sprawling car lot signified a large congregation. Abdullah winced at the sight. Next was a Kingdom Hall, of the Jehovah's Witnesses, which Abdullah explained was a fairly recent spinoff of the Christian blasphemy. "Their beliefs are entirely unquranic," he explained, "and don't even stress figures like Jesus and Ibrahim that are in the Christian and Jewish books. Instead, they focus on prosaic figures, who lived in the United States over a century ago."

"It sounds like a cult," stated Ahmed. "Like the Masons."

"They believe an angel gave their founder golden plates on which were holy revelations."

"Well," answered Ahmed, "that sounds a bit like Mohammed and the Koran. Totally blasphemous, though."

They passed the historic Ivy Hill Cemetery, filled with Christian heathens of the past 200 years, as they saw it. A little further on Abdullah was astonished to see yet more churches. "Alexandria must be a very religious place," he admitted, "however mistaken in its beliefs."

There was the King Street Church, part of the Church of God, a Tennessee-based evangelical organization, and the First Baptist Church, with a very large worship center and a parking lot big enough, it seemed, to hold enough cars for a pro football game. Abdullah felt ill. "I thought my escape would be a precursor to Paradise," he exclaimed, "but this line of infidel houses of worship is a Hell!" Ahmed eyed the pallor of his forehead and said, "Do not worry, Sahib, we're almost at our destination."

He turned off King onto a backstreet of well-kept suburban homes, past Quincy, Cleveland, and Roosevelt Streets, all named after American Presidents. Ahmed slowed and carefully eyed the street before him. He was glad it was nearly deserted. Except for a young woman walking her dog by a driveway of the sixth house on the left of the block. Ahmed, wishing the car to be seen by no one, waited until she disappeared around the corner. Then he motored to the home's driveway, and went up it. Abdullah looked across the street, and was dismayed to see yet another house of Christian worship, the Alexandria Presbyterian Church and, at the far end of Roosevelt, a local branch of Washington's Masonic headquarters, the Alexandria Scottish Rite Temple! Was this a trap of some sort, he wondered, here in the very lair of the enemy? As Ahmed maneuvered around to the rear of the house, his companion cried out: "Why is my hiding place encased in this desert of errant beliefs!?"

But even as he said that, he saw that the tall wooden fence about the house would keep out the eyes of the curious. And the neighborhood was obviously a quiet one. Ahmed told him the mosque's imam believed such a sedate and heavily Christian locale was an ideal hideaway for a jihadi.

He asked the escapee to wait, and went outside to knock on a side door of the low-slung suburban house. He spoke briefly with its residents, a middle-aged man and a woman of similar age, both from Yemen. He walked briskly back to the car, opened the door for Abdullah, and stated, "Quickly now, all things are set. Welcome to your safe house, to your new home, for now at least!"

After giving brief introductions, Ahmed returned to his vehicle, and undertook the plan to dispose of it, and for himself to go into hiding too.

Chapter 3 – Echoes of Civil Strife

Several days later, as prison authorities, police, and the FBI mounted a continuing search for Abdullah and Ahmed, Ted and Harmony planned to attend a gathering on a controversial topic. The City Council was holding a meeting that morning on what to do with Alexandria's Appomattox statue. As a local historian, Ted was to speak as an authority on the matter. Most of those testifying to the Council would talk about the statue itself, but Ted hoped to transform the debate by bringing up a much broader topic.

Before the lunchtime session, Harmony wanted to take publicity photos for Ted's "Tour of America's Most Historic Street." That is, Prince St., one block south of King St., and named in colonial times for the Prince of Wales, the traditional heir to the British throne.

Harmony walked there from her townhome apartment. As a morning rain had wettened the town's biking paths, Ted, instead of cycling the two miles from his duplex, drove over. He found his usual free street parking spot on St. Asaph St., named for the patron saint of Wales. The pair met four blocks from City Hall, on a notable stretch of Prince St. one block west of S. Washington St. It is replete with sumptuous, antebellum townhomes, and marked by sharp reminders of the Civil War.

Standing together, sweating some from the day's humidity, they took to admiring a structure that resembles a doll house. It is the three-story Patton-Fowle House, dating from the War of 1812. Its front door's portico of thin white columns stands below a small, second-floor balcony fronted by wrought-iron fencing. Unusual for Old Town, where space is at a premium, a front lawn, parted by a patch of white slate, sets the house back from Prince St.

No one seemed home and Ted, taking a chance, walked through the open front gate onto the lawn. He took a close-in cell photo of three rows of five windows each that artfully dotted the front wall, which was capped by a small, semi-circular aperture.

Such a house owes its grandeur to its architect, who was probably Charles Bulfinch, the designer of the old Alexandria prison and rebuilder of the U.S. Capitol Building. When Ted first viewed the townhome, and noticed the Patton name, he crossed his fingers that, as a historian with a special interest in the military, he'd find a link to the famous Second World War general. He knew that George Patton had a Virginia Confederate ancestor, and had been tutored in the military arts by a former Confederate colonel from northern Virginia. And he was aware that Admiral William "Bull" Halsey, also prominent in the second global war, had lived in a still-existing house on Old Town's Queen St. Could the famous Patton have also dwelled nearby while stationed in the capital region?

In his research Ted found, alas, that a different line of Pattons, who were Alexandria planters, had built the house. A "planter" had been the politically accepted term for a plantation owner, usually an owner of slaves as well as arable land. In fact, the Patton in question, Robert, rented another home to a notorious slave trader. At the time of the Civil War, a wealthy merchant family, the Fowles, resided at the Patton-Fowle House. Confederate sympathizers, they'd owned other impressive properties along the street.

Ted and Harmony moved up Prince to a graceful brownstone that Ted believed had housed a pro-South cleric, the rector of St. Paul's Episcopal Church, an extant structure a few blocks away. He searched for its street number, and at length spotted the numbered sign on the wall behind its porch. The numerals were in shadow, impossible to read, so he stepped on the deck for a better look, while Harmony, unsurprised at Ted's disregard for propriety, stayed on the sidewalk. As he examined the sign, the front door opened, and a withered, white-haired man emerged. He wore long, baggy pants and a coarse cotton shirt held up by suspenders.

Ted was surprised the man, though definitely of an at-risk age, was unmasked. The elder noticed the uninvited visitor, and shuffled over. Ted was also surprised the man didn't seem angry over his trespassing. Instead, his eyes were dreamy, intent on some faraway place. But he raised an index finger at Ted. 'Uh oh,' the historian thought, 'here we go.' But the elderly gent said something unexpected.

"Humanity is doomed," he intoned, speaking at Ted yet somehow past him. "Man's greed and corruptible seed, his fallen nature, is leading to disasters world-wide." He stopped two steps from Ted, then turned back to the door. Seemingly speaking to the house now, he stated, "The rivers are rising, there are rumors of war, dog soldiers are baying, the streets will flow with blood! Mankind's violent, selfish ways will be the end of all!" He entered his abode, his words echoing, and the screen door slammed behind him.

Ted walked back to Harmony, who stood still and wide-eyed. He shrugged his broad shoulders, wrote down the address to look up its history later, and they two headed back up Prince.

As visually impressive as the Patton-Fowle House is the dwelling across Prince from it, the Swann-Daingerfield House. Daingerfield as in the street that Abdullah and Ahmed had driven by. The home was originally designed in the spare, spartan Federalist style, made of simple brick with few flourishes to door or windows. An early owner was Henry Daingerfield, Alexandria's wealthiest man, born in 1800 and dying right after the Civil War.

The son of a sea captain, and manager of the town's riverside warehouses, Daingerfield readily took to waterways. Following up on George Washington's Potomack Canal upriver from Georgetown, he supervised the Alexandria Canal that ran up to Georgetown itself. Remarkably, Daingerfield's canal flowed through the center of a bridge, the aptly named Aqueduct Bridge, later replaced by Georgetown's Francis Scott Key Bridge. A peninsula jutting from today's Reagan National Airport north of Old Town, Daingerfield Island, is named for him.

After the Civil War, the house was transformed by its new owner, Thomas Swann, with changes that reflected the transformation of America. The once-fledgling nation confined to the Atlantic Seaboard now stretched to the Pacific. On the verge of Great Power status, by the 1870s it was entering a Gilded Age of great wealth. Schools, homes, government offices, and businesses redesigned themselves in the opulent style of the "French Empire". The Empire of Napoleon's nephew that yielded the Louvre and the boulevards of modern Paris. Thomas Swann added an extra floor to his abode, and a large ballroom for soirees, and built the mansard roofs, typical of the Empire style, which curve back gracefully from the top floor's edges, with the dormers pushed out and highlighted. The once simple steps leading to the entrance became a great, roofed balcony of four arches and a balustrade.

Like many grand homes in Old Town, its personal history as well as its architectural past spanned different eras and social mores. Henry Daingerfield, like most merchants in Alexandria, owned slaves. However, in 1827 he and fellow importer-exporter William Fowle—

yes, the same man who had Bulfinch create the masterpiece across the street—freed five persons, including a teenager and a nine-year-old girl, "out of our desire to confer a Boon and a benefit upon our slaves." Perhaps Daingerfield had been influenced by the War of 1812. During that conflict several of his slaves escaped, when a Royal Navy fleet briefly occupied Alexandria.

Two generations later, various members of the Daingerfield clan, which had spread throughout the South, fought as Confederate officers. In fact, public service, military and civilian, ran deep in the family. Henry's relation, William Henry Daingerfield, also from Alexandria, moved south by southwest to become, remarkably, the mayor of San Antonio, when it was part of the independent Republic of Texas.

The Old Town Daingerfields eventually sold the large, attractive property. Around the turn of the 20th century, it was bought by St. Mary's Academy, a school for teenaged girls managed by the Sisters of the Holy Cross. The Academy was a spin-off of the town's Catholic basilica, St. Mary's, dating from 1795. The nuns added two large wings, in the same lavish, post-Federal style. They instructed middle-school students there until the 1940s. For an almost ten-fold increase in price, the Academy sold the now-extensive property to Alexandria Hospital, which kept its educational focus, as a School of Nursing. The Hospital and School moved out to the suburbs starting in the 1960s, and in the following decade the place became a private home, in the original Swann house, with the rest turned into condos. Full circle, the main dwelling again a sumptuous private residence, now worth millions.

As Ted and Harmony admired the splendid dwelling, a bit of sun peaked through the dark clouds cloaking Alexandria that day. In the sudden light, they noticed aerosol paint splashed on the home's façade, and they stepped over for a closer look.

"Racist!" the graffiti screamed. "Your Swann Song Is Coming! Oppressor! Die!! Soon!"

Gazing at the graffiti, her amber eyes glowing, her mouth open with surprise tinged with some concern, Harmony asked, "Did the owner do something wrong? Maybe said something offensive online?"

Her full lips parted in a smile. "And whoever did this should have used Spellcheck. He, or she, must be pretty ignorant. Swan is a pretty basic word."

Ted, deep in thought as he looked over the scrawl, shook his head. "The opposite is probably the case. I'd say whoever defaced this is quite knowledgeable."

He caught Harmony's quizzable look, and pointed to the small plaque which gave the official name of the house, "Daingerfield-Swann".

Normally very observant, Harmony had missed it due to her focus on the graffiti.

Her piercing eyes glanced over its text, which gave a summary of the home's history. "Is a Swann the current occupant?" she asked.

Ted's smile was almost a smirk. "Thomas Swann," he intoned, "was—and there are many contenders—was perhaps the most bigoted man in the history of the Potomac region."

Harmony Jain knew her friend was about to give a brief history lecture. She stood waiting.

"Thomas Swann, Swann Jr.," began Ted, "was the son of the man, with the same name, who originally built this place, in the early 1800s, before the Daingerfields took it over.

"Not Rodney Dangerfield," he smirked, and Harmony smiled.

The historian continued. "The younger Thomas Swann spanned the antebellum, Civil War, and post-war, the Reconstruction times. And he was mostly terrible throughout." Ted Sifter paused.

"But popular throughout the region too. A plantation owner, he started his public career as the federal attorney for Alexandria, working in the old courthouse right across Washington St. from here. He gravitated to Baltimore, and got himself elected Mayor in the 1850s. By aligning himself with the Know-Nothing party."

Harmony snickered. She had heard of that long-disappeared faction, but couldn't keep a straight face on hearing its name.

"Did the 'Know Nothings,'" she quipped, "also not use Spellcheck—or never learn to read or spell at all?" She wondered if, from hanging around Ted, she was starting to tell jokes like his.

"Very funny," replied Ted dryly. "The Know Nothings were a political party, a big one for a time, who opposed Catholic immigration, at a time when the Irish Catholics, and Germans, Catholic and Protestant, were swarming into the country by the millions. The Irish starting with the Potato Famine in the 1840s, and the Germans after democratic revolutions in Europe were crushed, in the late 1840s. In fact, the revolutions broke out in 1848, and those coming here were called the '48ers', the year before the '49ers', the people who hurried off to the California Gold Rush." Harmony listened, quietly now, and intrigued. She had an East Asian ancestor who had come to San Francisco, according to her family's lore, around that time.

"In fact, some of the 49ers were 48ers. Like Levi Strauss; in the gold mines outside San Francisco he came up with Levi's, or dungarees, to keep the dung and the mud off the legs of the prospectors."

Harmony laughed. She loved how Ted often turned a historical narrative into a funny or intriguing anecdote. Still, she was curious about the original point of his story.

"And Swann?" she asked.

"Forgive me for going on a tangent," said Ted, smiling, the laugh lines at the edges of his mouth visible, "as I often do with history.

"In the 1850s, America was a Protestant country. Overwhelmingly Protestant. And there was lots of resentment against the masses of foreigners, many of them uneducated, and not speaking English, wading into the country.

"And many of them liked to drink. The Germans, who started all those breweries, and the Irish, well, they became notorious for drink.

"And it wasn't just a stereotype. Their rates of alcoholism were so high they sparked the movement toward Prohibition."

Ted paused, smiling some. "I can say that——"

"——Can say that," interrupted Harmony, "because your great-grandmother was Irish, and she bootlegged whiskey to customers in Manhattan." Harmony had heard this story more than once, and so she finished the apology for him.

"That's right," said Ted. "She liked her 'Manhattans'."

"As for Swann, he took full advantage of the sentiments of the time. He allied himself with gangs of 'nativists': laboring men of mostly English descent. They hated the Irish newcomers—both groups competed for the same jobs and for neighborhood turf. The English or 'Yankee' mobs, they attacked Irish gangs in Baltimore, in the runup to that city's mayoral election. In 1857, or '59, I forget.

"It sounds like the riots in *Gangs of New York*," Harmony interjected.

"Like in the movie, with the Yanks versus the Irish there too, during the Civil War."

63

"Yes," Ted, "during the *Un*civil War. With the 'Italian' actor, 'Leonardo' DiCaprio, playing the Irish gangbanger, and the 'Irish' actor, Daniel Day Lewis, playing the Anglo-American thug."

He grinned. "Now that's good acting!"

"So Swann got himself elected mayor—" continued Harmony.

"—Of 'Charm City'," noted Ted. "But he didn't stop there. During the Civil War, as a Know Nothing, he backed the Union, and Lincoln's Republicans."

"But weren't they," asked Harmony, "the party of abolition? On the side of the blacks and abolition and, toleration?"

"Yes, mostly," replied Ted, "but Swann's two-step made sense, kind of. The Know- Nothings were a sort of nationalist party, so they backed those in favor of a strong, unified Nation. Unionists, like Lincoln.

"So, to your point," Ted went on, "after the war, one might have expected Swann to back civil rights for the freedmen. Instead, after getting elected governor of Maryland, he backed 'Jim Crow', and laws that barred black fishermen from the Chesapeake, from harvesting oysters there. 'Separate but *un*equal'.

"Racist gangs, segregation, racist laws," Ted summarized. "Thomas Swann may have been the most bigoted man in the history of this region." He winked. "Though, as I said, he's had some very stiff competition."

Harmony waited. She knew Ted often had an intriguing follow-up to his tales. He didn't disappoint, as they stood examining the ugly message painted on the wall.

"Swann's brother, by the way, Wilson Swann, could not have been more opposite, in temperament. He freed all his slaves, all 40 of them, and paid for their education and their lodgings. And after moving to Philadelphia, he joined the Union League. Which, as its name suggests, backed the Union during the 'Late Unpleasantness'. People, even people on the same side, fought the Civil War for different reasons. And when things became more 'pleasant', after Appomattox, Wilson Swann, like many abolitionists, joined the temperance movement." Harmony shot Ted a quizzical look.

"Yes," he continued, "the teetotalers who aimed their fire at those same unruly, hard-drinking Irish immigrants that the Know-Nothings had targeted. Lots of reformers who were anti-slavery were also anti-drink. "Wilson Swann starts to sound more like his brother. However, with liquor he waved more of a carrot than a stick. Instead of attacking or barring immigrants, he built water fountains for them. In lots of cities, these so-called 'temperance fountains' were alternatives to the dark, dirty pubs of the Irish. Wilson Swann was a reformer to the core. He was even a leader of an early Society for the Prevention of Cruelty to Animals.

"It would be interesting to find out what gave two brothers such very different personalities." Ted winked again at Harmony. "One could almost write a book about it."

Harmony offered a lopsided grin. "I think you should stick to your general history of Alexandria for now. Besides, you already have a stack of a hundred new book ideas."

The two turned their attention back to the hateful graffiti about a hater. The color of the inscription was a bright red, and it marred the meticulously restored and painted pine wood wall. The current owner, like so many denizens of historic Old Town properties, had an evident love for the place. Fingering her Nikon Coolpix, Harmony clicked photos of the house proper, and of Ted, and then the ugly scrawl.

Ted shuffled over to the wall, and flicked his fingers on the painted graffiti. Harmony cautioned, "You know this is a private residence, right?" Ted answered, "Just for a second..."

At that, the big door to the broad entranceway opened, and out stepped a grey-haired, bespectacled man. Dry lips were cloaked by a cloth mask he'd pushed hurriedly over his face. He grasped a thick hickory cane, and brandished it as one would a sword.

Ted pulled back his hand. "I'm sorry, sir," he said sincerely, if coolly. Gesturing at the graffiti, he noted, "And I'm sorry about what happened here." Harmony held her hands low, almost in supplication, for her friend's misbehavior. The owner took a step toward them, then realized they were unmasked, and took a quick step back.

The owner was unhappy, more at the scrawl than at the trespassing or the lack of masks. "I've spent a fortune renovating this place," he stated, grimacing. "And a smaller fortune conforming to this town's rules, its strict rules on historical renovation." He turned bleary eyes to the graffiti. "And now this!"

"It's terrible," Ted agreed. He added: "I noticed that the graffiti 'artist' wrote 'Swann' and..."

"...I know all about him, and the background of this place!" the homeowner barked, with a Maine accent that seemed to make him even angrier. "Intolerant before the Civil War, intolerant after it. But he was the mayor of a big city, and this has also been home to a school of nuns, and a school for nurses. And I'm the most tolerant person alive. That's one reason I chose to move here to Alexandria.

"Why did some nutjob pick on me?!" He angrily wiped sweat off his forehead with a handkerchief.

The fellow sure knew his history. Ted was about to give him a business card for his history tours, then thought that inopportune. Without

saying anything more, the owner disappeared within, after slamming
the door. Ted and Harmony heard the turning of two locks.

"I guess he doesn't want to talk to us," noted Ted.

"Two locks," noted Harmony. "He's worried."

Stepping aside from rain puddles, the pair walked a block west on
Prince St. to complete their photo shoot. They came to a three-story,
sandstone townhouse, dating from 1854, with an attached conservatory,
and a spacious, gated garden facing the sidewalk. The original builder
had evidently been a man of wealth and taste. In fact, the owner had
been William Fowle, of the same family that resided at the Fowle-
Patton House. During The War Between the States, Fowle, a person of
Southern sympathies, had departed Alexandria, when it came under the
Union Army's occupation, or liberation, depending on your point of
view. He and his family stayed until conflict's end in the Confederate
capital of Richmond, Virginia.

Like so many large buildings in Alexandria, especially those owned by
backers of the South, the Union Army seized Fowle's home and turned
it into a hospital. Ted often started his Civil War tours from outside its
evocative garden, where wounded Federal soldiers had recuperated
under the shade, succored by the sweet scent of flowers. Indeed, a
corporal from Pittsburgh had written lyrically to his mother: "Lying on
the cool grass here, and under the shade of the sycamore, I cannot help
but recall the shades of my lost companions, their spirits residing
evermore under the bloody clay soil of Virginia..."

As Ted leaned his back against the iron fence, Harmony aimed her
Nikon at him and the stately home from different angles. Finally, Ted
remarked, "It's getting near time to wrap things up and head over to
City Hall."

But then they turned to the sound of a heavy door slamming shut from an exquisite townhouse on the opposite, south side of Prince. Leaving the entranceway was a stout, elderly woman, in black pants and a patterned sweater, with light gray hair and a determined, if glum, visage. Holding a bouquet of roses, she began heading eastward down the block as if on a mission. As ever, she limped, pushing herself along with a cane, as her right foot had been amputated due to diabetes. Ted recognized her immediately as the woman who occasionally opened up the building for an unusual start to his Civil War tours. For the townhouse, which had been part of the same Union hospital complex, hosted a small but intriguing museum of the Confederacy. Its proper name was the R.E. Lee Camp Hall. And the 70-year-old Bertha Stuart was one of its managers, and a head of the local chapter of the United Daughters of the Confederacy. Its members were descendants of rebel soldiers, and its main mission was to maintain artefacts, memorials, and memories from "The Lost Cause", as its critics often termed post-war proponents of the Confederacy.

Stuart liked to point out that she was not descended from Rev. Stewart, a Confederate-sympathizing minister of 1860s Old Town, but was related to J.E.B. Stuart, the dashing, gaudily dressed Confederate cavalry commander. There was then a controversy on whether to rename Alexandria's J.E.B. Stuart High School, due to this rebellious association. Ted had sometimes passed the school, a few miles up King St., when swimming at the nearby Lake Anna.

Ted called out to Bertha Stuart, who continued to walk doggedly ahead even as she craned her head back at him and Harmony. Normally she was friendly, appreciative of his interested in her museum. But she just nodded blankly and plowed forward.

Harmony recalled when Ted had brought her into the R.E. Lee Camp Hall on one of his tours. The stolid stack of reddish-brown brick, dating from 1852, had been the home of a prosperous doctor. It is closely connected to the Confederate Army's 17th Infantry Regiment, which mustered near the site of the future Appomattox statue on the day a large Union force entered Old Town. The 17th was made up of citizens from Alexandria, who fought, or were wounded or died, in battles from the start of the war, such as Bull Run, or Manassas as they called it, to the very end of the conflict. Among its ranking officers were Arthur Herbert, the co-founder of the town's Burke & Herbert bank.

The Camp Hall is said to be haunted. From the many wounded soldiers who breathed their last there in the hospital complex. Union ghosts in a Confederate camp. The fine townhome next door is haunted too, it's believed. By the ghost of an Alexandria mayor, John B. Smoot, who died there on Christmas Day, 1887, in his residence. According to city lore, the stricken magistrate, whose family ran a vast lumber yard near the future Torpedo Factory, fell out of a window to his death. In a scene out of Hitchcock's *Spellbound*, Smoot was smote, impaled, on the spikes of a gate. The Smoot family endures to this day in Alexandria as a seller of building materials.

The elegant Hall was linked, during the Civil War, to a church minister involved in one of the most searing and divisive events in Old Town history. Harmony listened attentively, if somewhat anxiously, as she glanced at her watch, as Ted retold the tale.

The cleric in question, Rev. Kinsley Stewart, was in 1862 the prelate of St. Paul's Episcopal Church, just four blocks away on Pitt St. The Episcopalians were formerly called Anglicans, as in Anglo or English, being members of the Church of England, until the American Revolution tarnished the King's Church, leading to the name change.

Their house of worship, built in 1809, was the second major Episcopal institution in town. The first was the lovely Christ Church, to whose congregation George Washington and Robert E. Lee belonged. The Episcopalians, of well-connected, English ancestry, were often wealthy. For St. Paul's, they could afford to bring in "the Father of American architecture", Benjamin Latrobe, to design it. The result is a minor masterpiece, a Greek Revival work with three grand exterior arches that echo three smaller arches behind the altar within. Though drawing on medieval inspiration, Latrobe created plain, open pews straight out of the early Reformation, and smooth exterior walls that are strikingly modern.

As with most Alexandria churches during the war, its congregation was "secess", or Southern in inclination. This presented Rev. Stewart with a dilemma.

As part of the Episcopal liturgy, the minister delivered a prayer, a plea for divine protection and inspiration, for the President. No doubt Stewart, as a cleric of a town on the very knife edge of North and South, reflected: 'Who was the President, and of what nation?' Was the Chief Executive to whom he and his flock owed their allegiance President Lincoln, of the United States? Or to Jefferson Davis, President of the Confederate States?

Rev. Stewart was secessionist in his thinking, if seemingly moderately so—he didn't flee to Richmond, or take up arms—but he faced a Hobson's choice. If he uttered a prayer for President Lincoln, he'd alienate most of his flock. If he uttered praise for President Davis, he'd enrage the large contingent of Union soldiers in town. Then came the rub. The Union officer in charge of Alexandria directed the town's ministers to pray for the well-being of Mr. Lincoln.

The Reverend might have made a good politician in another time and place, for he tried to steer a middle course. During worship services on Sunday, February 9, 1862, he was presiding at the altar. He came to the President's prayer. The congregation filling the pews watched him expectantly. And watched as he skipped over the prayer. Neither lauding, nor by implication slighting, the Union leader or the Confederate one.

But as with many political non-decisions, his action pleased neither side. Especially the Union soldiers in the church, on hand for a confrontation. Their leader, 26-year-old Captain Elon Farnsworth, was the nephew of a politician from Lincoln's state of Illinois, and a staunch Union man. With his fellow Illinois troops in attendance, and with Confederate sympathizers in the pews around them, he called out to Rev. Stewart, and demanded he read the presidential prayer. For President Lincoln. Stewart didn't, so Farnsworth in a loud voice recited the Presidential prayer himself. Moreover, he and his soldiers rose up, and strode to the altar. They grabbed the cleric and, with Stewart's young daughter clutching to his vestments, hauled him down the aisle to the exits, as the Reverend continued to call out the service litany! As the group started to depart the church, one soldier was struck, not by a bullet, but by a prayer book hurled by an irate female worshipper from the upper gallery. The soldiers detained Rev. Stewart, until ranking officers ordered his release.

He turned out to be less neutral than he might have appeared. Stewart received and sent vital intel to General Lee about a big Union offensive planned for the lower Potomac region. As for Captain Farnsworth, tragedy ensued. He was killed the following year, during a pointless cavalry fight at Gettysburg after Lee had already been bested there.

The startling seizure of a minister in his church deepened anger toward "them Yankees" among most of the town's citizens. The rancor grew when Union cavalry turned St. Paul's into a stable, with the horses damaging Latrobe's beautiful construction. After the war, the town sued the federal government for restitution. The case was settled in Alexandria's favor—in 1913. The resentment over this incident and others endured for generations, even up to the dawn of the civil rights era, and perhaps beyond.

More immediately, the "Battle of St. Paul's Church" triggered a bizarre skirmish between secessionists and Union troops at a fire station and newspaper office a few blocks down Prince St. Their photography session over, Ted was about to relate that intriguing incident to Harmony when she reminded her friend he was running, as usual, "on Ted time", and they would be late for the City Hall presentation.

Now mindful of the event awaiting them, they began walking briskly down Prince St. The two again reached the Patton-Fowle House side, and up ahead they saw Bertha Stuart.

The limping woman had paused with much indecision at the stop light and busy intersection at South Washington St. To her right was the Lyceum, the town history museum. In front of her, in the center of the crossing, was the Appomattox statue. A skillfully sculpted bronze figure of a Confederate soldier lost in thought, it honored the rebel soldiers from Alexandria who died in battle. Given the soldier's somber expression, it signified perhaps the cost of war as well.

When they reached the crossroad, with Washington St. spilling out in either direction, Ted was reminded why he often took his War Between the States tours there. Indeed, it was one of his history sweet spots. This stretch of boulevard had, among other things, an astonishing collection of Civil War-related sites, including churches that had stood on opposing sides of the great national divide.

Down to his left was the ornate, almost candy-cake façade of the Methodist church. A Southern Methodist church during the war, its congregation was secess, and so Union troops seized it. As with St. Paul's, they made the consecrated place a stable for their cavalry and draft horses. The equines banged up and soiled the floors. As with St. Paul's, the church authorities filed for compensation from the federal government. And again, they had to wait until 1913 until they were compensated. Not coincidentally, that was during the first year of the Woodrow Wilson presidency. Wilson, who resegregated the federal work force at that time, had grown up in Roanoke, Virginia, up above the Shenandoah Valley shattered and impoverished by the war. The son of a Confederate doctor, he determined to right some of the wrongs, as he saw it, still outstanding from the conflict.

On the other, southside of the crossway is the longstanding, block-long federal courthouse. In 1917, it was the site of a trial of suffragettes, including the noted Alice Paul, imprisoned after protesting outside the White House in a time of war. And jailed with other female demonstrators in the dank Lorton, Virginia prison, until outrage at the ladies' mistreatment there led to their release. And to a change of heart in President Wilson, leading him to back, despite states' rights qualms, a federal constitutional amendment guaranteeing women the right to vote in federal elections.

A block south of the courthouse is another place of worship, the Baptist Church, which was very much secess, as a Southern Baptist congregation from 1861 to 1865. The Union occupiers/liberators made it a hospital too. In its case, the wounded pouring into town from the many battles in northern Virginia included Confederates. They were put into the church hospital along with the Yankees. Yet a kind of apartheid system reigned. Injured Union soldiers got the upper floors; Confederates were consigned to the basement. And when Southern belles brought flowers, fresh food, and clean underclothes to the recovering rebs, Yankee soldiers blocked their way. Union sentries may have feared the sympathetic ladies would smuggle in weapons or other contraband. But the prohibition on giving gifts to the stricken, like the damage to the Methodist and Episcopalian churches, and Rev. Stewart's detention, long left a sour feeling in many Alexandrians.

Ted looked a block further down Washington St. to a very different religious institution, one on the way to "the Bottoms", a formerly black neighborhood of modest workmen's houses. This is the Beulah Baptist Church.

On its brick walls is a plaque with the date of its construction, 1863, significantly, the year of the pivotal battle of Gettysburg, where Alexandria's one-time favorite son, Robert Edward Lee, met his decisive defeat. By then, thousands of "contraband"—escaped slaves who were not yet legally free citizens—had fled to Alexandria from farms and plantations. Among those proffering them the greatest support were black Protestant ministers. One of them, the Reverend Clem Robinson, directed the construction of that church, which also hosted a popular school he established.

The contrast with the imposing Baptist Church and the ornate Methodist Church is marked, and telling. It's constructed of plain brick, two stories high with a slanted roof. The front wall has a modest stained-glass window, with two larger, bricked-up window spaces on either side. These recessed windows make it seem as if the congregation ran out of money for the glass. A prosaic canvas awning is propped above the two wooden front doors. The walls sag some—

they look worn and tired and dusty, as if reflecting the hardships of those who prayed and took solace there a century and a half ago. The free and recently freed blacks of Alexandria were cash-poor, so a humble church had to do.

Along with Rev. Robinson, other notable figures are associated with that place, such as the remarkable Harriet Jacobs, a North Carolinian of mixed ancestry who escaped slavery and became an author, notably, of *Incidents in the Life of a Slave Girl*. The tireless Jacobs set up many of the other schools for the Civil War Era blacks surging into town.

Ted briefly sketched the church's story to Harmony, and added, "Beulah means 'Promised Land' in Hebrew—or 'Land of Your Own.'"

"That seems fitting," she nodded.

"Yes...Beulah became a common, almost stereotypical name for black ladies, a century ago." Ted recalled watching movies from the 1930s, or televisions shows dating from the 1950s, where 'colored ladies', often cleaning ladies, often had that name.

His blue eyes drifted further down toward the bottom of the Bottoms on Washington St., and toward another venerable African-American institution, the Roberts Memorial United Methodist Church. Though the current church dates from the 1890s, by the 1830s its congregation had a chapel there, set up with the aid of a white Methodist Bishop, a Robert Richford Roberts. Famous figures visited it, like Frederick Douglass, and Booker Taliaferro Washington. 'Booker T, the black educator,' Ted thought smiling, 'not the 1960s rhythm and rock band.' Once, in researching an Eastertide article on the historic churches of Old Town, Sifter had sat in on the Sunday services of the Roberts Church. To his astonishment, behind the pulpit of the female minister was an actual baptismal basin. Looking rather like a bathtub, but for a more ethereal purpose, for cleansing one's soul instead of skin. Ted had been raised in a far more restrained, Roman Catholic tradition, where a priest baptizes an infant by pouring a small amount of sanctified water onto a baby held over a baptismal fountain. But this Methodist church seemed much more Baptist, Southern Baptist, in every sense of the term. In it, full-grown adults who caught the Holy Spirit immersed themselves in view of their family, friends, and congregation, then emerged from the immersion born-again. When he examined the tub, Ted was reminded of the scene in the film, *Oh Brother, Where Art Thou*, with its mass baptism of the devout in a river, to the angelic singing of "Go Down to the River to Pray".

"I think," said Harmony, interrupting Ted's reverie, "that you could dwell all day on this stuff. But we can't."

Ted nodded absently, his attention returning to the Appomattox statue and to Bertha, who was still standing on the corner. The intersection was normally one of the busiest in town. But Harmony noted the traffic was light, "as it has been," she said, "since the start of the epidemic." The adjoining streets, still wet from the rainstorm, had few pedestrians, and those few were masked and wary of anyone coming near. On the other side of the town's history museum, the Lyceum, a popular Italian restaurant seemed closed, perhaps due to the virus or to financial woes from the shutdowns. There Ted had treated Harmony on her birthday to an operetta performance, a delightful supper and singer affair. But the music and the Florentine treats now seemed in a distant past.

The two crossed over Prince St. and paused in front of the history museum and eyed Bertha. She remained at the intersection, silent and still with her flower bouquet, seemingly trying to make up her mind on whether to walk over to the Appomattox statue.

Before the Civil War the Lyceum had been a lecture hall, where the momentous issues of the day were examined. In fact, the noted abolitionist, President, son of a President, and ex-President-turned-Congressman, John Quincy Adams, spoke there. Quincy Adams, a Boston intellectual, was not a popular figure in the earthier, more rustic South. It was his fate to run for President against the most popular man in the country, indeed in the first half of the 19th century: Andrew Jackson, born in a Carolina wilderness, and the hero of the 1815 Battle of New Orleans. Twice Quincy lost the popular vote to Jackson, though he won the Electoral College tally once, before losing to Old Hickory in the rematch. "We've never," went a wry comment of Ted's, "had any Electoral College disputes since." As a federal legislator In his old age, Quincy Adams was especially suspect in much of the South for pushing an end to a "gag order" that forbade congressional debates on slavery. But he wouldn't push that pressing issue under the rug, and after years of trying, he got the gag order rescinded.

It was not entirely incongruous that Adams of Quincy, Massachusetts spoke at the Lyceum. The place had been founded by a noted Quaker educator of Alexandria, Benjamin Hallowell.

As a member of the Society of Friends, Hallowell saw slavery as an offense against God, a refusal to obey the command to love one's neighbor. In Alexandria, where so many with differing views on that matter lived, worked, and studied cheek by jowl, Hallowell's connections reached across the spectrum. As an instructor in mathematics at a school run out of his home, a prize student was a young Robert E. Lee, who Hallowell prepped for West Point. And prepared him well, as Lee graduated with the second highest marks in the Military Academy's history (a score of 1995.5 out of 2,000), and was later commandant of the Academy, presiding over students such as future Union General Philip Sheridan.

Another Lee connection to the intersection was his nephew, Fitzhugh Lee, the postbellum Governor of Virginia. A Confederate general who'd headed up his uncle's cavalry, he actually battled Sheridan in the verdant Shenandoah Valley, 80 miles to the west of Alexandria. And as a post-war Governor, Fitzhugh Lee delivered a speech in May 1889 before an immense crowd in the intersection, to mark the unveiling of the Appomattox statue. He spoke of 'valiant soldiers from both North and South, now united as citizens of the same Nation, with a glorious future ahead of them.' Around the same time, Gov. Lee offered similar remarks at the college his uncle had administered, West Point. After the younger Lee's death, *The New York Times* commented, "There is no man in the South and no man in the United States, who contributed more than Fitzhugh Lee to forming, after the division of the Civil War, 'a more perfect union.'" As the Tennessee Civil War historian Shelby Foote put it, the Northerners and Southerners of the time made a 'gentlemen's pact', whereby Southerners would accept their defeat and the primacy of the Union, whereas Northerners would ease the sting of their errant brothers' loss by acknowledging their courage as warriors. The Appomattox statue was in some ways part of that unspoken accord. The statue's sculptor was himself something of a compromiser. He was Caspar Buberl, a Czech immigrant who played, if you will, both sides. In the years before his Appomattox figurine, he created an astonishing, 1,200-feet-long set of friezes on the exterior wall of D.C.'s massive Union Army Pension Building. Each foot of it has a representation of a Union infantryman, mule driver, artillery hauler, or cavalryman. It housed the Pension Bureau, then the largest federal agency, which paid out the benefits to the 2,128,948 million soldiers, and their widows, children, and other dependents, of the gigantic federal army. The individual Southern states paid pensions to Confederate soldiers or their widows. Today the structure, with its breathtaking atrium, is the National Building Museum.

The construction supervisor for the Pension Building, composed of over 15 million red bricks, was Union General Montgomery Cunningham Meigs. In the pre-war and during the conflict, Meigs, a brilliant architect and logistician, supervised construction of the great Rotunda that now graces the top of the U.S. Capitol Building. Incredibly, the man who chose him for this prestigious task was the then-Architect of the Capitol, and Secretary of War, one Jefferson Davis—the future President of the Confederacy! Another of Meigs' personal ties was as astonishing. In the pre-war he was a close friend of fellow federal officer Robert E. Lee. During the war Meigs, a staunch abolitionist, despised Lee as a traitor. His rancor hardened when his son, John Rodgers Meigs, named for a founder of the U.S. Navy, was killed during a skirmish with Confederate troops near the Shenandoah. Montgomery Meigs had seized control of Lee's Arlington House estate, formerly the plantation of George Washington's grandson-in-law, via Washington's marriage to Martha Dandridge Custis Washington. Meigs began turning the extensive properties into a cemetery for the Union war dead. To ensure the Lee family would never get the land back, he directed the burials begin in the rose garden of the Lees' Arlington House. His intent was fulfilled. The grounds are now Arlington National Cemetery.

Though the story is ever more complicated, with nuances, shades, of gray, and blue. Before the war Lee, who at the time revered his service in the federal army, took two long years off from it to manage Parke-Custis' sprawling lands, including Arlington House. The purpose: to make the lands profitable. The reason: To permit the freeing of the 200 slaves working there, as Parke-Custis had indicated in his will. For under slavery's abstruse and absurd laws, servants had to be held as collateral for payment of debts. James Madison, Thomas Jefferson, James Monroe, and other indebted Virginia planters had faced that situation.

Lee famously wrote a friend of Lincoln's, Francis Preston Blair, at the start of the war: "If I owned the four millions of slaves in the South I would sacrifice them all to the Union." He added, "but how can I draw my sword upon Virginia, my native state?" (Historians still argue whether Lee ordered an Arlington House slave who had escaped whipped on recapture.)

And Lee, along with being an admired soldier, must have had a talent for business, as he made the estates profitable. The slaves would likely have been freed by him sometime after the outbreak of the war. And they became free after Union troops seized the estate. Lee manumitted, or freed, his several personal slaves during the conflict.

As these thoughts about the Appomattox statue, the war, and more swirled through Ted's active mind, he and Harmony kept their eyes on the Bertha Stuart. She finally decided to move off toward the statue. With one hand clacking her hickory cane on the moist pavement, and the other grasping the bouquet, she slowly stepped up to the artwork. Up to its southern side, a side the Confederate faced, a side she had deliberately chosen, which contained the names of the Alexandrians who died in battle for their South. Bertha paused and looked around— to check for traffic, and to see if anyone hostile was watching her. A tense woman by nature, she'd been unusually nervous over the past several weeks, after getting threats to the museum and her person. She looked about, but without noticing Ted and his friend.

Sifter had sometimes wondered who occasionally left flowers at the site. He figured it was one or more members of the Daughters of the

Confederacy, and most likely Bertha. He and Harmony watched her
bulky form squat down to place the bunch of roses under the names of
the deceased. A bus and a sedan passed slowly by in either direction,
one to the north, and one toward the south, partly obscuring the scene.
Ted wondered what the occasion might be. He knew that Robert E.
Lee's birthday, once celebrated throughout the South, was January 19,
a day before his own birthday. 'Both Lee and I were Capricorns,' he
reflected. 'Mountain climbers, stubborn and relentless.' But it was then
late in the spring, the traditional time to begin military campaigns.
Perhaps the woman was honoring a battle in northern Virginia. 'What
the date of Fredericksburg or Chancellorsville?' Ted tried to recall.
Suddenly, a thin, masked figure draped in black darted out from the
northeast side of the intersection. The person, Ted noticed, had
emerged from near a venerable row of businesses. They had been built
by John Lloyd, a merchant descended from Quakers who was Lee's
cousin-in-law. The person, of average height, grasped an umbrella,
which was open, which was odd, as it had stopped raining long before.
He, or she—it was hard to say from the person's masks and thin
physique—rushed over to Bertha, and reached down to grab the
bouquet. Two city buses, both bereft of passengers, their drivers
masked, passed by in either direction, again obscuring the scene. Ted
and Harmony stood watching wide-eyed.
Bertha was about to lay the roses down when she heard the fast-moving
footsteps approach. Glimpsing the interloper at the last moment, she
froze, and held on hard to the flowers' moist stems. The figure in black
stopped, reached down, and pulled hard on the bouquet.
Bertha pulled back, thorns pricking several of her fingers. The figure
pushed the point of the umbrella toward the woman. She in turn barked
out something—Harmony couldn't make it out given the traffic noise—

and menacingly patted a hand on a bulge of her pants pocket. The black-clad person jumped back in fright, stood up straight, and then stepped back into the street proper, as a vehicle closed in from S. Washington. It was a hearse, from the Demaine funeral home down the boulevard! Startled, the would-be flower snatcher barely dodged the car. The person slipped, and nearly fell. The interloper then quickly ran off in Nike running shoes to the old courthouse's parking lot, and disappeared around the side of the building.

It had all happened in seconds, faster than a stunned Ted and Harmony could react.

Bertha, red-faced, looked around, and saw Ted, and gave him an emotionless gaze. He called out to her, "Are you all right?"

She said nothing and, now sitting in the street, placed the bouquet with trembling, bleeding hands flat against the statue base, underneath the names of the dead. She rubbed her pricked fingers, and a few drops of blood fell onto the roses' red.

Ignoring the two onlookers, Bertha Stuart crossed to the far side of Washington St. Determinedly, yet nervously, she walked past a building that housed a society of military engineers, evocative of Lee and Meigs. Pacing fast despite her limp, she went past the Murray-Dick-Fawcett House, 'where Washington dined and slept', then disappeared from view near a townhouse built by Confederate sympathizer William McVeigh.

Ted was still trying to take the incident in when Harmony asked: "Did you see the symbols on that person's shirt?"

"The what? Uh, no. I didn't make it out. It happened so quick."

"Though I couldn't figure out the sex," Harmony continued.

"Neither could I," Ted answered. "The clothes and masks covered up too much of the body."

"That's not what I mean," she replied. "Normally you can tell, from the person's gait. But in this case I couldn't."

"Okay," Ted answered. "But what about the shirt?"

Harmony looked at the spot near the statue where she'd first noticed the person's apparel. "It was like a circle, with three arrows."

"Huh?"

"Three downward arrows."

The image clicked in Ted's mind. For years, he'd noticed members of Antifa strutting around the capital area, usually in downtown D.C. They were often dressed, it seemed, for battle, with helmets, elbow and knee pads, and draped in black, ninja-like attire. And shirts with a small black flag and a larger red flag, or the three arrows. He knew the latter represented symbols of three things ardent anti-fascists opposed back in the 1930s: monarchs, Nazis, and Stalinists. The last before many of them switched to backing Stalin.

"The person was Antifa," Ted told Harmony.

"Sometimes," he added, "I feel like we're on the verge of a second Civil War."

Because of their cramming in a photo session before the Council meeting, not to mention Ted's history tangents, and the strange statue incident, the two were now very late for the meeting. They rushed past the brooding rebel statue down Prince St., past the Murray and the McVeigh homes, and turned left onto Pitt St., named for the British Prime Ministers, William Pitt, the Elder and Younger, who had sympathized with the American Revolution. They passed the so-called "tenement house" of Martha Washington, bought for her by George as an investment property. Striding fast, they crossed over to the main thoroughfare of King St., and went by the large city block of the Alexandrian Hotel. With its four stories of red bricks, and tall side chimneys, it was supposed to mime the Federalist style of the original buildings there.

As she paced alongside him, Harmony noticed again that Ted was "dressed up" for the coming occasion, or as much as one who only wore formal attire for very formal occasions. Speaking before the City Council, apparently, didn't qualify. A pair of relatively new hiking shorts and a blue Land's End shirt with a very short collar would have to do. Nor did the day pack loosely affixed to his shoulders strike a Brooks Brothers note. "I like to dress and feel comfortable, like I'm in the outdoors," Ted would tell her. For the City Hall event, Harmony was more fashion-conscious, with a close-fitting, flower-print cotton dress cut off halfway up her supple calves, and her dark-brown hair pulled out into two bows somewhere short of pigtails.

They raced past the hotel's Jackson pub, presumably named for the secess owner of the Civil War hotel on that site, and past the hotel entrance, where two glum Eritrean immigrant doormen stood wearing double masks. For a moment they thought the two striders were coming to their hotel, and they rushed over to help, until Ted and Harmony rushed by them. The men had no guests to help lug their baggage, no tips to collect, little money to pay their mounting bills in what they had seen as a land of opportunity. They wondered and worried if the nearly empty hotel would shut down entirely from the malaise.

The lodging seemed suffused with sadness, current and past. The violent owner of the antebellum hotel there had shot a Union officer to death in a stairwell. And once chock-full of historic dwellings, this block had been bulldozed during the "urban renewal" of the 1960s. The current hotel structure had been a Marriott where Ted, before his move to Alexandria, had stayed for a writer's conference during the week of the Space Shuttle *Columbia* disaster. With other guests in the Jackson bar, he'd watched in horror the breaking news of the crew's catastrophic descent to Earth.

Chapter 4 – Addition versus Subtraction

Soon the duo was across from City Hall's Market Square, and near another modern setting, not the accustomed historic one. Across King St. and along N. Royal is a set of drab, low-level office buildings, with facades of a faux colonial style, another product of the urban renewal program. There was a Celtic souvenir store, a shuttered hamburger place, a chain drugstore, blasé office spaces, and a taco joint. As with many other urban centers in the 1950s, local residents and businesses fled to the suburbs, pulling the rug out from the venerable commerce of Old Town. The response of the city and federal authorities was to put a wrecking ball to dozens of dilapidated but historically rich Colonial, Federal, and Antebellum Era town homes and stores. The result, as with D.C.'s Pennsylvania Avenue renovations in the late 20th century, was more modern and less shabby, but less vibrant and evocative. They crossed over to Market Square, with Ted barely checking the traffic, and not at all the stop lights, before crossing. This habit again concerned Harmony, particularly as two police cars were moving quickly up the street. Ted had told her his practice came from growing up in New York City's congested streets, where busy people crossed when the coast was clear, not when it was legal to cross. Harmony wondered if this was really true, or one of the oddly humorous beliefs and superstitions her friend possessed.

The cop cars turned the corner, and the street fell completely, eerily, silent again. Down the steep slope of lower King St., just a few bistros of Restaurant Row were open, with just a few customers in the makeshift, outdoor seating that maître d's desperate for customers had thrown together. They walked across the bricked pavement of Market Square, a public park about 75 yards on each side.

With the town's 1749 founding, the Market Square became, in English fashion, the town's commons, a smaller version of the great Commons in Boston, and a major marketplace for the region's growers.

Washington had trained his colonials there for the French and Indian War, and his Continentals for the American Revolution. The Square once had rows of business stalls, a jail, a slave market, and a produce stand run by a civil rights prophetess, Alethia Tanner Browning. With the profits from her sales, she bought her own freedom, and those of over a dozen enslaved relatives, one of whom set up the region's first middle school for blacks. The Square told many tales across its 270 years.

At its center, normally an attraction for tourists, the large water fountain was turned off, and its surrounding basin drained of water, an effort to "stop the spread" by discouraging gatherings. However, on the north end of the Square, next to City Hall, Ted and Harmony heard the chants of a sizeable crowd.

A group of protestors, about 100 in number, were milling about the City Hall entrance. Many were from Black Lives Matter and social justice warrior groups, and a few clad in black seemed to be from Antifa. Others were lawyers from the courthouse across King St., or clerics and congregants from local churches, especially churches with black or progressive ministers or congregations. Many had placed banners in front of their churches with such slogans as, "Hate Has No Home Here", or "All Are Welcome From Everywhere". Some were holding up signs with similar messages.

Long a genteel Border South town, Alexandria was still a rather staid place. So it was jarring to come across a loud demonstration in Market

Square. Indeed, the mood of the crowd was very angry. Ted and Harmony went by two protestors, a young black woman and young white man, both in jeans, both with masks slung around their necks, who were "getting in the face" of two Alexandria police, a white female and a Latino male, stationed outside the Hall. The male protestor stood three inches from the face of the male cop, as the female protestor, from a few steps away, recorded the encounter with her iPhone.

The male protestor screamed: "You fucking pig! You killer!" Spittle flew from his lips, dotting parts of the cop's face not covered by his mask. "You're not so tough now, are you!? You're a coward, a murderer! You pig!"

It was as if they were trying to bait the cop into a violent reaction, and capture it on video, and hope the resulting images went viral. Observing the encounter, Harmony asked Ted: "Are you sure you want to do this?" Yet he seemed cool, even cold-blooded, as he usually was in a tense situation, and more so when Harmony was present. His innate sang-froid, and his protective instinct, was kicking in. He fully extended his arms, which were rock-steady, and said sarcastically, "My hands are shaking."

They approached City Hall's rear entrance. Its main entry point, at Cameron St. on the giant Hall's opposite side, had been closed. The goal of that was to have everyone enter in one place, where security guards could ensure everyone was wearing a mask. Either side of the entrance had lines of rainbow flags, to demonstrate the City Council's support for LGBTQIA+-#. Passing these ensigns, the duo looked up at the immense American flag draped on the south wall. High up on their left was the white clock tower with its soaring steeple, fashioned 205 years before. It looked just like a church steeple, and tourists often mistook it for such. Up across Royal St. was venerable Gadsby's Tavern, dating from Washington's time, the site of inaugural celebrations for the first six U.S. Presidents. There in 1816 had occurred the death of a mysterious young woman, rumored to be Aaron Burr's daughter, and said to haunt the place since.

Ted took from a pants pocket a flimsy, blue surgical mask, which he had reluctantly purchased via Amazon, $6 for a package of 24. As he slipped it across his chin, grimacing, with his nose uncovered at first, and his mouth barely so, Harmony laughed, knowing his disdain for the cloth preventatives. He had argued, convincingly, based on medical reports when the pandemic broke out, that masks discouraged people from focusing on a larger concern: proper health practices, such as diet and exercise, to prevent comorbidities like diabetes and heart disease that posed a far greater risk to those infected.

Ted pushed opened the entrance door, holding it for Harmony, and muttering though the thin fabric, "God, how I hate these things, I can't breathe." His friend took note he had unwittingly used the three-word phrase that had become nationally famous due to the death, while in police custody, of a black man in the upper Midwest. Harmony essentially agreed with Ted, having read that standard cloth masks were unable to stop viruses, and could lead to the buildup of molds, bacteria, and viral infections in the mouth, throat, and lungs. Still, most buildings in the capital region had strict mask requirements. Thus the duo, like everyone else, conformed upon entering.

The security guard, a stocky young woman with a double mask, looking bored even through the face covering. Standing at a table next to a metal detector, she glumly asked for their IDs. City Hall hadn't required an ID check before. Ted figured the requirement was likely due to the protestors and the controversial issue behind the meeting.

Indeed, the guard had a Motorola two-way radio on her hip, and a voice crackling from it announced that additional police were coming to Market Square from a precinct outside Old Town.

Ted told the guard they were on hand for the Council meeting.

"You can't go in there," she stated, her eyes turning sharp above the masks. "It's standing room only, with a line out the door." She moved her head in displeasure. "And way over the Covid restrictions."

Ted replied: "I'm one of the speakers." Feeling embarrassed about his attire—he hardly looked like a speaker—he started to pull his prepared remarks from his daypack. From her small brown shoulder purse, Harmony pulled out a printed meeting schedule.

"He's listed on the agenda," Harmony said. "She's with me," Ted added.

The guard looked them over, and slowly nodded. She reached into a drawer, and gave them two badges.

"Put these on, they'll get you in." She waved them down the hall to the elevators and stairways leading up to the Council chambers.

Ted had visited the City Hall and Council rooms before, for research on a book, and he led the way. They passed along a green-carpeted hallway speckled with city administrators, members of activist groups, and reporters. The latter were scribbling into notepads or sitting on the carpet keying stories into laptops. A TV reporter with the face of a supermodel and decked out in Armani apparel watched her crew set up camera lighting.

As one would expect from the town hall of a historic town, the place had many tales attached to it. For instance in 1872, 54 years after its construction, a fire had burned down much of the structure. The rear of City Hall was wrecked, and that just seven years after the Civil War had upended the region. The city fathers, including John Daingerfield, of the same family that acquired the Swann-Daingerfield House, ponied up some of the $8,000 for the City Hall reconstruction. The railroads had replaced King Cotton as the dominant industry in America, and loans for the balance of the rebuilding came from Alexandria and Baltimore railway concerns. Fueled with this money, the city, as in its glory days with Latrobe and Bulfinch, brought in the capital's best architect. Namely, Adolph Cluss, the designer of D.C.'s Eastern Market, the capital's answer to Boston's Faneuil Hall marketplace. Cluss also created the National Portrait Gallery's grand Hall of Creation honoring America's most famous inventors, and Dupont Circle's Charles Sumner School, named for an abolitionist New England Senator, and built for the children of former slaves.

In his tours, Ted referred to Cluss as "the 'good Adolph.' We all know who the 'bad Adolph' was. Adolph used to be a common name for German or German-American boys. But around 1945, for obvious reasons," he'd smile slyly, "German moms stopped giving their sons that name."

The 'good Adolph' was part of the wave of German immigrants who made their way to America after Europe's failed democratic revolutions of 1848. And for his reconstruction of the burnt-out City Hall, Cluss pulled off a double feat. For the less-damaged south side, he restored the original spare yet stately style. Mostly simple brick, but with tall chimneys, a broad slanted roof, and a portico on top that evoked the Georgian architectural stamp of the old colonial capital of Williamsburg, Virginia. Retained were the spacious side halls, as well as Latrobe's steeple.

But on the ruined north side, the good Adolph created in effect a second building, one that gloried in the most admired architecture of its time. With a massive mansard roof perched atop four stories, and with blue tints contrasting with the predominant red brick, that side of City Hall looks much like the Louvre. Cluss drew on France's "Second Empire" imperial style, then all the rage. In effect, he took the latter-day Swann-Daingerfield House design, and placed it on a far greater canvas. Its regal look contrasts sharply with the simpler, Federal Era townhouses across from it on Cameron St.

When they neared the open double-doors of the Council, Ted and Harmony heard the intermittent roars of a contentious gathering. A City Hall security officer and a city policeman gave them hard glances before they appeased them with a flash of their badges. They walked inside tentatively.

The meeting space was a crowded cavern. Below a high ceiling and toward the right wall were twelve rows of high-backed seats, made of thick brown wood like church pews, each with ten seats for a row. A middle aisle separated them from a set of six rows, with five seats across, that ran along the left wall. Almost all the spots were occupied, while other attendees stood in the middle and side aisles or leaned against the side walls. The crowd reminded Ted of the packed Easter services at Old Presbyterian, but rambunctious, not respectful, in mood. Running along the front of the hall on a long, raised dais of three-foot-high mahogany were a dozen or so City Council members and key staff, as well as the Mayor and Deputy Mayor, all in neat business attire, and sitting in upholstered swivel chairs. It was a wet, humid day, and very humid and uncomfortable in the chamber, as the air-conditioning hadn't been turned on for the summer. Occupying the center seat was the energetic City Council Coordinator Avril Forstandt. Right below the elected officials was a long table with microphones and straight-back seats for those addressing the Council.

Catching the eye of anyone entering the chamber was the outsized drawing of Old Town's 19th-century layout, as viewed from above the Potomac River. About 15 feet by 15 feet, it was mounted, like a precious artwork, in a thick wooden frame, and hung from the high wall behind the dais. The illustration so dwarfed the Council that the viewer seemed drawn into a time portal of Alexandria's past.

The town's gridwork of streets—King St. in the center right, and then Prince and Cameron on either side, and Duke and Queen alongside them, was plainly visible. The artist had drawn ships berthed in the port, then one of America's busiest, with their sails pulled down and their rigging prominent. Plying the river were steam-powered vessels, possibly U.S. Navy ships. Also depicted near the waterfront were many warehouses, and some factories, a reminder of just how industrial Alexandria had been, unusually so for a Southern town.

To Ted's learned eye, the depiction was clearly from the time of the Civil War. At the top of the illustration, where the George Washington Masonic Temple stands today, was the broad plateau of Shuter's Hill, and the faint outlines of dozens of military tents below a fort at the summit of the strategic rise. This had been one of the three main Union Army encampments in town. For years, Ted had tried to find remnants of one of the other camps, a few blocks west of King St. nearer the river.

The commercial buildings that had once dotted Market Square could be seen. Latrobe's tower astride City Hall was visible enough, as were tall trees in the rear garden of the Carlyle House mansion across from it. However, Alexandria was and is a sizeable place, and such a drawing could only take in so much. Details of other noted buildings were missing, or the buildings missing entirely. Christ Church was little more than a smudge, and the Old Presbyterian Meeting House, despite its prominent church tower, couldn't be seen at all. Toward the west, the old, circus-tent-like roundabout for switching trains, near today's Eisenhower Avenue, and so vital at the time for Union Army logistics, did stand out.

As they stood staring at the picture, Harmony and Ted couldn't but help but think of J. Swift's "treasure map", with its faded markings and absent sections. Whereas their map was missing most of the north section of town, the City Hall drawing depicted it clearly. Ted could make out the Old Cotton Mill on N. Washington St., and several of the Lee family homes just down the road from it. As ever, he was astonished at the number of antebellum Lee properties. And just across from the Carlyle mansion—he strained his eyes for it—yes, there it was, a blur of paint that would have been the Bank of Alexandria. Ted knew the large building was there during the Civil War, but the artist, out of ignorance or haste, had neglected it.

That sparked something in Ted's mind. Their chart, while leaving out some prominent buildings, as did the city map, had drawings of all the merchant banks of the time. As if trying to give them special emphasis. Something to consider after giving his speech.

He and Harmony walked slowly up a side aisle. Ted saw the place on the wall where there had been another noted illustration: a drawing of a grizzled Robert E. Lee, post-bellum. Lee had been removed, after some Council members objected to having an image of the Confederate general in the chamber.

The duo paused to listen to a woman giving a speech from the speaker's desk. The elderly lady was the sister of an officer at Christ Church, the latter formerly the church of Lee, and Washington. She was herself a prelate of a church in the Takoma Park neighborhood of D.C. And she was inveighing against the Appomattox statue. Of

English and Welsh ancestry, the woman was short, thin, and prim, with a pinched face and scrubbed white hair, and attired in a tight-fitting pants suit. Harmony remarked, "She has a lean and hungry look." Ted recognized her as someone who, at a public meeting some years, before had strongly urged the removal from Christ Church's altar wall the inscribed names of Lee and Washington.

Ted often took tour groups to that place of worship. The knowledgeable docent there would proudly point out the burnished brown plaques behind the pure-white, wineglass-shaped pulpit. Inscribed by architect James Wren's hand, they contained Old and New Testament precepts, including the Ten Commandments and the Golden Rule. On a recent visit, Ted had noticed that some of the ink had badly faded on the admonitions condemning murder, and urging benevolence.

The prelate was saying, "For so many years, whenever I've driven through Old Town," she said, in a strident, high-pitched cadence, "I have had to view, that statue, that monstrous reminder, of slavery and oppression." A large majority of the audience clapped loudly and shouted its approval for her denunciation. The speaker wiped sweat from her brow and went on. "It is a giant slap in the face, of every Alexandrian, who recalls the centuries of oppression, of oppression and servitude, which it represents." Most in the audience rose to their feet, and applauded or raised up fists.

"This symbol of hate was constructed, not reconstructed, during the times of Jim Crow and racial separation. It was, and is, a homage to those who strove and fought to preserve slavery and white supremacy! It is defended by the very same people who defended the Robert E. Lee statue in Charlottesville, Virginia. Where a valiant woman was run over and killed by a mob of neo-Nazis, and neo-Confederates!"

The noise of the listeners rose to that of a sport arena during a rock concert, as they cried out and stomped their feet in approval. Indeed, the floors of the cavern-like hall shook. Ted and Harmony stood watching and listening with keen interest.

"This vile work of 'art', this Confederate statue, makes it impossible to put our painful and sinful past behind," the prelate went on, her voicing rising. "And to stride forward, united, as one people, of many cultures, multi-cultures, into another future, one that will never again tolerate such injustice, such inequity—such *privilege*!" She spat the last word out like a curse. The crowd roared its agreement, the enraptured listeners stamping their feet again in angry approbation.

Ted would have gone up to the speakers table, where others scheduled to talk were sitting, but the center and side aisles were jammed with spectators, sitting or standing, and shouting out their solidarity.

Luckily, Harmony noted that three radio reporters had just vacated their seats, so the duo slipped past seated listeners to those spots. Ted figured he could wait there for a while, until things cleared out or calmed down a bit after the prelate's jeremiad.

To thunderous applause, the church lady concluded her remarks. Sitting next to her was a 52-year-old man of English, Scottish, and Hispanic descent who was adjusting his microphone with shaking hands. He was of medium height and girth, though with a paunch from his sedentary work; his hair, carefully combed, seemed an exact match of black and gray strands. This professorial-looking fellow was outfitted as if he were teaching in class. He wore a light-blue, Van Heusen open-collar shirt, pressed and belted Docker pants, and brown, thickly leathered Oxford shoes. He stood up and stretched, cleared this throat, mopped his forehead, and sat down again, shuffling carefully prepared notes.

Ted recognized him as Sherman S. Gordon, one of the leaders of the Washington Area Civil War Lecture Series. A historian and college professor, Gordon sometimes joked he was leading a "Lost Cause" for the preservation of antebellum and Civil War memorials.

Gordon had such history in his blood: he was descended from a Confederate officer on his father's side, and from a Union Army fundraiser on his mother's side. His maternal grandmother had suggested his first name, in honor of the conqueror of Atlanta. He'd taken a DNA test that seemed to confirm most of his known ancestry, and also indicated he had a bloodline that was 6 percent Moorish or African. He wondered if he might have had a slave as an ancestor, or a Barbary pirate. His tanned face, which bordered on nut brown, suggested—along with a predilection for golf, one of the few sports still open to the public—the 25 percent of his inheritance, courtesy of a Panamanian grandfather, that was Latino.

At a signal from the City Council chair, he glanced at the packed seats of the attendees, then at the officials on the dais. He adjusted a microphone and began. "I recognize, and appreciate, the passion and commitment, of the previous, the previous speakers," he began hesitantly, his left palm pushing down on his text. "However, I believe that one must be careful to put the Appomattox statue in context." He was careful to refer to the formal name of the statue, not the loaded term Confederate. A few muffled boos and hisses sailed down from the audience.

Professor Gordon nervously licked his lips. "First the term: Appomattox. Appomattox was a rebel *defeat*, not a victory. Where the war ended, in effect, with Lee surrendering, surrendering his battered force to General Grant. The statue shows a soldier thoughtfully, even forlornly, facing south, to the South, ruminating on the war. Probably thinking about its costs, its triumphs, its tragedies, and its losses. All that blood that had been spilled. Some of those losses, the names of the soldiers killed in battle, from this very town, are etched on the statue." The crowd was silent now but not, Harmony observed, happy with the speaker's words.

Gordon wiped a handkerchief across his nose and went on. "So it is not a victory statue, it is not an expression of defiance, actually, but a meditation on the war. A war that some believe is America's greatest saga, our nation's most important and influential event." Much of the crowd now began to hiss and boo.

The professor's mouth and throat felt dry. Unsure of himself, Gordon plowed ahead. "And we should remember how the statue was unveiled. By the Governor of our state, a former Confederate general, and yes, a Lee—who, who had reconciled with the Union."

On hearing "Lee", the audience was triggered. It stomped its feet violently. Listeners smashed their fists on the armrests of their seats. Amid the din, it was hard to make out the speaker's words. Harmony was reminded of a family story about an elderly in-law, an elementary school teacher who'd been silenced during China's Cultural Revolution.

"In his remarks," Gordon attempted, "Governor Fitzhugh Lee—whose family was related by marriage, I might add, to George Washington— this Lee praised, he praised, the valor of the soldiers, of both the North and South, now united again in one people, I mean, as one people." Wading through the shouts hurled at him, Gordon stated, his voice quivering: "In a time of such, such divisiveness, isn't that a message worth preserving?"

The audience roared its opposition, overwhelming the speaker's words. Gordon waited a while, until the tumult slackened some, and continued.

"One should add that the Lees were then presiding over a state that was ahead of the other Southern states, and some Northern states, in educating their children." The audience's negative reaction to this reached another crescendo. Gordon wasn't sure if anyone could hear him.

"And that the Lees," he said, in a louder voice, "believed education was the key to uplifting the South, from the destruction of the war, and from its own backwardness." The speaker stopped, barely able to hear himself, then started again.

"In fact, Fitzhugh Lee's uncle, after the war, took on the presidency of Washington and Lee University, actually college, a college then, for this very purpose, in Lexington, Virginia."

Gordon stopped again as several in the audience threw rolled-up balls of paper at the speaker. Some in attendance were in fact part of a social media campaign to rename Washington-Lee University, and to remove from the campus grounds Robert E. Lee's grave, and even his horse buried next to him. Attendees shouted out: "Racist! Hater! Hitler!" One person threw a banana, which whizzed surreally across the hall like a boomerang, before dropping harmlessly onto the dais.

The City Council members sat silent. Some officials worried about the speaker's safety; most agreed with the reaction of the crowd.

Flustered and a more than a little afraid, Gordon struggled to keep talking. "I—I should add that the elder Lee, in that capacity, severely reprimanded students who roughed up blacks near the school..."

In the hubbub, Gordon wasn't sure if his allotted time had run out. He turned toward the Council, whose members met his eyes with blank or stony stares. The Mayor, his long legs stretching under the dais, was tight-lipped. Gordon stopped, took up his notes, and fell back into his chair, met by a crescendo of hoots and insults: "Fascist! Fry the pig! Go home! Nazi!"

The professor got up and walked slowly to the other end of the table. He dropped down next to the prelate. Her face was blood-red; she shot him a baleful look.

In between glances at the crowd and the besieged speaker, Harmony and Ted scanned her printout of the speakers' schedule. He was next. "Are you sure you want to do this?" Harmony asked again, this time expressionless, which meant she was hiding her feelings, fearful of what might happen to Ted.

He shot her a crooked grin. As usual in times of stress or crisis, he felt little fear, but instead a quiet thrill. As for the wild state of the chamber, he ardently believed in his own approach to the statue, and the general issue it raised, and was willing to take the risk of speaking out.

For his tours, he'd email himself an itinerary and notes to jog his memory. For his talk, he emailed himself his remarks. He also grasped an extra, paper copy of them. Ted excelled at improvisational remarks, but thought it wise, before the Council and its audience, to offer prepared text. In case he did get flustered and forgot himself.

He rose, and walked quickly down the right-side aisle, his long legs taking the long, carpeted steps two at a time. He reached the speakers table, and sat across from Gordon and the church officer. Gordon looked at him with sad eyes, while the prelate, sweating from the humidity, and her face still flushed, looked at him with curiosity. The City Council members tried to keep poker faces, but looked down upon Ted with impatience and traces of disdain. Gordon, visibly shaking, got up and left the chamber through its rear exit, a spitball sailing over his head. A burly policeman accompanied him out.

City Council Coordinator Forstandt had to take a private phone call outside after Professor Gordon's talk. So the Deputy Mayor, standing at the dais, banged the gavel to continue. Ted knew him in passing. His name was Sean Morenis, 40, a man of varied Irish, African, and Hispanic ancestry. Cool in manner, but emotional underneath, he was the nephew of a long-time state senator from the region, and known to be an advocate for removing "uncomfortable aspects" of the city's past. Morenis, his rather ill-fitting attire masking a somewhat muscular physique, gave Ted a look of studied indifference.

"Mr. Sifter has the floor," he pronounced into his mike. "We're behind schedule. So, let's keep to it: Five minutes, no more."

Ted was momentarily taken aback at the surprise reduction of his allotted time. His hands fumbled with the microphone. Inept with the simplest technical matters, it took him half a minute to adjust it properly, his lanky figure bending down slightly. Several Council members glared down at him with annoyance. He stole a look at the audience, and glimpsed a wall of stony faces. He also glanced at Harmony. Her face was impassive, but she was rapidly tapping an armrest with her long, tapered fingers. During this brief interval, Ted figured out which parts of his prepared remarks, the best parts he thought, he would deliver.

His lower back wet with sweat from the humid hall, the historian began.

"Instead of focusing solely on the Appomattox statue, I'd like to look a little further abroad, and propose a compromise. A bold compromise, I believe. To think outside the box. To outline a proposal that all Alexandrians, I think, of all different views, might find agreeable."

He was happy to find that his voice, a bit high-strung at first, quickly calmed down, and hit its normal, middle register.

101

"Instead of removing, or keeping, a single statue—why not add statues, many, many statues—and memorials, and works of art, and monuments?

"About people from all aspects of the Civil War, and the antebellum and post-war periods, as all of that played out here in Alexandria." The audience, he noted, was quiet, if puzzled, which was good.

"Why don't we add," he stressed, "to the rich tapestry of our town's history, of our nation's history, instead of focusing on just a single aspect of it?

"Let's create more statues—of runaway slaves, rebel spies, builders of schools for the freedmen and women. And Federal officers, rebel soldiers, Union Army doctors and Southern nurses, African-American ministers, and more." Like Gordon, Ted deliberately didn't use the explosive word "Confederate", substituting "rebel" or "Southern" instead.

"In short, mementos of everyone who took part here in America's greatest story, its greatest drama, the Civil War." The crowd stirred, with some people making muted, mostly negative, comments.

"Let's honor such people who are linked to our town. Persons such as the great Harriet Jacobs. She was the escaped slave who, like Anne Frank, in the Europe that the Nazis had seized, hid out in the attic of a relative, hid for years, to escape the slave catchers trying to find her. A woman of mixed ancestry, black and white, like many civil rights leaders have been. Like Frederick Douglass, also of mixed ancestry, she authored an autobiography that informed countless readers of the evils of slavery."

Though he had his talk more or less memorized, Ted glanced from time to time at the notes he'd sent to the email app of his phone.

"Harriet Jacobs," he stated, gazing up at the ceiling dramatically, "should be a household name. When thousands of so-called 'contrabands' escaped from plantations to the Union lines in Alexandria. A dire shortage of shelter, of medicine, and education ensued. Harriet Jacobs organized the building of homes, hospitals, and schools for thousands of these displaced persons. Years later, she went on to found a college in the South, where women could attend, one of the first schools in the nation for this, along with our own Thompson school.

"Certainly, she deserves a statue of her own! And why not place it across the street from the existing one of the Southern soldier at Washington and Prince Streets?" At this point there were more audience murmurs, again mostly negatives, but some positive "yeahs" and nods of affirmation as well.

"Then there's someone like John Janney, of the distinguished Quaker family of businessmen in the Old Town of old. Everyone here has heard of Quaker Lane, west of Old Town, and Janney's Lane; they are named after the Janney family and its religion. John Janney actually managed the secession conferences that took Virginia out of the Union"—the listeners began to boo, and Ted's voice rose—"and he *opposed* secession." The booing stopped.

"Janney warned that leaving the Union would be a disaster for Virginia, and for the United States. 'I've done everything in my power,' he said at that time, 'to try and avert this catastrophe.'

"And there were actually two secession conferences. In the first one, Virginia actually voted to *stay in* the Union. Then came Fort Sumter, and President Lincoln's call for 75,000 volunteers to 'suppress the rebellion,' which a lot of Alexandrians thought meant bloody battles on their doorstep. And so, in the second secession conference there came the break with the Union. However, John Janney still opposed leaving. In the end, he stood with his State, while opposing its decision."

Ted paused; the room was silent. He added, "Surely a statue of that man would provoke thoughtful reflection on that momentous period.

"In fact, the city could place DOZENS of statues and memorials throughout Old Town, that relate to that great conflict. For figures such as Booker T. Washington, the former slave, of mixed ancestry, turned founder of Tuskegee Institute college in Alabama." Ted was careful to pronounce Tuskegee, a tongue twister, correctly, as "TusKEEgee".

"That esteemed educator spoke after the war at the African-American Roberts Memorial Church, on Washington St. He founded a university that would give us the first black squadron of fighter pilots, that took on and defeated Nazi pilots over the skies of World War Two Europe.

"Why not a statue of Booker T. near that church?"

A few clapped, but the crowd sat mostly in silence, surprised at this discourse, unsure what to make of it. Listeners looked at each other for a hint of whether they should respond positively or negatively.

Harmony noticed this, and realized Ted was winning a victory of a sort. He was prodding people to think about the various sides of a complex issue. 'He should be a college professor,' she thought, 'or a speechwriter.'

"Then there's the spy, a local spy," Ted went on, "with an unusual name: Benjamin Franklin Stringfellow. Born and bred around Alexandria. Some years before, PBS did a TV series based on actual events in Alexandria during the Civil War. A major character was Stringfellow." Most in the crowd, who had never heard of him, looked at Ted with puzzled interest.

"When you drive west out along Route 66, near Manassas, you may have noticed an exit called Stringfellow Road. It's named after him."

Ted had been hesitant to mention this man, for fear he'd trigger a movement to change the name of the exit. But this story was too good not to tell.

"Stringfellow spied for the rebel side, at the Carlyle House," he stated evenly, as the crowd murmured negatively, "at our town's largest and oldest mansion, and one of its biggest tourist attractions. Now it's a museum, in part, of Civil War history." Ted spoke rapidly, to defuse the negative reaction. "After the war Stringfellow joined the Federal Army—the Union Army, in effect—as a chaplain. With the signed approval of Northern Presidents of the United States, supporters of civil rights. Presidents like Ulysses S. Grant, the former commander of the Union Army." The murmuring remained, but was less negative in tone. "Stringfellow, as his name suggests, had a slender frame: in fact, he would sometimes disguise himself as a woman to elicit information from Union soldiers." Ted paused, remembering his bad speaking habit of ignoring the audience. But he knew a speaker should continually gauge his audience's reaction. He looked out into the hall. His listeners seemed wary, unsure: interested in what he was saying, but uncomfortable. Many were frowning, but listened keenly. A few laughed at the remark about Stringfellow dressing up as a woman.

"This man, who got his education at the Episcopal High School just west of here, wound up as chaplain with another President: Teddy Roosevelt, and his Rough Riders, at the famous Battle of San Juan Hill, in Cuba.

"Surely a character like that merits a statue," Ted stated.

Some listeners, he saw, shook their heads negatively, so he added quickly, "And there's also George Lewis Seaton, the son of an enslaved woman, freed by Martha Washington at Mt. Vernon. George Seaton was a pathbreaker: in the wake of the Civil War, he was one of the first

105

blacks elected to the Virginia House of Delegates, in Richmond—the former capital of the Confederacy. A master carpenter, Seaton built the Odd Fellows Hall here, on South Royal St.

"The 'Odd Fellows': what a wonderfully descriptive name, for the fellows who were the 'odd men out' during segregation. They were a fraternal organization for African-Americans, and usually professionals or skilled workmen—doctors, carpenters, architects—during the time of Jim Crow. George Seaton also built two schools for the freed men and women of color. Not least, he had twelve children."

Ted thought of something. He couldn't resist. "Twelve kids, wow. How about that? A dozen children. Perhaps it was George Seaton, and not George Washington, who was the true, Father, of his country!"

At this a number in the crowd guffawed.

Ted stopped, then stressed: "But seriously: From a slave at the first President's plantation, to becoming a state legislator, in one generation! Why not craft a Seaton statue to stand outside the other Odd Fellows Hall, which is right down the street from Christ Church? Surely such a man deserves it!"

Ted stole a glance at the church prelate; she was frowning and shaking her head. Deputy Mayor Morenis, he noticed, was grimacing, his hand gripping hard the gavel. Whatever their thoughts of Seaton, they evidently didn't like where Ted was going with this. He plowed ahead.

"That latter Hall was founded, by the way, by Martha Washington, in the early 1800s, as one of the town's first schools. For women. During the Civil War it was prison run by the Union Army, where disloyal civilians from the region were detained. After the war, ironically, Confederate veterans held meetings in the place.

Ted sensed his window of opportunity before a less-than-friendly audience might be closing. He stated quickly, "In fact, the city could erect dozens of statues and markers and memorial inscriptions about its unparalleled history. It wouldn't cost much, or maybe anything at all. Historical societies, and government grants, might pay the expenses." He paused for added emphasis, and said:

"Think of it: Alexandria could transform chunks of Old Town into an Outdoor Museum of the Civil War! With walking paths for different aspects of the war: escaped slaves, rebel spies, Union doctors, the dilemmas that women faced during the conflict, the role of Quaker merchants and educators in ending slavery, the Union fort that stood near Jones Point and the Wilson Bridge—the possibilities are endless indeed!"

The audience stirred. But Ted was too caught up in his talk to tell if the reaction was good or ill. He was a little nervous, but mostly excited at being able to offer such remarks in a public forum.

"Washington D.C.," he added, rushing his words, "already has something like this, through its Cultural Tourism project. It's built walking trails for different topics in the city's history throughout its downtown. For instance, a walk on Abraham Lincoln and the Civil War.

"It is even possible," he stressed, moving toward his conclusion, "to make Alexandria comparable to Gettysburg, or to Richmond, Virginia, or to D.C. itself, as a nationally recognized destination for Civil War tourism. What an opportunity to examine all aspects of that story! We could draw in millions of dollars of tourist revenues to the town!" He took a breath, as Council members fidgeted, and peeked at their watches or stared at their phones. The prelate was wearing an ugly expression, but his focus was riveted on another major point.

"And why stop with the Civil War? We have scores of buildings from the colonial and Federal periods, that are linked to figures like George

107

and Martha Washington and with Lafayette. Why not develop an open-air museum of the American Revolution as well?! And, given the Torpedo Factory and the former homes here of famous military figures, like Admiral 'Bull' Halsey, we could have trails too for the Second World War, and for—"

"—I object to this!" shouted the prelate into her microphone, startling everyone. "This is so way off topic," she sniffed. "We're supposed to be debating the *removal* of the Appomattox statue. And not *adding* more statues like it!"

The loud crack of a gavel reverberated through the hall. "I must agree!" intoned Morenis. "And, Mr. Sifter, you're over your allotted time. We have a few more speakers to get to, and I won't have the urgent matter of the statue's removal delayed another day!"

Most of the audience applauded. The prelate preened, her pinched face aglow with spiteful triumph.

Trying to stay even-tempered at his sudden dismissal, Ted grabbed his notes, and walked back into the audience to sit down again next to Harmony. Along the way he observed the attendees, who seemed relieved at hearing from the prelate and the City Council Vice-President, and thus sure now on how they were supposed to look upon Ted's views. Negatively.

As he sat down, Ted quoted Lincoln's self-deprecating remark after his delivery of the Gettysburg Address: "That was a flat failure."

Harmony shook her head. "No." She rolled her shoulders as she considered the event. "I was carefully watching the audience reaction," she said in her mellifluous voice. "I think a lot of people liked your idea, or at least were willing to entertain it. That's why they were so quiet, relatively quiet, during your presentation. They listened to you with interest, and with surprise." She punched him lightly in his arm in a sign of approbation. Once again, she was impressed with how eloquent and persuasive Ted could be, with an individual, or before a large audience, and in this case an unfriendly one.

The next speaker was, like Ted, rather off the point. An educator, she was a stout, 37-year African-American woman. As a highly paid consultant, she'd developed curricula for the school board of a nearby Virginia town along the trendy lines of Critical Race Theory. She plunged into her talk, putting forth a plan for changing the names of Alexandria's streets, particularly those named after Confederate officers, but many others as well. The audience met her notions with bouts of sustained applause. Along with the removal of the Appomattox statue, she zeroed in on the figurine's cross streets: Washington and Prince. "Washington smacks of slave ownership," she intoned, "and Prince suggests imperialism." With a wink, Ted whispered to Harmony, "I think 'Prince' suggests catchy pop music." The speaker added that the terms Washington and Prince "reflected the patriarchy." The woman also went over her allotted time, but the Council was more tolerant of her. Harmony almost laughed when she saw Ted's pained expression during this talk. Changing the historic names of streets was the very opposite of what he proposed. "A narrow, reductionist approach, instead of a far-sighted, expansionist one," as he once it put in his professorial way.

And both she and Ted viewed Critical Race Theory as, well, racist. Its teachings impugned one race in particular, and to very young, very impressionable school children. As if they were being taught to hate one another, and their nation's heritage, and for the most superficial and irrelevant of reasons: skin color.

The two looked at each other, nodded silently, and got up to leave. Ted had a tour to give, that is, if anyone in the virus-stricken town showed up for it, and Harmony was late for her job at Amazon. They walked up the aisle to the front entrance, some spectators giving Ted hard-eyed stares, one or two giving him the thumbs up, but with most fixed on the current talker. The historian left, a prophet without honor in his own town.

Chapter 5 – Rebel with a Caustic Cause

Wilhelm "Willy" McVeigh steered his Ram ProMaster cargo van down the same road that Abdullah Hamaas had taken. The six-foot-three, 195-pound former soldier and military contractor was lost in thought. When he saw the place, on the plateau of upper King St., he braked hard, his vehicle screeching. He cursed. The last thing he wanted was a random encounter with the police, an incident of the sort that had done in his near-namesake, Timothy McVie, a man he'd admired for bold action, but disdained for his sloppy tactics.

McVeigh prided himself on his precision, discipline, and technical skill. Those attributes that served him well in the Army artillery, and as a contractor in Afghanistan and Africa. He hoped they would aid him again in the challenging days to come.

Ivy Hill Cemetery is modest in size, and most of it runs down a slope from its entrance, so it was easy to drive past it on the roadway without noticing. McVeigh decided against parking his supersized van in the few parking spaces near the graveyard's entry point. 'Too visible,' he thought. So, wheeling around, he hunted for parking in the suburban streets on the other side of the road. The King's Cloister Circle, a plush, private community in a cul-de-sac of finely kept homes, had only permit parking. So McVeigh drove past the Mormon Church and parked at Melrose St., a block further east toward the George Washington Masonic Temple. On that cloudy afternoon, the street was quiet, except for a lone, teenaged pedestrian. McVeigh crossed to the other side of the street to avoid him.

Due to the viral plague, the Ivy Hill graveyard was itself, apart from its eternal denizens, almost deserted. He slipped through the front gates and past the utility building's work shed. Its door was open; he saw the shed was chockfull of tools. He idly wondered if it contained instruments he might employ in his operations, then dropped the notion of theft as too risky. He strode past the porched administrator's building dating from antebellum times. It was unclear if the building was closed. In fact, the middle-aged male docent was in his office within, writing out a map of the cemetery's highlights—for none other than Ted Sifter. The historian had been researching the place for a possible tour, and the friendly docent, a descendent himself of several of the cemetery's more notable residents, would graciously leave the information for Ted to pick up later that week.

McVeigh, with long, powerful strides powered by muscular legs, moved away from the admin building toward the graves. He grasped a map of his own making that he'd scribbled off the cemetery's website. As a youth, growing up in central and northern Virginia, he'd often visit the haunts of his ancestors, inspirations, and grievances, and Ivy Hill was a prime location.

He went by an unusual facet of a memorial: a rectangular trench of water, filled by a firehose spigot, and leading to a 14-foot marble obelisk. The white shaft was topped by a funeral urn, and graced with an elegant frieze of a woman reposed in sorrow. Modern, freestanding shelves containing the cremated ashes of recently deceased firemen contrasted with this memorial from a distant era. It commemorated seven firefighters who'd died fighting a terrible blaze and explosion in 1855, at a china shop a block up from the King St. waterfront. The fire, perhaps set by arsonist, ignited the store's cellar, which contained a cache of dynamite for a construction site. Firemen who'd been on the

scene for hours dousing the conflagration were blown to pieces. The
tragedy affected the whole town, and thousands attended the funerals of
those killed.

The memorial was rededicated in October 2001 for the 345 firefighters
who lost their lives in the World Trade Towers attacks. An event that
Abdullah had marked with celebration, and McVeigh too, as he thought
America got what it deserved for following a "Zionist" foreign policy
with its invasions of Afghanistan and Iraq.

Thirty yards beyond the memorial is a large granite cross marking the
grave of John Woolfolk Burke, a founding member of the Burke &
Herbert banking clan. Woolfolk, literally "sheep cloth people," is a
name that could have only been coined in Scotland, the land of
Alexandria's founders. A namesake scion of that financier, Dr. John
Woolfolk Burke, had the means to take a voyage in 1912 on a ship
called the *Titanic*; he survived, and lived until 1959.

The first John Woolfolk Burke had a prominent in-town role in the
Civil War, and like other Burkes had very prominent relations buried at
Ivy Hill. These include Nicholas Trist, the U.S. envoy to Mexico
during the Mexican-American War. His wife, buried alongside him,
was Virginia Jefferson Randolph, the granddaughter of Thomas
Jefferson and Martha Wayles Jefferson, and the last person born at
Monticello. Her daughter, Martha Jefferson Trist, was John Woolfolk
Burke's wife.

As he stepped past the broken ground about the graves, McVeigh
dredged up his disdain for Jefferson. 'He actually believed, at least
much of the time," McVeigh reflected, "that bullcrap about 'all men
created equal.' And he backed it up, by banning the slave trade from
Africa, and abolishing slavery in the Old Northwest, from Ohio to

Minnesota.' McVeigh grimaced. 'No wonder Detroit and Milwaukee are such dung holes today. Jefferson, ahead of his time indeed.'

He walked about 75 yards west on the manicured grass to a high, peaked tombstone. It held the remains of perhaps the Confederacy's most able male spy, Benjamin Franklin Stringfellow, the very man Ted had referenced in his speech. McVeigh had mixed views of him, and fully negative views of his wife, Emma Green Stringfellow, who lies beside his remains.

Before their marriage, Emma Green was the daughter of a pro-Southern merchant, James Green, the owner of a large furniture factory in Old Town. He also owned a large hotel built on the former, and future, front yard of the Carlyle House. 'When the War of Northern Conquest came,' McVeigh ruminated, 'those damn Yankees seized the Carlyle Hotel for a hospital.'

This happened as James Green declined to take an oath of allegiance to the Union government, even when offered compensation for use of his hotel. So far, so good, in McVeigh's view. But then Emma Green, he thought, decided to work as a nurse at the hospital 'where,' McVeigh fumed, 'she helped save the lives of many Northern invaders.'

Actually, McVeigh was mistaken, for Emma was never a nurse at the mansion hospital. He fell into his mistaken belief by watching the television series, *Mercy Street*, which inaccurately portrayed her in that role.

Perhaps she somewhat atoned somewhat for her betrayal, he reasoned, when she aided her beau and future husband, Stringfellow, with his espionage at the Carlyle Hospital and elsewhere in Old Town.

Along with his undercover work, Stringfellow was a scout for Confederate units in northern Virginia, mostly for J.E.B. Stuart, after whom the Alexandria high school was named. One time, while scouting out terrain near the camp of the future head of the Federal Army himself, U.S. Grant, Stringfellow got within a short distance—shooting distance—of Grant.

According to a version of the story, the General was outside his tent, without guards; he was a sitting duck. Stringfellow, not believing his luck, eyed his prey, patted his pistol, and considered his next move. After a pause that must have seemed eternal, he kept his weapon holstered.

'It would have unethical,' reflected Stringfellow years later, 'to shoot a defenseless man.'

'That damn fool,' thought McVeigh bitterly, recalling the account. 'He might have turned the war around with one bullet! Some ethics!'

The ex-soldier gazed at the grave of Emma Green Stringfellow, which lies next to her husband's. After the war they married and had six children, two with middle names of Stuart and Lee, but one with the name of Stanton, Lincoln's Secretary of War. Stringfellow also "found religion", contemptible to a strict materialist like the atheistic McVeigh. As he thought further about it, McVeigh felt just as angry with Stringfellow's public acts after the war. He not only reconciled with the Union, he actually joined the Federal Army! As a chaplain, as Ted had discussed in his speech. 'To the end, too much the coward to pull a trigger,' judged McVeigh.

Incredibly, at age 58, Stringfellow found himself in Cuba, during the Spanish-American War of 1898. Along with other former Confederate generals turned Federal generals, including Gov. Fitzhugh Lee. "Bobby Lee's own nephew!" McVeigh muttered. He reflected further: 'And he served alongside, worst of all, the nigger Buffalo Soldiers in that army. Better to be caught as a Confederate spy, back in '63, and hanged!'

He took a final look at Stringfellow's peaked tombstone. Civil War lore
had it that such graves had a sharpened summit to stop mocking
Yankees from sitting on them. 'Maybe a myth,' thought McVeigh.
There were so many myths about the war, he figured. He spat on the
tombstone, and moved on.

After ruminating on these Confederate dead, McVeigh changed his
planned route through the cemetery, and saved the main reason for his
visit for last. He knew there were other graves relating to the
secessionist cause only about 200 yards away.

With his powerful stride, he rapidly approached flat, open land, about
80 yards long and 40 yards across, covered by grass and edged by
Southern red oaks, sassafras, and hickories. Tombstones 150 years old
or more were scattered about. He passed markers of the Fowle family,
the merchants who, like the McVeighs, had built some of Alexandria's
most sumptuous, antebellum homes, photographed recently by
Harmony and Ted. He eyed the one for William H. Fowle, the son of
the merchant who'd fled to Richmond, his house transformed into a
Union hospital. The younger Fowle was a Confederate veteran who'd
lived until 1903. McVeigh winced at the thought of the grand
townhomes, marks of Southern Civilization, long since swept away
from their builders, gone with the wind.

Nearby was the tombstone of the wife of John Douglas Corse, the
brother of Montgomery Dent Corse. The latter, the owner of a towering
mansion at 504 Prince St., lived a life out of pulp fiction. An
Alexandria merchant banker, he'd fought for the Federal army, serving
with its 1st Virginia Regiment, in the Mexican-American War of 1846.
Thirsting for more adventure, and wealth, he moved to the newly
conquered American territory of California, as a "49er", one year after
the war's end. After seeking another fortune there, he returned to his

Old Town business. When the Civil War broke out, he headed the town's Confederate 17th Regiment, as in the Bertha Stuart-run museum named after it. He was an infantry colonel and a brigadier general in a litany of battles that defined the war in the Eastern Theater: First Manassas (Bull Run); Second Manassas; Antietam; Fredericksburg; Gettysburg (with Gen. Pickett's division, but luckily for him on a different mission during Pickett's Charge); Cold Harbor, or Grant's disastrous "Gettysburg in reverse"; the siege of Petersburg near Richmond; and all the way to Appomattox. When Lee surrendered, Corse was detained and sent off for detention in Boston with a clutch of 15 Johnny Reb generals.

Their ill luck was to be passing through staunchly Unionist Pennsylvania when word came, on April 15, 1865, of Lincoln's assassination. A local mob formed, thirsting for revenge. But a valiant squad of Union soldiers saved Corse and the others from a lynching. Then Corse—McVeigh remembered this part of the story with disgust—took the oath of allegiance to the Union, and resumed to his financial work in Alexandria. But he had gotten what he deserved, figured McVeigh, when five years later he was blinded during an overflow meeting at Richmond, Virginia's Jefferson-designed state house, to decide whether a pro-Northern or a pro-Southern mayor should run the city. Proceedings were interrupted by a calamitous collapse that killed 62 people, and maimed Corse.

Smiling at the thought of 'turncoat' Corse's personal tragedy, McVeigh went by a fenced-off patch of ground, with an obelisk in the center, that marked the graves of the Hooe family, the one Ted humorously pronounces as "Who" in his tours. He next passed the tombstone of a Janney, not the secession conference leader, but Major Eli Hamilton Janney. He was the inventor of a metal coupler that, by letting railroad cars easily connect and disconnect, saved countless engineers and passengers from being crushed between railway cars. This Janney had served on Robert E. Lee's staff as a supply officer. Indeed, all about were Confederate ghosts, and their victories gained and lost, which seemed to fuel McVeigh's bottomless fury. He spotted the grave of Frank Hume, a rebel soldier injured at Gettysburg, and a descendant of Scottish barons and a man distantly related to philosopher David Hume. Steeped in the Civil War history of the place, McVeigh knew that Frank Hume, though successful in the postwar as a politician and distiller (the two seem to go hand in hand), was a bungling soldier. As a Confederate scout in Maryland, he once tried crossing the Potomac on a coffin, while paddling with a fence post—and got stuck in the middle of the stream. Opposing soldiers on either side of the river bent over with laughter at the sight. 'Perhaps his incompetence,' thought McVeigh, 'came from his mother, a cousin to U.S. Grant, that overrated butcher of troops.'

McVeigh frowned at the name Hume, as in the Scot David Hume. It reminded him of other thinkers of the Scottish and English Enlightenment, like John Locke, who'd inspired Jefferson about natural law, and the natural equality of all men at birth instead, as McVeigh viewed as "self-evident", the inherent superiority of certain men and certain races over others. In the endless struggle for life, he believed, marked by the rightful slaughter of the inferior.

Towards the end of the 'Confederate clearing', McVeigh came upon graves linked to the Burke tombs near the cemetery entrance, and through them to the Burke & Herbert Bank. Two of them were Herbert relatives and noted rebel officers. William W. Herbert was on the staff of Gen. Lewis Armistead, who led the spear point of Pickett's doomed charge, his troops advancing the furthest, before he fell fatally wounded. 'If only General Longstreet, that Yankee lover,' thought McVeigh gloomily, 'had attacked harder the previous day, there would have been no need for pitiful Pickett's attack!' Many historians of the South had for generations believed this about Longstreet. Ted believed the error lay with Lee, who himself admitted right after the assault, "It's all my fault." As for McVeigh, he despised Longstreet, who'd lived in the South for years, before working with the Federal government post-bellum.

William W. Herbert's older relative, Col. Arthur Herbert, was a colonel with Alexandria's 17th Regiment. His wartime career paralleled Corse's, in whose unit he served. He too was Forrest Gump-like in his ubiquity, fighting from First Manassas to Appomattox. During that period, he was the "Herbert" in the Burke & Herbert Bank, which closed during the war, as one owner was a Confederate colonel and the other a known rebel sympathizer.

The war brought a harrowing experience for banker Burke. Rebel guerillas attacked wagon trains and railways supplying Union troops throughout northern Virginia. In response, the Union Army stationed Southern hostages on supply trains to deter attacks. As a well-known banker, Burke made an effective hostage, and was forced to stand on the prows of onrushing locomotives.

McVeigh might have continued to refight 'The War of Northern Aggression' in his mind, but his discipline kicked in. He had lingered too long in that part of Ivy Hill. It was time for his main task.

He left the clearing, and fell back into his measured strides, one of the marks of his years in the military. His hulking form went down the Old Vault Road, a paved, narrow path lined with lovely hickory trees and leafy maples. The foliage formed a hairpin turn down a valley path.

There the past and present warrior encountered an elderly man, a retired Pentagon administrator, shuffling along with two brown-and-white furred collies. He was the first person McVeigh had seen in the graveyard. It was strange that cemeteries seemed even more deserted during pandemics.

Instinctively, McVeigh thought of the easiest way to slay the man, if need be. The elder, his mask pulled down his face, was fragile: a twist of his scrawny neck would be a quick means of dispatch. With so few people about, the thick forest surrounding them might hide a body for days.

But this fellow was no threat. McVeigh averted his face as they passed; the old man, lost in his thoughts, didn't realize anyone was near, even when one collie stopped, sniffed, and snarled in a low, rough voice at the stranger, leading the other canine to follow suit. McVeigh momentarily tensed, then strode ahead unnoticed.

A third of the way down winding Valley Road, the path flattened out, and he neared his destination. His pulse quickened. Intent on his goal, he didn't notice the smell of sassafras wafting through the early summer air. He seemed oblivious to natural beauty.

He entered a more recent section of the cemetery. New tombstones, their markings clearly readable, lined the way, down from a hillock of ancient burial sites, the inscribed tributes to their deceased worn away by time.

McVeigh reasoned the grave of the famous person would be commemorated somehow, and he was right. Two small bundles of flowers, only a little withered, lay on either side of the headstone. And what might have been mistaken as children's toys were stuck in the soil behind it. In fact, whoever had placed them there had mistakenly dropped a toy car, probably from the store where the other items were purchased. The trinkets appeared at first sight to be thick pens.

'But this was no mere scribbler,' thought McVeigh, 'but a man of consequence, the world's leading authority in the hardest field of hard science.'

He recalled a visit years before to Congressional Cemetery, to view the rumored hiding place of Lewis Powell, the Confederate veteran who, on the night of Lincoln's murder, severely wounded William Seward, Lincoln's Secretary of State. There he also paid his respects to the cenotaph, or honorary marker, for South Carolina Senator John C. Calhoun, the apostle of slavery and secession. McVeigh had then stumbled upon the grave of the Civil War photographer, Matthew Brady. Brady, though a Yankee from New York, had sent his staff photographers out to battlefields to photograph the generals and soldiers of both sides. Admirers had humorously left miniature plastic cameras on his grave site, as well as rolls of old-fashioned film.

For the personage at Ivy Hill, admirers had pushed toy rockets into the earth. They were tiny replicas of the great Saturn V rocket, the largest ever built, that the man and his staff, Germans for the most part, had designed. McVeigh saw that someone had also stuck small flags of black, red, and gold in the ground as well.

The visitor blanched. This was the flag of contemporary Germany and, as he saw it, the degenerate Weimar Republic of the 1920s.

The emblem indicated the national origin of the engineer, later a naturalized American citizen, who lay in the ground beneath.

Werner von Braun.

Examining the gravestone, Wilhelm McVeigh straightened out his large, muscled frame, and took in a deep breath of pride for the chief designer of the first rocket to the Moon. Followed by a frown. For the emblematic display of the rocket scientist's later-life allegiances disturbed him.

Not so much the allegiances themselves. He figured they were an act, a façade, to enable von Braun to continue his scientific work, after Germany's 1945 surrender, with the resources of an American superpower.

In any case, he had brought along things that would make amends. He looked up and down Valley Road to make sure no one was around. He slipped his right hand into his tactical pack, grazing past the Glock 29 concealed in a shoulder harness. He took out a handful of small model rockets. They looked like the Saturn missiles.

But they were actually their *precursors*: the mammoth V-2 Vengeance rockets that von Braun had developed for Adolf Hitler. 'The good Adolf', in his mind.

McVeigh much admired the engineer's handiwork for the Führer. And for his use of thousands of doomed *Untermensch* as slave workers to construct the missiles.

'The right kind of labor force for the right kind of work,' he smiled in reflection, while he stood by the toy rockets next to the grave.

His day pack contained other items. He pulled out two.

After pushing the Federal Republic's flags down below the soil, he replaced them with ensigns of a black, twisted cross, emblazoned on a white circle surrounded by blood red. The flag of the nation to whom he felt the strongest allegiance: Nazi Germany.

His main chore done, McVeigh started the stretch run of his circuit loop around the cemetery.

He strode up a paved slope to far older graves. One plot of level land held resting sites of the illustrious Fairfax family. And many Harrisons, some related to the founding Virginia family that gave America two Presidents, William Henry Harrison and Benjamin Harrison.

While ignoring the warble of the nearby glacial creek, McVeigh paused at the graves of a couple whose lives he considered admirable early on, yet nearly treasonous later. On a tombstone of darkened granite was inscribed Burton Harrison, the private secretary for 'the President', as McVeigh saw it: Jefferson Davis. McVeigh's countenance lightened for a moment, then glowered, as he remembered reading about Harrison's post-war work as an epitome of Yankee industry: running the mass transit trolley lines and horse-drawn omnibuses in, as he believed, the debased, polyglot mix of New York City. It was true Burton's wife, Constance Fairfax Cary Harrison, had been a noted poet, and the designer of the Confederate Battle Flag, the Stars and Bars. But she was proud of her family's blood ties to Jefferson, and boasted how the 9th Lord Fairfax had freed his hundreds of slaves, and even set aside funds for their education.

'Such outrages,' McVeigh reflected. 'There is so much restitution to be made.'

Down the looping path were other venerable resting places, including that of Beverly Randolph Mason, a Confederate soldier and a great-grandson of Founding Father George Mason. In McVeigh's mind, the Mason tribe had improved over time. George Mason had demanded, and over time had brought about, the end of the slave trade from Africa, a huge step toward eventual abolition. Whereas the grandson, James Mason, the Confederate ambassador to Great Britain, had done the right thing, McVeigh believed, by backing secession and King Cotton's slave plantations.

The former soldier approached the end of the path. And a brick structure cut into the hillside that separated the older part of the cemetery from the newer.

It was The Vault. A common structure in antebellum graveyards, in the days before excavation machines could quickly dig graves. In wintertime the frozen ground made such digging difficult. Thus a corpse might remain in The Vault for days or months before a proper burial could be had. The chamber held tiered, temporary resting places that resembled bunk beds, where corpses kept a strange communion before springtime's thaw, when the shad began to run in the Old Dominion's rivers, and the shadblow and serviceberry trees shot out their blossoms, and the now long-dead finally met their final resting place.

Far from feeling queasy at the thought of The Vault's eerie old innards, the idea of a pile of dead lying together amused McVeigh. He looked fondly upon the ancient receptacle of death. It reminded him of certain camps of concentration from the 1940s.

The self-styled warrior reached the exit of Ivy Hill, steering clear of a happy young couple that had appeared near the firemen's memorial. He crossed King St., thinking of the ordinance in his van. Soon he was driving into Old Town, to refamiliarize himself with the city of his youth, and the potential targets of his adulthood.

Chapter 6 – A Splash and a Dash to Desolation

Ted swam harder, while peeking ahead every eight or ten strokes, to keep himself aligned with the big orange buoy. Occasionally he stole a look at the flag poles on the pier that signaled the wind direction. On the triangular swim course, one lap was with the wind and easy, one lap was into the wind and choppy, and the third one neutral. He veered left to avoid hitting a block of wood, flotsam from the recent rains, then stroked back on course.

He wanted to make the turn into another loop before the organizers closed the river course down for the evening. As each lap around the three buoys in the Potomac was 400 yards, it meant the difference between completing 2,000 versus 2,400 yards. He'd been slowed by a rotator cuff injury, and been basically swimming with one and a half shoulders. His normal distance of 3,600 yards or so for the 75-minute open-water workout had fallen off. Getting in that extra 400 yards would be a sign his injured arm was healing.

As he approached the buoy marking the start and end of the course, he turned his eyes to the pier where the swimmers exited. If there were a group of strokers at the exit ladders, the club manager might have begun pulling the athletes in. There were half a dozen soaked figures clinging to the ladders, or already standing on the long concrete pier. Ted picked up speed as he reached the buoy, then twirled around 180 degrees to get around it fast. He glanced up, and almost smashed into a kayaker, who'd positioned her craft to block any swimmers from heading out again. His workout was over, at a disappointing 2,000 yards.

And his shoulder, and the back of his right knee—sprained the previous summer on this very course—were sore.

Ted breast-stroked over to the dock. As it had been an unusually warm and humid month, the river temperature had spiked, so he'd swum without a wetsuit. While hanging onto a rung, he pulled his suit up a couple of inches. He was in good shape for his age, but not in peak shape. Hitching up the waist band hid some of the belly fat. On deck, embarrassed by his lack of speed, he joked to the manager, who was chatting with one of his ultra-distance swimmers, that he was training for the Olympic Trials.

"The Senior Olympics?" remarked the manager gruffly from behind his mask.

"The Special Olympics?" said the ultra-swimmer, the cloth mask dipped below his

nose, breathing easily after his long, fast swim.

Ted laughed at the first comment, while noting silently the second remark was in bad taste, especially at this venue, which often hosted Special Olympics swimmers. He washed some of the Potomac off him at a make-shift shower, then limped up the dock ramp, his left knee stiff, his rotator cuff achy, up toward the broad expanse of National Harbor.

The few spectators on the 275-foot-long pier looked with curiosity and some disbelief at the athletes toweling off and slipping on their clothes. They figured it was defying death, or serious illness, to swim in a river with a reputation for being filthy. Particularly during a pandemic! But in fact, a river quality group had recently awarded that stretch of the Potomac a "B" rating, way up from the "C minus" of a few years before. Indeed, for 12 years now, over 10,000 swimmers had checked into the swim club's thrice-weekly workouts. Ted, one of the original

126

strokers, had never gotten sick from working out there, and he knew of only a few who had. And they had usually swum after heavy rains the previous night, when runoff carried dirt and trash and animal droppings into the river. Out of caution, he usually waited a full day after a storm before swimming. Especially now—who wanted to get stricken by the virus?

He hung out with the other swimmers and triathletes for just a few minutes. The sun was setting across the river on the Alexandria horizon, and he would have to bike the five miles back home in the dwindling twilight. And "hanging out" was hardly the term for it. After and before a swim, everyone was masked, and Ted couldn't wear even a loose cloth mask for a few seconds without feeling he was choking. So he stood on the other side of the pier, watching the others, but saying little, ardently wishing the pandemic, or at least its most rigorous restrictions, would go away. The virus was making communication difficult everywhere, even with his swimmer buds.

Ted snapped a small rearview mirror onto his eyeglass frame, and sidled onto his hybrid, Specialized-brand bike, and pedaled slowly up the pier. Across a narrow inlet to his right rose the harbor's 180-foot-high Ferris wheel, at the end of another long dock. The giant arc was motionless. Normally filled with pleasure seekers, the pandemic had closed it.

A dark cloud covered much of the Potomac's Virginia side. Ted imagined a storm approaching, and a lightning bolt striking the Ferris wheel, and was glad it was shut down for this night at least. He looked at another Harbor attraction, the immense and hilarious "Awakening" statue. Seventy-two feet of gray steel, cast in the image of a colossus, a half-buried giant in the sands of a narrow, artificial beach, rising up out of the earth from a deep sleep. Originally located on Hains Point across from Fort McNair, where the John Wilkes Booth conspirators had been hanged, it had been moved here as a centerpiece of National Harbor. Normally, gleeful children romped, like Lilliputians on Gulliver, atop the giant's silvery hands, knees, and feet, and his bearded, open-mouthed face. But today, as for weeks, the harbor was practically empty. Just up from the gargantuan statue, a concert stage with a wide-screen display that normally offers free weekend movies and shows had long been blank. Closed too were most of the restaurants along the river strand, and the pubs up the steeply banked roads leading to Oxen Hill, Maryland. And several blocks downriver, Ted knew from frequent bike rides in the area, the vast Gaylord hotel, convention center, and indoor mall were shuttered too.

This made him all the more grateful that his swim group, unlike many sports clubs, had remained active. The virus was not transmittable in water, according to the science, and the swim manager used this argument to keep his group operating. Indeed, the swim team was expanding its workouts and races. Addicted to daily exercise, Ted figured he would have gone crazy without the swims, and the modest amount of sports and socializing they did provide.

He turned north onto the asphalt trail flanking a narrow, pebbled beach. Six hundred yards ahead was the mammoth Woodrow Wilson Bridge linking Maryland to Virginia. On his inland side was an animal carousel, often filled with shouting children. Now, with the machinery shut off, the carved lions, bears, unicorns, and dragons decorating the seats were crushingly silent.

Ted was an officer in local bike and runner groups that had urged the bridge construction authority to put a cyclists and pedestrian trail along the mighty span. The builders had outdone themselves with two paved lanes that ran along its 1.4-mile length. This proved a great boon, and especially for the mostly black community in mostly black, Prince George's County, on the span's Maryland side, across from the mostly white community of Old Town on the Virginia side.

To Ted's delight, the bridge had become a vast outdoor gym. Each day, hundreds of runners, walkers, cyclists, and families pushing strollers and walking with their children went from one end to the other and back. And for a county suffering from a "plague of obesity", with related diabetes and heart disease, such a spur to exercise was especially welcome. And even more so during a viral pandemic in which the obese, who had a disproportionate number of "comorbidities", made up a disproportionate number of hospitalizations and deaths. Ted had for years been part of outreach to "underserved communities" for sports like triathlon, but nothing had worked better than simply building a trail alongside a bridge.

As he pedaled forward slowly, his legs stiff from the swim, and a bit bored, Ted started to think about the history of the region. Prince George's County, Maryland, like Washington, D.C., had long been a regional center of African-American life. After Lord Calvert set up Britain's lone Catholic colony among its American dominions, enslaved African blacks made up much of the work force for Maryland and Virginia's cash crop, tobacco, the use of it gleaned from the native Piscataway Indians. The names of nearby towns, such as Port Tobacco, reflect this. Among Europe's royalty and social-climbing merchants, stuffing one's nostrils with snuff became a fad and then a mark of class and success, and then a long-enduring habit of pipe, cigar, and cigarette among kings and commoners alike.

Gentry like Calvert managed vast plantations and grew fabulously rich. On the wonderfully named Oxen Hill above the future National Harbor, where slaves and freemen drove their oxen and mules, the Addison family was the region's potentate. By the American Revolution, they owned 14,000 acres of land, as well as dozens of slaves, at and beyond their Oxen Hill manor.

After the American Revolution an Oxon Hill minister, the Rev. Walter Dulany Addison, took his New Testament literally like the Quakers. He freed his slaves, and called for every other owner to do so. Yet a namesake descendent would fight for the Confederacy, with Alexandria's own 17th Infantry Regiment. Some of the huge Tidewater mansion masters, like their kind throughout the South, tended to tradition, leaning to King George during the Revolution, and to President Davis, not Lincoln, during The War Between the States. Rev. Addison became the chaplain of the U.S. Senate, and presided at Washington's 1799 funeral. Yet Washington was not technically the first American President. That was a distant relation of Addison, a Maryland merchant named John Hanson. He was picked as President of the Continental Congress, which ran the loose central government under the Articles of Confederation in the years immediately following the Revolution.

Ted wheeled toward the long incline that led up to the bridge. As always, the view back towards National Harbor, across a broad, shallow bay, was magnificent. The sparkling neon lights of the Ferris wheel shone through the mist of the evening. He stopped to take it in, glad the proprietors kept the lights on at night despite shutting down the great disk itself.

Suddenly he heard shouting behind him, friendly shouts. Two triathletes from the swim club had found a restaurant open, the only restaurant open at the Harbor. A bunch from the swim group had decided to have dinner there. These two had spotted Ted rolling slowly along, and ran him down to ask him to come along.

Ted hesitated. Dinner meant he'd cycle back home in pitch dark, probably on wet pavements. Maybe in a rainstorm. Conditions he disliked. Maybe in an early summer lightning storm, which he loathed and feared. But he was aching for more companionship during the loneliness of the pandemic lockdowns. So he pedaled over to the Irish pub restaurant to join the others. There appetizers and drinks led to dinner, and to dessert, and to other drinks and side dishes. And hours of hearty, face-to-face conversation sorely missing in recent weeks.

Ted was among the last to leave. His companions were driving home to Maryland or into D.C., and not Virginia, so it was back to his bike. By the time he neared the bridge approach again, it was past midnight. His head was clear, but his body bone-tired. He rode through air so humid it was almost dripped rain. The night was inky black, with clouds blocking the starlight. He clicked into lower gear, and carefully pedaled up the wet pavement of the steep ramp. Halfway to the summit of the bridge, he stopped, and clicked on blinker lights attached to the handlebars, the straps of his day pack, and the front and back of his bicycle shirt. 'I look,' he joked to himself, 'like a winking Christmas tree, in early summer.'

Even with the tall sound barriers separating the interstate from the trail, normally it was noisy from the rumble of traffic. That evening, due to the lockdowns and the telework spurred by the China virus, the traffic was light, the pathway almost quiet. At the summit, Ted passed some markers detailing the geology, fauna, and species of fish in the Potomac Basin, as well as the holly, sedum, and other plants native to the region. Startled, he suddenly braked at an example of such. A deer, and two of her fawns, appeared in front of him. They commenced munching on some actual flora.

They'd probably come up from the Maryland side, which had an expanse of untracked forest near inlets across from National Harbor. That area was very different from the urban landscape on the Virginia shore. Still, it was a solid thousand yards from where the creatures might have gotten onto the trail. An impressive trek. The lovely animals looked curiously at Ted and his blinking lights through large, almond-shaped eyes, as he dismounted and walked his bike past them. 'Caught like a deer in, not in headlights, but blinking lights,' he reflected humorously.

From the top of the bridge, it was mostly downhill to Old Town, and in the gloom and the wetness Ted went cautiously, and more so when a light rain began falling. His mind again wandering due to the tepid pace, he mused whether the recent demands in Alexandria to change the names of anything associated with the Confederacy would extend to this bridge named for Woodrow Wilson. The 28th President had permitted a White House showing of the silent movie film *Birth of a Nation*, a homage to the original Ku Klux Klan. Ted disdained those and other aspects of Wilson. But as a historian, and given that Wilson was a President who, whatever you thought of him, had significant achievements—the Federal Reserve, the income tax, victory in the First World War—he figured the name should be retained.

Near the end of the bridge, Ted's hands began to ache from gripping the handlebars during such a time-consuming ride. To his right side, cast in darkness, was the St. Mary's Basilica Cemetery, sanctified in 1795. A tall cypress tree among the graves pierced the night like a darkened blade, its edge point reaching out toward the George Washington Masonic Temple, murkily visible in the distance, its bright lights dulled by fog. To his left was the sound barrier, even higher there to spare the town the roar of rumbling trucks.

Then, in the stillness of that night, Ted began to hear the wail of police and ambulance sirens. Which grew louder as he pedaled on.

He also became aware of a persistent beep from the Samsung Galaxy in the back pocket of his cycling jersey. Due to the rain, he'd placed it in a plastic bag, making it harder to hear the beeps. Only one person would buzz him like that.

Twenty yards from where the bridge ends at South Washington St., he got off the bike. Just ahead to his right were the glow of swirling lights, from the cherry tops of cop cars.

He spoke into the phone, his breathing deep and regular after the snail-like progression of his ride.

"Hi, Harmony. What is it?"

"You've haven't heard?" Her voice was unusually high-pitched, and very tense.

"Heard what?"

"Where are you? Bike riding, probably?"

"Actually, I am. Coming back late from the swim, and dinner. I'm near the Virginia end of the Wilson Bridge, not far from home." He peered ahead toward the swirling lights.

"Then I'm about a hundred yards from you." Harmony's voice was anguished, almost breaking. "At the Freedmen's Cemetery."

From her tone, and the police lights, Ted sensed his stomach growing tight, like before a challenging race.

"What the heck are you doing there? This late at night?"

"Well, I saw the news, and I had just had to come down here and—"
Her voice broke off. Harmony wasn't much for crying, but Ted heard sobbing. He felt scared.

"I'll be right there."

Chapter 7 – A Jihadi's Jitters

Abdullah Hamaas now found himself unable to stay still. It was true that at first, simply from not being in jail, he had reveled in his relative freedom. Just to be done with the prison routines, to take meals when he wanted to, and to pray without prying eyes upon him. And to check the news of the world on the cable TV in the safe house, or on one of the burner phones that the escape driver Ahmed had given him. These things made the terrorist almost giddy. It was as if he were floating, like Elijah, like Muhammad, up to Paradise.

Ahmed had disappeared, put up at a safe house in Detroit. The authorities had questioned the owner of Ahmed's workplace, but reluctance to appear Islamophobic had slow-walked their investigations of his mosque. Meantime Abdullah was surprised at the newscasts about his disappearance. For several days, the escape had been an important story. But two decades after September 11, terrorism was no longer the pressing, obsessive issue it had been. As Ahmed had predicted, the media's attention quickly dwindled. Abdullah sensed that a diminished effort by the police and FBI to recapture him would parallel that lack of interest. Moreover, the media was obsessed with the pandemic.

Abdullah sized up American society and culture. Its attention span was short, its people ever eager to move on to the next sensational story. Abdullah thought this had to do with the corrupt, money-grubbing nature of the infidel society. A perceived crisis of any kind, he figured, meant higher ratings, and more money, for the social-media firms and the news networks. Instead of focusing on the eternal truth of Allah, they fritted away their time on the latest passing fancy. At the same time, Abdullah was ecstatic the decreased fear of terrorism was spurring leaders of both the political factions to demand American soldiers quit Afghanistan. That, Abdullah was convinced, would bring victories for his old comrades in the Taliban, and likely lead to the outright liberation of the country. Which could bring a big increase in Acts of Allah, or "terror attacks", as the unbelievers called them. He hoped to soon do his part in that again.

His terror cell at the Alexandria mosque warned him that he must stay in place for a time. Along with burner phones, its members communicated with him via a new, "dark Web" app, FaxSimile, that seemed impervious to snooping lawmen. They informed Abdullah they were making plans to transport him to another city, perhaps for a new act of jihad. Despite the public's waning interest in terror, he was still too "hot a property" in northern Virginia, the place of his escape. In another locale, he could safely engage in violence.

Yet Abdullah Hamaas, who had exhibited such discipline in prison, found himself increasingly impatient and restless in his new abode. His host family, devout Wahhabi Muslims, had set up a small room for him in their basement, a lodging that he found claustrophobic. He could venture outside to the little lawn, surrounded by a tall fence of solid pine wood. But such visits only reminded him of the short, daily intervals when the inmates were let out into the prison yard. He felt like he'd merely substituted one kind of incarceration for another.

Further darkening his mood were the teenage son and daughter, Khaani and Liyana, 17 and 15 years old, of the pious parents. The father and mother had concocted a cover story that Abdullah, who they called Amir, and jokingly "the Emir", was a distant relation, and a Koranic scholar and eccentric mystic. He would be staying with them before heading to Mecca and Medina on a hegira. They introduced them to

135

him briefly, after he had shaved off his beard and cut and dyed his hair, and applied a lotion that lightened his skin. They told them to leave him alone in the basement, so as not to interrupt his constant praying and meditation. The ruse seemed to work. The teens exhibited little interest in "the Emir", indeed a mild derision about his piety, and left him alone. The parents were confident they would say little, or anything, about him at their school.

But to Abdullah's horror, and the parents' ongoing chagrin, Khaani and Liyana had become largely "Americanized". They spoke English perfectly, in the colorless, modern local accent, and had forgotten much of the Arabic taught them growing up. Khaani, a middle-school running back, often wore a gray University of Virginia pullover. He dreamed of playing football at the college, and beyond. At the dinner table one night he shocked his parents, by stating he was probably getting a tattoo on his shoulder. A tattoo of an alluring young woman. When he was told about this, Abdullah had almost screamed in wrath at such a sacrilege, before restraining himself, and muttering that "such graven images are an absolute affront to God."

The parents told Abdullah they had exploded in righteous anger at the idea of a tattoo, and one with a debased depiction of womankind. He sensed, however, from the teens' negative reaction about the matter, that they saw their elders as hidebound and irrelevant. Worse, Liyana actually brought a "boyfriend" back to the house one night. The young man was an infidel and an abeed, a youth of partially African blood. Worse still, he knew, she had begun seeing him without first informing her parents.

The mosque's maintenance chief, the man who'd installed the passenger seat in the escape car, had placed security cameras on the lawn and in the living and dining room of the home's first floor. These devices wirelessly transmitted video images to Abdullah's room below. Although he had little chance of escaping out of a basement back door if police arrived, the cameras allowed Abdullah to keep an eye on things while the family members were away, and even to quietly observe the family members when they were at home. At first he felt shame about his eavesdropping, then began to rely on it as a link to the outside world, and a break from his suffocating, solitary existence.

On the video feed, he watched in disgust one evening as the daughter introduced her acquaintance to the parents. He was 18, old compared to her, and had already graduated from the high school. He seemed respectful enough, for a pagan—until he asked the father if he could have a beer. In a Muslim house! And for this encounter Liyana wore a dress well up from her ankles, like a prostitute! Abdullah assumed she was having carnal relations, out of marriage, with a non-believer. He wondered what he would do if she brought the boyfriend back to the house for such a purpose while the parents were away. He might not be able to control his rage. At least the father had come down hard on the children after the tattoo and boyfriend incidents. But this only seemed to alienate them further.

Abdullah began to worry whether the two youngsters doubted his cover story, and suspected he was the prison escapee. His parents had ordered them to leave him in peace, but it was clear the impious youths paid little heed to their elders. He made sure they didn't nose around his basement abode.

Given his dissatisfaction with the house, and his growing restlessness, Abdullah determined to risk a look about town. The parents had given him a spare key to their second car, a 2012 Toyota Camry, in the event he had to attempt a quick getaway. So one afternoon, while the father was at work, the mother visiting a relative, and the teens at school, he drove out of the neighborhood's cul-de-sac.

He had pulled the red brim of a Washington Nationals ballcap well down his forehead. He'd double-masked his face, after learning from a news video that many people, incredibly, drove while masked. As he drove along, he nervously rubbed his chin, still feeling weird from the absence of the beard that had long covered his face. And at the light-colored hair he observed in the rear-view mirror.

On his way to Old Town, he went slowly, careful to try to follow, and indeed to remember, every rule of the road, as he hadn't driven since his incarceration. Being stopped by a policeman could spell disaster. But if that happened, he wouldn't go back to jail. In his person he carried, courtesy of the mosque, a small-caliber handgun, and a sharp Turkish blade.

Proceeding down King St., he was angered again by the many churches, and imagined their replacement with a row of mosques and minarets. After passing the Washington Masonic Temple, he drove past Diagonal St., where he and Ahmed had seen the 'pagan' drum circle after the prison escape. He entered the west end of Old Town. The neighborhood was evidently prosperous, filled with specialty boutiques, women's fashions shops, antique stores, and restaurants heralding cuisines from around the world. There was a Moroccan and a Japanese bistro, and an attractive old theater turned into a Patagonia store, as well as a fire station dating from the 1770s. But almost all the places were shuttered, the street almost devoid of traffic and pedestrians. 'This fits my purpose,' thought Abdullah, 'I can stay invisible.'

The afternoon had waxed warm, hitting 87 degrees, and was Tidewater-humid. He fumbled turning on the air conditioning as he turned onto

Patrick St., as in Patrick Henry, then took a right onto Princess St. He went by three-story townhomes from Revolutionary War and antebellum times, with an occasional grand mansion, usually at an intersection down from modest workmen's homes, now themselves highly desirable houses. Unknowingly, he passed by an apartment complex that had long before replaced a mansion that its owner, the unpredictable pirate-turned-merchant, J. Swift, had ordered rooted up by its foundations, and moved to another city.

Abdullah drove on, past a scattering of funeral homes and small, well-maintained churches with African-American congregations, in the old Civil War neighborhood known as Haiti. It had been named after the 1790s slave revolt on that island nation, and for the freed American blacks who'd settled in that locale.

A few blocks further he was startled, in such an opulent town, of Colonial Era manses and gentrified neighborhoods, to drive by a slum. Or public housing, an "affordable housing project", as the Americans called it.

A tiny one. No more than a city block wide, and two blocks long, near Pitt and Princess Streets. "A boutique slum," Abdullah laughed to himself. The place seemed like an indulgence, like residential alms for the poor, in a town so affluent.

Fascinated, he parked the Camry in a side street off Princess, a block for well-off professionals residing in restored townhomes. He locked the doors, and double- and triple-clicked the lock button of the key. It would be a catastrophe to have the car stolen, and a housing project might be a crime-ridden place.

He looked around warily; the side street was empty. He tucked the handgun in a waistband, and pulled on an old sweatshirt and hood he'd found in the rear seat. He tugged the masks up toward his eyes, and walked to North Royal St.

The public housing came into view. Five rows of two-story residences, with small plots of scrubby-looking grass in between. A few children's bikes were scattered on the lawns, along with some barbecue pits. There was no bustle, no one in sight, which somehow made that hot afternoon even hotter. The contrast with the gleaming townhomes lining the streets across from the project was jarring. Abdullah knew northern Virginia had long ago had many plantations, and it seemed it still had its gentry and its servants.

He walked a block to another identical chockablock, squat residences with scrub grass in between. Here there were a small number of people outside. In the doorway of a residence nearest the street was a white-haired, heavyset black woman, with the doting, loving air of a grandmother, watching a cute little girl with ribboned hair, who was playing with a doll on the lawn. A third of the way into the grassy lot were three black men stridently conversing. Garbed in ragged T-shirts and baggy shorts, they were in their middle or late twenties, Abdullah judged. Two had thin cloth masks pushed down on their necks; the third was maskless. Though it was the middle of the workday, they weren't working. They were kaffirs, he judged, probably pagans, probably users of liquor or worse.

Something, maybe his experience in watching battles take form in Afghanistan, made Abdullah uneasy, and urged him to make himself inconspicuous. On the opposite sidewalk he stepped behind an elm tree and a Subaru SUV, with just his hooded head peaking out.

The man furthest from Abdullah, the largest of the three, handed a small, wrapped package to the man closest to the onlooker. Thin, almost emaciated, he took the package, and shook it. Then, with a lightning-fast motion, he pulled a pistol from his shorts pocket, and fired a bullet in the big man's stomach! The victim gasped in shock and agony, and fell over onto his side, his belly fat rubbing on the lawn, the grass staining red. The man in the middle was stunned, his expression frozen, expecting to be shot next.

Across the lawn, the child screamed, and wailed woefully. The old woman, despite her heft, jumped up and grabbed the girl with surprising speed, and hauled her inside the home, the door slamming shut. To Abdullah's alarm, the man with the gun rushed in his direction. 'Allah, what should I do?' he thought frantically. 'What if I'm caught up in this? I'll be doomed!' He reached for his own gun. However, the shooter veered suddenly in the middle of N. Royal and, not seeing Abdullah, sprinted toward the north end of the slum. He disappeared behind one of the low-slung buildings. The uninjured man just stood where he was, his legs quaking, a dark stain appearing in the back of his pants, as the legs of the stricken man quivered, then became still.

Abdullah knew the police would show up soon. He might be pegged as a suspect. He went back to the car as quickly as he could without running, without seeming to be a man in flight. Sweating, anxious, he glanced at the windows of the townhouses. Despite the sound of the gunshot, he could see no one looking out a window. The town was as dead as ever. No, more so, as death had taken a life from the housing project. As he unlocked the Camry's door, he glimpsed a pink piece of paper attached to the windshield. He saw that he had, in his preoccupation with locking the car, errantly parked it in a handicapped zone. He was actually relieved at the expensive ticket, as the car could easily have been towed. Not to worry: the owners of the safe house would be mailed a summons long after he'd left their home.

He drove off, as fast as he could without arousing suspicion. He swore at himself for putting himself in danger, and pledged to stay put in the safe house. But it was a promise his restless self would find difficult to keep. Soon he would find himself back on the byways of Alexandria.

Chapter 8 – Stalking a Prey

The predator, with considerable patience, had waited for the right time at the right place.

The killer knew it had to be done at night, under the cover of gloom. The fiend had waited until the moon had waned. And a night that was damp and misty. Had been casing the site for weeks. Knew it was an ideal place for the deed, as it had few visitors; in fact, it was usually deserted. And a decent proportion of the few who did come, given the place's purpose, were of the desired ancestry.

In examining the site, the predator had checked the lines of sight from the few residences that were close enough to afford a close view of the place, or for their occupants to hear a scream. It would be unlikely for anyone to see or hear what happened.

It seemed not at all unusual to cover up the face, to cloak the identity, as everyone those days was wearing a mask. Carefully pushing the hair under a skull cap, and placing a close-fitting cap over that. After much research, the predator had purchased, using a fake identity, a close-fitting shirt and trousers of synthetic material that would leave no fibers behind. And boots covered with similar materials. And a day pack to hold a rope and a hunting knife. And a 9mm Springfield Hellcat pistol, with a modified Odessa silencer. In the event the knife didn't suffice. And the predator had continued the 90-minute daily workouts, focused on weight training. After all, an encounter might come down to a hand-to-hand struggle. And this particular encounter would be followed by a need for brute strength.

"'Vengeance is mine, saith the Lord,'" the would-be killer would breathe during the dead-weight lifts, then laugh, "and vengeance is coming quick."

The first night, the predator parked on Franklin, a sleepy residential backstreet, and walked the four short blocks to the old cemetery site. In the late-night hours S. Washington St., quiet during most hours, and quieter from the pandemic, was deadly still. The human hunter walked around the perimeter of the small, historic grave sites, thinking over the approach, the attack, the retreat. The place stayed bereft of visitors. "Patience," the predator muttered, "there is plenty of time."

The following night, the fiend parked two blocks away, believing it wise to alter the routine slightly. On approaching the mound of block-long earth and grass marking the Freedmen's Cemetery, the hunter noticed the thicket of trees and bushes behind the grass of the graveyard. The predator reasoned the vegetation might provide cover for a significant stretch of an approach, and exit. Standing still on Church St., the fiend took out a small but powerful LETMY 90000 tactical flashlight, hooded to focus its beam forward. Glancing behind to ensure there were no watching eyes, the killer entered the thicket. The boxwoods were dense from the growth engendered by the approach of summer, but the way forward was passable. The predator stepped along a thin path amidst the vegetation, trying not to let thorns from the barberries catch onto the clothes. After a minute of creeping through the bushes, the predator emerged onto the gravel path leading to the memorial. There was someone there, examining the statuary. Perhaps the hunter was in luck!

The predator stepped onto grass that muffled the sounds of footsteps, and felt for the dagger, the pistol, the rope with its slick coating. Then the interloper stopped. A second person had emerged from behind the memorial's thick stone and wrought-metal construction. Two were two much to handle; a solitary victim was required.

Besides, from the faces illuminated by the dull glow of the streetlights, and from the sound of the voices, they were the wrong race. Things would have to wait. The predator turned about, and walked down the strip of lawn to the thicket, then through it again, stepping carefully through the darkness. And crossed into Church St., and Columbus St., a name the predator disdained, and back toward the car. Where the hunter was taken by surprise, by an elderly woman walking her cocker spaniel. But, fixed on her pet's sniffing and licking, she hardly noticed the passerby.

"Three times the charm," the predator murmured, "and sometimes, three times the harm, and patience is a virtue indeed." And on the third night a return journey was made.

The weather had again turned damp, both lessening the odds of a visitor yet offering opportunities. It was drizzling, which would keep some people indoors. But it also meant, if a prey entered the hunting ground, there was a smaller chance of being seen during the approach, or of a third party observing the deed itself.

This time the hunter parked two blocks away on Green St., next to a shuttered business, and across from two darkened homes. It was not far from the Greene Funeral Home, the site of the former race track. The predator made the short walk along the Washington St. boulevard, past the Monticello Lee apartments, and past the gate of St. Mary's Cemetery, with its chalk-white statue of a protective angel standing by the first grave inside the entrance. The name "Good" is inscribed on the headstone, which is dwarfed by a large granite cross. The predator grinned at the inscription. Then across Washington, then a slow walk down along the street adjoining the memorial.

Tense with anticipation, the predator realized luck might be at hand. From the dip of Church St. street could be spied, at the Freedmen's Memorial, the flickering of a cell phone. Someone was taking flash photos of the site. The person likely had more than a passing interest in the place, and might linger.

The observer stopped on the far side of the street, making sure no one was watching from the darkened residences, and peered at the memorial to see if anyone with the visitor. No one was in sight. The fiend crossed over to the thicket, and elbowed through the brambles, moving cautiously. Still, a foot stepped awkwardly on a thick root, and the predator thought for a moment that an ankle had turned. No, the joint had snapped back into place, as it sometimes did during the five-mile runs to build stamina and strength.

The predator emerged from the foliage and stepped along the lawn bordering the gravel path. Two-thirds along the way, a small, night-vision monocular was pulled from a fanny pack. The fiend peered through the eyepiece, and waited. The visitor, unaware he was being watched, turned briefly toward the direction of the observer, then turned away. He was a young man, and appeared to be the right ancestry. The observer pocketed the eyepiece and quickly strode along the grass to the top of the path. There, the knife was taken from the day pack, and placed on a utility belt, within easy reach.

The predator turned onto the sidewalk of S. Washington. The streetlamps were gray in the drizzle. The droplets were growing bigger, heavier. 'Need to hurry now,' the attacker thought, 'lest he decide to leave during a downpour.'

Down the boulevard was the parking lot of the eight-story Hunting Towers apartments, named for the hunting grounds where George Washington had stalked game. The apartment windows are some 130 yards away, making it nearly impossible for a resident to get a good read on visitors to the Freedmen's monument.

Though breathing heavily from excitement, the predator did not break into a trot, but with quick, silent strides moved the 60 yards on the wet brick sidewalk to the entrance. The fenced opening was 25 yards from the wrought-iron memorial. Once on the grass of the Freedmen's Cemetery, the predator slowed. Below him were the unmarked graves of fleeing slaves who had reached Union lines during the Civil War; many of them had perished from the privations of war.

Looming in front was a strange, wide shaft of metal swirling up 10 feet to an iron circle seven feet in height. The ring was ragged and twisted, like a crown of thorns. Statues on it and on the ground depicted desperate figures kneeling or bowing down. Standing in the halo-like circle, at the summit of the shaft, was the statue of a black man, with a worried visage, yet proud and erect. On the ground 20 feet to the right was a kind of concrete box, open-aired yet bunker-like, garnished along its top with a horizontal line of thick, thorn-like steel. Inside it were inscriptions describing the plight of the fleeing freemen. Most of the quotations were from Harriet Jacobs, the humanitarian who'd set up schools and hospitals for those Civil War Era escapees.

The unlucky visitor had slipped behind one of the memorial's displays. Before him rose the sculpture of an empathetic black woman reaching her hand down to the figure of an enslaved man.

The predator slinked across the lawn, and slipped behind the memorial. He stepped up to the statues, and stated in a low, friendly tone: "Hello. Anybody there?"

Stepping out in the gloom was a man, about 30 years in age, under six feet tall, neatly dressed, with short, kinky brown hair. He had on no rain slicker; his hair and clothes were damp. He wore no mask, making his facial expressions evident.

"Yes, there is," he replied softly, laughing a bit in a good-natured way. To the predator, he appeared to be of Latin and African descent. Dark-skinned. More African than Hispanic. There was no one with him. This would do nicely.

"A fellow history enthusiast, I see," said the predator, walking up to the visitor, adding, "African-American history."

"I suppose," the man smiled. He noticed that this other man, though carefully masked, didn't seem to mind him being maskless. "I've never been to this place, never saw it up close before."

"It's impressive, isn't it?" purred the predator. Though he actually thought the unusual group of sculptures ugly, the inscribed slabs plaintive, the whole thing a cheap and thrown-together sop.

"It's very moving," said his prey.

"Oh, and did you see the best part? Over here," he said, pointing, "the thing that links the woman to the man below her."

"What's that?" said the prey, curious. He was a somewhat naïve and trusting fellow, and that night he was utterly unsuspecting. He stepped over to the rear of the statue, which blocked the view of anyone who might be passing along Washington St.

The predator gestured to a spot at shoulder height, midway up the artwork. In the dark, the visitor stepped over to it, looking at the metalwork intensely.

"Where is it?" he asked. "I don't see it."

The predator stepped behind him. "Oh, it's right in front of you. Look closely." The tall, muscular figure grasped the knife. Then thought of a better, quicker, quieter move. Putting into play a maneuver learned in martial arts classes. The fiend drew back his right hand—and chopped

148

it hard against the carotid artery of the visitor. The latter blacked out immediately, and dropped to the ground.

His attacker dropped down to him like a jackal. He cradled the young man's neck on his lap, and grasped his skull. With a powerful turn of his arms, he broke the neck.

He was elated at this swift success. He rose, and stole glances toward Church and Washington Streets. And St. Mary's Cemetery, its alabaster angel dimmed by the mist. He could see no one, hear no noise. No one could see nor hear him.

Moments later, a landscape worker's truck did come rolling down the boulevard. But the driver didn't slow or stop, and disappeared into the fog of Old Town.

Now the real work could begin. The predator took out the rope, and grabbed the knife again.

Chapter 9 – The Garish Gallows of the Sodden Night

Ted cycled off the bridge's bike path, tapping lightly on his wet brakes. He wheeled slowly into the soft glare of S. Washington St. He rubbed rain drops from his glasses with wet fingers. Across the road was a startling sight.

A half dozen police cars and ambulances, scarlet lights whirling and ablaze, had been hurriedly parked near the gate of the memorial. Dozens of police and emergency personnel stood around the statue, the concrete memorial, its grounds, and the sidewalk. Some of the cops were shooing away a few fast-arriving reporters to protect the crime scene. One of those sent back slipped onto the wet grass; two pulled out cells to contact their newsrooms.

This sight was unusual enough, but the portable klieg lights the cops had set up to illuminate the sculpture revealed something far stranger, and horrific.

Atop the soaring work of art, a dead man was hanging from a rope attached to the metal ring. The corpse dangled alongside the sculpted freeman. The deceased's shirt was ripped open, his pants legs torn, and even from across the way Ted could see his limbs had been horribly mutilated. The victim's face looked African-American. His bloodied face was slack-jawed.

It looked for all the world like an Old South lynching.

Fixing his eyes on the dead man, Ted walked his bike across the road. And jumped aside when a van from a TV station barreled past, before making a screeching U-turn to park along the curb.

Ted felt his phone buzz. He looked at the text:

"Do you see me?"

Harmony was waving from outside the entrance gate.

Ted waved back and headed over. As he neared her, he looked toward the corpse. From closer up, he could make out puncture marks on the chest, legs, and arms. It looked like someone had gone over the fellow with a pitchfork.

But that registered only after Ted took in the gruesome sight of the man's face. His head was at a brutal angle, swiveled away from the neck. He had African, and maybe Hispanic, features too, but the post-mortem pallor and the bright lights made his skin look bluish-white, the blood having drained away. He looked like an albino black man. A light rain was falling, and the rain mixed with the blood, and dripped down in a sickening, yellowish hue.

Standing on the sidewalk, Harmony's svelte, five-foot-seven frame was cast in shadows. But on reaching her, he saw that her light bronze skin had flushed with an almost greenish hue. This happened when she grew very excited, or dismayed.

"You got here quick," he began.

"When I saw it on my news feed," she said, her voice almost squeaky from emotion, "I jumped on my bike." Her townhouse apartment was just eight blocks away.

"Who could have done this?" she muttered. "Why?"

"It's a terrible thing," he answered.

She noticed that Ted seemed calm, at least on the surface. That trait of his of being icy-cool in a stressful setting. Though his face had a cast of concern, his breathing was deep and regular. The moisture on his cheeks was from the mist, not from a sweat produced by fear.

Ted had another trait, of going into places where he didn't belong. Almost unthinkingly, he walked away from Harmony, and went through the open entrance gate and toward the memorial. Harmony hesitated, then followed.

On the lawn between the statue and Church St. to the right, Ted saw his Alexandria police acquaintance, the thick-bodied detective, Dmitri "John" Greco, scribbling onto a notepad. Several of the younger cops near him were keying into iPads.

Greco looked at Ted, and frowned. But he didn't tell the historian to leave. "Don't get any closer, Sifter," he said, his gruff voice thick with tension. "And they'll probably kick you out any second." He saw Harmony, nodded almost imperceptibly, and looked away.

Harmony was surprised the detective had allowed her and Ted to remain. It must be true what Ted had told her, that he'd helped Greco out with some previous cases and the detective was grateful.

A few steps from the duo, Greco spoke into his phone. In between siren blasts, Ted caught much of what he said: "…dead perhaps an hour…broken neck BEFORE the stabbings, we think…a {garbled} knife…no bullet entries…rope burns {garbled]…no sign…foot prints?…blood loss massive…arterial {garbled}…African-Am…"

The detective slid his cell into his trousers, and said matter-of-factly to Harmony, "John Doe for now. We found no ID on him…"

Though surprised he had spoken to her, Harmony answered, "And it could be a while, as there seem to be no video cameras in the cemetery." She waved her hands beyond the statues. Indeed, there were none. Greco looked hard at her, then nodded. She was probably right.

Ted took a step toward the detective, spread out his palms, as if in supplication, and told him, "This will have a terrible impact in town, and downtown," meaning D.C. As he often did, he was thinking of the social or historical implications of things, not the thing or the person itself. Greco looked at him quizzically.

"This could cause Alexandria to explode," Ted explained. "The murder, the slaughter, of a black man, a minority, in a town, a region, already on edge."

He thought of something else. The horrific image facing him seemed familiar somehow. He couldn't place it. But he had an excellent memory for persons, dates, and the other errata a historian dredges up. He knew it would come to him eventually. He mumbled absently: "I've seen this before."

The cops were about to try to find out who the victim was, for a policeman and a policewoman had stationed tall ladders next to the corpse dangling from the ring of metal. With difficulty, they loosened the noose from the top of the seven-foot-high arc. During this the female cop stopped, and gagged, her vomit splattering onto a statue below. The other cop kept tugging at the rope. Two emergency personnel workers clambered up the ladders to assist him.

Finally, the noose gave way. Those atop the ladders grabbed the corpse, blood dripping onto their masks, necks, shirts, boots. Then all four, grunting, their backs aching, lurched down with the body to the sodden grass.

Chapter 10 – Anatomy of a Kill

The predator first made sure his victim would never wake again. He turned the young man over, face up. He got out his Ka-Bar 1213 dagger. He bent down, arching his body away from the neck, and dug the long, stainless-steel blade into the man's jugular. The victim gasped, his eyes still shut. His killer stepped away from the spurting fountain of blood.

The unfortunate's eyes opened for a moment. His receding thoughts took in the dim figure of the sculptured woman on the metal ring. Was she an Avenging Angel? Surely not a Guardian Angel. His eyes twitched closed, never to know the image was an allegorical figure of Compassion.

The predator waited for the flow of blood to subside. He looked about, sweeping his eyes up and down Washington St. and Church St. All around him was darkness. He was confident no one had seen him, none were watching. He got back to his work.

He cut open the dead man's shirt and trousers, exposing the flesh. A terrible image came into his mind. Of a terrible event, from long ago. His pulse, already high, raced higher. He pushed the memory aside. 'Focus, I should focus, focus,' he told himself. He took deep, slow breaths; his heart rate slowed.

The predator started with the chest and stomach, bending over, stabbing and slashing with quick cuts. A dozen times, with blood still flowing from the still-warm corpse. Then he cut and gashed the face. Then he kneeled near the man's legs, and quickly slashed them, again and again.

"Finally, *the piece de resistance*," he mumbled, his heart beginning to race again. Then suddenly he stopped, and crouched low. An Uber sedan emerged down Washington St., near the Hunting Towers. Driving fast. Good, the killer thought. The driver was unlikely to look this way, and unlikely to notice anything if he did.

As the vehicle faded through the dark mist into town, the killer grabbed the rope. It was weighted on one end. He tossed that end through the iron mesh at the top of the ring. He tied the other end around the dead man's neck, fastening it securely.

Now came the hard part. His weight training would serve him now. In fact, he had practiced the procedure at his home, by throwing the laminated rope around an attic rafter, then groaning and sweating and hauling up 160 pounds of weight. He pulled and grunted and pulled, and steadily hoisted the body to the top of the sculpture. The corpse dangled alongside the male statue at the top, the allegorical figure of Hope. He laughed at the irony. Both the faces of the sculpted man and the murdered man now looked out onto Washington St.

The predator secured the rope to the feet of the female figure. He pulled on the cord; it held. He gazed upward. The rope was snug; the corpse swung slightly in the mist. The killer gloried in the ghastly sight.

Time was even more of the essence now. The whole procedure had taken only minutes, but seconds seemed eternal with a sudden concern he'd be spotted. He wiped the knife and placed it in a lined pocket. He padded his gun, to make sure it hadn't fallen out during the slashing and hoisting. With the shrouded flashlight, he checked the ground for anything else of his.

He allowed himself one more look of admiration at the dangling corpse, a mangled, blue-white specter in the soft glow of the moistened night.

He made his way back along the lawn and the gravel path. The predator entered the thicket, his light speckling the way forward.

At the edge of the bushes, he paused. Church St. was bereft of passing vehicles. Only a couple of lamps shone from the houses of the George Mason apartments; he could discern no one at the windows.

Quickly he walked back to the car. He encountered only a stray dog which, sniffing blood, crossed to the other side of Franklin Street to avoid this strange man with a strange scent. After a furtive glance about, he placed his day pack and his fanny pack into a large plastic bag in the car trunk. Elated, yet again forcing himself to focus, he drove home, scrupulously observing every traffic law.

The predator drove into the garage of his house. Inside, he peeled off his trousers, shirt, shoe coverings, gloves, hat, masks, and skull cap. Although it had been a relatively clean killing, there might be bits of blood and other material on the exterior of his stuff. All the items were stashed in the plastic bag, tightened securely. He would dispose of the material later. He knew just the place for it.

On that warm humid night, he took a warm shower, scouring his face and hair, torso and limbs. A passage from the Christian Bible came to him. Of Pontius Pilate unable to wash his hands of guilt from consigning Jesus to a brutal beating, then death on the cross. And he recalled a passage from the theater, where Lady MacBeth could not rid her hands of blood-stained spots. He laughed. He had no guilt. He felt refreshed, a conscience vibrant and clean.

From an ablution, an absolution, of blood.

Chapter 11 – On Closer Inspection

The police had opened things up a bit. A local Fox News TV crew and three reporters from *The Washington Post* strode by Ted and Harmony, toward the crime scene tape strung around the statuary area. Ted watched them, and Harmony, watching Ted, realized what he was thinking. She knew that, because he wrote free-lance articles on tourism and history, he kept handy a press card from the Washington Journalists Association. It was a simple paper card, not even laminated, but he sometimes flashed it to get into media-related events.

Harmony had at times found herself with Ted when he decided to do something that was stretching, if not breaking, the boundaries of the law or accepted behavior. Her practice was to object to his idea and then, despite herself, go along with it.

"I wouldn't do that if I were you," she told him.

Ted paused for a moment, realizing his mind had been read. "Just getting a little bit closer," he replied, "would give us a much better look." Using the reporters ahead of them as a "cavalry screen", a military term Ted liked to employ, to shield them from unwanted eyes, they stepped toward the statue. Harmony was nervous, but she saw that Ted not only looked calm, but acted like he belonged there as much as anyone. She wondered at this trait of his, of being able to fit in immediately with strangers or a novel locale.

A burly young cop checked the IDs of the newspaper reporters, and waved the TV crew in close to the police tape. He glanced from Harmony to Ted, and barked at the latter: "Who are you?"

Ted flashed his press card, and said, fibbing some, "We're with the Washington reporters' group." The cop replied brusquely: "Don't get much closer. And don't stay long." He added: "And don't even think about crossing that tape."

Using the journalists to cloak their movements, the duo crept up toward the crime scene. The wounds on the victim, glowing in the klieg lights, were now starkly clear.

Ted had visited this cemetery many times, sometimes on the way back from a swim. In recent years the history of slavery had become a "growth industry", and Ted had long incorporated tales about slaves and early civil rights leaders into his tours and books. He believed in giving all sides of a historical drama, whereas for generations the story of the enslaved had been, as Frederick Douglass put it, "the half not spoken." Ted reflected on the graves of the scores of freedmen and women, right underneath his feet, and the many children who'd succumbed to diseases ravaging the freedmen's encampments in the neighborhood here. And now this horror.

His eyes riveted on the corpse, dangling from its ring of symbolic metal thorns. Some of the blood of the dead man had dripped on the adjoining statue of Hope. Apart from the atrocity itself, Ted was troubled by something else. He blocked out everything else, focusing on the bloodied body. That image, a disturbing image, and akin to an old photograph, flashed again in his mind. Then the image disappeared, like the memory of a dream that fades when waking up. He figured the figment would come back to him. Or would it? His almost photographic memory was drawing a blank. He felt a twinge of fear. It seemed his mind was deliberately trying to erase, not recall, the image, like when it tries to forget a nightmare. Abruptly he turned his gaze away from the corpse.

Harmony broke into his thoughts again, remarking: "He was a bold killer."

"You mean the extreme violence?" asked Ted, focusing his eyes back on the dangling body.

"I mean, to walk into this cemetery, carrying his victim maybe, and stringing him up here, then walking out the front gate again. I bet somebody saw him, and he'll be captured soon."

Ted pondered this. He knew the visitors to the cemetery were few, though the numbers had been growing, before the pandemic, given the growing interest in the slavery saga. He looked at the grass around the statuary, and tried to make out if it had been disturbed. The thicket of police made that difficult. "It's quite possible," he said, "that he, or she, killed him here."

"That would be an unusual woman," replied Harmony, "to have the upper body strength to hoist a body up to the top of the statue."

"Unless there was more than more killer," replied Ted. His ability to look at a crime from many different angles was a reason the local police not only tolerated Ted, but used him as a resource in some of its investigations.

"We're assuming," he continued, as the duo gazed at the desecrated memorial, "the killer or killers entered and left through the front entrance. I wouldn't have."

"What do you mean?" Harmony replied. She looked at the metal fence surrounding the visible part of the cemetery. "How else could he get in here?" Then she briefly recalled a night the previous autumn when Ted had taken her to Old Town's long-abandoned railway line under the Wilkes Street tunnel. It had been a full moon, in a rather romantic locale, and they had nuzzled together.

"You don't mean a secret passageway, do you?" She knew archeologists were finding additional graves of freedmen and women under the grass and sidewalk. In fact, specially colored bricks on the sidewalk marked the sites of individual graves. Could they have discovered a tunnel too?

"Not secret, just not obvious," Ted answered. He pointed to the high ground of the cemetery behind the memorial. "The surrounding fence only goes so far. The far side is open-ended, and heads along a gravelly path. Hidden from view. I found it when poking around here, doing research for a tour. If I were the murderer, that's how I would approach."

Harmony said, "Maybe we can take a look there next, and—"

"—Who the hell are you?!" screamed a harsh male voice.

A tall, sallow-faced man with furtive eyes, garbed in a business suit, pricey coat, and wing-tipped shoes, stood before them, blocking their view of the statuary. Both Ted and Harmony, both news junkies, recognized him as Andrew "Andy" Cabell Comitas, the 38-year-old Associate Executive Assistant Director of the FBI's Washington region. He stared at Ted, walked quickly over, and checked his 'press pass'.

"You don't have the proper credentials for this!" he hollered. "Get out of my investigation!" Ted knew that "Andy" Comitas, who'd reached a high status in the FBI at a young age, was exceedingly ambitious. His eyes were already set on the post of FBI Director, if not higher in the Justice Department. He was said to be ruthless toward anyone posing a threat to his advancement.

Harmony's face blushed from the verbal lambast. Ted stood silent, expressionless, icily eyeing Comitas. Harmony sensed he wanted to throw a punch at the FBI man, "go Eight Avenue" on him, as Ted would say, and she prayed he wouldn't.

Yet despite her concern, she sized up the two. They were roughly the same size, both sturdily built, though the lawman had a modest paunch, while Ted was in very good shape. She figured Ted could take him.

But before Comitas, or Ted, could say or do anything else, they heard footsteps behind them.

John Greco approached the FBI man slowly, but deliberately. The short yet sturdily built detective looked at Comitas with a set, emotionless face.

"They're allowed here," he stated. "On my discretion." He looked at Ted. "They'll be leaving soon."

Comitas nearly snarled. He stared down at Greco. "They're leaving *now*! On my order." He sucked in his stomach, and rose up on the tips of his wingtip shoes. "This is *my* crime scene. The FBI is taking over from the locals, the local authorities."

Harmony had read about MS-13 gangs crossing over from D.C. into Alexandria, and how Comitas and Greco had clashed over which of them had jurisdiction over the hoodlums.

"On who's authority?" shot back Greco, his sharp green eyes glistening like a reptile's. "I wasn't informed about it."

The contrast between the two men's attire was marked. Greco with his off-the-rack trousers, patent-leather shoes, cloth raincoat, and a too-small straw hat, and Comitas with his dress shoes and dark business suit with a cashmere overcoat.

"The Director's orders," snapped Comitas. "With backing from the Attorney General's office." He pushed back his dark brown locks, hair gel sticking to his fingers. "The AG approved my request within this very hour. This is a big story, nation-wide, international—we won't take any chances." He looked toward the TV crew, then back at the detective. "Your police will be reporting to me." Even in the darkness and drizzle, Harmony could see Greco's face redden. He started to say something, then bit his lip, then started to speak again. But Comitas, eager for an interview, walked away toward the TV journalists. Looking over his shoulder, he glared at Ted, and shouted, "Out of here!" They looked at Greco, who stayed close-mouthed. He turned slowly, and walked back toward the statue and to a forensic expert examining the murdered man's wounds.

Harmony thought Ted would stay, if only to spite Comitas, and was surprised when he said: "Let's go." They left through the front gate and retrieved their bikes.

Ted normally took a path home that paralleled the Interstate, while Harmony would ride through Old Town to her studio loft. But Ted, with a mysterious look on his face, said, "Follow me." Harmony got on her carbon Felt race bike, which she'd taken to get quickly to the crime scene, and Ted got on his heavy aluminum hybrid. They rode away from the lawmen and the reporters and went slowly up Church St. Harmony didn't have long to find out what Ted was up to. Along the rear of the cemetery, out of sight of the investigators, Ted motioned her to stop at the thicket of bushes and trees.

On the sidewalk, Ted placed his bike against a No Parking sign. He asked Harmony to shine her powerful Bontrager bike lights onto the edge of the growth. She looked nervously up the hill toward the cemetery. "Ted, I don't know if this is a good idea." But she carefully walked a path of illumination along the edge of the little forest. Ted followed the line of light, the embedded cleats of his bike shoes crunching softly on the sidewalk. He looked hard for footprints, or for a broken branch or twig. They got to the edge of the thicket, then reversed course, with Ted entering the thicket, and closely examining the ground and the vegetation. Nothing.

They were wet, upset, and exhausted. Ted called off the search. They departed, promising to get back in touch with each other the following day.

The next morning, not long after dawn, Harmony was in bed. Awake, and red-eyed, after a sleep punctuated by nightmares of a man torn to pieces by wild hounds grasping knives in their paws.

She heard her phone vibrate. It was Ted.

"Hard to sleep last night," he announced. "I went back to the thicket right before dawn. Found a little piece of cloth on thorns. Maybe nothing, maybe something."

Harmony was swiftly awake. "Turn it over to the FBI?"

"No" Ted responded. "I'll make it a gift for Greco. He looked like he could use a break."

"You know," said Harmony, "when the police, and FBI, look for footprints around the back of the park, they may find some from your bike shoes."

"Well then," replied Ted non-plussed, "I better turn this cloth over to Greco right away."

As he hung up, she could hear his smile through the phone. She didn't smile, as the nightmare came flooding back to her.

Chapter 12 – Rediscovering a Satanic Shrine

Soon after his visit to Ivy Hill Cemetery, Wilhelm "Willy" McVeigh embarked on a more ambitious pilgrimage. He went bushwhacking through a Maryland forest, a few miles north of the National Harbor pier of Ted's swimming group. Off to a place of true heroes, as McVeigh saw it, unlike the rebel turncoats like Stringfellow, and Burke & Herbert, who reconciled with the Union after the Confederacy's fall. But his destination hadn't been easy to find. For the location of the shrine in question was a state secret.

It all went back to summer 1942, and a dangerous mission, initiated by the Führer himself, to sow mayhem and destruction in America, on which Germany had declared war seven months before.

It was a critical time. The Wehrmacht was surging eastward, from the Donbas, the Don river basin, in the southern Ukraine of the Soviet Union, its goal the capture of Stalingrad, and the vast oil fields near Soviet Georgia.

It was still months before large numbers of U.S. troops could arrive in England and North Africa. But America was already sending huge amounts of supplies to Britain and the Soviets. The "Arsenal of Democracy", as President Franklin Roosevelt cynically called it, thought McVeigh, was shipping trucks, airplanes, food, and other necessaries to Moscow, no democracy but an arch foe of the Nazis. Russia was reeling from the German invasion, but America might help it survive.

So, to wreak havoc on America's means to make and transport war supplies, Hitler and his foreign intelligence agency, the *Abwehr*, sent saboteurs into the U.S. That summer, U-boats landed two squads of four men each off Long Island and Florida. They brought along tons of explosives. They were ordered to blow up dams, bridges, canals, munition plants—the infrastructure critical to democracy's arsenal. Teams of other deadly saboteurs would follow in their wake. They were specifically ordered, and McVeigh smiled as he recalled this, to blow up Macy's department store in Manhattan, because the emporium was Jewish-owned.

However, and McVeigh grimaced as he recalled this, while trudging along a country trail bracketed by oak trees, the operation was betrayed by two of the saboteurs. One contacted the FBI headquarters in Washington which, after verifying the outlandish plot, soon hunted down the other six men. A military tribunal followed. The whistleblowers got prison sentences; the other six the death penalty. Which in 1942, at the Washington City Jail near Congressional Cemetery, meant the use of "Old Sparky", the descriptive nickname for its electric chair.

Their execution presented President Roosevelt with a problem. With prescience, he feared the placement of their remains in a public cemetery might encourage sympathizers to turn their graves into a Nazi shrine. So he directed their burial to take place in a little-known potter's field, deep in a forest above the Maryland bluffs opposite Alexandria. It was to that site that McVeigh was making his way, on a hot and humid morning, through dense woodland.

The former soldier had become aware of the graves from a story published a decade before. On how repairmen from the Potomac Electric Power Co. had found wreaths that neo-Nazis had placed at the burial place. The Park

Service removed the unwanted mementoes, and the location of the graves was deleted from web sites and other parts of the public record. But McVeigh became fixed on finding the graves. He'd hired a "black hat" hacker to sift through the electronic files of the National Archives for the final resting sites of the saboteurs. The hacker was a purple- and red-haired, nose- and mouth-ringed young woman who reminded him of the cyber sleuth in *The Girl with the Dragon Tattoo*. She was curious why her client might want the unusual information, but thought it wise, as with most of her customers, not to ask. Especially with this muscular man with a military bearing and a facial expression that screamed, 'Don't even bother to ask.' Besides, he paid her well in finding what he wanted.

For a forest thick with brambles and thorns, McVeigh wore a long-sleeved hunting shirt and fatigue pants that hugged his hunting boots. He little cared if he left evidence of himself along the trace, as he expected no one else to come there in a long time, long after he had left the region. The day was warm, and humid—typical Tidewater weather in late spring or summer—and he wiped trickles of sweat from his forehead. He'd tightened the frame of his sunglasses to stop them drooping from the sweaty brim of his nose. He carried concealed, just in case, a Glock 29, and a small box of 10mm ammunition. But his main cargo was in the knapsack. The special gift inside was heavy, but he was a vigorous man. Surely it would be worth the exertion.

He read the GPS coordinates from a Samsung cell strapped to his left wrist. He preferred a phone from Korea, a nation of hardy fighters, to one from Apple, a U.S.-based firm, and thus, as he saw it, the product of a degenerate, mongrelized land. 'I should dub the Koreans 'Honorable Aryans',' he joked to himself, 'as the Führer called his Imperial Japanese allies.'

McVeigh saw from the map image he'd crossed over the Maryland border, and was now in the Blue Plains area of D.C. Not much further to go, he thought, sweating yet smiling, as he entered a faint trace in the woods.

He stopped short, as a deer and her fawn shot across the path with remarkable speed. The mother paused, and eyed him impassively, coldly. 'Was this human a danger to her brood?,' she seemed to be thinking. McVeigh almost wished he'd brought along one of his hunting rifles. Deer bones, he reflected, had once been a sacrificial offering among the ancient Nordic tribes he admired. But a gunshot in even a practically deserted woodland might bring unneeded attention. Besides, he had a much better honorific than animal remains. He trekked on, and the deer, thoroughly alarmed, fled with her charges. Mopping sweat from his neck, McVeigh stopped for a rest under a linden tree. '*Unter den Linden,*' he said to himself, recalling the boulevard in one of his favorite cities, Berlin. He pressed the photos section of his cell, and displayed the original tribute to the saboteurs. On a small granite slab were carved the words:

"In Memory of the German Abwehr, Executed August 8, 1942".

The memorial stone also listed the six men who'd been electrocuted. 'Such fine Nordic names', McVeigh reflected. 'Heinrich, Haupt, Werner, Hermann, Thiel.' Then he frowned at Thiel. That was the same name of a traitor in German intelligence who'd given the British a lead on Germany's heavy water plant in Norway, leading to its destruction by commandos. It had been a key component in a potential nuclear weapons program. 'If only Berlin had built The Bomb first,' he mused. 'World Empire Gained!'

The slab's inscription ended with the phrase, "Donated by the N.S.W.P.P." The National Socialist White People's Party. It was the successor, evidently even more race-obsessed, to the National Socialist Workers Party of America, better known as the American Nazi Party. McVeigh pocketed the phone and, tramping onward, encountered a wall of bushes blocking the path. He took a machete from his belt and slashed at the undergrowth. He was sweating profusely now, but shrugged it off, thinking of the special knowledge he'd gleaned from the nose-ringed hacker. The authorities had recently put out disinformation, fake news, about the graves of the saboteurs. They wanted the public to think a stream, a small tributary of the Potomac, had washed away the graves. In fact, they were still there, weathered, but intact.

He reached a clearing, then a copse of trees, and eyed the GPS. He was close. McVeigh smelled the odor of a westerly breeze carrying the stench of a sewage treatment plant. It was a huge facility for handling waste from the Anacostia River, a far larger Potomac tributary. 80 years before the Navy had built weapons there that helped defeat the German U-boats and the battleships of Imperial Japan; some of the toxic wastes from manufacturing the arms still lined the river bottom. McVeigh hardly noticed the smell, so excited he was at nearing his destination. He angled to the left, plunged into waist-high forsythia, cursed at a thorn that pricked an ankle—and he was there!

Before him was a tattered graveyard, the potter's field from long ago. A clearing about 15 yards long and 70 yards wide, blocked off by a decrepit, five-foot-high metal fence, with strings of rusted barbed wire running along the top. In the little cemetery were six stone tombstones stretching left to right, unmarked except for numbers, which read 276 to 281. The place was utterly quiet, bereft even of springtime songbirds. The smell of the wastewater fumes drifted in.

Only the side of the graveyard facing him had a fence. So McVeigh walked through low bushes to get around it and come up to the graves. He took off the knapsack, took out a burlap bag, and took from it a marble slab, two feet long and one foot wide.

'Where to place my fine personal memorial?' he wondered.

He picked one of the middle tombs, of a saboteur, who'd loudly sworn continued allegiance to the Third Reich on the day of his electrocution. Savoring the moment, McVeigh placed the slab on the side of the tombstone.

It read: "In Memory of Our Race Heroes, Who Gave Their Lives, For Fatherland and Führer, August 8, 1942". Then it listed the six names of those executed. Then the final phrase: "From an Admirer, Still Inspired by Their Vision. Inspired into Aktion." He considered the German spelling for the final word a nice touch.

He sat squatting by the graves for several minutes, as if in prayer. Indeed, he thought of Valhalla. The destination of any Nordic warrior perishing in battle.

He got up, his mind filled with admiration for the slain saboteurs, loyal to the end, and with burning hate for those who killed them. He left the graveyard, sweeping his feet back and forth to erase his boot prints. Yet there was little to worry about. By the time anyone found his tribute, the rest of his mission would be long fulfilled.

Chapter 13 – Considering the Case

Ted and Harmony were relieved to find a restaurant that was actually open, and especially this new, open-air place right on the riverside. The airy setting took away a bit of the horror of the Freedmen's Cemetery. The broad Potomac spread before them, the water calm for the time being, despite the intermittent clouds and the strong tide flowing upriver all the way from the Atlantic.

The owner of the Starboard bistro was plagued, so to speak, with bad luck. Picking the Ides of March, March 15, for a grand opening asked for trouble, and trouble came. A week before that date, as cases from the pandemic soared, he was forced to hold off the launch until May, and with restrictions.

Thus at lunchtime the two sat at their small table by the riverside bar, with empty tables, per the regulations, between them and any other guests. Who were few, as tourists and residents had largely abandoned eating out, or going outside for almost anything.

Harmony sipped an ice tea while checking her cell for updates.

"You care more about your news feed," joked Ted, "than feeding yourself."

Harmony smiled slightly, her normally glowing countenance bleak. "The Freedmen's murder is the Number One story in the country," she announced. "Maybe the world." The pupils of her iridescent eyes widened. "But there's no news about the identity of the killer. Or killers."

"I know," said Ted, glumly. "I checked with Greco before getting here."

"'Every agency of the federal, city, and state law enforcement,"
Harmony quoted, "'is looking into it.'" She shook her head firmly.
"There's no way the killer will get away."

Ted replied, "Maybe. Maybe not. The online *Washington Examiner* had
a breaking story, a leaked story, about the piece of clothing I turned in
to Greco." He paused. "It isn't leading anywhere. They traced the
fabric to a pair of pants in the inventory of River Armaments. It's an
Army-Navy store that was on the Old Town waterfront for years." A
professorial look came over him. "It once unwittingly sold explosives
to bank robbers, bank robbers up in Canada. And it's said it furnished
some of the weapons for the Iran-Contra deal, a big scandal back in the
'80s.

"Nowadays the store is up on upper Duke St., by the big Post Office. It
has computer records of three people who've purchased those type of
pants in the last ten years. It's a rare item." Ted stroked his left cheek as
he recalled the details. "Let's see. One person is deceased. And one is
an elderly woman, with health problems, Greco told me. The third was
a male, apparently from Portsmouth, Virginia, with a fancy name.
Harry, Henry or Enrique something, last name Williamson...I
remember now: Enrique Victoriano Williamson, the Fourth!

"No check or credit card record of the purchase, was probably in cash.
No one with that name came up in any database. Yet."

"Did the clerks at River Armaments remember selling it to him?"
Harmony asked.

"No. They're unlikely to remember it, as the sale was three years ago.
And that name sounds phony. Victoriano Williamson. Probably made
up by someone who didn't want to be traced."

"You say the story was leaked?"

"Yes, and I suspect by 'Associate Assistant Director' Comitas. I think he wanted to make Greco look bad by showing that the clue 'Greco discovered', the clue I gave him, hasn't panned out."

Ted shrugged. He asked, "Is there anything more on the victim?"

Harmony peered at a news story. "His name was Cordero, and Carl, or Carlos." She glanced back and forth between her friend and the phone. "He went by 'Carl'. Of Latino and black background. He lived in Manassas, Virginia." Her face fell. "He has, he had, a wife and three young kids.

"And beforehand, before his kill—his murder, he met friends at Southerner", Harmony continued, referring to a restaurant a block up Washington St. from the Freedmen's Cemetery. "And after eating there he told his friends he was going 'walk off some calories and beer,' before driving back to Manassas."

"I'm surprised," said Ted, "that Southerner is open."

"Outdoor seating only, like this place," replied Harmony. "Or takeout, 'no contact' between waiters and customers."

At the mention of Manassas, Ted the historian inevitably thought of the Civil War's first major battle, fought just 35 miles west of Alexandria at Bull Run, as the Federals called the town, or Manassas, as the Southerners dubbed it. A bloody, day-long fight that presaged four years of carnage.

"His friends," Harmony went on, "heard nothing more of Carl, until they heard the news of his death."

"Anything about any of his friends having an argument with him," asked Ted, "and being under suspicion for some reason?"

"It doesn't mention it," answered Harmony. "It seems they all left the bar for their own homes." She scanned the text. "Of the towns listed, none of them live in Alexandria."

Ted was still worried about civil strife resulting from the killing. He asked: "Was Carlos, or Carl, Cordero active in politics?"

Harmony flicked with both thumbs through an article. "It doesn't say here. At least not much, it seems. Worked in a realty firm in Annandale," she related, referring to a suburban town between Manassas and Alexandria. "'He was a real family man, it says, everyone is shocked someone could do this to him...'"

As Harmony continued, Ted seemed distracted. He was still trying to recall the image of a murdered man that had flashed through his mind at Freedmen's. "Yes, an awful deed," he replied absently.

Harmony stated, "One more thing. The FBI thinks it's identified the murder weapon used, from, from the, the cuts on the body. A kind of dagger, 'often acquired by the Marines and other military outfits. It leaves characteristic wound marks'." Her thick eyebrows arched as her face fell. "Maybe the killer's an ex-military man."

"Could be. Maybe he got the dagger at River Armaments. Maybe he's the 'Williamson' guy. The cops will check that."

To change the grim mood, Harmony placed her cell's browser over a barcode, and it popped a menu onto her screen. Ted, a klutz with most things technical, listened to her explain how the online ordering worked. "It's actually easier, and faster. And with the China virus, no messy fingering of greasy paper menus, no germs."

The two asked a double-masked waiter to refill their drinks, and sat back to enjoy the setting. The bistro was set on a dock jutting into the river, affording a grand view of the Woodrow Wilson Bridge a half mile downstream. Sunlight poked through low clouds above the bridge, the rays glistening off its white-colored span. A sailboat glided with the prevailing wind and current upriver. To their left, the core of Old Town jutted out from the upriver shore. Behind them was another brand-new restaurant, with usual offerings of Southern cuisine—baked catfish, honeyed grits, collard greens, apple cobbler—yet it was shuttered from the plague.

Ted had mixed feelings about these new constructions. The restaurants, and the block of expensive condominiums behind them, built in faux, colonial-style brick, had replaced crumbling warehouses from the 19th and early 20th century, built back when Alexandria was an industrial hub.

"The city," Ted told his friend, while gesturing at the condos, "only saved one of the historic warehouses from the wrecking ball. And they're turning that into a pricey food court."

"Yes, I saw that coming over here," replied Harmony. "Chef Josef, the fellow who runs those trendy places in Georgetown; he'll be the manager."

Ted knew this was a common dilemma for any town with venerable, but run-down, real estate. Sometimes the only alternative to leveling a historic property, and replacing it with an office building, was to transform it into something new, while retaining some of the original architecture. Still, Ted believed the town's insatiable hunger for tax revenue tipped it into knocking down some salvageable structures, to replace them with luxury residences or corporate quarters.

"Well," commented Harmony, gesturing downriver, "at least digging out the foundations for the newest hotel unearthed the 'treasure ship.'"

"That's true," Ted smiled. A busboy from Guatemala arrived with his order of fish and chips, and Harmony's salmon salad. Ted thought it opportune to reach into his daypack for a copy of the "treasure map". Harmony had made high-quality xeroxes of it at work, while locking the original in a secret passage of her 18th-century townhouse apartment. Supposedly, escaped slaves had hidden there during journeys along the Underground Railway.

Ted spread the map on the table, careful to stop the westerly breeze from spiriting it away.

"Mr. Swift was a very odd character," he commented, staring at the street pattern of the chart.

"I imagine so," said Harmony with a wink. "He was after all a pirate."

"That, and a lot more," said Ted, winking back. "You know, his reputation as a pirate was widely known, for a century after."

"You mean Robert Louis Stevenson."

"Yes." During a private tour of Old Town, Ted had shown Harmony the humongous J. Swift mansions, one of which was now owned by the Burke & Herbert Bank. During their walk around Swift Alley there, he'd informed her that Stevenson, in writing his classic *Treasure Island*, partly based his famous, peg-legged character, Long John Silver, on Mr. Swift.

Ted couldn't resist: "Though it would be hard for a peg leg to be Swift."

Harmony laughed aloud. Unlike most, who mostly groaned at Ted's puns, she enjoyed his love of wordplay.

Ted smirked, squirted ketchup onto his fries, and examined the map.

"For a chart of Old Town in the 1780s, it seems incomplete."

"What do you mean? We know it's missing sections."

"I don't mean the parts that have been torn away, or badly smudged. But the parts that are there, yet are missing stuff.

"Like the old warehouse district we're in now: In Swift's day, it was already a landfill with lots of businesses. And the west end of town: the middle part of the map ends at Pitt St., just four or five blocks from the river; just beyond it were the townhouses of many wealthy people."

175

"Yes," answered Harmony, her graceful neck bent over as she peered at the chart. "But, like you said, Mr. Swift conducted lots of his business in Old Town, Old Town proper, which is most of the map. The core of it, really."

"That's right," Ted replied, looking thoughtful. "Swift was a highly accomplished, if eccentric, man—an achiever in different paths of life. Like other movers and shakers of this region: Jefferson, Dr. William Thornton, a physician and an architect of the Capitol, and Washington, that soldier, surveyor, and businessman. Swift doesn't strike me as someone who would jot out a map on a whim, as opposed to a specific purpose." His blue eyes glowing, Ted studied the map for the hundredth time. "It's seems like a specialized map," he thought out loud.

"Share me your mind," said Harmony, as she chewed on a piece of spicy salmon.

"Well, Swift's focus seems to be the main businesses in the center of town. There's William Herbert's bank near the Carlyle mansion. As opposed to the Herbert, the Burke and Herbert Bank, at King St. and Fairfax St. That was built later. This map also has City Hall's Market Square, the town's center of business at that time. Also the Athenaeum, then a major bank. And also William Ramsey's general store, at the foot of King Street on the waterfront—"

"—But, like you said, the map doesn't show the tobacco warehouses," interrupted Harmony. "And tobacco was the big business for the whole region at the time, wasn't it?"

"Actually, no. Tobacco was in steep decline throughout the Tidewater, by the time of Swift's map. That crop wears out the soil. It made the region's original fortune, from selling it to all those aristocrats pinching snuff back in Europe. Then the tobacco business went belly-up." Ted paused, thinking of his Presidents tours. "That's why guys like Jefferson died broke and in debt. They'd inherited or acquired tobacco lands, which made no money by the 1770s onward. The smartest investors, like Washington, moved their money into other things: grain, cotton, distilleries, factories, canals." His left hand hovered over the chart. "This is like a commercial map of town."

Harmony was finishing up her lunch but Ted, as he often did when fascinated by a topic during a meal, had ignored much of his.

"That makes sense," she noted. "Swift was really rich, and he had a lot of money to play with, to invest. He had to put it somewhere." As she spoke, Ted's gaze was diverted from her and the map. Seeing this, and seeing what had caught his attention, Harmony reached under the table and tapped him hard on the leg.

Ted had noticed the "Mysterious Stranger", as he had nicknamed the attractive, enigmatic woman who was passing by.

The young lady in question was draped, as usual, in dark clothing. Colors that she wore even on hot days. The attire seemed to match her otherworldly psyche. The previous summer, a few weeks before he met Harmony, Ted had learned of her in an unusual and puzzling way. One evening, as he sat with his laptop at home, a social media site had mysteriously popped her curvaceous image onto his screen. The site noted they shared interests, in hiking, education, and foreign languages and travel, and suggested, as they lived near each other, they should meet. It was odd, as the message didn't come from a dating site, and indeed didn't have an identifier of any kind. Out of curiosity and, to be sure, due to her beauty, Ted had thus contacted Cassandra "Sandra" Benedita. And they had agreed to meet one fine late afternoon not far from where he and Harmony were now dining, in the new riverfront park at the foot of King St.

From social media, Ted found out Sandra's family lived in São Paulo, and she was teaching French and math at an Arlington, Virginia elementary school.

Ted did have qualms about meeting her, as her Instagram posts revealed a woman with a strangely superstitious set of beliefs. She was fascinated by Tarot cards, astral projection, crystals, and other New Age practices. In one online post, she showed off her colored shirts for chakra practice. Where one puts on variously tinted apparel on alternating days to enhance mood and "purge toxicity from body and spirit." Highly intelligent if offbeat, Benedita wrote poetry, in English, Portuguese, Spanish, and French, about new meditation techniques she'd come upon. And, like so many who spend a lot of time on social media, she was constantly posting pictures of herself. These photos were always flattering, yet seemed to be from someone crying out for attention and approval.

Not that an admirer would object to the photos. She dressed impeccably, drawing on a large ensemble of tasteful, expensive clothing. And her physical attractiveness was undeniable: long locks of raven-colored hair, wide lips highlighted with crimson lipstick, high, rounded cheekbones pressing against soft, creamy-brown skin, supple calves, and a wafer-thin waist swelling out to broad hips.

Their first meeting, on a bench at the riverfront, had gone well. In person, Sandra Benedita said nothing about mystical practices, but chatted pleasantly and prosaically, if self-centeredly, about her trying experiences as a teacher. After a freezing school year in Ontario, she'd gotten a posting in Arlington, a town with a far more congenial climate, and obtained lodging on the edge of Old Town. There she felt at home culturally, as it reminded her of centuries-old cities in Latin America and Portugal. She savored taking walks around Old Town and its adjoining riverfront parks. Perhaps it was that which triggered an algorithm, given Ted's own affection for urban hikes, that informed him about her.

In fact, after their initial chat, Ted took her on a history tour of the nearby neighborhood. In the weeks after, they'd taken several walks in Alexandria and one along the Georgetown riverside. Then things fizzled out, and Sandra drifted into, then broke off, a relationship with a young fellow from Rio. A stocky, plain-spoken mechanic who seemed the opposite of her, though in this case the opposites failed to fully attract.

Thereafter, Ted spotted her from time to time on Alexandria's cobblestoned backstreets, or on the waterfront walking down from her North Alexandria home near the old riverside power plant. She was always alone, with an ethereal expression on her face, and ever attired in silky dark, usually black, clothing, which is how Ted imagined how the "Female Stranger" of Old Town legend would have dressed. Thus the nickname, "Mysterious Stranger".

The Female Stranger was a glamorous lady with a hidden identity who had died back in 1816 from a terrible illness, after her lover had procured her a room at Alexandria's Gadsby's Tavern. She was buried, with a poetic epitaph on her tombstone, at a venerable Episcopal Cemetery south of Old Town. Ted had memorized a fragment of the poem:

"How loved how valued once avails thee not

To whom related or by whom begot

A heap of dust alone remains of thee

Tis all thou art and all the proud shall be."

When the contemporary "Mysterious Stranger" glided past the restaurant in her finery, Ted couldn't help but notice. And Harmony couldn't help Ted noticing. She thought of the famous ad of the boyfriend looking back admiringly toward an attractive woman while walking with his annoyed girlfriend. Thus the rap on the leg.

"I wonder where she was during the cemetery murder?" asked Ted, trying to change the subject.

"You don't really suspect her, do you?" asked Harmony, dubiously.

"I don't think," Ted replied, turning back to Harmony, "that she's very high on the list of the FBI's suspects."

"Oh please," said Harmony. "Don't remind me of Comitas. What an arrogant jerk!"

Ted was glad he and she were back in, well, harmony. "Greco agrees with your view of him," he noted.

They got the check from their waiter, and Ted got a leftovers bag and paid the bill. They headed off from the riverside, Harmony back to her Amazon office, and Ted up toward Prince St.

As he walked away from the restaurant, Ted noticed some recently placed inscriptions in the footpaths of the new restaurant and condominium projects:

"1840s – Millers, stonemasons, butchers, ironsmiths," stated one.

"1823 – Site of a tannery and slaughterhouse," read another.

Given his profession, Ted was always pleased to see a city put historical information at a public place. But he also viewed these short, occasional notations as throwing a bone to skeptics of new waterfront construction, a toss-off to people who wanted more of the ancient buildings preserved.

He came upon a tiny bit of lawn dubbed "Roberdeau Park". This green space is so small it's laughable. However, it helps complete a scenic walkway that runs from the northern end of Old Town to beyond its southern endpoint near the Wilson Bridge.

The Roberdeau in question, Ted was aware, had been a ranking supply officer in Washington's army. General Daniel Roberdeau had expertise in mining, and he supplied the Continental Army with lead for making bullets. Like countless other officers under G.W.'s command, Roberdeau had settled after the Revolution in Old Town, at an extant townhouse property just two blocks away on Lee St. Ted sometimes started his "Washington and the American Revolution" tours at it.

Yet more interesting than the General's war work was the employment gained by his son, Isaac Roberdeau. The younger Roberdeau was starting out in the world when the capital city of Washington was just taking shape. He obtained a position with a noted colleague of his father—a military engineer and portrait painter of Washington, and the man Washington tapped to design D.C.: Pierre L'Enfant. Isaac Roberdeau was hired as a construction manager, and he and his gang of workers began to carve out the roads around the planned Capitol Building. Not at Old Town's Shuter's Hill, which Madison and Jefferson had explored for that purpose, but at Jenkin's Hill, soon to be called Capitol Hill.

The problem for Roberdeau, Jr. was his boss was impatient and stubborn, traits that did not endear him to the powers that be— Washington, Jefferson, and the three, well-connected city commissioners—who outranked him when it came to building the new city. In constructing New Jersey Avenue on Jenkins Hill's southern fringe, Roberdeau's work team came upon a townhouse that blocked the way. Instead of checking with its owner, L'Enfant simply ordered Roberdeau to tear the place down. Which the young man did, all the way down to its stone foundations. Unfortunately for him and his boss, the house's owner was a member of the Carroll family—the Catholic clan that was the richest, and most politically powerful, in Maryland. A family that had granted the federal government the very land on which Capitol was being built!

Whenever he recalled this story, Ted would think of the phrase oft repeated in his Catholic elementary school: "Charles Carroll, of Carrollton, the only Catholic, signer, of the Declaration of Independence." The Carroll in question, a Mr. Carroll of Duddington, wasn't pleased with the destruction of his house. He got an injunction against L'Enfant at the Maryland state house in Annapolis. And he fired off an angry letter to President Washington.

The Father of His Country wasn't happy either. The matter not only irked a politically potent family, it put the fledging federal city under a cloud. G.W. wrote L'Enfant a letter urging him to obey the city commissioners, while writing another missive offering Carroll a rebuilt house or financial compensation. Meantime the city commissioners ordered Isaac Roberdeau to obey them, not L'Enfant, and to rebuild the house. The young Roberdeau refused, and the commissioners responded by putting him under arrest!

Things got even worse. L'Enfant refused to print street maps to promote the new city, again against the wishes of Washington and the commissioners. Finally, a flabbergasted President Washington directed Jefferson, his Secretary of State and point man on the capital's construction, to fire L'Enfant.

Ted enjoyed telling this story because, among other things, it illustrated how things had sometimes gone terribly awry from the very start in D.C., and in Alexandria, which at that time was part of the capital city. The historian reached Lee St., with the Roberdeau home right down the block. He intended to look over some workmen's townhouses near it as research for his next book. The carpenters, masons, and iron workers who'd dwelled there helped construct the mansions of the town's early elite, while residing in far more modest abodes which, however, were worth up to a million dollars each today. Ted had plenty of material on Old Town's movers and shakers, like Swift and Washington, but less on persons of more humble standing.

He was about to chat with the current owner of one such townhome, when he heard the same shriek of sirens that still rang in his mind from the Freedmen's Cemetery murder. As before, both police cars and ambulances screamed out alarms. And a fire truck with a flashing light went flying by him, down Lee toward Prince St.

Chapter 14 – Agony at the Athenaeum

The destination for the EMS was just five blocks away, and Ted, ignoring tightness in his left knee, and following the route of the blaring vehicles, quick-walked there in less than 10 minutes. The familiar intersection, one of his history sweet spots, came into view as he reached Prince.

Looming on his left was Mayor Hooe's mansion, on his right the far more modest wood frame house of General Marsteller, and just beyond it, Captain's Row, descending down its cobbled streets toward Col. Fitzgerald's riverside park. Left of the Athenaeum was the broad Southern porch of the grand Fairfax mansion of Sally Fairfax, who'd instructed Washington on the arts of the gentleman. And across the way the townhome of Colonel Michael Swope, an officer of Washington's army who'd been taken prisoner, then exchanged for the son of none other than Ben Franklin, one William Franklin, the Tory royal Governor of New Jersey.

All this was taken in unconsciously, for Ted's attention was riveted on the outlandish scene at the Athenaeum, the old merchant bank, turned Civil War hospital, turned art gallery. Cop cars and ambulances, their engines running and lights whirling, lined up along or over the curbsides of Prince and Lee. Gallery administrators, sad-faced, several of them weeping, were being interviewed by police outside the thick-columned, Greek Revival entrance. A larger group of cops gathered down Lee St. at the gallery's small back yard. Ted headed there, stopping first to text Harmony a photo of the scene. She replied instantly: she wanted to come over, but was in a meeting to interview a candidate for her IT developers team.

A small crowd of masked locals, while keeping six feet or more between them, had gathered on the sidewalk next to the back yard. Ted slipped on his thin cloth mask and rushed past them, getting angry looks for intruding on their zone of safety. He peered through an unlocked iron gate outside the yard. He then stepped inside quietly, gambling the policemen wouldn't kick him out. He saw Greco and others stooping over a body.

It was a horrific sight. The body of the gallery's night watchwoman lay on moss-covered bricks two or three feet from the servant's entrance. Her dark-blue work clothes were dirty and torn. The woman's head was face down, looking away from the Atheneum and twisted in a grotesque angle to her right, pushing her still-open eyes and bloodied forehead off the brickwork. Her lifeless brown eyes seemed to be staring right at Ted. The deceased appeared to be of African or perhaps Afro-Caribbean descent. Ted thought absently to himself that many of the region's security guards were of that ancestry, and sometimes studied for a degree, often in IT, during their usually uneventful working hours. Twenty-seven feet above the body, in the gallery's attic, the glass of a large window had been shattered. Ted heard an FBI man muttering into his cell that the guard had apparently been thrown to her death.

Ted made eye contact with Greco, and figured that was the end of his close-in observation. But he surprised Ted by simply shaking his head, and stating in his deep voice: "Can you believe this?" Nonetheless, as more FBI agents arrived in a van, Ted deemed it wise to step behind the crime scene line that Alexandria police were stringing along the Athenaeum's sidewalk. He still had a view through the open gate. The agents and police, like everyone in town, all wore masks, and this somehow seemed to make them less impressive, even powerless. He listened as Greco asked the gallery's manager, Katherine Warren, what valuables, including artwork, were kept in the attic. Kate Warren, an energetic, 34-year-old woman in a colorful dress with a Salvador Dali motif, was trembling. Normally smooth-spoken, with an Ivy League accent, she mumbled a response: "Nothing, Officer, no. Nothing of value. Most, most of our prized items, um, are displayed, on the gallery floor. With, with a few stored, stashed away in the attic. Some very old things are, are kept there, papers and such, but none of, our, uh, prized art." Greco scribbled a few of her words on a notepad, relying on his excellent memory to remember the rest, and thanked the obviously stricken woman.

Ted quietly took other photos of the scene, and texted them to Harmony, whom he pictured, correctly, as sitting impatiently in her meeting, wanting it to end, wishing she could be with him at the scene of the crime. In fact, at the interview Harmony mentioned the watchwoman's death to the prospective hirer, who without blinking turned the conversation back to his knowledge of SQL*Plus code.

As a local guide, Ted knew the back story of the stately Athenaeum, including the long period where it had been one of the town's three premier merchant banks, namely the Bank of the Old Dominion. The story he often told tour guests was how its Civil War owner, fearing Union Army confiscation of its deposits, including those of a customer named Robert E. Lee, had hidden away the money for the balance of the war, then returned the full amounts after Appomattox.

Ted had an extremely active imagination, and he let it run. Could some of those funds, he wondered, somehow been left undiscovered in the attic? Did an intruder, or an employee running an inside job, somehow

learn that part of a fortune in cash and securities had been hidden there?
It seemed unlikely, as he had read that all the money to the penny had
been returned to its depositors after the Civil War's end. And that was
so long ago.

A more prosaic, and likely, explanation was that a burglar and the
guard had stumbled upon each other, and a scuffle and tragedy had
resulted. Yet he knew most murders involved people who knew each
other: had the intruder been romantically involved with the guard? Or,
was the death of the watchwoman connected somehow to the assault on
the harborside watchman? Were two guards assaulted in separate
incidents too much of a coincidence? Or was the death tied to the
murder at Freedmen's Cemetery? The dead watchwoman was a
"minority", as was the man killed at Freedmen's and, indeed, as was
the injured watchman at the ship excavation site. The implication of all
that could explosive, and might tear the town to pieces. Then of course
there was the chance there had been more than one intruder.

As Ted mulled over the possibilities, an armor-plated SUV pulled into
a small space along the curb. It bumped slightly into an Acura TLX
owned by a local resident.

Comitas stepped out from the vehicle. His eyes, peering above a black
N95 mask, shot Ted a death stare. The FBI officer strode over to the
back lot to talk to Greco. The much taller agent bent over the stocky
detective. An image of a slender tree, bending in the wind over a stout
brick wall, entered Ted's mind. Comitas spoke briefly and brusquely,
then stepped over to the body. The agent whom Ted had overheard
gave the FBI official his opinion the guard had been pushed to her
death. Comitas, looking back and forth from the corpse to the attic
window and back again, nodded, though whether he agreed was hard to
say.

Ted watched Greco slip away from Comitas with evident distaste, and follow the Athenaeum's manager to the front of the gallery. Ted walked surreptitiously behind them. Glancing at the rows of pricey townhouses on Lee St. beyond the Hooe mansion, he recalled the joyous Halloween festival its residents put on every year, except pandemic years. Hundreds of adorable kids in costume walked with their parents from one elaborately decorated house to another to gather their candy treats. In sparkling autumn sunshine, residents got fully into the spirit, constructing steam-breathing paper dragons, mechanical Frankensteins, and broom-sticked witches flying along the clothes lines of alleys. The annual festival, with its good-natured, faux-horror themes, was in startling contrast, Ted reflected, to the real horror of recent days.

Greco and Kate Warren paused on the steps of the entrance columns of pink Aquia sandstone. The same material from a downriver Virginia quarry that Scottish masons, Irish mechanics, and free and enslaved African-Americans had cut and hauled and molded to build the White House, the Capitol Building, the Smithsonian Castle, and other noted edifices in D.C. Bracketed by the wide Doric columns holding up the tympanum, the blank stone triangle above the pillars, the manager wiped her teary face with a handkerchief Greco offered her. Ted slowly walked along the sidewalk listening as Greco asked her more questions. He picked up most of what Warren said. Still visibly distraught, the woman stated: "...I, I can't say—I don't remember if I saw that a light was...in the attic, when I arrived."

"What time...you get here?" queried Greco.

"Before six, a little before dawn." The woman rubbed her eyes. "I always arrive early...open things up...things to get done before the employees come." She swallowed. "Like I said, I had trouble...the door, getting it open. I...turn the key many, many times."

"Yes," said Greco, "one of my men found scratch marks around the keyhole. Maybe the door...forced open." Ted moved a bit closer, the conversation becoming more clearly audible.

He saw that Miss Warren's face was flushed bright red. "So I went inside, and maybe that's when, I noticed that, the light was on." She rubbed the handkerchief across a runny nose. "I don't know, I'm sorry, sir, maybe it was when I went upstairs." The detective placed a meaty hand on the woman's shoulder. "Take your time. Take a breath. Tell me what happened next."

Warren, her flaxen hair looking withered like autumn straw, exhaled, and continued. "I always look through the whole building, when I enter. Not that we've had anything stolen, but just out of habit. Or duty you might say. I went, through the gallery, the main floor, first. It was as it always is—nothing had been disturbed.

"Maybe it was on the second floor, I mean the attic, when I definitely noticed the light on there. I make sure, of course, that all our lights are turned off before leaving, at the end of the day, or when the gallery closes." Her pale, watery eyes regained some of their focus. "I knew something was amiss as soon as...went in. The place was a mess." On her forehead, she touched a light bruise that Greco was about to ask her about. "I bumped my head from the low ceiling...my excitement. I saw boxes that were opened, shelves, things on the shelves, knocked askew.

"We rarely go up there, you know, to the storage space. I saw clouds of dust in the light, dust that had been kicked up. Then I saw the broken window and, and, I looked below." Her voice broke. "Raiza had been with us for just eight months...Everyone liked her. She is, was, studious, loved our artwork and..." Warren's throat caught again.

"That's more than enough for now, ma'am," said Greco, looking sympathetic yet grimly determined at the same time. He helped Warren sit down on the pitted sandstone steps.

Meanwhile, Ted saw Comitas come quickly around the corner from the back lot. Pulling up the collar of his suede Nobis raincoat, he strode up to Greco. Ted tried to blend into the background. He turned to the side, pushed a sports cap down on his head, and pulled his mask up from his neck, well up over his broad, eagle-like nose.

The FBI man literally buttonholed the Alexandria cop, tapping on the buttons of his blue, Men's Wearhouse shirt, almost touching his badge. Greco clenched his fists, then slowly unclenched them.

"It seems like we've got a maniac on the loose!" Comitas almost shouted as he peered down upon the detective.

"Maybe," Greco said in a flat tone, while gritting his prominent jaw.

Comitas nearly sneered. "It has to be the same guy. Same as the Cemetery!"

"No obvious racial motive here," Greco replied evenly.

'Well, it was a black woman from Dominica, the Dominican Republic. You should look for a motive. *We'll* find one, for sure." Greco began to respond but Comitas, having made his point, walked quickly away.

Greco noticed Ted nearby. His face cast in concrete, he glanced at the historian, then started to step back toward the lot to reexamine the corpse.

On a whim, Ted walked over to the gate of a small service alley on the side of the Athenaeum, between the gallery and the Fairfax mansion. He expected the gate to be locked, but it was open, the sturdy lock cut cleanly in two. Was it possible the authorities, in their haste, hadn't seen this?

"Detective Greco," Ted called out as quietly as he could. "Did you see the gate?" He pointed to the side entrance. "The lock is broke." Greco gave him a sharp, surprised look, and walked over to take a look.

He and Ted stepped up the narrow alley dating from the 1780s. At a basement window, they found evidence of tampering. In a scattering of mud outside it, Greco kneeled down, and found what might be part of a footprint. He took a photo with his cell and, unclipping the Motorola analog radio off his belt, ordered a forensic man to come over.

He looked up to see Ted staring at him. "Thanks for your help. But this is a crime scene, you know."

The historian took the hint and, his mind swimming with thoughts, headed back home.

Chapter 15 – The Late Unpleasantness

Alexandria had so many buildings and incidents relating to the War Between the States, Ted had found, that it was impossible for any one tour to encompass them all. So he broke the town up into parts, giving separate Civil War-themed tours in each. Most frequently he would begin near the Appomattox statue, starting perhaps with a brief visit to Bertha's small Confederate war museum. His most recent tours had begun from there, so this day he started from the north edge of Old Town, at the Old Cotton Mill, a block-long condominium where workers had once spun the cash crop of the Old South's economy. The Mount Vernon Cotton Factory, as it was formally known, is a massive, four-story building, and elegant for a former industrial facility. It has a slanted roof, dormer windows, whitewashed brick walls, porticoed entrance, and a commanding cupola, capped by a weather vane, that soars over North Washington St. And it has an amazingly varied history. The site is atop a hill that crowns a steady rise up from the Potomac, affording it excellent drainage. The British and colonial forces, in the French and Indian War, under General Braddock and Major Washington, as well as Generals Washington and Lafayette, in the American Revolution, bivouacked troops nearby on the dry high ground.

The land parallels the former King George St., long since renamed Washington St., a major byway just a few blocks northwest of Alexandria's wharves. A logical place to place a factory to process the "white gold" of the antebellum. As the Tidewater soil didn't take to cotton, the stuff was imported from plantations in Carolina and Alabama that grew it in abundance.

By 1860, cotton was America's most profitable industry, bigger than the railroads, and the Old Cotton Mill was a top local employer. One hundred fifty people, mostly female, toiled there in 11-hour days, paid about $180 a year for spinning the material that was typically picked by unpaid field hands. The complex was huge, with almost 4,000 spindles and 125 looms, even a small "picking house". Picking was hard, dirty work, often performed in the South by blacks or poor whites, giving birth to the expression, "Keep your cotton-picking hands off me!"

As a massive enterprise operated by Southern interests, it was destined after 1861 to be either a Union hospital or, in its case, a Confederate prison. Up to 1,400 captured rebels were jammed into cells there. They were so badly treated the commandant was dismissed.

King Cotton was dethroned in the war; British India and British-influenced Egypt became major growers of the stuff. The Mill was transformed into a brewery and bottling plant, by an immigrant, a German of course, a Herr Portner, who built a sister installation a block away. By the 1910s, as the Model T and the suburbs rolled into adjoining farmlands, the place was turned into a spark plug factory. More recently, the International Association of Police Chiefs, one of the countless lobbies in the capital region, acquired it for headquarters. Now, inevitably, as with most enduring, admired structures in town, it was being converted into condos.

During all its iterations, the Old Cotton Mill had one constant: a ghost. Actually a wax figure, of a man who'd faced a horrible death back in July 1854. As a profitable piece of property, the place needed a watchman. Irish immigrants were pouring into America, with many of them becoming policemen or security guards, and the Cotton Mill hired a young man as one.

One terrible morning, the fellow was found dead outside the Mill, his skull crushed in. The local gendarmes learned that, the night before, a neighbor had heard a man with an Irish accent, presumably the guard, arguing with another man. The latter screamed, "You damned Irishman, you have been interfering with me!" A loud smack was heard. Presumably a blow, presumably from the other man, presumably the killer.

An investigation followed. The police were stumped. No credible suspect was found.

Frustrated, the cops employed a stratagem. They had a large wax dummy made to mimic the murdered guard. They placed it in the windowed cupola on the roof of the Mill. They hoped the murderer might come by and, seeing a figure in the accustomed spot of the watchman, conclude he'd survived. And might make his way inside to finish his victim off. The police staked out the Mill, night and day, but the killer, perhaps wary of a trap or aware of the ruse, never returned. The case remains one of the longest-running, and strangest, unsolved murders.

Remarkably, even as the memory of the horrific deed faded away, the wax figure stayed. Perhaps the Mill's owners wanted to keep it to ward off other felons. Later owners kept it as a weird yet amusing totem. When Ted was starting up his tours of Old Town, back when the Mill was being renovated for the police chief's association, he heard about the eerie sentinel. Curious, he went to the construction site and, ignoring the Keep Out signs, slipped through the spacious backyard and into the building. There he chatted with a hard-hat from El Salvador who, instead of kicking him off the property, offered to take him up to see the wax dummy. They mounted four creaky flights of stairs to the cupola, an abandoned elevator shaft to their side. They entered a top-floor doorway, and there it was. The still-recognizable figure of a man, but with the waxen face horribly disfigured, having shrunken and expanded for 165-plus years from the baking Southern heat and the drafty winter cold.

From a certain vantage point across N. Washington St., one can see the dark, spooky "Ghost of the Old Cotton Mill", especially at night, as more recent owners have installed lights to illuminate the cupola after dusk. Ted began, or ended, his Halloween tours, and some of his Civil War tours, with this view of the bizarre figurine.

In fact, on the day of his tour, Ted took his small group across the street to look up at the waxen ghost. But on that day, the Ghost of the Old Cotton Mill could not be seen.

"That's odd," he told his guests. "When I drove by here just last week, I parked at this spot, to get a good look at it. And I got it."

"They must have moved it," said a guest, a gray-haired history and culture lover typical of Ted's clientele.

"I guess so," the guide replied, but he was puzzled. In checking out the construction site before the tour, Ted had noticed that work was proceeding at the back lot, but the building itself, including the cupola, was shut down. The ghost should have stayed put. 'Unless,' he chuckled to himself, 'a real ghost is involved!'

Ted shrugged it off and continued the tour. In the style of a university lecturer, he stated: "The Cotton Mill represents a key economic cause of the Civil War: the slave plantations in the Deep South that grew the cotton. Let's take a look at the military side of the war, and the family most associated with the Confederate army."

Incredibly, or perhaps fittingly, just one block south on Washington St. was what locals called "the Lee Neighborhood", at least until it became impolitic to mention the name Lee. Several dozen relatives of Robert Edward Lee had lived within several blocks of each other in that little district, in the time before, during, and after "The Late Unpleasantness".

They first walked to a handsome, expansive house at the bottom of a cobblestoned stretch of Oronoco St. The future general was raised there in "Lee's Boyhood Home", as noted by the historical marker on the sidewalk. The tour goers admired the garden, one of the largest in town, and walked back up to the other side of Oronoco, to its corner with Washington St., and the Lee-Fendall House. There young Edward also spent a great deal of time, an orphan surrounded and raised by the seemingly endless number of Lees who resided nearby.

Ted spoke of the antebellum resident after whose family the house is partly named. Philip Fendall II, himself a cousin to the Lees. Fendall was an attorney for the most powerful politician of the pre-war period—Kentucky's Henry Clay. Clay was the congressman who twice averted civil war, with the nation at a boiling point over slavery, through his congressional Compromises, of 1820 and 1850.

In 1820, by bringing Missouri into the Union as a slave state, and Maine as a free state. Ted noted, to his guests' surprise, that Maine had become its own state after seceding from Massachusetts. Yes, a Northern state had split away, not from the Union, but from another state it disliked, some 41 years *before* the Civil War. Among other things, Maine was angry at how the rest of New England had failed to properly defend it from British attacks during the War of 1812.

In his Compromise of 1850, Clay brought California, swelled with settlers by the '49 Gold Rush, into the U.S. as a free state. At the same time, he appeased slaveholders with a more stringent Fugitive Slave Law, which empowered slaveholders, and federal marshals, to go after escaped slaves, including those who had fled to Northern states. As might be expected, many Northerners were enraged at this infringement on their turf. Some feared the South was trying to impose its own economic system on everyone else.

21 years prior to the 1850 law, Philip Fendall II handled a famous case of an enslaved woman which involved Clay, then Secretary of State as well as the owner of the woman. Amazingly, this lady, a Mrs. Charlotte Dupuy, sued Clay in federal court for her freedom. Claiming that her transfer from the previous owner to Clay was invalid. Ted outlined this and asked the guests, "Who do you think won the case? The Secretary of State, or the slave suing him?" Not surprisingly, the woman lost in court to the powerful, influential politician and his well-connected lawyer, Mr. Fendall. Still, Clay freed the woman some years later. And he may have had a guilty conscience about the matter. For a component of his 1850 Compromise was to ban the buying and selling of slaves in Washington, D.C. This finally ended the slave trade, if not slavery outright, in the capital of a democratic republic. Another factor might have been that Clay may have had children with one of his female "servants", a liaison that could have heightened his sympathy for such folk. The "peculiar institution" was a peculiar one indeed.

After telling the Dupuy story, and how the Lee-Fendall abode became a Union Army hospital during the Civil War, Ted pointed out the townhome right across Washington St., a carefully maintained beauty that takes up a full half block. It is the antebellum house of another Lee, who championed an unusual attempt to get a grip on the burning issue of involuntary servitude. And he took the group over to this former home of Edmund Jennings Lee, Sr. As they crossed the street, a guest noted that, "given the murder at the Freedmen's Cemetery, a Civil War tour seems more appropriate than ever."

If the Old Cotton Mill typified the Old South's economy, the Edmund Lee home seemed to embody its social structure. Fronting Washington St. is the three-story stone townhouse, really a mansion in elegance and extent, with a red-brick front, eleven windows, a soaring chimney, and a wisteria-draped colonnade. Behind it is a second, more modest dwelling, made of wood; presumably it contained the children's rooms. Behind it is a third house, even shorter in length, though wider, and presumably for relatives or out-of-town guests. Behind that is a fourth, much smaller home, with just two windows, and resembling a large shed. That was, presumably, for slaves or, after abolition, for house servants. During Edmund Lee's life, both free and enslaved blacks lived in the domiciles at various times.

"This place was not so much *Upstairs, Downstairs*," said Ted, referring to the British television show that was a precursor to *Downton Abbey*, "but '*Frontways, Backwards*.'" A glance at the long edifice illustrated the pecking order of the Antebellum Era. Unlike the Cotton Mill, this Lee home remains a private residence, having ducked for now the condominium conundrum.

Its best-known owner, Edmund Jennings Lee, was a true "BMIOT": a Big Man in Old Town. From 1810 to 1840, he seemed to take up every important position. He served as town Mayor, as President of the town Council, and Clerk of the Alexander Circuit Court, the current quarters of which are across from City Hall. He helped run the Alexandria Academy, a public school across from the Lyceum and the Appomattox statue, that Washington himself endowed. He also had the closest ties to powerful figures in the new Federal government, as he was the brother of Charles Lee, President Washington's second Attorney

General. He was also the brother of Light-Horse Harry Lee, an esteemed cavalry general for General Washington and the father of Robert E. Lee.

Edmund Jennings Lee was also a leading force in a strange something called the American Colonization Society. This was a generations-long attempt, kicked off in 1816, to send freed African-Americans back to Africa. Thousands of blacks, many of them educated, and with the monetary aid of the Society, state organizations, and the United States government, set up their own West African country, named Liberia, or Free Land. A Who's Who of Southern and Border-South statesmen backed the effort, including Clay, retired Presidents Jefferson and Madison, and then-President James Monroe. In fact, the capital of Liberia is named Monrovia after him. Today, the country has a population of five million. Earlier, the British Empire set up its own country in West Africa, Sierra Leone, for some of its own free blacks. The American Colonization Society was a rare point of agreement among certain Southerners and Northerners on slavery. Some Northern abolitionists and missionaries, for instance, welcomed the idea of a nation for free blacks. Yet Ted suspected there were mixed motives behind the oddly named Society. There was an idealistic one, of setting up a land of liberty. It flowed out of a successful movement, pushed by the likes of songwriter John Newton, composer of "Amazing Grace", to ban the slave trade from Africa, which President Jefferson and King George III both did in 1807. Politics makes strange bedfellows, and seldom more than in that case. The British, pushed by the great parliamentarian William Wilberforce, went further, and banned slavery outright in their Empire in 1833, while the U.S. dragged its feet on that far larger reform. Yet U.S. politicians could assert, short of calling for abolition, that they were taking real steps through the Colonization Society to help blacks.

Supporting Liberia also provided a safety valve for a simmering issue. Free, educated blacks, who were increasing in number, were pushing for outright abolition. Sending them to Africa drained away some of that impetus. Abraham Lincoln himself supported the transfer of American blacks to Africa or to Panama. The brilliant scientist Matthew Fontaine Maury suggested Brazil as the destination. Naturally, the large majority of African-Americans rejected such schemes, pointing out they were as American as anyone else.

Ted found it ironic that post-bellum black leaders, such as Marcus Garvey, irate at the slow progress of civil rights, led a Back to Africa movement, in a kind of revival of the Liberia idea. Astonishingly, the American Colonization Society itself didn't formally dissolve until 1964, at the height of the Civil Rights Era, and 99 years after the Civil War's end.

The Society's failure to achieve one of its aims, averting civil war, was reflected in Edmund Lee's sons. One, Edmund Jennings Lee, Jr., became a Confederal general; another, Cassius Lee, named after the Roman who led the plot to assassinate Julius Caesar, may have been a Confederate spy.

Ted's group was astonished how this little two-block section of Alexandria had been a microcosm of the Border South before and during the Civil War. The Old Cotton Mill, Bobby Lee's boyhood home, and that of Edmund Jennings Lee and the other Lee properties, including the Lee-Fendall House and even the former, private law office of Charles Lee. And on an urban hillock where troops from three major wars had encamped or set up hospitals. Ted was surprised, and quietly pleased, that those intent on scrubbing Old Town of any reminders of the Confederacy hadn't yet turned their attention to the "Lee Neighborhood".

Getting to the other major Civil War sites in town normally meant going south on Washington St. But though the motor traffic on the boulevard was fairly quiet due to the pandemic, Ted disliked its mostly modern appearance, which took away from the 18th and 19th-century ambience of his events. Further, for a long city block there were almost no historic locales, which was most unusual for Old Town. This bothered Ted, who prided himself on pointing out three or four historic spots on almost any block of his itinerary.

So he took his masked guests back across Washington, back down the cobblestones of Lee's childhood home, and onto quiet, residential St. Asaph St. Some of the guests, given the day's humidity, slipped their masks off their mouth and noses, while one couple, already irritated at a few who weren't not wearing one, looked on with annoyance and angst. The group soon reached the Old City Jail, the predecessor to the Alexandria Detention Center, and now a very attractive, and expensive, townhouse.

"Alexandria was such a rich merchant city," Ted noted, "that it could afford the very best. Even for its prisons. To build it, the city council hired Charles Bulfinch, the man who rebuilt the Capitol Building, after the British burnt it down." He smiled, and asked rhetorically: "The Royal Marines burned it in 1814, two years after what war began?" The guests, masked or not, replied, "1812!" "Ah," he joked, "my guests are expert at mathematics, and arithmetic, as well as history."

Their host noted Bulfinch had also designed the charming Fowle-Patton mansion, the one Harmony had photographed, and a planned stop later in the tour. Ted added that behind the tall, whitewashed wall of the condominium was the old prison yard where the jail's gallows had stood. Condemned criminals were put to death on its scaffold. Though the gallows were long gone, the souls who'd died there had not vanished, perhaps, as the yard was said to be haunted. The group moved on, reflecting grimly on the executions of long ago.

Ted had picked this route for another reason than to avoid traffic and to point out the Bulfinch prison. One block down from the jail are several very old homes along the side of a very modern asphalt parking lot. "Take a look at this parking lot," he told the guests, "and keep it in mind. Now follow me." He took the group around the corner to Queen St. He stood outside the door of the corner home, and spread out his long, stringy arms. To the surprise of the guests, his limbs exceeded the narrow width of the building.

"Welcome," he announced, "to perhaps the narrowest house in America! Alexandria's own, 'Spite House'."

"'Spite', as in 'out of spite.' Built to get back at a noisy neighbor. In this case, the owner, a Mr. John Hollensbury, a City Council representative. He filled in the former alley here with a very narrow Spite House. According to one tale on how the little home came about, he did this to stop his noisy Irish neighbors from riding and carousing through his alley late at night. To stop their drinking and singing, and their robbing him and his family of sleep."

He paused a moment to let that sink in, then continued. "The noisy neighbors were among the Irish immigrants pouring into Alexandria in the early decades of the 1800s. The nightwatchman at the Cotton Mill was an example. The newcomers were mostly poor, and poorly educated, and Catholic, and entering a town dominated by wealthy English and Scottish businessmen, who were Protestants. A town already inhabited also by African-Americans, slaves or the newly free, competing with the newcomers for low-paying jobs." Ted stopped to take a breath. "This was a recipe for friction. And certainly so for Hollensbury. Who had the alley walled up, and turned it into a tiny house, a Spite House.

"A few years ago, a nice couple then living here invited me inside. Along the side walls, they showed me the marks of carriage wheels, that had scraped across the bottom of the alley walls, which were now the inner walls of the home!" Ted remembered to look at his audience, and gauge its reaction. The guests were open-eyed. They had never heard this bizarre tale. That was good. He loved it when attendees were learning something new about history.

"And this spiteful citizen of Old Town didn't stop here. Remember the parking lot I showed you? It's said a group of Irish families lived in houses there. Another Alexandrian of British and Protestant descent, a home builder named Mr. Robert Brockett, had the homes knocked down, leaving an empty yard in their place. Today it's a parking lot, ringed by the fine, courtly buildings that Brockett built."

He concluded, "The moral of the story? Well, apart from it's wrong to be spiteful, it seems America was fracturing in multiple ways by 1861, and not just in a slave versus free, or North versus South, or a factory versus farm, divide. There was also, if you will, a 'North versus North' split. Or a 'Pope versus Minister' split, of native-born 'Yankees', mostly Protestant, against Irish, and German, arrivals, mostly Catholic. "In many ways, old Alexandria typified those divisions. It was a wild place indeed."

It was time to get back to the Civil War itself, and related matters, so he took the guests up Queen St. back to Washington St., and crossed over to Alexandria's first library, dating from 1794, and still in operation. It was a locus of civil strife and civil rights history.

The Kate Waller Barrett Library was, originally, the site of a Meeting House and burial ground for the town's influential, and abolitionist, Quaker community. Ted explained how the Society of Friends got its odd nickname. Critics conflated them with another splinter, Christian sect, of so-called "holly rollers" given to trembling and shaking, or "quaking", at services, when struck by the Holy Spirit. Though actual Quaker gatherings couldn't be more different. They're rather informal get-togethers of acquaintances for friendly, if spiritually related, conversation.

In the years after the American Revolution, Alexandria's erudite town fathers acquired the cemetery grounds, and built a lending library there. This was when America already had the highest literacy rate in the world, and when Alexandria was in the forefront of education, particularly for women. Appropriately the library was named after a lady, Dr. Kate Waller Barrett.

A descendent of Virginia founder John Smith, of Pocahontas fame, and born on a plantation, Barrett had sympathy for persons on all sides of the Civil War, particularly for widows and displaced women. She made mighty efforts to preserve the state's history from that time, and her eponymous library has a fine collection on the Old Dominion's early years. But her greatest exertions were for "fallen women".

At a time when a female's social standing went rock-bottom after an out-of-wedlock birth, Barrett, a medical school graduate, was the force behind the National Florence Crittenton Mission, with its goal to aid single, unmarried mothers. Barrett's townhouse on 408 Duke St. still stands, and a recent owner hung a "Don't Tread on Me" flag from it, a hint that the multifaceted Barrett also headed Old Town's chapter of the American Legion.

The Old Town Horror

Just 14 years after the broad-minded lady's death in 1925, her namesake library witnessed an event that would, over the next two decades, be mimicked with tectonic consequences around the South, and the world. On August 31 of that year, Ted told his guests, five neatly dressed young black men entered the library. They followed a strategy laid out by a 26-year-old, Alexandria-born attorney, Samuel Tucker. The men wanted to fill out library cards, but were denied the privilege. So, they picked out books, and sat down to quietly read them. This caused a ruckus, as the library in 1939 was a segregated, "whites only" place. Local cops arrived to arrest them.

Old Town seemed to prove a rather genteel place, even in its bigotry. The young men were released, with the help of a prominent, local white lawyer named Armistead Boothe. He was a Rhodes scholar and "courtly Southern gentleman". His first name evoked the General who ordered the raising of the Star-Spangled Banner above Fort McHenry, and his son, Lewis Armistead, who fatally led the spearpoint of Pickett's Charge at Gettysburg. Armistead Boothe, definitely no relation to John Wilkes Booth, would later foil those resisting the peaceful integration of Virginia's schools.

After Tucker's band of would-be readers were freed, Ted went on, the town tried compromise. It built a small, blacks-only library on the west end of Old Town on Wythe St., named for Jefferson's abolitionist law professor. That library, named for a black minister who was the grandson of a Martha Washington slave, was a separate, but unequal, place.

Yet Sam Tucker had set the ball rolling. By the 1960s, such "sit-down strikes" for racial integration became common at lunch counters and department stores, in places like Greensboro, North Carolina, and the

Hecht's department store in downtown D.C. These non-violent actions, appealing to everyone's better angels, helped much to bury Jim Crow. Ted explained all this to his listeners in front of the library entrance's glass window, with its motif of the rays of a stylized sun radiating out wisdom. He displayed a vintage photograph of the sit-down strikers being led by police out of that very entranceway. Over 80 years later, the entrance and window looked exactly the same.

"Yet much has changed," stated a guest.

'Or has it?' Ted would wonder, after the events of later that day.

Right across Queen St. from the library is a townhouse archetypical of Alexandria's stance as a place straddling South and North. Ted pointed out another typically elegant, Old Town house—three stories of red brick, with multiple tall chimneys and rooftop dormers, and an unusually large backyard. "It's called the Lloyd House," he noted, smiling, and taking a deep breath, "but it could well be dubbed the, Lloyd-Hooe-Hoffman-Hallowell-Robert E. Lee-Underground Railroad-House.

"How's that for a mouthful!?"

The Lloyd family of merchants, cousins-in-law to Robert E., owned the mansion from the 1830s until the 1930s, and the Great Depression. The city saved it from demolition during the urban redevelopment era of the 1950s. It was originally built by John Wise, a savvy businessman, hotelier, and builder of what became Gadsby's Tavern. Then it was acquired by the Hooe family, the same bunch that gave the town its first mayor. Another early owner was Southern industrialist Jacob Hoffman, whose workers manufactured rope there for the harbor town's ships.

But the most intriguing of its denizens was an educator, Benjamin Hallowell, who set up an antebellum school inside. In this learned town, this noted Quaker, no doubt taking inspiration from the library down the street, also built the town's lecture hall, the Lyceum. In his school Hallowell taught mathematics and science, and his prize student was a young Robert E. Lee, who walked or rode to school from his boyhood home just down the road. Lee burnished his knowledge of physics with Hallowell before entering America's then-preeminent center of engineering science, West Point.

The irony seemed stark. Hallowell was a Quaker, and by definition for abolition, while Lee was a chief commander of the Confederate Army. The dividing line between Lee and Hallowell became evident when word arrived of Lee's crushing 1863 defeat at Gettysburg. Hallowell wrote: "Although Robert E. Lee had been one of my students, in great favor...when I heard that {Union} General George G. Meade had arrested his progress and driven him across the Potomac to his own State {of Virginia}, my heart rejoiced! It was impossible to avoid it. It was an instinctive outburst in favor of right, justice, and freedom." Hallowell's son Henry, it is thought, along with other Quakers in town, maintained their homes and businesses as stops on the Underground Railway. Some abolitionists gave shelter to fugitive slaves during the day; at night, the escapees would slip out under the cover of dark to restart their trek to the free northern states.

Another irony, and complexity. The full name of Hallowell's son: Henry *Clay* Hallowell. He was named for the slave owner, albeit strong Unionist, who had blocked the Dupuy woman's courtroom bid for freedom.

The Lloyd, or Hooe, or Hoffman, or Hallowell, or Lee, or Underground Railroad, House, Ted pointed out, showed how different Alexandria was for a Southern city of its time. And not just because of its strongly abolitionist links. But because its broad backyard once abutted on a most unusual commercial facility—a rope walk. In the 19th century, laborers created rope for ships by walking, like human spindles, along a path with cord attached to their persons, with the twine intertwining as they went along, thus forming rope.

Old Town's Northern-like industry didn't end at Jacob Hoffman's rope walk. It extended to the sweet tooth. One block up from the Hallowell school and across Columbus St. are some of the extant buildings of the old McLean family sugar and candy factory. The complex stretched a long city block to Alfred St., named not for Batman's butler, but for the original unifier of England, Alfred the Great, and thus an icon for the colonial British town. In giant, boiling vats, enslaved workers poured in sugar cane shipped in from Cuban plantations. The crop formed part of the "triangle trade" between the Caribbean, the colonies, and their mother country. Out of the processing came cane sugar and molasses. Made into candy or added to ice cream. It may be a coincidence, or not, that a confectionery store stands next to the Alfred St. side of the former sugar factory. The latter now consists mainly of apartments and offices, along with a Sugar House Day Spa, but the Legos-like heap of brick and iron is clearly industrial in appearance.

Along with tasty confections, two good things emerged from the cane sugar enterprise. One is that the McLean family freed their slaves working there. The other is that descendants of that family, flush with the profits of their produce, founded the attractive town of McLean Virginia, 15 miles northwest of Old Town.

There was more about the Lees at the next stop of the tour, and more of Washington too. Namely, the lovely Christ Church, its 1765 construction financed via sales of tobacco. The designer was James Wren, architect of the equally impressive church in Falls Church, Virginia, and cousin of Christopher Wren, architect of London's grand

St. Paul's Cathedral. These churches were built to last. Christ Church looks like it did when constructed, while Christopher Wren constructed St. Paul's dome so sturdily that Nazi bombs bounced off it during the 1940 Blitz.

Christ Church's very entranceway, Ted knew, revealed to its visitors a schism between the old Old Town culture and the new. On the iron fence of its gate hung a large Black Lives Matter banner. Other banners along the lines of "Hate Has No Place Here" also draped from the railing. Like many old-line Protestant denominations in America, and in Europe, the Episcopalian Christ Church had become increasingly political, and progressive, in its public stance, even as the sect's congregations have dwindled. Some said this was due to the rise of alternative, evangelical churches, while others attributed it to a general decline in religiosity in America.

The BLM ensign partly cloaked from view a mound of earth behind the fence. The ivy-covered rise, 21 feet long by 18 feet wide, contains the remains of 34 Confederate soldiers, some of them from northern Virginia, who perished in hospitals in town, after being wounded and captured in nearby battles.

Christ Church was Southern in its sympathies before, during, and long after the conflict, though not, as the banners showed, currently. Before the war, R.E. Lee made a major endowment to the already historic church. Historic due to the American Wren, and to the many noted colonials who attended services there, the most notable being Washington. The first President also made a significant endowment. For generations, the name of Washington and of Lee were prominently stenciled on the wall behind the church altar. However, as part of the growing movement to delete anything Confederate, or things suggesting slavery, voices had been raised to remove Washington's and

Lee's names. Some Alexandrians had opposed this, noting Washington
freed his slaves via his will, and Martha freed hers several years after
her husband's death. And, as noted, Lee freed his personal slaves in his
lifetime, and arranged to try to free the many more owned by his wife
via her father, George Washington Parke Custis, the late owner of the
Arlington House estates and the grandson of Martha Washington
herself.

In the middle of the small Christ Church cemetery, Ted explained to his
small, masked group the old Old Town view of things. "The Union
troops, as they did with other 'secess', or secessionist, churches in
Alexandria, were not on their best behavior here." He pointed to the
tombstones, which start near the entrance gate by the Confederate
mound and go past the six-story steeple of the church to its Columbus
St. entrance. The grave markers were once more extensive, but many
disappeared at the hands of the Northern occupiers. Union soldiers
hauled away gravestones for road stones or for the front steps of
officers' homes. Some Unionists took away the fine, raised tomb of
Col. Marsteller, the supplier to Washington's army. The church altar's
silver communion chalice was pilfered. Another theft was books, from
the library down the street. They made their way to the Smithsonian
Castle's museum, where many were destroyed in a fire. The Castle was
restored by City Hall architect Adolph Cluss, who himself worked with
the Federal forces. During the conflict, pro-Confederate worshippers
shunned the church, while Union Army chaplains held services inside.
The historian took his guests to the tombstone of a soldier who was
also very controversial in town, but for an entirely different, and *outré*,
reason. Near the church's east wall is the worn yet faintly legible
gravestone of Colonel, and Mayor, Charles Simms. Ted had trouble
finding it, before spotting an oxidized metal rod with a small, circular

top indicating the grave of a veteran of the American Revolution. Though not also a veteran of the War of 1812, Simms notably participated in it. The British, while burning down the Capitol Building and White House in the war, sent a fleet up the Potomac to demand Alexandria's surrender. Otherwise, its admiral threatened, his Royal Navy warships would level the town. Mayor Simms, though a war hero of the Revolution, surrendered. Without a fight. As he had no militia, no regular Army troops, and no sailors and fighting ships. Mayor Simms also let the Brits walk off with as many barrels of tobacco, corn, and whiskey as their Royal Marines could carry, and pilfer at least 20 cargo ships from the harbor.

His inaction was condemned as cowardice. The Mayor was vilified in cartoon and caricature. The martial reputation of General Washington's town suffered. Simms' action, however, saved from certain destruction the town, its stunning architecture, and its Revolutionary War legacy. When Ted asked his guests what they would have done in Simms' shoes, most agreed they would have had Old Town spared, for the future enjoyment of countless tourists like themselves. The Mayor chose the better part of valor.

From Simms' humble grave, Ted and the group stepped across the cemetery's compact grounds to a raised tomb. Instead of the usual, simple headstone, it was a four-sided stone box, six feet long and several across. The obvious expense of its construction signaled a deceased person of special worth. In this case, a well-known actress, Anne Merry Warren, "the ornament of the American stage". She died in 1808 at age 39 after giving birth to a stillborn child. A common occurrence then, when death stalked maternity. Like "the Mysterious Woman", Warren passed away at Gadsby's Tavern.

Ted touched the raised tomb's covering slab, and told a "horror story" not uncommon in the Antebellum Era.

"Sometimes at night," he began, "an admirer or family member might come to a grave like this to say a prayer, or to place flowers. Sometimes, to the visitor's shock, the slab on top of the tomb would start to move. And then be pushed aside entirely. Then, as the observer stood frozen in fright, a figure would slowly rise from the tomb. The visitor, legs suddenly unfrozen, would sprint out of the graveyard, fearful of looking over his shoulder.

"Meantime, the figure would step out of the stone box, and look around warily. If there was moonlight, the ebony face of the figure might be more easily discerned. For the figure was African-American. And not a tomb raider. Nor someone who'd mistakenly been buried alive." Ted paused dramatically.

"The figure was an escaped slave. Hiding out, as some fugitive slaves did, in graveyards. During the day. Before coming out at night to make their way North. Sometimes, during the long daylight hours, in having to relieve themselves, or desperate for something to eat, he would leave his stone hideaway, in a break from the horror, the seeming eternity, of hiding in a tomb. To face another possible horror, of being caught, and sent back to his master. In any case, such a ghostly person would scare the bejesus out of any unwitting observer. And be scared as heck at being observed!"

With that, Ted took his guests to the remarkable metal plaque on the wall of the church entrance. It honored six men, all colonels in Washington's army, who served as the pallbearers at his funeral. All were esteemed residents of Alexandria. They were: George Gilpin, a cousin of Martha's, who sold George the grain for his Mt. Vernon distillery; Charles Little who, with some irony, helped the distiller

212

President Washington put down the "Whiskey Rebellion" of tax protestors; Dennis Ramsay, one of the "midnight judges" appointed by outgoing President John Adams to foil his successor, Thomas Jefferson; William Payne, who George shrewdly befriended after a fistfight; Philip Marsteller, the German provisioner to G.W.'s army; and Charles Simms, the hero of 1776 and the goat, not G.O.A.T., of the War of 1812. There were more colonels at Washington's funeral than kernels of corn in the mash of his distillery.

Ted's favorite tale of these men was that of the aptly named William Payne, as in "Pain in the neck". He told his guests the story, which goes along the following lines.

Payne and Washington, at the dawn of the Revolution, backed different candidates to Virginia's House of Burgesses, in Williamsburg. One day, while then-Colonel Washington was training his militia in Market Square, he exchanged heated words with Payne, of a prominent family from the west end of King St. Words led to blows, and Payne knocked the Colonel to the ground.

Washington's men were astonished. George stood six feet two, very tall for his time, and possessed immense strength. No, he couldn't toss a coin across the Potomac, but he could manhandle a heavy cannon about the battlefield. The militiamen were shocked their commander got knocked down, and they were apoplectic at Payne. They surrounded him to deliver a beating. From the ground, Washington waved them off. He addressed his tormentor. "Sir, I request your presence tomorrow at dawn."

The soldiers, and soon everyone in town, knew what this must mean. A duel of honor, possibly to the death.

At sunrise the next day, hundreds crowded Market Square. A grim-faced Payne arrived, got off his horse, and walked slowly to a soldier standing in front of Washington's campaign tent, which was set up in a corner of the Square. The soldier pointed to the tent, silently signaling Payne to enter. In the dim light within he saw Washington sitting in his campaign chair, the one from which he'd survey a field of battle. The Colonel silently pointed to a table in a corner of the tent. Payne saw two objects, which he thought at first must be dueling pistols. Instead, to his surprise, he realized they were two wine glasses. Washington then addressed him.

'Mr. Payne, I must say that yesterday I let my temper get the better of me, and I must say you got the better of me. But, instead of continuing our disagreement, I'd like to take a different tact. I ask that you share with me, not a dueling ground, but a bottle of fine Madeira.'

Sometime later the two men emerged from the tent, a bit woozy, arm in arm.

Sometime later the Revolution broke out, and Washington recruited Payne into his Army. He acquitted himself well, rising to the rank of colonel.

After the Revolution, Payne returned to Alexandria, where he and Washington became bosom friends, for life.

So much so that, with Washington's death, Payne served as his pallbearer.

Ted enjoyed this tale because, among other things, it showed how shrewd Washington was. He could have gone through with a duel, and perhaps gotten himself killed, and just before the Revolution, at the very time his nation needed him most. Instead, he recruited Payne to the fight, which led to a life-long friendship. Instead of pursuing a pointless squabble, Washington had wisely turned an unfortunate incident to the advantage of all.

As Christ Church had no services at that hour, Ted knocked on the entrance, hopeful the docent was there. Sometimes the church guide was able to give his guests a quick, private tour. Ted's events almost always took place in the open, as befitting his love of outdoor recreation; it was a treat for his guests to visit the interior of a special place.

They were in luck. An elderly, smartly dressed lady named Lucinda opened the door. Her alert gray eyes looked at Ted with a questioning gaze. She recognized him, but seemed dubious about his humorous "Political Party" shirt, the "costume" for all his tours. It depicted a formal presentation of the Declaration of Independence in July 1776, but with Washington, Adams, Jefferson, Franklin, and the other powdered wigs of the Continental Congress sporting sunglasses and drinking from red plastic cups, as if at a frat party. Political "party" indeed. The lady was rather "Old South" and traditional, and mildly disliked the shirt for its irreverence toward the Founding Fathers, and was somewhat wary of Ted for sporting such informal attire in a church. Still, Lucinda tolerated him, due to his in-depth knowledge of Christ Church, and for bringing guests there to learn about it. Besides, she found the much younger man to be handsome.

She took the group down the left aisle to pews near the lovingly crafted lectern in front of the altar. Lucinda pointed out the Washington pew, where George and Martha sat during services. They were members in standing of the Episcopal Church—but not its predecessor the Church of England, run by despised King George.

Ted might have irreverently told how indentured servants or slaves, during a cold winter Sunday morn, would place cannisters of heated coals near the First Couple, to warm them up in the days before central heating. Or how Martha and the other fine ladies disliked the menfolk's uncivilized habit, in tobacco country, of spitting tobacco juice onto the church floors. The hems of their expensive dresses picked up rust-colored stains from the disgusting practice. The women led a minor revolution of their own by demanding sacks be nailed to the side walls, to permit a more sanitary deposit of tobacco juice.

In the presence of Lucinda, Ted restrained from presenting such insights. Instead, to enlighten his guests about the town's rich military history, he asked about the two world-famous statesmen who visited Christ Church back in 1941.

"Oh yes," the docent stated primly and proudly. "Just after Pearl Harbor, and America's entrance into the war against Japan and Germany, President Franklin Roosevelt came here with a special guest: Winston Churchill, the British Prime Minister. He had flown to Washington to discuss the wartime strategy of the two new allies." Lucinda had the perceptible Southern accent of someone who'd grown up in the Alexandria area before 1960 or so, before the Beltway road, the Metro rail, and the immigration and population growth that transformed it into a cosmopolitan place and, some thought, too "Yankee" a place.

"The two leaders came here to pray for divine inspiration," said Lucinda, drawling a bit, "and for ultimate victory. And Mr. Churchill must have liked being invited to a place modeled on an English country church."

"Though the English leader might have less liked," Ted broke in, unable to resist, "the homage to General Washington, the defeater of the English, that is in here."

Lucinda smiled slightly and indulgently at the interruption. Moving to another subject, she pointed past the raised, bright-white pulpit, mounted atop a short staircase in the English style. On the walls behind it were the hand-lettered tablets of the Lord's Prayer, the Ten Commandments, the Apostle's Creed, and the Golden Rule. The inscriptions were large enough to allow those in the front pews, such as the Washingtons or the Lees, to read them. The lettering was at least as old as the church, and though they had not been retouched, they appeared better than new, as age had transformed the original white coloring to a golden hue.

As Ted's eyes looked over the gorgeously rendered precepts, he noticed something that seemed amiss.

"Have the Washington and Lee tablets," he asked, "been covered over for restoration?" In 1870, golden-lettered marble plaques for the two famous Virginia generals were placed behind the altar. The congregants of the time, mostly Southern sympathizers, likely saw this as restitution, or pushback, for the Union occupation of and acts of theft at the church.

Lucinda looked embarrassed and a little annoyed. "I'm surprised you hadn't heard, Mr. Sifter, as you normally follow such matters so closely. They were moved some time ago."

"Moved out of the public eye?" asked Ted. He could guess the reason for removal of the Robert E. Lee plaque. "And Washington too?"

Lucinda blushed, the flush noticeable on her pale, wrinkled visage.

"The church and some city authorities pushed for it to be so. Because of General Washington's..." She paused, and took a breath.

"...Because of his servants."

"But didn't he free, his 'servants'?" Ted asked. Getting no reply, he asked: "Who in the city was for this? The Mayor?"

"No. Another ranking official, I can't remember who. I was told that he or she was quite adamant about it."

Clearly embarrassed, and attempting to make amends, Lucinda
motioned the guests back over to the Washington pew. With a smile,
she pointed out the small piece of golden metal inscribed with George's
signature. Ted wondered whether there was a similar signature for
Lee's pew, and if so whether it had been erased.

When Lucinda was finished, Ted led the visitors back to the
entranceway. He made sure the docent saw him slip some greenbacks
into the contribution bin. He was always happy to help out a fellow
history lover and her institution. As the guests left, he lingered with her
a bit, and asked about the removals.

She pursed the lips on her pale, prim face. "There've been many
changes of late," she stated simply, drawling out the words more than
before.

Outside, up past the Columbus St. entrance, was one of Old Town's
few prosaic streets, where stands the Ross Dress for Less store between
the church and King Street. So, to retain the 19th-century vibe, Ted
walked his group down Cameron St., past a townhouse that was once
part of the sugar factory, and then left onto N. Alfred St. That route was
much more pre-modern in atmosphere, including the larger buildings
from the old sugar cane complex.

At the end of Alfred was busy King St. As Ted led the group across it,
he pointed out the Light Horse tavern, named for Light-Horse Harry
Lee, and gestured toward the western end of King, and at the tall
outlines of the George Washington Masonic Temple.

King St. divides the northern side of Old Town from its southern part,
so they were now on South Columbus St. There Ted noted that
Washington, as a youthful surveyor, had laid out King St., and with
great skill. One February, while working in offices nearby, Ted took
lunch-time constitutionals up and down King, as it seemed the warmest

spot in wintertime Virginia. Why? It's said G.W. laid out the streets to have the sun strike them at the angle providing the greatest possible amount of light and heat.

Chapter 16 - The Current Strife

The group was halfway to Prince St., a block away, when Ted, and a guest's pet dog, perceived a low roar. It sounded like the rumble of distant ocean waves or the commotion from a faraway sports stadium. Then, three-quarters of the way up the block, he spotted Harmony, looking elegant on the stoop of an elegant townhouse. They had arranged for her to join the tour during her lunch break.

"Didn't you see the text I just sent?" she asked, concern in her voice. "I might have heard the buzz on my phone," Ted answered, "but I was caught up talking while crossing King Street." He introduced her to the guests: "This is my friend Harmony." She noted he hadn't used the term "girlfriend", probably from his innate shyness, she figured. Still, it was a trait he had largely overcome from years of giving tours and author interviews.

By then all the guests had heard the noise, which was growing in volume, and were wondering what it was. Ted pulled out his phone. Harmony's text read: "There may be trouble up ahead."

Ted, with a mix of worry, puzzlement, and excitement, said, "Let's take a look," and strode toward Prince St., with Harmony at his side. His guests followed, somewhat hesitantly.

They passed the Friendship Firehouse, with its steeple-like lookout tower, and tall double windows that resemble the pale stained glass of a Baptist church. The "1774" emblazoned below the tower and above the broad entrance marks its construction during a time of revolution.

It was now clear the noise was from a crowd. It got louder as the tour group reached Smuggler's and Corsair Alleys, their names hinting at J.

Swift-style pirates. Curses and angry slogans were audible ahead. The tourists reached the Virginia Tech College of Architecture, where Ted normally paused to prep his guests for architectural marvels, namely the glittering mansions next on the itinerary. But that not day. At the intersection with Prince on their right, and extending up past Patrick and Henry Streets, was a milling, raucous crowd of about four hundred persons. And it was heading in the direction of Ted's little group.

It was a mixed crowd, of blacks, Latinos, whites, and a few of Asian descent. Many had signs, with slogans such as "Death to the Killer!" and "Justice Now!" and "No to White Supremacy!" Harmony was struck how most weren't wearing masks, or had pulled their masks down below their chins. A group of blacks, with Black Lives Matter shirts, were in the forefront of the crowd on the opposite side of Prince. Ted noticed that some of the whites, mostly young men, wore the black pants and shirts, elbow pads, and helmets characteristic of Antifa.

Ted, Harmony, and the guests, wide-eyed and mouths agape, halted at Alfred and Prince. Down the latter street Ted and Harmony spotted Bertha, her face as drained of color as new-fallen snow. Her body was turned toward the United Daughters of the Confederacy museum, while her head was turned 90-degrees toward the approaching crowd. Ted and Harmony noticed iron grates in the first-floor windows, of the type to discourage burglars. Metal bars on windows had been quite common in Old Town 20 years prior, before its widespread gentrification and a big drop in crime. But these grates, they recalled, hadn't been there at the time of the roses and statue incident.

"Bertha must have just had them installed," Ted told her.

"Does she know something we don't?" Harmony asked.

"No," Ted answered, "she's just been reading the papers and blogs. She probably feels threatened after all the angst, and angry statements, in the wake of the Freedmen's murder." Indeed, some local and national activist groups had made threatening remarks. Several northern Virginia orgs had turned their verbal fire on Alexandria's Appomattox Confederate statue and Christ Church's Confederate graves.

Bertha, with surprising speed for her 64 years, and despite her noticeable limp, scampered down Prince. She took a quick look at the statue in the street ahead of her, and made a sharp right, disappearing behind Hallowell's old Lyceum on S. Washington. Ted looked where she had looked. He told Harmony: "You don't have to be a mind reader to know where the crowd is heading."

As those in the tour group looked on with wild wonder, the throng strode down the street, chanting, "No Justice, No Peace—But War!", and "Show Us the Killer Now!" On the wall of the UDC museum, several protestors spray-painted slogans and curses. At a nearby brownstone next door, once the home of the Confederate-sympathizing Rev. Stewart, they smashed the basement windows. The tour guests were shocked and scared.

"That's weird," Ted commented to his group.

"What?" asked a retired military man, after pulling down his mask to make himself clearly heard. "That there's no police in sight?"

"There's that," Ted replied. "But I mean the damage to those buildings. Very few persons, only historians like me, or die-hard Civil War buffs, know the background of those buildings. I'm surprised the protestors do."

Ted and, with some hesitation Harmony, began to follow the crowd, but the guests stayed frozen in place. Thinking quickly, their guide turned to them and said, "I suppose we'll have to suspend today's tour." He paused, and people seemed more relieved than disappointed. "If anyone wants a refund, just let me know, and I'll happily return the fee." A guest, a retired schoolteacher, stated: "Don't worry about that. Just stay safe." "Thanks for a great tour, Ted!" cried a woman nervously. All the guests turned about, and walked quickly back toward King St.

"Should we really we doing this?" Harmony asked, her body language tense, but her iridescent eyes fixed with fascination on the crowd.

"It's living history," Ted responded. "History in the making. How could I, we, miss it!?" He said this half humorously, half seriously, but also worried about what might be coming.

The crowd paused where Prince meets S. Washington, with the temple-like Lyceum of its pacific Quaker founder to its right. Before them, in the middle of the street, stood the Appomattox statue. With its soldier, his face resting on his chin, turned toward the South. His expression seemed more reflective than usual.

In front of him, and ahead of the mass of the crowd, was a group of a dozen people, mostly men, of different ages, mostly white, with a few who seemed Latino. They were in the intersection, and several carried American flags, while one held a Confederate banner. Some had signs with slogans that read, "It's Our History!", "Heritage Not Hate!", and "White Lives Matter Most".

This group seemed surprised by the appearance of the much larger group on the corner before it. The latter, angry at the sight, began chanting its slogans louder. The former, recovering itself, began shouting its slogans in return. The black lives protest group, being larger, drowned out the other voices. Almost in reaction, the white rights group moved toward the Appomattox statue, as if to defend it. Those in the front of the blacks rights group moved out toward them. The slogans of both turned to curses.

Harmony and Ted watched transfixed from the southwest corner of Prince and Washington. Harmony leaned into Ted's side while Ted put his arm around her. The traffic on both sides of the thoroughfare halted: drivers were both curious about the confrontation, and afraid to run over those in the street. "Still no police," Harmony breathed into Ted's ear. Protestors trained cell phones on those from the other side, watchful, perhaps eager, to capture an act of violence. Some drivers and passengers began videorecording the event as well.

Out of the corner of his eye, Ted saw a car, a black sedan, jerk forward from the left, from up S. Washington St., then stop with a screeching sound. He and Harmony watched the car then jump into the intersection, stop, lurch forward again, and then with sudden speed head for the statue. Two people, protestors from both sides, were between it and the sculpture.

"No!" shouted Harmony, burying her face in Ted's shoulder, then glancing up. They saw the car smash into the base of the statue. Before that, it knocked over a black protestor, and seemed to have hit a white female protestor, possibly running over her foot.

Harmony looked back at the scene. The black-shirted male driver was angry, but seemed angrier he had hit people instead of the statue. He backed up suddenly, halted, and sped off between the small space between the two groups, almost hitting three other persons. The car raced off down S. Washington.

The bottom of the Appomattox statue was banged up, but intact. Ted had wondered for years if some trucker might someday take the statue out. The car driver had just tried to. But the statue was bigger, and size matters.

"I wish I had taken the car's photo!" said Ted, reaching too late for his cell.

"I got the license plate!" replied Harmony. "Memorized it."

For a brief moment, both groups were stunned silent. Then a middle-aged man who seemed to be a leader of the white group screamed at the black rights group: "You bastards! Barbarians. Destroying our statue!"

"Racists! Privileged pigs!" shot back a white woman in the black rights group. Suddenly, in the middle of the street, the two sides rushed together.

Ted and Harmony watched astonished as a wild melee broke out. People kicked, clawed, punched, bit, and punched each other. Some smashed others over the head with the post of their signs.

From atop his pedestal, the figure of the rebel looked down silently, distantly, with a sad, thoughtful look. Below, drivers sat in their cars, stunned silent. Then several leaned out of windows to take videos again.

It was the Battle of Alexandria. Seemingly, of a second Civil War. Seemingly out of nowhere, police finally arrived. Some running in on foot, others came in cop cars, tops flashing, rushing down Prince and Washington Streets to the crossing.

Four black-clad police in helmets, body armor and machine pistols pushed past Ted and Harmony. Across the intersection, near the mobs duking it out in the street, similarly clad cops appeared. About half dozen of the brawlers, bloodied, bruised, clothes torn, had fallen to the pavement.

Ted and Harmony were surprised the cops, though some had bullhorns, did not order the crowds to disperse. They simply took out canisters of tear gas, and tossed them into the middle of the street fight.

Some in the brawl, gasping for air, stopped fighting. Others, surreally, coughed violently while continuing to fight. Most of the white rights group seemed to disperse. The crowd of black rights groups, though growing smaller, was still intact.

As the gas wafting about, Ted and Harmony clutched each other, and Ted pulled her up S. Washington St. toward King St., toward fresh air and, he hoped, safety. She pulled out a handkerchief from her purse, and Ted grabbed Powerade from his daypack. Ted poured the liquid onto it, and Harmony ripped the kerchief in two. Gagging, eyes tearing, they pushed the cloth over their faces and ran up the boulevard.

They paused outside the ornate façade of the Methodist Church. Ted couldn't help thinking that, in an earlier civil conflict, Union cavalry had occupied that secess church. Down Washington, clouds of tear gas obscured much of the Appomattox statue. However, to its left, they could see some protestors had moved over to the old post office on the corner. They threw bricks through three of its windows, before police in gas masks wrestled one less than peaceful protestor to the sidewalk, and cuffed him, while the other two ran off.

Harmony coughed, her eyes burning, their amber color stricken with red. "I can't believe what I saw."

Ted pointed and said, "There's more to see."

Chapter 17 – The Old Town Riot

From out of the swirl of gas clouds came a crowd, half-walking, half-running up S. Washington St. Protestors and rioters coughing, yet still furious from the brawl, and unbowed from the skirmish with the police. They streamed past stopped cars or spilled onto the sidewalk. It was the remnants of the black rights protesters. The hardcore, mostly Antifa and BLM or related groups. About 80 in number.

"Should we run away?" Harmony asked.

Ted pulled her into the overhang of the church's portico, and placed his body between her and the crowd streaming by. "No," he smiled grimly, "it's too late now. Besides, it is living history, and we are its witnesses."

From their cubbyhole, they watched the mass of people surge to the major intersection of King and Washington Streets, where it paused. The traffic light turned green and then red, to no avail, as drivers stopped their vehicles at all four corners. Some held tissues to their mouths to try to block the tear gas pushed by the westerly breeze. Others rolled up their windows and turned up the air-conditioning, but the revolting odor still penetrated their cars.

The riotous demonstrators seemed confused about where to go next. Then a black man in a black T-shirt, a white man with a helmet and dark shirt, its shoulders bulging from shoulder pads, and a third, tall man of indeterminate race, wearing long pants, a full-length shirt and his face almost completely covered, ran into the intersection.

They all pointed east, down King St., toward the waterfront. The mob took off in that direction. Most ran along on the street or on the southside sidewalk; some loitered momentarily outside a Banana Republic. Then they moved on to a Vietnamese Pho restaurant alongside a Thai noodle spot. The previous owners had been put out of business by the virus shutdowns, and by the high rents and taxes in town; the new owners were hoping, once the pandemic lifted, to prosper in their new country.

On the opposite side of King, Ted and Harmony walked past a shuttered restaurant that had been turned into a national political campaign headquarters. Harmony was still coughing some, while Ted, who had a nasal drip from his Potomac River swim, now compounded by the tear gas, hacked long and loud, to Harmony's concern. They paused outside a Chipotle's on the corner of St. Asaph. Eyeing it, and the Asian eateries, Harmony said, with a hesitant smile, "Ted, this is your 'Culinary Corner'." He often ate at these cheap but nutritious places after a long swim or bike ride, for "recovery food". Though at the moment his stomach was queasy.

Across the way, the crowd quick-walked past a Starbucks. Those with signs brandished them, and the chants began again, of "Show Us the Murderer," "No to Privilege!", and "Our Lives Count!" The throng continued down King, slipping around stopped cars and buses. A man pounded his fist on the hood of a Hyundai, shocking its driver. Another man grabbed and shook the radio antenna of an old Ford Mercury. The two observers warily followed.

The three persons who seemed to be the leaders continued to show the way. Though it was hard to say for sure, as they were often lost in the swirl of the moving mass of people. At King and Pitt Streets, across from a French boulangerie, where the scent of newly baked bread finally supplanted the stench of tear gas, a man pointed to the southwest corner of a five-story, red-brick hotel. It was the Alexandrian, formerly a Marriott.

On that site in 1861 stood the Marshall House hotel, famed in Civil War lore, and marked by a plaque in a niche of the hotel wall. Ted was stunned the crowd was being directed to it. Its leaders' knowledge of The War Between the States seemed as specialized as his own. He recalled the bloody tale referenced in the text of the plaque.

The Marshall House owner, James W. Jackson, was a fiery secessionist in a pro-Southern town. From the roof of his hotel, he flew a gigantic Confederate flag. It was so big the newly elected President, Lincoln, could see it through a spyglass from the roof of his White House. It was a thumb in Honest Abe's eye.

The President directed a friend and head of his personal security, a Union colonel with a wonderfully alliterative name—Elmer Ephraim Ellsworth—to take a regiment of troops down the Potomac to Alexandria, occupy the strategic town, and haul down the rebel ensign. On May 24, 1861, in the month after Fort Sumter touched off the war, Ellsworth and his men disembarked at the waterfront, and his superbly drilled troops marched smartly through Alexandria, to occupy key sites like the telegraph office.

Residents and workers, most of them secessionist, warily peeked at the troops from behind the shuttered windows of warehouses and homes. African-Americans, slave or free, almost all Unionist, warily wondered what would happen to them.

Ellsworth's regiment, the 11th New York Infantry, had style. Each man strutted wearing the Arab turban, bright blue vests, and red pantaloons borrowed from the Zouaves, France's dashing colonial troops, known for a distant war at a place called Crimea.

Meanwhile at Prince and S. Washington Streets, the site of the future
Appomattox statue, men of Alexandria mustered at that crossroad. A
battle between them and the Zouaves, on the streets of Old Town,
seemed likely. But a regional commander, Robert E. Lee, judged they'd
be outnumbered and outgunned. So they marched out of town to fight
another day. Actually many more days, for the Alexandrians fought in
almost every significant battle of the Eastern Theater until, well,
Appomattox. When they laid down their arms and returned to their
hometown. And over time formed the Mary Custis Lee-17th Virginia
Regiment Chapter of the United Daughters of the Confederacy,
the R.E. Lee Camp Hall. Housed in the Prince St. museum now
operated by Bertha Stuart.

Early that 1861 morning in May, Ellsworth and his gaudy host marched
up near the Marshall House. Accompanied by a lieutenant, a corporal,
and a reporter, Col. Ellsworth mounted the four flights of stairs to the
hostelry's roof. The giant rebel flag was hauled down without incident,
and the Stars and Stripes, with 34 stars for all the states, South and
North, hoisted up. Then the Colonel and two fellow troopers started
their way down the stairwell. Mission accomplished.

Not quite. At the third-floor landing, a door flung open. James W.
Jackson emerged. With a shotgun, double-barreled, double loads. The
hotel owner blasted a hole in Ellsworth's chest, killing him.

The Colonel's enraged corporal shot Jackson, and for good measure ran
him through with his bayonet.

Both Ellsworth and Jackson lay dead on the blood-soaked floor. They
were perhaps the first two fatalities of the Civil War, and certainly the
two most prominent in the public eye. At Fort Sumter, despite a fierce
rebel cannonade on the besieged Union troops, no Federals had been
killed.

The two slain men were lauded in their regions. "Remember Ellsworth!" shouted Northerners, who hailed him as "the first to fall" in a righteous cause. Patriots prized as holy relics the bloodstained splinters from the stairway where he fell. Lincoln presided over tributes for his slain friend in the grand East Room of the White House. In Border South Old Town, not to mention further South, James Jackson was the hero who was hailed.

An Alexandria grand jury convened. It ruled the hotel owner was in his rights, by defending his property rights, including a rebel flag flying atop his place of work.

For many years a commemorative plaque hung in the hotel niche. As Ted would tell his tour, it reflected the town's majority opinion in 1861. It read in part: "JAMES W. JACKSON was killed by federal soldiers while defending his property and personal rights...He was the first martyr to the cause of Southern independence..."

Thinking about this, Ted realized why the crowd had been led, rolling like a ship on the ocean, up to the plaque. He and Harmony watched as an Antifa member sprayed it with red paint, and another hurled two bottles of piss into it. "Or maybe acid," Harmony observed, as a smoky mist emanated from the plaque.

A middle-aged female pedestrian, keeping her terrorized terrier tight on its leash, strode by them, and shouted through her mask: "Where are the police?!" They had disappeared. Or, at least for now, the crowd had outrun them.

Harmony and Ted walked at the back of the crowd down King. Most of it went to the corner of Fairfax St.

"Oh," said Harmony, "I hope they leave the tourist center alone."

It was once the townhouse of William Ramsey, a town founder and Scottish merchant. By the 1930s, it had nearly fallen apart. Then

Ramsey's great-great-great-granddaughter began an effort to restore it. After a turn as a brothel in the Second World War, public-spirited groups had restored it a decade later. Now it's the Tourist Information Center.

Ted, standing tippytoe, looked over the heads of the protestors, thought he saw a leader pointing out their next focus of attention. Even in seeing the masked person from the rear, Ted thought the figure looked like someone he knew. In the chaos, he put the thought aside.

At the Burke & Herbert headquarters across from the Ramsey House, a male rioter, after much effort, managed to dent the front-door window with the handle of a sign. Meantime a young, black-clad woman with dyed indigo hair slid open the night deposit box, and poured red paint down its slot. In the windows above, employees, including at least one descendent of co-founder Arthur Herbert, a colonel with the 17th Virginia, as well as many black staffers, two of whom were descended from those freed at Mt. Vernon, watched the assault with eyes as wide as the Wilkes St. tunnel. The male demonstrator threw down the signpost, and stepped into the hallway of the double-doored entrance, just after the bank manager on duty locked the second door, stymying him. For a moment, Ted wondered how James W. Jackson might have responded to all this. Or Col. Elmer Ephraim Ellsworth.

But there was little time to think, as the crowd descended the steep decline of lower King St. to Old Town's densest concentrations of restaurants. Ted swallowed hard. All of them were in historic homes, former warehouses, and venerable stores, and other choice locales in what had been one of America's busiest port cities.

Because of the pandemic-related restrictions on indoor dining, the restaurants that were open had set up outdoor dining, with tables and chairs covered by canvas tents that had transparent, plastic windows. A modest number of tourists and locals had ventured there to eat lunch, some for the first time since the virus struck. The diners had heard the ruckus approaching them, or had been texted by friends about what the media was already calling the "Old Town Protest" or the "Confederate Riot". Some hastily left; the owner of a new Mexicali restaurant yelled at his staff to "Shut the place now!" Customers and waitresses and the maître d's stood next to the sidewalk tents, and looked up King St. with nervous anticipation.

From the Burke & Herbert Bank, Ted and Harmony watched the crowd rumble onward. A husky black man in his twenties, seemingly without direction from any leader, lurched across the street to an Italian restaurant on the northeast corner of King and Fairfax. Ted featured the 19th-century place in his military history tours. It was originally built by a thieving ship captain who was consigned, according to legend, to a Market Square stockade. In the Civil War it became a house of ill repute, servicing some of the hundreds of thousands of homesick Yankee soldiers funneling through the capital region, hundreds of miles away from their wives or girlfriends. During Prohibition, it was a speakeasy, selling illicit rum in a Southern realm otherwise known for its blue laws. At the time of the Second World War, a German sympathizer operated a wireless radio from its basement, sending intel on the region's military installations to U-boats prowling off the Chesapeake. The spy didn't have far to go for sensitive information, given the vast Torpedo Factory down the street churning out munitions for America's own undersea vessels. The emporium became most famous, however, for a piano player expert in ragtime, the proto-jazz genre largely invented by African-American musicians like Eubie Blake and Scott Joplin.

To the shock of those seated outside, the young man, wearing a Diversity, Equity & Inclusion shirt and a red, black, and green Africa cap, entered a sidewalk tent containing four tables. Maskless, he strutted from one table to the other, smashing his fist on each, shaking plates and glasses, shouting, "We must have justice now! No justice, no peace—just war!"

Looking at this through a tent aperture, Harmony winced with every fist smash. The guests, some of them elderly, were filled with fear. Except for one middle-aged white man who gave the interloper a fist bump. Peeling away his masks, he shouted, "I support your cause, one hundred percent!" Smiling, he took cell photos of the intruder, and posted them, hoping they'd go viral, which they quickly did.

The rest of the demonstrators continued down to the other side of King, to an art gallery, where some of them paused. Ted winced. He knew its operators, and loved the place, which specialized in realistic, neo-traditionalist paintings. On many Fridays, it put on an open house, with appetizers and wine, to highlight the work of a fledgling artist. He'd brought Harmony there on one of their nights out. Given that it was originally the townhome of one of those ubiquitous colonels from the American Revolution, he started some of his George Washington tours there.

Its managers, a young man and a young woman, liked the publicity Ted brought the gallery, and admired his knowledge of their building's rich history. The place had been named for George Gilpin, a town official and entrepreneur and an officer in Washington's army who had introduced the other George to his cousin Martha, leading to their epochal marriage. Gilpin was also one of the six pallbearers for Washington's funeral commemorated on the Christ Church plaque. The

gallery operators had beautifully redone the circa 1800 home with glass
skylights and pinewood floors, while retaining the original stone walls.
Ted and Harmony crossed the street and tracked the rear of the crowd
again. Seemingly on cue from a tall female leader, a rioter took a chair
from a restaurant table and threw it at a gracefully arced bay window
by the gallery entrance. The window cracked, but held. Demonstrators
milled about outside and cried out slogans.

"I hope," said Harmony, "they've locked the front door." As she spoke,
Ted looked up the street, and saw Michael, a dreadlocked gallery
employee, emerge from the Italian restaurant. He was speaking to its
owner. Unaware of the mayhem, they had emerged, horrified, to see the
mob in front of their places of work.

Ted thought fast. He had once helped Michael take out paintings from a
showing. Artwork was stowed in the gallery's basement, in a humidity-
free room, and was removed via a side door to a narrow alleyway.

"Distract them!" Ted yelled to Harmony, as he sprinted toward the side
alley. Harmony was stunned silent for a moment, then guessed what
Ted was up to. She jogged to the middle of the street, stopped,
gulped—and pressed the emergency button on her cell. A loud,
repetitive burst of noise, intended to foil a sexual assaulter, shot from
the phone. Many in the crowd turned from the gallery to her, as she
shouted: "The police! The police are coming! SWAT team! I got an
alert! Tear gas too. Alert!" The people in the mob paused, with some
still feeling the effects of the tear gas at the statue. They talked
excitedly with each another on what to do.

Ted raced to the alley, grabbing a restaurant chair along the way,
figuring he'd break a rear window to enter the place. At the basement's
side entrance, he gave the latch a try, and was elated to find the street-

level cover unlocked. Tossing aside the chair, he stepped into the cellar
and, his left knee aching, ran up the stairs to the gallery.

He walked briskly through the main room toward the entrance. On the
walls to either side of him hung hundreds of thousands of dollars of
paintings and illustrations by up-and-coming artists. He looked through
the glass windows near the entrance door to the mob outside. Smiling,
he heard the dull thudding of Harmony's phone alert; the ruse of hers
had worked.

The protestors were still staring in her direction, or looking down and
up King for the police. Ted rushed to the door—both locks were
unlocked. As he locked them, he feared someone would burst in first.
Luckily, only one rioter was looking into the gallery, but he was
looking, with admiration, at the paintings, not at him!

Without turning, Ted jogged steadily backwards, like a cornerback
warily giving space to a fast receiver. He raced down to the basement,
scrambled up the steps of the side entrance, and closed the cover, much
relieved to find no one in the alley.

Harmony's alarm stopped; he suddenly felt afraid for her. He ran
around to the entrance, and found the throng had moved its attention
away from Harmony, who had moved to the other side of King.
However, its focus had turned back to the gallery. A 25-year-old man
in a red Che Guevara shirt smashed open the bay window with a brick.
Its sill displayed illustrations from the latest show. The man ripped a
watercolor of a New York City street scene off its placeholder, and
ferried it away. Meantime a young woman with violet hair and black
pants and an Extinction Rebellion shirt tried the door knob. "It's
locked!" she cried. As some considered entering through the bay
window, the crowd saw a **masked, hooded** leader point them down to
the end of the street, where King meets Union St.

Ted rushed over to Harmony and grasped both her hands. "That was some trick!" he lauded.

"They never saw you," she replied in wonderment. And in admiration, "That was fast!"

The mob moved near a newly opened Mediterranean eatery at the intersection's southeast corner. Well, almost to the corner. The recent heavy rains had flooded Union St. This happened often, as the lower part of Old Town was practically at river level. In fact, kitty-corner from that intersection, at the side of the Torpedo Factory, was a sign that showed the high-water marks of the flooding Potomac in various years. This deluge was minor in comparison, but it did keep most of the crowd above Union St.

Ted's heart sunk again. The Mediterranean place had been the first in town to reopen, starting with take-out soon after the pandemic began. Then, as most places stayed closed, it expanded to outdoor and limited indoor dining. To raise the spirits of its customers, and of Old Town's generally, it played terrific pop music from large speakers propped on open windows. Ella Fitzgerald, the late Tom Petty, the Hayde Bluegrass Orchestra, and many more.

Its venue is stunning: a former warehouse that looks more like a little city hall. Two massive stories lead to a reinforced roof held up by brick columns. White pillars climb up along the first floor and front the French windows, with high, thin glass panes shooting above.

Built in 1872, it replaced the customs house of the busy port that collected the tariffs on imports which Hamilton had set up to gain the revenue for the new federal government. A tax that, Ted figured, was a distant seed of the Civil War, as Jefferson's Southern planters and Western farmers hated the tariff, which raised the cost of the manufactured goods the agricultural South and rural West had to import from Europe.

Locals believed the site was "cursed", in the commercial sense. Over the decades, multiple restaurants had set up shop in the attractive space, only to quickly close. Probably because of its location, with dense traffic passing by at all four corners, and with the dearth of street parking nearby. And then the pandemic. And now this rolling riot. However, the protestors alongside the bistro were not tempted to break the frail thin glass of its windows. They seemed distracted, confounded, by the flood, though the waters were but a foot or so deep. The crowd, including a leader or two, stood at the curb, staring at the roiling Potomac just on the other side of the small park fronting Union St., with the massive Torpedo Factory complex on their left.

Rudderless, the mob shifted left to the northwest corner of Union and King, with Ted and Harmony just behind them next to a popular ice cream shop, now shuttered at the very start of summer. She gestured toward the corner building just down King.

"William Ramsey's store, right?" said Harmony. Ted was surprised she'd remembered him telling her that. The man whose home would become the tourist info center had his main business, a general store, and now a women's clothing store, at that spot. It hadn't reopened yet. Its lights were out, its front door locked. A sign hanging on a window by the front door contradicted its closure, stating primly, "Do not bring ice cream inside. Our floors and dresses are precious."

Then two young black men in loosely hanging jeans and shirts festooned with the images of rap stars appeared from around the corner of N. Union. They ignored the sign. After jimmying the door knob, they sauntered inside. They were later identified by the enterprise's video cameras: they were not protestors or rioters, but youths with rap

238

sheets, police records, from the Old Town housing project. The younger of the two grabbed an armful of satiny dresses, and the other, a couple of years older, grabbed a big, expensive handbag and tossed dress shoes into it. They departed quickly, and sloshed through the flood waters up N. Union St., again soaking their $265 Nike Air Zooms.

By then, though some of the mob had dispersed, the protest leaders had regained their confidence. A woman and, was it a man?—Ted wasn't sure—signaled the 50 or so people remaining to follow them across the flooded street. They waded through filthy water up to their ankles. "They're going for the coffee shop," stated Harmony, now standing with Ted outside the clothing store. "Yeah," he said with restrained anger, "the ground floor of the Fitzgerald warehouse."

There soared the full half-block of one of Old Town's great relics. The tobacco warehouse of Colonel John Fitzgerald. The Irish-Catholic immigrant who'd served as General Washington's aide-de-camp in the Revolution and then, like so many other colonels, had settled in Old Town post-war. He went into the tobacco business, the town's early mainstay, and prospered mightily, as his cavernous warehouse, built in 1795, still evinced.

Ted greatly admired the building, with its two stone chimneys poking through a vast, slanted roof. A distinguishing feature is a top-floor pulley hanging out into Union St. With it, men hauled tobacco barrels up to the attic, a relatively dry place above the often-flooding Potomac. For years, the city had debated whether to keep the traditional name of John Fitzgerald Square for the intersection. But some in the town government complained that Fitzgerald had owned slaves, and that tobacco had been based on the Southern plantation system. The term Waterfront Park was bandied about as a new park took shape between the warehouse and the river. For now the locus remained a place without a name.

Suddenly it hit Ted anew, and harder. The sites on King St. the rioters were attacking weren't being targeted by chance. Their actions weren't random, but deliberate. Based on the antebellum, and bellum, history of the locales. "The Marshall Hotel," he muttered aloud, "the Burke & Herbert bank, the tobacco warehouse."

"Huh?" said Harmony.

"They're all connected," said Ted. "Whoever is organizing this, and someone, or some persons, *are* organizing this, has an expert's knowledge of Old Town history."

Harmony nodded slowly, then shook her head doubtfully, and said, "It feels pretty spontaneous, and dangerous, to me."

The operators of the cafe in the warehouse's first floor had anticipated the flooding. They'd placed sandbags along the foundation stones of the ancient building to stem the waters from seeping in. But they hadn't anticipated the rioters.

Before Ted could respond to Harmony, they saw a muscular youth pick up one of the stuffed, 40-pound sandbags, and toss it through the cafe window.

Ted bristled. He felt like punching someone. "More destruction in Old Town," he noted grimly. "And maybe another confrontation," said Harmony, who pointed to four heavily armed policemen splashing through the water toward the warehouse from the Torpedo Factory.

Not seeing them yet, two thin, black-clad youths took soda bottles from a daypack. The bottles were filled with liquid, capped with straw, and had fuses. Molotov cocktails. Ted was stunned silent. Harmony gasped. They lit the kerosene-filled receptacles, and tossed them through a window of the coffee shop. A portion of the cafe, and thus the venerable warehouse, erupted in flames. Two other rioters lit three more of the incendiaries.

The armed cops had warily neared the Starbucks. As the firebombs were tossed, they paused in the watery street, just in view of the mob. One cop raised up a pistol, and fired off two shots into the air. The mob froze.

Then a siren was heard, at first faintly, then loudly. Suddenly from around the corner of Prince St., several blocks down Union, rushed an eight-wheel fire engine truck, from the modern fire station a block from the Athenaeum. It came roaring toward the rioters.

The mob was trapped. Some in the crowd jumped from the flooded street to the café's sidewalk. The police scurried over to the north wall of the warehouse, temporarily out of sight. The fire truck roared to the cafe, and braked, but not before it kicked up a huge wall of water onto the troublemakers, dousing the pyromaniacs and their Molotov cocktails.

Two burly firemen, a white man and a Hispanic man, emerged from the driver's compartment. They tossed aside two skinny Antifa youths, and knocked down a man in a BLM shirt. They raced into the cafe with portable fire extinguishers, and contained the blaze.

The police slipped up a rear side street, Wales Alley, and rounded the corner onto Union, guns, batons, and Tasers at the ready. Surprised, the mob scattered. Cops nabbed a few of the lawbreakers, including the man who'd pilfered the gallery painting. Protestors flew off in all four directions, some sloshing through dirty, thigh-high water toward the river. One of the policemen thought, 'They remind me of wharf rats. The really big kind at a harbor.'

Harmony pointed to two of the cops in front of the warehouse. "Tear gas cannisters!" she cried out.

But as the cops decided whether it was still necessary to throw them, she and Ted scooted fast up King St., and away from any further danger, eyewitnesses to the Old Town Riot.

Chapter 18 – Religious Liberty, Medieval Medicine

Ted was glum about the prospects for his next event. Two of his flagship tours, a Lincoln and the Civil War walk in downtown Washington, and a Lafayette Square Tour of Scandal and Assassination across from the White House, had been effectively shuttered, after protests and riots near the Executive Mansion that echoed the ones in Alexandria, as well as those that erupted around the nation. People were also skittish about attending another of his major tours, on the history of espionage, in Georgetown, after widespread looting and burglaries there.

Even with the pandemic, Ted had continued his tours. But the riot and the deaths at the Freedmen's Cemetery and Atheneum had plunged an already frightened, gloom-ridden town into a deeper malaise. Ted himself was further upset at the killing by a fentanyl pusher of the young man at the housing project. He was dismayed it got far less publicity than the other incidents. It reminded him of the slaughter each weekend on the streets of Southside Chicago, which exceeded by many multiples the much-publicized deaths of suspected felons in police custody, but which garnered infinitely less media coverage.

In Old Town's historic core, some people weren't venturing outside at all, and relied on delivery services for food. That day, the number of guests who'd RSVP'd for his tour had fallen to a handful. And he knew from experience that only half or those, or less, might actually show up. Along with Meetup, his pre-paid RSVPs, via Eventbrite, Atlas Obscura, PayPal, and Airbnb Experiences, were almost nil.

Still, for weeks he'd advertised his Old Town tour of George Washington and the American Revolution, which he hadn't given for some time. He was disturbed, but strangely stimulated as well, by the recent outrages, rather as he had felt after 9/11. He felt rather like a soldier on a battlefield, a man shaken out of everyday tedium. And he figured a tour would spur, as it almost always did, his research and writing, and raise his spirits.

He did, however, switch its starting point, the "history sweet spot" near the Athenaeum, with its towering townhouse of Mayor Hooe, and the porticoed mansion of Sally Fairfax. Guests might be put off by the yellow police tape, and its reminder of the recent fatality, that still surrounded the backlot of the Athenaeum gallery.

So he stood in bright, early afternoon sunshine at another oft-used jumping off point for his G.W. tours. Where St. Mary's Basilica and the Old Presbyterian Meeting House adjoin on S. Royal St. He liked this spot, across the street from the two churches, for its stunning visuals, and for its juxtaposition of two startlingly different cultures. He found to his left St. Mary's, the church endowed by Col. John Fitzgerald, of Fitzgerald Park fame, and Washington's aide de camp. It is a soaring, Gothic Revival basilica, of lovely, light-colored stone, trinities of windows and entrances, and a side spire of slit apertures evocative of a medieval castle. Its 133-foot belfry can be seen far down Royal St. The Catholics had spared little expense in creating their rococo wonder.

Yet immediately to Ted's right was the spare parson's home of the Presbyterian Meeting House. It was far lower in height than the basilica, darker in hue, and fashioned of plain brick. And it was a "flounder house" of the type often built by the Scottish merchants and prelates who'd founded Alexandria. From the side, the minister's home looked like a giant triangle that had been cut in half, or a flounder fish sliced in two by a fishmonger, thus its nickname.

The story was too good not to be true. Supposedly the "frugal" Scots built their homes to be one half the size of a typical house, by the simple expedient of cutting it in two. Because, if the square footage fell below a certain amount, they'd be exempt from paying property taxes! Cheap, frugal, pennywise, wily, thrifty, or business-savvy—pick your less-offensive term of choice for the canny old Scots of Old Town. The contrast between the two cultures—one Catholic and baroque, representing the more emotional and stylish traditions of Southern Europe—and one Protestant and spartan, typifying the more restrained, cooler, and commercially-oriented customs of Northern Europe, couldn't be starker. Yet instead of warring against each other, as they had in Old Europe—during the Thirty Years War and the English Civil War, for instance—in Alexandria, as in America generally, they lived peacefully and even, as in this case, cheek by jowl, joined at the hip. Ted would point out that Washington, and Jefferson, were in good measure responsible for this concord. Those leaders worried a religious war might come to America, such as the one in France, between Catholics and Protestant Huguenots, which had torn that nation apart in the late 1600s, within the historical memory of the two Founding Fathers.

As President, Jefferson wrote a famous letter of support to dissident Baptists in New England, where they faced oppression from that state's dominant religious group, the Puritans—the enduring, derisive term for that region's Presbyterians.

Jefferson wrote that America should abide by a "separation of church and state." Not as an attack on, or a call for, a ban on the public practice of Christianity, but as an admonition against an official state religion, like the Church of England under King George, the Lutheran faith in the German-speaking lands, or Catholicism in Spain and Italy. In remarkable response, the rural Baptist community had brought together all their cows, and milk maids, and with the aid of a giant wine press, had produced the world's largest cheese. The so-called Mammoth Cheese, 1,235 pounds worth. Which they shipped by sled in winter to Jefferson's Execution Mansion as a gift of gratitude.

President Washington penned a related letter, to a non-Christian group, members of a synagogue in Newport, Rhode Island, the colony whose religiously inspired capital, Providence, was named by Baptist Roger Williams. Washington elegantly wrote the Jews there that all good citizens, including people of differing faiths, were welcome in the newly democratic America:

"...Happily the Government of the United States, which gives to bigotry no sanction, to persecution no assistance, requires only that they who live under its protection should demean {exhibit} themselves as good citizens, in giving it on all occasions their effectual support...May the children of the Stock of Abraham, who dwell in this land, continue to merit and enjoy the good will of the other Inhabitants; while every one shall sit in safety under his own vine and fig tree, and there shall be none to make him afraid..."

On religious tolerance, Ted would note, Washington and Jefferson were sagacious, and in large result the U.S. avoided the pitfalls of the Old World. On matters of race and ethnicity, however, the road ahead proved more difficult. Indeed, a very old reminder of that was in a mundane spot just behind him.

Ted turned his gaze from the churches to a paved, narrow alley leading from Royal St. to a parking lot for St. Mary's. In the antebellum, the lot had been the place of a school for the female Catholic parishioners. It

was another example of how much Alexandria stressed education
almost from its start, and for women as well as men. But it also
illustrated the terrible divide on race and region at that time. For the
most famous, or infamous, graduate of this Academy for Young Ladies
was a woman who'd grown up in the Maryland countryside of tobacco
plantations. And who later ran a boarding house in downtown D.C. A
lodging where John Wilkes Booth and his fellow conspirators met to
plot, at first, the kidnapping of Abraham Lincoln. And later, when that
ploy failed and as the Confederacy collapsed, the President's
assassination. For the woman in question was Mary Surratt. Later tried,
convicted, and executed for her role in the Lincoln conspiracy. The
only American woman executed in the 19th century.

On the tour, Ted would say, tongue in cheek, that her ghost was
sometimes seen in the parking lot. Somewhat more seriously, he'd note
other tour guides claimed to have seen her ghost where she was hanged,
at today's Fort McNair in D.C.

Ted had arrived at the churches at 1:15 p.m., 15 minutes before the
tour's starting time. He liked to arrive a quarter hour ahead, to chat with
the guests and put them at ease while sizing up their personalities and
interests. But the minutes went by without anyone arriving. Ted
checked his phone for messages; there were none. He checked his
email: Three people had changed their Yes RSVPs to No. Only three
Yes RSVPS remained, and one pre-paid reservation.

Royal St. was empty of pedestrians, despite the welcoming weather,
which was warm and partly sunny for a change. His Garmin timepiece
read 1:30 p.m., then 1:40. No one arrived. He figured he'd wait until a
quarter of two, then call it quits.

From behind, seemingly out of nowhere like a ghost, and startling him,
came a voice. "Hello, Ted." It was Saul, one of the biggest fans of his

books and tours. The gray-haired, stoutly built man was outfitted in tailored shirt and cuffed pants. Ted hadn't noticed his characteristically quiet approach. Saul looked up and down Royal St.

"Are we it?" he said, smiling faintly, his owlish eyebrows raised in a questioning manner. "Maybe so," answered Ted, scanning his cell futilely for new messages. "It's about 1:45 already, so why don't we start?"

They ambled across Royal to the gate of the Old Presbyterian Meeting House. Ahead of them was a small graveyard dating from the town's founding. "Let's begin with one of Old Town's most historic, and lesser known, spots," said Ted, adding dramatically: "The Tomb of the Unknown Soldier, of the American Revolution!"

Ted took a step forward, but Saul stayed where he was, looking doubtful. He explained, "I'm not allowed to enter this, this cemetery." He looked uncomfortable, and embarrassed. "Let me walk around the block, and meet you at the front of the church, at the cemetery exit."

Ted thought a moment, then understood. One time, another Jewish friend of his had been visibly uneasy at walking through a Christian cemetery. He remembered that Saul belonged to a Conservative branch of Judaism. According to a strict rabbinical interpretation, apparently, such graveyards were unhallowed ground, and should be avoided.

Ted said he understood, and took a step forward, then stopped as Saul said to him, "Look. There are no other guests. If this isn't worth your while, and it isn't, why don't we call this off? So that you're not wasting your time." Ted smiled and said, "But you were the only one who prepaid." "Don't worry about that," Saul smiled back. "They'll be plenty more tours." He began walking down Royal St., and called out over his shoulder, "Enjoy your day."

Ted knew his friend was right, but he was still disappointed, and restless. He decided to least get some exercise, despite the busted tour, with a ramble about Old Town. The historian continued through the Old Presbyterian Meeting House cemetery, dating from 1774. The church's four stories of rectangular brick with a wooden bell tower and lookout made the humble parson's home seem earthbound. It reminded him of Boston's Old North Church, and with reason, as it was also a hotbed of the American Revolution.

Out of respect, Ted took off his Jamestown, Virginia Triathlon ballcap, and walked through the scattering of graves of Scottish town founders, such as John Carlyle of the Carlyle mansion. He noted the flat gravestone of William Hunter, and its inscription honoring the founder of the St. Andrews Society in America, for persons of Scottish ancestry. Ted reminded himself to create a tour of the Scots of historic Alexandria. Or perhaps the Celts of Old Town, bringing in people of Irish ancestry, like Col. Fitzgerald, or the revelers who so annoyed the builder of the Spite House. And persons of Welsh descent, for whom was named St. Asaph St., after the patron saint of Wales. He thought he could pitch the idea to tourists visiting from the British Isles and the Republic of Ireland.

On the high wall separating, not church and state, but the Presbyterian churchyard from the Catholic basilica grounds, was the Tomb of the Unknown Soldier. Not the famous graves, of four separate wars, at Arlington National Cemetery. But Alexandria's own. The Unknown of the American Revolution. It was a highlight of Ted's tours there.

After the First World War, Britain and France each created an honored tomb of an unidentified soldier. The United States decided to create such a monument for America's fallen. The first Tomb of the Unknown at Arlington National Cemetery, created in 1921, was of an unidentified

U.S. soldier from the Great War. The Second World War, Korea, and Vietnam followed, and no doubt more will come.

In the 1920s, Alexandria citizens who were restoring the Old Presbyterian Meeting House determined that their town should have its own Tomb of the Unknown. They figured that, for its size, Alexandria had as great a military legacy as any. It was the hometown of Washington, and the Lees: Light-Horse Harry and Robert E. The submissive actions of Colonel Simms in the War of 1812 was downplayed, before its recent revival as a comic-opera episode in the town's past. Although no one was then thinking of taking down statues of Confederate soldiers, officials chose the American Revolution, a unifying event for all Americans, as the period to honor. Old Presbyterian, having been a focus of Revolutionary sentiment, was the fitting locale.

However, as Ted would explain on tours, they needed an unknown soldier. During the First World War, and at least until DNA analysis could precisely identify a dead trooper, there would have been many deceased, unidentified soldiers to choose from. But in 1928 the American Revolution had been over for 145 years. There were graves of unknowns from then, but where, and where in Alexandria?

It happened there was one just a stone's throw from the Old Presbyterian graveyard. Of a soldier from the Revolution, who'd been buried in an ammunition crate, and originally discovered way back in 1826 during construction work on St. Mary's grounds. For the new memorial, the remains of the man were transferred to Old Presbyterian. On April 19, 1929, on the anniversary of the 1775 Battles of Lexington and Concord, the Tomb of the Unknown Soldier of the American Revolution was dedicated. This was done with much ceremony: There were religious services in the Meeting House, and then high officials of

the federal and Virginia governments, with the U.S. Army band
playing, paid their respects to the Unknown.

Unlike at Arlington, no solitary sentinel performs around-the-clock
guarding of this grave. This seems unnecessary, as this Tomb of the
Unknown remains, well, relatively unknown. A simple waist-high iron
fence protects three of its sides, and a wall the fourth. An American
flag flies from one of the corners. And on the slab topping the grave are
inscribed phrases that might bring any patriot to tears. Written by the
Clerk of the House of Representatives and author of "The American's
Creed", William Tyler Page, they read:

"Here lies a soldier of the Revolution

Whose identity is known but to God.

His was an idealism that recognized a Supreme Being,

That planted religious liberty on our shores,

That overthrew despotism,

That established a people's government,

That wrote a Constitution setting

Metes {measures} and bounds of delegated authority,

That fixed a standard of value upon men above gold

And lifted high the torch of civil liberty

Along the pathway of mankind.

In ourselves his soul exists as part of ours,

his memory's mansion."

His eyes straining, Ted read through the faded message—he was
always moved by it. After finishing, he looked up above the grave at
the small circular window on the rear wall of the parson's house. He
smiled on seeing the opaque window, its pane oddly split in two by a
thin vertical rod, as he recalled the tales of some fellow guides.

Tour guides of historical locales can be superstitious. Probably because they discuss legendary figures who died long ago, they often believe in ghosts. Guides familiar with Old Presbyterian had sworn to Ted they'd seen the spirit of the Unknown Soldier in that window. This apparition always appeared at night, and Ted wondered wryly if the sightings occurred at midnight when the moon is full. But the soldier was most likely to show himself, he was informed, when visitors to the graveyard behaved improperly. By laughing or cursing, or disrespectfully keeping their hats on in a sacred place. Perhaps his friend Saul, Ted mused, was being properly cautious in avoiding this ground.

He left the graveyard through the narrow path that runs between the Meeting House and its "wall of separation" from St. Mary's. He paused, as always, at the tombstone of Dr. James Craik. He was Washington's physician, remarkably, from the French and Indian War in the 1750s up until the night of his famous patient's death in 1799. Ted looked through the windows of the Meeting House, noting the spare yet elegant ground-floor pews and upper gallery. Outside the pathway, on S. Fairfax St., he paused below the plaque above the church's twin-doored front entrance. On the entrance rails below it were broad banners reading, "Hate Has No Place Here", and "Intolerance Is a Sin". The messages seemed to underscore the recent deaths, though they'd been in place for over a year.

The plaque commemorated a 1798 religious ceremony there that reflected the pressing concern of the time, the prospect of an all-out war with France, America's former ally from the American Revolution. During the Administration of John Adams that followed Washington's, the U.S. fought an undeclared naval war with France, the so-called "Quasi War". But it was in fact a real war, with many engagements between the small, fledging U.S. Navy and the large, well-established

French fleet. In fact, President Adams founded the U.S. Navy at this time to protect the nation from foreign superpowers. Further, Washington was brought out of retirement, to head the U.S. Army, in tandem with Alexander Hamilton, in the event of land battles.

But Adams was no warmonger. He may have worried a full-scale conflict with the powerful French might wreck the new American republic. So he prepared for a wider war while at the same time pursuing peace. He sent his Secretary of State, John Marshall, the future Supreme Court Chief Justice, to Paris to negotiate.

And Adams and Washington attempted divine intervention for peace. The current and former Presidents took part in a national day of prayer and fasting in the hope of ending the growing rift with France. Indeed, Washington attended a special service at the Old Presbyterian Meeting House for that purpose.

The Presidents' prayers, and sincere desire for peace if possible, worked, after a fashion, after a while. Following two years of quasi-war, the U.S. and France agreed to end hostilities. Thus the commemorative plaque. In its 240-plus years of existence, the U.S. has never fought a declared war with France, the foreign nation most critical to securing American independence. Further, for much of that period France has been a valued ally. Give Old Presbyterian some of the credit.

Ted continued down the usual path of his Washington tour, going up S. Royal and turning right on Duke, while thinking over the "treasure map". As ever, he loitered for a bit at the impressive townhome, dating from 1796, of Dr. Craik, just two blocks from his grave. He liked peering through the home's gated alleyway to the back garden. With its narrow passageway shadowed from the sun, the garden dimly visible in the distance, it looked like a time tunnel back to colonial days.

Dr. Craik was the Forrest Gump of Washington's era. During the French and Indian War, when accompanying the colonial Colonel Washington to Fort Pitt on the star-crossed expedition of General Braddock, Craik tried and failed to save the life of the wounded British commander. During the American Revolution, at the major battle of Brandywine in Pennsylvania, he helped save the life of the man who was perhaps the most important wartime leader after Washington. This was the Marquis de Lafayette, the key liaison to America's key ally of France. Fortunately for the Marquis, stricken with a gunshot wound to the leg, two men came to attend to him. One was James Craik. The second was a young Virginia sharpshooter, who'd abandoned his studies at William and Mary College to join the revolution. This was James Monroe, the future President, who as Chief Executive feted the Marquis at the White House, and recast President's Park as Lafayette Square.

Dr. Craik's final famous treatment was his worst, for it came at, and contributed to, George Washington's untimely death. The first President had finally retired to Mt. Vernon, while still serving as titular Army chief due to the Quasi War. One afternoon, Washington rode out midday in cold and rain to inspect his extensive estates. On his return to Mt. Vernon, instead of changing clothes and taking a warm bath, the man of duty sat at his worktable, writing out correspondence, then lingered to dine with Martha.

The next day, despite a hoarse throat, he supervised slaves who were removing trees near the mansion house. That night, he very much caught his death of cold. By contracting an extreme inflammation of the throat. Probably his epiglottis, the flap of tissue at the back of the throat, that opens up to permit breathing, had swollen up like a balloon. He was unable to eat or swallow, and barely able to breath.

The plantation's overseer, at Washington's request, bled him, of more than a half pint of blood, a now-discredited technique that the patient believed had helped quell some of his previous maladies. For his throbbing throat, Washington was given an admixture of vinegar, which nearly caused him to choke to death.

To treat the stricken man, three respected doctors arrived at the plantation. One was a physician from the Rose Hill estate near Port Tobacco, Maryland, a Dr. Gustavus Brown, the former Surgeon General of Washington's army. The second, whose home was next to Sally Fairfax's near the Athenaeum, was Dr. Elisha Dick. The third was Craik, himself a former Army Surgeon General, and like Dick a personal physician of Washington's.

Dick and Craik prescribed remedies then common. The first was an enema. A baleful liquid, probably mixed with toxic compounds like lead, was forced up into the patient's bowels, then expelled. The idea was that an enema would force out whatever harmful substances caused the malady. Unsurprisingly, the treatment didn't work.

Others were attempted. Painful plasters were placed on the patient's feet and legs. A poultice of Spanish fly, a poisonous ointment concocted from dead beetles, and famous as a supposed love potion, was applied to the exterior of the throat. More healthily, the sufferer was also instructed to gargle with a sage tea and vinegar mix. But nothing worked.

So Dr. Craik turned back to another remedy: bleeding. But not with leeches. Washington was a strapping man. Pinpricks wouldn't do. So the doctors opened up his veins, and drew out at least 32 ounces, and up to 80 ounces, of blood. The sources on the amount differ, but it's clear a large fraction of Washington's vital red stuff was siphoned away. The procedure might very well have killed him. (Incidentally, bleeding, with leeches, has made a bit of a comeback. Medical researchers believe the insects, if applied in a limited and controlled way, can alleviate blood clots and other circulatory woes.)

At one point in the treatments, Dr. Dick proposed a modern technique. Being up on the latest medical procedures, he advocated making a small incision in Washington's throat, to help him breath and to let him take in water and broth. A tracheotomy. But the other medicos rejected this novel approach as too risky.

Frustrated, the doctors again tried an emetic, this time for Washington's throat, to induce vomiting. The potion, which contained toxic mercury, didn't help either.

Washington seemed to have had enough. The great man told Craik: "Doctor, I die hard; but I am not afraid to go; I believed from my first attack that I should not survive it; my breath can not last long."

Sensing death was near, he finalized his last will and testament, and gave instructions to his personal secretary, Tobias Lear, about ensuring a proper burial. The hands of the clock near his deathbed stopped at 10:30 p.m., the second evening after the fateful ride about his estates. Today the clock is in the possession of Old Town's George Washington Masonic Temple.

It was a sorrowful end for a hero who'd given a half century of his life to public service.

The tragic tale always astounded Ted's guests. He figured, 'No matter how bad the pandemic is, or how uncertain the response to it, one has to be glad one's living now, in an age of modern medicine. And not at the mercy of the doctors of Washington's time.'

Ted next turned up Lee St., passing the home and garden of George Johnston, an influential Alexandria attorney at the dawn of the revolution. He was the protégé of a talented young lawyer with a gift for oratory, his most famed remark being: "Give me liberty, or give me death!" Yes, Johnston sponsored Patrick Henry, later Virginia's Revolutionary War governor, and its greatest orator. Ted admired the meticulously maintained house, but chuckled knowing he'd never afford the $5 million asking price. 'Unless,' he quipped to himself, 'we find Swift's treasure.'

The historian reached Lee and Prince, "America's most historic street". The yellow police tape had been removed from the Athenaeum, but the art gallery remained closed after the death of the security guard, lending the place a continuing aura of dread. Ted walked past it, feeling glum about the deceased guard, and knowing there had been no breaks in that case. Still, he had heard the injured waterfront guard had fully recovered.

Chapter 19 – Mysterious Observers

Ted passed the mansion of Sally Fairfax, admiring as ever its grand Southern porch, and the adjoining, far more modest townhouse of Dr. Dick, which inevitably brought back to mind leeches and fatal bloodlettings. He passed the townhome that had been the offices of the pro-Confederate *Alexander Gazette* newspaper, burned by Northern troops back in 1862. And further up Prince an antiques shop, now occupying the former British post office where in the '70s, the 1770s that is, Alexandrians staged a Stamp Act tax revolt. Ted paused his long strides halfway up the block at a stunning Federal townhouse. He admired the three stories of Flemish bond brickwork highlighted by ten front windows and two arched entrances of fine white stone.

It had been the Bank of Potomac. And it had been, with the Bank of the Old Dominion, today's Athenaeum, one of the three large merchant banks tending to the city's deep-pocketed businessmen. During the Civil War, the Union turned it into government offices, of a most unusual sort. One of Ted's favorite Civil War stories had taken form there.

It involved, according to several accounts, a sickly-looking old man in tattered clothes and with a white beard and white hair and bushy white eyebrows, who'd stopped his horse and rickety carriage on the street outside the offices one day in 1863.

The decrepit man looked like he might fall ill, or worse, at any moment. However, a keen observer might have noticed he continually scanned the street, up and down, west and east, with alert blue eyes. He took particular interest in any troops on Prince St., and in the officials, staff members, and Union officers entering and leaving the former bank building. Far from being senile, the man actually had piercing intelligence, and he took careful note of everything in view.

At length the man, seemingly after a long and needed rest, goaded his horse into a slow trot. The carriage departed Old Town, and clattered toward the lines separating Union soldiers from Confederates. At a lonely place along his route, he brought the vehicle to a halt. He looked about carefully: There was no one in sight.

With dramatic flair, he pulled off his white-haired wig. And dispensed with the fake beard and eyebrows. Revealing an earnest, clean-shaven face. He stripped off his tattered clothes, and revealed the neat gray uniform of a Confederate colonel.

For the sickly old man was in fact the 30-year-old "Gray Ghost of the Confederacy", the legendary, notorious, Confederate raider and spy, John Singleton Mosby. A scout who once snuck through Yankee lines with his men to bag Union General Edwin Stoughton, in his pajamas, while he was slumbering in a Fairfax City home supposedly protected by his large force of Federals.

Mosby had been spying on the Old Town building, and for an excellent reason. For the bank offices had been transformed into gubernatorial offices. Very unique ones. When Virginia seceded, the Union Army took over the portion of northern Virginia closest to Alexandria and D.C. Although the bulk of the state was in rebel hands, the part that remained under Northern control required a Governor. And Francis Harrison Pierpont, the Governor of the Union's Restored Government of Virginia, put his offices in the old Bank.

Yet he wasn't the only official from a state there. Even though most of Virginia seceded, a big block of it opted to stay with the Union. Not the small, northeastern part close to the federal capital—it was largely pro-

Southern, and in reality occupied by Union troops. But the large, mountainous part to the far north and west with few plantations and slaves. West Virginia, as it came to be called, which moved to secede in 1861, not from the Union, but from the Confederate state of Virginia, in order to stay in the Union!

To become a state, it needed a constitutional convention, and a Governor, not to mention a state capital, as well as a state legislature and a Governor's offices. As a new state in the making, it didn't yet have any of those. So in a sense, until West Virginia formally seceded in 1863, Pierpoint, the Governor of the Restored Government of Virginia, northern Virginia, was also the governor of West Virginia. With a wink, Ted would tell his tour guests the former Bank of Potomac was the only place in America to host the Governor of two different states.

Due to its administrative control over so much territory, including turf facing the Confederate capital of Richmond, it became a place of great interest for Colonel Mosby. In his clever disguise he reconnoitered it, with the aim of kidnapping the Governor of two Northern states! And perhaps exchange Pierpoint for a host of rebel prisoners of war. However, Mosby, though a daring man, was hardly foolish. He determined that, given the thousands of Federal troops in Alexandria, and swarming over Prince St., a kidnapping scheme was too risky. He shelved the notion.

Ted stood outside the bank, lost in his thoughts, as he retold the story to himself as he would to his guests, like an absentminded professor, oblivious to anyone else on the block. Indeed, he was unaware that a person with a wiry physique and an alert manner was just across Prince St. Keenly observing him, and even more so the former Bank of Potomac.

260

After the war, Ted continued recalling, none other than Ulysses S. Grant had befriended Mosby, a slavery opponent who had quickly reconciled with the Union. When Grant ran for re-election as President in 1872, Grant took on Mosby as a political consultant to advise him on the Southland. Many Southerners saw him as a traitor eager to switch sides. Unfazed, Mosby later accepted a prominent position with the Feds: U.S. consul to Hong Kong, of all places, where he became a scourge of corrupt American officials there.

His long life in war, politics, and diplomacy included a stint in California commerce, working for railroad tycoon Collis Huntington. While in the Golden State, he befriended the precocious boy of a wealthy family, a youth with a fascination for the military. Mosby would take the youngster out on rides, where they'd reenact Civil War battles, with the boy playing the part of General Lee. He went on to attend the U.S. Military Academy, to fight in the first American motorized unit (during the Pancho Villa Mexican border war), to represent the United States in the pentathlon (with its shooting and sword events) of the 1912 Stockholm Olympics, and to train and command, in the First World War, the first U.S. armored unit. And to lead, during the Second World War, a mighty mechanized army, fighting from North Africa to Sicily to France to Belgium to Germany.

For the youth that Mosby had befriended, and taught the art of surprise attack and swift maneuver was—and when telling this tale, Ted would flash a photo of the boy turned man, recognizable to all—General George S. Patton.

The historian liked to relate the Mosby story due to its message, among others, of national reconciliation, and because it illustrated how young a nation America was. After all, in the Civil War there were people alive who could remember the American Revolution. And there were people alive in the Second World War who could remember the Civil War. And a few ancient veterans were still around who could remember fighting with Patton. And some people are alive today who carried the glories, as well as the grudges, of those past times.

The trim, athletic man watching Ted from across the street was driven by emotions, if not exactly grudges. He recalled seeing Ted observe the aftermath of the Athenaeum death, and talk with the policemen there. And now this historian was at another site of extreme interest to him. The previous night, in fact, the observer had crept through the alley of the former Bank of Potomac residence to explore its back lawn and rear windows, before heading a few blocks away to another venerable structure, and for the same purpose.

The observer tugged on the wig that covered his dark, curly hair. His clothing—jeans, a light-blue cotton shirt, a gray ball cap, and Adidas running shoes, along with the obligatory masks—were non-descript. To hide from view, he stood behind a mature elm tree, while snatching looks at the building. His next act was coming together in his mind. But he was worried about this inquisitive fellow outside the old bank.

Was it a coincidence, him being here, or was this fellow on to him? More importantly, were the police, with whom this man seemed to have some kind of working relationship?

He felt the nerves tingle in the top of his stomach, a sensation common to his dangerous profession. He took deep, regular breaths, and calmed himself down. He would continue with his plan. There was too much at stake, far too much to gain. 'And perhaps lose,' he thought.

Luckily, the lanky tour guide outside the building seemed lost in reflection. The observer imagined that, if need be, he could approach him stealthily and knock him unconscious. But Ted, lost in a reverie, didn't glance his way.

After looking over the building some more, and solidifying his plans, the observer walked quietly up Prince St., and onto Pitt St. He sauntered past the alluring townhomes of Revolutionary congressmen, a plantation owner, and Quaker businessmen. He filed some of these places away in his head for possible future exploits. And he'd soon return to the former Bank of Potomac.

Chapter 20 – Excavations, Ignitions, Arrests

Oblivious of the departing stranger, and smiling in remembrance of the Mosby/Patton tales, Ted started walking again up Prince St. Due to his walkabout, he was starting to get hungry. For years, his friends were amazed at how rarely he ate at home. At least until he met Harmony. For a long time, along with his tours, book writing, and IT work, he had pursued the workouts of a long-distance triathlete. This meant a regimen on most days of a 3000-yard swim, or a 25- to 50-mile bike ride, or a run ranging from 6 to 10 miles, if not a track workout of middle-distance repeats. After the injuries to his knees, he reluctantly stopping running, and added hikes or long walks to the mix, and took to racing in "aquavelos", the swim-bike variant of triathlon.

After an arduous workout, he'd be famished, yet needing to swiftly get back to research and writing. So he'd compiled a set of food joints offering healthy, rapidly prepared "recovery foods". Several, including a Mexican burrito and a Thai noodle place, were nearby. While pondering such "gourmet" choices, Ted turned onto St. Asaph St. He passed a restaurant, formerly another one of Old Town's famous, old-timey fire stations, whose large arched windows betrayed the entrances and exits of its one-time use. Its food was tasty, but too expensive and took too long to prepare. Then, a bit further up the quiet street, he reached one of the most remarkable, if tiny, parks in the nation.

He entered the front yard of the Murray-Dick-Fawcett House, the name referring to the various people who owned it in the Federal Era, circa 1800. It's a former ranch house, dating from the 1700s, after landowner John Alexander had lent his name to the region, when what was to be

Old Town was still farm and forest. The home's contemporary owner had peeled away many layers of paint to reveal the slanting roofs and red-timber side walls which, if not original, dated from Washington's time.

The "Dick" in Murray-Dick-Fawcett was "Doctor Dick", as Ted called him, part of the team that plied the fatal remedies on the ill-disposed Washington. The physician had his home here as well as the one next to Sally Fairfax's manse. "Fawcett" was another of Old Town's prominent families, who intermarried with the Hooes, that mayoral First Family of Alexandria, and the Leadbetters, the Quaker family that helped run the town pharmacy. "Murray" had interesting employment, and a renowned client. Patrick Murray was one of George's stablers; Washington, a superb equestrian, trusted some of his horses to Murray's care. And possibly his military uniforms for haberdashery work. Sadly, Mr. Murray went broke, and Doctor Dick acquired the place.

Many places in America boast that "Washington Slept Here". There was no doubt of that at the Murray-Dick-Fawcett place. During his more prosperous years, Murray would often invite the Washingtons over for dinner. They slept there too at times, given the displeasing prospect of a long carriage ride at night along bumpy country roads back to Mt. Vernon. It could also be said that "Washington shat here," Ted might note irreverently to tourists, as the house had three privies dating from the first President's time. Just holes into the ground really, with stone toilets at the top, in a room right behind a wall. "There was no running water back then," the tour guide would joke. "You might say they turned off the Fawcetts."

Ted wandered around the current owner's front yard, not trespassing this time, as it was open to the public. As usual, it was littered with bric-a-brac, which had been brought out of the house, which was being renovated, as 250-year houses often are. Strung about were rocking chairs, chess sets with sculpted, extra-large pieces, bound sets of yellowed magazines like *Southern Living* and *National Geographic*, and living room tables, most serviceable, and some of them antiques of oak or mahogany. The collections of many owners, most fairly well off, over many generations.

The present owner of the venerable abode had made a distinctive and generous offer to the town, which had long desired to possess his lodging as a historic site. He was an elderly man, of an age when many have thought out their will and testament, and to whom they might leave their earthly possessions. Ted had met and chatted with the fellow, after he found the historian scoping out his exterior walls, in trying to figure out what was new and what was restored.

The owner obviously loved the rich heritage of Old Town. He decided to bequeath the place, and not only for future generations, but for the current one as well. Under an agreement with the city government, the front yard of his home was made a public park for the remainder of his life. Visitors were free to come through the yard's gate, and sit on the antique chairs set up on the lawn. To get a good and unencumbered view of the colonial ranch house where Washington, and many others, had lived, visited, dined, or slept. Further, on the public-spirited man's death, his house would be deeded to the city, as a history museum. Ted had never heard of a public-private partnership of this kind, and one so personal.

In the little front-yard park, Ted approached Wright "Rick" Richards, the 45-year-old, hard-hatted manager of the current restoration. Around them was the usual potpourri: venerable furniture, out-of-print books, and old-fashioned toys, the latter to delight children who wandered in with their parents.

Near a set of rocking chairs, Ted noticed a new excavation next to the west wall, "the privy wall", a narrow ditch with moist, red-clay soil flung up around it. As he stared at the hole the restoration boss stepped over to him. Slipping down his mask, the hearty fellow shouted, "Hey Ted, how goes it?!" Rick started to slap the historian on his shoulder but, thinking he might not be "keeping a safe social distance", drew back. Smiling, Ted reached out his left hand, and the two men fist-bumped. In a pandemic, this seemed a safer, yet still friendly, way of greeting.

He and the manager shared an interest in Old Town ghost stories, and they swapped a couple of hoary tales of residents who had been killed, or committed suicide, or who had otherwise met a horrible end in historic dwellings, which their restless spirits had supposedly haunted ever since. Rick told him of one such place, an ancient townhouse where he had been laying down wood floors in its attic room, where long before a woman had accidentally burned herself to death on the morning of her wedding. Ted knew the place, which now hosts apartments and a ground-floor gelati shop across from Market Square. With some embellishment and changes for dramatic effect, Rick's story went something like this:

'It was not long after the Civil War, when countless people went hungry. Alexandria was distressed, depressed. Most had cheered on, or fought for, the Confederacy, and many had family members who'd died, or been maimed, in the many battles around the region. The black population, on the other hand, had been largely pro-Union, and liberty had come for the newly free, and sunnier prospects for the already free. But those of African descent had much suffered too, from the dire privations of the war. Indeed, Ted had recently read through a book from a Connecticut historian, who estimated that perhaps a million African-Americans—there were about four million Southern slaves—died from the war's hardships, especially from a horrific typhoid epidemic spun off from the soldiers. Especially distressed in Alexandria were the fugitive slaves who'd surged into town—the very people commemorated at the Freedmen's Cemetery. They were largely bereft of the necessities of life that heroines like Harriet Jacobs strove to provide.

Still, for all of Alexandria, there was finally peace. And it was springtime. The weather was warming, laurel and redbud were blooming. The town looked forward to a seasonal, national, and municipal rebirth.

A much-anticipated marriage symbolized the town's hopes for more peaceful and prosperous times. Laura Schaefer was a town beauty, betrothed to the handsome and successful, if somewhat impatient, Charles Tennyson. Though a local hero, he was no relation to the English poet Tennyson, famous for the Pickett-like "Charge of the Light Brigade". Everyone in town looked forward to his nuptial celebrations.

Before the wedding, Laura stayed at the towering townhome near the southern end of North Fairfax St. In her silken white wedding gown and its stunning, 15-foot-long trail, she was giddily attended to by bridesmaids and the maid-of-honor. All were besides themselves with glee for the church ceremony to come.

However, the impetuous groom, Tennyson, did something no man is supposed to do on the morning of his wedding. Unable to restrain himself until the big event, he made a surprise visit to his betrothed. As he arrived at its threshold of the townhome, surprising the bridesmaids,

Laura rushed up to the top floor to hastily arrange her coiffure and clothes.

She stood before a long mirror, a kerosene lamp at her side so she could better judge her appearance. She felt behind her, making sure the pearl buttons on the back of her dress were in place. Yet as her alluring visage stared back at herself, she smelled something. Smoke.

At first she ignored it, perhaps thinking the scent was from the kitchen, and stayed intent on making herself look her best for her beau.

But the smell got stronger. And stronger. She stared at the mirror, and saw smoke right behind her. She looked down at the train of her dress. To her horror, she realized that the long, thin attachment had snaked its way back to the fireplace. A fireplace that was still aglow from the embers of a blaze set the previous evening.

Her train was on fire!

She twisted about to get a better view, and knocked the kerosene lamp down on the back of her dress. In seconds she was ablaze from the train to her back.

Laura Schaefer tried frantically to put out the flames, to no avail. Her dress was very long, too long for her to extinguish every spark.

Besides, silk is a very flammable material. Tongues of fire ran up and down her clothing and her body.

In a panic, desperate to escape, she rushed to the door, and pulled hard on the knob. But the door was stuck!

The flames had now reached the top of the dress, and were licking at the creamy-white skin of her lovely neck. She pulled on the knob again, ever harder, but the door remained stuck. She screamed, but her room were so far up that no one on the first floor heard her shouts. She pounded on the door with her fists, she stamped her feet. She kicked the door in agony as the fires scorched her shoulders. She howled, and pounded again, and again, as the blaze reached the hairs of her head. Finally, the cacophony from above was heard downstairs. Alarmed, Tennyson went racing up the narrow flight of stairs to the room a full three stories above. At the top landing, he heard the pounding, heard the screams, saw smoke coming out from underneath the door.

Now it was his turn to pull on a door knob. But the damnable thing wouldn't budge! He cried tears of rage, as he heard the agonizing cries of Laura, calling out again and again. Then, with a herculean effort, he yanked open the door.

As he did, Laura, by then a ball of fire, rushed by him, and went tumbling down the stairs, like a fiery comet crashing down to earth. The wretched bride-to-be ended up at the foot of the steps, her lily-white wedding dress blackened, her fair maiden's skin ruined. Soon she died from the burns.

Later that terrible day, a broken Tennyson met a friend, the manager of a liquor shop down the street. He was given a stiff drink, which he drained, and asked for another. As his friend turned his back and reached for the bottle, he heard a gunshot. Tennyson had pulled out a pistol, and taken his own life. A life no longer worth living, he felt, after the death of his beloved Laura Schaefer. A day the town had looked forward to with so much joy had turned to horror.'

After finishing the story, Rick informed Ted that once, while on a construction job, he had actually worked outside the room where Laura was so horribly burned. One winter evening, he'd finished redoing a floor. It was a long, back-aching job, albeit well-paying, and he labored well past sunset. As he was finishing up, he remembered a contract laborer of his was supposed to have repaired the interior room. He decided to check on the workmanship.

With a downcast expression, Rick told Ted how he tried to pull open the door, but found it was stuck. He pulled and pulled: no success. He checked if the door was locked. It was not. He pulled hard again; no success. It was almost as if he was reenacting Laura Schaefer's final actions. Rick rocked back on his heels, and the stocky fellow pulled and pulled with all his weight. When the door suddenly opened, he almost fell over on his back.

As he regained his balance, a great rush of very warm air, on a very cold night, came pouring out of the room. Yet, as the heat touched his face, he felt a clammy cold.

"I'm not a superstitious man," he said to Ted. "But I swear that the gust was a ghost, the ghost of Miss Schaefer." Normally happy-go-lucky, Rick seemed crestfallen from the retelling.

Perhaps the general atmosphere of dread in town was affecting him, Ted figured. To change the subject, the historian gestured toward the hole in the ground near the privy wall. "Are you propping up the place?" he queried. He knew the foundations were centuries-old, and might need fixing.

Rick's countenance turned from gloom to puzzlement. "In truth, I couldn't tell you," he said. "I noticed it when I arrived this morning. But me and my Salvadoreans didn't dig that hole." Ted was surprised. Rick continued, "I know it wasn't there yesterday. I was examining the privy and the wall, and I would have noticed it. It's as if it appeared out of thin air." He shook his head hard. "The hole touches the foundation stones, chipped away at them some. I just can't figure it." He grinned. "Maybe it's the ghost of Laura Schaefer. Or George Washington." Ted didn't grin.

The manager excused himself to return to work. Ted, rubbing the stubble on his chin thoughtfully, stepped over to the hole. A ring of fresh dirt surrounded it. He noticed what seemed to be finger marks from where the digger would have hoisted himself back onto the lawn. Long, slender fingers. Of a woman, or a thin man. Next to them were footprints. Actually, just portions of prints: It looked as though someone had stamped over them. Still, Ted recognized they were from running shoes similar to his. He placed his ASICS shoes next to the print. The digger's shoe was smaller than his. Ted is 5'11-3/4''. He estimated the digger was 5'7" or so. A shorter person. And strong, able to pull himself or herself up from a deep hole.

Wondering about the strange excavation, he left the yard, and turned from St. Asaph to Prince St., heading west. Across the way was the hulk of the federal courthouse, fronting a large parking lot. It was testament to a most remarkable court case.

In 1917, a group of highly educated, smartly attired women, operating out of their offices near the White House, staged loud protests outside the Executive Mansion. They were suffragettes, demanding the right to vote. Two months prior, the United States had entered the First World War, and the protestors held up banners reading, "How Can You Fight for Democracy Abroad When You Don't Allow Voting at Home?" President Wilson, and many Americans, did not appreciate denunciations of the Commander-in-Chief in a time of war. Justice Department officials indicted the suffragettes, including Alice Paul, their haunted-eyed, 28-year-old leader.

The women were tried in the Old Town courthouse. Thirty-three of them were convicted, incredibly, of blocking a sidewalk, and were consigned to a dank Lorton, Virginia prison. Their treatment was horrific. Guards smashed the head of one suffragette against an iron cot. When Paul went on a hunger strike, eggs were forced down her throat through a tube. The inmates were forbidden medical care.

That was the bad news, Ted reflected. The good news: Negative publicity about the brutal treatment made newspaper headlines worldwide. An outraged press pushed Wilson into backing a Constitutional amendment giving women the vote in every state.

These thoughts of long-ago woes vanished as Ted approached the intersection with S. Washington. In the middle of the street stood the symbol of the current strife, the Appomattox statue. But it looked very different. The torso and boots of the soldier were splashed with red paint. The base of the statue was scarred from where the car had hit it. Trash lay scattered about its base. Moreover, on the northeast corner of the intersection, the large windows of an enterprise were boarded up. The smell of smoke lingered near it.

The Lyceum was, he was relieved to see, undamaged. But alongside it on Prince St. was a strange contraption. A flatbed trailer truck with a long metal rail rising up at a 90-degree angle. At the rail's top was a video camera, its lenses trained on the statue. It was prepped to record anyone who tried to deface, burn, or topple the artwork. Ted knew of similar video hoists that had been set up in Richmond and Charlottesville, prior to riots and demonstrations that led to the hauling away of Civil War statues. But it was jarring to see this in his own town.

Feeling low from the killings and the mayhem and their aftermath, he walked past the familiar sight of the Fowle-Patton manse, and the less-familiar, yet disturbing markings, scrawled on the Swann-Daingerfield House.

After grabbing a snack at a little grocery, he came to Bertha's museum, the Robert E. Lee Camp Hall. Ted thought this was one of the most impressive-looking structures in town. The open, rust-red shutters of the 12 large windows pressed against the lighter red of the bricks, giving an appearance of solidity and strength. Still, perhaps due to his New York City upbringing and his Swiss-German ancestors who fought for the Union, the building also struck him as a bit forbidding. He walked across Prince toward the former Union Army garden of the house where convalescing soldiers had written so eloquently of their dead comrades. 'I wish the iron grates between the garden and sidewalk were wider,' he thought, 'to afford a better view.'

Then his reflections were broken by the whoosh of vehicles approaching, roaring to a crescendo, and screeching to a stop across the street.

Out of four vans stepped muscular, hard-faced men with submachine pistols and flak jackets, emblazoned with the letters "F B I". The tall figure of Associate Assistant Director Comitas stepped quickly if awkwardly out of the final van. Two Alexandria police cars rushed from either side of Prince St., and pulled to an abrupt halt in front of and behind the vans. The husky figure of Greco stepped out of the one to Ted's right.

The armed men ran to the entrance of the dark brownstone of the Confederate museum, guns pointed at its polished mahogany doorway. Comitas, pistol drawn, his pale face flushed, stepped to the door and banged on it, paused impatiently, then banged it again. After a few seconds, he punched in a number on his iPhone. He got a connection, and shouted, "We know you're in there! Come out, out peacefully, while you have the chance!"

Ted felt a buzz on his own cell and thought it was Harmony. 'How could she know about this?!' he wondered, and looked at his text.

"Can you help me? I don't know what to do," it read. "I'm so scared."

It was Bertha, the museum's operator! Ted was speechless, textless. Had she spotted him from a window? He was on amicable terms with the lady, but hardly the close friend or family member to contact at such a time.

Comitas motioned to a burly agent, who took a crowbar to the door. Historic hinges snapped apart. The FBI man slowly pulled the door open, cursing when a splinter entered his hand. Other agents, machine pistols brandished, rushed inside.

Peering through the window panes, Ted saw the agents spread throughout the townhome's first floor. Finding no one, they rushed up to the second floor, the locale of the small museum.

Later Ted learned they found Bertha, stricken, cowering, her back to a wall underneath portraits of Lee, A.P. Hill, and Stonewall Jackson. Now, through the open entrance, he saw armed agents walk the handcuffed old woman down the staircase to the ground floor, and the entranceway's stone steps.

Behind them, a female agent came out carrying several laptops, apparently Bertha's. As Comitas stood motionless on the stone stoop, they packed her, sobbing, into a van.

Ted's eyes went from Bertha to Comitas, who was looking directly at him. The tall man's jaws were gripped with fury. "I saw you watching us!" he shouted out. "You'll be the next one we look into!" Ted, normally cool when confronted, was shaken by the FBI man's angry implication.

Comitas walked to the van and took a rear seat next to the arrested woman. The vehicle pulled away quickly, made a sharp left onto S. Washington St., and headed to the J. Edgar Hoover Building in downtown D.C. for an interrogation of Bertha. Some of the agents stayed inside the house to conduct a forensic examination.

One of the Alexandria police cars at the curb slowly drove away down Prince. The other backed up, turned, and stopped directly in front of Ted. Greco's broad figure got out. His olive-tinted cheeks were flushed. "What the hell are you doing here?!" he demanded.

"Pure coincidence," answered Ted, shaken again, almost stammering.

"Seriously."

Greco looked away sharply, not believing nor disbelieving, his dark eyes staring toward the Appomattox statue at the corner, and the video crane observing it. "You better be damn careful, Sifter. This is deadly serious stuff."

"I know it is," Ted replied evenly, having recovered his aplomb. Then with some emotion, he added, "And I know that woman enough to figure she wasn't involved in the murder. Or murders."

The veteran cop gave Ted a piercing stare, and started to walk back to his vehicle. Ted figured Comitas was pressuring the detective, which no doubt got under his skin. Greco stopped, and turned to the historian. "If you know anything about this, you better—" He paused, gaining control of himself, recalling their work together. "—I would, appreciate it, much, if you told me." And he went slowly over to his car.

Chapter 21 – A Wolf's Lair

For his stay in Alexandria, Wilhelm McVeigh had picked below-the-radar lodging. He first booked a room at the Traveler's Horse motel on Route 1, aka Jefferson Davis Highway. It was a couple of miles south of the Beltway and southeast of Fort Lyon. The worn, one-story lodgings stretched for 90 yards along a pot-holed parking lot next to a small, abandoned bank. The hostelry had been built back in segregation days, before the forever-busy Route 95 became the main north-south highway in Virginia.

At first, it seemed just the right spot, as it was almost deserted. Just a couple of derelicts and a few itinerant salesmen with limited expense accounts took up rooms there. Those within the few cars moving along Jeff Davis Highway might have thought the motel itself, with its busted neon signs, had been abandoned.

McVeigh was able to park his van behind the lodgings, out of sight of the thoroughfare, and visible only from a little-used access road. He could remain anonymous. And he had to laugh at the motel name's reference to Robert E. Lee's horse Traveler. A bit of the Old South, just as he liked it.

He paid for seven days, in cash, handing the bills to the daughter of its East Indian proprietor. She paid no attention to him behind her mask, and certainly wouldn't recall his features behind his double mask. 'She must be from South India,' McVeigh judged from her dark skin. 'An *Untermensch*, maybe a Dravidian, not a light-skinned Brahmin, and Aryan, from north India.' As he handed over the money, he sneered from behind his cloth coverings.

But one night, McVeigh had a scare. Rain turned into a torrential downpour, lasting for six hours. As often happens, those sections of Alexandria barely above river level and closest to the Potomac were flooded. Hardest hit were the nearby Old Town, Belle Haven, and Cameron Run neighborhoods. This caused many residents, their yards and basements swamped with river water, to relocate to hotels for the night. Brand-name, Old Town lodgings like the Hampton Inn and the Alexandrian were full up. Some displaced homeowners resigned themselves to staying at Traveler's Horse.

McVeigh was horrified at the lodgers filling up the place, who even took the rooms to either side of his. His van, which had been the only vehicle in the rear parking lot, now had multiple cars and work trucks plopped alongside it. The chances were still slim anyone would grow suspicious of him, but the chances had increased. For each day he was "in the wild" casing out targets, with a van laden with guns and explosives, the risks increased. 'I need another place to stay,' he decided.

Early the next morn, before any other lodger was awake, he packed up. As it would be suspicious to just take off, he got the balance of his money back, from the same East Indian woman, who seemed permanently fixed in the motel office. Her attention was on a sexy TikTok video, so she handed over the cash without even looking up. Figuring the poorer, northern part of Old Town might have similarly cheap, low-profile lodging, McVeigh took his van in that direction. Curious to see how the area along the north waterfront had changed, he drove along N. Royal St., passing the public housing project, and went over to the riverfront's former warehouses, now demolished, or converted to low-rise offices, or to new residences modeled along Colonial Era lines. At several intersections, train tracks ran along the streets up from the Potomac. He neither saw nor heard any trains, however, and wondered if the freight lines were still in service. If they were, he mused, they could make for a spectacular bombing, if he could board a railroad car and pack it with explosives.

Near a paved-over canal lock, he reached Abingdon Drive, named for the sprawling plantation that once reached up to today's Reagan National Airport. He swerved left to avoid a set of railway tracks next to a bike trail. He braked the van to a stop at the crossing, and was astonished by the expanse to his right.

Rising into the sky above the Potomac was the town's abandoned, coal-powered power plant. Its five mammoth smokestacks, like the funnels of the *Titanic*, topped off a 161-foot-high complex of corrugated iron and concrete.

Curiosity overcame McVeigh. He left the van on Bashford Lane, after first ensuring the parking space was legal. 'It just wouldn't do,' he chortled to himself, 'to have a tow truck haul away the ordinance hidden inside.'

The vast, desolate place was even more deserted than the rest of the pandemic-gripped city. Deathly quiet, abandoned and unused for years. And though the former, 514-megawatt facility must have been worth many millions, if only in scrap metal, there was no security checkpoint, no guards. Realizing this, a notion took shape in his mind.

After picking the lock to a chain wrapped around the gated entrance, McVeigh had made a quick examination of the grounds. Coming upon a broken window at the plant, he crawled inside, and examined a portion of the interior. On the first floor of the main building, he found a plant manager's long-deserted office. 'This could do very well," he thought.

That night, he had returned, draped in black and with night-vision goggles strapped to his head. He made several trips from his van, taking along necessaries and some ordinance. Although moldy, the office was otherwise in fine condition. It had an old table, a settee, a small desk, and two chairs. It had windows which, though smeared with dirt and grit, afforded a view of the grounds. It was in a corner of the structure which could permit a window escape if he detected someone's approach from within the building. Further, he could leave his van in the adjoining, out-of-the way neighborhood, which had no metered parking.

The decaying coal plant was the perfect night-time hiding spot. 'It's just like The Joker's lair!" he grinned. An ideal place to lay low for a some nights while planning destruction of the kind which a comic book villain would relish.

Chapter 22 – Media Sensation

Late on the afternoon of Bertha Stuart's arrest, Ted was back at his duplex a mile south of Old Town. Images of the riot clung to his brain, and Bertha's perp walk, as well as Carl Cordero's murder. He tried tying the Freedmen's death to the attack on the waterfront watchman, but his head ached, and his brain seemed frozen. Normally one who fell asleep "before his head hit the pillow", tired out from work and workouts, he had tossed and turned in his sleep the previous night. He stared idly at his text app, wondering if he should finally return Bertha's message, then realizing how absurd that was, as her cell had been seized, and she was likely in a prison cell.

Just then, he got a text from Harmony. "You might want to come to Market Square—it's quite the circus. I'm there across from the Carlyle mansion."

Ted felt too tired to bike over, so he took his RAV4, infrequently used as he biked so much to get around town. The City Hall plaza of Market Square is on the north side of King St., so he parked a few blocks north of it, on N. Fairfax St. near the housing project.

Locking the car, Ted thought of the recent murder there. He'd read the authorities had few leads, and in any event seemed to be spending all of their time on the Athenaeum and Freedmen's cases, especially the latter. They seemed to have forgotten about the terrorist's escape.

To briefly scope out the little slum, he cut across the shabby-looking grass of a building's courtyard, and walked over to the site of the drug murder. Its crime scene tape was gone, all traces of blood gone, its courtyard deserted. It was like the murder had never happened, already forgotten, like thousands of other pointless deaths 'in the ghetto'. An Elvis song in that vein ran through his mind.

Now sad as well as tired, Ted walked under a bank of gray clouds back down Royal, and approached Latrobe's magnificent City Hall from its rear. At the intersection with Cameron St. was the familiar sight of Gadsby's Tavern. Ted enjoyed showing tour guests the ice storage well outside it. In the days before refrigeration, John Gadsby's indentured servants, slaves, and freemen would pick-ax ice out of the frozen Potomac, then haul the frozen stuff the three blocks up to his emporium. After tossing the ice in the 11-foot-deep cistern, they'd cover it with heaps of straw, and hope the frozen stuff would last through the following summer.

To Ted's left soared the "modern" side of City Hall, dating from 1871, rebuilt after a great fire that year. Ted recalled how the building avoided complete immolation. According to city legend, the other side, facing Market Square, had been saved by chance, from a traveling circus that happened to be in town. The cirque had a trapeze artist, a master of the high wire. Seeing the roof of the City Hall ablaze, he climbed atop it. He balanced perilously on the slanted roof while firemen and citizens formed a bucket brigade below him, and pulleyed up pails of water and sand. Teetering topside, he poured the cooling liquid and the quelling sand onto the flames. Thus helping save much of Latrobe's original creation, including the grand spire. But not the south side, rebuilt by the estimable architect Adolf Cluss.

Ted turned left on Cameron so he could admire up close Cluss' glorious French Empire style. Passing the old Lee and Duvall townhouse and tavern, he rounded the corner to Fairfax St., and went by the City Hall's old meeting hall.

He glanced at the former tavern of George Wise, who built and sold John Gadsby his other public house. He passed William Herbert's massive old Bank of Alexandria, then being extensively remodeled, and looked at the excavations and piles of insulation material.

He heard crowd noise and amplified voices coming out of Market Square. But he couldn't resist first ambling past the front lawn of the John Carlyle mansion, the former Union Army hospital. Whenever he passed it, Ted thought of the scores of wounded soldiers who'd been placed on sidewalk planks there after a major battle. As physicians with blood-stained shirts stepped amidst them performing triage: Ordering the lightly wounded moved to convalescent hospitals, denying those too far gone any treatment, and indicating those in the middle, to be brought into the mansion or its adjoining hotel for intensive care, and possibly amputation, possibly without anesthesia, and definitely without modern anti-infectives, in the dire years before the nostrums of Lister and Pasteur took root in America.

'And now we seem in the midst of another civil war,' he mused, unable to shake off the recent deaths and rioting. He recalled the words of General Lee: "We are adrift in a sea of blood."

Ted's head cleared and his mood shifted on seeing Harmony's graceful form and keen, sparkling eyes. She was standing across the street from the Carlyle manse, at City Hall's southeast corner. As Ted walked up, he noticed the "circus" she'd referred to.

The City Council had ordered built a wooden platform 40 yards long on the side of the main City Hall entrance. To Ted, whose "scandal tours" of the past described grisly events like hangings, the construct looked like a scaffold. On it stood dozens of FBI agents, city police, Council members, mayoral administrators, and reporters, all carefully masked and struggling to maintain a safe distance. The Mayor was out of town, to "set an example," he pronounced in an online statement, about the "extreme caution required with face-to-face contacts during the continuing health emergency."

Chairs and raised microphones had been set up along the platform, with a lectern and a Hydra's head of microphones plopped in the center. Off on the sides were loudspeakers powerful enough for a local Wolf Trap music hall show. FBI vans and federal government trucks jammed with communications gear were parked on the adjacent streets of N. Fairfax and N. Royal. A scattering of masked spectators, residents, and reporters not deemed important enough for the scaffold stood watching from the Square, while carefully staying six feet apart.

"We're in the middle of the country's biggest story," Harmony told Ted. "The FBI has set up its murder investigation center, right here."

"It looks," said Ted, "like the city has put its media center here."

"That too," replied Harmony.

"Andy" Comitas was at the podium, preening, two masks pushed down to his neck, as he finished up an address. "To repeat," he was saying, "we already have persons of interest under investigation, or in actual custody." His red vest stood out from his white silk shirt, bracketed by the dark jacket of his pinstriped Washington power suit. "We will bring, we are bringing, the full force of the federal government to bear on this case."

He rocked on his heels, while thrusting forward his chin, making him look bigger and more aggressive.

"The Bureau shall not rest until, as it always does, until it gets its man! Or woman."

Harmony nudged Ted. With a slight smile tending toward a look of concern, she told him, "He better not see you here. I think you're on his Most Wanted List."

"Yes," replied Ted dryly. "You can expect to see my picture at the Post Office soon."

"That's so 'Twentieth Century'," she replied. "More likely you'll be on the FBI's Facebook page."

"That's so last year," answered Ted. "On TikTok, most likely."

Comitas finished, to the crackling applause of City Council members and spectators. Some of the reporters joined in the plaudits, which Harmony and her friend found odd, given the avowed objectivity of journalists.

Ted looked over the King St. side of the Square, and saw it lined with media vans and trucks, some with large satellite dishes. "Yes, we're the number one story on the planet," he said. Harmony, a news hound like Ted, answered, "It's funny. The escape of that jihadi has been almost forgotten."

"Not to mention," stated Ted, "the housing project killing."

Deputy Mayor Sean Morenis put out a hand to shake that of Comitas, then pulled it back with embarrassment, realizing he was being non-hygienic. "Out of an abundance of caution", he gently fist-bumped the FBI man instead. Morenis then spoke emotionally about the Freemen's Cemetery murder.

"That heinous, that unconscionable, act," he intoned, "proves that we have not at all overcome the terrible misdeeds of our oppressive past. Racism and hate pervade society today as it did 160 years ago!" Overcome with emotion, his chest rose and fell deeply as he inhaled and exhaled. He wiped his forehead with a tissue, and spoke in a voice loud enough to be heard through his two masks, "This city, built on slavery and marked by lynching, must be completely transformed. And the time is now! The time for waiting, centuries of waiting, has long passed."

Ted, a professional communicator, was surprised by the style of his talk. Previously he'd found Morenis to be pedantic, dull, but this time he was fiery, and persuasive.

Harmony was less admiring. "It is terrible, but I wish they'd also talk about, and condemn, the rioting."

They watched City Council Coordinator Avril Forstandt deliver, as was her wont, very energetic remarks. While speaking she gestured forcefully, her muscles rippling and visible underneath her business suit.

The speakers that followed were less compelling, though, and Ted saw that Harmony was fidgeting. "Why don't we get dinner?" he asked. Harmony readily agreed.

Most of lower King St. was shut down due to the disturbances, so they headed to upper King, where some restaurants, despite the virus, had open-air tables as well as widely spaced interior dining. They ended up on the 800 block of King St., at a fine Greek restaurant. It was one of Ted's, and Harmony's favorites, because of the moussaka and lamb pilaf, and its house band of Greek folk musicians. It was far more subdued than usual, however, as live performances had been suspended. Their table was in a back alley next to the Morrison House hotel, whose dead-on Federalist style had initially fooled Ted into thinking it was built in the time of the American Revolution, instead of the mid-1980s. Just a few customers were present, with many scared off both by the pandemic and by the threatening clouds roiling above the town early that evening.

Ted glanced back toward the Hotel and playfully smacked the top of his head. "Duh. I can't believe I never thought of it," he told Harmony. "Thought of what?" she responded.

"The Morrison Hotel must be named, I bet, after Jim Morrison."

Harmony wasn't familiar with the name, and she pushed forward her full lips, and freckled nose, in a questioning way.

"He grew up in Alexandria," Ted explained. "He was a singer for a famous rock band. During the glory days of rock and roll, around 1970. Jim Morrison came up with some stand-out songs." Ted tapped his forehead again. "Double duh. 'Morrison Hotel' was one of their tunes."

"I wish I heard more of him," said Harmony, holding a forkful of feta-speckled lettuce to her mouth.

"Maybe not. He was a weird dude. Something about being a, an exhibitionist on stage. Got busted I think. Died young, like Jimi Hendrix. Drugs, I guess…But, yes, some famous performers from that era came from here. Cass, Mother—" Ted struggled to recall the name—"A woman singer from the 'Mommas and the something: Mama Cass Elliott, that was her name, came from here too."

As was his wont, Ted speculated on the historical basis of the topic at hand.

"The Mamas and the Whatevers were a kind of folkie group, and The Doors—Morrison's band—were a bluesy rock band. Both rootsy, Americana. The fact they were from Alexandria, between the North's jazz bands and music studios, and the South's bluegrass and blues, must have influenced their sound."

"Or," interjected Harmony, "you're over-speculating, as you often do. Or just making it up. Sometimes I can't tell."

"Neither can I," he answered.

They laughed, and a masked waiter brought over their entrees.

The two talked about the rolling riot they'd witnessed.

"It could have been much worse," noted Harmony, sipping an ice tea with lime. "Thank goodness no one was killed. And no building burned completely down to the ground."

"Yes, but I don't agree with you, with your view it was spontaneous," said Ted, as he examined the colonial-style walls of the Hotel. "I think I recognized several of the leaders. Kind of. A man, and maybe a woman. I can't quite place them."

"What's happened to your famous memory?" teased Harmony. "Your 'encyclopedic' memory, that you show off on your tours?"

"It's true," he replied, sucking on a cube from his ice water. "My memory's been off of late. I think it's the pandemic, the lockdowns. The lack of social interaction."

"I can do something," said Harmony coquettishly, "about your lack of social interaction." They laughed again, and dug into the food.

"With big meals tonight and tomorrow," joked Ted between bites, "we're likely to get fat." And they began talking about their dinner the following night with their friend Anthony "Tony the Pony" Hill.

A native of Loudoun County, Virginia, he was an avid equestrian, like so many in the Virginia foothills, and a fellow history enthusiast. Sandy-haired, about six foot tall and hefty, he had worked with Harmony as a marketing chief in her previous IT firm. Where he was the life of every office party and happy hour. Switching careers, he had set up his own real estate firm, which specialized in buying, fixing up, and selling historic Old Town homes.

The affable fellow went by various nicknames: Tony, Pony, Tony the Pony, or "A.P. Hill", a reference to a Civil War Confederate commander to whom, he believed, he was distantly related. His regard for history and horses had led him, 10 years prior, before Old Town home prices had completely skyrocketed, to purchase the stately Cameron St. townhouse of Light-Horse Harry Lee.

As the two finished their dinner, they agreed to go on a bike ride early the following evening before heading over to Tony's. Harmony texted him their plans, and Tony quickly replied: "Why not come straight to my house, and shower here? Bring change of clothes in your day packs; I'll lay out soap, shampoo, towels. Btw-I'll be adding hickory to the barbecue!" His townhouse, like so many venerable homes in the historic district, had a large number of rooms, including multiple bathrooms and showers. As in the days of Light-Horse, of "Southern hospitality", the place was conducive to hosting, both in its spaciousness, and in the modern-day geniality of its owner.

Chapter 23 – Cyclists of the Condemned Powerhouse

Very late the following afternoon, Ted and Harmony were on the north side of Old Town, wheeling along on their Trek and Felt carbon bikes toward the Mt. Vernon Trail. They rode past the abandoned railroad tracks that once delivered wood pulp to the printing plant of *The Washington Post*. The town, while vocally in favor of a "green city", had long allowed untreated trash to flow into the Potomac. After many complaints, Alexandria was turning the riverside block in front of the old facility into a water treatment plant. Glancing at the signs touting the cleaner Potomac to come, the two rode onto the paved Mt. Vernon Trail. They went past the rusty fences, off Slater's Lane, of the mammoth, abandoned power plant that hugs the river. In another attempt to bolster its environmental stance, the city had shuttered it years before.

Ted had varied feelings on this. The closure made for somewhat cleaner air over Old Town. But shuttering the plant, as opposed to say, installing better smokestack scrubbers, had eliminated one of the few sources of blue-collar jobs in a town abounding with lawyers and government officials. The closing seemed especially negative for the employment prospects of blacks in the housing project and the poorer neighborhoods extending from north Alexandria to south Arlington. Ted knew that area was historically an impoverished place of shacks, swamps, former slaves, and "places of entertainment": saloons, bordellos, distilleries, and gambling dens. Indeed, in 1904 the "Good Citizens' League" of progressive-minded folk had empowered strong-armed men to take axes to the center of the illicit businesses, located in

Rosslyn, Virginia, a hamlet across the Francis Scott Key bridge from Georgetown. The entertainment strip was torn apart and cleaned up, with considerable violence. Rosslyn fell into a dusty backwater, hosting the remaining houses of dubious repute, which serviced sailors and leathernecks from the Washington Navy Yard and the Marine Barracks, until the construction of the metro stations in the 1970s drew in mini-malls and affluent "young professionals".

They took a side street to the west side of the power plant, and rode past the facility's chain-link fences. Ted noticed via his clip-on, rear-view mirror that Harmony had fallen behind. "It's unlocked," she called out, slowing down. Curious, Ted stopped altogether, and Harmony too.

He saw how Harmony had again proven how sharp-eyed she was. Almost anyone else, in passing by, would have thought the entrance gate to the complex was secure, as a long chain with a large steel lock was wrapped around it. But the lock was unlocked. Ted shook his head, amazed Harmony had noticed this while riding by on a bike.

"Maybe they're starting to renovate the place," he said. "I heard they may make the plant into a mixed development, with homes and businesses."

"I read," countered Harmony, "that was years in the future."

"Maybe," mused Ted, "a vagrant made his way in." He gazed down the concrete and corrugated-metal walls of the complex, three city blocks long, as long as an aircraft carrier, its four shuttered smokestacks atop copper scaffolding and thick, concrete walls. "I've always thought this deserted space would make a great lair for The Joker." He eyed the unlocked lock thoughtfully, then looked over the grounds again. "Hmm, there's no security around."

Reading his mind, Harmony stated, "You're in enough hot water with the police. That might get us arrested." Glancing at her Apple watch, she continued, "If we're to get in any kind of workout, and not be late for Tony, we have to go now."

Ted filed away his notion, and they took off. They got back on the Mt. Vernon Trail, and were soon gliding past Reagan National Airport. The wind picked up, as it often did in that locale, and Ted recalled a story the original aerodrome, for biplanes, was put there to take advantage of the strong prevailing winds. They passed the spot in 1949 where the pilot of a fighter plane, a surplus craft from the Second World War, had crashed into a DC-3, scattering the body parts of 55 souls over the Potomac and the George Washington Parkway. They went on to Gravelly Point, at the edge of an expanse of flat, windy lawn where families, most of them immigrants, took their kids for a free treat, to watch the jet planes landing and taking off, the giant titanium birds and their deafening engines flying just a few hundred feet above the onlookers. At the far, north side of the grass was the 14th St. Bridge, the successor to the Long Bridge of antebellum days, where a woman fleeing from the dreaded Yellow House slave pen hurled herself to death instead of returning to servitude. And where in January 1982 a jetliner crashed into the bridge and fell into the icy Potomac, killing 78, and leading to spectacular rescues, as a helicopter crew skidded its craft into the river to pull passengers out of the freezing water. 'So much death across so much time,' reflected Ted gloomily.

They rode over the span's bike and running path, and Ted's spirit rose with the magnificent upriver view of Rosslyn's new skyscrapers and Georgetown University's spire, and straight ahead the granite obelisk of the Washington Monument and the marbled dome of the Jefferson Memorial. Once on the D.C. side they saw the scaffolding set atop the

Memorial, a restoration project to remove river fungi that had spread
across its top.

Then on to one of the District's better-kept secrets, the three-mile loop
around the peninsula of Hains Point, a mecca for the region's cyclists
due to the light motor traffic there. As they neared its municipal golf
course, they passed fences blocking off the long-shuttered public
swimming pool. "I can't believe it's still closed!" called out Harmony.
The city, and municipal contractors, had spent over three years
renovating the dilapidated, 50-meter outdoor facility. Apparently, a
year into the project, engineers found structural flaws in the new
design, and had to start over again. Then apparently found the elevated
water table of the land next to the Potomac might prevent construction
at all. Ted figured millions of dollars had been wasted, but it seemed
neither the city government nor the builders had been brought to
account. He and Harmony, enthusiastic swimmers both, were chagrined
at this loss of the popular athletic facility.

As they rode together they approached the peninsula's midpoint, where
the course veers sharply right to head back upriver. The prevailing
winds are northwesterly, and normally the turn there brings a fierce
headwind. But that evening the gusts were racing upriver, carrying gray
thunderheads toward Alexandria. Bent over, they pedaled hard and,
realizing rain was in the offing, decided to head back. With the sun now
low and the sky darkening, they passed again over the bridge and then
up the Mt. Vernon Trail.

When they went by the shuttered power plant on their return, they
reached the street near the unlocked gate. It had started to rain some,
and they slowed down, wary of the slick ground and gravel scattered
about.

Ted's bike suddenly veered, almost throwing him onto the aerobars. He swerved again, his bike wobbling uncontrollably, and halted. His front wheels hadn't slipped, but his rear tire had flattened, probably from a bit of wire or glass mixed into the pieces of gravel.

As Ted looked over the tire, Harmony eyed the gate. She called out: "Look! It's been locked up again." Indeed, the lock was now secure. "A custodian must have come by," she added.

"That's odd," stated Ted. He looked down a hundred yards of the complex, and saw no one. "Just came by to lock the gate?"

The rain was coming down harder. "Look, it'll take me an hour, given my mechanical expertise," he told Harmony sarcastically, "to fix change the inner tube. Why don't you go ahead to Tony's? I'll take the bike up to Wheel Natural." This was a mom-and-pop bike shop on the north end of town that friends of Ted's operated. "There're probably no customers there with this rain. The mechanic will fix it fast, and I'll meet you and Tony quick." As Harmony got ready to go, he clipped several small blinking lights onto her rear shirt pockets, to make her more visible to any drivers out in the gloom.

Chapter 24 – The Mound of the Rebellious Dead

Harmony took off, and Ted slowly rode toward the bike store. Then, worrying he'd bend the rim of the wheel, he got off and walked the bike. It was a miserable trek. The sun had set, and rain poured down, soaking him through. And when he got to the bike shop, the mechanics had closed early from a lack of customers. Ted felt bad for the small business and hoped, for the sake of his pals who ran it, it would survive the pandemic.

He took out his cell to text Harmony about his delay, and heard a robotic voice announce, "Phone is malfunctioning; place it in a dry place." It was wet from the rain. He stuck the device inside his day pack, cursing that he should have done that when it started pouring. No chance of calling an Uber now. He headed on to Tony's, rolling his bike along by hand.

It was very dark, with a cold light rain dripping, as he got to a hundred yards from the intersection near their friend's house, off Cameron St. and N. Washington St.

Despite a mist, the graveyard of Christ Church was visible to his right. Tony's home was across Washington and several doors down on the left. A light from the great church's top floor cast a dim, spooky glow on the damp nighttime air. Ted got back on his bike, thinking the short distance that remained wouldn't damage the wheel. He carefully rode up the boulevard, thankful the rain and the pandemic made car traffic nearly non-existent, and the cycling safer.

Then he spied the blinking lights of cop cars and EMS vehicles.

'I guess some poor driver did go out in this mess,' he told himself, 'and did get into an accident.'

The vehicles, about eight of them, a huge number for Old Town, were pulled up outside the church gate.

'Right across the street from Tony's,' Ted thought, and felt his stomach churn. "Right where Harmony would have turned left!" he muttered aloud. He suddenly pedaled hard, like at the start of a time trial, and almost fell over from the flat tire. He recovered and, after reaching the church property, threw his Trek down at the corner of the graveyard's fence. He eyed the parked vehicles in front of him.

Cameron St. jutted to his right along the north side of the cemetery. This was the area that had been part of the cemetery, but ravaged by Union soldiers, its tombstones pilfered, its graves robbed. According to local lore, it and the adjoining private homes were haunted, disturbed by restless spirits whose resting places had been defiled. Fearing something awful had happened to Harmony, Ted felt as though an evil specter from those houses had seized him.

He walked slowly up the sidewalk. Through the cemetery fence he caught glimpses of policemen. They were standing on and around the mound of Confederate dead. Ted felt his spirits rise. He figured that, in the wake of the Appomattox statue fracas, someone had desecrated the site of the rebels' mass grave. 'So this isn't about Harmony,' he reckoned, relief pouring out of him.

His relief was short-lived. Getting closer, he realized some of the cops, cloaked in darkness and mist, seemed to be examining something on the mound, a person perhaps—or a body. Behind the police, looking like grim, giant eyes were the gray tombstones of Lyndon Johnson's Treasury Secretary and wife. Like Washington and Lee, they had endowed the church, and the church had named its gift shop after them.

EMS personnel stood outside on the sidewalk, next to the wide Black
Lives Matter poster hanging from the church fence.

Ted felt panic again. 'This is odd,' he thought. 'If the person were
alive, the EMS would be attending to him—or to her.'

Then he saw her. Not Harmony, but the 'Mysterious Stranger', seeming
to appear out of nowhere, striding across Washington St. away the
church. She was dressed, as usual, in dark, tasteful attire: designer
jeans, a black, silken blouse, and a brown leather jacket, with leather
boots, and an expensive handbag. She seemed oblivious to the hubbub
about her. The Stranger, her boot heels clacking, walked onto Cameron
St., and disappeared, like a ghost, behind the line of cars on her side of
the street, across from the house of Robert E. Lee's father. The police
officials, their attention on the prone figure, didn't notice her.

Ted's attention riveted back to the mound. A knot of cops at the
entrance clogged up the approach, so he stopped 50 feet away, and
peered through the fence rails. Some of the law enforcement officers
seemed on fire from their glow-in-the-dark vests.

Ted's heart sunk further as he realized these were FBI agents, no doubt
investigating more foul play. 'Could he, *she*, have been murdered?!' he
screamed to himself. Harmony had been on a bike, but she could have
entered the graveyard for some reason. Perhaps on a whim, to explore
it, just as he might have done. Maybe she had noticed something
strange happening there. Ted felt his legs lock up. He realized he was
literally frozen from fear. With an effort of the will, he forced himself
to walk forward, and get a closer look at the mound.

A local policeman shone a bright flashlight on the figure lying on it.
The bulky cop looked like Greco, but Ted couldn't tell for sure. The
figure wasn't moving, and its arms and legs were twisted in an
awkward position.

Then Ted perceived that the shape on the ground was a man, not a woman. He felt a huge relief, then felt guilty about feeling good about someone else's tragedy. But his heart fell again when a policewoman shone a bright light on the man's face.

Even from 50 feet, Ted could see, from the light's glow, that the poor fellow was dead. And that his face had been horribly bruised, and viciously cut up. To his horror, he saw that one of his eyes had been gouged clear out of its socket. It hung disgustingly, by its optic nerves, strung out along the man's cheek.

Once again, as at the Freedmen's Cemetery, an image popped into his head, of a terrible event from long ago. But a different event. And once again, he couldn't quite place it. As if his brain was refusing to recall a horror. A horror that sooner or later he would have to face.

Then, peering again through the grating, and focusing on the dead man's face, he almost fell over from the sight.

The murdered man was Tony Hill.

Ted reeled backwards, stumbling back to his bike. He felt sick. Phlegm boiled up from his stomach and licked at his throat. Their friend: massacred.

Then his stomach, and head, cleared some. He remembered his cell. He ripped it out of his daypack. It was working again, and he had a text. From Harmony! From 40 minutes before.

"Where are you?!" it read. "Tony isn't home. His door was open, next door too."

She was referring to a rundown house next to Tony's, whose absentee owner left it unlocked and insecure.

The text continued:

"I am in its basement. The floor is an OCEAN OF BLOOD.

"Where's Tony?? Where are you? Please come!!"

Without checking for passing cars, Ted ran blindly across Washington
St., and hurtled down Cameron. He glanced across the street, for the
Mysterious Stranger, but she'd vanished into the darkness. He rushed
by Tony's house, and through the open door of the neighboring home.
He was sweating hard, his knees ached. His racing heart felt like a
ticking bomb in his chest.

At the entrance he flicked the light switch; one overhead bulb faintly
glowed. He saw rats, wharf rats by the size of them, scurry away on the
filthy wooden floor of the abandoned house. In a daze he stepped
through the living room, into the parlor, and to the staircase below.
Feeling his way through the dimness, he heard stirrings in the
basement. And moans. He held up his cell, its thin beam making for a
weak flashlight, and stepped carefully down the dusty steps, which
creaked in tandem to his gimpy knees. He cursed himself for not
knowing how to put his phone in flashlight mode.

At the foot of the stairs he saw a brighter light, and movement, and
thought for a moment it was an animal.

It was Harmony, in a back corner of the basement. There was a long
dark blotch on the pitted stone floor. The pool of blood. She was on all
fours, her cell turned to flashlight mode, examining the premises for
further evidence of the mayhem that had taken place. Her hands and
biking pants had picked up some of the blood.

She looked up, saw the blurry image of a man approaching, and
shuttered audibly. 'Has the killer come back?!' she asked herself in
horror. Hands shaking, she shone the light on Ted's face and, exhaling
with relief, toppled onto her side, from nervous exhaustion.

Ted pulled her up and hugged her, blood smearing his bicycle attire.
They went over to the other corner, where the floor was dry, and leaned

together against a wall. Harmony's face was smeared with blood and sweat.

"Do you think it's the same killer as at the Freemen's Cemetery?" she blurted out, almost in shock. "Was the person whose blood this is, was he killed? Was it the owner of this place, that old woman?" She breathed harshly, her hands trembling.

"Harmony," Ted began, relieved she was alive, but dreading what he had to tell her. "I just came from—

"—When I got to Tony's house," she broke in, gasping excitedly, "he wasn't in.

"Weird," she continued in a low voice, almost to herself, "weird he didn't text. I went around to the back, and the barbecue was all set up. Then I heard noises, it sounded like an argument, coming from next door, from this basement—"

"—Harmony, I—" Ted tried again, but, as in a dream, or nightmare, she kept talking, not hearing, as if he wasn't there.

"—I wasn't sure what to do. I texted you, no answer. I called you, no answer. No answer.

"All alone."

She stared across the basement at a black wall. "Maybe I should have called the police. I waited. Probably for too long. Still no Ted, no you." She leaned into him. She paused for a moment, then shone the light onto her left hand; the manicured fingers were speckled with blood. Ted opened his mouth to say something; no words came out.

"I went to the front of this house," Harmony went on. "The door was stuck. Locked? I don't know. I pushed hard, really hard, a few times, and it opened." She looked down at the blood on the floor. "The place seemed deserted as usual. I came down here where I'd heard the noise. Saw all this. Shocked. Investigated," she went on in a stream-of-consciousness way. "Texted you. No answer. Who was attacked here? All this blood..." Her voice, choking, trailed off.

Ted took her bloodstained hand, rubbed it, and placed it by her side. He hugged her by her shoulders.

"I've terrible news." He took a step back. "There *was* a murder, and, it was...it was Tony, who was killed."

At first Harmony didn't cry, but reacted with a kind of stunned despondency. After recovering somewhat, she asked, "How? Where?" And tears began streaming down her cheeks.

And Ted told her about how he came upon the body and the police at the Christ Church burial mound.

"He must have been killed here," Ted said absently, before being gripped by a flood of emotion about their friend's horrific end. He tried to focus on what to say next, and what to do, and steadied himself some. He couldn't bring himself to mention the mutilation. He said, "The killer must, must have quickly taken his body, somehow, to Christ Church."

Harmony, though sobbing, thought of the practicalities of that. "Well, he, or she, had the cover of darkness," she said softly, as if speaking in a dream. "And of rain. And the Confederate mound is only a half block from here."

"If the murderer carried the body," Ted added, "he would have to be strong, athletic." He pulled out a tissue and wiped some of the tears from Harmony's face.

"Or the killer," answered Harmony, "could have placed, placed Tony..." She paused, and cried, but her voice, seemingly detached from her emotions, sounded clipped, logical. "Could have put the, the body in a car. Driven the car in seconds, to the cemetery gate. Dropped the body and driven off." She stopped again, thinking, her nose all clogged up, then started talking again. "There's hardly any traffic, any pedestrians around here, anywhere in town."

"I think the church has video cameras," replied Ted. "But maybe not at the far end of the graveyard, by the mound. Maybe only at the church's entrance, the main entrance, on the other side."

They both fell silent. Harmony wiped at the tears on her round, full cheeks, smearing them with the blood on her hands. She said suddenly: "He went down fighting."

"What do you mean?" replied Ted.

She twisted her back away from the wall, and shone her cell's bright light along it. It illuminated a splattering of blood. "I also found buttons on the floor. From a Brooks Brothers' shirt. It didn't register at the time. Of the kind Tony likes, liked, likes, to wear," she said haltingly, her voice thick from her clogged nostrils. "They must have struggled, the killer ripping off the buttons." Her head dropped to her bosom in sorrow. "I wish I'd found stuff from the killer. It would help better in finding out who he is."

The duo stared at each other, and said almost simultaneously, "So what do we do now?"

Ted laughed a sad little laugh. "Well, we contact the police, and the FBI. It's not like they're far away. Though they may suspect you, for a while at least, about what happened here."

"They'll suspect you more, and for longer," responded Harmony. "You were at the Freedmen's site, and the Athenaeum. And the waterfront. And here. And 'FBI Guy' hates you."

"That's ridiculous to suspect me." Ted paused. "But I will contact Greco, and not Comitas, about this."

He clicked on the detective's cell number, and instantly got through.

"Greco: Hello, horrible night again. Yes, it's Ted. I have info about the Christ Church killer. And maybe the, the murder scene too."

"I'm at the church now," replied John Greco, his voice gruffer than normal. "How do you know about it?" Suspicion seemed to leap from his comment.

"I walked, biked, by there. Harmony too. Come to the house next to the Light-Horse Harry Lee house." Harmony told Ted the street address, which he relayed to Greco. "It's just half a block away. You'll find me and Harmony there. We're in the basement now. We think we found where the murder happened." There was a pause, as the detective processed this information. Greco said, "I'll be right over."

Ted told Harmony, "Let's go outside. If they do suspect us, it's better to meet the police on the sidewalk, instead of by this sea of blood."

As soon as they got to the wet, darkened street, police cars alerted by Greco came rushing up. Cops stepped out, and the duo told them about the stairway to the basement. Several officers stayed with them while others hurried inside the house.

Greco arrived moments later, striding purposefully up from Christ Church. He stared at them silently, his Shantung straw hat pushed to a sloppy angle on his head. In the drizzle, under the glare of a streetlight, his watchful eyes, peering out like those of a reptile, saw the blood on Harmony's hands and blouse, and saw some more on Ted's hands and bike shirt.

His squat, powerful figure took a step toward them. "This seems like a hell of a coincidence," he told them. He got into Ted's face. "I'll ask you something outright. Did your friend Tony have any sympathy for hate groups? He lived in Lee's father's house—was he a neo-Confederate? Neo-Nazi?"

Ted was stunned.

Thinking back to the riot, he answered, in a hard tone, "He was *not* a member of Antifa, or BLM, or the Aryan Brotherhood, or *any* violent group." Greco didn't take to the answer. His green eyes turned to small points of light as they searched Ted's face, like those of a cop running a harsh interrogation.

Watching this, Harmony said, "He's, he was, apolitical. A realtor. Just a history buff, like Ted." Tears began flowing again. "And the nicest, guy. He wouldn't hurt..." She choked up, unable to further speak.

Greco exhaled in frustration at Ted, then winced in empathy for his lady friend. He said he would be asking them plenty of questions. Then, turning his broad shoulders away from the pair, he walked over to a female police sergeant. He spoke to her in a voice that was low and inaudible, but resonant. It seemed to send powerful sound waves down the stricken street.

Wiping her face, Harmony looked up to see a black Ford RAM van rush up Cameron St., and come to a jolting stop.

Comitas got out. He gave Ted and Harmony a look of fury, and strode over to Greco. His open, cashmere overcoat swirling about his hips, he bent down into the detective's face. "A ton of bricks is gonna come down on us for another murder!" His stance reminded Ted of a tall boxer trying to get in close to a shorter yet brawny and dangerous foe. Comitas waved his right hand at the twosome. "You're detaining them, right?!"

Greco was upset with all concerned, but tried to stay under control. In a deep, measured voice he said, "I've already made arrangements to take them in for questioning."

Ted started to say something, and Greco cut him off. "Questioning, not arrest." He stared at Ted and Harmony and ordered, "Come along, this way!" Comitas, his overcoat flapping from a sudden gust, revealing his red suspenders, gave Greco a brutal look. But before he could react, the policewoman had taken Harmony by the elbow and walked her to a squad car, with Ted following on their heels. They got into the back of the vehicle and the historian thought, 'Protective custody.' The image of Charles Guiteau, the assassin of President James Garfield, popped into his mind. He had begged police to throw him in jail before a crowd lynched him over the assassination. The trio drove away, leaving Comitas, tight-lipped and furious, on the sidewalk, his polished, wing-tipped shoes glistening in the rain.

Another FBI van pulled up, and Comitas directed its agents to go inside. Greco had already entered the cellar, determined to have his officers begin the forensics first, and deny the FBI from taking over this incident completely.

Two hours later, a weary Greco arrived at the police station. Ted and Harmony wore hospital-like scrubs, their bloodstained clothes kept as evidence. Greco questioned Harmony at length about her experience at Tony Hill's and the adjoining home. He took special note when she described the carnage in the basement. Greco excelled at detecting lies and phonies; in her case he could detect none.

During the interrogations, he got a report on the background of the victim. No known ties to extremist groups. Quotes from neighbors about "such a great guy." A police record consisting of two parking tickets, from five and eight years ago. Preliminary forensic: Death by stab wounds, arterial bleeding in the neck; post-mortem cuts to the legs, arms, and eyes, one eye ripped out; no fingerprints found yet, still collecting possible DNA from assailant(s); also, fragments of footprints in the blood, smeared over in a possible attempt to erase tread marks. And nothing substantial yet from the Christ Church scene.

Greco grimaced in frustration, muttering: "Not a quick, open-and-shut case. Like the others."

The husky detective grilled Ted on his trek from the power plant to the church; he noted pointedly there was no one to check out his story. But he figured that even if Ted were lying about the flat tire, which he didn't think he was, he could hardly have gotten to the scene of the killing before Harmony.

He told the stricken, strung-out pair they could leave. Leave with a warning. He looked at them wearily, his burly form drained of energy. "I don't think the two of you are involved," he stated hoarsely, "but I'm not as sure as I was with the Freedmen's slaying." He spoke slowly, picking at his words. "If something else happens, I don't think I can protect you." He shook his head in anger. "Wouldn't want to, given this vile case. The consequences..." his voice trailed off.

"Good night. Leave. Get out."

They took a Lyft to Harmony's Old Town apartment. They showered away the blood, but none of the angst. Exhausted, yet strained to a high pitch by the night's events, they sat on Harmony's living room floor, backs against a sofa, Harmony's head pressed against Ted's shoulders, his shirt soaking up her tears. They bemoaned the fate of their friend late into the rain-and-blood-soaked night.

Chapter 25 – An Unwanted Intrusion

Robert Lowell IV was not atypical of Alexandria's modern gentry. A Yale-trained lawyer, he'd worked briefly at the State Department, then long-term for a politically connected law firm on K Street, a center of lobbying in downtown D.C. He made partner, took in seven figures, and after retirement worked as a highly paid legal consultant. Now 72, the trim, well-tailored man lived with his wife Evelyn, a former fine arts professor for the University of Maryland, in one of Old Town's most eye-catching homes, the former offices of two states' governors. With their children long having left the nest, they found the place overly large but, as lovers of history, culture, and architecture, they wouldn't have lived anywhere else.

Disturbed by the violent events in town, and even before by the lockdowns and the pandemic, they'd decided to spend a week at their second home on the Eastern Shore of the Chesapeake, in the toney village of St. Michaels. The Lowell's' eldest son had arranged to have two of their grandchildren meet them there.

However, a crisis had erupted in Robert Lowell's consulting firm concerning an important client. An import-export firm in Los Angeles had been hit by a ransomware attack, and demanded legal advice immediately about a member of the board who was evidently part of an inside job.

Lowell, normally restrained and diplomatic in manner, could have kicked himself. He'd neglected to take along his laptop that contained the files on the client. Due to his own failure to set up a secure connection, he couldn't access them remotely. He had to drive back to

retrieve his MacBook, a four-to-five-hour headache. That evening, he'd
left Mrs. Lowell at their seaside house, and took his 2019 baby-blue
Mercedes S-Class back over the Chesapeake Bay Bridge to Alexandria.
On Prince St. that evening, the night before the Christ Church killing,
Lowell found plenty of parking. Old Town, normally bustling in early
summer, seemed abandoned. It was almost like the long-gone days of
the cholera epidemics in the Washington region, when persons of
means would escape to the relative safety of the countryside, leaving
the poor in their close urban quarters to face a greater risk of disease.
Rather as, during the current pandemic, the less affluent continued to
work at construction sites or food processing plants.

Pulling up to the curb outside his house that evening, Lowell saw he'd
made another mistake. In the rush to get out of town, he'd neglected to
suspend his subscription to *The Wall Street Journal*, *The New York
Times*, and *Barron's*. He was old-fashioned enough to read their print
versions. A dozen of the papers had piled up in his driveway, a sure
giveaway to any would-be robber he was out of town. Though he was
not too worried. There hadn't been a serious burglary in Old Town in
months. There was the incident down Prince St. at the Athenaeum, but
he was convinced that was foul play, probably from a personal dispute.
He had read the authorities had evidence showing it was unrelated to
the Freedmen's killing. A second autopsy had been performed on the
watchwoman, which indicated she had died from a fall, and not from
any trauma she had received before plummeting to her death. Lowell
hadn't heard of the murder at the housing project.

The newspapers strewn outside reminded him of his wife's recent
rummage sale. Their front stoop, driveway, and backyard had been
filled with items accumulated in their manse across generations of
owners. Lowell briefly recalled the eccentric old man, with a stooped

back, full beard, and whitened hair, who'd purchased the most items that weekend. They were all stowed in ancient containers: Moldy chests and rusty old toolboxes that were practically worthless. They seemed to hold almost nothing of value; his spouse was happy to unload them. Lowell was about to enter though the front door, glad he'd at least remembered to leave the exterior light on. He reached into his pocket, fumbled for the house key, and couldn't find it. He searched all his pockets, for naught. Another blunder—'Am I getting old?' he thought. 'No, I *am* old!' Then he recalled placing the key in his cutoffs while on the Eastern Shore, then changing to a pair of Lands' End slacks for the drive back without transferring the key.

He felt crushed, thinking he'd have to motor back and forth to the Shore again, or get a locksmith, or even break into his own home. Then he remembered Evelyn kept spare house and car keys in the small shed adjoining the back yard.

He walked to it, slowly. At his age he found it hard to see in the dark, and the lights of his neighbor, who'd left town herself, were out. At length he stepped into the shed, muttering a curse at not finding the light switch, and felt for the key on a board over the door. After grabbing it, he stepped carefully outside, and glanced up at his home's first-floor side window.

He saw a circle of light, like that from a flashlight, run diagonally across the pane. Then nothing. He wondered if he had seen the reflection of something in the sky. He stared at the window for some time, but saw nothing else. Then he heard, or imagined he heard, a noise from within the home. As Lowell walked back to the front door, he considered calling the police, then dismissed the idea as an overreaction.

Inside, the intruder had been planning his action for some time. Studying the house from across the street. Going to its garage sale on the chance it would garner him what he wanted. It didn't, but he had learned more about the house. And he had gleaned from a neighbor, while listening intently behind his wig and beard and double mask, that the Lowells planned to go away for a week. And, he overheard Evelyn Lowell complain that their security system wasn't working. Fixing it would have to wait for their return. 'Excellent,' he figured. 'A lucky break.'

The newspapers left outside the home confirmed the Lowells' absence. He chose their fourth night away, in the middle of the vacation, and during a continuing rainy period that would help cloak his movements outside the home and in nearby streets.

He parked his 2015 Subaru Impresa, modest but reliable, a hatchback useful for his tasks, two blocks away on Wolfe St. There he slipped on the beard and wig.

Despite the disguise, despite the darkness, he was still wary about being seen. He had a habitually nervous manner, which contrasted with his innate courage. With his characteristic, rhythmic stride, he passed through the damp, deserted streets to reach the Prince St. manse. He stopped to turn away from a passing car and pretended to read something on his cell. When the block was quiet again, his taut figure strode to the home's driveway. He was pleased the lights of the neighbor were out.

A previous reconnaissance had shown the basement windows along the sides of the house had iron bars, but that those in the back yard did not. He entered through the middle window, and eased himself down onto the floor. 'No need to twist an ankle,' he told himself. He was in the latter stages of his fourth decade, and not as limber as before.

He had overheard Evelyn say that, despite the yard sale, the basement was still filled with the detritus of decades. Looking over the boxes and piles of junk, he saw this was true. It was 10 p.m., and he would give himself, if need be, until 3 or 4 a.m. to search. And if needed return the following night. It was a long shot, but his other exploits had made him financially secure, and this one was a labor of love.

'The basement, and then the attic,' he figured. 'Cache both for items of interest.' He knew it would be tedious work, like trying to find a golden needle in a stack of dried-out hay. But it would be worth exponentially more than the trouble and the risk if it panned out.

The intruder had brought along a backpack with tools, snacks, a drink, flashlights, and night vision goggles. He wore latex gloves of course to leave no fingerprints. But about 11 p.m., he quietly cursed himself, while laughing softly at the absurdity. He had forgotten a basic item: An empty bottle to urinate in if the need so arose. It was bad form, and bad workcraft, to piss in the toilet of the owner. Perhaps he was too finicky about such a thing, but in his orderly way he felt he was right. And perhaps because of the tension he felt at the break-in, and definitely due to his swelling prostate, the need to relieve himself was pressing.

He knew from the house schematics the residents, instead of building a furnished basement with a bathroom and bedroom, used the cellar only as a storeroom. Two of their five bathrooms were on the first floor, the rest upstairs. His flashlight twinkling, he mounted the stairs. 'Leave the toilet *exactly* as you find it,' he reminded himself. He'd made a mistake, but it was a small one.

But as he stepped through the living room, he glanced out the window to the alley—and froze in his steps. Through the parted curtain, he'd noted a male figure walking slowly toward the backyard. Even in the dim light, he'd recognized him from the yard sale as the house's owner. 'He's back in town?!' the intruder thought, stunned, almost frantic for an instant, before calming down. He'd been surprised before; it was part of the game. 'But why did he come down the alley instead of the front door?!'

He thought quickly. 'There's no back door. To get something from the shed?' As he considered this, through the side window he saw the man walk back up the alley, toward the front of the house. He flicked off his flashlight; he should have done that on spotting the man. Still, the owner hadn't spotted him, he thought. He stood motionless, listening intently. Then he heard the sound of a key in the front door lock.

'Maybe the owner forgot his house key and retrieved a spare key.' The intruder figured, 'The basement. Go back down to the basement.' But he hesitated. 'I might be trapped there, if he's here to stay.' He took a step back, then forward. He was rarely so indecisive. 'I can get out a basement window; I can cut my losses now…But if I leave now, he might hear me…Maybe I can hide and wait it out…'

As he hesitated, he stepped back and forth in the darkness, his movements echoing his indecision. His foot got tangled in a shoe rack, and he toppled. He fell onto an Afghan covering the hardwood floor, and banged an elbow on the floor, as slippers, running shoes, moccasins, and brown leather office shoes went flying.

'Did the owner hear this?!' his mind shouted. Despite that moment of clumsiness the intruder, a gymnast from his youth, had superb coordination. He scrambled up smoothly, into a squatting position, his lean, sallow face pointed towards the door, his alert ears quivering.

Outside, Lowell stepped onto the porch. He started to open the front door—and heard the crash. The attorney froze. His highly pitched, patrician voice called out with a tinge of fear: "Anybody there?"

The intruder could not believe his bad luck. How klutzy of him! In any event, he had to act fast. In the dimness, he scampered up toward the door. He banged his shin on a settee, stopped for a moment, silently cursed, trying to calculate how much noise he had made this time. Then stepping gracefully, like a cat, his legs like springs, he made it to the side of the door, as Lowell swung it fully open. The intruder held his breath.

Lowell, confused and nervous, mistook the low pattering of feet for the fluttering of birds. 'Did an oriole fly in as I opened the door?' he wondered. He stepped inside, then turned to flick the light switch. As he did, the intruder stepped quickly, smoothly from behind the door. The latter thought furiously, hopefully: 'Can I slip outside, escape, without him noticing me?!'

He reckoned he could not. He took a step behind Lowell as the owner swiveled his head to peer into his darkened home. The intruder figured, wrongly, that Lowell was twisting his head over to look at him.

He had the flashlight in his right hand. He raised it up. And he brought it down on the owner's head with what he hoped was a just moderately severe blow. Lowell collapsed, his forehead smashing into the wood floor. 'Too hard,' thought the intruder. The memory of a similar act not long before and not too far away entered his mind. He crouched down to examine the man.

He was out cold, or worse. He examined him with the light. He made out a gash on the right temple.

He needed to flee. But he had to know. He gently kicked the man on the side with his Arc'teryx trail running shoes. Lowell uttered a low moan.

'Thank God,' the intruder thought. 'He's not in a coma, not dead. At least not yet.'

He stepped outside, light on his feet, ready to run—he imagined he'd see a crowd of Alexandrians lined up to see what was happening. But it was late at night in a town forlorn and much abandoned. All he could see was a jogger making her way north on Prince St. toward the Murray-Dick-Fawcett house. He pranced across the street and, despite himself, despite telling himself to remain calm, ran to his vehicle. A rush of adrenalin kicked in. He was worried about the botched entry, and the condition of Lowell, but he moved along like a gazelle, becoming almost giddy, having escaped some danger, knowing he'd soon encounter other perils, another thrill. His kind of work was addictive.

Like Mosby of old, he fled through Old Town to a secluded spot, a mostly forested and completely deserted area on S. Lee St. He parked his Subaru near a World War Two Era victory garden, just five blocks from the Freedmen's Cemetery. At the site of the former Union Army fort that had guarded Alexandria from Confederate raiders. As Mosby had done, he stripped off his wig and beard. Then he drove back to his townhouse not far away.

On route, guilt gripped him. He pulled over, and grabbed a burner phone out of the glove compartment. Disguising his voice, he told the receptionist at Inova Hospital of an incident on Prince St. After making certain she had the correct address, he hung up. He'd later learn, like other close readers of the news, about the "foiled break-in". And, with relief, about Lowell's quick recovery.

Chapter 26 – It's All in the Name

The meeting was large, so large they held it in the garden of the Lee-Fendall House, instead of the small conference room within, whose close quarters were deemed likely to spread the virus. But even in the open air, all the attendees wore masks, and many of them two masks. They sat apart from each other, six-to-ten-feet-distant, abundantly cautious, on the dozens of wooden folding chairs set up on the lawn. Despite the general atmosphere of gloom in town, and the emotional issue at hand, the weather had lifted that day, letting sunlight pour onto the attendees. The white picket fence and tall shade trees of the half-acre garden dampened the noise of any traffic on N. Washington St. With its gingko and magnolia trees, the latter 170 years young, its roses and English boxwoods, and manicured lawn, the locale often held wedding receptions, and hosted field trips for school children. But possibly not that year, with marital parties skittish of the plague and the public schools limited to online instruction. And behind their cloth face coverings, none of the docents, municipal officers, journalists, historians, and concerned citizens could smell the usually lulling scent of the early-summer blooms.

In walking to his place of work that day, Lee-Fendall's chief administrator, Ashby Hume, had looked with interest and some concern at the 75 protestors from social justice orgs strung along N. Washington. Many held signs reading, "Erase the Racist Past Now!" and "No Names for Haters!!" They shouted out slogans in loud unison, and walked up and down the block in almost military formation. Three blocks down Washington St. from Lee-Fendall, the 38-year-old Hume had noticed police and FBI vehicles strung along the sidewalk of Christ Church. Investigators were still combing the Confederate mound and the graveyard for evidence. Forensic specialists had done an autopsy on the battered body of Tony Hill, and sent flesh and blood samples to the FBI Crime Lab in Quantico, Virginia 40 miles to the south.

In the aftermath of the Freedmen's Cemetery murder, the vestiges of Alexandria's Confederate past, or anything deemed associated with it, were rendered verboten. An online petition, signed by 45,000 persons worldwide, insisted on the removal of the historic marker, down the cobblestoned street from Hume's workplace, for "Robert E. Lee's Boyhood Home". And the hastily convened meeting at Lee-Fendall resulted from the demands of ranking City Hall and City Council officers, and irate protestors from in and out of town, for another name change.

And so Ashby Hume, a graduate of the College of William and Mary, Virginia's oldest university, stood addressing those seated in the garden along the semicircular rows of chairs. Ted was among the attendees, and Hume was among the first of a series of speakers. Though the rising sun behind the lecturer cast a warm glow on the attendees, their mood was mostly dark. Hume, a soft-spoken man who enjoyed the quiet life of a researcher and public administrator, was surprised his workplace had become a battleground in a culture war.

"We would certainly take under consideration alternative names to our institution," he told the audience, his mask slung down his neck. "I understand why the name Lee has become a lightning rod in contemporary disputes. And that some are now objecting to the name Fendall as well," he said with sincerity.

"The point has been made that Philip Fendall, the owner of this place in the antebellum period, was an attorney for Henry Clay, while he was

Secretary of State. And at a time when Clay was being sued by the slave, by the enslaved woman, Mrs. Dupuy, for her liberty."

Ashby Hume paused. Those facing him, from the city Government, local news organs, and community groups, blanched at the reference to the infamous court case, which Dupuy had lost, consigning her and her family to further years of servitude. Among the onlookers, jaws were clenched, lips were pursed, and eyes glowered. And out on the sidewalk, on the other side of the picket fence, protestors clapped rhythmically to the cadence of their shouted slogans.

Hume, himself the descendent of a Confederate spy turned post-war public citizen, had doubts about the burgeoning movement to remove statues and alter the names of institutions linked to the "Lost Cause". But he thought it his duty, as the manager of such a place, if not as the descendent of rebels, to at least give the other side.

"I might note, however, in the defense of the Lee-Fendall House," he went on, "that the term Lee does not necessarily refer to Robert Edward Lee." His audience seemed surprised, almost startled, at this remark, and skeptical. "The Lee family was protean, and influential, at various times across the long sweep of Virginia's history."

He stopped to gauge the reaction of the listeners. It wasn't favorable, but he swallowed and plowed ahead, somewhat pedantically, as if he were reading lecture notes to students. "Richard Henry Lee, for instance, was the senior member of our state's delegation to the Continental Congress. It was he who cast the vote for Independence, for America's then-largest, and wealthiest, and most learned, and most influential state. Jefferson, though writing the Declaration, writing most of it, was actually a junior member of the delegation." At the mention of Jefferson, some of the listeners frowned, and a few gave a thumbs-down.

"Then of course there's Light-Horse Harry Lee, Robert's father. He was actually a noted 'Federalist', a proponent of a strong Union." Hume paused again. Though a pleasant breeze was blowing through the assemblage, the listeners had begun to fidget, and many grimaced. They were resistant to hearing to anything positive about a Lee. Further, the horrific murder next to Light-Horse Lee's house, and the dumping of Hill's body at Christ Church, was fresh in everyone's mind, adding to their angst. Hume had heard that some in the town's government feared the more recent murder might have been the work of a left-wing activist, a revenge attack for the Freedmen's Cemetery killing, which was evidently the work of a right-wing extremist. The arrest of someone on the opposite side of the political spectrum might slow the town's ongoing effort to purge the town of its racist antecedents. And that could not stand. Meantime, out on the sidewalk, there were further grumblings, and shouts of "Justice for Yesterday, Today, Forever!"

Hume moved on to a historical example he hoped would meet with more favor from the audience. "There are many, many instances of this famous family. Take the Admiral, Samuel Phillips Lee, Robert E. Lee's cousin. He stayed with, served with, the Union Navy, and married the daughter of a key advisor to President Lincoln. The ships of Admiral Lee blockaded the Confederate coastline. They stopped the South from exporting its cash crop, the material woven at the Old Cotton Mill down the street from us.

"There were many, many Lees," he went on. "Some thirty-seven Lees lived in this place. The Lees are, or were, the most prominent family in Virginia's history."

Someone yelled, "They were *racist!*"

Someone else yelled, "They were *privileged!*"

Hume blushed, coughed into his hand, and continued.

"And, and, it isn't just the Lee name, of course, that is associated with this place," he continued, somewhat stiffly, though less so than the faces of his listeners, which seemed to resemble stone.

"This is the House of Lee-*Fendall*. Actually, at least two Fendalls of note. Philip Fendall the Second, or Junior, did defend Henry Clay against the enslaved lady Dupuy. That is true. But like his friend and client Clay, Philip Fendall Junior was a Unionist, he was for a strong federal government—and for a Union that would endure forever. In no way a secessionist. He also opposed slavery. And even as his cousin Robert E. Lee fought for the Confederacy, two of Fendall's sons fought for the Union. And one fought for the South. Brother against brother." Hume licked his dry lips. He stated in a low voice, "Those times were—*complicated.*"

A voice called out from the assemblage. "But he *owned slaves*! Didn't he?!"

Thrown off guard, Hume stopped, and broke out in a sweat. He started to, then decided against, mentioning Fendall's involvement in the American Colonization Society, the effort to send freed slaves to their own African nation. It had been an action against slavery, of sorts, but this audience might not interpret it that way.

He took a long drink from his bottle of Evian, and heard his cell buzz for the third time since the start of his talk. Stealing a quick look, he saw he'd gotten two threatening texts, including a death threat to his daughter, a young teen at Arlington's Washington-Liberty school, recently renamed from its former appellation, Washington-Lee.

Hume swallowed more water, and continued in a strained voice. "And the elder Fendall, Philip Fendall, Senior, the First—sorry if that's a bit confusing—who built this place, yes, probably with the help of slaves, he, he was unionist, or Federalist, as they called themselves, at the start of our country. He was the cousin of Arthur *Lee*, our diplomat, along with Ben Franklin and John Adams, to France, during our American Revolution." He inhaled deeply, and managed to speak in a normal register again.

"Fendall Senior was a friend of Washington, and helped him build the Potomack Canal, not far from here, north of Arlington." His throat cleared, and grew stronger, as he warmed to his subject. "The idea behind such 'infrastructure projects' was pure 'Union': Build canals and roads, and later railroads, to bind together the disparate States, for a 'more perfect Union' if you will. Fendall even served as a director of Hamilton's Bank, the Bank of the United States, a kind of early Federal Reserve. And for the same purpose. To make the American economy, and nation stronger, and more unified."

Yet his audience sat restlessly, if mostly quiet, and unmoved by these remarks. 'Economics is the dismal science indeed,' Hume thought, 'and rarely interests an audience.' He plowed on.

"My, my main point is that deleting the Fendall name or the Lee name from our museum, may be undercutting all of those other Lees, all the Fendalls. And, and perhaps, getting rid of a big chunk of our state's history, the worthy as well as the controversial.

"And they weren't the only famous people to live here. One of the greatest labor union leaders of all time, Mr. John L. Lew—"

At this point the City Council Coordinator, Avril Forstandt, even without raising her hand to gain the floor, rose up from her folding chair to interrupt Hume. Six-feet-tall, blonde, ramrod straight, with a strong physique, she drew everyone's attention. Forstandt raised out her right arm, and cried out: "The time for careful consideration is past; the time for decisive action is NOW!" And she thrust her hand forward as in throwing a knife.

Stunned by her outburst, Hume tried to continue, haltingly. Forstandt sat down, and folded her arms rigidly. Hume intended to speak about labor unionist John L. Lewis, on the museum's many outreach programs, on the "servants of color" who'd worked in the house, and on the "peculiar institution" in which many were enmeshed. But after a few more minutes, he grew nervous again, especially about his daughter. He was also irritated at the audience's response. 'I deserve better than this,' he reflected. 'I've made this institution my career, my life. I'm being treated like a servant.' Midway through his remarks on Lewis, he abruptly ended his talk and sat down.

The next speaker was Wilhelmina Boudinie, a researcher of Hispanic, Belgian, and African-American ancestry. The Council had hired her as a $295-an-hour consultant on ESG governance, particularly the notion that racism was endemic in America from its start. Part of her contract was to generate reports pointing out alleged, inherent bigotry in the town's institutions and infrastructure. For this gathering, the 48-year-old Oberlin College graduate outlined the many Alexandria road names with apparently antebellum or Jim Crow ties. Her aim, and that of the City Council, was to kickstart a process of replacing those road signs with the names of social justice figures.

Displaying a series of maps plastered onto posters, Boudinie outlined the 35 or so streets, alleys, or lanes that the former, largely pro-Confederate town may have named after Southern soldiers or officials. These included Pierre Beauregard, a U.S. Army hero of the Mexican-American War who became the Confederate commander at the First Battle of Bull Run, and Jefferson Davis, the former federal Secretary of

War, U.S. Senator, and Architect of the Capitol who went on to be the President of the Confederacy.

Ted listened to the presentation with interest, and some annoyance. As a Civil War buff, not to mention a historian on the period, he had always thought it, well, historical, that some streets in and around Old Town were named after Southern officials. Hailing from New York, the Confederate names seemed exotic to him. They reminded him of the traffic circles in D.C., almost all of which were named after Union generals and admirals. It seemed to make history, a sometimes distant and dusty thing, alive and immediate.

He did agree however, with Boudinie's call for changing the street name of Floyd, a Confederate general who'd been an antebellum Governor of Virginia, and whose father had been the state's Governor as well. Both Governors were villains, in Ted's view. The elder Floyd, though privately favoring gradual abolition, had thwarted a state conference on manumission, on the gradual freeing of Virginia's slaves, that Thomas Jefferson Randolph, a grandson of Thomas Jefferson, proposed in 1832. The initiative might have freed the state's slaves over time, as Northern states like New York had done. If abolition had happened early on in Virginia, the South's most influential state, it might have changed history, and for the better, even possibly avoiding civil war.

John Buchanan Floyd was, in Ted's view, worse. The younger Floyd defended slavery, and with the Civil War looming, sent weapons from the Old Dominion to the Deep South states, in preparation for the coming war, in which he was appointed a Confederate general. Further, crooked colleagues of his siphoned off federal funds from, of all things, the Pony Express.

After the race consultant's talk, a question-and-answer session took place. Ted, displaying his mischievous streak, played devil's advocate with a remark that was more of a short speech than a query. The historian raised his hand, was called on, and stood up straight. He stated:

"Thank you much, Professor Boudinie, for contributing to this debate. It seems the assumption is all those men were evil, uniformly evil. I'd agree that's the case, or almost so, with Governor and General John B. Floyd. But aren't there exceptions? Wheeler, for example, General Joseph Wheeler. He rejoined the federal army after the war, and became a two-star general in the Spanish-American War. Fought alongside Teddy Roosevelt's Rough Riders of Native-Americans and ranchers, as a three-star general, where he admired an attack by the all-black Buffalo Soldiers." Ted paused for emphasis. "That's sounds pretty All-American." He detected some frowns among the listeners, but plunged forward.

"And several of those proposed for deletion held high federal positions. Very high. Breckinridge, for instance, John Breckinridge, was Vice President of the United States. And Tyler Street might be named after one of several rebel officers—or after *John* Tyler, a U.S. President." Deputy Mayor Morenis shook his head, and said to Forstandt, "I know this guy. He's the one from the City Hall meeting, who called for retaining the Appomattox statue, and adding statues of black Am—, for adding other statues." Forstandt snorted in disgust.

Ted continued. "And the Janney street name is linked to John Janney, the head of Virginia's secession conference who *opposed* secession. He warned it would lead to catastrophe." He paused. "It did." Ted noticed town officers exchange annoyed glances, and gesture at Ted to get to his point, but he went on, while glancing occasionally at a list of noted persons he'd emailed to his cell.

"Then there's Mosby, Colonel Mosby—a notorious Confederate raider, but later an advisor to Ulysses S. Grant, the former head of the Union Army! And Longstreet, General Longstreet. He warned before the war the North's citizen-soldiers, once motivated and organized, would make ferocious foes. Afterwards he too served the reunited nation under President Grant, and took lots of grief from Southerners for his 'treason'." Ted saw the audience's restless reaction, and quickened his pace.

"Also Maury—Matthew Fontaine Maury. Before and after the conflict, he was one of the greatest scientists in American, no, in world history. Maury was the father of oceanography, and the godfather of atmospheric science—climate science if you like."

Ted noted an angry titter in the crowd, as some started to object to his lengthy 'question'. "Get to the point!" shouted a community organizer. Boudinie was herself wringing her hands, and contemplating how to react.

Ted stated, "Let me finish up. Some of the names proposed for deletion are especially problematic—because we're not sure whom they're named after. Armistead, for instance. That street might be named for Lewis Armistead, the Confederate general who fell at Gettysburg. With great pathos, in fact. As he lay dying he asked about his friend from the pre-war, asked for Union General Hancock, later a presidential candidate. Or is 'Armistead' named after his granduncle, George Armistead, who ordered the flying of the 'Star-Spangled Banner' at Fort McHenry?

"Then there's Herbert. Does it refer to the Confederate Arthur Herbert, or does it reference the two-hundred-and-twenty years that Herbert, and

324

Burke, our town's bankers, have been in business? And have granted
loans to so many of Alexandria's entrepreneurs. And, does Pierpont
Street refer to a rebel musician, the fellow who wrote 'Jingle Bells', by
the way, or to the war-time, *Union* governor of Virginia?"
The audience had turned sullen, so Ted ended with a wry comment,
while suspecting it wouldn't move his listeners either.
"And lastly, one cannot but help mention the name of Hume, the same
as today's host. During the war Frank Hume was a rebel spy, true,
though a bungling one. But after the war Hume was the force behind
D.C.'s Memorial Bridge, the one leading from the Lincoln Memorial,
the monument honoring the great President, and the span leading to
Arlington National Cemetery, the graveyard that honors all our war
dead. And his home is the site of the historical society for our sister
city, Arlington." As catcalls began to break out, Ted ended his
"question" without asking one, and dropped into his folding chair.
There was uneasy silence. Except for Forstandt. She called out, "Ms.
Boudinie, you don't have to answer that, that 'question'. Besides, we're
out of time, thanks to Mr. Sifter, so let's end this Q&A session. And
bring out our next speaker."
Ted had little interest in this topic, namely the legal and administrative
expenses, versus the apparent public benefits, of changing street names.
He got up, and on the receiving end of angry glares and a few boos, he
left Lee-Fendall to tackle a pile of work for his book on Alexandria's
history. He learned afterwards, from a news link Harmony sent, that the
meeting ended with a decision to rename the Lee-Fendall House at an
unspecified time. "Liberty-Equity House" was the leading contender
for the new moniker.

Chapter 27 – Lafayettes, Lowells, Lees

A few days after the Christ Church atrocity, Ted and Harmony were walking together down Duke St. Ted had his cloth mask in his pocket, while Harmony's was slipped down her neck. On that cloudy, humid midafternoon, Harmony clasped an umbrella, while her friend, who disdained the things as an encumbrance, had a little Totes stashed in his daypack. Despite the prospect of more rain, and much more the demise of Tony weighing on their minds, the fresh air of their ramble seemed to do both some good.

The historian had a destination in mind, and had asked the adventurous lady Jain to come along. A lover of surprise, he mysteriously declined to reveal their destination.

They strode past a Fairfax mansion where the Marquis de Lafayette had stayed during his grand 1824 'nostalgia tour' of the United States. Alexandrians had gathered in the thousands to hear the hero, who was then one of the last living links to the American Revolution. When the Marquis found the city fathers had neglected to build a speaker's platform, he simply walked across Duke St. to the Benjamin Dulany mansion—and gave his address from its front steps. He also appeared before the U.S. House and Senate, as the first foreigner to speak to both houses of Congress. At a congressional dinner the old soldier made a prediction, a prophecy, really, that the United States 'would one day save the world.' In 1917-18, the U.S. surely helped save France, from Imperial Germany. And in the 1940s it helped liberate France, while helping save the world from Nazi Germany and Imperial Japan.

In listening to the Frenchman's oratory on Dulany's steps, some in that crowd recalled the unusual parties that Dulany gave in his abode. Ted told Harmony that the festivities were a reminder that Alexandria, not too far from the frontier of that time, was a rough-and-tumble place. Benjamin Dulany loved hosting parties, loved to dance, and the hard-drinking fellow of Irish descent insisted that any wallflowers among his guests perform the minuet, or an up-country jig. When someone refused, Dulany would take out a pistol, and fire at the reluctant hoofer's feet! The guest immediately broke into a quick-step. At one soiree, Mrs. Dulany complained the discharge of firearms indoors was unworthy of a good host. Mr. Dulany responded—by locking his spouse up in a closet for the balance of the fest!

The town let his misbehavior pass, and evinced unusual tolerance toward the irascible Celt during other outrageous misbehavior. Namely, his loyalty to King George during the Revolution, in a town that fiercely favored separation from the mother country.

How did a Tory like Dulany avoid being stripped, tarred, feathered, and run out of town on a rail, the normal punishment for Loyalists? Well, right down the block from the Dulany mansion is a remarkably preserved stable dating from the late 1700s. That stable sheltered a horse who was sold to an important personage. The person in question was George Washington, and he rode Dulany's half-Arabian stallion throughout the battles of the Revolution. Aware of the equestrian connection between the royalist and the American commander, the townspeople let slide Dulany's fealty to that other George, the King.

Ted and Harmony went up St. Asaph past the antebellum and bellum John Janney home, and at the Murray-Dick-Fawcett ranch house turned right onto Prince, "America's most historic street". They ambled down a block laden with the townhomes of other Revolutionary War acquaintances of George Washington. Out of one stepped a masked, middle-aged couple. On seeing the unmasked pair approach, they literally jumped back in horror onto their stoop.

"Maybe they think we're the murderer," quipped Ted, and Harmony glumly answered, "I don't know if they have their priorities straight. I'd be more afraid of a killer than of catching a virus while walking outdoors." As they shook their heads Ted remarked, "The Bank of Potomac home is one block down, directly on our left." They discussed the article they'd read in the *Alexandria Gazette*, about the night-time assault on the house's owner.

"I'm glad," said Harmony, "he wasn't badly hurt, that Mr., Mr. Lovett?"

"Lowell," corrected Ted. "Yes, he was lucky. You know, today's *Alexandria Gazette* is obviously descended from, or at least borrows its name, from the old *Alexandria Gazette*, a pro-Southern paper that was printed on Prince St. at the start of the Civil War." His face took on an abstracted look. "And I wonder if Lowell is related to the old textile mill family of Massachusetts, and the city of Lowell there. I bet they've sent plenty of lawyers and politicians down this way."

Harmony smiled indulgently at Ted's love of words and their historical connections, however strained at times. "The police, and the FBI," she commented more practically, "seem to have dismissed the incident. 'FBI Guy' was quoted downplaying it. He said it was unrelated to the murder, I mean, murders." She grimaced with the memory of the atrocities.

"Maybe, maybe not," replied Ted, becoming serious. He took out a copy of the J. Swift map and held it out toward his friend. He looked at the Athenaeum site on the chart, and thought of its many roles over the eras: art gallery, financial institution, hospital, depository for Robert E. Lee's savings, Methodist Church. They walked slowly together, side by side, Ted's hip occasionally bumping into Harmony's waist, as they once more scrutinized the map.

"Not related to the murders," he said, "but maybe related to the Athenaeum death."

"What are you talking about?" asked Harmony.

"Most people have speculated," Ted said evenly, "that Tony's murder," and then his voice dropped a register, as he choked up, "that Tony's death, was some kind of revenge for the Freedmen's slaying." He coughed to clear the phlegm from his throat, as Harmony wiped away tears that had burst forth at the mention of their late friend.

Ted noted how the police and FBI had yet to turn up much evidence at the Christ Church graveyard. The killer had mostly stuck to the brick pathway, apparently, and had left no footprints. The hard rain that night may have erased them, and other possible clues. And the Church's video cameras, Greco had been dismayed to find, did only cover the grounds around the main church entrance and visitor center. And not the gateway and mound at the far end of the cemetery where the body had been dumped.

"They think it's a revenge attack," Ted continued. "That may be so, or not. Maybe a fake…" His voice trailed off, then picked up again. "But there was a connection, I think, between the Athenaeum incident and the assault on Mr. Lowell."

"But they seem very different," commented Harmony, glad to change the subject away from Tony. "The house break-in was an obvious robbery attempt. A petty crime."

"Was it?" asked Ted. "Perhaps the robber, the attacker, whatever he is, knew Mr. Lowell."

"That's a guess," chided Harmony. "And the Athenaeum was no simple burglary, and maybe no robbery at all. It was a murder, or manslaughter."

"Now you're the one speculating," chided Ted. "It could have been an accident." He thought a moment, and cleared his throat, while rubbing some tears away. "I think the Athenaeum and Lowell events are connected—and maybe the attack on the riverfront watchman too!"

They stopped between the adjoining homes of Sally Fairfax and Dr. Elias Dick, Washington's lady friend and Washington's physician, respectively. As Ted held the J. Swift map, and Harmony called up a contemporary map of Old Town on her cell, the historian laid out his theory.

"The Athenaeum, back in Swift's time, was a merchant bank. A very important one. And Lowell's home, before it held the offices of Civil War governors, it was another of Alexandria's main banks, a very profitable one.

"If I'm right," he continued, "the pattern of crime will hold for the town's other banks from the antebellum period."

"Now you're the one speculating," Harmony commented. "But I admit there's some logic to what you saying."

"There were just a handful of these big banks," Ted went on. "So it shouldn't be hard to check them all out."

"What were the other ones again?" Harmony asked.

"Well, the obvious one to look at is the Bank of Alexandria, the original Herbert family bank, next to the Carlyle House. But since we're so close, why don't we pay a visit to the headquarters of the Burke & Herbert Bank?"

Harmony objected, pursing together her full lips in a kind of pout. Her freckled nose flared, as if she sensed something that didn't smell right.

"But you told me, on one of your tours, that bank wasn't set up until the 1850s, just before the Civil War. That was long after J. Swift died, wasn't it?"

"Yes," Ted answered, "and today's headquarters wasn't built until the 20th century. But that building is famous, among historians and archivists, for the records in its attic, from long before the Civil War, to the periods after it. Probably including artefacts from the original Herbert bank too, the Bank of Alexandria."

They turned onto Fairfax St. They could see the bank two blocks north on the corner of King.

"About two decades ago, for instance," Ted went on, "the Burke & Herbert managers found a treasure trove for history buffs in their attic."

"I think I read about that," said Harmony. "Something about Robert E. Lee's daughter?"

"Good memory!" Ted remarked. "Yes, Mary Custis Lee. There were a series of letters between her and her father, many written after the war. Rediscovered in her luggage, stored in a top-floor 'silver room'. That's what the bank calls its storage space for really valuable stuff.

"The letters shed light on Robert E. Lee's thoughts on rebuilding the South, the status of the former slaves, education in the South, and so on. He thought education was key, for lifting up his region, which is one reason he became head of Washington and Lee College, in the Shenandoah, in Lexington, Virginia. His letters are controversial because, though Lee had freed his personal slaves in the war, he did not have, how do you say—he lacked, 'modern views', on civil rights."

Harmony noticed Ted had lapsed into his professorial mode, before falling silent and watchful as they neared the complex of the Burke & Herbert Bank buildings. First on the right, before Swift's Alley, were the towering townhouses of the man himself, J. Swift. Built from the proceeds of his piracy, or privateering, during the Revolution, as well as his canny business investments. Burke & Herbert had purchased the mansion on the south side of the alley, while the one just northeast of it was still a private home.

Ted and Harmony entered the small parking lot adjoining both structures. They were said to be the fourth and fifth largest mansions in town, after the Carlyle House, a Fairfax mansion down from Tony's Light-Horse Harry Lee home, and the Smith-Vowell mansion, formerly of Robert E. Lee's attorney. Ted had long wanted to see the backyard of the private Swift home, he said to Harmony, "but its gate, facing the parking lot down the alley, is always locked."

He winked mischievously at Harmony, and leaving her standing alone and surprised, strode down the byway. Recovering herself, Harmony followed, also eager to see the yard, but concerned Ted was about to break the law.

She ran gracefully up to him, her strong yet tapered calves quivering, her running shoes sounding softly on the bricks. They turned into a narrow side alley that was the sidewalk of a private home. They were trespassing, with Ted once again exploring without permission the courtyards and lanes of a historic spot. If caught, he'd explain he was simply being curious about a place of historic interest. Which was true, and it usually got him off the hook. And sometimes, after a friendly chat with the placated owner, he'd garner another guest for his tours, as well as inside information on an intriguing locale.

In this case, no one seemed at home. Perhaps its occupants, like so many others, had split town to dodge the malaise.

They reached a small gazebo with a flowery garden. Scattered about were signs of the season: enchanter's nightshades, white Indian pipes, and lightly purpled Virginia roses. There was the thickly sweet smell that Ted found distinctive of Old Dominion gardens.

Harmony was the first to see, and point out, the little excavation. Ted thought of the Murray-Dick-Fawcett dig—the dimensions of the hole were almost the same. They walked to it past a few sweetbay magnolia leaves lying on the grass.

Harmony took Swift's map, looked about the ground, and out of the corner of her eye saw Ted moving forward.

"Stop!" she cried.

He was about to step near the dig, but she'd spotted footprints there. He might stomp all over them. Ted looked down. About two-thirds of a footprint were visible, and portions of others.

"The soles seem almost like those of ballet shoes," said Harmony, recalling her childhood training in dance. "Very light shoes," said Ted, "good for moving about quickly."

They were similar to the portions of footprints Ted had seen at the Murray-Dick-Fawcett house.

Ted took several steps back, and examined the map.

He placed his finger on the part of the chart where the garden between the Swift mansions might be. Harmony stood on the tips of her toes, peering over his wide shoulders. "Look," he said, "right about here." Right about where the two were standing. The chart had a small smudge. "Indicating an 'X', perhaps?" asked Ted. "Or an abbreviation for a small building, or an alley name." They couldn't tell.

Careful to sidestep the footprints, they looked down into the hole. If there had been anything there, the digger had taken it. They both took photos of the hole and the prints and returned down the alley unseen.

"You might be on to something after all," Harmony told Ted excitedly. "Should you tell Greco?"

"Not right now," replied Ted. "Let's pay a visit to the bank."

They went back onto S. Fairfax St., where it intersects with Swift's Alley. They were now close to another one of Ted's "history sweet spots": the corner of Fairfax and King. It boasts the Swift mansions, and down Swift's Alley toward the waterfront, the late-1700s homes of Lawrence Washington, G.W.'s esteemed brother, and Col. George Gilpin, Martha Washington's cousin. Both dwellings are right down the cobblestoned path from the Burke & Herbert headquarters, which is modern-looking and seeming out of place in comparison, though over a century old. It is across S. Fairfax from the Leadbeater-Stabler "apothecary", or pharmacy, a drugstore and general store of abolitionist Quaker families built in President Washington's first term in office. Martha Washington shopped there, and the place is particularly noteworthy for its Lee lore.

It's said "Bobby Lee", a Federal Army officer in 1859, was shopping there when he heard of John Brown's raid on the Federal arsenal in Harper's Ferry, Virginia. Brown's intent: Seize the weapons, and ignite a slave insurrection. The War Department directed Colonel Lee, and Lieutenant James Ewell Brown Stuart, "J.E.B." Stuart, another future Confederate general, to muster a company of U.S. Marines to put down Brown and his band. They did, and Brown was captured, tried for treason, and hanged. His raid terrified the South with fears of an armed slave revolt; it was a precipitating event of the Civil War. In thinking of this Ted recalled the controversy of several years prior, when the school board in Fairfax County changed the name of Alexandria's J.E.B. Stuart High School to Justice High School.

According to another story, Lee was also in Stabler-Leadbeater's in April 1861, shopping for paint for the Lees' Arlington House, when he learned of the attack on Federal forces, at Fort Sumter in Charleston,

South Carolina. THE precipitating event of the war. The pharmacy would later be popular with the Union soldiers who, depending on your point of view, occupied or liberated the town. Blue-clad troops who had fallen ill queued up outside to buy one-cent, alcohol-laced lozenges for their coughs and colds.

In 1933, the Stabler-Leadbeater business went out business during the Great Depression, to be transformed into a distinctive museum of early American medicine. Other noted town enterprises such as Gadsby's Tavern nearly went belly-up during those hard times. Burke & Herbert stayed flush.

Harmony and Ted lingered at the intersection outside the entrance to that bank. Kitty corner across King from the old Quaker pharmacy was the William Ramsey House visitor center. And next to it the tall warehouse turned Italian ice shop where Laura Schaefer burned to death on her wedding day. And just a few feet away was the site of the horrific, early-20th-century lynching. And not far from it had occurred a related, opposing, and highly ironic event.

On his Civil War tours, after relating the experience of Lee at Stabler-Leadbeater, Ted would often tell the remarkable tale of what took place on King St. in 1902. Its focus was an elderly, well-dressed woman who was shopping in town on a Friday the Thirteenth afternoon in June. Shopping just as many today frequent the antique shops and furniture stores along the town's Main Street. The story goes something like this. The lady was bone-tired and, on entering a horse-drawn trolley to get to her destination, sank into a seat with her heavy bags. Soon the trolley conductor approached her. He said, 'Excuse me, ma'am, but you're not allowed to sit here.'

The lady was annoyed, and replied, 'Sir, I've had a long day. I'm tired. I'm not moving.'

The man persisted: 'Ma'am, again, I'm sorry, but under the law you are not entitled to this seat, and you must move.'

The classy lady, 66 years young, replied: 'Sir, I've been shopping for quite some time, in warm weather. I'm worn out. Lugging these heavy bags around is not an easy thing. I'm resting nicely here. I'm not moving.'

The conductor pointed to the front of the trolley. 'But ma'am, this is the *back* of the trolley. White women can't sit here. You're supposed to sit in the *front* of the car.'

'Not back here with the Negroes.'

It was the time of Jim Crow in the South, including the near South of northern Virginia. And the lady had violated a new local ordinance by sitting with the black folks in the back. Including the black maid who had accompanied her to the shops.

When, after a few stops, the lady alighted from the trolley, two magistrates of the law detained her. The policemen took the woman to the precinct house. Probably the police station in rooms on the east side of City Hall. Where one can still see the markings for the precinct on the wall.

A rumor was spreading around town about the woman, and a crowd was forming. Men who had served with the lady's father began protesting her detention. They informed the magistrates about the fame of the femme they'd collared. She was quite well-known in town, and throughout the South.

"Do you know who you've arrested?!" a spectator demanded of the police.

"That's the daughter of Robert E. Lee!"

Indeed, it was Mary Custis Lee, the General's oldest daughter. And the great-grand-daughter of Martha Washington.

An independent woman, who'd never married, was well-read, and even more well-traveled, having visited over 25 countries in Africa, Europe, and Asia. She was the daughter who had corresponded at length with her father before his 1870 death, and whose letters wound up in the Burke & Herbert storage room.

What accounted for her behavior that day? She had grown up with enslaved persons at Arlington House in the pre-war, and may have held benign views of them. She was a worldly lady, and perhaps her outlook was ahead of its time. Or perhaps she was simply exhausted that day, and took, and kept, the first seat she could find. She might not have been aware of the recent ordinance about segregation on public conveyances. Incredibly, such laws were only taking hold in some Southern states 37 years *after* the Civil War. Surely she was annoyed with having to separate from her servant.

Whatever the case, the precinct officer was chagrined. That his men had arrested the daughter of the esteemed head of the Army of Northern Virginia, with whom Alexandria's 17th Infantry Regiment had valorously served. Miss Lee was released, 'under her own recognizance'. She was instructed to show up in court the following day. She didn't. The authorities didn't pursue the matter.

But the newspapers got wind of the amazing event. Of how the daughter of the most famous Confederate general had tried, wittingly or not, to break the color line of the Old South. The story made headlines around the globe.

37 years later, 74 years after the Civil War, black Alexandrians would try to permanently end segregation in town, with a sit-down protest at the segregated Old Town library. And, in so doing, sent the ball rolling to end it everywhere.

Chapter 28 – The Thief of the Ancient Attic

Outside Burke & Herbert, Ted and Harmony slipped on cloth masks,
with Ted grumbling about their efficacy. Harmony glanced at the night
deposit box, and saw the paint that had marred it during the Old Town
Riot, or Confederate Riot, depending on various people's points of
view, had been scrubbed away. They entered the bank of Mary Custis
Lee's correspondence. They walked up to the office of an assistant
manager, Alfred Herbert "Herb" Harrison, Jr.

Ted assumed, but wasn't sure, Harrison was related to the Herbert
family that founded, and still partly managed, the bank. And perhaps to
the Harrisons of Virginia, whose descendants gave the country two
Presidents. He knew Herb Harrison from previous visits, including one
when Ted was looking for a booklet the bank had published for its
centennial back in 1952. The work, though short, had a treasure of
information on early Alexandria, especially anecdotes on the Civil War.
Ted found an entertaining story how pro-Confederate co-founder John
Woolfolk Burke and a Philadelphia Yankee lass had conspired to
preserve funds for the restoration of Mt. Vernon.

The lovely young lady in question, though a Northerner, was working
on the planned renovation of Mt. Vernon, a property she loved. She
agreed, at Burke's suggestion, to sneak the $100,000 in rebuilding
funds through lines of Union pickets into Washington, D.C. The money
was hidden under the egg carton of a picnic basket, the eggs procured
at the Saturday farmer's market in Market Square. Whenever a Federal
soldier thought of inspecting her basket, the lass would smile demurely,
and the love-starved trooper, far away from lady friend or wife, would

wave her on. At the downtown D.C. bank of George Washington Riggs, then the capital town's richest financier, she placed the egg basket on Mr. Riggs' desk. Though loyal to the Union, Riggs was a friend of Burke's and other Southerners and, like just about everyone, North and South, an admirer of George Washington. He kept the money in a safety deposit box for the balance of the war. When the guns fell silent, he returned the $100,000 to Burke, who returned it to the folks running the overhaul of Mt. Vernon.

As a transplanted Yankee himself, Ted found fascinating the book's point of view of white Alexandrians toward the North's 'occupation' of the town, as they saw it. And how some 'Negroes' had 'taken advantage' of the liberties granted them after The War Between the States. Ted thought this might have been a veiled reference to the widespread disorder, and perhaps an increase in theft and violent crimes, in the devastated, post-bellum South.

Herb Harrison, 41 and sandy-haired, was in his window office, sitting behind a Green Company furniture desk from the 1850s. On the walls were photos and paintings of previous Burkes and Herberts who'd managed the bank, and to whom he was indeed related on his mother's side. These distinguished-looking men, in attire that ranged from early Victorian to contemporary, seemed to stare right down at the visitors. Ted darted his eyes from the portraits to Harrison and back, trying to see a resemblance. For a second he thought of *The Hound of the Baskervilles*, and how Sherlock Holmes had detected a resemblance between the book's villain and a picture of an ancestor. But even with his overactive imagination, Ted saw none.

Harrison was of medium height, with a paunch spreading out from his innate stockiness. His face was "blunt", that is, open and friendly, made more inviting by a broad forehead, made more prominent by thinning hair. His countenance was generally well-proportioned except for his prominent, dark eyebrows, which seemed to catch a visitor's attention. His skin, often ruddy from golf, boating in the Chesapeake, or from Caribbean vacations, was pale from the lockdowns and the travel restrictions. His expression, normally inviting and curious, seemed anxious.

On his desk were photos of his wife Rodriga and their three children. The two boys were attending the highly regarded Thomas Jefferson High School for Science and Technology, then in a battle over ethnic quotas and academic standards. The oldest child was a female freshman at the University of Virginia, soon to battle over a venerable fountain bequeathed by a Confederate alumnus, none other than Frank Hume. Ted introduced Harmony to Harrison. As with most men, the manager's eyes sparkled in admiration for her exotic beauty.

"What can I do for you today, Mr. Sifter?" stated Harrison, with a forced smile. "Open an account, for you or for this lady, or are you here for another of our booklets?

"Or," and his smile completely left him, "are you here on a matter relating to Detective Greco? I know you've helped him in cases before." He paused and looked away, recalling a recent article featuring that policeman. "Our town certainly has some troubling cases these days."

"Actually," said Ted, "I had a professional question, as a historian. About your attic vault, and some of the old documents it might still contain."

"It's funny you ask," said Harrison, turning back and suddenly lowering his voice. "The other night we had, had a, an incident, upstairs." He stopped, embarrassed, his broad face reddening.

Standing inside the doorway of the office, Ted and Harmony
exchanged glances, their eyes glistening with curiosity.

Ted chuckled. He told the banker: "That's like saying, 'I have a secret,'
then refusing to reveal it."

Harrison looked at Harmony questioningly.

Ted stated: "Anything you might share with me, you can share with
her. Harmony can be trusted implicitly; she's the perfect colleague and
confidante." Harmony's round, tawny-tinted cheeks blushed at
Ted's praise.

"Well Ted," said Alfred Herbert Harrison, straightening up in his
chair, his hands on his plump middle, "it's embarrassing, for me. I
suppose I could tell you, given your keen interest in the history of this
place. I've followed your work in the news, and I feel I can trust you.
And I'll take your word about this fine lady here." Without prompting,
Harmony closed the door to the office.

The banker exhaled; his face tightened in remembrance. "Several
nights ago, I left here, as usual, at 5:30 p.m., after locking up. You
should know that I, like many bank managers, hardly work 'banker's
hours.' I arrive daily at 7 a.m." Ted nodded. He remembered his last
visit to the bank, when Harrison seemed a whirlwind of nonstop labor.

"One of my end-of-day tasks," he continued, nodding at Harmony, "is
turning out all the lights in the building. There's a switch for the first
floor—this floor—and one for the second floor, the 'attic' floor. We
have a basement, but it's rather dank and dark—it was under the shore
of the Potomac, I think you know, when the original Mr. Herbert was
setting up shop down the street from here. So we don't keep anything
down there, and we keep its lights off day and night.

Stroking his chin, Harrison stared up at the ceiling, stoking his
memory. "You might recall the other night was rainy. Like almost

every night this week. I'd stayed late to work on some mortgages—you know how the Amazon headquarters has made the home market here red-hot. I didn't leave until around 9:30."

His geniality returned for a moment. "I often take a scooter back to my townhouse on upper Duke St. I daresay I look odd, in my banker's suit, shooting along Fairfax and Royal Streets. But it's fun, and just a short hop to my home. It reminds me a bit of sailing off St. Croix.

"But since the streets were wet that night, I took a Lyft. The driver, an Ethiopian man I think, yelled at me for not having my mask on. On the way, I was thinking about the day's events, uneventful events, at the bank." Harrison seemed relieved, as if making a confession, by relating the story to his visitors.

"Suddenly I felt very nervous, because, for the life of me, I couldn't recall if I had turned the bank's lights off or not. I could imagine Mr. Herbert—THE Mr. Herbert—arriving at dawn and finding the lights to the building still on. He hardly works banker's hours too, and he keeps and expects high standards.

"Still, it's hardly unsafe to leave the interior lights on, and at first I thought I'd arrive extra early the next morning to turn them off. But the thought of the lights blazing out into the street for anyone to see—and we have a number of managers from our branches who live nearby in Old Town—made me change my mind. Between Patrick and Henry Streets, I told the driver to take me back. On our return I thought some more, and I recalled I'd turned off the attic switch, but not the ground-floor one.

"So I was surprised, when the driver dropped me off, across the street at Stabler- Leadbeater, to find the lights for both floors were on. I entered, with my special pass key. I remember thinking, 'Maybe another ranking manager noticed the light on, and has come in to turn it off, but flicked both on first.'

Harrison took a breath. "There are two ways to get to the second floor. Through the stairwell, the usual way, or via an old elevator. The kind that office buildings and department stores had back in the day. Which had an employee who actually stayed in the elevator all day and operated the thing! And we have such a lift, for just one floor up. Such an extravagance! And we have always been a very profitable concern. "The second floor has been used for our most wealthy customers, to keep their jewels and such in safety-deposit boxes, or in larger containers if need be. Many of our deposits"—and Harrison lowered his voice to a more confidential tone, even though the door was closed—"are 'old money', trust funds and the like from wealthy Alexandrians who've lived here for generations."

The banker's voice returned to its normal register. "I took the stairs as usual. The attic's light switch is on the second floor. You can actually turn the lights for both floors off and on from a master switch, from a teller's booth across from my office, but I was naturally curious about the upper light being on.

"The second floor is made up of a long corridor with locked offices, some of them no longer used. They lead to the 'attic': a large storage room on the north side, facing King Street. That's where Mary Lee's letters to her father were discovered." Harrison scratched the light bristles of his chin. "There must be scores of boxes of documents, and personal items too, in that storage space. I'm sorry to say we've never done a full inventory of it all." He looked at Ted. "Perhaps our town historian would like to perform that task some time."

"I'd be happy to," Ted said quickly, anxious to hear the rest.

"We really focus on business," continued Harrison, "and not on our rich history. Anyway, my heart fell when I reached the top of the landing. The doors to most of the offices were open! Forced open, as many hadn't been used for years and are locked shut. I peered into several: One was in disarray, with boxes opened, and several knocked to the ground. I glanced down the hall to the storeroom, and the door was closed. However, when I tried the door knob, the door swung open. I looked inside, and the place was in disarray. Not a mess, exactly, but changed. Some of the boxes had been moved, some of the boxes were open. There were a few papers and personal items, like old wills and even mementos like family medallions, strewn along the floor. But that wasn't what really caught my attention, because—"

"—No one," asked Ted, "ever enters the storeroom?"

"No, well, almost no one," answered Harrison. "An occasional researcher, people like you. I was here for the last one, just a couple of weeks ago. He was following up on some work he was doing, he said, on some correspondence of General Washington." Harrison looked at Ted. "I believed our historian knows that Washington was a client of William Herbert."

"I do," said Ted with sudden interest. "Who was Washington writing to?"

Harrison thought hard. "What is happening to my memory of late? I think this virus is making our minds soft, or distracted. Or maybe it's being online so much. Oh yes, now I recall it. The correspondent had a funny name, a famous name.

"Jonathan Swift."

Ted and Harmony were silent and bug-eyed.

"But not the man who wrote *Gulliver's Travels*," Harrison added. "But a very wealthy merchant in, in colonial times, I think. Jonathan, or Jay,

Swift. He must be the man after whom Swift's Alley is named. The bank now owns one of the houses there."

"I know," said Ted. With excitement he asked, "What did this researcher look like?"

"Oh, I remember that—he really stood out. At first, I thought he was one of our elderly, 'old money' clients. He was white-haired, with a long gray or grayish-white beard. And he stooped, and had a limp."

"Did he say anything else about his work?" asked Ted.

"Oh yes. He said he was actually doing the research for somebody else." Harrison paused in thought. He smiled. "My memory is coming back to me. My wife's from St. Louis, Missouri, and I thought of that when I heard his name. Bobby Louis Stephens. No wait. Bobby Lou Stevenson."

Ted blinked hard. "Or more formally," he said, "Robert Louis Stevenson."

Harrison shot them a surprised look. "The novelist's name."

Ted looked at Harmony and whispered, "Well at least our man has a sense of humor."

Harmony shook her head in wonder. She recalled Ted's story about Jonathan, or J., Swift's life after his privateering. Desiring even more wealth, he'd journeyed out to Tennessee and Kentucky, where he prospected for gold. Those states have limited amounts of gold or silver, Swift was disappointed to learn. But Robert Louis Stevenson, in his great adventure tale, *Treasure Island*, drew on the story of the pirate turned prospector in crafting the immortal character of Long John Silver.

"Robert Louis Stevenson indeed," muttered Ted, smiling.

Harrison got back to his main story. "As I left the storeroom, I heard, bizarrely, the doors to the elevator close."

"It's still in use?" asked Harmony, surprised.

"The owners keep it in working order to give 'fun rides' to major clients. A bit of nostalgia. Anyway, I rushed down the corridor to the stairs.

"When I reached the bottom of the staircase, huffing and puffing I might say, the front door to the bank was closing. I was diverted briefly, to check if the intruder had gone behind the teller's windows, to the safes and the cash drawers there. They were locked shut; everything seemed in order.

"By the time I rushed outside, the fellow was way up Fairfax St., apparently. I think it was him. I think it was a he. I looked up and down King St., and down South Fairfax Street, which were faintly lit by the streetlights, and saw no one else. A figure was running away from here fast, I think he had light hair..."

Ted interrupted: "Light hair," he asked. "Or white hair?"

"Now that you say that," Harrison responded, "I did get, or thought I got, a glance of him just before he went out through our doors. I had a bizarre impression—of an old man with white hair, but moving fast and gracefully like a young man or woman, like an athlete.

"But by the time I saw him again, assuming it was him, he was way up North Fairfax Street. He got near the Carlyle House," Harrison continued, "and the old William Herbert bank. Then he disappeared from view."

Harrison ended his arresting tale almost breathless. Harmony and Ted gazed at each other amazed. The banker pulled out a handkerchief and dabbed his forehead. "My Lord, retelling it is like reliving it. I'm sweating like I did coming down the stairs."

He grew somber, and looked at Ted in the eyes, then Harmony. "You can see why I am embarrassed to talk about this. It makes me, and maybe the bank, look bad. You *must* promise to tell no one else."

The two visitors replied simultaneously, almost in one voice: "You have our word!"

Harrison smiled. "I know I can. It feels good to get it off my chest again.

"I did tell Mr. Burke about it when he arrived. Honesty is the best, you know. I wasn't fired, obviously. Nothing of value had been taken, it seems. Maybe nothing at all."

"But how," interjected Harmony, "did the thief, this intruder, get in?"

"Did he," asked Ted, "climb up the walls?"

Harrison again looked embarrassed. "It was quite clever, actually. There's a narrow alley between the bank and the restaurant next door. Leading to Swift's Alley. We're not certain, but apparently he jumped, or lowered himself with a rope, from the roof of the restaurant to the roof of our bank. There's an old sky light—it hasn't been used since the early 20th century—on our roof." Harrison flushed. "It's practically welded shut from rust—or so our security team thought. Either it was not hooked up to our alarm system, or the burglar disconnected the alarm somehow. And got the skylight to open. Our people are looking into now, and—"

Ted interjected: "—So you haven't contacted the police?"

Harrison' embarrassment turned back to concern. "That's why I have to ask you two, reiterate it, insist on it, really, that you not tell anyone about this." He nervously rubbed his jaw. "There's never been a robbery of the Burke & Herbert headquarters. Our reputation for serving our clients is legend. We even tried to stay open during the Great Depression, when FDR closed the banks for a time.

"If a story emerged that someone snuck into our flagship bank, and through the negligence, perhaps, of our security team, our reputation could be besmirched.

"And believe me," Harrison added, tapping his oaken desk for emphasis, "we'll find out how it happened. We're bringing in some top private security consultants for that purpose."

Harmony and Ted both felt bad for the banker. Ted said, "Mr. Harrison, don't worry.

Nothing you've said will leave this room. Not from us, never."

Harrison smiled weakly, nodding his head, and twisted in his chair away from them. Their conversation was over. His guests left.

The duo, silent and thoughtful, walked down King St., and paused outside a shoe store, at the ground floor of a former warehouse for the bustling colonial port, and later a prison for Confederate captives.

"This confirms your theory," said Harmony. "And it's no theory, but a fact."

"Yes," said Ted. "Our 'cat burglar', if that's what he is, is actually a bank robber. Of a most unusual kind. Who robs banks from long ago."

"The Bank of Potomac, where the owner gets a knock on the head. The Bank of the Old Dominion, at the Athenaeum, where the guard is thrown, or falls, to her death. Burke & Herbert, where luckily our pal Herb Harrison was not assaulted.

"He does seem like a cat burglar, you know. Jumping or slip-lining down to the roof. And accustomed to costumes, to disguise."

"And," Harmony replied, "if you tie this person to the watchman assaulted at the waterfront excavation…"

"…Then that person was looking for something on the map," said Ted with a crooked grin, as he pulled out the copy of it. "He got to the ship first, he likely has his own copy of the chart, and maybe a better, a more complete one.

"He is looking for buried treasure," he continued. "Like J. Swift, like Long John Silver, the inspirations for 'Bobby Lou' Stevenson."

Harmony, her face flushing, suddenly thought of something. "Could he have been on one of your tours? They're so detailed. Was that how he learned of J. Swift, and, maybe, Swift's lost fortune?"

"Perhaps," answered Ted. "He certainly knows a lot about the history of Old Town. I'll think about it. Problem is, thousands of people have come on the hundreds of tours I've given."

"Perhaps," said Harmony, smiling, "you're the burglar."

Ted smiled ruefully. "The police, and the FBI, might just think so. Or worse."

"Try to remember," urged Harmony, "if someone like that was on one of your Alexandria tours, it might lead to a breakthrough." She bowed her head sorrowfully. "And try to remember that image you told me about, that popped into your head when you saw the corpse, that body hanging down from the Freedmen's statue."

"I wish I could remember to forget that," Ted joked sadly. "I'll think that over again, yes."

He gazed at the map. "It's like the burglar is following a path along the chart to do his break-ins. If you follow it, and know the history of the town's merchant banks, you get a good idea of where he'll strike next."

Chapter 29 - Disposing of the Evidence

Jerry Connors had long fallen on hard times. In his opioid haze, he couldn't remember when they had ever been good. His parents were from the hardscrabble section of far North Alexandria, close to the border of Arlington, and long the poor, forgotten lowlands between two noted towns. Nowadays it was a district of apartment complexes and squat frame houses populated by many Central American immigrants, illegal and legal. Before it had been home to slaves on the run, settling there during the Civil War. There had relocated some of the gambling dens, dank bars, and red-lit bordellos that sprang up to service the Union Army's soldiers.

North Alexandria remained déclassé, its shacks replaced in time by car dealerships, a vast water treatment plant, and 'Arlandria''s ubiquitous apartment, and later condo, complexes of cheap, low-rise, but sturdily built World War Two housing. Built for the legions of military officers, administrators, and female workers flooding into the region, its end point the vast Pentagon, "the world's largest office building", its construction starting in 1941, as the great world conflict neared its height. In recent decades there emerged the business office complexes of Pentagon City and Crystal City, both much dependent on military largesse, and most recently Amazon's East Coast headquarters.

Jerry's parents were alcoholics, and their son, though a handsome and active lad, was unwanted. He was shunted to a granduncle, after his mother died in an auto accident and his father took up residence in the family car. In the mid-1980s he dropped out of Alexandria's George Washington Middle School, on the southern fringe of the city's north end, during the crack epidemic spilling out from the District of Columbia. In between classes, as something of a rebel, he'd snort the regular white powder instead of the crumbly stuff. He kicked the habit, regained it, and kicked it again. In his early adulthood, he settled on his father's preference for Scotch whiskey. Jerry next drifted in and out of warehouse jobs near the worn commercial district west of Old Town. In the 1990s, a Christian charity for the homeless near Wyeth St., once the locale of slaughterhouses, took him in. He worked for some time at its discount clothes and furniture shop, helping bring in income for the Catholic charity. But thefts in the store, and the returning lure of Doctor Jack, pushed him back to living in the street. In the 21st century, he left alcohol and coke behind, and found a far more powerful way to forget the world: fentanyl.

He was now 51, his face badly sunburnt, yet with a full head of dark hair and features that retained the handsomeness he'd had since childhood. He was trim, from lack of regular food, and retained a certain vibrancy when not stoned, leading some passersby to wonder how such a man how fallen so far.

After two years of on-and-off drug treatment and lodging at another religious charity on N. Washington St., he'd moved into his own place, so to speak. A 'rent-free' domicile. In his youth, the Metro stop at Huntington, Alexandria, near George Washington's old hunting grounds of Cameron Run, was brand-new, and he'd sometimes take the subway there to see a girlfriend. Maybe it was that fond memory that drew him there again.

Outside the exit of the station is a steep hill with a stretch of woods. The high ground, which commands the approaches to Old Town from the south, was a strategic point during the Civil War, and there the Union Army constructed Fort Lyon. It was part of an array of 68 bastions to protect the federal capital and environs. Another was Fort Ward, just northwest of Quaker Lane and Janney's Lane to the west of Old Town, and known today for its Civil War reenactments. The present site of George Washington's Masonic Temple atop Shuter's Hill had two fortresses: Fort Dahlgren, named for the Union commandant of the Washington Navy Yard, whose son was killed in a failed raid to capture Jefferson Davis; and Fort Ellsworth, named for the Union officer killed after hauling down the Confederate flag at Old Town's Marshall House.

Though no rebel force dared approach impregnable Fort Lyon, the troops there suffered horrific casualties. On June 9, 1863, less than a month before Gettysburg, a lieutenant at the bastion ordered his men to use priming wires to clean away gunpowder that had dried and caked onto cannon shells. A mistake. The wires ignited bombs that blew up thousands of rounds of ammunition and 16,000 pounds of gunpowder. Twenty soldiers were blown to bits, and twenty more were wounded or horribly maimed. In a role of Comforter-in-Chief, President Lincoln visited the disaster scene the following day.

The long-abandoned fortress, its remnants overgrown by foliage, lies in a two-mile stretch of woods on the western edge of the Metro stop and its multi-story garage. A narrow trail runs through it, but few know of it and fewer still walk through it.

Reminiscing about his long-lost love, in traipsing through that small forest one afternoon, Jerry stumbled on a shack that a previous vagrant had put together, then abandoned. It was sturdily made, of wood, plasterboard, sheet metal. It was wide enough to lay down in, and even to pace back and forth some, while dreaming of other places, dreaming to forget.

And if an occasional stroller happened by and spotted the ramshackle lodge, the visitor would never disturb him. No one had ever called in the illegal occupancy to the police. It was an ideal place for a lost soul to dwell.

Jerry Connors kept his few possessions—some clothes, soap, a rusty razor and cracked mirror, thick blankets, pairs of charity sneakers, a battery-powered lamp, a hammer and nails—in the makeshift shelf of a side wall. He'd taken over the refuge for the better part of a year. For food he'd forage in the garbage dumps of the Latino supermarket just across Telegraph Road, and in the backlot bins of the all-night diner just down his hill. That 24x7 place was known for its large and delectable portions, and there Jerry often found nearly complete dinners, not long after they'd been tossed out.

After his search for discarded food, he might sit at either entrance of the Metro complex, pleading for dollars and dimes. Alexandria has few vagrants, and an almost genteel approach to them; he was the only beggar there, no one told him to get lost, and more than a few gave him change. The only trouble was the one time he was robbed, from a man living in the public-assisted housing near a shady 7-11 on Huntington Avenue east of the Metro. He wasn't hurt, except for bruises from a few punches, but his $43.53 of alms were pilfered.

Growing up in Alexandria, Jerry had heard tales of the Fort Lyon explosion. Sometimes his sleep, already roiled by the dread opioid, was upended further with nightmare images of Union soldiers, with missing arms or fingers, their faces burned like charcoal, entrails hanging down the lower limbs, sleepwalking like the undead through the woods near his shack. Sometimes he's wake up sweating bullets, his thoughts ringing with the strange image of a colonel, his head replaced with a cannon shell, with a modern alarm clock on its side, ticking away, ready to explode, but never going off. In his delirium, he'd wake and point a flashlight into every corner of the hut, before finally realizing there was no officer and no bomb.

Yet this unfortunate man had a new friend who brought him a bit of comfort. Jerry saw him again one morning, when he awoke from his drug-addled slumber, worse than ever from visions of hideously injured blue-belly soldiers, shards of shrapnel sticking out like scarlet arrows from their faded-blue blouses. Outside his thrown-together abode, blinking his eyes against the sun peeping through the oak trees to the east, he spotted him. Looking as he had before. A tall man, vigorous in his step, which contrasted with his apparent age.

For his visitor had a long beard, and long, shaggy hair, that contrasted with his tight-fitting shirt and pants. He wore sneakers, strange sneakers that had plastic bags around them. And he had a backpack slung around his right shoulder, with a plastic bag popping out from a partly zippered pocket.

The tall man winked at him in recognition through his masks, and stopped a few paces from the shack. He reached into a pants pocket, and pulled out a package of bar soap and two $20 bills. He gave them to Jerry, who thanked him and went back inside his shed.

The stranger looked around cautiously: As before, there was no one in sight. There were also no visible footprints on the trail. He walked through a first, and then a second grouping of maple trees, and on to a welter of bushes.

He brushed aside some leaves, and picked up an entrenching tool he'd purchased in cash from the River Armaments military surplus store two miles away on upper Duke St. He found the soil loose in this unseen spot, not tangled with roots as it was near the trees. He patiently dug out a hole five feet wide and three feet across. He lowered the bag, which stank, into the ground, and shoved the soil back. He smoothed out the surface, and covered it with twigs and handfuls of grass. He was confident no one would discover the blood-soaked clothing, scraps of flesh, and broken, red-specked knife. It was a secure dumping ground. And his gifts to the vagrant were a tiny price to keep it that way.

A thought came of an old movie, one of extreme violence. He thought of an actor in that film, whose ancestor, a cousin of the Lees, once ran a tavern in a Lee property, two blocks down Cameron St. from the Confederate mound. He recalled a famous line from the film. He muttered aloud a little joke about it, altering the words a bit: "Nothing like the smell of rotting human in the morning!"

Grinning, he left his secret spot, his eyes glazing over, his feverish brain already thinking of his own next act of extreme violence.

Chapter 30 – A Mason-ic Temple

Old Town was in shock over the murders at the Freedmen's Cemetery and the Christ Church burial mound. And over the string of violent incidents from the waterfront to the Athenaeum to Lowell's house to the Appomattox statue. Dread pervaded the normally placid town, regularly voted in magazines as "One of the Ten Best Small Cities in America". Until the plague brought its restrictions and lockdowns, followed by the high-profile crimes.

Many had stayed indoors due to the virus. Now, many more locked themselves inside. More restaurants and shops shut their doors, for the time being, or forever. Schools had closed, and shifted to "distance learning", making the town, usually marked by its many young parents and school-age kids, seem barren. At home, parents wrestled with children restless or listless from spending their school hours on computers.

The unusually wet weather during this time added to the atmosphere of doom. More of the most affluent citizens left for their second homes in the Blue Ridge or at the Atlantic or Eastern Shores. The few pedestrians found on the cobbled and brick-lined streets during the day, and the fewer still during the night, would hurry away from someone coming toward them, for fear of the disease, but also from terror, that the person approaching might be a killer. Unease was worsened by the double- and triple-masks that people were wearing, making it impossible to make out a person's face, to get a sense of his or her intent. It was as if every day had become Halloween: the movie, not the autumn festival.

The town had long hosted popular, nocturnal 'Ghost Tours' of historic sites. After the pandemic struck, the size of the tour groups had been limited, "out of an abundance of caution". Now the tours were suspended outright. Caution abounded.

Ted continued with his own tours, despite the mere handful of guests showing up. Though he felt little outright fear himself, he did think of arming himself, with a knife, or by concealing on his person his 9mm Ruger pistol, acquired despite the city's recent restrictions on handguns. Harmony, worried about coming home late from Amazon, considered purchasing a Springfield Hellcat, a concealed-carry weapon popular with women.

The social isolation arising from the China virus affected everyone, but some groups more so and, in Ted's mind, unnecessarily. School children, for instance, who were cut off from their playmates. The elderly in nursing homes, in effect quarantined, their family members and friends forbidden to see them, to hug them, and in terminal cases to mourn with them.

Another group especially affected were teenagers and those in their 20s and early 30s who, like the very young, had little risk of getting very sick. At an age where they would normally be at concerts, bars, out on dates, or watching or playing sporting events, the lockdowns rendered many frustrated and depressed.

This had been a factor, Ted suspected, in the riot along King St. It began to play out again, along with other things, several nights after the "Christ Church Killing", as it was now being called.

While some thought the murder of Tony Hill had been a revenge slaying, others were persuaded it was a "head fake" by whomever committed the Freedmen's murder. This was especially true of BLM and Antifa members, still enraged, as almost everyone was, over the first slaying.

That evening, a crowd from both groups and related orgs gathered at Ted's favorite history sweet spot, the corner of Cameron and N. Fairfax Streets just above Market Square and the Carlyle mansion. Organizers had set up a barebones speaker's section, with a microphone, a lecturer's stand, and portable stereo speakers, at the northeast corner of City Hall. The location was deliberate. A plaque on the wall there honored George Mason, the father of the Bill of Rights. He penned some of his famous writings, possibly including drafts of what became first ten amendments to the U.S. Constitution, in a meeting hall within. However, Mason, whose plantation house at Mason Neck still stands just 16 miles down the Potomac, had been a slave owner, a fact not lost on the demonstrators. In fact, the stated goals of their rally were, one, to demand the swift arrest and prosecution of the Freedmen's Cemetery killer and, two, the immediate removal of the Mason honorific.

Ted watched the rally at his home via Facebook and Rumble livestreams. From his knowledge of City Hall history, he thought the organizers could have chosen a different, and more apt, locale very close by. The choice that was made occurred because their views of the Founding Father were skewed.

It was true George Mason owned slaves. However, unlike some others who decried slavery without really believing so, Mason was sincere. And he backed it up.

Mason was the most articulate opponent of slavery at the time of the American Revolution. In a remarkable reflection on Southern aristocrats like himself, he wrote: "Slavery {is} that slow poison…daily contaminating the minds and morals of our people. Every gentleman here is born a petty tyrant. Practiced in acts of despotism and cruelty, we become callous to the dictates of humanity, and all the finer feelings of the soul. Taught to regard a part of our own species in the most abject and contemptible degree below us, we lose that idea of the dignity of man..."

After the Revolution, Mason underscored his fine phrases with a call for a far-reaching reform that would have world-wide impact. At that time, Mason had been a strong proponent of a "more perfect union" for the newly independent states. However, he had qualms about the new federal government being set up. He feared a strong central government might crush the rights of the people, as King George's ministers had done. In return for his influential support for the Constitution, he demanded a formal bill of rights spelling out liberties on which the federal authority could not infringe. A deal was struck in which James Madison, his fellow Virginia gentleman, agreed reluctantly to approve those rights in an early session of the new federal Congress. Thus the first 10 Amendments, authored by Mason, came to be. And so was born "freedom of speech," "the right to bear arms," "freedom of assembly," and the rest.

But George Mason had another major concern that gave him pause about the proposed Constitution. It was mostly silent on slavery, which he loathed, and wanted ended over time. To give this noble goal a push, he called for a ban on the slave trade, the capture and transporting of slaves from Africa into the new United States.

This proposal of his failed. At first. But in 1807, 15 years after his death, his colleague Jefferson, then President, signed the ban into law. Many at the time thought it sounded the death knell for slavery. They were wrong, in part due to an invention called the cotton engine. But it was a major milestone in the path to abolition. After the formal ban, there was considerable smuggling in the Southern states to get around it. But for decades the U.S. Navy, in cooperation with the Royal Navy, strongly interfered with the illicit trade.

In Ted the historian's view, the logical next step should have been a ban on the internal slave trade: the buying, selling, and transport of enslaved persons from one U.S. state to another. A most baleful form of "interstate commerce" which, among other grievous things, broke up American families, with many mothers and sons and nieces sold on the auction block, never to see one another again. Alexandria's slave pens along Duke St. became a national center of this vile practice. In the years before the Civil War, thousands of sold-off slaves were marched down to the waterfront late at night, when most residents were blissfully asleep. Those shackled were loaded on ships heading for the huge slave market in New Orleans, where they were sold again or transported straight to the vast cotton fields of the Lower South.

A ban on the domestic slave trade would have been a logical, and just, extension of the ideas of such Southern reformers as Mason and Jefferson. But alas, in the runup to the great conflict, the South lacked the leaders of the founding generation, Instead, it had men like Alexander Hamilton Stephens, and Jefferson Davis, the Vice-President and President of the Confederacy, respectively, who justified slavery, and even called for its expansion.

Mason would have ardently opposed such a wayward turn. Still, as Ted noted in his tours that passed the historic intersection with its Mason plaque, George Mason *was* a slaveowner. To balance the good points of Mason, or any enlightened planter of the time, with this negative aspect, he liked to tell a story, one he had first heard at the Mason Neck plantation, today a beautifully preserved mansion house and grounds rivaling that of Mt. Vernon. The story was related by a talented African-American docent, who played the part of a female slave.

The story goes something like this:

'Near dusk one day, when George Mason was late in life, and slowed by gout and other infirmities, yet renowned for his knowledge and wisdom, a young servant was walking along a path at his master's Mason Neck estate. With some trepidation, the lad found himself outside the rusty iron gate of the plantation's graveyard. The youthful male slave might have noticed some scraps of burlap scattered along the dirt trail on which he was walking. But his attention was riveted elsewhere. For he heard voices, strange voices coming from within the graveyard, sounds that stopped him cold. He was a somewhat superstitious youth, and had been worried about approaching the cemetery, and certainly didn't 'whistle past the graveyard' as he walked up to it.

Now he cupped his left hand to his left ear, and listened intently. He heard a male voice, speaking softly, but firmly, and speaking thus: "One is for me—and one for you." The voice went on in that vein. "That's one for me, and one for you." Another male voice seemed the echo the first voice. "That's right. I get one. That's good. You next, then I get another. Keep going."

The servant, along with being superstitious, had an active imagination. He assumed the two personages, their voices resounding in the twilight—as the sun was starting to set, when the spirits of the dead come out—were the Devil and one of his minions. He judged they were splitting up the souls of the recently deceased, and taking them into their possession, and down into Hell.

"That's one or you, and one for me. One for you—and one for me," the first voice continued.

The servant broke out in a chill. Terrified, he tried to run away.

But you may have heard of the expression, "frozen in fear". The slave found that the muscles of his legs were locked up, and he couldn't move.

Meantime, the utterings from the graveyard continued.

"One for you, and one for me."

"That's right, good, give me another!"

With a mighty effort, the enslaved youth willed his muscles to relax. He began to walk, then stride along the path, then run, then sprint. He raced along, faster than he had ever run before, toward his shack in the middle of the plantation, not far from his master George Mason's mansion house.

He ran along, in great fright, his neck and eyes turned back toward the cemetery, not watching where he was going, fearful at any instant the two satanic spirits would come flying out toward him to seize his soul. Suddenly, he smashed into something, and came to a complete halt.

Was it Satan who had blocked him?

He looked up, and saw he had run into his master, George Mason himself!

The famous planter looked down at him, more with concern than anger, even though the impact of their collision had stung his ample belly.

"Why John," he said to his servant, for that was the servant's name. "John, what is ever the matter? I never saw you so frightened. I never saw you with such a sweat. It's as if you've seen a ghost!"

And the servant John explained that he hadn't seen a ghost, but that he had *heard* two of them, speaking within the graveyard.

"Master Mason," he cried, "it's the Devil Himself, and his servant, divvying, splitting up, the souls of the dead!" John gasped with terror, and went on. "Taking one, and then another, for themselves, to bring them down to the eternal flames of Hell!"

George Mason's concern turned into a bemused smile. He was known for being paternalistic toward his charges. He was also known, like his friends Ben Franklin and Thomas Jefferson, for being a man of science, an apostle of the French and American Enlightenments. As such, he deemed it his duty to replace superstition with logic and reason.

He gently chided, "Come now, John. Surely those were no Devils that you heard. I am certain there is a rational explanation. Come walk with me back to the cemetery, and I will prove it to you."

John was very afraid of going back there, but Master Mason's reputation for good sense was known to all and, besides, no slave could turn down a suggestion from a master. So the two walked slowly but purposefully back to the rusty iron gate of the graveyard.

When they arrived, they heard voices. They stood together, stooping slightly, with John's left hand cupped to his left ear, and Mason's right hand cupped to his right ear. They heard:

"One for me; and one for you. That's one for me, and another for you."

"That's right. So good, keep going. Split 'em up!"

Master Mason stared at John. Servant John stared at Mason.

And both men, terrified, both their legs unfrozen, sprinted away from the graveyard, and from the terrifying voices of the Devil and his henchman.

But if Master Mason, and the young servant John, had been more observant at the cemetery gate, they might have noticed some bits of burlap bag and some crushed pieces of tubers on the wagon path there. For, some hours earlier, two other servants had passed by the graveyard, and found a sack of potatoes that had fallen off a cart. The cart, from another plantation, was long gone. There was no way of returning the sacks and its contents to its owner.

So the two servants decided to share their lucky find, and divvy up the potatoes between them. Yet they feared that, if they split up their hoard in public view, in front of the graveyard, someone might spot them and accuse them of stealing. The punishment for a slave stealing something could be very harsh.

So they dragged the sack of potatoes into the cemetery and, behind a few tall tombstones, split up the food.

"That's one for me, and one for you…"

But John the servant and George the master didn't know this. Their imaginations, even in the Age of Enlightenment and Reason, had gotten the better of them.

And they kept sprinting along the dirt path, John toward his shack, and George toward his mansion.

They both ran very fast. And surprisingly, Master Mason, though elderly, and heavyset, and afflicted by gout, pulled ahead of John. Even though the servant was a young man, of thin yet muscular build, without infirmities, and very quick.

George Mason, despite his prominent paunch, ran faster, and pulled further ahead of servant John. And when he got to his mansion house, he raced inside. And ran to his bedroom, and threw himself under the mahogany posts of his bed, and stayed there trembling for the rest of the night.

And John came running behind him, saw his master run into his mansion, and kept running to his shack. And raced inside, and ran to his straw bed, and threw himself under the rough cotton covers, and stayed there trembling for the rest of the night.

And so it is said:

That this was the only time.

In the long history of the antebellum South.

And of antebellum Virginia.

Yes, this was the only time.

That a master:

Outran his slave!'

The story is amusing, with a moral lesson. But Ted knew the protestors, if they were aware of the history of the City Hall locale, might harp on a terrible event, one not at all funny, that had taken place there over a century before, just a few years before Mary Custis Lee refused to budge from her segregated seat on the trolley.

Chapter 31 – All Lives Shattered

Just as Ted was thinking about this, his live feed showed a rally speaker who was bringing up that very subject. A rector from a local African-American church was at the microphone. His was a black church dating, like so many in the region, from the 1860s, a time of war and of freedom. Rebuilt several times due to fire or renovation, it was now located in West Alexandria, several miles up from the old Joseph Bruin slave jail and office, and the Franklin and Armfield slave pen. During its fledgling years, it may have been a stop on the Underground Railroad.

Ted had often driven past a large banner that the rector's colleagues had gotten placed on the wall of a building facing Washington St. It listed the names of blacks who'd died in recent years while in police custody. Some of the people were true victims. But others, such as a drug dealer, a drug addict and counterfeiter, and a man who violently assaulted a cop, had been the ones at fault, or largely so. Ted thought it misleading to put the names of felons on a display that was supposed to memorialize people who had been actually wronged. He also thought the banner ignored a situation that led to far more black deaths than police actions. Namely, the killing of blacks by black criminals, often in the inner cities. But the rector was silent on this, which struck the historian, as a concerned citizen, as unfortunate, and a missed opportunity.

About 35 years old, of medium build, and a shade shy of six feet, the rector looked out toward the intersection, and the old Wise Tavern townhouse across the way. The protestors momentarily stopped chanting, and put down their signs as he spoke, and listened closely. Just a few local police, their arms folded, stood across Cameron St. The rector, a man of African and partly Irish ancestry, pointed angrily to his right, toward the east wall of City Hall.

"It was just yards from us," he stated, "where one of the worst excesses of racism in our city's, in America's, history took place!" He waved toward the site of the former police precinct office of the building. "He was a young black man, arrested without evidence, and brought to the jail in this very structure. Accused, without evidence, in the Year of Our Lord, 1897, accused without cause, of a sexual assault, on a young white woman." Although fairly youthful, the pastor had picked up the unique cadence of traditional gospel preachers.

"A setup, a setup, by the racist Alexandria mayor of that time!" At this the crowd began shouting angrily. "He refused to hear evidence, that would have exonerated the young man. He stirred, he stirred up hate, hate amongst the townspeople!" Some of the listeners raised their signs back up and shook them hard.

"He refused to bring in extra guards, to protect the young man." The rector paused dramatically.

"And so one night a mob, a racist mob, a lynch mob, gathered at the police station, just yards from where we stand today." He raised his eyes to the sky, as if addressing God Himself.

"And this racist mob *broke into the jail*! And they pushed aside the few police, that the racist mayor, had provided, provided 'for protection'. They broke into the cell of this poor young man, unfairly and *unjustly* thrown into that jail, that very jail that stood just yards away from us!

"And that pitiable young man feared for his very life. He feared for his life, and he tried to hide. He climbed up, up to the ceiling of his jail cell, trying to hide. He pulled himself up, and pulled up his legs, trying to hide. But they saw him, they spotted his legs, his legs dangling down. Despite his trying to hide, trying to find refuge.

"And they grabbed him, and they beat him, and they dragged him from his cell. And they dragged him from the jail, and they took him right past this very spot, where we stand today!" The crowd erupted in a frenzy of shouting and leaping about, as the preacher inveighed, and broke out sweating.

"And they dragged him, they dragged him down the street, the street right behind you. To a lamppost, a lamppost!—on the very corner of the block behind you. On *Lee* Street.

"And they strung him up, this innocent boy, this young man, they strung him up, they HANGED HIM, like a common criminal, *this young and innocent man.*" The fury of the crowd reached a boiling point.

"They *hanged* him! But they did *worse.*

"They MUTILATED him! They cut his body up, with dozens, with hundreds, of cuts: bloody, hateful cuts, from their knives. They desecrated the body of that innocent boy. And they left his precious flesh, his body, the Blood of this Lamb, they left it to rot, hanging from that lamppost!" The rector paused, as if drained of his last ounce of strength. He ended softly, "They left his body there."

At this, some in the crowd pushed past the rector, knocking him against the brick wall. Some carried makeshift weapons: a wrench, some two-by-fours, rocks, and a couple of baseball bats. They surged to the old police site. They smashed its window, and cursed at the fading words "Police Station", etched high up on the wall.

On his sofa, Ted sat up straight, and on his laptop watched in fascination at these actions, which a videographer at the scene was capturing. Her jagged images were like the shaky cam footage of a spy thriller.

The throng surged back to the microphone stand. There a young white man and a young white woman dressed in black tossed pails of red paint onto the George Mason plaque.

Half a dozen people called out to the crowd, and waved them down toward the waterfront. Ted was surprised to see City Council and mayor's office administrators among this group. In the jostling throng, and with many wearing masks, it was hard to clearly identify some of the city officers. Ted wondered if they had been among the leaders of the King Street riot. In any event, the crowd, which had swelled to over one hundred people, rushed down Cameron St., as the demonstrators shouted and shook their fists. The videographer, gripping tightly her camera, followed closely.

The street there drops down sharply toward the harbor. To the protestors' right was the small rise leading to the Carlyle mansion. Constructed some 270 years before by carpenters, slaves, free men of color, architects, indentured whites, blacksmiths, glaziers, and more. At the southeast corner, where Cameron meets Lee St., stands a lamppost. As if on demand, as if created by a 3-D printer, a black male protestor raised up a six-foot papier-mâché replica of the Appomattox statue! A braided-haired female protestor, evidently of Hispanic descent, then produced a long cord of rope.

By then, the rector had caught up to the others. To Ted's amazement, the man of the cloth took the rope, and wound it around the neck of the effigy. As protestors smashed the figure with fists, knives, and stones, the female demonstrator took the rope and hoisted the effigy up to the top of the lamppost. The crowd erupted in a great cheer, which echoed in the rear garden of the Carlyle House.

Then a young man in black clothes and wearing a helmet and elbow pads, the same man who had thrown the paint at the Mason plaque, shouted out: "Follow me to the Mason house!" About half of the crowd went with him back up Cameron St., while the rest milled excitedly about the effigy. At the "history sweet spot" on the corner, the crowd followed the young man onto N. Fairfax.

The videographer had positioned herself in the midst of the crowd, so Ted continued to get a fairly good view of things. He asked himself what the 'influencer' had meant by the "Mason house". He knew the area intimately, and there was no George Mason house there. Then Ted realized what was up. The Mason family of the early 1800s had strong business links with, and marital ties to, the Thomson family, wealthy merchants from Georgetown. When he mentioned this in his Georgetown tours, Ted would joke the Thomsons weren't related to John Thompson, the famous black coach who'd led the Georgetown Hoyas to a college basketball title. Indeed, Ted knew, historians sometimes confused the Thomsons with the Thompsons, a prominent Federal Era family in Alexandria.

Alexandria, not Georgetown. Thompson, not Thomson. Could the irate crowd be mistakenly heading to the former Thompson School just up the block?

Ted felt sick. It was the last place such a protest-turned-riot should target. A school there, established in the 1840s, was one of the first for women in Virginia, indeed in the nation. Further, its principal was Hallowell, the Quaker professor, who was anything but a bigot. The place was little-known, except to history lovers like himself, and was a venerable property, that reflected the town's architectural and educational heritage. Moreover, Ted knew, from his Civil War research, the school had been a hospital for *Union* soldiers.

To his dismay, as he stared at his HP laptop's screen, he saw the throng turn into an alley, leading down to the side of the property. He recalled that side of the Thompson building, one of the prettiest parts of any structure in Old Town. It has a stately loggia of period windows and five recessed archways behind a narrow, fenced portico. It's part of a red-brick, three-story building, now a townhome and a condo, which makes up much of a city block, and which was then being renovated. Ted waited anxiously for the camerawoman to turn the corner, to see if the crowd would damage the edifice. The videographer, as if swept by the current of a raging river, was carried close to the loggia. Through her lens could be seen black-clad men, apparently from Antifa, and three or four black men, possibly with a Black Lives Matter-related group.

Ted was stunned to see the latter holding Molotov cocktails in their hands. 'Are they from the same group that tried to burn the Fitzgerald warehouse?' he asked himself. His eyes studied the video feed: The men seemed to be searching their pockets for lighters. The historian wondered where the police were.

He got a text from Harmony:

"Do you see what I'm seeing? Near City Hall!"

'Yes, I do,' Ted thought. He reached for his cell. He was about to key in "9 1 1".

Then he heard through the audio feed the warbly sound of sirens, a shriek that got louder and louder.

The crowd got suddenly quiet. Those with the Molotov cocktails had lit them, however, and were readying to hurl the incendiaries through the windows of the loggia.

On the video feed, the images became blurry. Had the camera operator messed up the focus? No, Ted saw, a film of water was on the lens, dripping down from it. The videographer struggled to keep the crowd in view, then turned the device to her rear, back up the alley, to a group of darkly clad figures that were hard to make out. Then she swiveled her lens back to the crowd again. Ted could make out that the clothes of the rioters were soaking-wet. And that those with the Molotov cocktails had dropped the bottles, which sputtered weakly with little smoke on the pavement. The camera view switched back to the rear again.

The blurred shapes came into sharper focus. It was men from the fire department, once more from the Prince St. station. Hosing down the rioters!

Ted learned later the firemen and their engines had been placed on standby, per a request from Greco. They waited on Queen St., out of sight of the demonstration. When it turned violent, and threatened the Thompson school, the firefighters had rushed into action. And doused the would-be pyros with a stream of high-pressure water.

Ted's face broke into a wide grin. He watched with satisfaction at the aftermath, as the rioters who remained took off up and down the alley. Angst over an atrocity, a lynching in the past, was one thing, but taking out anger on a former women's school and Union Army hospital and architectural marvel was another thing entirely. Before clicking off the video stream, Ted saved it, making a mental note to later examine the images to try to identify more of the demonstration's leaders. And perhaps pair them with the instigators of the Old Town riot.

Chapter 32 – An Arresting Development

Harmony bicycled over that night to Ted's duplex a mile from Old Town. It was past 10 o'clock, as she had worked late at Amazon and Ted had given an evening tour of Fort Washington, Maryland. They aimed to brainstorm about the crimes afflicting Old Town, and decide on their next move about the "treasure banks". The weather was grim: Gray-black clouds and sprinkles of rain threatened a downpour. On the way over, Harmony skidded on her Felt bike but managed to keep gliding along.

She rolled to a neighborhood of modest homes down the hill from Fort Lyon, the decayed fortress near Jerry Connors' shed. The bricked, two-story residences looked much like the inexpensive but well-built dwellings that had been thrown up all around Alexandria and Arlington during World War Two. The homes in Ted's neighborhood, however, were built in 1947, just after war's end, to cope with the baby boom triggered by the returning servicemen.

On Harmony's arrival, Ted wiped down her bike and hoisted it up the front steps and into his living room. They sat down on the couch of that small space, their legs lightly touching. This part of his house led to a tiny dining room across from a faux-granite counter to a very small kitchen. History books and magazines, research material for his work-in-progress on Alexandria, were stacked high on a settee, which stood next to a high-backed vinyl chair and a metal work desk. Placed on it was a HP Envy laptop, which was opened to three browsers: one a video feed, a second for research on the new history book, and the third showing an itinerary for a military history tour of Old Town. On the wall above the workstation was a reprint of a Leonardo DaVinci sketch, for an unfinished painting, of the Madonna and Mary Magdalen, with the baby Jesus and a young St. John the Baptist. Ted, an aficionado of Renaissance art, liked the preparatory drawings, "cartoons" as they are known—of masters like Leonardo, Dürer, and Raphael—even more than their famed finished works.

Two bicycles, a Fuji carbon and a backup aluminum bike, for racing and commuting, hung from a wall rack. His Specialized hybrid, for riding about the city, leaned against a high, cheaply made bookshelf that should have been consigned to a fraternity house. Harmony's bike leaned against his. The bookshelf held anything but books: water bottles, bicycle parts, hats from the many foreign countries he'd visited, and a jumble of old running shoes.

Not for the first time, Harmony looked about the small living space and imagined how, with just a few flourishes, a woman's touch, she could make it much more homey or *heimat*, to use one of those unusual terms that few people have ever encountered outside a book, but that Ted sprinkled throughout his conversations.

The second floor of the duplex had a small bedroom, bathroom, and den, where Ted kept copies of his 10 published books and, as an indie businessman, stacks of tax records stretching way back past the IRS minimum of seven years. Above the second floor was an attic, and below the living room a half-finished basement. From time to time, he and Harmony discussed renovating the cellar into an Airbnb lodging for tourists visiting the capital region, as both as money maker and a tool for promoting Ted's tours. They joked that Harmony, with her green thumb and love of fresh vegetables, would also take over his back lawn. And extend his tiny vegetable garden into the park outside the back lawn, transforming it into a small farm.

As Ted sipped a Dogfish IPA, and Harmony a Sauvignon blanc, they went over what they'd gathered from their Burke & Herbert interview. "It seems obvious," reiterated Ted, "where our 'cat burglar' will strike next."

"Shouldn't we tell the police?" inquired Harmony.

"We should," Ted replied with a wink, "but I'm on their 'wanted list'." He added, "Actually I did tell Greco of my suspicions earlier today, and he seemed interested. But he's been blindsided by the Christ Church, um, by the incident at that church."

"I do not believe," said Harmony, trying to block out an image of a torn and bloodied Tony Hill from her mind, "that Bertha Stuart was the killer. Maybe connected somehow, but not the murderer."

"I know her enough," replied Ted, "to doubt she was involved in any way."

His friend shook her head sadly; her braids of dark hair quivered. "It's a shame the authorities seem to have few clues on who the murderer is."

"Or murderers."

"You really think there's more than one?"

"The killings may be too involved for any one man." He tapped Harmony on her knees and got up. "But there is a pattern, as with the banks, that does suggest a single individual."

"What do you mean?" Harmony frowned. "You're being mysterious again."

Ted walked over to the kitchen. Though he habitually got takeout, he actually liked to cook. Being a creative person, he enjoyed mixing and matching various foods and spices. But being single, he rarely got to cook for others. But that evening, for Harmony, he was trying out a new concoction: of rice, chicken, eggplant, and spinach. Into the spice mix he added turmeric, ginger, and mustard. With the viral plague, he had begun to cook more at home, and to add more tasty, and anti-infective, seasonings to the meals.

Still, he was hardly a master chef in a state-of-the-art kitchen. He baked the eggplant in a microwave, while juggling the rice, vegetables, and the pre-cooked meat in a frying pan.

At 10:55 that evening, he was placing multigrain bread with chopped garlic into a toaster oven. Harmony sat on the sofa, scanning her news feed, the scent of the spices and eggplant making her nose flare and her stomach rumble.

Suddenly she was startled—by a loud banging on the front door.

"Open up!" cried a harsh male voice from the other side. "Open up now!"

The banging and the yelling could be heard clearly in the kitchen. Ted was reminded of a terrible flood in the neighborhood a decade before. His home bordered Cameron Run, a tributary of the Potomac. Before a levee had been built five years prior, the stream had at times overflowed during torrential summer rains, inundating the cellars of the bordering homes. During one deluge, which wrecked his half-finished basement and nearly reached the ground floor, Ted had been rudely awakened, at three in the morning, by a fireman banging his fists on his front door, yelling at him to evacuate.

Harmony, her mouth wide open, stared at the door, which was shaking from the pounding. "Do you hear!" shouted another voice, of another man, higher in register. From the kitchen, Ted vaguely recognized it. At the stove he looked through the kitchen's glass-paneled door to the back lawn, and saw two men standing in the grass.

Two men with guns.

The thought popped into his head, 'They're cutting off an escape route.' He heard the first voice again reverberating through the living room: "Open up! Now!!"

Ted went quickly back through the living room, glancing with puzzlement at Harmony. He opened the door.

Outside were seven men and one woman. Three were on the porch stoop, and the rest on the small front lawn. Most were clad in black, heavily armed, with pistols and submachine guns, and wearing tactical gear: helmets, body armor, and knee and elbow pads. Their body language was threatening. All wore masks.

And FBI insignia.

Two were not in paramilitary garb, but in the dark business attire of Washington officials. One was Comitas, and the other his young female aide, a Miss Hillary Harris. Comitas took a legal document in a folder from his aide, an attractive lady of African descent.

He pushed through the doorway past Ted, the others following. Comitas pulled down his mask, and glanced in disgust at Harmony, frozen in surprise on the sofa. In moments, the small living room was crowded with jack-booted men and machineguns. Then, on a signal from the FBI official, some of the agents trotted up the steps to the second floor.

Ted stood surprised, but surprisingly cool as well, as he stood next to Harmony, then moved a step closer to her in a protective stance.

Comitas, not at all cool, waved a warrant in Ted's face. His own face had a look of triumph.

"Theodore Paul Sifter," he intoned, waving a warrant, "you are under arrest. For involvement in the deaths of Carlos Cordero and Antony Hill."

Ted knew the FBI had its suspicions about him and the man slain at the Freedmen's Cemetery, but was stunned into silence at the mention of Hill.

Harmony was shocked into speaking up. "Arrested for the murder of his friend?" she declared, in an accusing tone. "Tony Hill!?" She looked at Comitas like she would a lunatic. "You have to be joking. You should be ashamed!"

Comitas glared down at her. Harris, uncertain, asked her boss, "Do we arrest her too?"

The FBI man snarled at his assistant, "Just him for now!" He stared back at Harmony. "But we have lots of doubts about her as well!"

He took a step over to Ted's workstation, and tapped hard on the cover of the laptop. He turned to two of the agents and barked, "Confiscate this computer. And search the house for any other laptops!" An agent grabbed the device and Ted's cell, which was power-plugged into it, went clattering onto the floor. Comitas reached down and pocketed it. Soon several men were heard rummaging upstairs, going through the storage room, while others went into the kitchen and down the basement steps.

Comitas turned back to Ted and told him, "You have the right to remain silent." He didn't even finish the rest of the Miranda warning. He tapped the side of his pocket containing Ted's cell, and said, "We have text messages between you and Bertha Stuart. We have video of you at Burke & Herbert, and photos of you and your lady friend at the house next to Hill's at the time of his death. Not to mention DNA samples of her there. And footprints of the both of you at the rear of the Freedmen's cemetery. And plenty of other evidence to hold you for now—and convict you down the road!"

Harmony looked up at Ted, normally so talkative, but now tight-lipped. And eerily calm. He simply stared at Comitas. Later he told her he did have an urge to "go Eight Avenue" on the FBI man, and sock him in the mouth, but fortunately restrained himself. Ted had learned that expression from his father, a gruff military veteran who'd grown up in an extremely tough neighborhood on Manhattan's west side.

While gazing at Ted, Harmony felt the phone in her pocket buzz. She slipped out the device; it was her news feed. She had programmed it to alert her in the event of breaking news.

There was a special bulletin. She read it with surprise, and a kind of relief.

Coolly, with a trace of contempt, Harmony looked up at Comitas. She stated: "You've got the wrong guy." She held up her phone. "And I can prove it."

Comitas stared at her derisively. Harris mimicked her boss' angry, skeptical look.

"There's just been another murder," said Harmony. "A horrific murder. "A woman was killed at the Old Presbyterian Meeting House. She was mutilated. And the body dumped onto a historic tomb."

Everyone in the living room was stunned silent. Ted looked at Harmony with a mixture of shock, relief, and appreciation. Comitas took a step toward her, to check the message on her phone, then stopped. He pulled out his own cell. He saw that he'd gotten a message about the slaying 10 minutes before, just before entering Ted's house. But caught up in the vindictive pleasure of the arrest, he hadn't seen it. He glanced back and forth at several agents who'd returned to the room. One had a box of Ted's tax records.

Comitas avoided looking at Ted and Harmony, and broke into a cold sweat. His young deputy, confused, looked at him for instructions.

Finally, he shouted up to the second floor: "Everyone out! Out! And over to the Pre—the Presbyterian, this Meeting House!" He stomped to the kitchen, screamed similar words down to the basement, and stomped back. He turned to Harris, and asked, "What is this 'meeting house'? A community center?" Looking uncomfortable in her Washington garb, a blue pantsuit with a wide-collared jacket, Harris looked blankly at her boss.

Ted leaned on the arm of the sofa, close to Harmony. He stated evenly: "The Meeting House is the name for a Presbyterian church, back in Washington's day."

Comitas looked away from Ted. One of the armed agents gestured toward the historian with the stub of his machine gun, and asked his boss, "What do we do with him?"

"Arre—" he started to say, then stopped. Comitas wiped his brow with his hand. He loudly exhaled. In a quiet voice, he said, "Let him go for now."

Harris waved the warrant in front of her ample chest. "What do I do with this?"

Comitas exploded. "Stick it in your purse!"

Other agents, bewildered, ran down from the second floor and up from the basement, the wooden stairs buckling from their heavy steps.

Ted couldn't resist asking one: "Did you find anything?"

Harmony, more practically than comically, stood up, and took Ted's laptop back from an agent. And Ted got his cell back from Comitas. The latter seemed unsure what to do next, before a frantic determination overcame him. "Come on!" he screamed. "Let's go!" He turned to his embattled aide. "Find this Meeting House address on Google Maps!"

Ted, almost lolling now on the couch's armrest, stated: "It's at Royal, between Duke and Wolfe Streets, two blocks up from the little Safeway supermarket." Then Ted's insouciance faded, as he wondered who had been killed. Harmony silently prayed it wasn't another friend.

The SWAT team, swatted down, stormed out of the duplex, leaving the door open.

Harmony took a deep breath. Ted looked over to the kitchen. Through the dining room partition he could see a pot boiling over, and meat beginning to smoke.

He shouted, "I'll turn everything off! Go to my car. Let's get to the Meeting House!"

As they climbed into his RAV4, Ted looked out onto the street. His neighbors across the street, one a Pakistani family, the father a friend of Ted's, and the other an extended family from El Salvador, were standing on their front lawns, and staring at him. Later they told Ted they had never taken him for a criminal, and were relieved when the FBI agents seemed to leave as quickly as they had come. One of the other neighbors though, a grandmother from Oregon, had nervously locked her door at the sight of the gun-toting federales.

In the darkness, Ted drove out of the neighborhood and hooked a left, with the steep hill leading to Fort Lyon on the right. He raced down Route 1, Jefferson Davis Highway, then hurtled past the Woodrow Wilson Bridge interchange, and turned onto Green St., a residential block just north of the Freedmen's Cemetery. The Green St. named for the industrial family that had owned the Carlyle House and hospital of the Civil War, and whose furniture factory on Prince St. had been turned into a Confederate prison.

The overhead streetlights on Green had been out for months, so Ted slowed down near the Greene funeral home. It was not named after the street or the pro-South furniture family, but for the family that operated the funeral parlor. Like other such establishments in town, African-Americans had long owned it. Back in antebellum and Jim Crow days, it was the kind of business, looked on askance by whites, that offered a way up the economic ladder for blacks. In recent years the management had, and especially so for undertakers, quite the sense of humor. During Halloween it placed giant plastic Frankensteins and other famous horror figures on its front lawn. In other times of the year, giant plastic dinosaurs, blown up to gargantuan size and beloved by kids, were put near the entrance. As Ted drove by he thought, 'Nothing but real-life horror now.'

At the S. Washington St. corner, Harmony looked over to the right, where she glimpsed a corner of the Freedmen's Cemetery. As Ted waited impatiently for a couple of cars to pass at an intersection, his cell buzzed. Harmony picked it up. There was a text from Greco. She read it aloud: "Don't know if you're the killer, Ted, or Nostradamus. I will see you at the Meeting House."

Harmony commented, "I think you're making a believer of him." Her face grew fearful. "Who could have done it?"

"I talked to Greco yesterday about the earlier killings," Ted replied, as he jumped the light, and veered onto S. Washington. "I told him there is a pattern, a pattern emerging about them. He had calmed down from the, the incident at Christ Church, and seems to have started to see things the way I see them." He shrugged. "We'll know more when we find out how this new victim was killed."

Death was all about them. The Freedmen's Cemetery. The funeral parlor. Green's, but another one too, as Ted drove past the Demaine funeral home. A large, white-painted brick building with a tall thick chimney, possibly for cremation, that reaches much of a block down

Gibbon St. A sign on it reads, "1841". But Ted knew its roots went back further. An earlier incarnation had crafted Washington's coffin, after his horrific death in 1799.

Ted turned a right, then made a hard left onto Royal St., despite a no-turn sign, and went as fast as he dared down the residential neighborhood. The spire of St. Mary's Basilica poked through a patch of fog, which creeped along the back streets like a squadron of ghosts. He screeched to a halt, and parked at the starting point of his George Washington tours, across from St. Mary's and the Old Presbyterian Meeting House.

Chapter 33 – The Tomb of an Unknown Assailant

In daytime, the soaring, light-hued, crenelated Basilica lifts the spirit. That night, however, under threatening clouds and wrapped in mist, it took on the aspect of a Transylvanian castle.

Due to Ted's knowledge of the local roads, and his frenetic driving, he and Harmony reached the Meeting House before the FBI. They approached the unlocked entrance gate together. As they walked slowly up the brick path to the small churchyard cemetery, they passed the diagonal walls of the ruling elder's spare "flounder house". On their left a tall masonry wall separated the Meeting House grounds from the Basilica. Ted archly noted in his tours that it formed a "wall of separation", not between church and state, but between "church and church". Across the path, resembling the elder's domicile, was another ancient house, evidently holding administrative and school offices, with a wall plaque identified it as Fellowship Hall. Strewn on the ground, and incongruous, given the grim reason for their visit, were children's lawn toys. Under a curtain of clouds were a swing, a plastic choo-choo train, toy cars, and a portable sandbox. They seemed shrunken compared to the dark walls of brick above them.

In front of the duo rose the Meeting House itself, dating from 1774, built as the American Revolution was breaking out. Ted had lived for some time in Boston, where he'd become familiar with its Freedom Trail, and the Old Presbyterian always reminded him of the Old North Church, of Paul Revere and William Dawes fame. "One if by land, and two if by sea." Normally darkened during weeknight, the first floor of the Meeting House was aglow, its lights switched on to help the work of the police.

Greco's team was already there. The detective, though shaken by another murder, took some quiet satisfaction in having beaten the FBI team to the spot. After parking on S. Fairfax St., his police had passed under the plaque honoring George Washington and John Adams' Day of Prayer and Fasting. And past a much more recent, rainbow-colored banner, now an emblem of irony that stated, "Hate Has No Place Here". Guns at the ready, they'd passed along the narrow walkway sidling the church, stopping first at a blood-speckled tombstone of Dr. James Craig, the man partly responsible for Washington's ugly, bloody demise.

With trepidation, Ted and Harmony moved forward, and the small, rectangular graveyard, about 60 yards across and 40 yards deep, came into view. The brick path continued snaking through it to the Meeting House. Tombstones, about 15 in number, lay scattered across the moist lawn, to the right of the "wall of separation". Ahead and to the right was a blood-spattered table grave, of the town's co-founder, John Carlyle. On their left next to the wall was a boxed tomb with a short fence around it. At first glance, it seemed to have a funeral sculpture of its deceased atop its six-foot-long granite box.

Greco's group had scattered about the cemetery; cops were bent over, carefully examining the grounds. Two policemen held tightly to K9s as the animals, sniffing and snorting, strained at taut leashes.

Ted and Harmony heard the rustle of coats and the tread of footsteps behind them. It was Comitas and his entourage. The FBI man was shaken by word of the latest murder, and by the embarrassment of his errant arrest warrant for Ted. On the way over, while fumbling with Google Maps, he'd ordered a flustered Harris to start the process of withdrawing the warrant. Now, as he walked hesitantly into the churchyard, unsure of his footing in the darkness, he wondered if word of his blunder would leak to the press. 'I'll make sure Harris keeps her mouth shut,' he thought, 'and make it up to her. But I don't know if I can trust the SWAT team members to keep quiet, or Ted's damn neighbors. Headline: 'FBI Official Persecutes Tour Guide.' What a Debacle!' Then his worried mind was torn away to the grimmest of sights.

The attention of the federal agents, and of Harmony and Ted, was riveted on the fenced-off grave. Ted knew it very well. The Tomb of the Unknown Soldier, of the American Revolution. "Alexandria's Own". With the small, circular glass window above it, where guides had sworn they'd seen the Unknown's ghost. The flat top of the three-foot-high boxed grave inscribed with the poetic inscription: "Here's lies a soldier of the Revolution, his soul known only to God..."

Everyone was staring at the thing piled over the inscription. Greco's cops had set up a portable light stand, which glared down upon the stone reticule.

On it was a woman, or what was a woman, now a grotesque form.

A corpse of a rotund, middle-aged lady, Caucasian, chest-down on the slab, the body tilted toward the other graves.

Her neck twisted and punctured and broken, her face ghastly, drained of blood. Her mouth, turned toward the cemetery lawn, was agape, the teeth protruding horribly, like a deceased soldier in a Matthew Brady photograph, swollen from the summer heat after a Gettysburg firefight. Along with being murdered, the woman had been desecrated. Her skirt and panties had been pulled down to the ankles, and her buttocks were disfigured. The air about her was putrid.

Ted, Harmony, and the FBI squad walked slowly to the tomb as if sleepwalking in the dank night. With each step the butchered figure grew clearer, more terrible in its aspect.

They saw her anal cavity had been violated. Not sexually. But with dirt, shoved up the orifice. Her oral cavity too. Down her throat dirt and, something black, looking like oil, had been shoved. The throat had a large puncture wound on it, a little below the Adam's apple. A large spider scurried across the incision. Flies flew about, illuminated by the lights, alighting on the rear end, mouth, and eyes.

A rookie cop working the light for Greco staggered away from the gruesome sight, and vomited on the wall of separation.

Ted nearly reeled. He looked at the battered body through the corner of an eye, as if watching a horror movie whose violent scenes were too terrible to view. The face of the woman, distorted by her death agonies, was hard to recognize. Ted looked askance, then forced himself to look at it with both eyes.

He recognized her.

It was an acquaintance, Lillian Harper, a docent at the Meeting House. Ted again made himself to stare at her. There was no doubt about the identity, despite the ravaged flesh. The body of a woman in her mid-50s, medium in height, heavyset, white hair, the wrinkled, freckled face of an aging Scotch-Irishwoman.

She and Ted share, or shared, a kinship for the town's historic churches and resting places. Lily Harper had taken Ted on two tours of the newer, but still venerable, Presbyterian Cemetery, along with the Episcopal and Methodist ones, on the southern edge of Old Town, a third of a mile northwest of the Freedmen's Cemetery.

Much of Ted's knowledge of these cemeteries had come from Harper. She had dedicated herself to broadening the public's knowledge of them. She had been helping expand the church's congregation which, as a secess church, had lost many of its male members from battles during the Civil War, and hadn't recovered until well into the twentieth century.

Ted tried wishing away this horrible new sight, but he couldn't. It wasn't a nightmare, but real.

A strange notion came to him. Although he knew it couldn't be true, and tried not to look, he felt compelled to gaze at the window above the tomb. He saw, or thought he saw, the fleeting image of a ghost: the haunted spirit of the Unknown Soldier.

Who appears, according to the sworn accounts of tour guides, when the hallowed ground about him is dishonored.

Like Ted, Harmony was stricken by the sight of the woman. She grabbed her knees, as at end of a brutal road race, and felt her stomach nearly retch. The memory of the horrible night in the basement next to Tony Hill's house flooded back into her mind, and merged with this new horror. Ted took her hand and, picking their way around crime scene tape, they staggered toward Greco's team. It was huddled around the John Carlyle grave.

Greco's prominent jaw was set, his emotions held somewhat in check. Harmony did notice though, even in the gloom, that his graying hair seemed grayer. Greco gazed blankly at Ted, and told him, "We may actually have some decent clues this time." He pointed stiffly to the slab of Carlyle's raised table grave.

There were splotches of red matter on it and, Harmony and Ted saw, there were more sprinklings of blood leading from it along the stone walkway toward the corpse on the Unknown's Tomb.

Ted's broad shoulders hunched over; he too felt like throwing up. But he regained focus in looking over Carlyle's slab. He said to Greco: "It's almost like a sacrificial offering." Ted thought of Abraham offering his son Isaac up to Jehovah.

"Yes," replied Greco. "She was probably killed here, on the Carlyle slab, then dragged over. Carried, in fact. There are traces of foot marks on the lawn, but not a body dragged along it."

A grim Greco tried in the dim light to look into Ted's eyes, their robin's eggs color evident even at night, trying to read through those azure windows into his soul.

Harmony read Greco's thoughts. Although her hands were trembling, she told him evenly: "Comitas is our alibi, if that's what you're wondering. We were with him when we got the news."

Though this latest slaughter seemed to confirm Ted's theory, Greco had been wondering how he got to the graveyard so fast. And now he wondered why they had apparently arrived with Comitas and his team.

Ted asked: "Did you identify the murdered woman yet?" As Greco shook his head, Ted added, "Because I can. It's Lily Harper, a docent in this church." And Ted briefly explained who she was and how he knew her.

Greco took this in. The two were standing by a window looking into the plainly decorated, yet somehow regal, pews and balcony of the Meeting House. One of the pews near the altar was lit up, by a portable light, and by the flashlights of police giving it a look over. Greco gestured toward these officers, and informed Ted there were signs of violence in the church.

"It seems Harper was knocked unconscious, or worse, inside. No sign of a struggle: maybe this Lily Harper was caught unaware—or maybe she knew the killer."

Ted noted, "That's the pew where President Washington sat when attending services here."

Greco, intent on reconstructing the crime, continued: "Then the killer took Harper outside. A strong man, to be able to do that. Over to Carlyle's grave, apparently for the coup de grâce." His tone grew more severe. "Judging by the amount of blood and skin fragments on and around his raised tomb."

"Killer, or killers?" asked Ted.

"The indications are a single killer."

"The prints: a big man, or small?"

"So far, vague outlines of parts of a shoe or boot. I'd say big, maybe 6-feet to 6-feet-two.

Greco paused, his wide forehead wrinkled in thought. "An odd thing. The path of the crime, from the church to the Carlyle tomb, past an old grave of a William Hunter, to the Revolutionary War Tomb, seems clear enough. But we also found bits of blood on other graves. And more than a bit on one. A new one. Of a Dr. James Crack."

"Craig," corrected Ted. The historian looked worried, his eyes hard, a growing awareness of something overtaking him. "And no," he added, "that's a very old grave. So old its lettering faded away, and the church replaced it with a newer one.

"James Craig was Washington's doctor."

Both men fell silent for a moment. Greco scratched the side of his right temple and said, "What else can you tell me?" Ted remarked thoughtfully, "Well, Hunter is known for founding the Scotch-Irish, the St. Andrews, Society.

"And as for Lillian Harper..." Ted shook his head sorrowfully and cleared his throat. "...The Harpers were famous in the history of Alexandria. Their ancestor, Captain John Harper, and his children, and their many grandkids, practically founded Captain's Row."

Greco blinked hard and stated, "The street near the Athenaeum."

"Yes," replied Ted, "right at the top of the street. Near where the watchwoman died."

The detective focused his laser stare at the historian. "But you told me you think the Athenaeum death is unrelated to the two murders. Now three murders. Assuming the watchwoman wasn't murdered."

Ted looked past Greco's thick shoulders, and toward the tombstone of Dr. Craik. Then he looked back toward the Tomb of the Unknown. "I'm more convinced than ever," he told Greco excitedly, "that the murder here is unrelated to the Athenaeum death. And that it *is* related to Tony's Hill's murder, and likely the killing at the Freedmen's cemetery. In fact—"

The two turned to noises coming from the direction of the Unknown's Tomb.

There Comitas and his men weren't their normally confident, bustling selves. The klieg lights had cast the agents' long dark shadows onto the Tomb, shadows which seemed frozen by the gruesome sight of Lily Harper.

But then Hillary Harris had cried out, and swooned, swaying for a moment near the wall, then falling onto the lawn. After she hit the grass, Comitas took a step, much too late, in an apparent attempt to catch her fall. He seemed to do it out of show, as he was too far away to catch her. As Greco and Ted looked on, one of the first responders tended to Harris. He pronounced the young lady unconscious, but unhurt, the lawn having softened her tumble.

Next, from both South Royal and Fairfax Streets came another sound, the roar of approaching vehicles.

"It's the media," stated Greco with distaste. He looked upon them as jackals, sprinting to the scene of another fallen animal. And he felt mortified, as he hadn't yet been able to figure out, for their benefit or anyone else, the identity of the predatory beast. He strode toward the church entrance, partly to check on the investigation near the Washington pew, partly to escape reporters' hostile questions. When the scribes entered the cemetery, they turned on a bewildered Comitas. After these two loud interruptions, Ted decided for now not to tell Greco of his latest idea, related to Dr. Craig. It was almost too wild to believe; he needed to think it through first. And he was simply exhausted from a long day and a wild night. As after Tony Hill's murder, he felt like he'd been on the losing end of a heavyweight match, spent and bruised in head and body. He could tell Harmony felt the same.

The duo took a last look at the graveyard. They were ignored by Comitas, who seemed to have forgotten Ted's arrest, or was trying to forget his embarrassment. Tight-lipped, white-faced, he was telling the journalists to back away from the crime scene, "so that I can examine the corpse." He bent over the bloodied body, coughing up phlegm, as he held a silk handkerchief to his nose and mouth. Miss Harris had been propped up on the grass, still attended to by an emergency worker. Harmony saw the gleam from the portable lights bouncing off the window above the Tomb, and for an instant thought she saw a flickering ghost, not of the Unknown Soldier, but of the ravaged face of Lily Harper. Then the figment was gone.

The pair walked down a little path on the church's south side. Above, dense clouds obscured any moonlight or starlight. At least the rain was holding off.

Harmony begun to sob from the stress of the horrific things seen in recent days. They both walked in a daze to S. Fairfax, then around the block past a parson's house, and slipped into Ted's SUV. The two drove back as in a fevered dream to his home, then collapsed like dead persons on the living room sofa.

"This is like one of those reoccurring nightmares in school," sighed Harmony. "When you dream you haven't prepared for a test, and it keeps happening over and over."

Placing his arm around her shoulder, Ted responded, "I have one of those. I'm in a speeding car, out of control, about to crash, but the car keeps going, and going, and death is certain, it seems, but the car keeps going."

"Maybe when we wake up tomorrow," said Harmony, wiping away tears, "this nightmare will finally start to lift."

Ted blew a sad breath out of his mouth. "One can hope. Or it may keep going, and going."

Chapter 34 – Reconnaissance Missions

Willy McVeigh arrived in the heart of Old Town. Given the prominence and historical significance of City Hall, it was one of the obvious targets for devastation with his bomb, which was a mass of fuel oil mixed with a large amount of ammonium nitrate. It could be a homecoming of sorts, he told himself, making his mark on the government center of the region where he'd been reared. The time had come to case out the right place, to determine the where and the how of such an act.

After parking on Princess St., he walked along the edge of the public housing project, contemptuous of the men, young and old, loitering on its stoops. 'This might make a good backup target,' he noted, laughing with the memory of the recent killing there. With almost no one on the sidewalks, he strode, masked, in raincoat, corduroys, Army boots, and a soft camo Desert Shadow hat, down to Market Square. Down Lee St., past some restored warehouses from the days of tobacco and rye farming, and past some new condos for the present-day town gentry. Past the Federal Era house where resided the pugnacious admiral of the Second World War, William "Bull" Halsey, when stationed in Washington.

Starting at N. Fairfax, at Ted's sweetest history sweet spot, McVeigh made a circumference of City Hall. First going west on Cameron, along the side of the building reconstructed by Adolf Cluss. He was one of the "48er's" McVeigh disliked, a German who claimed to find "freedom and opportunity" in America, and who worked with the Union Army, instead of staying home and helping build the power of the Fatherland, or at least shunning service with the Yankees. Then down N. Royal past Gadsby's Tavern, and the Revolutionary War cannon nearby cleverly turned into a water fountain. Past the sterile-looking, little-used commercial buildings that during the "urban renewal" of the 1960s replaced the decaying, Colonial Era businesses and residences. Turning left at King St., and the modern Alexandrian Hotel, on the site of the Marshall Hotel, with its echoes of the first fatal firefight of the Civil War.

"The first Civil War," grunted McVeigh, hoping to help spark a second. On past the benches and the spacious fountain of Market Square, before turning back onto Fairfax St. at the Ramsay House tourist center, past the old precinct rooms in the City Hall where the second-to-last man lynched in Alexandria had spent his final, terrified hours. 'Too bad there wasn't more vigilante justice,' McVeigh thought, 'to keep order among the *unter* race.' And then the Carlyle mansion where so many wounded Union and Confederate men had their limbs amputated, or breathed their last. Ending his 360-degree walk at the former meeting house on the Hall's northwest corner. Where it's believed George Mason crafted some of his Bill of Rights after foolishly, as McVeigh viewed it, calling for an end to the import of slaves from Africa. 'Better here than there: Put 'em to use,' he reflected. He noticed the plaque honoring Mason was still smeared with paint from the other day's disturbance.

Despite the recent riots, the security around City Hall was practically non-existent, McVeigh noted with satisfaction. He'd seen just one policeman, and not a single security guard. And that after a spate of murders too. And Market Square was itself a wide-open, unguarded space. He literally spat with contempt at the blindness of the authorities. 'Very well, then,' his train of thought continued, 'they won't know what hit them.'

He confidently took another turn around the building, in the reverse direction. He again went by the underground garage where City Hall ended and Market Square began. But suddenly a policeman appeared, out of the Italian ice store across Fairfax, where Laura Schaefer had met her fiery doom. He was a muscular cop, with a strong, well-defined jaw and prominent cheekbones. McVeigh slowed and turned his head away, then slowly turned his head back. The cop was striding purposefully away towards King. He watched him make a left at the tourist info center, and disappear down the sloping sidewalk toward the waterfront, and the black rain clouds drifting up the Potomac.

The bomber was fairly sure the policeman hadn't noticed him. Not that it should have been a big deal if he had. But he liked to play scarce with the law.

The parking garage beckoned. He walked down its ramp, past the payment booth, and entered the dark, cavernous space. Slowly, methodically, he determined whether the garage extended underneath the City Hall. With his long stride, he paced off 28 steps, too few he estimated. He walked back up the ramp to the sidewalk, looked around for cops, saw none, and marked off the same number of paces. At step 28 he reached the City Hall, at its exact start at the southeast wall. "Damn it!" he muttered. The garage did not reach underneath it. A prime method of taking down a building, employed by the World Trade Center attackers, before their plot turned to hijacking planes, was denied him.

For this target, he'd have to position his van somewhere outside the Hall, as Timothy McVie had done in Oklahoma City. And as Zawahiri and Al Qaeda did at Saudi Arabia's Khobar Towers in 1996, and against the American embassies in Kenya and Tanzania in 1998. McVeigh intended to survive his attack, like McVie, and unlike bin-Laden's minions, though he admired the latter for their courage and willingness to self-sacrifice for their cause, however errant.

From his viewpoint outside the garage, McVeigh saw it would be hard to get his vehicle into Market Square on City Hall's south side. Though open-aired and the size of a football field, the Square is walled off in most places by four feet of concrete and brick. Behind the walls are more obstacles—thickets of shrubbery, plants in large heavy pots, and heavy benches of stone. There are five pedestrian entranceways, consisting of six steep concrete steps. Even if the vehicle could make it up the steps, he'd have to motor past the large fountain and up to the side of City Hall. He'd be totally exposed getting into Market Square. Too risky.

McVeigh walked back up S. Fairfax, and then went left on Cameron again to examine the opposite side of City Hall. He told himself, 'Must park the van during working hours, to kill the most city employees. And in a place that won't draw much suspicion.' Cameron St. had the typical sidewalk framed by a six-inch-high curb. He could readily drive his vehicle onto it. However, during the working day and into the night, cars would be parked along the street. When the time came, he might not be able to drive the van on and off the sidewalk. And of course, rolling up onto a sidewalk would draw the attention of any onlooker. Too much risk and uncertainty.

At the end of the block he reached the main rear entrance of City Hall. The entrance the town authorities had closed it due to the virus, forcing everyone to enter from the Market Square side for a mask check. Though the French Empire façade was visually appealing, McVeigh thought, he cursed again at its architect, the 'race traitor' Adolf Cluss. 'And what a first name for such a scoundrel!'

He turned purposefully onto N. Royal, and halfway up the block he stopped. 'This is more like it!' he thought. A sign read, "No-Parking Zone—For Deliveries Only". Even better, he found, many cubicles were near the street-level windows. A detonation here was certain to murder or maim any workers inside. McVeigh smiled at this. Then frowned on realizing that the teleworking sparked by the pandemic might keep many of those workers at home. 'Oh well,' he concluded, 'you work with what you're given.'

He peered down Royal St. and at the ugly modern buildings across the way. The street was quiet. He figured the actual number of deliveries to City Hall were much fewer than to a place of business. On the appointed day, if there were a delivery truck, he would simply wait for it to leave. Then roll up onto the sidewalk, set the timer, and quickly walk away. He'd disguise the vehicle as a delivery company van. No one would deem it odd to park such a vehicle there.

After leaving the van, he'd head toward the north side of town. He'd strip off his outer layer of clothes, stuffing it into his backpack, in case anyone had spotted him at the site. That would muddy the description an observer might give to the police. He would have left a getaway car near the public housing. 'Steal it, or rent it beforehand?' he pondered. 'Either way, I'll screw on one of the fake license plates.' He might even leave some fake evidence falsely implicating the black residents. Maybe leave a can of ammonium nitrate by a doorway, and tell the cops about it from an encrypted site. 'Wouldn't *that* be fun?!'

A federal target, such as a government courthouse, might be preferable, but City Hall was a definite possibility. For now, he put it at the top of his target list.

During his stay in Alexandria, McVeigh mostly avoided restaurants and their ubiquitous video cameras, and instead dug into MREs or survival food kits he'd stored in the van. That day, however, he was famished, and wanted to grab a snack returning to his van for the next reconnaissance. So, after adjusting his two masks, and pulling the camou cap down over his eyes, he entered a French brasserie at the southeast corner of the courthouse complex. It was open for limited seating, but that didn't matter. Only a few customers, McVeigh was glad to see, were braving the pandemic. They were scattered about the tables of the brasserie's spacious dining room. Every second table had a sign telling diners not to sit there.

He ordered a sausage and cheese croissant and a black coffee, paying in cash. He was pleased to find the mostly African and Caribbean workers, many from former French colonies, paid him no heed, though he disdained having to interact with such underlings, such *Untermensch*, and he actually muttered the word aloud to the unwitting cashier.

He idled outside the bistro, munching and sipping. He walked down King St., scrutinizing City Hall some more. He reached the corner at Pitt St., where a garage behind the French bistro caught his eye. He had thought only City Hall had an underground garage near Market Square. Curious, he walked to the two-way entrance ramp and looked at its payment booth, 30 yards down a ramp. The driveway was wide enough for two trucks, much less one van. He strode down it, and saw the entrance and the exit were automatically operated. 'No payer in a booth I'd have to deal with,' he reflected. On his right was a window, behind which was the office of the parking garage manager. He had his back turned to the window, feet propped up on his desk, as he surfed the

Internet. The security was laughable. After all, who'd expect an attack here?

McVeigh stepped down into the garage. It was vast. He walked in a straight line from the entrance ramp to the far wall, along the line of Pitt St. He counted off 64 steps. He was pretty sure this took him close to King St., and later out on the sidewalk he would confirm it. Moreover, the garage stretched far up along King St. too, probably out to St. Asaph St. Almost the entire courthouse was above the garage! A powerful bomb, placed in the right spot, would take down a big chunk of the building. He could time the detonation for 10 a.m., after everyone who worked on site had arrived.

Back out on Pitt St., he checked a wiki to look up the court's responsibilities. His spirits fell a bit. Being a municipal courthouse, much of its work was mundane. It did handle some felonies, but more so such things as marriage licenses and birth certificates, land records, and civil suits.

Still, it was a major public building in a well-known city close to the federal capital. It was right across the street from its City Hall. He added it to his "short list" of targets. Satisfied for now, he headed back to his lair.

Chapter 35 – Pressure at the Presser

At noontime, the city government, the FBI, and local police held another press conference. This one was shorter, and took place in the City Hall meeting space, not outside in a larger venue, as public opinion had shifted. The Mayor, who said he'd been stricken by the virus, decided to stay at home due to the illness, and to duck criticism at a public event.

Ted was at home working on his Old Town history book, though Harmony watched the event on livestream during her lunch break at Amazon.

Along with reporters and city workers, worried citizens jammed the gathering, filling up the seats in front of embattled City Council members at the dais. One woman held a sign, "Why Won't You Protect Us?!" and another, "Riots Are Not the Answer!!" The owner of an Irish pub on King St. pulled down his mask and shouted out, "We're all terrified! Our customers are too scared to come out to us! When will you catch the murderers?!" Indeed, the general feeling in the town was changing from rage and shame over the initial, evidently racial killings to even deeper emotions of self-preservation and fear.

When three Black Lives Matter members tried to interrupt the gathering with shouts of "Defund the Police!" and "Fry the Pigs!", some in the audience outshouted them. Shaken by the response, the trio, escorted by security, left the hall.

Standing at a lectern, with a bank of microphones placed before him, Associate Assistant Director Comitas added to the gloom by giving on update on the investigations. His preening self-confidence had taken a hit after the Old Presbyterian slaying. Looking wan, and thinner, his striped pants sagged, and he adjusted his suspenders to pull them up. Sounding like an overgrown schoolboy caught cheating, he announced wanly: "We have released the suspect Bertha Stuart from custody." His face reddening, he licked dry lips. "We were unable to find any hard evidence, any evidence, that connects her to the Freedmen's slaying. Or to the Christ Church killing."

A reporter from the *Alexandria Paddlewheel* newspaper interrupted him. "But we were told Stuart had sent racist, inflammatory texts and emails to radical organizations. Expressing her neo-Confederate views."

Comitas glumly stated, "I, we think, that it's safe to say, that she has Confederate views. Her ancestors fought for the Confederacy." He couldn't believe what he saying as he uttered it: "But that's not a crime." Fingering the lapels of his Brooks Brothers jacket, he continued. "Despite her dubious beliefs, there is no evidence in her life, past or present, of advocating, or engaging in, violence. Further, she has air-tight—she has credible, alibis, for her whereabouts on the nights of those two murders.

"And on the night of the Old Presbyterian murder, for that matter," an embarrassed Comitas added. Each item on the growing litany of horror, he realized, made him and his team seem more inept.

"And the death of the Athenaeum guard," he went on, sounding like a penitent in a confessional ticking off a list of sins. "We now have a full and completed DNA analysis of her and her clothing, along with the clues we have gleaned from the site of that fatality, and the other sites. And none of that has been tied to Bertha Stuart." He swallowed. "And nothing has yet to match up with other potential suspects."

A reporter from the local ABC TV station stood up from the second row of seats, and called out: "And what about the other evidence? You've been very slow in releasing any clues you have gathered." Deputy Mayor Morenis called out from his chair: "That's right!" His words redounded through the hall like thunder. Embarrassed, he lowered his voice, but continued sternly. "We have asked you, Mr. Comitas, and more than once, to provide us with any clues your team does have. Your presentation of such has been," and Morenis curled his lips in distaste, "very, very slow."

Comitas felt sweat well up between his wrists and his jacket sleeves. The politicians, who were his staunch allies not long before, were turning on him.

"I have to say, and this is not an excuse," he replied, "that we're faced with a killer, or killers, of unusual skill. The perpetrator has, have, left less of a 'footprint', I don't mean footprints, but indications, clues, of his, or her, identity, identities, than one would expect, expect from scenes of such violence. DNA fragments for instance. We do have portions of footprints, in fact, at several of the crime scenes, but no match—no exact matches, at this point." He paused on hearing loud grumblings from the audience.

"We have found some indications," he continued, coughing to clear his throat, "about the criminal or criminals, at the scene of the Freedmen's and Hill, the Anthony Hill, slayings, but nothing that has yet led to a breakthrough. And let me point that our investigation of the Presbyterian Meeting Church incident is still in its early stages.

"I, I must urge, ask for, patience. I'm confident, given the massive resources that we are applying to these cases, of an unprecedented amount, that a break-through *will* come soon enough."

City Council Coordinator Avril Forstandt ran a hand through her dirty-blonde hair, and pushed back her swivel chair. In a screeching voice she stated: "You've told us that you have some fifty agents on these cases. Not to mention your vaunted crime lab. And yet you seem to have almost no solid evidence or actual suspects!" A murmur of assent rose up from the attendees.

A reporter from the local WMAL radio station shouted out, "Is it really too early for a breakthrough at Old Presbyterian? What about the blood, the trail of blood, along the path of the graveyard that journalists noted? And the blood on the headstone, in the church, and at the Tomb of the Unknown? Surely you have some leads from all of that?!"

Comitas stood silent and nervous. An FBI forensics scientist next to him bent down to a microphone to answer, "Unfortunately, the killer or killers wore gloves, apparently, and masks, and maybe protective clothing, and we haven't located clear fingerprints, nor a murder weapon, at any of the crime sites mentioned. Nor at the Athenaeum, if that was a murder.

"As for the Meeting House, the killer stuck to the stone steps and footpath, leaving, maybe, only a couple of portions, segments, of footprints. We're not sure at this time if they were of the perpetrator." The expert paused, looking as embarrassed as Comitas. "Our team, or the local police team, may have stepped on top of the footprints that were—"

At this Comitas bent back over the microphone, as a loud murmur ran through the reporters. He began to speak, "As for the little amount of fiber and DNA evid—" but a *Paddlewheel* journalist had stood up, and cried out: "—It was leaked to us, apparently from someone within your team, that the FBI suspects a local author, a historian, of the crimes." Listening in, Harmony almost choked on her ramen.

"Then that story," the reporter went on, "seemed to go down the rabbit hole. Can you tell us more about that suspect at least?"

Comitas' stomach roiled. Sweat poured from his wrists onto his soft, alabaster hands. He'd hoped the reporters would have missed that blunder. He fervently hoped they wouldn't ask about the arrest warrant.

"I, I have nothing to say on that. I can neither confirm nor deny the various—rumors—that have been making the rounds. Most, all, most are without substance."

"What a horse's ass!" muttered Harmony, using an expression of Ted's. 'Is he trying a smear job?!' she asked herself.

Reddening further, the FBI man added, "I will say we, we have moved on, to look at other susp—to look at other possible persons of interest. But I can't, I shouldn't, go into any details at this time…" His voice trailing off, he stopped, and turned toward the dais, where a Council member had created a stir.

Forstandt was pounding a table with her right hand. The 37-year-old paused, her bright-blond highlights standing out more than usual under a stage light. "It is not my special area of expertise, Mr. Comitas. But some of us in the city government are starting to think that solving murders is not *your* area of expertise! Perhaps a tougher, more capable hand is needed at the helm."

The tall, statuesque lady stood up. Forstandt had been in an awful mood even before the meeting. She had recently had an ugly romantic breakup, including a shouting match with her ex that very morning. Staring at Comitas, she said icily: "Yes, perhaps it's time for some heads to roll among the law enforcers. Some of your agents, for example, who have not been producing results." She added sarcastically, "We wouldn't want, after all, to replace the head of the investigation himself."

Comitas felt the sweat soaking his lower back, and wished the inquisition would end. "I assure you, madam, ma'am, that I, that we, are doing everything humanly possible, to solve, and end, these outrages." He lowered his voice, and said in a confidential tone, "And let me say that the head of the Department itself, just last night, has pledged even more, more human and material resources for the solving of this, these crimes."

He was shocked at the tone of the press conference. 'They're setting me up as a scapegoat!' he cried to himself. Panicking, he tried to redirect the criticism.

"And I have to say, madam, Ms., and members of the Council, and media, that our own agency has not been completely satisfied, with the cooperation and results it's obtained,

from some of the local law enforcement authorities. In fact, this tardiness, and lack of participation, may have violated certain statutes."

The Council members and the reporters seemed surprised at this statement. Comitas wondered if he'd blundered again, and gone too far. "Of course," he added hurriedly, "we have been impressed by the great majority of the men and women in, Virginia, in the Alexandria police forces, and among the Fairfax County enforcement, law enforcers.

"And of course," he added, looking at Forstandt, "by the cooperation from the local government officials."

The more savvy journalists and politicos were keenly aware of the FBI man's target. Forstandt, the other Council members, and the WMAL and ABC reporters looked over to a group of Alexandria police officers standing in the rear of the dais, and looked for the head of their investigation. But they couldn't spot Greco among them. He was away investigating, and would soon delve into a possible break in the case.

Chapter 36 – An Out-of-Town Conspiracy

They sat on a colorful Afghan at a back room of the Wahhabi mosque, just six miles from Abdullah's safe house. On the other side of the wall behind them, congregants prostrated themselves in prayers, unaware of the illicit meeting taking place just feet away.

On hand was Abdullah, Ahmed the escape driver, the mosque's imam, the mosque's accountant, and a visitor from a Pakistani-funded "civil rights advocacy group" in Jersey City, New Jersey. The man from Jersey had big news, but first Suleiman, the imam, chided Abdullah.

"I have been informed," said Suleiman, a dour man with a white-flecked beard, "that you have not, as had been promised, kept strictly to the safe house."

Abdullah, sitting on the carpet with his legs crossed, straightened his back. He was rather expecting this, but was still nervous. The others watched intently, silently.

"Despite giving your word," Suleiman continued, "you have been engaged in walks and drives about town. This not only puts you in danger, but also the family that so generously and at its own risk granted you lodging. Worse, you are endangering our mosque, and its congregants and its leadership." He frowned, his dry, thick lips twisting into a snarl. "And above all, Allah forbid, you may be putting at risk the mission that our friend Mehmed has come to tell us about today."

He then recited in Arabic a Hadith commentary about the perils Mohammed faced in leading a military campaign back in 627 A.D. Among its themes were the dangers of betrayal. The others in the circle looked at Abdullah with a mixture of unblinking surprise and disappointment.

Abdullah wondered if the imam, an intelligent and cautious man, had quietly placed observers outside the home to follow his movements. Or perhaps a member of the mosque's inner circle had spotted him in Old Town. Chagrined, he almost tried to make an excuse. He thought about telling this group of the devout about the wanderlust that had seized him after the prison escape. Despite his vaunted discipline, he found himself unable to stay indoors all the time when he had the opportunity of going about Alexandria, albeit at considerable risk. 'These men have never been in prison like me,' he reflected, 'enduring long and hard years of isolation from the world.'

He looked up at the others. They were staring at him with concern. He decided to act contrite, and to certainly not tell his listeners of the action he was contemplating.

"Imam Suleiman, I should, and will, make no excuses." He bowed his head. "It is difficult to abide by the confines of a second prison, if you will. But I will from now on obey your wishes, and the desires of everyone else in this sacred place, and of course the will of Allah."

The religious leader's face remained stone-like. "When you hear what our friend Mehmed has to say," noted Suleiman, "I doubt you will again endanger our activities. No, indeed, you must not, you cannot."

His implicit threat was clear. Even the life of a lion like Abdullah might be forfeit if he put a vital operation in peril.

The imam told those gathered to leave, except for Abdullah and Mehmed, the New Jersey visitor. When the three were alone, he turned to Mehmed, and nodded.

Originally from the slums of Islamabad, Pakistan, where a Saudi-funded charity had saved him from a life on the street, Mehmed was 42 years old. He'd spent a decade and a half working for, and then operating, jihadi cells in Newark and Hoboken, New Jersey. Like Abdullah, he recruited black criminals, who'd done time in Jersey and New York prisons. However, most of his men were immigrants, legal and illegal, from Pakistan, Kashmir, and Afghanistan. And several of the most seasoned operatives were from Chechnya and Syria.

Short and thin, dressed in dark slacks and a bright silken shirt, his black beard closely cropped, Mehmed looked more like a furniture salesman than a terrorist. He suppressed his own concern about Abdullah's meanderings. He knew of his efforts in Afghanistan, and before that in Alexandria, and in prison. The man's courage and skill were undoubted. He saw his departures from the safe house as a sign he was eager for another mission, whatever the cost. He figured he would gladly join up for the Manhattan Plot.

"As we all know," Mehmed smiled slightly, several gold fillings glistening, "we soldiers of Allah are famed for our patience." He cleared his throat, and switched over to classical Arabic, the tongue of Muhammed. "We follow very long timelines. Where the infidels obsess over the most ephemeral pleasures—a daily stock price, the sight of a harlot on a video, a few months or years of a war—we operate by a calendar that is centuries long.

"For 1,400 years we have struggled and bled, conquered and lost, and conquered again. Almost a millennium and a half. Yet that is a mere pittance of time, for Allah and his Creation are eternal, and our own reward shall be an eternity of bliss."

The imam and Abdullah listened in silence, impressed by the visitor's oracular oratory. A golden tongue belied his outward appearance.

"And in New York City, where the faithless pigs obsess on one date only, our glorious day, to use their calendar, of September 11, 2001, we have been active amid that metropolis for 40 years. And are active still. "Years before that 'September 11,' we assaulted the World Trade Towers, with a truck bomb in the building's underground garage. The infidels, with their tiny timelines and child-like impatience, forget that. In 1993, our gallant ally Ramsi Yousef directed the detonation of a car bomb in its garage. A plot brilliant in its simplicity, much easier to undertake than the complex series of airplane hijackings that happened eight years later. Brother Yousef's plan failed, but only by a little, and only after wounding a thousand of the infidels."

Mehmed paused, smiling. "It's astonishing that our enemies forget that great blow, remembering only the airline attacks, due to their endless, pornographic replaying of the videos of the Trade Towers crashing down."

His face had a look of prideful determination. "Of course, instead of giving up after one 'failure', we tried and tried again, on the same site, again and again focusing our efforts, on the place at the center of our foes' endless pursuit of lucre, of the false idols of worldly wealth, the Golden Calves of greed.

"Finally, our persistence was rewarded, through the genius of Osama bin Laden, Allah bless him forever, and the fearless Mohammed Atta, Heaven praise him, through the great stroke of 'September 11'. A blow that drew Great Satan into his endless wars of Iraq and Afghanistan, where he's losing the will to fight in less than 20 years, his ultimate defeat in those holy Muslim lands inevitable."

For a moment, Mehmed's tone became sober. "Still, the infidels have shown some persistence of their own, we must admit, in that hallowed place of our New York triumph. Unlike in Afghanistan, where they make plans to flee before our indomitable Taliban. But in New York, they have rebuilt the Trade Towers, guided by the Jew architect Daniel Libeskind, and to an even great height, making a new, ultra-modern Tower of Babel and Baal. They built it to a height of 1776 feet, after their year of Revolution, an abortion birthed in the very height of their pagan 'Enlightenment', which overthrew their own Abrahamic faiths with the blind worship of Science and Material Things, which they place before the creations of Allah, worshiping them as if they were Allah Himself!"

He paused, licking his lips like a predator contemplating a prey. Abdullah and Suleiman were transfixed by the sweep of his rhetoric. Now he got to the main point.

"Our plan is to attack this so-called Freedom Tower, and to reduce it to rubble like the Towers before it." He took on a look of leering triumph. His listeners opened their eyes in wide wonder.

"Now it is true the security behind this new Tower of Babel is far greater than that of its predecessor. And it is unlikely we can take over airplanes as readily as before." He stopped and smiled, briefly imagining himself as a falconer eyeing his desert prey. "But there are multiple 'lines of attack' that we are considering. One of them shows great promise. I can reveal that we have more than a few of our own people who have attained employment in the Tower. But we need more soldiers. And the team of holy warriors that I'm assembling must be of the highest quality."

His brown eyes sparkled as he turned his eyes to Abdullah. "Which is why I am recruiting you for this sacred task. Despite a certain, a certain hardheadedness, you have proven yourself in our struggle, both abroad, and here in Great Satan's very lair."

Abdullah grew excited at the prospect of moving to the New York region to take part in another world-shaking event. After Mehmed completed his pitch, and the imam prodded him, Abdullah solemnly pledged to "behave himself" in Alexandria, in the brief period before leaving town to join Mehmed's band of jihadis.

Still, inwardly he knew obeying the imam would be difficult, and probably impossible. Something had come over him, was possessing him. The restlessness since leaving prison. For reasons that were indecipherable, but real nonetheless. He felt himself yearning for another act of war before departing Alexandria. But would that be a selfish action of vengeance, he asked himself, a result of the years he'd been walled up in prison? 'No!' he firmly believed. 'The hand of Allah Himself is guiding me. His will be done!'

Abdullah knew it was wrong, a sin, to deceive the imam, and the esteemed visitor from New York. But he believed Allah would forgive him. He wouldn't tell his colleagues what he was contemplating, what was driving his very soul. He prayed it wasn't the deceiver Satan misleading him. But he knew he could do nothing less.

Chapter 37 – Casing the Complexes

McVeigh figured Old Town would be his place of attack, but he wanted to thoroughly examine other potential targets. He drove past the West End of town over to Eisenhower Avenue, into a desolate locale on the site of the old Union Army railway line and round house, long since ripped apart and replaced with non-descript, high-rise apartments. Overcast skies added to the solitary feeling of the area. 'I knew the D.C. region was humid,' he told himself, 'but for days it's felt like mid-summer.'

After leaving his van on Hooffs Run Drive, he walked a third of a mile to the Alexandria Detention Center. McVeigh had examined its blueprints at the Kate Waller Barrett Library. He almost retched over the memorial there to the original civil rights sit-down strike of 1939, which had led to the widespread integration of American society. The library had a small but superb history and current events research room. His interest in the jail was sparked there, by reading of Abdullah Hamaas' escape and the failure of the federal, municipal, and state authorities to find him. Would a prison with such lax security be relatively easy to attack? Maybe not, as security should have been tightened after the high-profile escape. But perhaps only tightened for a short while, as speculation about the Muslim terrorist had faded in the wake of the murders in town.

McVeigh was aware the prison's inmates contained a sizeable number of Aryan Nation gang members, who were at odds with Black Muslims and other black or Islamic inmates. McVeigh dreamed for a while of blowing up a prison wall to help the skinhead gangbangers to escape,

413

while blowing up some of the blacks, but dismissed the fantasy. Better to simply bomb the place, a symbol of the federal authority he loathed. If white nationalists were killed in the event, 'along with the niggers and the Arab sand flies,' he figured, it was simply the price of war. Actually seeing the prison walls and entrances that day confirmed his initial qualms about an attack. He could probably force his van through the entrance gate, and possibly get to the main jail to detonate it, and then likely take down an entire wall, perhaps killing or maiming dozens of prisoners, guards, and administrators. Pandemic or no, there would be plenty of people inside a prison.

However, it would be a suicide mission. And as an atheist, he looked askance on the ideology of Islamic bombers, however courageous, who blew themselves up partly due to the belief they'd be rewarded with Paradise in another world. Though the notion of an eternal Valhalla for Aryan warriors, he admitted, as with an eternity of bliss for Muslim or Christian ones, did have a romantic appeal.

No, he preferred to mimic his near-namesake, Timothy McVeigh, and walk safely away from a planted bomb. To fight another day, and to strike another blow against the federal Leviathan, and the Jews, international bankers, darkies, and other *Untermenschen* controlling it. He must survive an assault, and not get caught through a bonehead blunder like Timothy McVeigh's arrest for driving without a license plate.

After crossing the prison off his hit list, he piled back into his van and drove toward other potential targets by heading up Mill St., near the same route Abdullah and Ahmed had taken. A complex bigger than City Hall caught his eye: the vast quarters of the U.S. Patent and Trademark Office. When he was a youth in the area, the Patent Office had been in Arlington's Crystal City. He hadn't known of its move to the outskirts of Old Town. Actually Ted, soon after moving to the capital region, had written a booklet for the Patent Office on its new facility.

McVeigh drove up and down Dulany St. Then, as he motored slowly along the parallel road skirting the glass-and-steel buildings, he grew more impressed and intrigued. By the buildings' extent, and by the world-famous agency itself, one integral to globalist financiers, the moguls he believed dictated the life of the world. Bombing it would make a powerful statement, akin to the assaults on the World Trade Towers and the Pentagon.

The very names of the office buildings he saw inscribed on the exterior walls would underscore his message. They were Edmund Jennings Randolph, the first Attorney General of the U.S.; the race mixer Jefferson, the first Secretary of State and the Patent Office founder; Henry Knox, the first Secretary of War, as in Fort Knox, the storehouse of the U.S. gold supply; and James Madison, the author of the U.S. Constitution, with its absurd list, as he viewed it, of rights, instead of a superior man's duties and prohibitions.

McVeigh rounded the northern parallel road onto the southern one, and they joined at the entrance to the headquarters. An African-American security guard on its broad steps eyed him; McVeigh thought suspiciously so. He immediately drove off, to explore some of the side streets that seemed under less scrutiny.

These were designed in the wake of the 1995 Oklahoma bombing and the September 11 attacks. The buildings were mammoth, fortress-like constructions of concrete, mortar, and steel: materials aimed at limiting damage from big explosions. The exteriors and entranceways did have a lot of glass, to allow light into the workspaces and atriums. Exploded glass flung into the interior, McVeigh reasoned, would wreak much bloodletting. And the sidewalks lacked the heavy metal posts to stop a truck or van's approach. Yet the building entrances had those protective posts, as well as a half dozen sizeable steps each, on which stood two additional rows of metal posts.

'No,' McVeigh analyzed, 'driving my van to an entrance here would be impossible.' There were wide ramps for disabled persons leading to the entrances that might be wide enough for a small truck, but they turned at too sharp an angle for any large vehicle to get through.

He drove on. An attack would have to be along the side or rear of a building, where the damage would be far from optimal. Moreover, McVeigh noticed there were few delivery trucks along the concourse. If he left his bomb-laden van there, it would stand out, and security might quickly discover and disarm the explosives. He placed the Patent Office at the bottom of his hit list.

McVeigh continued motoring up Mill Road, his windshield wipers throwing aside a scattering of rain. Just south of upper Duke St., he ran into another surprise, and possible target. To his left spread out the massive Albert V. Bryan United States Courthouse. He had been unaware of it too. Several decades before, its offices were moved from the smaller Martin Bostetter Courthouse located near the Appomattox statue.

In its new abode, the Bryan courthouse had long been the scene of high-profile prosecutions of terrorists, foreign and domestic, including Zacarias Moussaoui and Chelsea Manning. And the trial of Abdullah Hamaas, whose bold escape from the prison a mile away McVeigh admired. 'He's accomplished much, despite being a member of a subhuman race,' he mused. 'Perhaps Abdullah is one of those Central Asian types, like the Brahmin of northern India, or those Afghan

fighters descended from Alexander the Great, in whose veins flow the
martial Aryan blood.'

Running his eyes along the forbidding walls of the courthouse,
McVeigh reflected ruefully that if authorities managed to arrest him,
he'd likely be tried within. But he vowed not to be caught, and if
cornered to go down fighting, like the Norsemen of old, and to take
many lawmen down with him.

He fretted that driving his truck nearer the building might draw
unwanted attention again. So he parked a couple of blocks south on
Eisenhower Avenue. Even though he found it distasteful to leave his
vehicle on a road named for the man who crushed the Wehrmacht.

Back at the courthouse, he walked slowly around its city-block-wide
expanse. He tried to seem nonchalant while clicking photos of the
entrances.

Unfortunately for him, the Bryan courthouse is constructed, as is the
Patent Office, like a fortress. Built eight years after Oklahoma City, the
walls were placed back from the street to minimize damage from a
street explosion. Dark metal posts, three feet high and resembling big
fire hydrants, are at intervals along the buildings' sidewalks, making it
very hard to drive a large vehicle up to a wall. He did find an alley
behind the main buildings unprotected by barriers. However, to enter it
he'd have to drive past a security guardhouse that is manned around the
clock. He could not find a point of vulnerability to inflict considerable
harm. He crossed the Albert B. Bryan Courthouse off his list.

Once back in his vehicle, he went back up Dulany St. Rising up behind
him was the Motley Fool investing firm headquarters, in the former
AOL-Time-Life building, the latter's businesses shattered by changes
in technology. He crossed Duke St. past the real estate company in the
antebellum building of the Franklin and Armfield slave traders.

It was impossible to miss the next point of reconnaissance. The 333-foot-tall George Washington Masonic Temple was like a Saturn V rocket scraping the gray clouds above old Shuter's Hill, at the western end of King St. Once considered as a possible locale for the Capitol Building, the little mountain had ended up with a less significant but still magnificent edifice, composed during the 1920s and 1930s with masonic skill out of tons of stone and steel.

As he had for Jefferson, McVeigh held a special animus for Washington. In his will George Washington freed all 123 of his slaves. Which encouraged his wife after his death to free many others. Thus did America's first First Family set a terrible precedent, in the mind of the would-be bomber, pushing the nation to miscegenation and degeneracy. Adding to his disdain for the monument, he'd read its cornerstone had been placed by President Calvin Coolidge, an advocate of civil rights, while brandishing the same Masonic trowel with which Washington had laid the cornerstone of the U.S. Capitol. As did the Nazis, McVeigh considered the Free Masons, along with plutocrats and Jews, as instrumental in Germany's defeat in the world wars. Symbolically at least, damage to or destruction of this place would be hard to surpass.

He turned into the roadway looping across and up the Memorial's steep, terraced hill. Near the top is a giant concrete "G" for George, encircled by a giant freemason's compass and ruler. McVeigh drove slowly by the entrance, with its six plain Doric columns, capped by the triangular tympanum typical of Greco-Roman, and American, public buildings. High above was the magnificent tower, actually 15 towers, of steadily decreasing width, piled one upon the other, mimicking the great Lighthouse of Alexandria, in Egypt, a symbol of the accumulation of knowledge against the darkness of barbarism.

McVeigh had figured the enormous, artfully constructed Memorial would prove invulnerable to assault, but wanted to find out for himself. And indeed, the broad stairways leading to the entrance made him drop any hope of an attack. His van might get up the lower, less steep of stairs, 12 in number. But beyond were three more sets of steps, with the second and fourth sets steeper than the first. Their angle of ascent was too much for his vehicle to climb. He'd need a tracked conveyance like an armored car. Further, such an ascent would take place very much in the open, suicidally so.

As he drove back down the terrace road, he knew the George Washington Masonic Temple was off his target list.

Weary from the wide-ranging reconnaissance, he headed back to his hideaway. He brought in some more personal items, making the abandoned office somewhat more livable. He looked forward to laying low there, in solitude, before making his attack.

Chapter 38 – The Lion's Lodge

As ever, on the occasions Ted felt down or listless, he had a solution. Sports. He'd go biking, or swimming or hiking and, no matter how tired or low in spirits before, he felt revived after. Harmony was the same way. And both were very out of sorts after the death of their friend Tony, and then Ted's acquaintance Lily Harper. So they opted for an early evening bike ride.

Once more they headed up the Mt. Vernon Trail, past the abandoned train tracks and converted warehouses of upper Old Town. Past the 400-yard crescent-shaped bay of Founders Park. And the luxury townhomes, miming the colonial style, along the river park. They walked their bikes over the restored lock of the canal that once streamed all the way down from Georgetown. They rolled slowly past bizarre waterfront statuary of faux-marble pillars and disembodied faces that was supposed to resemble ancient Roman ruins. As if lost travelers had shipwrecked in America at the time of Caesar, to construct a solitary temple on a distant shore.

Both cyclists had an informal rule to never exactly repeat a ride, so they chose a different route from the previous jaunt to Hains Point. They'd ride up the Mt. Vernon Trail to Arlington, then take the Custis Trail, as in Martha Custis Washington, and head up the steep Arlington Heights. Those hills, which once provided as a vantage point for Confederate scouts during "The Late Unpleasantness", would offer a stiff workout. Hard enough, they hoped, to forget their woes for a time.

Their route took them again past the massive, shuttered coal plant that hugged the river north of the "Roman ruins". The former Pepco property, built in 1931, provided blue-collar jobs during the Great Depression and beyond. It had been closed years before from concerns about pollution wafting out of its smokestacks. To prettify a section of the closed industrial facility visible from the river trail, some multi-colored murals, hundreds of meters long and some six-feet high, were created. Originally, the wall paintings depicted scenes from colonial and Revolutionary War Alexandria that focused on hometown hero George Washington. The Carlisle House, Christ Church, the George Washington Masonic Temple, and master mason George Washington's laying of the U.S. Capitol Building's cornerstone were among the things depicted.

However, some local community groups and politicos objected to this honoring, as they viewed it, of a slave owner and representative of a ruling class which oppressed women and 'peoples of color'. So the mural was replaced with a 'more inclusive' and environmentally friendly theme. The new paintings depicted Alexandria residents of various ethnicities and ages in pristine settings: Rowing human-power craft on the Potomac, practicing yoga under the spotless rays of a cleansing sun, plugging in electric vehicles at a charging station, and so on. Ted thought the new mural colorful but, as a tour guide with a specialty on the American Revolution, disliked the cancellation of the George Washington scenes.

"Couldn't the city have retained the old mural," he mentioned to Harmony, as they rode close together, "while adding the new one?"

"That would have been pretty cool," she replied, realizing Ted had made a similar pitch about the Appomattox statue.

Beyond the lengthy mural the bike trail dipped almost to river level, and entered a series of short, sharp turns. Ted remembered a friend who'd crashed there, breaking her leg, and he flashed Harmony the cyclist's signal for slowing down. Then on to a straightaway, where they reached the north end of the coal plant, fenced off behind an 80-yard-wide swatch of broad-branched maple trees and thick bindweed bushes.

Here Ted experienced a common calling of men experiencing the passage of time. As he signaled another slowdown and pulled to a stop by the trees, Harmony laughed, knowing from prior workouts his purpose.

"I must pause to relieve myself," he told her, grinning.

"I couldn't tell," she replied with a wink. Harmony figured Ted's imminent action resulted partly from a full bladder, and partly from his anti-authority streak. That apparently including peeing on a public property that hadn't placed a port-a-potty on premises near an athletic trail, far from any tavern or other establishment with a public loo.

Ted walked his bike through tall grass to where the leafy maples could shelter him from the eyes of passersby. "You hardly need to hide," Harmony called out. "There's almost no one on the trail today."

"I would want any lady passing by to swoon," he gibed, "or any fella passing by to get jealous."

She followed him for 20 yards or so, causing him to look over his shoulder and say, "Are you going to watch? That might leave you 'prostate' with laughter." Harmony laughed hard indeed as she briskly walked away. Behind her she could hear the flapping of cardinals' wings. While smiling at the chirping, she realized she had never seen the coal plant so up close. As she stepped along the tall barrier separating it from the woods, Harmony was impressed once more by its size. It stretched for perhaps 300 feet to her left, and well out of view. Each smokestack sat atop its own building, equivalent to a 16-story skyscraper, attached to each other. A vast array of metal scaffolding hung from three sides of the structures. The walls and roofs contained tons of corrugated tin and sheet metal. She made out large, freestanding circular basins, apparently to hold water. The installation looked more like a fortress than an industrial facility. 'And you could hide a military base in there,' Harmony thought. She eyed rusted, metallic stairwells at the nearest end, permitting access and egress in the days gone by. Once a hive of bustle and noise, the complex was now as quiet as a country graveyard.

With tree branches brushing against her bike shirt, worn half-zippered over her sports bra, Harmony neared the southern end of the fence. There it met another fence, near the grounds of an apartment building rising over the Potomac. She reversed direction, and looked toward the trail, which was completed hidden by the foliage. She turned back to look at the coal plant, and her sharp, amber-colored eyes noticed something.

A small part of the fence looked different. She sniffed. She could sense the early summer pollen, the fragrance of flowers. But there was something else that smelled different too.

"Ted!" she called out. "If you're done, you might want to look at this."

After 'cleaning' his hands with leaves, he walked over.

"Do you see, what I see?" Harmony asked melodically, almost singing her words. She pointed in front of her.

Ted wasn't sure if she meant the fence, or the ground beyond it. He saw nothing.

Her slender waist bent over, Harmony pointed again, and tapped the fence's intermeshed wire. It moved a bit from its position.

Ted saw. He reached down and touched it. It moved some more.

"Has it been cut out?" he asked. He leaned over and grabbed a chunk of the fence's wire rectangles—and pulled out that part of the fence.

The piece was three feet wide, and somewhat bigger from bottom to top. Starting about two feet from the ground.

"Big enough for a man," Ted noted.

Harmony stated: "And they think this place has no visitors."

Ted examined the wire. "It's been cut pretty cleanly, by a tool or a machine of some sort."

Harmony replied, "That's not all." She touched a speck of white where the cut-out area met the rest of the fence. She sniffed it again, hard, like a Chesapeake Bay retriever smelling a beached alewife fish. "It smells acrid."

Ted took a look, and a sniff. He could barely detect the odor. They noticed that the white flakes were on other portions of the fence near the cutout.

"A poison?" Harmony asked, half-seriously.

"An explosive?" Ted asked, more seriously. Then less seriously, "But that's a stretch, isn't it?"

He tasted a flake, despite fearing it would burn his tongue. It did, a little, like a jalapeno, and he spit it out.

They looked at each other quizzically. And said, almost simultaneously, "Should we find out?"

Ted grinned. Harmony became hesitant. "That's trespassing. And you're in big enough trouble with the authorities."

"Not nearly as much as before," he replied. "I'm in the clear actually."

"There are probably video cameras watching the buildings," Harmony countered.

"Maybe, maybe not," replied Ted. "The place seems so, so deserted. Besides, if FBI Guy catches us on video, I'll say what I normally say under such conditions. That I'm a historian, exploring a local landmark."

Harmony said dubiously, "I could lose my security clearance." Twice
in her career she'd obtained Top Secret clearance, though to her
disappointment she'd never worked on anything hush-hush. Losing it
might lose her job at Amazon, which at times involved military
contracts. "I don't know about this, Ted." But hers was a job she kind
of wanted to lose, by leaving, as she found her work increasingly dull.
While this little mystery was intriguing. She felt her reluctance weaken.
Ted had stopped listening to her. He had put the cutaway back in place,
but now he took it off again and put it against the fence. He stepped his
left leg through the opening, then the rest of him. He glanced back at
Harmony, who stood motionless, and he began walking toward the
plant, which now seemed even bigger, and more ominous, than before.
He heard steps behind him and realized that his friend's curiosity, and
desire to be in an adventure with him, had overcome any qualms. Being
more meticulous than Ted, Harmony put the cutout back in place
before rushing up.

They stepped through grass, moist and overgrown from the recent
rains. They got to the edge of the plant and its loading docks. The doors
were locked with heavy chains. The chains were rusted, and looked
fragile. Ted pulled hard on them, but they wouldn't budge.

They gazed far down the side of the plant that paralleled the river. At
the end there seemed to be an entrance.

"Too far," said Ted. He eyed a metal stairway nearby with crumpled
steps leading to the second floor.

"I wouldn't," said Harmony. But he tried it, and the steps, though dirty
and worn, held. In seconds he was clambering up, and he heard
Harmony climbing up behind him.

On the steel landing they found three doors. All were locked tight. There was a series of windows to their left, and another window around the corner to their right.

They tried the first window on the left; it was latched tight. They walked along the landing and Ted randomly tried the fourth and fifth windows. Sealed tight. Nervous someone might spot them, they were ready to give up. As they walked back to the steps, Ted checked the second window on a whim. With several tugs, he raised it. It was unlatched.

"Maybe," said Harmony, "someone forgot to latch it in closing the place up long ago."

"Maybe," replied Ted. They both thought of an alternative explanation. Ted climbed over the sill to the other side. The sill seemed less dirty than he expected. Ted pulled Harmony inside, and they brushed away some dust.

The interior of the old warehouse was still somewhat visible from the late-day light filtering through the dusty windowpanes. The stark outlines of a Bobcat forklift, its yellow paint peeling away, appeared below them like a petrified raptor. Industrial lamps hung down from the ceiling, covered by conical shrouds, their lamps unlit, their plastic covers cracked. Balsa wood cartons, like those at a produce market, lay about, their frames splintered. In the southeast corner was a puddle the size of a small pond, slowly growing from a leak dripping down from the ceiling's corrugated tin. The floor was marked by dirt, litter, dead insects, dust. Harmony whispered to Ted, "This place would make a great hangout for the cartels or the Mob."

The duo jumped three feet down to the warehouse floor. Ted's left knee ached from landing on the concrete floor. "I bet this place gives off quite the echo, echo, ec—" he whispered jokingly. "But we'd be wise to be quiet." Indeed, Harmony was very worried about encountering the fence cutter, whoever he might be, and in such an eerie place. Ted was less concerned, telling himself, perhaps fatuously, that they could make a quick retreat back outside if they came upon anything dangerous.

The northwest corner had a large, walled-off office, evidently for a foreman or floor manager. They crept up to its metal door, Ted going first, feeling protective toward his friend. He thrust his left hand forward to try the knob, then froze mid-air, as Harmony hissed: "Stop!" He turned to see her pointing her left index finger to the floor. Ted took a step back toward her, and looked. There were footprints in the dust. Recent footprints. Not their footprints. The prints led to and from the office!

Ted bent over the faint markings, peering through the dim light. Harmony shone her cell phone light on them. They looked like the prints of boots. Hiking boots? Army boots? The feet of the wearer were larger than his size 10. "Their owner," he whispered, "is, what, six-foot-two, six-three?"

"The same as at Old Presbyterian?" answered Harmony.

She and Ted looked at each other, their ears cocked, listening intently. They heard nothing. Ted stepped cautiously back to the door. A worried Harmony walked right behind him, peering over his wide shoulders. Ted reached out his hand to the knob.

Harmony said softly, "I don't know if you should do that." Ted paused, fingers on the knob, listening hard. Harmony crouched down, and stared at the bottom of the door. In the crack between it and the floor, no light was filtering through. She listened harder, could hear nothing within.

Ted turned the knob gingerly.

The door wouldn't open.

Harmony felt relieved. Ted felt frustrated.

He tried to turn the knob harder. It wouldn't turn. He pulled hard. No luck.

He straightened himself up, and stated quietly, "Maybe its window outside is open." He walked briskly to the warehouse ledge, pulled himself up, and went out the way they'd entered.

Harmony, surprised at his sudden departure, nervously waited in the growing gloom of the warehouse. What if someone came upon Ted while he was outside? She'd be trapped. But she was more worried about something happening to him.

After a few minutes, Harmony heard a low noise from within the office. She saw the knob turn. She tensed, expecting Ted to appear, but maybe someone else.

The door opened. It was Ted. The room behind him was illuminated by the late-day sun. He shot her a look of surprise.

"Wait 'til you see this!" he breathed.

Careful to step over the dust and the prints, Harmony stepped inside the office, closing the door behind her. She saw a worn, yet tidy, lived-in place. The floor seemed swept clean. On it, near the window, was a foldable cot, military-style, low to the ground, with a sheet, a wool blanket, and a small pillow. Next to it was a little table with a wash basin, a bar of soap, a razor, and a towel. Just inside the door to her right was a little stand with some MREs and bottles of Powerade and Monster energy drink.

Ted turned to examine the cot, but Harmony's attention swerved to a stand pushed up against the office wall. On it were a few books and magazines. And some little toys and miniature flags. She immediately recognized the man on the cover of the book set in the center of the small stand. He was the author of the book.

The book was *Mein Kampf*.

Harmony felt a curtain of dread fall upon her.

"Take a look at the flags," said Ted, breaking in on her thoughts. The emblems, she saw, was small, but discernible. They were Nazi Germany flags, adorned with the swastika, or the death-head's emblems of its S.S., the unit that staffed the extermination camps.

Harmony eyed a photo next to the book. "That's a handsome young man," she said. "Is that him?"

Ted took a glance, and his lower jaw dropped in surprise. The photo was of a clean-shaven fellow about 25 years of age. He was handsome, strapping, posing for the photographer with his back against an iron wall.

"That's not our guy," he stated. "That's Lewis Powell." His eyes widened at the retouched Matthew Brady photograph. Seeing Harmony's quizzical look, he continued, "That photo's over 150 years old. Made to look newer. Powell was the other assassin on the night Lincoln was killed. He went after Lincoln's Secretary of State, William Seward."

"You mean like in 'Seward's Folly'?"

Ted grunted. "That came later, when Seward purchased Alaska. But on that terrible night, as John Wilkes Booth was shooting President Lincoln, Powell tried to murder Seward. Almost did. Sliced him up bad." His face took on a reflective look. "Cut him with a long dagger." He thought of Freedmen's and Christ Church and Old Presbyterian. "He was, like Booth, quite skilled in the use of a knife."

He commented, "This guy is an admirer of the worst of the white racists, on either side of the Atlantic."

"He must be the murderer," said Harmony. Ted didn't answer. After looking over the items, while careful not to touch them, they examined another corner of the room. It held a modest-sized metal case, about four feet across and three feet deep, and a second, somewhat smaller one. The latter's lid was askew. They looked it over. It contained a metal powder. Harmony sniffed at it, and nodded.

"The same substance," said Ted, "that you found on the fence?"

"Yes."

"I remember it now from research I did on a case for Greco. It's gunpowder."

"This is a strange place to keep gunpowder."

"Maybe not for our 'Joker'," said Ted grimly. He reached toward the larger case.

"Shouldn't you wrap a tissue around your hand before touching it?" asked Harmony.

Ted paused, arm in the air, and reflected. "I doubt our Nazi here has the apparatus to detect fingerprints. Besides," Ted smirked, "we're probably not in his database."

"But when Comitas' men dust for fingerprints," she rejoindered, "they'll find yours."

"Yeah," said Ted wanly, "but I'm not a suspect now. He might even befriend us after we tip him, or Greco, off about this."

Ted saw Harmony's worried expression, and gave in. He pulled out napkins from a pocket and wrapped them around his hands. Being careful to not move the case, he held it down with one hand while trying to open it with the other. It didn't budge. Then Harmony held it down with her bike glove, while Ted tried lifting the lid up with both hands. No luck. "Maybe it's locked or something," he noted, as both eyed the smaller case.

It was designed like a toolbox, with a removable top shelf and a deep bottom. They stared at the top. Along with the gunpowder, it contained bullet shells, and a lengthy piece of steel with a long slot cut into it.

"That looks like a knife sharpener," breathed Harmony. "When I was a kid in Malaysia, a man, the knife sharpener man, used to come to our door. Nowadays of course, people just buy a new set of utensils."

Ted lifted up the top shelf. Harmony gasped.

They saw three daggers, some grenades of different types, and two handguns, a Glock 29 and a 9mm Luger. One of the knives was a serrated MTECH Extreme 5-inch hunting special.

Harmony contorted her lips. Usually lovely, they looked like someone had scarred them with a blade. She said slowly, in a low tone, "Was that used to cut, to cut into Ton—, into the victims?"

"Could be," said Ted, lost in his thoughts. But neither he nor his fellow sleuth could see a trace of blood on it. "Maybe wiped them off carefully," he muttered. Ted gingerly put back the top shelf.

"Maybe we found our murderer," he said.

"And maybe our robber too," she replied.

Ted squinted. "Or maybe not." He looked skeptical. "The killer doesn't quite fit the profile of a devotee of the *Führer*. Slayings at Revolutionary War and Civil War sites. No, the murderer seems rooted in the history of *this* town, not central or eastern Europe.

"And if I'm right about the robber, he has a different motive altogether, something else than murder."

Harmony was growing more nervous, more so as she saw Ted becoming almost relaxed in this office of horror, as if he was simply on one of his research jaunts around Old Town.

"I think it's past time," she said, "that we got out of here. And told the authorities what we've found."

"Yes," said Ted, looking up from the containers, like a professor looking up from his class notes. "You're probably right. I'll take some quick photos of these things first."

As he was pulling out his cell from his bike shirt, Harmony cracked open the door, and stopped cold. Her torso stiffened with tension, as if she'd sensed a wild beast emerging from a jungle.

She quietly closed the door and stepped back in a quick, smooth motion. Ted was reminded of the way she gracefully handed out energy drinks when volunteering at races, moving about like a ballerina. He started to ask, "What?" But she pirouetted like a spinning top, and stabbed her lips with the index finger in a plea for silence.

"Someone's coming through the window! Maybe THAT man!" she hissed. "I don't think he saw me!"

Ted thought fast, real fast. There was one escape. He knew there was a direct path from the window back to the plant's landward gate, on the opposite side from the river.

He pocketed his cell, stepped to the window, its exterior gray from years of muck, and motioned Harmony over toward him. Before moving, she had the presence of mind to turn the lock to the door knob. Ted turned the window latch. It was stuck! Harmony looked at him, her cheeks flushing from fright. Ted imagined he heard steps in the warehouse heading their way. Maybe he wasn't imagining it.

He tried the latch again. It turned! He pushed open the dirty window, wincing as he heard it creak a bit, and climbed through. It was dark outside, near sunset. As Harmony followed Ted through the open window, she caught her bike shorts on the latch, and almost tumbled headfirst into the ground.

Ted caught her. He gazed through the window at the door knob. It wasn't turning. Not yet.

He closed the window. He couldn't close the latch from outside of course. Would the Nazi not notice, or think he'd forgotten to latch it? Ted stole another glance. The knob was turning.

The duo sprinted to the western gate, the hard plastic of their bike soles silenced by the grass, with Harmony ahead and Ted, his left knee flaring up, coming up behind. As they climbed over the fence gate, Ted stole a nervous look at the window in the distance. As near as he could tell, it was still closed.

They kept running for a block up Abington Lane, until they were out of sight of anyone who might be watching from the plant. They hoofed it in their bike shoes back to the trail by way of Slater's Lane, along the far northern end of the coal plant. After running down the Mt. Vernon Trail, their feet aching from the inflexible shoes, they reentered the woods where their adventure had begun, fearing an armed and angry killer might be lurking behind a tree. But the place was deserted. They hopped on their bikes and, with the sun below the horizon, cycled slowly back to Old Town, and Harmony's townhouse apartment. At a stoplight on the way, Ted punched a number into his cell.

"Telling the FBI?" smiled Harmony grimly, still sweating from the close call.

"Not quite," smiled Ted. "We have quite the scoop to tell our friend Greco."

Chapter 39 – Research Rendezvous

Ted and Harmony gathered at her place in the late afternoon to discuss their next moves. Ted preferred meeting there instead at his duplex, as did Harmony. His place looked as ever as a stereotype of a bachelor's, and writer's, abode, while Harmony's place in contrast was tidy, and far homier, indeed, more harmonious. In fact, her lodging was a steal that any apartment renter would die for.

It had fallen into her lap two years before after she'd gotten the Amazon job and moved to Alexandria. At a business lunch a top executive, in mentioning an imminent move to Seattle, mentioned he'd be renting out floors of his Old Town townhouse. The asking price was a bargain for the property in question, part of a 4,642-square-foot home, a mansion in fact, dating from 1809. When Ted first visited Harmony there, on the 400 block of Duke St., he was astonished, as he knew the building's story. It reflected, like so much of Old Town, the check-to-jowl relationships of pro-Southern and pro-Union families in the antebellum.

Early on, the home was the property of Richard Bland Lee, the first Virginian elected to the first U.S. Congress, and an uncle to Robert E. Lee. Richard Bland Lee's son, with the same name, a colonel in the Confederate Army, is buried at Ivy Hill Cemetery. The mansion home was later acquired by Elisha Janney. He was of the noted Quaker family, partial to abolition, that included John Janney, who managed, while partial to the Union, Virginia's secession conferences of 1861. In walking by the house one time, Ted reflected: 'Only in Old Town would powerful people on opposite sides of the great national divide live next door to one another, or sometimes in the same house. A House divided indeed.'

Harmony leased the top floor of the four-story edifice. Her windows abutted two antique chimneys. Spacious dormers rising from the roof afforded a grand view of Old Town and beyond.

Late that afternoon, Ted arrived on his bike. He entered its Greek Revival doorway, feeling dwarfed by the massive white cornice above, which contrasted with the small, wrought-iron, Regency rails below. After being buzzed in, he climbed a grand staircase to reach the upper landing, where he savored the pungent yet sweet aroma from Harmony's kitchen. As he heard the clatter of pans in an oven, he looked over the living area.

The polished wood floors were partially covered by a colorful, Middle Eastern carpet. The walls had reproductions of paintings from widely varying places and times: The Italian Renaissance, the Chinese Tang dynasty, 19th century Americana. A cherrywood showcase, an heirloom from her grandmother, had glassed-in shelves from which peeked generations of family photo albums. A new bookshelf held university texts on engineering science and business management, as well as travel books on Southeast Asia, Central America, the Greek islands, and East Africa. A Felt racing bike, cleaned and oiled, was snugly attached to a wall rack.

Hearing footsteps, Harmony called out, "I'm almost done." Ted walked over and saw her taking off the oven mitts. A Malaysian chicken concoction, with coconut rice, lay on the stove. Ted's mouth watered. "You know," he said, "it may rain later, but it's only cloudy now, and warm and mild. We could take this to the dormers."

Harmony's nose wrinkled in delight, and they carried the victuals out to an open window. The owner kept a bunch of old Sports Authority folding chairs in the attic space; they put two of them at a bridge table on the south side. After setting up the repast, they gazed out toward the Woodrow Wilson Bridge; its span seemed diminutive in the distance. The mighty Potomac coursing under it was for the most part darkened from the clouds, though some of the waves glistened from rays of the descending sun.

As they dug into the food, they briefly went over the murders again. Ted shared a rumor, "on good information" he said, about the FBI investigation. "At Christ Church and at the Tomb of the Unknown, they did find sweat samples on the body of the victim, sweat that differed from the victims. But the FBI's crime lab botched the tests, I heard, and mucked up the samples. So they can't identify the person or persons from the sweat."

"That's incredible," said Harmony. "It's supposed to be the foremost crime lab in the world."

"But that's not the worst part of it. My source," and Ted, looking conspiratorial, lowered his voice, "my source swears the supervisor of the lab work was an ex-lover of Comitas. She was kept on the job despite her incompetence in the lab."

Harmony could guess who Ted's source was, but didn't mention Greco's name. "That would be a huge scandal," she said.

"It would be," replied Ted, "if it wasn't covered up."

Anticipating the next, pressing subject, he told her he'd informed Greco of the coal plant office, and its disturbing contents.

"Did they raid the place?!"

"Greco didn't tell me much, but I gather they haven't yet. But that a big chunk of the Alexandria police department will very soon come hard down on that place."

Though she didn't want to, Harmony brought up the Christ Church slaying of Tony, and the other killings. Her voice choking up, she stated, "I could surely understand the Freedmen's murder as a racist attack, and Ton—and, and, the Christ Church, matter, as a revenge attack. Or a feint." She put down her knife and fork. "But the killing at Presbyterian, at Old Presbyterian, doesn't make sense." She lost whatever appetite she had. "And the mutilation. Mutilations again. What, what fiend, could possibly do that? Our 'Joker' could, I guess. But why churches and graveyards? What's the point?"

Ted shook his head. "Yes, it's hard to fathom. But I think I've figured out the reason behind that mutilation. And maybe Tony's too."

Harmony stared at him with wide, teary eyes.

Ted looked away. "Let me tell you later. Let's finish eating. It's getting late. And I have some research to do."

To the south they could make out the treetops of the African-American Heritage Memorial Park along Hooffs Run, near where "contrabands" fleeing their owners in the Civil War had set up shanties and shacks. The park was an entry point to a vast complex of church cemeteries, established outside of congested Old Town after an epidemic in the early 1800s. Further, the National Cemetery there holds 3,500 Union Army dead. In contrast, the various Protestant graveyards contain prominent citizens who were fiercely loyal to the Southern cause. Cheek-by-jowl opponents in life, resting nearby forever in death.

As Ted finished off the succulent chicken and rice, he said, "The cool breeze is so nice, after another humid day. The Wilkes area looks inviting." Harmony pointed a fork into the distance and, her face expressionless, asked: "You're still not thinking of going out there, are you?"

Previously, they'd discussed whether it was safe for Ted to continue his far-flung research about town. The next topic for his book was the historic graveyards south of Old Town, and he had tentatively planned to go there after dinner. With Lily Harper deceased, Ted would have to finish his investigations there himself. And he was determined to do so. "The killer strikes at night," he told Harmony. "Usually late at night. And I only plan on a couple hours of poking about the tombs. I should be done around sunset. Besides, Greco may nail the killer by tonight, if the killer is the coal plant guy."

Harmony frowned, but figured protest was futile. Once Ted had made up his mind about anything history-related, he was impossible to budge.

"I suppose that's right," she said evenly. Then added quickly, "And I'll go with you."

Ted smiled inwardly, while outwardly hiding his reaction. Which was two-fold. He thought in fact there was some danger in venturing out in the evening, so he worried about Harmony going. But he felt even more it'd be great to have her along.

Harmony broke into a wide grin. "We can bike over."

Chapter 40 – A Cemetery Stalker

He left his borrowed car near the Lee recreation center, in one of the many vacant parking spots along Franklin St. The street was named after the Founding Father whom it seemed everyone could agree to like. Except perhaps the prudish, those aware that Ben Franklin was at times a nudist and definitely a womanizer. As well as the person in question, who would have disdained the freethinking Dr. Franklin as a non-believer. The rec center, just seven short blocks northwest of the Freedmen's Cemetery, had been closed from the pandemic, thus freeing up street parking.

Although Abdullah intended to strike at night, he arrived while it was still light to get a lay of the land. He felt for the arc of solid metal, tucked into the scabbard under his untucked shirt. He checked the charge and the camera of his cell, to ensure he could take video evidence of his strike.

After his arrival in New York, he might post that—the recording could go viral, inspiring many faithful around the world. The imam might not like it, but he'd be in another city by then.

Though in his mid-40s, Abdullah paced along with the easy lope of an athlete in his prime. His years of strength and cardio workouts at the Detention Center had rewarded him with an enviable physique. He was hooded, triple-masked, his muscled body draped in black. From online maps and a brief, previous visit during one of his wanderings about town, he'd learned something about the confusing jumble of 11 cemeteries, of mostly Christian denominations, scattered across 135 acres and two centuries of burials. He knew where he would most enjoy striking, and started his search there, near Jefferson and S. Payne Streets at the southeast edge of the necropolis.

A few days before, by chance, he'd come across the smallest of the cemeteries. Not easy to find, it was hidden from S. Payne St., a setting which would cloak the movements of a killer. The path leading up from the street resembled one of the dirt and gravel trails, quickly blending into the countryside, often seen in old Southern towns. But at its terminus, with lush maple trees flanking either side, was a modern graveyard, just 45 yards across and 70 yards deep.

When he had first encountered it, Abdullah's reaction was a mix of surprise, revulsion, and excitement. There were neat rows of tombstones, with about 15 in each row. Many had Stars of David or Hebraic script carved on them. It was Alexandria's Jewish Cemetery: Agudas Achim, roughly, "Band of Brothers".

It is the city's most recently resting place, established in 1933. That year was significant, and Abdullah felt, like Willy McVeigh, that he might carry on a 'grand tradition' in full flower at that time. It was the year Hitler took power, and many Jews began fleeing Europe. Orthodox Jews arriving in Alexandria at that time founded the place. As he walked alone among the memorials, he was disgusted again. 'This is truly polluted soil', he thought, 'a pigsty.' He was also disappointed. As in the first time he visited it, the cemetery was deserted. No victim to be had.

Then a novel thought struck him. About an assault that could be far better than a mere knifing or a beheading. He looked again at the gravestones. It was indeed a newer place, a 'working cemetery' as the infidels called it. In fact, judging from the dates of the deaths, many of the burials were very recent. He made a mental note about this. If a burial was upcoming, he might be able to plant an explosive device beforehand, and time the bomb to go off during the services. 'An improvised explosive device', in the jargon of Great Satan's military. The thought of the angst and mayhem which that would generate quickened his pulse. Such an attack would take preplanning, however. He did prefer something quick before his departure to the sacred soil of lower Manhattan.

The Agudas Achim cemetery was enclosed, segregated from the other graveyards. He walked through of a thin line of oak trees to find himself among the other cemeteries. In the dimming light, the jihadi swerved his head back and forth, like a U-boat periscope scanning for merchant ships, but could see no prey. He went past the wide lawn of the Penny Hill Cemetery, a kind of potter's graves for the indigent of the 1800s, including many blacks, a kind of Freedmen's Cemetery, but not directly related to the Civil War. The unmarked grave of Benjamin Thomas, the black teen lynched near Market Square in 1899, is said to rest, uneasily, on these grounds. Wooden crosses for its impoverished denizens have long since molded away. There were none of the marble obelisks and raised sandstone graves that marked the resting places of the opulent. Not that such things matter in eternity.

Amidst the lengthening shades and shadows Abdullah could see none among the living. He stepped past the adjoining Home of Peace Cemetery. He assumed it was part of the Penny Hill plots, but if he had examined the headstones more closely he would have discovered Jewish-American names. For it is Alexandria's earliest Hebraic graveyard, founded by Reform Jews before the Civil War.

He veered left and northwestward toward the center of the vast expanse of the dead. The gravesites were now greater in number, and a greater possibility presented itself of finding a living visitor to send to an untimely grave.

Chapter 41 – Sunset Searches

After hurriedly finishing their repast, Ted and Harmony took a final look toward the cemetery complex in the distance, and at the sun slipping down toward the faraway horizon. Leaving behind Harmony's china plates and porcelain cups for cleanup later, they scurried down the stairs, Ted carrying Harmony's Felt bike. To make good time, they rode down Henry St., parallel to Patrick St., a normally busy thoroughfare now practically devoid of traffic from the infections and murders. They turned onto Commerce St., cutting diagonally to the southwest. The pair passed a long, low building, now private residences, of a little-known, former slave pen, at the intersection of the aptly named Commerce and Payne Streets. The Commerce of Pain indeed. The same block had one of Old Town's abandoned ice houses, which had doubled as a mortuary, before refrigeration rendered its secondary functions obsolete. An entrepreneur was smartly turning legacy into lucre by building an ice cream shop within.

They crossed Duke St. onto Daingerfield Road. This short byway is so modern, sterile, and non-descript, on the back side of a Residence Inn and a public storage site, that Ted always loved the contrast when encountering its terminus at Jamieson St. The underground stream there, which once ran freely through from the west end of Old Town, goes free again above ground, turning the city's concrete into a bucolic brook, of moving water sheltered by a thick canopy of trees. The stream flows under the abandoned Orange and Alexandria railway bridge, where it morphs into Hooffs Run to the south. Cattle diverted along Diagonal and Daingerfield Streets had once hoofed their way past here. Indeed, the wonderfully named Hooff family had set up a

ranch and slaughterhouse on an adjoining pasture watered by their
stream. There cattle drives out of a Wild West movie would end, after
starting as far away as the Shenandoah Valley.

Harmony and Ted paused at the ancient stone bridge, and gazed about
and across Jamieson St. onto a distinctive landscape. To their left was
the Douglass Cemetery, named for Frederick Douglass, containing
recent African-American graves. Strangely, the tombstones were
located on the lawn of an apartment building, the past and the present
jumbled jarringly together. To their right was the forest where Hooffs
Run meandered through the bottomland of the African-American
history park. To their front was a low iron fence running along
Jamieson and marking the boundary of the main cemetery complex.
Ted thought of Andrew Jamieson, a Scottish baker whose waterfront
business turned out tasty crackers, beloved by Queen Victoria, who
imported them all the way to London. It seemed one of the few place
names in Alexandria that wasn't connected to something dire or under
dispute. Beyond Jamieson a broad expanse of headstones stretched into
the shadows ahead.

The plan was to pedal the short distance to the adjoining National,
Episcopal, and Presbyterian cemeteries, for Ted to check on some
research items. Then back to Harmony's to clean up. She judged the
agenda too ambitious for the little daylight left.

The African-American park, with its overhanging holly and hackberry
trees and scattering of graves, was spooky in normal times, and more so
now, as the darkening sky seeming to heighten the lingering dread from
the murders. Despite their supposedly "fun" outing, the duo felt
nervous.

They slowly pedaled on a path through the woods, a shortcut to
National Cemetery, their first research stop. Reaching a leafy overhang

of Southern oak trees, Ted regretted not having left sooner. Under the canopy, it was as dark as midnight. They got off their bikes and felt their way along. Ted's night vision wasn't great, so he followed Harmony, who had under all conditions had unusually sharp 20/15 vision. Ted would joke she should try out for a professional ball team. For Ted Williams, he'd note, maybe the greatest of all hitters, had the same visual acuity, and was actually able to see the spin on an approaching ball.

They moved past four worn, unmarked headstones, put back in place decades before by the town's archaeologists. Those scholars had discovered the remnants of an African-American graveyard dating back to least the 1890s. Ted winced in recalling that, in the 1950s and 1960s, the locale became a town dump. The graves had been disturbed. Some believed that restless spirits, unable to find peace, haunted the place. In visiting before, Ted had sifted through the soil, and found coffin handles, and oyster shells for decorating graves in African and Caribbean tradition. Perhaps they were stepping atop such things now, which was tempting fate, to pay such disrespect to the dead.

They went down a short, paved path, and heard the gurgle of Hooffs Run. Due to all the rain, it was higher, and louder, than usual. They walked by historical plaques outlining the freedmen's village of yore. Ted imagined the harsh conditions, including malaria and cholera from the insects and germs and viruses of the marsh. Then the image of the murdered man hanging from the Freedmen's Cemetery statue came to mind, and he banished that thought.

It seemed longer, but after just a few minutes they went up a rise and reached the National Cemetery. The tree line ended; there was more light. They pedaled slowly through the Civil War graveyard, and the thousands of headstones, including the remains of over 225 Colored Troops, all stretched out in graceful rows.

To Ted the irony was obvious. A historically Southern town, hosting a large Union Army cemetery. Rows of identical, white-tinted tombstones, turned dark by the dusk, stretched into the distance. During a recent research tour of Gettysburg, Ted had learned the designer of "National", or Union, cemeteries, had insisted on an identical tombstone for every soldier, be he a private or a general, black or white, rich or poor. No raised graves nor fancy mausoleums were permitted. The notion, quite related to the conflict, was that everyone *was* created equal, had equality of citizenship and soul, and should repose the same way as everyone else. Surely in death everyone was equal indeed.

Passing a reviewing stand, they went over to the most noted graves. These were the four Union soldiers who perished, in a horrific Potomac shipping accident, while keeping a watch for Lincoln's murderer. In his research, Ted hadn't been able to find all their names, nor the full circumstances of their deaths. As Harmony looked with worry at the darkening sky, Ted bent over a historical plaque about "Booth's Bloodhounds", and snapped a photo of the troopers' names.

When they moved on, Ted worried the front entrance would be locked. His concern stemmed from the authorities discouraging people from visiting public spaces, including cemeteries. Supposedly to prevent groups from gathering and spreading the virus. Indeed, officials had taped off playgrounds, boardwalks, and volleyball courts throughout the region. Ted considered this odd, since outdoor recreation of various kinds was a healthful practice. Such restrictions would have seemed especially weird there, in a place whose buried denizens posed zero risk to the living. In any case, Harmony found an open gateway near the administrator's stolid red stone lodge.

They walked their bikes into the vast necropolis. The church graveyards had been established, Ted told Harmony, during a time of great distress, the yellow fever outbreak of 1803. Washington's physician, Dr. Elisha Dick, whose enemas and bleedings helped put the first President into an early grave, wrongly ascribed the pandemic to spoiled oysters. Dr. Walter Reed wouldn't peg the actual transmitter, mosquitoes, until 1900. Yellow fever forced half of Alexandria's 6,000 residents to flee to the countryside; over 200 perished.

Bricked, uneven pathways fanned out westward from Wilkes St. into the array of cemeteries. When Ted had first encountered the name Wilkes, a major street stretching out of Old Town, he'd wondered if a relative of John Wilkes Booth had been prominent in Alexandria. He knew the hanged Lincoln conspirator Mary Surratt went to a school in town. But this Wilkes was John Wilkes, a lord mayor of London, radical member of the British Parliament, and eventually a British Prime Minister. Although an ugly-faced man, he was a relentless womanizer—as well as champion of the poor and of free speech. He'd taken the side of his fellow 'extremists', the colonials staging the American Revolution. Ted laughed inwardly as he recalled the story of Charles Fox, another ardently pro-American Parliament member, who dressed up in General Washington's buff-blue uniform to highlight his sympathies.

Soon they were amidst the graves of St. Paul's Episcopalian, as in the church where Union troops arrested Rev. Stewart for declining to pray for President Lincoln. It was the worship house of wealthy persons of English descent, a status suggested by the expensive, elegant obelisks adorning many graves. Ted had always found it hard to identify the more famous personages there, as the tombstone inscriptions were so weathered. Still, he and Harmony located some such congregants. They found the grave of Montgomery Corse, the Confederate general who was almost lynched, after surrendering, on the night of Lincoln's killing. Just three plots away they hit upon the resting place of W.H. Marbury, of the clan of strongly pro-Federal advocates. It was Marbury of Georgetown, a judge appointed by President John Adams, who wrangled with Secretary of State James Madison at the Supreme Court in the famed *Marbury vs. Madison* case. Much to President Jefferson's dismay, the Marbury precedent established the authority of Chief Justice John Marshall's Court to review, and invalidate, the actions of the President or Congress. In the hometown of arch Federalist George Washington, many Alexandrians staunchly backed this view, and the new, stronger federal union, even as they would secede from it several generations later. Washington and successor Adams appointed to the federal courts many Federalist judges, such as Marbury and Dennis Harper, the son of Captain Harper, ancestors of Lily Harper.

Next to W.H. Marbury is a "J. Entwisle", sometimes spelled Entwistle in town archives, and Ted chuckled to himself, 'WHO might that man be!?' And then two graves down was the ranch family itself, the Hooffs, like the "hooves" of the cattle they herded.

Ted was pleased: He was finding plenty of material for his book and for a new tour. **Harmony was less happy.** After passing the small graveyard of the Trinity United Methodist congregation, she noted the stone hands carved into some tombstones. A strange image struck her, of the hands of deceased spirits reaching back out to the material world, to offer inspiration, or terror.

Creeping off from Wilkes St. was the bricked Hamilton Avenue, named not after Washington's "right hand man", but for a Scottish tradesman in a town founded by Highlanders. They passed clumps of dilapidated headstones encircled by worn-down iron posts. Along two parallel north-south lanes sprawled the granite and marble headstones of the "newer" Old Presbyterian cemetery. Ted and Harmony grimaced in reminder of the Harper atrocity at its Old Town church. Gated off and immaculately maintained by its caretaker, it contains graves of those who died after the very old burials at the Old Presbyterian Meeting House, before the congregation moved its funerals out of town in the time of cholera. Still, some graves were very old indeed, such as Robert Allison, Jr., who'd died in the War of 1812, at the Battle of the "White House", Virginia, which skedaddled the British out of their temporary occupation of Alexandria.

Bikes in tow, the pair headed southward on Hamilton Lane, near another, long-abandoned Methodist cemetery, many of its headstones crumbled or fallen over. Ted paused to take a photo of a connection to Native Americans that reminded him of his research into Tammany Hall. That was the corrupt New York political club, cofounded by Aaron Burr, which was a bulwark of the 19th-century Democratic Party. Tammany borrowed its trappings from the Empire State's Iroquois tribes, which practiced a form of democracy. Some of the Hall's leaders even dressed up in Native-American garb. In Old Town, these public-spirited folk dubbed their group the "Improved Order of Red Men", which morphed more into a fraternal than a political organization. Ted leaned down to a headstone, calling out, "What a great find!" The marker was inscribed with the abbreviation, "I O R M", and the images of a war club and tomahawk.

Smiling, Ted guided Harmony past tombstones garnished with a more common symbol, the compass and measuring rule of the Masons. It was no surprise a cemetery in the hometown of master mason George

Washington would hold the graves of so many masonic lodge members.

But the historian was more interested in a far rarer organization. He stared through the growing darkness, and pointed to a tombstone with the markings, L F T, standing for "Love, Friendship, and Truth". That was the sign of the distinctively named Society of Odd Fellows, which included local African-American chapters, professional societies in the days of segregation.

Harmony was amazed as ever at Ted's knowledge of local esoterica, but voiced concern at the gathering dusk. They had barely reached the heart of in the complex, and had more many places to search. Ted could have explored through the night, but he agreed they should turn around and come back another time.

He stepped over to grab his bike, propped up against the fence of a family gravesite. He had pedaled a total of 50,000 miles over the past decade, and even in the twilight had a practiced eye for anything out of place on two wheels. And something did seem wrong with his hybrid. He touched the rear spokes, and cried out, "Oh shoot! A flat!"

Harmony jogged over, and saw a visible cut in the tire. "That's a bad one," she noted. "It'll be an Uber for you to get back home tonight."

Ted thought he might crash at Harmony's instead. He added, "And it's the rear wheel. It would take me forever to replace the inner tube."

With a determined look Harmony said, "I can try." An IT person, she was pretty mechanical, more mechanical than Ted. "That's all right," he answered. "I can bring it to the Wheel Natural shop tomorrow."

Ted kneeled by the bike for a closer look. "I guess this settles it about leaving," he called out absently. "We should go back now. Walking out will take longer than riding." And he peered some more at the wheel.

But Harmony was doing something characteristic of her observant nature, one often captured by curiosity. Something had caught her eye deep within the cemetery grounds. 'Is that a person way down Hamilton Lane?' she asked herself. Almost unconsciously, and without telling Ted, she started striding down the Lane into the darkness.

Chapter 42 – Mysterious Strangers

After leaving the Home of Peace, Abdullah headed northward past another scattering of African-American graves. It was growing even darker from the elm, red oak, and cherry trees overhanging parts of the expanse. He approached the gated, southern fringe of the Old Presbyterian graveyard. He knew he should stick to the brick paths, but the restlessness that had gripped him seemed to seize his soul. Veering left, he tramped northwestwardly past long-forgotten souls, like a wandering ghost in the gloom.

Unwittingly, he traipsed over the large burial lot of Anthony-Charles Cazenove. His family, despite a name that is a variant of Casanova, had been affected by military and religious strife, not romantic adventure, and across four centuries. Of French origin, it escaped the slaughter of French Presbyterians in the St. Bartholomew's Massacre of 1572. Family members side-stepped the slaughter by guillotine of French revolutionaries in the 1790s, and found refuge in Switzerland. They made their way to America where A.C. Cazenove formed a business partnership with another French-speaking Swiss immigrant, future Treasury Secretary Albert Gallatin, the financier of the Louisiana Purchase. In Alexandria, Cazenove founded a second enterprise with another noted family of French roots, the DuPonts, makers of gunpowder and later, the behemoth chemical concern that made, among other items, napalm. The twin clans set up a firm on lower King St. that imported clothes, and buckshot. Cazenove's son had a bloody duel with a son of William Fowle, of the Fowle-Patton House, leaving the younger Fowle blinded. One of Cazenove's daughters married Gen.

Archibald Henderson, the longest-serving commandant of the U.S.
Marines Corps, a man who quelled the bloody D.C. race riot of 1857. A
grand-daughter married a first cousin of Robert E. Lee, and resided in
the Lee-Fendall House.

Unaware of the violent legacies beneath his feet, Abdullah strode on,
peering ahead, disappointed at seeing no potential victim in the
necropolis, indeed, no one at all. The imam's warning to lay low rang
in his mind, and began to undermine his determination. He was sinning,
he knew. Still, would a modest sin be cancelled out by a larger, nobler
act: a righteous act of violence against the infidel? Then again, what if
he were somehow captured or killed before the New York mission,
which promised an incalculably greater success?

He was unsure of himself in this strange place. Yet all about him, if
only he knew, were graves representing even more American turmoil.
If he had known, he would have taken comfort, knowing the locale was
a fitting place to add to the toll.

He trod over the sunken graves of the Vowell and Smith families, who
supplied Robert E. Lee with his personal attorney, who successfully
sued the federal government for compensation after the seizure of the
Lees' Arlington House estate. Even as those grounds, laden with buried
Union, and Confederate, remains, were already being transformed
into Arlington National Cemetery.

Abdullah stepped over the mound marking the resting spot of Dr.
Dick, one of the bleeders of the fatally ill Washington. He stepped by
the site of the Marstellers, for centuries provisioners of military
supplies to Germanic dukes, then to Washington's army.

With each futile step, Abdullah Hamaas' guilt and frustration grew, and
his resolve weakened. Except for the dead, there was no one about.

Then, as he was about to turn back to the cemeteries' southern exit, he spotted her.

'Is she dining here?!' Abdullah asked himself in amazement. Even in the gloom, he could see the person was a woman, a beautiful woman. She was kneeling down at what appeared to be a table, supported by posts in its middle and the four ends. 'Could she have brought a folding picnic table here?' he wondered skeptically.

The terrorist stopped cold, aware his chance may have come. He realized he must step silently. Though the woman, this beautiful woman, seemed oblivious to all about her, as if in a trance. She wore a long dark garment, black shoes, and a dark shawl over her head. Eyeing the scarf he wondered, 'Could she be a Muslim?' Then he must spare her. 'But why would she be here amongst the infidel dead?'

In fact, the lady was Ted's 'Mysterious Stranger'!

Abdullah stepped quietly to the left, to come up behind her. He perceived she had on a colorful scarf, of a type popular with women, Christian women, from Spain and Latin America.

'This would be perfect,' he thought. 'A dark-skinned man has been killed in town. And a white man and a white woman. The murder of a Hispanic woman might send the town over the edge entirely.

'Yes, suspicion and loathing in every group! It could tear apart not just this town, but all of America! Perhaps the imam, bless him, has underestimated me!'

As the terrorist crept closer, he saw the woman was not reclining before a dining table, but a table marker, a long stone rectangle set over a grave. On which a deceased's loved one could have words of loss and affection inscribed.

Abdullah stopped, fascinated. The woman, in a low but clear voice, was praying! From the Bible?

453

'No, wait,' he realized. 'That wasn't a Christian prayer. Perhaps no prayer at all.' She was reciting something.

Just feet away, he reclined his head, listening intently:

"...To the memory of a Female Stranger," she was whispering.

"Whose mortal sufferings terminated

"On the 14th day of October 1816

"Aged 23 years and 8 months.

"This stone," she continued, "is placed here by her disconsolate Husband

"In whose arms she sighed out her Latest breath

"And who under God did his utmost,

"Even to soothe the cold dead ear of death."

The Mysterious Stranger, Cassandra Benedita, paused, and daubed at her eyes with a silk kerchief. She was weeping at the words, and at recalling the tragedy of long ago.

She took out a small candle from her Armani pocketbook, and placed it next to three others on the table marker. Abdullah watched in wonderment as she lit each candle, placing one at the start of each of the four stanzas of the commemorative poem.

The Mysterious Stranger stretched out her elegant hands along the stone table, from the first candle and on to the last, then drew them back. She closed her eyes, her long, dark eyelashes dipping in the slight evening breeze, and breathed heavily, and softly, as if asleep. She seemed almost to be holding her own séance, communing with the dead. With the spirit of the long-gone woman to whom she felt a kinship.

Then, in a low, murmuring voice, in an English accented with her native Columbian Spanish, she began again:

"How loved, how valued once, avails thee not,

"To whom related or by whom begot,

"A heap of dust alone remains of thee,

"Tis all thou art and all the proud shall be."

For this last phrase, her voice became higher-pitched, full of sorrow
and regret. She seemed ready to break into tears.

Abdullah didn't know it, but those final lines were by Alexander Pope.
After Shakespeare and after William Tyndale, the main translator of the
King James Bible, perhaps the most quoted poet in English. Pope's
lines had been borrowed by the deceased women's "husband",
probably her lover in fact, as part of this inscribed honorific.

And Abdullah didn't realize it, but the female visitor obviously did, that
they were at the famous Tomb of the Female Stranger. Subject to
endless speculation about the deceased's identity since her untimely
death over 200 years before.

Ted well knew the story, and its many versions, and sometimes told it
on his Old Town tours. Of the lovely young lady of lush attire, who'd
arrived deathly ill at Gadsby's Tavern one chilly autumn night in 1816,
her face and identity covered by a shawl. Accompanied by a handsome,
well-dressed man, distressed beyond measure by his beloved's malaise.
He obtained a room at Gadsby's and arranged for doctors to visit her.
Who were puzzled, during their treatment, at her refusal to remove the
face covering or give her name.

She soon died from the illness, and her presumed lover stole out of
town—without paying for the room or the medical aid.

Ever since, many have speculated on her identity. Ted's favorite
suspect was Theodosia Burr Alston, the alluring and brilliant daughter
of Aaron Burr, and at the time the wife of a South Carolina governor.
The former Vice President, disgraced for slaying Alexander Hamilton,
had raised Theodosia like a son, affording her the best classical

education. At least one author has averred Mr. Burr's love for his daughter crossed over into carnal relations, and that Hamilton's hinting at this enraged Burr enough to demand the fatal duel.

Though most historians conclude the unfortunate woman was not a Burr. It is true Theodosia disappeared after a Chesapeake Bay shipwreck, and might conceivably have made it to shore with a lover, and they might possibly have made their way to Alexandria, a riverport in the Chesapeake basin. However, Old Town is 200 miles from the mouth of the Chesapeake, and the shipwreck occurred a full three years before the arrival of the Female Stranger at Gadsby's. Yet it is the kind of tale that is so good that one wants it to be true.

The unnamed woman was laid to rest at the graveyard of the Old Presbyterian, then new, having opened just seven years before. The table marker was erected over her grave. Some claimed to have seen the ghost of the Stranger hovering over her mortal remains. At Gadsby's, the lady's afterlife appearances are said to continue to this day. Believers aver these visitations take on physical manifestations. Inside the room where she suffered and died, candles and lanterns are lit and then snuffed out, apparently without human intervention. The room number on the outside of her door, Number 8, may appear lopsided, as if moved by a hidden hand.

At the Wilkes Cemetery tomb, the modern Female Stranger held her hand over the last lit candle, as if detecting a warmth from beyond the grave. She parted her luscious lips as Abdullah listened in, his pulse quickening from the deed he was contemplating.

The Stranger, her eyes closed in reverie, took up again the words of the memorial poem:

"To him gave all the Prophets witness that,

"Through his name whosoever believeth in Him,

"Shall receive remission of his sins,

"Acts 10th Chap 43rd verse."

Across two centuries, many have speculated why the presumed lover
ended his poem with these words. That he was a believing Christian,
even if sinful, seemed clear.

Perhaps, some thought, his affair with a married woman filled him with
guilt, as did her untimely death. And he attempted to atone with those
closing words.

But to Abdullah, those lines meant not atonement, but blasphemy. He
recognized it as a quotation from the New Testament, from the Acts of
the Apostles.

To him, referencing "all the Prophets" defamed The Prophet himself,
Mohammed, and by implication, Allah Himself.

Suddenly enraged, Abdullah reached inside his loose shirt for the short,
curved scimitar.

Just the night before he'd sharpened it to a diamond-like edge. It made
the perfect weapon for a beheading.

With firm and quiet step, he emerged behind the Stranger. His boots
rustled some leaves from the previous autumn, but the woman was in
such a trance she didn't hear his approach. He raised the Turkish blade
up high…

…Harmony had walked swiftly away from Ted and his bike. Far from
accepting the end of their walk, her thrill-seeking self spurred her into
another exploration. She left him at his flat tire, and was 70 yards down
Hamilton Lane before she thought of looking back. Then, while
striding fast, something caught her laser-like eyes.

At first, she thought they were headlights, from the traffic of the
Wilson Bridge beyond the cemeteries. But no, such illuminations

would be cloaked by the high sound barrier girding the highway, and by the tall trees enclosing the graveyards.

'More likely flashlights,' she thought, 'some other visitor here.' But the faint glow wasn't steady, like flashlights, but flickered. 'Like candles!' she realized, as she moved onward. 'But who in Heaven's name would light candles in a graveyard? What is this, Halloween in early summer?!' She quickened her stride.

The idea of graverobbers then entered her mind. 'A silly thought, but still…' She figured she should call out to Ted. She looked back, and he was already covered by the spreading dark. She thought she could detect a metallic glint near his bike, or hers, but wasn't sure. 'His flashlight, or a reflection from the final rays of the sun?' she asked herself.

Harmony kept pushing ahead, her bike shoes clacking, and found herself over a hundred yards up the Lane. The lights ahead were clearer now. They were definitely candles, she perceived. And at least three of them, she estimated. Did she see a fourth?

Harmony Jain squinted, and seemed to make out shapes underneath and behind the lights. The candles seemed to be floating on air. Or were they on a platform of some sort? And just behind them was another shape, something dark. At first, it seemed like a black, triangular blanket. Then, as she moved closer, Harmony saw it was a figure, a person, bending down near the candles. 'Maybe this *is* a grave robber,' she told herself, half seriously, half in jest.

She was 30 yards from the table grave when the dark triangle resolved itself, into the shape of a woman. Harmony stumbled, from a loose brick in the path, and kept going…

…In the north end of the cemetery, a frustrated Ted finally looked up from examining his bicycle wheel. He didn't have a small "pinch flat", but a ripped tire. And the wheel's metal rim might have bent.

"It looks like one for the bike shop for sure," he said out loud. "And maybe a new wheel." He heard no reply, and looked over toward Harmony's Felt. She wasn't there. "Shoot!" he muttered. She had just taken off, as she sometimes did. As he often did, just blindly following an impulse. It was an endearing trait, he supposed. Though annoying at times.

Then the fear that had gnawed at him when entering the cemeteries redoubled. At dusk, Harmony had taken off by herself, into a graveyard, with a killer or killers on the loose.

"My God!" Ted exclaimed. He rose up and, with tingling of fear in his stomach, began running into the darkness of Hamilton Lane.

Meantime Harmony, 20 yards from the table grave, made out another dark shape, one behind the female stranger. It was a man, standing up behind her, his form partly illuminated by the candlelight. 'What an unusual couple,' thought Harmony, striding apace. Then she stopped. Would they resent her presence? Then she spied another flickering light. A fifth candle? It was a metallic glimmer rising up above the woman. Harmony *saw*. It was a knife!

And the woman seemed oblivious to it.

The man was about to stab her!

Meanwhile up the path Ted ran, his right knee aching. He made out the figure of Harmony ahead. She was walking fast, and his damn knees would take him some time to reach her. He started to call out, then paused when he saw her stop cold.

And heard her yell.

"NOOoooo!"

Her cry echoed along the countless mounds of the dead.

Ted felt the pit of his stomach convulse. He sprinted down the Lane...

...Abdullah had his victim lined up. He would plunge the blade into her jugular: a quick, fatal blow.

He remembered his cell. First the kill. Then the ritual beheading, captured on video. A wonderful capstone to his mostly frustrating, wasted years in Alexandria.

He fully extended the sword above his head. His right hand gripped it firmly. The woman had begun reciting the blasphemous poem again. As his fury grew, he saw she was still unaware of the Avenging Angel above her. He grinned. Abdullah pulled back his hand three inches, the muscles in his biceps tensing. He was ready.

Then came a piercing cry.

"NOOoooo!"

His arm froze and, startled, he looked up the Lane. A woman was standing on the brick path, no more than 20 yards from him. Her mouth was still open from her shout, her lips, as in an Edvard Munch painting, twisted in shock and fear.

Abdullah shifted the hand holding the blade as the woman below him, her trance broken, began to lift up her head. He glanced down at her throat. The shawl had fallen over her jugular vein, concealing it.

Abdullah hesitated, trying to figure where the vein was. He struck out his free hand to rip away the shawl.

As he did, he looked up the Lane again. The woman there now seemed to be the one in a trance. And instead of being terrified, she seemed to have taken on a blank, even calm, expression: a determined, almost fatalistic one. And she was walking his way again!

As Abdullah stood, sword in hand, he saw, and heard, another figure in the gloom.

Someone who was running down the path behind the approaching woman, his footwear soundly on the bricks.

Abdullah growled in frustration. To the startled Stranger it sounded like the roar of a wild beast. He brought the sword down to his chest, and smashed its handle across the woman's cheek. Her head crashed down upon the table grave, blood spilling from her mouth across the poem.

Harmony saw this. Her pace slowed as she came within five yards of Abdullah. Though outwardly calm, she thought she was in a nightmare. In an encounter, weaponless, with a wild animal ready to devour her.

The Stranger's head and neck were on the tablet; she was moaning. Abdullah smacked the back of her head with a fist—then rushed toward Harmony. She, and he, heard a cry from behind her.

"HARmoooooony!' shouted Ted, racing up the Lane, pumped up by adrenalin, fear, and concern.

Abdullah bull-rushed Harmony. As he did, she stopped, cringed, and held up her arms to protect her head. As he closed he raised the sword high above his left shoulder, then sent the blade slashing down.

Ted had closed to within five yards. He saw the flash of the sword, and shouted out a wild animal cry. He pulled down his head to his chest, and sprinted at the terrorist.

As Abdullah slashed at Harmony, she reflexively ducked down to her left, away from the blade. The sharp metal hit her, but missed the neck where her tormentor aimed. Instead, he cut her some between the right elbow and biceps, with his arm smashing into her side. The force of the blow knocked her down. Blood from her wound dripped onto the bricks.

Even as Abdullah swung the blade down, he saw Ted closing fast. The latter was aiming his broad shoulders at Abdullah's left side, away from the blade.

Abdullah pirouetted like a bull fighter, twisting his body leftward, making Ted miss. As Ted rushed by, Abdullah stuck out a leg, tripping him. As he fell forward, Abdullah smashed the sword handle into Ted's tailbone, sending him hurtling.

Ted felt like he was in a bicycle crash with his body flying over the handlebars. Instinctively, he threw out his hands. He landed, stunned, on his chest and arms.

Abdullah took quick stock of what he had wrought.

Harmony was on the ground before him, gasping. Ted a few feet beyond, woozy, dazed, and the Stranger unconscious, or worse, her head and upper chest prostrate on the table. He judged he could finish off all three of them. The woman nearest him, who was the most conscious, and thus posed the most danger, would be first. Then this man. Then the praying woman could be disposed of more leisurely.

Or maybe not. Some of the caution of his military training came back to him. The bullrush of the man and the appearance of the other woman was alarming. Did they have friends or family with them, possibly right up the walkway? Had someone else heard the commotion?

He was sweating hard, and thinking fast, somewhat confused. Did these two call for help before rushing at him? Contact the police? He couldn't be sure.

Killing three people, instead of the lone, helpless woman at the table grave, he thought quickly, confusedly, would take little time, but perhaps just enough time for the police to get here, and capture him, and prevent him from joining the noble mission in New York. On the other hand, he thought furiously, 'Shouldn't I kill any witnesses?!'

As he tried to decide, he heard the woman on the ground moaning. To his surprise, she began to rise, like a ghost from one of the graves. Ted, though silent, had gotten over the initial shock of slamming into the ground, and started to stir too. And the woman on the table grave as well.

Abdullah made up his mind. He ran. Fast. Away from Hamilton Lane, high-stepping over graves toward the northern edge of the cemeteries. Harmony got to her feet, shaking her head to clear her mind, and feeling pain in her injured arm. She saw Ted get on his knees; he didn't seem badly hurt. She looked toward the Stranger, who was in bad shape. Harmony heard the sound of someone running, and saw the attacker heading toward Jamieson St. Reflexively, she started to jog toward him, very slowly at first, then faster.

Ted stood up groggily. He eyed the woman at the table grave, and in his confusion and in the darkness thought it was Harmony. 'Is she dead?!" he shouted to himself. He staggered over, elbows aching, palms bruised, and slowly raised the woman up by her shoulders. It was the Mysterious Stranger! She was breathing, yet bruised and bleeding. He lay her carefully down against the tablet. His mind cleared. He heard noises from the north of the complex. He saw a female figure running steadily that way. He recognized Harmony's running gait. Well ahead of her he could barely make out another figure. The man he had bull-rushed! And no doubt had attacked the Stranger. And attacked Harmony too!

Ted was momentarily unsure. Should he stay with the injured woman? But he had to help Harmony. He started walking fast, then running, toward her. As he did, he reached for his cell, to call 911 for an ambulance. He had to stop for a second to get the phone out of his bike shirt. As he did, he dimly perceived the attacker reaching the St. Paul's Episcopal cemetery, near the grave of James Mason, the Confederate diplomat, not far from the Jamieson St. exit. Harmony had closed on him, and then, growing wary, had run over to the other side of

Hamilton Lane to keep her distance. Ted realized this and thought, 'Smart. He might have a gun. Still, from that range he might easily shoot her!'

Ted grabbed his cell, and cursed. He had, as usual, many apps open, and couldn't immediately find the phone app. He began running again, glancing at the phone, then staring ahead. His right knee ached, his lungs felt like he'd run ten miles, but he made up ground rapidly. He saw the attacker climb over the railing onto Jamieson. Harmony stopped at a gate 40 yards away from the man.

The historian ran up and over the grave of General Corse and rushed up to his friend. She was gasping from exertion, and held two fingers to the gash on her arm.

Ted touched her hand and said, "How badly are you hurt?"

Though breathing hard, she answered in a level voice, "I don't really feel it." The adrenalin was masking the pain for now. Her arm was bleeding, but not as much as before. Together they watched the assaulter cross the Hooffs Run Bridge, and head into the path paralleling the stream that went back into Old Town.

As they spoke, Ted looked at his cell, found the phone icon, and was about to press it when he heard Harmony cry out.

"He's getting away!"

"Let's get him!" reacted Ted. 'Maybe,' he thought, 'he's Tony's killer!'

They rushed across the street. Up and down Jamieson, there was no one in sight. Few of the houses along the way had lights on. There were few cars along the curbs.

It was as if the atmosphere of a graveyard had bled into the adjoining homes.

Chapter 43 – Phantoms in the Watery Night

At the Hooffs Run bridge, they stood on the side of the stream and stared down the path. It was wrapped in darkness; there were no streetlights along the little-used space.

A short but steep embankment led down the paved way to the running water. Across from them, just below the bridge, was a brick shed, a utility shack. The kind of structure that maintenance workers might open up perhaps once a year. Oddly, its door was ajar. Had the attacker been in it?

Then they saw a dark shape move near the end of the path, where it approaches Duke St., and where the stream exits from a pair of arched, concrete tunnels. From that point Hooffs Run is underground, streaming below Duke St. from Old Town.

"It's him!" hissed Harmony, her bright eyes peering through the dark. "He's moving down the path to the stream!"

Ted could barely make out his form. They ran down the path in pursuit, their bike shoes clattering on the asphalt. Where the figure had entered the stream, they heard splashing. The man was swimming toward the tunnels!

In the darkness, Ted began climbing over a short fence between the path and the stream.

"What are you doing?!" blurted his friend.

"Call 911! Get help for that woman! And tell the cops to get here fast!"

Harmony couldn't believe it. She watched Ted skitter down the embankment. Seconds later, he dove into the stream! More of a bellyflop, actually. But he was a good swimmer, and made slow but steady progress toward the archways…

…As he had headed to the path along the stream, Abdullah felt frustrated at the unlucky, unexpected arrival of the man and the woman. Things were all set for an easy kill, and a beheading, and viral, Internet glory. Then these two had intervened.

Brave people too, making a rush at him, instead of fleeing. Now they were pursuing him. He, who had been the predator moments before. If they got close enough, or even not, they would scream, call out, alerting the neighbors or any police passing by. They might be calling the authorities at this moment! He might be captured, which might lead to the unmasking of the mosque, the imam, even the New York plot. He had erred, he had sinned, that was clear. Allah was punishing him for his vanity. He prayed he might escape, if only to spare his colleagues capture and prison. If his prayers were answered, he vowed he would thereafter focus totally on the Freedom Tower plot, and neglect his foolish Old Town schemes.

The two in pursuit, he felt, were a most dangerous kind of foe: Courageous, energetic, and able to improvise. He thought back to Afghanistan, and to the U.S. Marines and British Special Forces who possessed similar traits.

Yet they were only civilians. And he had at least followed the basic tradecraft the day before of studying the streets around the cemeteries. He decided against escaping along Jamieson. Its east end ran past an apartment building and its strange, small adjoining cemetery, and then to busy S. Washington St. Its west end was a better possibility, as it went over to the Patent and Trade Office buildings. Largely deserted due to telework, they were a ghost town at night. But streetlights lit up their exteriors. He might be spotted, maybe by police, who might be already on the way.

When he got to the bridge, breathing hard, sweating, scared of being caught, he looked back at the cemetery fence. He saw, or thought he saw, a human form or two. He thought he heard a shout. Yes, two forms. And they began moving. Toward him! That annoying duo. Those mysterious strangers. Abdullah started running down the path. He knew this way wasn't ideal either. It ended at busy Duke St. Or relatively busy, at night during a pandemic. The street would be lit, but the traffic should be very light, he judged. But it was a broad boulevard, and if those two pursued him there, they might spot him, and pursue him, along its expanse.

He was two-thirds of the way to the water tunnels when he heard them. Voices down the path. He turned and saw their shapes. He could confront them, and probably kill them. But that man might give him some trouble. And that heinous woman might run for assistance. She was fast; help might arrive before he got away.

A quick escape without any more fighting was best. He looked at the stream. Could he? Yes, he could slip down there, and hide in the water. It was about 10 feet across, and he figured it shouldn't be too deep. His pursuers might not see him enter the stream. As soon as they left, he'd get out. He wasn't planning on this but, in the fury of the moment, it seemed a logical move.

The iron fence along the path was only three feet high, with no barbed or razor wire. He climbed over, and stepped fast down the slope, and entered the water. It was cool, not cold.

Tolerable. But that was not what worried him. The water was higher than expected, neck-high, and was moving along fast. From all the rain of the past week. It was hard to walk in, better to swim in. But he was a weak swimmer now. There had been no pool in the prison. His swim training to blow up the Wilson Bridge was two decades in the past. He took some slow steps forward, then doggy-paddled, with much effort, against the flow and toward the tunnels.

He paused, his feet touching the bottom, and looked up the slope to the path. He stayed down low, just his nose and eyes above water. He barely suppressed a cough after swallowing some of the water, which was dirty—the stream coming from the town was little better than sewage. As the current swirled past him, it was hard to stay in the same place.

Again he cursed himself for disobeying the imam. He deserved this for his sin. Again he swore to never disobey again, and to succeed in his New York mission—if Allah forgave and gave him the chance!

Then he heard his two pursuers. He looked down the water course, and saw something—it was the man, he was climbing over the fence! When his pursuer got to the water, he might very well be spotted. If he hadn't been already.

To keep an eye on Ted, Abdullah walked backwards, the stream pushing against his back, his hamstrings and lower back straining from the effort. His movement was further hindered by having to keep his head so low. He saw his nemesis enter the water. But he seemed to be having the same problem with the current. 'Good,' thought Abdullah, 'otherwise he might catch up to me in seconds.'

But then he was startled to hear a shout from above.

There, Ted! He's there! Just ahead of you!"

'It's that horrid woman,' Abdullah thought. 'Ted must be the name of this infidel pursuing me.' Frightened, the terrorist walked backwards hard against the current until his hamstrings burned. He neared the entrance to the tunnels. He heard splashes behind him. His pursuer was closer. Had this Ted spotted him? Would his wretched companion enter the water and pursue him as well?

Abdullah turned and looked into the tunnels. The water flowed from subterranean cisterns that were under a stone platform with a door at its rear. In front of him were steps leading up to the platform. Might the door provide an escape route? Or lead to an inescapable trap?!

The splashing behind him stopped. Was his pursuer worried about confronting him? 'He should be,' thought Abdullah. 'He might meet his doom here.' Seizing the moment, he scampered out of the water and onto the steps. His legs were heavy, his soaked clothes heavier still. He slipped and almost fell.

He turned awkwardly and saw that the man had stopped swimming, and was not far from him. His head and neck were out of the water. He was looking up at the platform; he seemed to spot Abdullah.

'How to stop him?' Abdullah thought in a frenzy, and came up with an idea. He shouted out: "I have a gun. I'll shoot it!"

Ted was standing up, water swirling by his chin, trying not to be swept downstream while trying to spot the assaulter. His ears were sopped up with water, and he heard only a portion of the man's shout. Something about a gun? Was he about to shoot?!

Acting on instinct, Ted ducked under the water, and let his feet go. He floated downstream about 15 yards, enough he hoped to throw off the attacker's aim.

Abdullah made his move. He rushed up the steps to the door. He breathed a prayer, and tried the handle. The door was unlocked! He entered.

In the soft red glow of an infrared light, he perceived a corridor. It went forward for about 40 feet until fading into blackness. Where did it lead to? To a dead end? In which case, he was trapped. Like a rat. A sewer rat.

He took shallow breaths in the dank air. Surely, he thought, such a corridor was there for a purpose. It must lead somewhere, it must have an exit. He turned the latch to lock the door. His drenched phone was useless as a flashlight. He began feeling his way along the passageway. Meantime Ted came to a stop in the water and then, worried about bullets, lunged to his left. He stopped again, keeping as submerged as possible. He heard Harmony call out from the pathway above: "Ted, where are you?!" He said nothing, no wanting to give away his position, and wishing Harmony would stay silent, and not give away her position. He waited about half a minute. The police should be arriving soon, assuming Harmony had got through to them.

He quickly thought things through. It was ridiculous, he surmised, to continue confronting a violent thug without a weapon, in a place where it was very hard to see and to move about, and when there was likely help on the way. He let himself drift down the stream for another 25 yards. Then he stroked over to the shore. Crouching, he slipped back up to the fence. Harmony was there. He looked back toward the tunnels. He saw no one.

Harmony stared into Ted's bloodshot blue eyes. Ted looked at her wound, stained with blood, and hugged her hard around the waist. "I'll be okay," she said. He whispered, "He's escaped, I think, into an underground chamber."

Despite their fear, they walked warily up to the end of the path, and to Duke St. They crept cautiously over to the sidewalk atop the tunnels. They eyed the Patent and Trade Office and the Motley Fool offices up the street, the George Washington Masonic Temple rising tall past the train depot, and the site of the antebellum slaving firm structure across

the way. The boulevard, devoid of traffic, of pedestrians, was as
deathly quiet as the cemeteries.

Hooffs Run went under Duke St., either across it or veering down
eastward toward the Potomac or, perhaps diagonally, toward Diagonal
St.

But they saw no sign of the attacker. Was he trapped in the
subterranean part of Hooffs Run? He'd disappeared, gone like a ghost
in the gloom.

Then they heard the shriek of sirens approaching. They saw the whirl of
lights down the cemetery side of the path. From the Old Town side of
Duke St., police cars came rushing in, and pulling up.

Out of one stepped Greco. Ted was glad it was him, not FBI Man.
Greco stared at Ted, who was soaked, and at Harmony, who was
holding her bleeding arm. He told the pair, "You certainly have noses
for trouble."

Ted, pointing toward the subterranean passage, told him urgently: "We
chased a man who attacked a woman in the cemetery. I chased him into
this tunnel!"

Greco blinked hard. He turned to the nearest cop, and ordered him and
two other patrol officers to climb down into the stream, and search the
tunnels.

It started to rain again. Ted told the cops to be very careful of the high,
rushing water.

"I already sent men to the cemetery, right after Harmony's call," the
detective told the historian. Harmony asked if Greco had a map of Old
Town's sewer system. He twisted his mouth in a strange expression,
half annoyed, half appreciative. This woman, as Ted often was, seemed
at times steps ahead of the authorities. Which seemed suspicious at

times. Though more often helpful. Greco called up the city's sanitation department. At that time of the evening, he got no answer.

Meantime, down below, the cops were thwarted in their search by the locked door. A fire engine was on the way from Prince St., and Greco would have its firemen force it open. After Harmony gave him a capsule description of the attacker—athletic, tall, masked, dark pants and long dark shirt, she thought, the clothes soaked of course, and probably a foreign accent—Greco put out an all-points bulletin. He ordered other police cars to the graveyard, and still others to block off the area up and down Duke St., up and down Jamieson, and the west end of King St. near the train station. "We'll get him," he said. "I hope."

As the firetruck arrived, Greco, Ted, and Harmony inspected the sidewalk above the tunnels. There was no manhole entrance to it there. But there was a manhole a half block down Duke. Greco instructed several firemen, and an armed cop, to go down it and do a quick search. After several minutes, they emerged from the manhole, soaked with filthy water, to report it was a storm water runoff chamber. It did not connect to the tunnels.

Then Harmony did something that, though in character, caught the others off guard. She wandered off again. She took off directly across Duke St., following the presumed direction of the underground cistern, assuming it flows in a north-to-south direction. Ted caught up to her, and she told him: "Maybe Hooffs Run swerves at some point but, judging from the little plateau here and in front of us, I bet it goes right across Duke."

Ted replied, "Maybe the tunnel tracks the stream. Let's find out."

Greco and a few cops and firemen followed the duo to the north side of the boulevard. Near the curb they came up to another manhole cover. Greco asked a fireman to check it out.

It began to rain hard. Water poured off Greco's straw hat. Soon everyone was as soaked as Ted.

The historian-sleuth walked ahead, reconnoitering the area, wandering about, as he always did when in a new place, trying to find something novel or unusual. It helped make him a good tour guide; it would have made him a good military scout. Harmony joined him, and they went up to patch of shrubbery next to a parking lot. They came upon another manhole, half-hidden by some plants.

Its cover was off.

They called Greco and the others over. They all looked down it. They saw no sign of anyone. Greco had an eager young cop go down to the depths below. A minute later he climbed back up. He announced, "I shined my flashlight down three corridors, sir. I could see nothing. But those tunnels go a long way, I think." Greco wrung his straw hat in frustration. Later a team of firemen and sanitation workers did a thorough search, but found no one, and no clues.

The assaulter had apparently gotten to this spot through the underground passage, and emerged via the manhole.

And then vanished into Old Town, cloaked by the rainstorm, and his own cunning. The all-points bulletin would turn up nothing.

Chapter 44 – The Sleuths Rebound

Ted met Harmony at her fourth-floor loft apartment the next evening. Sitting at her dining table, they reviewed their wild recent experiences while Harmony glanced at online news stories about the "Cemetery Stalker".

For the first time, their names had gotten play in the media. Positive play. How they had saved a woman from being murdered, how they had chased after someone whom many of the TV stations and blogs assumed was the murderer. Who had escaped from them and, what was more, had given the slip to the cops and the federal agents.

As a result, the media, and City Hall and the City Council, again tore into the FBI and the police. Reporters noted pointedly the federals had arrived very late to the incidents at Wilkes and Duke Streets. Things got even more heated when a forensics scientist at the FBI crime lab leaked preliminary findings of the Female Stranger crime scene. The rainstorm had erased most of the footprints and blood spots around the Stranger's tomb site, where the ground had been torn up from the attacker's struggle with Ted and Harmony. One discernible print was approximately the same size as partial prints from the Christ Church Confederate mound and from the Old Presbyterian crime site. However, indications of the kind of footwear worn differed in each case.

Angry editorials demanded the removal of Comitas. Council Coordinator Forstandt, the Mayor and the Deputy Mayor, and a full majority of the City Council called for the suspension of Greco. In an online posting, the Mayor even voiced tentative support for suspending the town's ban on the concealed carrying of firearms in public places. Then came the "good news". On its social media sites, the *Alexandria Paddlewheel* compared Ted Sifter and Harmony Jain to the hijacked airline passengers who, on September 11, had taken on the terrorists aboard Pan Am Flight 93. "This valiant duo, in mimicking Todd Beamer and the other brave private citizens above Shanksville, Pennsylvania, seem to be the only persons fighting back effectively against an ongoing public menace. The law enforcement authorities and our political leaders, in contrast, seem hopeless, clueless, and feckless, in the face of our dire civil emergency."

The "heroes", weary and shaken by the previous night's events, but also resolute, recalled the attack's aftermath. As the police were departing Duke St., an ambulance had taken Harmony, with Ted accompanying her, to Alexandria's Inova Hospital's emergency room. An elderly Lebanese-American doctor had disinfected, anesthetized, and bandaged her arm, after determining the wound was not serious. The knife had not cut into muscle, so Harmony was able to move her arm, with some pain. Apart from scraped elbows and hands, and balky knees sorer than ever, Ted was unhurt. Harmony was released later that night, and on leaving the hospital she and Ted came upon an orderly pushing a wheelchair, where sat a raven-haired woman with a sad, thoughtful expression. It was the Mysterious Stranger. Cassandra Benedita was conscious, and she gave Ted a weary look of recognition. She had welts on one of her cheeks, and bandages were wrapped around her neck and shoulders. The young lady appeared exhausted or drugged, probably both. If she wanted to express her gratitude, she was too weak to do so.

They inquired about her condition from an intern. The blow from the sword hilt, they learned, had bruised her neck and spine, but hadn't caused any spinal fractures. The blow to her face hadn't broken any bones. Two of her teeth were chipped. She was expected to fully recover.

Unfortunately, the traumatic incident had, temporarily at least, erased the attack from her memory. Much to the disappointment of the police and FBI, who hoped to gain information of the attacker, now an official suspect in the murders. They were also disappointed to learn, from questioning Ted and Harmony at the hospital, that neither had gotten a good read on the man. "It had been simply too dark," Harmony explained. Ted thought the assaulter had shouted at him with an accent that was "kind of Middle Eastern, or maybe Mediterranean." However, Comitas, who noted that Ted's ears were waterlogged at the time, discounted this. The FBI man was convinced the murderer would more likely have the accent of someone from the South or rural Midwest.

In Harmony's dining room, the amateur sleuths sipped takeout pho soup that Ted had brought along. Ted's Samsung phone, after its immersion in Hooffs Run, lay in a food container filled with salt. The aim was to drain away the moisture inside the cell, though Ted doubted it would ever work again. But he had to try. He had hundreds of tour and travel photos in it, and many images important to his historical research. Harmony had rigged up her hair dryer to blow air over it. With a fatalistic expression, Ted picked the phone up, and dramatically pressed the On button. To their surprise, it powered up and made a triumphant beeping noise.

"It's alive!" remarked Ted. "It's got its voice back." He looked over the apps. They were working fine.

"I wish I had photos of the attacker," he stated.

"I remember now!" said Harmony excitedly.

"Huh?"

"The sword man's voice. At the time, I was hurt, and, and was worried about you, about you getting out of that stream alive. I heard him shout at you, but it didn't really register." She licked her lips. "But I can hear him clearly now."

"Was I right? A Mediterranean accent maybe?"

"No. Further east. Middle East. Or even further east." She knitted her prominent eyebrows in thought, which made her look even more feline. "From my years growing up in South Asia, I swear I know that accent."

"Well, *your* ears weren't waterlogged," said Ted, unable to resist a jibe at Comitas.

"I know that accent," she answered firmly. "It's not Middle Eastern. It's Central Asian. Pakistani maybe. More like Pashto."

Ted looked at her iridescent eyes. "You mean the language of the Pashtuns. The main language of Afghanistan."

She looked at him in mutual comprehension.

Ted keyed his phone's first text message since its resurrection:

"Mr. Greco: If you haven't already, please check any DNA from the Stranger's tomb against the prison escapee. That Hamaas guy."

There was an instant response; the detective texted he'd focus his team on it. And asked Ted to explain why. Ted said he would get right back to him.

"Is Sword Man the killer?" Harmony asked.

"Maybe." Ted slowly shook his head. "But I don't think so. Not that killer. I'm convinced the other bloody attacks were the work of someone with deep ties to Old Town. I think there's more than one nut job running around the city. And at least one robber."

Indeed, despite the near-death experience at the cemetery, Ted was intent on investigating the last site in his robbery thesis. Earlier in the week, Greco had listened with interest to his theory, but declined to assign police to guard the place in question. He explained his force was stretched thin. And that patrols already went by the locale Ted had in mind, as it was so close to City Hall and to the Christ Church murder site.

Ted and Harmony agreed they would tackle the task themselves, and on that very night. The incidents at the Athenaeum, the old Bank of Potomac home, and at Burke & Herbert had all occurred at night or early in the morning. So they determined to arrive at the place around midnight. They spent the next few hours further deliberating the case, then taking a nap together on the sofa.

They awoke excited for their next adventure. As Harmony's arm was too sore to hold onto her handlebars, they left their bikes behind, and walked the half dozen blocks over toward Ted's "sweetest history sweet spot", the corner of Cameron and N. Fairfax Streets.

Old Town was as usual deserted, particularly so that late at night. The clouds overhead, paired with a light, intermittent rain, made the glow of the few lights in the side streets more diffuse than usual. Harmony wondered aloud if the warm, rainy weather was prolonging the viral outbreak. At S. Royal St. they passed the backyard of the old Arsenal, now a playground, but roped off to forbid children from frolicking there and perhaps catching the disease. At Prince St. they happened upon a lone jogger, triple-masked, and running with his dachshund. On seeing Ted and Harmony approach, the runner skittered across the street, though whether he feared an infection or a murderer was unknown.

They reached a wet and desolate King St., its stores shut down for the night or shuttered long-term. Speckles of rain looked like teardrops on the window panes. No police, nor almost anyone else, were seen. They crossed N. Fairfax, where Herb Harrison had spied the burglar sprinting away from Burke & Herbert. They left behind its stolid pile of art deco stone, so out of character with the street's prevailing, Colonial Era dwellings. They walked through Market Square, treading slowly past its fountain, its pool half-filled with rainwater, but its water pipes shut down to discourage gatherings on the public commons. They recalled the cold reception to the speech Ted gave inside City Hall. They passed the old police precinct house, the starting point of the recent fracas that ended up at the Thomson school, as well as the 1897 lynching that ended a block away on Lee St.

On seeing the weathered police precinct sign, Ted reflected on that racial murder of long ago. He suddenly stopped.

"That's it!" he cried, in a low but harsh voice.

"What is it?!" asked Harmony.

"The image, that awful image in my mind, from the Freedmen's Cemetery. It was of the lynching, of the lynching of the young man, over a century ago; he was being kept at the old precinct house here.

"My memory was of an illustration of the event, from a newspaper back then, that showed the youth hanging from the lamppost. It looked almost exactly like Cordero, the man hanging from the Freedmen sculpture. Or I should say the Freedmen hanging looked just like the illustration."

The two stopped, and stood a in silence for a moment. Then Ted, his face looking pale, spoke up. "The treasure aside, whoever's committing the murders is channeling, reenacting, violent incidents from the past. Old Town's past."

Harmony thought about it, and tended to agree, but was more worried about any immediate peril. "Well," she answered, "we're now a half a block away. We need to be careful."

A lone policewoman on patrol emerged from the northeast corner of City Hall. The duo stopped in their tracks. Technically, they wouldn't be trespassing; the Carlyle House grounds were open at all hours. However, they preferred to go about their mission without questioning or interference. The lady cop disappeared up Cameron St.

They entered the lawn of the grand Carlyle manse. The frontispiece of its restored stone and stucco walls was draped, as it sometimes was, with black bunting. Marking a tragedy of some kind. Perhaps the anniversary of the death of General Braddock, who had planned his disastrous French and Indian War expedition from inside. More likely, a bow to the town residents who'd recently been slain. A grimmer atmosphere near City Hall couldn't be imagined.

"Let's hope," stated Harmony, her sensitive nature oppressed by the surroundings, "that we finally find something to be happy about tonight." Ted said quietly, "We're certainly overdue for good news." He thought of their map, and how it seemed to be missing vital information about Carlyle's property. 'If only we had a complete chart!' he told himself.

Chapter 45 – The Intruder's Approach

The intruder appeared like a warm dark breeze, outfitted in black pants, dark brown shirt, dark green daypack, trail running shoes and black ballcap. He glided along gracefully, almost invisible in the gloom. After parking at N. Lee and Pendleton Streets, masks pulled tightly over his face, he had made for Founders Park. He looked around furtively for pedestrians or police, and saw none.

With a graceful, determined lope, he reached N. Union St., and the long-unused train tracks leading to the old Robinson Terminal Warehouse. Once a storehouse of grains, then of paper and pulp for the now-dying print edition of *The Washington Post*. In the digital age, it had become a humble depot for a kitchen equipment firm supplying the new and restored townhomes of Old Town.

Across Union St. had been the Hugh West tobacco warehouse, which preceded the founding of Old Town itself. Now it was the construction site of the wastewater treatment plant. The interloper strode from the pricey condos on Union and entered the park. He was glad for the lack of streetlights there, which was near the Colonial Era shipment point for tobacco, and slaves, who rolled the hogshead barrels of the savory stuff down to the river.

Clinging to the darkened riverfront, his sinewy form edged along the boulders and clumps of shade trees along the Potomac shore. The river was high from the tide and the rains. Plastic bottles and logs and pieces of driftwood outlined a recent flood's high-water mark.

He stepped carefully through the detritus; a twisted ankle would be ruinous to his type of work. He wondered if he should have taped his ankles. He passed the deserted volleyball court, girded by sagging plastic tape to discourage children from playing. A few Canadian geese were on the paved walking path, and skeins of ducks floated near the piers. For weeks almost no tourists had tossed them their customary scraps of bread. A ripple on the water indicated the splashes of catfish, also ever on the prowl for easy sustenance, but also denied it for now. Toward the south end of the park, some lights glowed along a boardwalk, so the intruder slipped back into the park proper, and returned to Union St. He just had a half block to go before becoming invisible again.

Despite his dangerous mission, he ever enjoyed walking outdoors, savoring the fresh air as he moved acrobatically along. To his left was the massive bulk of the main building of the Torpedo Factory. The World War One Era project, a 100,000-plus square foot complex that once manufactured weapons for the Navy's submarine fleet. The war ended before a torpedo could be launched. However, the Factory had great effect in the succeeding world war. Big initial problems— warheads that didn't explode, or that detonated too soon—were overcome. Some 5,000 machinists, designers, and administrators churned out 10,000 of the deadly cylinders, put to use against Imperial Japan's merchant fleet, largely sunk as a result. Starved of fuel and food from its overseas conquests, Tokyo's economy became a walking dead man even before Hiroshima.

A converted artist colony since the 1970s, the Torpedo Factory now has office studios for dozens of sculptors, painters, craftsmen. The intruder smiled in fond memory. The place was the scene of one of his most lucrative takeaways: hand-wrought, silver-and-platinum medallions of historical scenes. They'd brought in a five-figure sum.

To his right was another hulking Torpedo Factory installation, converted into a parking garage. Then he spotted a taxi parked in front of its entrance ramp, and halted. There was no way around it, except to go back into the lighted section of the park, or to reverse course and go around the block up Cameron St. He stared at the vehicle. The engine of the Ford Fusion was running, but he saw no driver. Had he gone into the garage? Taking a chance, the intruder quickly walked by, unseen. He approached the well-lit intersection of Union and King Streets, and his 'secret passageway'. This desolate back alley behind King St., dating from the Revolution, had various names. Near the Torpedo Factory it was known as Fayette Alley, as in Lafayette, with the "La" chopped off, as it often was in American locales named after the great Marquis. The heroic Frenchman who'd visited Alexandria during his grand 1824 reunion tour of the United States. Toward its top end it was dubbed Ramsay's Alley, after Scotsman William Ramsey, the Old Town founding father.

Fayette Alley and Ramsay's Alley have another, wonderfully expressive, moniker: Sharp's Alley. Before Hamilton set up his Treasury, lending America a currency of its own, townspeople would pay for goods with foreign coins like Spanish doubloons and Portuguese escudos. A gold coin might be worth, well, a pretty penny. Often worth much more than what a buyer was purchasing at Market Square or in the shops along King. So he'd cut the coin up with a sharp blade, into quarters perhaps: thus the term "a quarter". And stick the unspent quarter pieces in his pocket. But the metal edges were sharp, and might cut their way through his trousers. And drop onto the cobblestones of Sharp's Alley.

"Sharp's" had a second, ironic meaning. The back alley was the hangout of prostitutes and robbers, or "sharps", both keeping keen eyes on the shiploads of sailors, their pockets bulging with pay, on shore leave after a long voyage. The dark, out-of-the-way alley was the perfect place for assignations or robberies.

Yet the intruder felt safe there, at home almost. He sauntered up the cobbled path, framed by the high rear walls of warehouses-turned-restaurants. They had the wide, upper-floor windows for hoisting up tobacco, whiskey, and grains, hauled up and away from the dirt and damp of riverfront streets, or the flooding Potomac. Some still had pulley wheel boards sticking out from the roofs.

Garbage bins were pushed up to the back doors. Rats scurried about some of them. 'They look smaller than the wharf rats of several years ago,' the passerby noticed. With most restaurants and shops closed, and with little trash around, the creatures did seem smaller.

He examined the three-and-four-story buildings with a professional's eye. Most only had thin iron bars around their ground-floor windows. Access to the second floors, or even the third or fourth, was easy via the drainage pipes, or by climbing along the window ledges.

Some establishments lacked floodlights, and others had lights that weren't illuminating. After the pandemic, he thought, there could be many a cash register begging for a picking. But for now, he sought far greater lucre.

Up the sloping path, toward the end of the alley, Market Square became visible across N. Fairfax St. On his immediate left rose a former warehouse. Its bottom floor now an ice cream shop, a few floors below an attic room, reputedly haunted by the doomed Laura Schaefer.

But before reaching Fairfax, the intruder made a sharp right into another alleyway. Narrow and grimy, it looked like something out of the Paris of Quasimodo. He stepped past a dwelling with walls blackened from the 1871 fire that nearly gutted City Hall.

The house was a private residence. All its lights were out: The owners were either dozing or had fled town. At the end of the alley, the intruder looked about carefully, saw no one, and climbed over a low wall. He was soon at a higher wall near the boundary of the Carlyle mansion.

It may have been a remnant of an extension to the old south wall of the Civil War's Mansion House Hotel. Five decades before, a regional authority had taken down the hostelry-turned-apartment building. Recently a construction firm had been hired to inspect the crumbling extension with a possible eye to removing it. From previous reconnaissance, the intruder knew digging there had created an opening from the lane that ran up from Sharp's Alley. He stepped down carefully into the excavation and came up on the other side, the courtyard of the mansion.

His lean, compact form stayed low as he crept across the grass. A very light mist began falling. On his right was the black bunting on the façade of the great manse. He drew up to the street entrance, its gate askew as usual. He slowly closed it, after glancing up and down and across Fairfax St. There was a police car at the corner of King. The two cops inside didn't notice him, and they soon drove away up the block. For now at least, there was no one on N. Royal St., or in Market Square. The City Hall offices across the way were darker than the mansion's bunting.

Though excited for the evening's task, in general he wasn't happy how things had gone. The death of the watchwoman at the Athenaeum had brought on unwanted attention. Knocking out the lawyer in his Prince St. home might have caused another serious injury or death. And of course, the failure thus far to attain his objective.

He wished he had paid more attention to the map, and had changed
the order of his attempts. He had been too orderly, going methodically
from A to B to C, instead of heading right away to the best prospect.
His chart had indications of a possible jackpot at the Bank of the Old
Dominion (the Athenaeum), at Swift's Alley, or here, William
Herbert's old Bank of Alexandria. Not so much the Bank of Potomac,
Mr. Lowell's residence. Though his break-in in there, he recalled, was
partly due to events. To the owner's leaving town, supposedly for a
week. It was simply bad luck that he returned when he did. Though it
was good fortune he hadn't been more seriously hurt.

Moreover, while his chart suggested the Bank of the Old Dominion as a
possible location for the treasure, it did not indicate a specific place.
Thus his search throughout the art gallery, and the unfortunate
encounter with the guard. He also regretted losing another, more worn
copy of the chart at the waterfront, when the wind had swept it away. It
might have contained additional clues. Still, on his map, the former
Bank of Alexandria at which he now stood pointed to a very specific
locale. 'Not exactly 'X marks the spot,' he told himself, as he looked
up at its shadowed hulk, 'but close enough.' At this place, on his map
was scrawled, barely visible, the letters, "JSS".

At first, he'd imagined they meant "Jonathan Swift, 'S' something'."
Silver perhaps? 'Hah,' he had thought, 'like Long John *Silver*.' Then, in
examining the chart under ultraviolet light in his home's workroom,
he'd perceived that the second "S" wasn't an S at all, but a $, a dollar
sign. And he learned from his readings that Swift's horde likely wasn't
in cash—paper currency was still a rarity then. Most people, most
merchants, carried out transactions with metal, like the cut-up
doubloons that had given Sharp's Alley its name.

He rubbed his hands together. 'I expect a large amount of bullion here! And perhaps jewels!' His plan was to first locate the treasure, and quickly carry some away. Then come back several more nights until the whole hoard was his. And he was a rich man. And a retired thief. A retired prince of thieves.

The map marked a place that was on the side of the bank, thankfully. No searching through an attic or cellar, like at Lowell's home, or at Burke & Herbert, where he had hoped to find some insights on the terrain here. 'This has to be the location of the treasure!' he thought excitedly. Then the professional in him turned skeptical. 'It might have somehow been destroyed, or pushed over to another spot, during the, what, 240 years of renovations and excavations here.' He frowned. 'Or it might have been discovered by another treasure hunter of long ago.' Or from today. There was that nosy, annoying historian, or tour guide, or writer, whatever he called himself. The guy who knew the bank manager who had come upon him at the Burke & Herbert attic. And who had been observing Lowell's Prince St. house—and the Athenaeum. It seemed possible he might discover the secret hoard of Jonathan Swift. If anyone was capable, it was him.

He had turned into a threat. He and that ugly girlfriend of his, from Mongolia, or wherever she was from, who had foiled the murder attempt at the Wilkes cemeteries. Those two were everywhere, it seemed.

He smiled; he was treating them too harshly. 'They should be running law enforcement around here,' he figured, 'not the incompetents who are! They deserve grudging respect: They might have caught me long before.

'Well, after tonight,' the intruder consoled himself, 'I may finally know if my efforts have paid off. I am getting too old for this, too old for break-ins and lurking about rooftops. I want a peaceful retirement in the Caribbean or Costa Rica!'

What a crowning glory it would be to a largely successful career, of pilfering the rich, and giving their holdings to the less well-to-do, namely himself. 'Not a bad ending,' he reflected, 'for a kid who started out with nothing."

If he failed, he reasoned, so be it. He was trying his best, after getting the chance of a lifetime for any thief or treasure hunter. His career had been one of derring-do, of living on the edge of, or outside of, the law. His recent acts had just been more unusual instances of the same.

He bent down under dark, cloudy skies, his trim figure hovering above the lawn, and got to work.

There was no need to refer to the actual map in his pocket. He had it long before memorized it. He reached behind him, to his tactical daypack, and felt the sturdy instrument inside. He glanced once more along Fairfax, assured himself it was deserted, and slinked over to the south side of the former bank, its darkened walls like the battlements of an ancient castle.

It was now a construction site. After years of wrangling and indecision, he figured, Alexandria had finally come down on the side of its tax base. He had read that preservationists and historians, including that Ted character, had wanted to restore the three-story red brick pile to its exact, original appearance, when it was the bank to President Washington. And turn it in to a museum of finance, the only one south of New York. With a special wing for the accomplishments of Washington's "right-hand man": Treasury Secretary Hamilton.

But critics and developers noted there were already three museums within two blocks of there. At the Stabler-Leadbeater pharmacy, Gadsby's Tavern, and within the Carlyle mansion itself.

Not to mention the Lee-Fendall Museum six blocks away. All of these museums are small, and have modest attendance. Would another one, and one devoted to a rather technical subject, be worth it? The town decided no. 'After all,' the intruder thought cynically, 'luxury homes mean even more revenues for Alexandria.'

His map showed the line of demarcation between the bank and the Carlyle House. And halfway between Fairfax and Lee Streets, on the lawn of the mansion, was an actual "X". Not that kind of X. But an X with legible terms on either side of it.

It read, "1/2 bet Water FFX, 10 FT".

The intruder had been baffled by the scrawl, and had wracked his brains without a solution. The "10 FT" was clear enough: ten feet, though less helpful without context, without knowing ten feet down, up, or across. He soon figured out that FFX meant Fairfax. But he puzzled over "1/2 bet Water".

At first, he foolishly thought Swift might have referred to a wager on a boat race, on the waters of the Potomac. Perhaps a bet at one in two, or half, odds. Surely the skippers of that busy port city must have prided themselves on the speed of their sailing ships. Perhaps they held races to prove who was fastest. And the river shore was very near the mansion. But, in combing through late-18th century editions of town newspapers at the Barrett Library, he found no ads or articles about such events.

Then, while at the Georgetown waterfront one day, he happened to pass a tour—given by Ted Sifter himself—at the intersection of Wisconsin Avenue, a main thoroughfare, and K St., the street paralleling the Potomac River park there. He overheard the tour guide note the shoreline, now 50 yards from K St., had once lapped against K St., which had then been called, logically, Water St. Later on, landfill had pushed the shoreline back. The intruder knew much of Old Town itself was comprised of landfill that had pushed back the original Potomac shore. So he went to the Barrett Library once more to look up maps from the late 1700s. He found that Lee St. had *itself* been called Water St., before the tidal flats were filled in, and before the byway was renamed Lee to honor the Confederate general.

The cryptic scrawl then made sense. "Water" meant the former street name. "bet" must mean "between" Water and Fairfax. And "1/2", or halfway between. The treasure, if it existed, should be exactly halfway between Fairfax St. and the old Water St., today's Lee St. And as the chart indicated, between the bank and the mansion. And, surely, 10 feet below the surface!

The intruder knew there had likely been settling and movement of the soil there across two centuries, partly from renovations to both buildings. Thus he brought along a device useful in casing out properties. A thousand-dollar Equinox metal detector, with a digital reader, able to sense objects up to 15 feet away. He hoped it would indicate a hoard of bullion. If not, it would save him much effort and time.

Keeping his head down, Anthony Lercino, master burglar, now crept from the entrance gate to the lawn's antique cannon. The brass of the gun, a relic from the French and Indian War, shone slightly in the dark. Lercino moved past it, and past the plaque explaining the mansion's role as a hospital for wounded soldiers of the Civil War. Slipping on his night-vision goggles, he moved over toward the Bank of Alexandria. A light mist fell upon the lenses, and he wiped the droplets off with gloved fingers.

Many of the bank's windows had been removed, he saw. Workmen had run scaffolding up the brick walls, and dug holes along the foundations.

Long metal tubes for tossing out debris, like the arms of a giant spider, ran from the upper floors to the ground. Large gray circuit boxes hung from some of the lower walls, or were set on the ground for later installation. Near them was a Bobcat Mini Excavator, its yellow color glowing dully.

Lercino took out his Garmin GPSMAP. He expected it to locate the halfway point between the bank and mansion boundaries with space-age accuracy. The thief stepped softly down a grassy slope, the bank to his left, manse to his right. When the mansion was built in 1752, this ground was over a steep river embarkment, and it still dropped sharply down toward Lee St. He was grateful for the decline: The depression cloaked his form from any passerby glancing into the yard.

He crept past the entrance of the mansion's museum, closed down for weeks. A sole light bulb above its doorway flickered faintly in the mist. Ahead was the shingled dome of the gazebo bordering the mansion's garden. Normally a favorite place for wedding receptions and engagement photos, now rendered vacant by the viral dread. He took a quick look at his Garmin. "Almost there," he mumbled excitedly.

Behind the bank he passed by a tiny parking lot on the side of Cameron St., just down and across the street from the old Wise Tavern. It was very close to where the Garmin indicated the halfway point. His mind rang with the phrase, "1/2 bet Water FFX, 10 FT". His heart rate picked up. Perhaps the moment had finally come, after the harrowing series of searches. 'If not,' he urged himself, 'it's still worth it.' The thrill of the chase, the excitement of robbing the rich and confounding the cops. The enduring motivations of a lawless life.

He put on the headphones of the metal detector. He slid the long thin apparatus out to its full length, and switched it on. He took another look around to make certain he was alone. He bowed his head, as if praying, and listened intently.

Nothing. That was to be expected. It was unlikely, even with the GPS, that he was standing on top of exactly the right spot.

He took five golf tees out from a pocket of his tactical pack. He placed one on the location indicated, and the other four in the corners of a square, each of them one foot from the first tee. He moved the detector over the square.

Nothing. He wasn't disappointed. Not yet. He would progressively expand the square outward, foot by foot, and check its outer border each time. He moved the tees out another foot, and listened hard.

Had he heard a faint noise from a part of the expanded square? In the direction of the bank? He knew it might mean nothing, but his heart quickened another beat. He bent down and moved the pegs outward another foot.

He listened harder, blocking everything else from his mind. It *was* a sound! And the noise was growing louder. And definitely coming from the ground toward the Bank.

But wait! Was it a sound from the detector, or something else?

It got louder, much louder.

The sound of footsteps!

Then a blinding flash in his eyes.

Then utter darkness.

Chapter 46 – A Suffocating Atmosphere

Ted and Harmony noted the relative lack of police presence near City Hall. They had spotted one of Greco's men at the corner of the main thoroughfare of Washington and King, and saw one police car pass through that intersection. There was no trace of the FBI. Of course, there might be undercover agents around, but they saw no one. The streets were as empty as the funereal grounds of Christ Church.

"Maybe they're off cornering 'The Joker'," said Ted in a low voice. "Or running down the 'Cemetery Stalker'." Indeed, in following up Ted's tip, Greco's forensics team had made a preliminary match on clothes fibers found on the fence above the Hooffs Run stream. The fibers contained fragments of genetic material, which were a close match to the DNA of Abdullah Hamaas, the prison escapee. That case, which had practically gone into hibernation after the Freedmen's killing, had revved back up again. And it embarrassed the FBI and Comitas, whose crime lab had been beaten to the punch by Greco's much smaller one.

Inevitably, as they approached the Carlyle manse, Ted thought of its incredible, and often bloody, military history. Of General Braddock, and the young Major Washington, and their ill-fated fight in the Indian wilderness near Fort Pitt. And the Civil War hospital, with its doctors, amputees, and rebel spies. Including the town's most colorful character of the "Late Unpleasantness", the slender, fair-skinned Confederate agent with a grandiose name, Benjamin Franklin Stringfellow. Early Americans loved naming their sons after Founding Fathers.

The Carlyle House, as the city's largest mansion, and then a hotel
complex owned by a Southern advocate, was a prime candidate for
confiscation and rejiggering as a Union Army hospital. And the
Northern officers recuperating there offered a matchless opportunity for
a rebel spy to obtain intel.

Benjamin Franklin Stringfellow trained as a dentist's aide, and gained
employment as such at the mansion. He befriended Union officers
recovering from jaw and teeth wounds. From them he elicited valuable
information on Union morale, supplies, and deployments.

Being slim, as befitting his last name, as well as lightly bearded and
rather feminine-looking, Stringfellow sometimes impersonated a lady.
And danced with and beguiled captains and colonels at Union soirees,
his alert ears pulling in military secrets as well as the sweet nothings
whispered in his ears.

Yet his efforts were endangered one day, when a Federal agent
recognized him in a street not far from the Carlyle House. The Yankee
gave the alarm. The lanky spy sprinted away. Armed men pursued him.
He ran fast: If captured, he'd be hanged as a spy.

Exhausted from his desperate flight, and about to be seized, he spied an
open door and ran into a townhouse. Inside was a Southern belle,
sitting at a table knitting. The spy implored her for help.

Outside, the agents surrounded the house, making escape impossible,
and barged in to get their man. Yet though they searched everywhere,
from attic to cellar, from kitchen to clothes closet, they found no trace
of Stringfellow. They harshly questioned the lady, but she insisted no
one else was in her house. Stymied, the Yankees left the home in great
frustration.

In hearing Ted's telling of this tale, and having been informed of
Stringfellow's skill at shape-shifting from man to woman, many tour

guests would guess that Stringfellow was the woman, having avoided capture by dressing up as a femme.

In fact, he avoided arrest and the hangman's noose by hiding in the house—under the hoop skirt of the Southern belle! One can imagine Stringfellow's angst while crouching under the ruffled skirts of his protector at the same time she was undergoing vigorous interrogation. One can also imagine the discomfort of the lady.

Ted smiled in recalling the story—there had been so few lighthearted moments in recent days. Then, hearing the rustle of Harmony's clothes beside him, he snapped back to the present.

In the black of the night the duo passed through the Carlyle House entranceway, and carefully shut the gate behind them. Ted reasoned the burglar would first concentrate on the Bank's construction site. The renovation work might do some of the criminal's work for him, having dug up the ground and revealed parts of the building that had long been hidden. So they headed there first.

The pair passed by the war cannon. Ted wiped droplets of a light mist from his glasses. Harmony bent down for a moment, borrowed Ted's flashlight, and examined the moistened lawn.

"What is it?" asked Ted.

"The grass looks disturbed, like someone went by here. Recently."

"Well, it could be our man," said Ted. "Or it could be anyone who came by here. Though not very many people are out and about."

"It's hard to tell in the darkness," she replied, "but I think there were two people here."

She got up, wiping her hands of the grass and mud, and they continued along.

Ted wondered if he should have brought along his Sig Sauer P320 handgun. However, since purchasing the pistol, he hadn't attended gun training classes or visited any gun ranges. Due to a lack of time, and the lockdown of the facilities. In any event, the weapon might do more harm than good in the hands of an amateur. He had thought that, if they encountered someone suspicious, he might try to make a citizen's arrest. After reflecting on that unlikely scenario, and on the Hooffs Run incident, he figured they would simply call Greco, or 911, and let the authorities detain the culprit.

To aid in the renovations, the fence separating the bank property from the mansion's lawn and back garden had been taken down in places. They went through one of the gaps. Some of the bank's windowpanes had been removed. Some of the plastic sheet covers on the window frames had been torn away, possibly by the wind and rain or, Ted thought, possibly by an intruder.

Ted shone the flashlight into the vacant space within. The old partitions had been knocked down, allowing them to see clear through to the foundation walls on the other side. These, like the Wise Tavern's foundation stones across the street, were very thick, to protect against the ravages of the Potomac's former shore. They saw no one in the ground floor.

"There must be stairs leading up to the other stories," suggested Ted. Harmony questioned whether they should go inside a darkened construction site, where a robber, or a murderer, might be lurking. She replied, "Why don't we first check the renovations outside?" She pointed toward the scaffolds and the Bobcat. "They're doing a lot of work on these exterior walls."

She looked around nervously, imagining Comitas arriving to arrest Ted for the second time. And imagining a killer lurking about. Despite her innate courage, her hands trembled in memory of the Wilkes cemetery attack.

Her friend nodded absently to her suggestion, as a story about the
Carlyle's manse's construction flashed through his mind. Ted often
brought tour guests across the lawn to its walls. Where he told them of
a strange superstition that Scotchman John Carlyle not only believed,
but had put into practice.

From time immemorial, Britons have feared the black magic of a black
cat. The same creatures featured in today's Halloween. The creatures
were said to possess evil powers, but powers that could be deployed for
a positive purpose. So, when his workers were laying the foundation
stones for his new home, Mr. Carlyle issued an unusual order. That a
black cat be walled up among the stones.

Walled up alive. To die slowly, in agony. Like the unfortunate man in
Poe's *The Cask of Amontillado*.

The workmen, with distaste, carried out their master's directive. The
terrified cat slowly suffocated. Its shrieks and wails, its caterwauls,
penetrated the thick stones out to the laborers on the lawn.

It was Carlyle's belief the angry spirit of the killed cat would forever
haunt the house, and scare away any other evil spirits attempting to
approach. The trick may have seemed to work, as the Carlyle House,
well into its third century, looked as sterling as it did when first built.
Of course, throughout the house's history the story was viewed as mere
superstition, a colorful tale with which to entertain tourists. But in the
1970s, the mansion complex was grandly restored for the nation's 1976
bicentennial. The antebellum, and post-bellum, hotel that had stood on
its front lawn was torn down. The only thing remaining were traces of
the struts that had held up its southern wall: These left ghostly blotches
on the adjoining building, now the Burke & Herbert branch office.

Construction crews gave the entire mansion a workover. While repairing foundation stones, they made a startling discovery, in a wall of the manse.

They found a skeleton of a cat.

The black cat that John Carlyle ordered sealed up within.

Carlyle was superstitious, but the Carlyle cat story was true. One of the many stricken spirits, perhaps, that haunts Old Town to the present day. The historian's mind came back to the here and now. He and his fellow sleuth stepped carefully toward a Bobcat excavator, watching out for holes dug in the ground. Ted looked down the slope at the gazebo, then toward the mansion museum's shuttered entrance.

Then out of the corner of an eye he saw something move. Move very fast.

A dark shape, low and horizontal, was on the darkened lawn. It was sniffing and scratching at the ground. For a moment he wondered if a canine had escaped from its kennel. He heard heavy breathing, and he saw a pen prick of light. From a penlight—held by Harmony.

She was on the ground, on all fours, scampering back and forth for all the world like a bloodhound. Ted hurried over.

Harmony lifted up a hand, and pointed the light under her chin, illuminating her eager face like a Halloween ghost, then shone the light toward the grass. "Do you see it?"

Ted bent down. He saw the blades of grass—and flecks of red.

Blood.

The moist grass around it was disturbed here as well. The scarlet-tinged blades were matted down or torn up.

He took his flashlight and studied the ground. He noticed clumps of something near the stained grass. A viscous, dully colored material. Something like paraffin.

Harmony scampered ahead. Between the excavator and the mansion's front lawn she found a long metallic rod.

"A metal detector?" asked Ted. It looked like the device he'd seen men carry when looking for coins at Ocean City Beach. He picked it up and looked it over. He was surprised how light it was. "It's high quality," he said. And heard no response from his friend.

Instead he heard scurrying and sniffing again. Harmony, still on her hands and feet, had moved off toward the mansion's entrance.

"There's a trail of blood leading this way!" she hissed.

Like a squire of yore on a fox hunt, like John Carlyle, or Lord Fairfax, Ted followed his friend across the grass. Harmony paused at the front entrance steps, under the ominous black bunting.

"Does it stop here?" she called out, and with great energy began scampering back and forth again, in all directions, looking to pick up the trace.

Then she leaned up on her haunches, her hands suspended from her chest like a dog begging for food.

"Listen!" she cried. Standing behind her, Ted cupped his ears. Though his night vision was nothing like Harmony's, he had excellent hearing. He thought he heard a dull thudding sound, but couldn't be sure.

"I hear banging," said Harmony excitedly. "And maybe a voice." She got up and, bent down low, stepped around the corner of the manse. They crept down the narrow strip of lawn along the manse's south side. The noises, though still indistinct, were louder. Harmony suddenly stopped, and got on her hands and knees again. "More blood!" she exclaimed. She seemed almost happy at the discovery. She jumped up, and they rounded another corner of the mansion, entering the back terrace and garden. The gazebo was visible on the far side through the mist. There were signs of construction work at the manse's southeast corner, the very oldest part of Carlyle's creation.

Where the thickest stones had been laid, to prevent the floodwaters of the Potomac from undermining the foundation. The stones were damp and darkened from 270 years of weathering, but still held up strong. Except for some that were on the grass. Grass that seemed disturbed. Ted could now definitely hear a voice, and a low pounding noise. The words the voice uttered were indistinct, but they sounded desperate, like a cry for help. For a moment, Ted felt he was in a garish nightmare, as if Carlyle's cursed cat was screaming out from another world.

Harmony was on hands and knees by the foundation stones, at where the voice seemed to be emanating. Shining the flashlight ahead, she scooted 20 feet along the lowest part of the wall, then scampered back. She looked up and said, "The blood trail stops here."

Ted found the scene surreal, and unnerving. A voice was definitely resounding from within. A human voice. A recording? It was as if an evil spirit was trying to communicate.

He got on his knees and peered at the stonework with Harmony. He felt along the edges of the gray, flat granite stones. They seemed as firm as ever.

The voice became louder, sounding like a shouted scream. And they could make out several of the words.

"Help!...Die...Choke...Ch—Choking!"

Alarmed, they pressed into action.

As Harmony shone the light along the wall, Ted pulled and pushed at every stone within reach.

"Here!" she shouted, pointed the beam about three feet off the grass, several feet from where the voice seemed centered. "Look! The stones here are off a bit!" She shone the light down and back along the wall. "They've been moved."

"And put back in place!" Ted responded, and felt a terrible dread as he again thought of the legend of the cat. He pulled at the stones, his fingernails splitting, his fingertips bruised by the edges.

It was hard to move the stones: They had been skillfully put back into their slots, making the wall almost as impenetrable as before. Harmony clawed ineffectively at them with her uninjured arm.

Sweat poured down Ted's face as in an all-out bike race while he tugged, pushed, and pulled frantically. The voice within was quieter, the screams turned to moans. Was someone in there dying?

At last, Ted forced a stone to slide. Then another. He tucked very hard on one, leaning back with all his weight, and it pulled out entirely. This made the remaining slabs easier to get at. He and Harmony attacked the wall, pulling out one stone after another, their hands covered with muck. Harmony cried out, her injured shoulder stabbed with pain. She and he kept at it. The voice bleated: "Choking!...Ne— need air!...Help!!"

Then a section of the wall, about three feet by three, caved inward. They reached into the cavity, and pulled out the slabs. "That hurts!" moaned the voice inside.

The two sleuths worked like demons, like devils in the night, as if possessed by the spirit of a condemned creature, sweating, grunting, tossing out the stones that had toppled in. As they worked, the stones became looser still, and easier to remove.

Then they stood up straight, took a step back, and Ted shone the flashlight into the opening they'd created. It was horizontal, about the length of a person, and about two feet high.

Inside it, a man was lying on his back. A thin person, 5-feet, 7-inches tall, lay groaning in a niche, between the foundation stones and an impenetrable wall behind. His pants, shirt, and daypack were covered in dirt, his hair filthy.

Between his feet and the foundation below them were the bones of small animal.

The man coughed violently, and swept dirt from his eyes and mouth. "Thank you!" he uttered, in a terrified voice. "Thank you, so, so much. It's like a, a tomb!"

He reached behind his head with his right hand, and brought it to his nose to smell. His fingers were pasted with blood.

What had happened seemed clear. Someone had taken him here, presumably after knocking him out on the lawn. And had placed him in the niche uncovered by recent construction work—the very niche where the black cat had been killed 270 years before. Then that someone had placed back the stones. So that the victim would, on awakening, die a slow, agonizing death.

With a handkerchief, Harmony wiped some of the dirt off his pant legs. Ted asked him, "Can you move?" The man wiggled his legs, and shook his head in affirmation.

"We better call an ambulance," Ted told Harmony. She punched 911 into her cell.

"No! Don't!" yelled the man. And Ted knew immediately who he was, and why he didn't want any official to arrive.

Then the man, lying exhausted in what could have been his grave, exhaled deeply, as if breathing out his last traces of energy. Any fight he might have had left in him seemed to slip away.

He looked at Ted, whose face was lit up momentarily by Harmony's light, and said, "You're Ted Sifter, aren't you?" Ted nodded. "And that's your friend, right, Harmony Jain?" The man grimaced and groaned. He reached up to flick bits of rock from his dark hair. "I've been following you in the news, the, the news accounts." Ted listened to him intently. He was pretty good at identifying accents, but this man's English was neutral. He could have been from the Midwest. Or the Mid-Atlantic. He definitely wasn't the man from the Wilkes St. Cemetery.

The fellow paused. His angular face became expressionless. In the glow of the flashlight, any blood that was not on his face seemed to have been drained from his body.

"And you," he continued, "have been following me."

That clinched it. Ted had got his man. One of them at least. The Burglar.

Ted took Harmony's cell, and texted Greco. Then, with much effort, he and Harmony were able to gingerly pull the man out of the niche. They propped him up, as he cried out in pain, against the wall next to the aperture.

The black-haired fellow was short, with a lean musculature. In vigorous middle age, it seemed. He looked to be of southern European heritage. Harmony took the kerchief and dabbed at the gash on the man's head. He winced, his eyes swollen, and gasped. Harmony stared at his shoulder, and her eyes widened. She pressed a thumb and index finger together and pinched off a small piece of soft matter, almost invisible in the low light. She eyed it, nodded, and handed it to Ted.

It was paraffin. Wax. Ted asked the burglar where it came from. The man said he didn't know. Ted placed it in a small plastic bag in which he kept his tours' business cards.

The thief asked Harmony to wet the kerchief, and press it to his wrists and arms, which were bruised and cut from twisting about the slabs. He gritted his teeth as she did so.

"Thank you, ma'am. I guess I'll be all right."

Any past annoyance he had for Ted was gone. Injured and spent, the fellow was contrite, apologetic. He slowly turned his aching head from Harmony to Ted.

"My name is Lercino. Leon, Leonidas—Lercino. I thought I had evaded you, Mr. Sifter. But I see that, that in the end, you got the better of me."

Ted stared at Leo's sharp countenance, the hollow cheek bones resembling Ted's own. The thief's large brown eyes were starting to regain some luster. He had on a tightly fitted brown shirt and long black pants. His backpack was crushed between him and the wall. He sank to the ground, his feet splayed out on the lawn, and Harmony noticed his brand of North Face trekking shoes, of a small and narrow size.

"Who dragged you in here?" Ted asked.

Lercino stared into the terraced garden, and tried to get beyond the throbbing in his head.

"I don't know. I felt a blinding smash, a blinding flash. Then blackness. Like a deep sleep. Then suddenly I was awake and choking to death, in darkness. In Hell."

He spat out some dirt. "A, a horrible idea came into my head. Maybe I was dreaming at that point." His face, pale in the glow of Harmony's light, turned ashen. "I became a character in an old Hitchcock, Alfred Hitchcock show whose, whose cassette, I had seen as a kid." He stared a thousand-mile stare, and spoke like he was speaking to himself.

"A criminal, a prison inmate, would sneak out of prison, by hiding in the coffin intended for a dead inmate—an inmate who had just died. The idea was that the prison undertaker, an old man, would dig him out of a graveyard after the burial. Then he'd be free." Anthony Lercino paused to lick filthy lips, then spat out more dirt. Ted gave him his Powerade bottle. The burglar drank greedily from it, coughed some of the liquid out, then drank again.

"In the final scene, the inmate is in the coffin, six feet under. He's lying next to the other corpse. His air is limited, and he's wondering, wondering what's taking the undertaker so long." Leon paused, to catch his breath. "He reaches into his pocket, and pulls out a book of matches. He lights one. He puts, puts the match up to the face of the stiff next to him.

"He sees that it's the undertaker.

"The, the old undertaker had died, died in the, interim, and unknown to the inmate, his body had been placed in, switched into, the same coffin as his."

If a face could become grayer, Lercino's did. "That's how I felt. I knew—just knew—I would suffocate. I used to have nightmares about such things, and now I was living it." He looked up at Harmony. "Then this angel, this guardian angel, saved me." He managed a slight smile.

Harmony looked up from her cell, and smiled. She replied, with sympathy in her voice, "The ambulance should be here any minute."

Ted asked him, "So, it was you at the Burke & Herbert attic?"

Before Lercino could answer, Ted added, "And at the old Bank of Potomac residence?"

"Yes," the thief answered. "And the Athenaeum, and the waterfront." Lercino bowed his head slightly, then raised it up, and raised his voice. "But I did not kill, I did not mean the watchwoman to die, at the

Athenaeum!" Ted and Harmony were surprised by this sudden confession.

"We scuffled, and she fell. Maybe I pushed her some—but I didn't mean to push her through the window. I swear!" Lercino continued with sudden energy. "Maybe she slipped. It was dark. I swear it! I meant to, to disable her, then flee the building." He stopped and coughed loudly, uncontrollably. His hacking overcame the wail of sirens, which could now be heard in the distance.

As he regained his breath, Harmony became somber. She asked the thief point-blank: "Did you kill Tony Hill? Were you at the Lee house that night?!"

Lercino looked at her, as fresh sweat broke out on his filthy face.

"I did not commit the murders!" he implored. "Not of Hill, nor Cordero at the Freedmen's Cemetery!

"Nor did I attack that lady at the Unknown's Tomb. Of course, I read, read all about that, those things. But I didn't do it! I swear!

His face took on a pathetic expression. "Actually, I started to fear, slinking about town, breaking into old banks at night, that the murderer might kill me. Or that, if the cops caught me, I'd be blamed for the murders." He looked pleadingly at Ted for understanding.

"I believe you," the historian stated. "I believe you, about those murders." Sirens were louder, and Ted had another question before the authorities arrived. To confirm things. He stared into Lercino's eyes, which were sad and bloodshot.

"So, you were looking for Jonathan Swift's, J. Swift's, treasure?" Leon returned Ted's gaze with a mixture of admiration and disappointment. "Well, you did figure it out. I thought as much. I was hoping to hit the jackpot tonight. Maybe foolish, but my map gave me hope." He reached, wincing, into a pants pocket, and hauled out a copy of his chart, as dirt spilled out of the pocket. He handed it to Ted. He took it and took a glance. From the terrace, they could hear vehicles coming to a stop outside on Fairfax. Ted gave the chart to Harmony, who slipped it inside her blouse. Ted had one final query.

"So, you didn't you see who hit you?"

Still shaken by his near-death experience, Leon had a horrified look. "No, no. I heard noises approach. Steps I guess. Through my metal detector, I mean the headphones. The steps of someone big, powerful. I felt like I was hit by a prize fighter. By the rabbit punch, of a maniac."

The sirens' wail lessened. They heard footsteps approach, from either end of the manse. Greco's squat figure appeared first, from the nearest corner. He looked past Ted at Lercino, then at Harmony. He said to her, "Somehow I wasn't surprised when they passed me a message from you two." He turned to Ted, but then they all turned to the other corner of the mansion, as Comitas appeared.

The FBI man was dazed and out of breath. And more discomforted when he recognized Harmony and Ted. He started to walk over, but stopped and stayed silent as EMS personnel came hurrying past him. Ted and Harmony filled the medical personnel in on Lercino's general condition, then Ted told Greco how they had found him. Greco asked a few questions of Lercino, with Comitas listening in. He confessed to the detective, succinctly telling him about his break-ins. Then the med techs took the burglar away in a stretcher.

In the falling mist, Greco turned to Ted and said, with some gratitude, "I'm guessing your hunch was right."

Harmony broke in. "It was more than a hunch. He reasoned it out."

Ted laughed a bit and replied, "She found him."

Comitas walked over to them. His tall figure seemed shrunken. And as usual, he seemed perplexed. "Is this Lercino the murderer too? I mean the cemeteries murderer, at Freedmen's and Old Presbyterian and, and Christ Church?" He cleared his throat. "And the cemetery attacker, at the Female Stranger's tomb?"

Ted stayed tight-lipped. Greco stated, "I'll be sure to press him about that on further interrogation." The detective smiled slightly, and Ted figured he knew why. The FBI man's haughtiness was gone. He didn't ask a thing of Ted and Harmony, but looked away from them, out of embarrassment. He asked Greco, "You'll keep me posted, of course?" Greco may have nodded, maybe not—it was hard to tell among the shadows. "And of course," he continued wearily, "I'll continue my own, thorough, investigation."

Greco's forensics team arrived, to examine the niche and the grounds. Comitas' squad followed a little while later. The conversations ended.

As they walked back to the front of the mansion, Harmony whispered to Ted, "Did you notice the grass stains on Comitas' knees and hands?" Ted whispered back, "He could have just been examining the crime scene."

Harmony replied, "Or committing the crime."

Her friend pursed his lips together. His expression was Sphinx-like. "Could be, I guess," he finally responded. "After all: Lercino, Bertha, and me—the number of murder suspects is dwindling."

"Then of course," answered Harmony, "there's that man at the coal plant."

Chapter 47 – Skinhead Stakeout

Greco now had full confidence in Ted and Harmony. Through their actions, he had collared the burglar. He had a good lead on Abdullah Hamaas. And he expected to nail the mysterious man of the coal plant, possibly the town murderer. His cops would try to take him in his hideout, to connect him to the bomb material and weaponry discovered there.

'Finally!', Greco thought with relief, 'an excellent lead in what's been a maddening case.'

Still, his department's first attempt to identify the suspected killer via computer searches of his most likely profile, crosschecked with murderers and extremists in the Mid-Atlantic and beyond, had turned up little. The same went for searches of crimes committed with the kind of ordinance that Ted had photographed. Whoever this outlaw was, he knew how to cover his tracks.

Greco hesitated about informing the FBI of what Ted and Harmony had found. Its resources were far greater for tracking down a suspect. But it had messed up throughout the Alexandria investigations. It might screw up this takedown as well.

'And I admit it: It's personal,' Greco told himself. He disdained Comitas, as a bungler, and as a vain man who would hog credit for any success. 'No,' the proud detective figured, 'let's try this stakeout, our own stakeout.' If nothing turned up, he could fall back on the Agency's vast resources.

Greco knew he was taking a risk. If he failed, the city might cashier him. And, win or lose, Comitas might rage after learning he'd been left in the dark. But Greco simply smiled at that.

He and his team had carefully questioned Ted and Harmony, but they could relate frustratingly little about the suspect. Harmony hadn't gotten a good look at him at the power plant. They had moxie those two, Greco acknowledged, but despite Ted's praise of Harmony's observational skills, they had provided insufficient info to nail down the identity of the coal plant man or the Wilkes St. assaulter, assuming they were separate individuals.

Meantime the husky lawman had to make a quick decision. Namely, case the secret room at the power plant, and possibly stumble upon an armed, bomb-laden felon? Or simply observe the suspect's lair, and wait for him to either arrive at or exit the place? The second option—stand pat—was the easier one. But the first, while risky, might uncover intel about the man that might short-circuit further mayhem in town. Greco thought of a friend, a security consultant who had been a surveillance technician for the Green Berets. He'd founded a company that aided police with an apparatus originally developed years before by the C.I.A., and that had been increasingly refined through advances in IT. A device that could "peer inside" a closed room.

Not through X-ray vision like Superman, but by analyzing the minute vibrations on a window. A laser is directed at the window, and its beam bounces back to the device, which processes the data contained in the beam. The technique is sophisticated enough, under the right conditions, to pick up monologues or parts of conversations within the room. By transforming the telltale vibrations on the window into human text. The machine could also indicate if appliances or power sources are operating inside a room, and whether the sounds of a radio,

CRT, or cell phone are emanating from it. It has been a useful, if not foolproof, means of finding out if a dwelling or room is occupied, and what is happening within. And it wouldn't involve putting any of Greco's personnel in danger. He got ahold of the apparatus for immediate use. He would also put into play his police department's latest acquisition: a surveillance drone.

The detective, as lead investigator, had already placed an observation squad and a hit team in and around the coal plant complex. They had seen no sign of the suspect the previous night, but were tense with expectation he might arrive that day.

That morning was for once thankfully free of clouds and rain. Greco located his command post at the west entrance to the complex by the train tracks, near where Ted and Harmony had first noticed the gate lock, and near where they had made their office escape. Heavily armed officers were put on the far, southern end of the power plant, ready to rush over to the suspect's office abode. For ground surveillance, Greco placed male and female officers with bikes and garbed in cycling attire on the Mt. Vernon Trail, not far from the fence opening that Harmony had discovered. And he had plains clothes officers stationed on Slaters and Bashford Lanes west of the plant, to warn him of anyone approaching it. For now they reported back, via their Motorola CP200D portable radios, that the streets were empty.

While studying the window of the office through Celestron TrailSeeker binoculars, Greco nodded to two technicians. Stepping through a small section of a fence that cops had cut down, they went up to the vibration analyzer, which had been placed behind a stand of elm trees. Hidden by the foliage, it afforded a view of the window through which the two amateur detectives had fled. Pleased with the ideal weather conditions, the techies began operating the laser. Its beam bounced off the window and back to their equipment. Results were compiled quickly; the operators doublechecked the data. There were clear indications that no machines nor appliances were turned on inside the office. No voices were detected. The information indicated no activity in the room at all. The police could turn now to option one: Pay the locale a visit. Greco headed in a roundabout route across the lawn with his senior detective Bill Bradenson, chief forensics expert Paula "Brownie" Leeds, and several armed cops. They entered the same way Ted and Harmony had. Within the warehouse, their flashlights illuminated the tin roof as they stepped around the floor puddles, which had grown larger from the frequent rains.

At the door to the office, Greco and the others gripped handguns in case the noise detection device had erred. Greco willed away fear and led by example. Fearing a booby trap, he whispered to the others to get away from the door while he opened it. No need for everyone to get injured, or worse.

As his comrades watched intently, he carefully turned the door knob. No booby trap, not there at least. He pushed the door open. Unlocked. No one was inside. They all entered, still tense, still holding their weapons.

They found the place as Ted and Harmony had described it. Paula Leeds, the forensics specialist, looked for fingerprints. She had taken out a plastic pouch to retain any hair samples, but found none. "This guy is meticulous," she commented, "about leaving traces. He must keep on gloves and a head cap when he's here." Greco pointed to a small, battery-operated vacuum cleaner in a corner. Leeds checked its pouch: It was clean. "He must take the bag on leaving," she said, "disposing of anything outside." Greco commented: "It's almost like he's expecting us to come here."

On seeing the copy of *Mein Kampf*, Bill Bradenson grimaced. "Damn
it, we got a real nut job on our hands. And, I would say, from the
spartan look of this place, former military." Greco replied tersely, "Or
current." The idea of a foe with professional soldiering skills was
sobering.

"What's this?" asked the detective. He pulled out from under the cot a
small, framed color picture of an old, bearded man wrapped in animal
furs, his head topped with a helmet, from which projected long, twisted
animal horns. "Is this guy a fan of Chris Hemsworth?" he asked,
referring to the *Thor* movie character.

Bradenson's eyes widened. "No, and that's no joke. That's Wodin." He
saw Greco's questioning look, and continued. "The main ancient
German god, of war and magic."

Leeds took a look, and a second look, at the picture frame.

"Eureka!" she cried. Two brown hair follicles were wedged between
the picture and the top of the frame. She pinched them with tweezers,
and placed them in a pouch. "They might not be the suspect's," noted
Greco, "but we'll surely run a check."

She documented every nook of the room with a Pentax KP low-light
camera, which caught things Ted's photos had missed. Greco eagerly
examined the type and brand of ordinance; he'd have his analysts run
another computer check on them. Leeds found no other hairs, and no
skin, fingernail, nor toenail fragments. Another disappointment: The
suspect had used a file and acid to obliterate the serial numbers of the
weapons.

The team left the office, leaving everything as before. With one
exception. Leeds pulled away a tiny section of a sidewall, and placed a
tiny listening device behind it. She and Greco examined it up close:

They could barely see the bug, and no one else would if not knowing where to look.

They returned the way they came, going around the puddles, and climbing up to the second-floor platform and down the steps to the outside. They took a circuitous route around the grass, to avoid stepping near the pathway to the entrance. In exiting the office, however, they hadn't noticed a tiny sliver of wood the suspect had placed under the fraying rubber lining of the door. Anyone opening it would knock the sliver aside, alerting him he'd had visitors.

The team got back to Greco's command center. They gave the intel from their reconnaissance to a data analyst. Preliminary results came up negative. Greco felt pretty sure, however, that something would turn up. The possessions of the suspect were too unique to not find some match somewhere. Meantime Leeds rushed off to do genetic analysis of the hair samples.

The detective checked with the police watching the approaches to the plant. Nothing so far. The detective and his officers broke out Panera Bread sandwiches and Dunkin' Donuts coffee from a police van, and settled in. From long experience, they knew the waiting can be the hardest part. Usually.

Chapter 48 – Flight from a Trap

After another day and night of reconnoitering potential bomb sites, McVeigh had found himself exhausted. Instead of returning to his lair to sleep, he had simply crashed in his van, spending a restless night there. He woke up achy and weary, and figured a few hours of sleep on the cot of his coal plant hideaway would revive him.

A tenet of McVeigh's tradecraft was to always alter his approach to any destination. He figured going back to his new lodging via Slater's Lane, the direct route, was too obvious. So he returned by an indirect route. He had parked his van on N. Pitt St., well outside the metered parking in the heart of town. With so many of the business offices shuttered in this commercial part of Alexandria, it had been easy to find a parking spot, even for a large vehicle.

After arming himself, putting on his backpack, and adjusting a pair of face masks, he walked to N. Fairfax, checking at times whether anyone was tailing him. The dark-colored jacket he was wearing was too warm for that day, but he needed it to cloak some of his weapons. He realized he looked ridiculous, given his masks, in trying to appear nonchalant as he looked around. And anyone who did see him would have trouble identifying him. 'The county-wide directive to wear a mask outdoors is a boon for the warrior!' he thought.

At N. Fairfax and 3rd St., he took a short path leading to the Mt. Vernon bike trail. The hole he'd cut in the coal plant fence was just 750 yards to the north. This alternative route wasn't far from his lodging. Though he worried a bit about the weather. It had become mostly clear. Nice enough to bring some people outside. He preferred of course not to be seen by anyone. In fact, due to his altered approach, the plainclothes police Greco had stationed in the area didn't spot him. He hitched up his pack and walked up the bike trail, thinking of his potential targets. 'Yeah, a big federal building might be better, but the garage of the courthouse across from City Hall may be too easy to pass up.' He grinned at the thought of the court collapsing into the well of the parking garage, taking scores of people with it. His smile widened at the thought of the resulting media coverage, with clueless reporters and baffled cops speculating on the culprit. He'd enjoy listening to the newscasts and press briefings on his drive out of town.

He thought over his idea of adding to the mayhem. Of placing a delayed-action bomb in Market Square, timed to go off just after the garage bomb, as workers rushed out of City Hall to look at the wrecked courthouse. Planting a second device meant taking a second risk, but it might be worth it.

Chuckling, McVeigh continued along the path, pleased to find it still devoid of its normal bunch of runners, cyclists, and dog walkers. Just above the old canal leading to the Potomac, he passed the strange statuary park of fake, ruined statues and obelisks meant to evoke a fallen civilization.

'Will I help restore Aryan civilization?' he wondered, 'It was at the heart of the greatness of ancient Greece and Rome, before their tragic fall…Well, not that tragic,' he checked himself, smiling again. 'After all, it was Germanic tribes who conquered them!'

As he approached a clump of riverside trees south of the coal plant, he spotted the first person since starting his walk. A woman, about 30 years old and in bike attire, had her back turned to him. She was leaning her hybrid bike against a tree. She couldn't see him, he thought, and he would silently pass by her without notice. In fact, she saw him in the little rear-view mirror attached to her sunglasses. And as soon he passed out of sight around a hairpin turn, she radioed Greco's team.

"A big man,' she communicated. "Strong-looking: Could pass for a linebacker. Masked, dark clothes, military-style boots, big backpack. Caught glimpses of his facial skin: Caucasian. Walks with military gait, determined stride." She then hopped on her bike and, after following McVeigh from afar for a bit, sped up and passed him.

Greco had been waiting impatiently for info, and was intrigued by the officer's description. He estimated when the man might reach the cut-out part of the fence, and ordered two of his other cops, also disguised as cyclists and stationed on the other side of the coal plant, to start cycling toward the female cop and the man she'd spotted. That male and female team headed out.

As the bomber left the hairpin turn, Greco walked over to a tech at his command post. This was a young, scrubby-looking fellow, on loan from the Arlington police department's IT team. He was operating the small drone cruising in the sky above. Greco had been on hand for its maiden flight a year before, and admired its sleek design, and its camouflage exterior: a coat of cerulean blue paint with white-gray splotches. It was nearly invisible to an earth-bound observer.

Its operator flew the craft over the Potomac, where it made a crossing pattern 600 yards above the coal plant fence. Its muffled motors were inaudible except when the craft glided very close to the ground. The young man trained his high-speed, high-resolution Sony CMOS camera onto the riverfront path.

As McVeigh strode onward, the two cop cyclists went by him. But just seconds before, a bee had flown into the face of the male cop. Flustered, he wobbled his bike noticeably five feet before the bomber, as he pulled down his mask to flick the insect away. McVeigh, a very observant man by training and trade, noted the cyclist had a strong, chiseled face, then for the time being thought nothing more of it.

About a minute later, the bomber was opposite the coal complex. The lone female cyclist then passed him on his left. He recognized her as the one who had stopped on the trail. 'There are an unusual number of people out exercising today,' he noted.

The cyclists stopped about 70 yards north, and south, respectively, of the cut-out fence, out of the view of anyone on the path. The headsets within their bike helmets crackled slightly as they radioed Greco. The pair of cops backed up what the solitary cyclist had said. The detective also got video feed from the drone, whose imaging had pinpointed the suspect.

He told the cyclists to stay where they were for now, and sent them two other cops as backup. He also sent another officer, a burly male veteran of the force, out on foot to reinforce the lone woman rider. With him he had a tactical squad of six, most of them heavily armed. There was also a SWAT team south of the complex, and another in reserve a few streets back from the river. The murderer—if he was the murderer— was trapped. He could not escape along the bike path, and if he entered the coal complex, as expected, he'd be surrounded by overwhelming force.

At the trees in front of the cutout, McVeigh slowed his pace, looked around, then strode quickly into the bushes. He reached the opening in the fence, and made sure the piece he'd removed was as he had left it. The bomber went through the aperture, catching his backpack on a piece of wire, then pulling it free.

He was walking briskly to the warehouse office when the chiseled face of the male cyclist popped back into his head.

He had seen that face before, and recently. He stopped involuntarily. This was important, he sensed. He tried to remember. Where and when? He remembered.

City Hall. When he cased out the Market Square garage, a policeman had been on street patrol, walking down from the Carlyle House. It was the same man, the cyclist!

Was it a coincidence? Today could be the man's day off, he could be out biking: Many cops were fitness fanatics, after all.

He thought back to the other cyclist passing him. A black woman. She had looked at him, steadily, for a second or two, when she passed by. It was a cold, penetrating stare, as if she was trying to size him up. Not the look of a casual cyclist.

Was his imagination running away from him? The few people who knew McVeigh concluded he was cool in temperament, without fear, but he knew a healthy fear could keep one from an early grave.

Well, he couldn't stand just there, in the open, trespassing on condemned property. He began walking slowly toward the office door. McVeigh was an atheist, but a kind of Nordic pagan worshiper as well, who dabbled in the magic cult of the warrior god Odin. He looked up to the heavens, to the mostly sunny sky that day, and asked the sky god for counsel.

Then he saw it. A small blue object. A bird? There were plenty of birds of prey along this stretch of the Potomac. In recent decades, as the river basin was being cleaned up, vast gaggles of Canadian geese had migrated here, attracting the bald eagles that preyed on them.

Yet as he stared upward, he noticed with his sharp eyesight that the object was almost static, like a satellite, like Jupiter or Venus at night, moving very slowly against an unmoving background. The blue object headed past the outline of a small cloud, and disappeared, then appeared again as it moved through the cloud. He thought back to the CIA operations he'd undertaken in the Horn of Africa. He and his fellow soldiers had been aided by such objects.

It was a drone. A surveillance drone. Surveilling *him*.

McVeigh stopped again. In the middle of the lawn, he felt naked, unprotected. He looked toward the fence near the railroad, and saw some trees, but no persons. He thought of taking his small but powerful Steiner Kommander binoculars from his pack to gain a better view of the sky. But he already knew it was a drone, no doubt operated by law officers.

He had walked into a trap. Against an enemy with massive resources. They might well be waiting for him in his lair. Or hiding right across the lawn from him. Somewhere. Likely all around him.

He knew he would probably lose the coming encounter. He also knew he would not surrender. Death was the common fate of a soldier. It instantly became a question of the best strategy of best acquitting himself in the coming clash, and possibly survive, or at least go down fighting.

McVeigh thought hard and fast. His hopes of a mighty explosion at a public building were dashed. So be it. That was in the past. 'Focus on the future, no, not even that, but the present struggle, the battle facing me in the moment,' he told himself. 'Remember the *diktat* of Nietzsche. Let the will triumph over the challenge, even over death at death's moment.'

He tried to figure out the best plan of retreat, or attack. Behind the fence ahead was likely a force of police or federals. In or behind the warehouse too. He had already spotted two cops on the bike path. 'There was also that woman cyclist I passed by. Was she undercover too?' Even if that were true, that left only one law officer, if she was the only one, that he knew of, on the south part of the bike path. 'If I head that way, I might be able to deal with any opposition.' He thought of the weapons in his pack, of his military experience, and estimated he should have an edge over just one or two cops.

He needed to try to get past the initial, hopefully light, opposition, and get to a vehicle. He knew from studying maps of the area around his lair that, to the north, the area consisted of the bike path, the George Washington Parkway, and the Dyke Marsh along the river's edge. Assuming he got past any police on the trail, he'd be trapped between the highway and the swamp. And any traffic on the highway moved too fast for a carjacking.

If, however, he went south, and got past one, or several cops, he might conceivably make it back to his van. Along with providing transport, it would give him a lot of explosives and heavier weaponry. If the way to his vehicle were blocked, he could head toward Old Town. There were many vehicles there for the taking. True, he would be boxed in, in a dense urban setting. But there might be opportunities to take hostages, or to go to ground in an empty building and make a stand.

Grimacing, grinding his teeth, he realized his chances were slim. He realized the other alternative was to race over to the Potomac, and try to escape by swimming. He was a decent swimmer, and the water was now warm enough to survive prolonged exposure. It was about a mile and a half to the opposite shore. But that option was unrealistic. The current was strong, and the river filthy from all the recent rains. Besides, if he were able to swim across, in 45 minutes or so, the police would be waiting for him, as he crawled ashore exhausted. It would be much better to steal a boat somewhere. He knew one thing: Surrender wasn't a choice.

His head aching from worry, desperate to decide, he thought of the Alexandria Marina, with its scores of sailboats and motorboats. It lay to the north about a mile away. Perhaps he should break for it in that direction after all. Then he remembered, from his research into Alexandria, the motor craft and yachts berthed at the docks of Old Town's waterfront. While the Marina was typically crowded, and would have some recreational sailors there even during a pandemic, the waterfront was mostly deserted, even in the healthiest of times. In his quick, fevered considerations, he seemed to also recall there was a boathouse on the edge of Old Town, nor far from the coal plant. He couldn't be sure. In any event, southward toward Old Town it had to be.

But first, he had to be sure about his conclusion. He turned around, slowly, and headed back, slowly, to the fence. Though he felt an urge to run, he restrained himself. He wanted any coppers or federals watching to think he had simply changed his mind about returning to his lair at this time.

After getting through the fence, he crept into a thicket and got out his binoculars. He now had a clear view of the far fence enclosing the coal plant, and he trained his strong lenses on it. He saw the gate with the lock where he had made his initial entry. Not far from it were trees and hedges. He increased the magnification. He made out the images of people there. More than he had seen in town all day.

He focused on some of them as they moved about. Several had on gray-blue uniforms, like those of the police, or had donned military-style khaki.

His suspicions were correct. It was time to act.

From his backpack he took out two explosive grenades, a stun grenade, his Glock 29, a compact machine pistol, and his MTECH hunting knife.

He popped a magazine box onto the machine pistol; the Glock was already loaded. He put everything but the machine pistol on his belt, and placed it inside a flap on the jacket covering the belt. He slipped extra bullet clips into his trouser pockets. He left the pack behind in the thicket, as it would slow him down. He hated having to leave it, and the items inside, but he was *in extremis*, and in any case he didn't expect to use them again. He strode to the edge of the grass, looked down the path, saw no one, and started a quick-walk south.

Beforehand Greco, from his lookout, had been wondering what the hell the suspect was doing. There he had been, his hulking figure standing in the grass between the warehouse and the fence, completely defenseless. "Is he posing for a picture?" the detective had muttered. The suspect reminded him of an animal on the African savannah who stops suddenly after sensing danger. 'That's it,' he concluded. 'He *knows*.' He watched McVeigh turn about, then stroll back to the fence. Greco radioed his squads. He told the SWAT crew by the power plant to get ready to move toward the river, and gave the same instructions to his reserve force. He ordered the undercover cops on the trail to take up defensive positions, and to wait for the suspect. They were not to arrest him, but to tail him. He wanted him tracked if possible to another lair or to another stash of ordinance.

On getting the word, the two cops on the trail's southern side positioned themselves at the Promenade Classique, the faux-ancient ruin. The suspect, if heading that way, had to take the bike path that runs by there. The statuary has steps leading to a plaza of office buildings, which in turn lead the old railroad bed near Abingdon Lane. At the Promenade, 33-year-old Archie Henderson moved his bike up a set of stone steps, and leaned it on a giant, sandstone Impressionist Mouth. The odd orifice supposedly represented part of an image that had tumbled down from an ancient temple. Possibly one of the Gemini twins, as a second giant Mouth was a few yards away. Henderson stood 15 yards up the steps on the side of the first Mouth; his perch gave him a view of the path. Somewhat vain, he knew he had a handsome face with a chiseled jaw, and he flattered himself by imagining how he could have been the model for the statue. A fan of pop music, Henderson remembered a musician friend telling him the drummer for Fleetwood Mac had once owned a nightclub near the plaza.

His partner was a 31-year-old African-American officer named Alice Tanner. She happened to be a descendant of an enslaved woman who, by selling farm goods in Market Square two centuries prior, had bought the freedom of herself and her relatives. Tanner stood on the river's edge across from the Mouths, crouching behind some thinly limbed trees and rugosa rose bushes. From there she could see anyone coming down the path while remaining hidden herself. Once the suspect passed, she would tail him on foot, bike in hand, with Henderson following her.

As McVeigh approached the weird Promenade, he remembered there was a plaza above it. It wasn't the straightest route to his van, but it might provide a path away from the river.

He was moving toward the steps when he saw the male biker pop out from behind the Mouth and give him the once-over.

A coincidence, to run into a biker again? Unlikely. And was that the biker cop from before?

At that instant he spotted two young men in tan, long-sleeve shirts and khaki pants who had turned onto the path, having come up from a rebuilt portion of the old Georgetown-Alexandria Canal.

They looked up toward him, then suddenly looked away. Too suddenly.

McVeigh thought fast. He saw that the statuary blocked the view of the two men from the cyclist. He stepped to his right, out of the view of the men, grabbed the stun grenade, and tossed it at the cyclist.

The device went off with a sharp bang. The cyclist, stunned indeed, fell to the ground, reflexively tried to cover his ears, and smacked the sides of his helmet instead. Now McVeigh would find out if the two men were cops or simply pedestrians.

"Explosion!" he cried. "Help!" He moved back into the middle of the path, and saw that the men had stopped—and reached toward their hips, for the handguns under their shirts.

At that instant he heard a voice behind him shout: "Stop! Hands up!" After seeing McVeigh toss the stun grenade, Officer Tanner had whipped out her Beretta 92, and drawn a bead on the bomber.

McVeigh heard her shrill voice, calculated approximately where she was, and made an instant decision. He dropped toward the ground, grasping his handgun from the belt as he did and, after whirling about, shot her in the waist, just below the bottom fringe of her bike shirt, and the protective vest above it. Her gun flew out of her hands. She collapsed in agony, moaning.

The bomber then pivoted quickly and rolled over to a fence along the river. He eyed the two men, who had just begun, guns drawn, to advance toward him. He grabbed a grenade, pulled the safety clip and the pin and, leaning on his left side, tossed it toward them.

The two saw the spherical object coming, and momentarily stopped in surprise. At the last instant, they threw themselves to either side of the path as the M67 weapon landed on the river side, scattered a few feet— and exploded. The cop near the river was mangled; the cop further away was hit with shrapnel in the legs and had his right eardrum punctured.

McVeigh's combat experience was aiding him. Everything seemed to appear in slow motion; he was able to think out his moves in seconds. He looked to his right, up the steps, and the male cyclist cop was on the ground, semi-conscious, no weapon in his hands. He looked behind him, and the female cop, gasping, was crawling over a pool of her own blood, crawling to her fallen handgun. McVeigh, his hand steady, pointed his Glock 29, and shot her between her neck and jaw, nearly tearing the head off.

He rose and began running up the stairs to the plaza. A few steps from the top, he stopped. He could see across the open space, past its water channel and fountain, which was turned off to "stop the spread". He saw a police car on the courtyard's far side, next to the railroad tracks. Its siren was off, but its lights were flashing.

He scampered back down the steps, past the disabled cop near the Mouth, and sprinted south along the path. He approached the two stricken policemen. The one at the river fence was on his back, moving a bit, smoke emanating from his shirt, his gun many feet from him. Not a threat. The one across the path was sitting, red splotches on his pants and—pointing his handgun at McVeigh!

The bomber instinctively veered right, and felt something on his stomach as the sharp sound of the shot registered in his ears. His left side burned, but he was able to keep running. He glanced down: The bullet had struck him in the left side of his waist, and had passed through.

He stopped. The cop was sitting just seven yards from him. He was playing with his Beretta—reloading it?—then gazed up at McVeigh. The policeman had a look of grim inevitability, the look of imminent death. McVeigh calmly pointed the pistol at his head, and pulled the trigger—and the gun jammed!

The cop looked stunned. McVeigh just ran. Any second he expected a bullet to smash into his back. None came. He raced around a bend to the old canal lock and out of sight of the cop.

The fatty part of his waist burning, McVeigh sprinted across the short bridge spanning the lock and fled into Rivergate City Park. He was now on the fringe of Old Town. As he went along, he looked up Montgomery St. He saw three, maybe four, police cars, lights flashing, sirens sounding. He ran on the paved footpath along the river. He looked skyward, almost reflexively, searching for the sight of a drone, though he doubted he'd be able to see it. 'Mustn't worry about that,' he thought. 'It would be a recon drone not a weapons drone.' Then he heard a whirling noise, and spotted a helicopter coming up along the Potomac from Old Town. He couldn't tell if it was a police or a newsroom helicopter. 'Probably police, too early for the news,' he figured.

At the end of the park a low, wide building jutted onto the river. It was the boathouse he had vaguely remembered, one for the T.C. Williams High School sculling teams. Beyond it was the wide, river-line crescent of Founders Park, where the wharves handling tobacco were built in the 1730s. And just beyond it was Old Town proper.

McVeigh knew the police would almost surely cut him off, and even gun him down with rage for their fallen comrades, before he could get into town. But he also saw that, despite the pandemic, the scull crews had continued training. Three sculls were near the boathouse dock, though it was unclear if they were embarking or disembarking. As McVeigh raced along, his waist aching, his heart pounding and lungs burning, a crazy thought flashed through his mind: Could he take a scull, and oar it across the river? Maybe, though he doubted he could row hard with this wound. But the dock might have a motorboat. That might be his only real chance. If he could find transport of any kind, he'd take it.

He ran up to the side of the boathouse, the center of which is a storehouse for kayaks and sculls. The garage-like doors below the gray siding were open, as usual, on both the river and the park side, giving the impression of a beach house with a giant, open-air space.

The rowing team manager, a man in his thirties, and the men's team scull captain, all of 17 years, were standing in front. They had misheard the concussive sounds of the grenades, wondering how thunder could have sounded from a clear sky. They were chatting about whether the virus would cancel the annual regatta when they noticed policemen running from Montgomery St. along the far end of the park. As they ran past a row of pricey new townhomes, the cops held on stiffly to rifles and handguns. The two onlookers were startled at the sight. Some of the police began sprinting across the broad lawn between the townhouses and the boathouse.

Then the coaches' attention was turned to the tall, athletic man running toward them. He was breathing very hard, like a rower at the end of a tough workout. He stopped near them. Their eyes dropped to the bottom of his dark coat, on which were blotches of red. And to his belt, which could be seen through the loose flaps of the jacket. The captain thought he saw a dagger hanging from it and—was that a grenade!? The man looked at them, then at the garage opening, and raced into it, before they could say a word. They saw the police approaching fasts. McVeigh, his hips swaying from the bullet wound, ran through the garage. A trio of high school girls, their faces flushed with their workout, were walking through it. The bomber pushed one aside, and almost knocked the others to the ground. He rushed through the far opening and stood, chest heaving, before a wide dock. From it five piers jutted 40 yards into the Potomac. The swollen river had a strong, southward current; white tops foamed up, disappeared, and foamed up again. McVeigh heard loud voices from behind, shouts that echoed in the sound chamber of the garage.

"Stop! Surrender!"

The police had rushed up faster than he expected.

Directly to his right a scull of female teens was gliding into a pier. The exhausted young women were unaware of the drama before them. Standing next to McVeigh was an assistant coach, a stocky man of about 45 years. He had a daughter on the crew team, and another who had graduated with a college scholarship for sculling. He didn't notice the blood on McVeigh's shirt. But he was annoyed at the surprise presence. He told him, "Mister, guests aren't allowed here." Then he heard the cops shouting. Puzzled, he stared at the interloper.

McVeigh spotted the small motorboat of the crew's coxswain two piers over. The female coxswain, a student, was slowly bringing it to the dock. It was 10 feet out. He strode toward it.

He reached the boat as the coxswain bumped its front end onto the dock. McVeigh leapt into the boat behind her. He landed, grimacing with pain. She looked behind her, shocked. The assistant coach rushed over, and stopped about halfway to the motorboat.

McVeigh was deciding whether to push the coxswain onto the dock, toss her overboard, or use her as a shield, when four police emerged at the garage opening. They had rifles and pistols, and seemed ready to use them.

A whooshing roar became audible above and inland. It was the helicopter, hovering above the lawn on the other side of the boathouse. McVeigh looked to the south side of the dock, where he saw three armed cops running up it. They had approached via the boardwalk on the edge of Founders Park. He was trapped on both land sides. Unseen above, the drone's cameras captured his plight, and relayed it to Greco's team.

But the bomber knew how to work the boat. He grabbed the girl and pulled her to his side. His right arm worked the controls.

As a policeman shouted, "Stop! Put down any weapons!", he put the craft sharply into reverse. He roared backwards away from the dock, hit the side of a pier, then swung into the river.

About 40 yards out, the coxswain, athletic and strong, pivoted, and broke free of him.

A shot rang out. McVeigh looked down at his chest in surprise and sudden pain. A slug had smashed into his ribs.

On the dock, the assistant coach, in a shooting position, held his Springfield Hellcat handgun steady, wisps of smoke threading up from its barrel. Though the City Council had banned guns in parks, he had a conceal carry permit, and had put it to use. His brown eyes sparkled. It had been a tough shot, at a moving boat, but he'd pulled it off.

The police, however, were not pleased. They were under orders to try to take the suspect alive, especially as he might be the murderer, or part of a terror cell. Not to mention that the instructor might have mistakenly shot the girl. And they knew the suspect could hardly escape.

"Don't shoot!" cried a cop at the garage entrance, just 20 feet from the coach. "No more shooting!" The man, frustrated, and unnerved by the order, pointed his handgun down at the dock.

In the boat, McVeigh lifted up the girl, and tossed her in the river. As he did, the wound in his waist seemed to shoot down into his thighs. His chest throbbed from the other gunshot.

The coxswain's head dipped under the swirling waves, then bobbed up. She gagged after swallowing dirty river water. She was a strong swimmer, but the water was very rough. Indeed, a leader of the scull team had lost his life near there some years before.

The swim instructors and crew scrambled to put three long sculls into the river. Rowing at the highest cadence, they moved along faster than they'd ever done in a race. They reached the girl, carried by the strong current despite swimming against it, some 130 yards downstream. Grabbing her jersey, as she coughed out murky water, they pulled her aboard one of the sculls.

Meantime McVeigh had revved the engine to full, and reversed back out further into the Potomac. About 200 yards from shore, he slowed and turned, then steered with the current. Above, the helicopter, a police copter, whirled out over the river above him. From the south, a police boat, trailed by a Coast Guard cutter, came racing his way. The drone followed him, its operator wishing it was weaponized.

The bomber saw that a wild chase was in order. He also saw that his fuel gauge read low. He was bleeding in two places, badly from his chest. He found it hard to think straight. He guessed his only chance was to get to the opposite shore, and make it into the forest and scrub before a large force of police arrived. 'Try to find some shelter to hide in', he thought wearily. He had a small medical kit taped to his lower back, and he could try to patch himself up.

He turned the boat, waves smashing into the port side, which sent searing pain across his hips and ribs. He took off fast toward the Maryland shore. The shaking of the small, light vessel triggered more agonizing pain.

The police boat was too fast for him. It headed him off a hundred yards from the shore, near the array of solar power panels for the D.C. water treatment plant. The policemen's craft loitered, rising and falling in the swells, in his way. The Coast Guard vessel pulled up along his starboard side. Crewmen on both ships rushed on deck with automatic rifles. Several Guardsmen manned a small cannon.

McVeigh cut the engine, his boat slowing, as he figured furiously what to do. The skipper of the police boat grasped a bullhorn. "Give up!" he called out. "You have no chance!" The skipper paused. He had almost said, "Throw your weapons overboard!", then realized they might provide valuable evidence. "Throw down," he shouted, "any weapons you may have!"

McVeigh gasped and shuddered from the hole in his chest. He knew it was over. But he didn't consider surrender. 'May Valhalla welcome me,' he muttered over the sputtering noise of the engine. He readied his machine pistol and a final grenade.

He sent a spray of bullets toward the police boat, wounding slightly one crewman. A moment later he tossed the grenade at the Coast Guard ship. It landed 20 yards to its side, sending up a big splash and a flash, but causing no damage.

He gunned the engine, and dashed at full speed between the two vessels. He got to within 50 yards of the shore.

Whatever the directives to take him alive, the cops and the Guardsmen, having received fire, responded with a barrage of gunshots.

McVie was struck above his right hip, and in his left arm and his neck. He felt searing pain, then his vision blurred and the pain softened somewhat. He staggered onto the bow of the boat, and fell into the water, belly first, unable to extend his arms.

His last view was of the shore ahead. Too far ahead. As he floated face-down on the roiling waves, his last thought was imagining he was outside the Alexandria City Hall, blown up by his own bomb, after forgetting to get away in time.

Five days later, after a futile search by frogmen, his bloated corpse would emerge on moss-covered rocks below the waste treatment project, directly down a bluff from the secret graves of the Nazi saboteurs where he had made his final pilgrimage.

Chapter 49 – Victory Lap

"Have your heard?" Greco told Ted on his cell. The detective was more and more convinced Ted, and Harmony, were clairvoyants.

Tired out from the late-night prowling, his hands and fingers sore and bruised from rescuing Lercino, Ted had stolen a rare nap on his living-room sofa, blissfully unaware of the breaking news. On awakening, he'd uttered a short prayer which, though about 1,990 years old, ended with a phrase that seemed more applicable than ever: "Deliver us from Evil." He wasn't as sure about the "forgiving those who trespass against us." Then, his head propped up on a couch pillow, he'd gotten the call, and Greco filled him in on the wild chase along the bike path and the river.

The backstory for McVeigh was astonishing, Greco explained. Just hours before, Leeds had examined the hair sample. Crosschecking with the NYPD, her analysis found it belonged to a William, or Wilhelm, Frederick McVeigh, an Army veteran and former CIA operative. According to the dossier, after leaving the services he got caught up in a neo-Nazi group, only to fall off the grid somewhere in Pennsylvania eight years ago.

As he listened, Ted did a simple Find That Grave ancestry search on his cell for McVeigh. He found indications the bomber might be related to the antebellum merchant family that had moved to the Confederate capital during the war, then moved back to Old Town afterwards. He told Greco about this, with hesitation. He was fairly certain the police, and even more the FBI, would assume and announce McVeigh was responsible for all the murders in town. With a racial motive. It seemed to tie everything together nicely. But Ted's doubts about this had continued to grow.

Indeed, at a press conference in Market Square later that day, Comitas smiled at the sight of reporters from the national and international media, who hung onto his words. He had personally gone over the press passes for those gathered, and vetoed the presence of journalists who'd given him a hard time. He was happy to entertain the other scribes, and elated the City Hall and City Council officials had suddenly warmed to him and the other law officers again. Many of the politicos and reporters now viewed him, the FBI, and the police as saviors.

In part, he stated: "We now think it likely, in fact almost a certainty, that this vile character McVeigh," he said, pronouncing it as McVEE-gah, "is the man who committed the three murders." Deputy Mayor Morenis stepped up to him, and whispered something in his ears. "That this vile man McVeigh," he restarted, pronouncing it correctly, "is *our man.*

"It all fits. The murder at the Freedmen's Cemetery by a modern-day fascist. The slaying and dumping of a body on a Confederate grave mound to divert attention. The slaughter of a rector of a church known for its dedication to racial harmony and its opposition to hate.

"We're still analyzing evidence from all those sites, and other locales, and we are confident we will soon link the evidence to McVeigh."

To the applause of the officials, reporters, and local residents who crowded into the Square, while maintaining a minimum six feet of distance, Comitas announced: "We believe this period of horror, in this most historic town, has finally, thankfully, come to an end."

He took the credit with faint praise for others. "We want to thank the work of the local police and local magistrates, backstopped and supported at every turn by the FBI, the world's finest crime-fighting organization, for their role in running this madman to ground." Council members stepped toward the speaker's microphone, holding their hands high up to clap in celebration. From the side the Mayor, back in town to share in the glow, looked on approvingly. Among the officials, only Council Coordinator Forstandt seemed subdued. Another off note was sounded by a reporter from the *Washington Examiner*, who had slipped through the FBI man's protective screening.

"Associate Executive Assistant Director Comitas," she asked, while tapping a stylus on her iPad, "do you believe McVeigh has ties to the burglar, Anthony Lercino?" And before he could begin to think of a reply, she added:

"And was it McVeigh who attacked those private citizens, Mr. Sifter and Miss Jain, who have produced some of the leads in this case?" Comitas was caught flat-footed by the first question, and perturbed by the second. "We, why, we are continuing, of course, and with the local police, our investigation into Mr. Lercino. Uh, we have no direct ties, at this time, no ties, between him and Mr. McVeigh." Hedging, he continued, "Of course, new evidence might always be forthcoming. But no, not for now. Doubtful there will be. We got our man."

He paused, struggling to put together thoughts. "Let me answer, perhaps, another one of the media's queries. As for that Wilkes Cemetery incident, it is very reasonable to assume, the would-be killer there was *the killer*, Will, Wilhelm McVeigh. Fortunately, Miss Benedita survived, and is recovering nicely, I've been informed. Hopefully she will be able to shed more light, and identify her attacker as MacVe—McVeigh." He decided against mentioning Ted and Harmony's role in saving Cassandra Benedita's life. The reporter's mention of them was enough.

With forced confidence, Comitas stated, "Next question." He turned to a TV reporter whose query, on the FBI's cutting-edge technology in crime detection, he'd planted before the press conference.

Chapter 50 – Sifting Through the Clues

The next morning at his home "office"—his sofa and laptop—Ted forced himself to crank out a few pages of his next book. But his restless mind swung back to the matter of the neo-Nazi bomber as the putative murderer. The town was atwitter from the shootings and explosives at the Promenade Classique, the theft of the scull at the boathouse, and the bloody chase across the Potomac. The Coast Guard was then still searching the river near the wastewater plant for the body, and concerned swift currents were ferrying it all the way down to the Chesapeake.

Not far from the coal plant, Greco's officers found McVeigh's van. It was loaded with ammonium nitrate, and C4, as well as handguns, an automatic rifle, and boxes of ammunition. The amount of explosive was more than enough to take down a courthouse, a school, or a city hall, and kill scores. Alexandrians were breathing a common sigh of relief after the death of McVeigh, as well as the capture of Lercino. But Ted figured it likely McVeigh, though a killer, was not *the killer*. 'Doesn't really fit the history angle,' he mused. He glanced at his Garmin wristwatch, and saw it was time to meet Harmony.

He biked past the Woodrow Wilson Bridge, and through Old Town side streets and across King St. to the Carlyle House. In the front lawn Harmony was waiting for him. She wore a skirt with a rose flower pattern that seemed tailor-made to show off her tapered legs. She smiled brightly, and the contrast with their desperate effort to save Lercino's life at the back of the mansion couldn't be greater. They shared a brief hug, then strolled the two blocks to a Pitmaster southern barbecue place on N. Lee St.

After ordering, Harmony placed her laptop on the tabletop. Ted moved alongside her, and she pulled up photos of McVeigh. They studied his physical dimensions, and tried to match it with their recollection of the person at the Wilkes cemeteries.

As he played with a side of mac and cheese, his fingers scarred from pulling out the Carlyle House rocks, Ted's eyes jumped from one image of the bomber to another, and hoped for an "Aha!" moment of recognition.

"They may be the same person," he said, slowly chewing on the little food he'd taken. "Usually I listen to my gut, though my gut—"

"—Your gut is carb-loading!" joked Harmony, noting the baked potato he'd also ordered.

She smiled, and dug a fork into collard greens mixed with bits of bacon. Ted laughed, then asked, "And what about the voice? You said it sounded Central Asian, or such. I don't know. The accent, to me, sounded, like a mix. Maybe standard American, with a foreign tinge. Maybe he had a mask on. It muffles the voice, can make a Midwest American accent sound exotic."

Harmony shook her head vigorously. "I have excellent hearing, and I know that accent. Definitely Central Asian. Certainly Greco seemed convinced. Enough to go after the escaped prisoner again. Per your suggestion."

With her MacBook Pro she increased the resolution of some head shots of McVeigh. As they peered at the screen, leaning on each other's shoulders, the waitress came over to ask if they wanted another round of Flying Dog Dead Rise, a hearty ale from a brewery in historic

Frederick, Maryland. Wanting to keep their heads clear, they settled for ice tea.

"Notice anything?" asked Ted.

The freckles on Harmony's nose seemed to quiver. Her glowing amber eyes sharpened.

"They're not the same man," she pronounced. "The man I glimpsed at the power plant, McVeigh, is not the same guy from the Wilkes Cemetery."

"But Greco thinks they are. And also Comit—"

"Please!" She raised up the fork from a plate of baby back ribs, and wielded it like a knife. Now I *know* I'm right, if that man thinks I'm wrong!"

"Well," said Ted, wiping his mouth, "he and the local cops are pouring over those photos, and with far greater computer power than your Mac. And tracking down McVeigh's past as well."

"My laptop's at least as good as your 'Find a Grave,'" responded Harmony with unusual asperity. Like Ted, she was worried the authorities, as they had been through most of the recent mayhem, were on the wrong track. And might not find Tony's killer.

Ted grunted, and curled his lips in a weak smile. Although he was hungry from the exertions of recent nights, much of his plate was still untouched. As usual, when he was immersed in something, he was neglecting to eat enough. When Harmony would bug him about it, he'd joke, "I like to maintain my girlish figure."

"As you very well know," Harmony continued, "two of the killings fit the pattern of a Fascist from Hell. The murder in a progressive church, and the Freedmen's killing." Harmony was suddenly grim. It would take months, or forever, to get over the grisly slaying of their friend. She went on, slowly: "And the, the Confederate mound, that incident, that was throwing shade, I think. I suspect you, may be right about that. To maybe get the investigators off track…"

Ted looked at her in the eyes, hoping to break the sorrowful spell, but just felt sad himself.

He blinked hard and shook his head, snapping himself out of it.

"Yes, it, the incidents," he stated, picking through his words, "could fit the pattern, of a, criminal, with the opposite views."

She looked up from her vegetables. "Please, tell me again."

"Well, the killer desecrated a Confederate grave mound, and places associated with a man, actually several men, related to Confederate generals: Light-Horse Harry Lee, and—Hill." Seeing Harmony's face fall again, he stated quickly, "General A.P. Hill, one of Robert E. Lee's commanders, at battles like Antietam."

Ted cringed in looking at his crestfallen friend. Any mention of Hill was like stabbing an arrow in her heart. But he had to explain.

"And the way Tony—was treated. It was like the personal assault, on Light-Horse Lee, in Baltimore, during the War of 1812. He was, beaten, and boil—heated oil, was thrown, was put onto his face, blinding an eye. And he was cut up all around his body. It matches what happened to our frien—" His voice trailed off. Then picked up again.

"Also, the murder at Old Presbyterian, was at a graveyard of many of Old Town's founders. A number of who, were, among other things, they were slaveowners."

Harmony wiped away a tear. "So you're suggesting…" she started.

"…I'm suggesting the murder of our friend may have indeed been a head fake. To divert attention from the real motive. But not the motive the authorities think."

Harmony snapped out of her sad revery for their lost friend.

"But what about the Freedmen's Cemetery murder? Surely that was the work of—"

"—Maybe that," interrupted Ted, "was another head fake. A *first* head fake." He continued. "Maybe the balance of the evidence points to a killer on the opposite end of the spectrum from a far-right nut job."

"Far right, far left," answered Harmony, "they all seem the same to me."

"They are," said Ted, waxing poetic. "They veer off the deep end of the spectrum, and meet each other somewhere in the void."

Ted put down his fork, and rubbed his palms together. They were greasy, and his broken fingernails ached.

"It is something I probably shouldn't 'discuss at the dinner table.' We might lose our appetite. It's about the corpse atop the Tomb of the Unknown Soldier, of Alexandria.

Harmony stopped chewing, and listened. She hadn't heard Ted explain the killings in such detail at any one sitting.

"Lil—Lillian Harper's desecration, the way her body was, was mutilated. Her throat, her rear end, it was no accident." Ted spoke slowly, choosing his words. "There was another death, 220 years ago, that her death was patterned on, I'm sure. It can't be a coincidence."

And Ted sketched out the awful final night of George Washington, and the awful treatments for his illness. The bleedings, the enema, the proposed tracheotomy, and other "remedies". Eerily echoed by Lily's murder, and mutilations.

"That graveyard is all caught up in Revolutionary War history, and General Washington. That's how the killer must see it.

"He even dropped blood on Dr. Craik's tombstone. The doctor who administered the bleedings to Washington. That was no coincidence.

"It was more like, like, a deliberate leaving of a clue."

Ted's face tightened; his eyes stared down at the floor.

"This fiend is committing horrific crimes, in this history-drenched town, by reenacting terrible events from its past."

Chapter 51 – Midnight Oil

Lisa Jennings Bland pulled up on N. St. Asaph St. next to the Old Towne School for Dogs, and turned off her wipers and headlights. The thin, gray-haired, 62-year-old rarely worked at night and, with the virus, should have had much less work. But then the City Council had demanded the alteration of the name of her Lee-Fendall Museum. The assistant manager had many items to work through: Donors to contact, suggestions for new names, hiring contractors to change the signage and the exhibits, the legal papers for making such alterations, and more. Lisa Bland found it hard to work at home, but she could focus when in her office, with no one else around.

Down the sidewalk was the solid brick-and-steel construct of the former Portner brewery, transformed now into pricey condominiums. In recent years, in an echo of the city's past, the great-great-granddaughters of the founding Mr. Portner had set up their own microbrewery across town. Bland stepped slowly, careful not to slip on the fog-moistened sidewalk, past Virginia's former Red Cross headquarters, now also condos, and once a Second World War hub for getting blood plasma to wounded troops abroad.

She crossed St. Asaph up to Pendleton St.

There is confusion for whom that street is named. Because so many roads in Alexandria are named for Confederate generals, some assume that street honors Gen. Joseph Henry Pendleton, Robert E. Lee's head of artillery, and himself named after a noted scientist and friend of Abraham Lincoln's. Some mistake paintings of Gen. Pendleton, with his curly, gray-white beard and hair, for General Lee. In fact, Pendleton

St. is named for a U.S. Marine general of the 20th century, as in Camp
Pendleton.

The scholarly Bland knew all this, yet wondered if activists would
demand changing the street name anyway. Or indeed the street it runs
into, Washington, given that Founding Father's connection to
involuntary servitude. Indeed, Pendleton St. physically connects with
Washington St. at the Old Cotton Mill, so emblematic of the Old South.
Incongruously, across the way from it was a yoga franchise,
emblematic like the dog shop of Old Town's changing nature.

But one couldn't completely escape the past, Bland thought, thinking of
Wythe St., one block from Pendleton, and named for George Wythe, an
abolitionist and the law teacher of plantation owner Thomas Jefferson,
and a man possibly murdered for his anti-slavery views. Whether one
knew it or not, Bland believed, history has a heavy hand, and nowhere
more so than in Old Town. She herself was a distant descendant of
Confederate General Richard Bland Lee, and of his father, Virginia's
first member of Congressman.

She dutifully locked the doors to her 2013 Camry, to prevent a thief
from making off with the box of antique books in the back seat. But
locking up seemed silly. A criminal was the last thing she should fear.
Like some others, she figured the authorities had nabbed the murderer
the other night, at the Carlyle mansion. The news sites reported that this
Lercino character had been connected to a string of robberies, and to
that horrible death at the Athenaeum. She deemed it likely he had also
committed the murder of poor Mr. Hill next to the Lighthouse Harry
Lee home. And if not him, then that awful McVeigh character, who had
also been found out.

'I pray the town finally gets back to normal,' she reflected, while
walking up the cobblestones of Oronoco St. She knew it was not named

after the river in Venezuela, like many people assumed, but after a Native-American tribe that originally dwelled in what became Alexandria. The researcher in her wondered idly if there was some connection between the two, whether Indians in the distant past had migrated from South America through the Caribbean to the Mid-Atlantic. 'People have so many misconceptions and theories about history,' she mused. 'There are often hidden links between things that have been long forgotten.'

The irregularly fashioned stones were hard on her ankles, so she shifted over to the sidewalk, and stepped past the lush, extensive gardens of a private house from 1795, universally referred to in town as "Lee's Boyhood Home". The young Robert Edward Lee had lived there after the death of his father Light-Horse Harry in 1818, after his maiming by a pro-War of 1812 mob in Baltimore. Bland thought of this, which made her think anew of Mr. Hill's horrific slaying, next to Light-Horse's house, just three blocks away.

She passed the site of the Boyhood Home's historical marker, and from memory and for the thousandth time recited its inscription: "After Appomattox Lee returned and climbed the wall to see 'if the snowballs were in bloom'," meaning the garden's round clusters of white viburnum flowers.

Bland had lived in Alexandria long enough to remember when the house, where Washington supped and where Lafayette slept, had been a museum of Lee's life. The docents had been very elderly Southern ladies, of a "unreconstructed" type. They drawled with accents common in town decades before. They wore gingham dresses out of a Matthew Brady photograph of 1863. Bland pursed her dry, cracked lips in a wry smile on recalling when a black lady friend had visited the place out of curiosity. The docents looked upon her like a creature from another planet. They were polite enough, but plainly uncomfortable at having to entertain a visitor whom, they thought, maintained views on social history rather different from their own.

These days the Boyhood Home, like the fine clapboard house adjoining it, was a lovingly maintained private residence. Another museum in town had idly thought of acquiring it and merging it with hers, but the asking price, over $6 million, would have broken the budget. She had herself dreamed of the museums acquiring the Cotton Mill too, and the spacious Edmund Jennings Lee house across Washington St. from the Lee-Fendall House.

Lisa Jennings Bland was herself a very distant descendent of the Lee family, including Edmund Jennings Lee. The leader, along with President James Monroe and House Speaker Henry Clay, of the American Colonization Society, the oddly named organization that sent freed slaves back to Africa. She was a somewhat nearer descendent of the also-prominent Jennings clan, including black relations. A Paul Jennings had been a manservant to President James Madison. Few people knew of this ethnic connection, and the woman herself had fair and freckled skin.

It would have been nice, she believed, if the neighborhood of old Lee houses made up its own historic district. But the Cotton Mill had been bought out by condo developers, and the other homes remained in private hands. And the notion of a "Lee" District was now utterly out of favor.

As she stepped along, Bland looked up at the historical marker, and the quietly perceptive woman did a double take. She looked again, confused, and figured she was further up the street than she had thought. She stopped, and looked at the part of the white picket fence that the sign was opposite from. She was at the right spot, she realized. She looked for it again. But there was no sign of it, the sign.

Bland gazed down to the moist grass on the sidewalk, and saw the stump of the rusted metal post that had held up the sign. Someone had recently sawed through, or blow-torched through, the post, and carried it off.

The Commonwealth of Virginia, probably the most historically minded of all the 50 states, was noted for its thousands of historical markers. A state agency maintained them, but Bland couldn't recall an effort to take down the sign.

As she reflected on that, she crossed again over the 240-year-old cobblestones to the corner. At Oronoco and Washington, by the doorway of her Lee-Fendall House, she looked up at a lamppost, and recalled the unsettling history of the intersection. In the Second World War, the combative, bushy-browed head of the United Mine Workers, John L. Lewis, made the Lee-Fendall House his residence. And even though the nation was in the midst of the conflict with Nazi Germany and Imperial Japan, Lewis led a labor strike that paralyzed swaths of war-time industry. Perhaps Lewis thought the mine owners were taking advantage of the workers during the national emergency. In any event, enraged students from Arlington's Washington and Lee High School—now named Washington-Liberty—surrounded Lewis' home. At this very spot, protestors hanged his effigy from a lamppost.

At the entranceway, Bland shook her head at the violent, unpleasant episode. She turned her key in the door lock, but it gave her difficulty—she had to turn it several times, and push hard on the door, before it opened.

She went inside the threshold, the large townhouse and its offices eerily quiet, and turned on a couple of lights. Normally, she'd light up the whole place, but deemed it wasteful for someone working alone to do so. She slowly climbed the 135-year-old staircase to the second floor. Her office was a third of the way down a hall from the second-floor landing.

Long before, the home had been the scene of countless deaths. Like so many other large houses of Southern sympathizers—such as the related Lee and Fendall families residing there—the Union Army had seized it, and turned it into a hospital for wounded troops. Alexandria's myriad of large townhomes and public buildings was ideal for makeshift hospitals. About 30 of these structures treated the injured, including at times Union and Confederate alike.

Many had perished in this house, but one stricken Northern trooper had miraculously survived. Due to blood loss, he was given up for dead, until his physician, a Dr. Edwin Bentley, tried a radical new therapy. A transfusion. The soldier was the beneficiary of the first successful blood transfusion in North America. And the trooper was very lucky. At the time, blood types were unknown. The donated blood with which physician infused him happened to be the same type as his own. Otherwise the serum might have killed him. And many soldiers would die before the discovery of blood types 36 years after the war. Some believed the house, like other former hospitals, was haunted, by persons who died in agony from grisly wounds.

In contrast to rooms throughout the house restored to their 19th-century appearance, Bland's workspace was contemporary. She had an IKEA work desk, to which was bolted a workstation holding her Apple iMac. Next to it was a MacBook laptop. That night, the room was half-lit by one of the ceiling's fluorescent lights. It was "old-fashioned" however, in that the office was fully enclosed by walls, unlike the cubicles in most contemporary enterprises.

In setting up her office, Lisa Bland had followed an eccentric belief. Perhaps it was the spy novels and thrillers she enjoyed. She noticed how master agents, such as Jason Bourne, would position themselves in a house or a restaurant so that they could see, and react to, any danger that might approach.

Following this tactic, she had her desk placed on the sharp angle away from the door, and across the room from a window facing the street. That evening, as there were no other employees to interfere with her work focus, she kept her door open. Also, as an elderly woman, and as someone who sometimes stayed after hours, she kept a can of bear spray in the pull-out file of her desk. She hoped she wasn't being neurotic about that.

Bland also owned a lightweight, Sig Sauer pistol that an old boyfriend had given her decades before. Back when crime in Old Town was rampant, after the crumbling of the city's industries and "white flight" to the suburbs. However, the handgun had rested for years in a locked box in her home. Still, after Hill's murder on Cameron St., she'd taken a steak knife from the pantry where the museum kept its silverware for special events, and placed it in her desk drawer as well.

Working alone that damp night, she felt a bit claustrophobic, so she pulled up her window's plastic slats to permit a view of the small preschool and the Edmunds Jennings Lee House across Washington St. She settled into her unwelcome tasks. Changing the name of the museum seemed so insignificant, she sighed, compared to the workaday issues facing most people. But Bland was a hardworking, reliable manager, so she pushed aside her complaint.

'Well,' she figured, 'after we change the name, all this rancor will hopefully settle down.'

Chapter 52 – Museum Macabre

Most in town were disappointed with the return of inclement weather. But he relished the protection it afforded. Fog rolled in off the roiled Potomac, the white caps dimly visible to the few persons driving or walking along its shore. Mist cloaked South Washington and Oronoco Streets. He stopped at the streetlamp, near the long-vanished one where John L. Lewis' effigy had been strung up. With gloved hands he felt the leather pouch hanging from neck to waist, and the hard, rubbery coils within. He straightened out the plastic pullovers covering his boots. He tapped the dagger on one side of his belt, and the pistol on the other. 'Loaded for bear,' he mused sardonically. He stretched his well-conditioned physique, and walked on.

The incident the other night had been fortunate and unfortunate, he reckoned. Fortunate that another would-be victim had so readily presented himself, as he crossed over the lawn of the Carlyle House. Unfortunate that the man had lived, despite the flash of genius of walling him up in the masonry, in a recreation of John Carlyle's consigning a black cat to death within the mansion stones.

Unfortunate, in that Ted Sifter and Harmony Jain had intervened, and then Detective Greco. Those three were becoming more of a threat. But he had outsmarted everyone thus far, and could do so again. His blood lust was up—it was becoming stronger, almost irresistible. Thus the impromptu attack on Lercino, unlike his other assaults, which had been so carefully thought out. Like this evening's affair.

The other night, he'd come by to make an impression of the door lock. The next day, he'd gone to a lock and key shop on upper Duke St.,

along the stretch of road named for Confederate generals such as
Pickett and Wheeler. 'They should keep the name Pickett,' he told
himself, 'given his suicidal attack at Gettysburg.' It took the locksmith
just two minutes to make the key. Given his double mask, disguised
voice, and the collar of a long coat pulled up around his neck, he was
certain the locksmith, who in any event had been distracted with other,
more complicated jobs, hadn't recognized him.

This night, he was happy to find the neighborhood devoid of people. As
he stood at the crossroad, he reflected, 'This moment of retribution has
been waiting for 160 years. Or 400 years. Tonight the waiting will
end!'

He carefully unlocked the front door, and stepped quietly into the
antique parlor. He knew, perhaps as much as the museum managers,
how the ghosts of the Lees, and their kissing cousins the Fendalls,
haunted the place. Some 37 different Lees dwelled there from the
American Revolution to the turn of the 20th century. The Lee brood,
including an ancestor of Lisa Bland, had largely raised young Robert in
lieu of his deceased, war-hero dad.

The interloper thought of attorney Philip Fendall II, and his
representation of Secretary of State Henry Clay against the enslaved
woman Dupuy, when she had sued Clay, and had urged a court to grant
her manumission. "That poor, poor woman,' the man said to himself.
"She was denied her freedom for so many years." He often thought of
that lawsuit, and others like it, which usually tossed him into a fury.
True, Fendall had sided with the Union when the Civil War erupted
but, he raged to himself, 'that in no way made up for his previous sins!'
Earlier, after hacking into Lisa Bland's Gmail account, he confirmed
she'd be working there alone this night. There was so much less guess
work than at the Freedmen's graves, when he couldn't be sure if

someone, the *right* someone, would visit the place. This would be more like the sacrificial offering of Anthony Hill. He had learned that Hill was a direct descendent of Confederate general A.P. Hill, and that he would be at his home that evening. Which let him lure Tony Hill to the basement of the adjoining, vacant home. Though he couldn't have guessed that Jain would show up just afterward, and with Sifter in her wake. That was an unexpected coincidence. He might have killed the woman. No matter. One life, or many, he reasoned, meant nothing in pursuit of his cause.

Light from the corner streetlamp shone softly through the front door's frosted glass panes and onto the stairs leading upward. He ascended them slowly because the steps, dating from an 1885 renovation, might creak. They did, but the noise was muffled some by the Persian carpeting.

At the top of the stairs he paused. Immediately to his left, workmen had taken off a door from a room under renovation and placed it against the wall. White canvas sheets spotted with blobs of dried paint lay crumpled on its floor, with buckets of paint and small cans of turpentine placed by the window. His target was one more room down on the right. Shimmers of light glowed from it. He felt a thrill pour through him, the thrill of the hunt.

Lisa Bland was tallying the financial expense of the name change when she heard sounds down the corridor. Her boney fingers poised over the keyboard; she looked up from her iMac. 'Is it the settling of the old building?,' she wondered. That happened all the time. Then Bland heard another noise. Had another colleague come in that night to work on the name controversy? She tried to figure who that might be.

The noise stopped, but her lower lip stiffened in concern. Could it possibly be, she shuddered, *that someone else,* the fiend who'd been afflicting Old Town? She stared out the doorway, but saw nothing, not even a shadow.

She felt ashamed of herself. 'A scared, little old lady I am! Besides, the killer has been caught.' She began tapping out cost estimates again. She shouldn't let her imagination get ahold of her. Even silly horror movies still scared her, had given her nightmares as a child.

But then she heard other noises. Not the creaking, or perhaps the settling, of the stairs, but sounds on the hallway between the stairs and her office. A sound like footsteps, of feet moving slowly, carefully. She felt her nerves tingle.

Lisa quietly pulled open the workstation drawer, and reached within, feeling her way through a stack of folders. 'Damn it!' she said to herself, when unable to locate the spray can. Had she removed it? Had the cleaning lady? The fingers of her left hand trembled. She stilled them, and listened intently.

The noise had stopped.

'Was probably my imagination.'

Still, should she go into the hall to make sure? Should she call out? 'Ah,' she told herself, 'here is the bear spray.' She placed it on the side of the folders. But she was being silly, and would feel foolish in a minute, she was sure.

Yet then she heard steps. Definitely steps. Someone treading along slowly.

Her stomach tensed with fear. Should she ask who was there? Of course she should. It had to be a colleague. But something told her not to. She reached into the drawer, and grasped the can.

She was startled, on seeing a shadow fall onto the doorway, a shadow cast from one of the town's first electric lamps, installed in 1895 on the ceiling near the stairs.

She began to utter, "Who is—" when one half of a figure stepped partly into the doorway. Then with another step, the complete figure emerged in the half light of the room.

A rather tall man. Draped in black. Somewhat athletic-looking, though not particularly young, Bland estimated. Wearing two masks, the outer one almost fully covered his face, except for the eye openings. And in his right hand was—could it be? Lisa was startled by the man's appearance, and for an instant didn't recognize his implement.

He was holding a bull whip!

Lisa stared at him, and at it, her lips parted, her heart now pounding like a broken-hearted woman at a former lover's door.

His large frame filled the doorway. He stared back. He hesitated, surprised at finding her at a desk facing him.

He recovered. He stated:

"Don't struggle. I'll make this quick. Like at the Old Presbyterian church. I promise you'll feel little pain.

"And nothing from the mutilation."

She was stunned. He was, indeed, The Murderer. Here, in the museum, in her office, her safe place.

And she recognized the voice, didn't she? She had heard it before. And recently.

By "quick", she wondered abstractly, through her fear, did he mean the whip? Meaning it wouldn't hurt?

She saw him reach with his left hand to pull open his dark, tight-fitting jacket. He was wearing a belt of some sort. There was a pistol on his belt. In Lisa's mind flashed the words and images "gunslinger", and "Wild West killer".

The Old Town Horror

From next to it he drew a dagger. A long dagger. 'The knife used at the Freedmen's atrocity!?' she wondered in fright. Its sharp edges glinted from the overhead light.

Lisa Bland wasn't a particularly brave person, but she wasn't a coward. She acted on instinct. Yes, she was very scared: Her pulse raced at a level beyond counting. But she found herself pushing her chair back from the desk into the short space between herself and the wall. As she did, her left hand pulled open the drawer. She surprised herself by grabbing the cannister with a swift motion.

She was fixed utterly on the moment, on survival. So it was only then that her brain fully registered and identified the man's voice. Yes, she knew it well, having met him multiple times, even worked with him. Another wave of shock swept over her from this realization. But she kept pushing the chair back and firmly gripped the can.

Grasping the whip and knife, the Old Town Horror stepped forward. He came around her desk. He could hardly miss seeing the something in her left hand. An absurd thought struck him: Was she trying to stop him with a garden hose? Then an instant of horror, as he thought it might be a gun. But no, it wasn't that—before he recognized it, the spray hit him.

The smell was atrocious, and stinging droplets flew through the eye apertures of his masks. He felt searing pain. He was nearly blinded; he screamed. But he blinked hard, and hard again, and managed to regain some of his vision. He strode the few remaining feet to her, raising the dagger in his left hand, while keeping the whip in his upright right arm. In an urge of self-preservation, Lisa pushed down hard on her feet, and pushed the swivel chair to the right side of her desk. As she did, she pulled open another desk drawer. Her right hand grabbed hold of the steak knife.

Enraged, the killer came upon her, and swung the whip down with a sharp, short twist.

It lashed into Lisa's left hand, knocking the cannister down onto the rug. Coughing, gasping, but his eyes clearing further, he brought the dagger up high, and plunged it down toward her right shoulder.

As he did, she stuck the steak knife upward. It stuck below his left biceps, changing the motion of his arm, causing him to miss his target. He felt a sharp pain, lost the grip, dropped the dagger, and lost his balance. His left arm smashed down onto the desk.

Lisa and her chair swiveled, and backed against the desk, knocking into the two computers. The intruder stumbled into the woman, pinning her onto the chair.

She was almost face-to-face with the killer. She felt suffocated, by his weight, by the stank of his breath, and by the fear and horror roaring through her mind and soul. Blood from his arm wound dripped upon her dress and her leggings. She was dizzy from her racing heart and hyperventilating lungs.

The gas cannister had rolled across the carpeted floor and out of reach. So she flung out her arms and hands, and groped desperately for another weapon. She reached up for the knife in his arm, and it fell out of the wound, splattering blood onto the MacBook.

His body was now pressed down hard on hers. She struggled to breathe. She sensed an object next to her left foot. It was his dagger! But there was no way of getting to it. Unable to see past his body, she reached her right hand along the desk, searching for the steak knife.

The attacker had been stunned by the blade entering his arm, and from losing his balance. Then, as his body pressed against hers, his mind cleared. He rose, and prepared to smash his right arm and the handle of the whip down upon his prey.

Bland was able to draw in a deep breath as his abdomen pulled away. She knew she would likely die within the next minutes. She felt a sadness about this, but not despondency. She had to continue the struggle, whatever the outcome.

She ran her fingers along the table. She came upon a sharp object. Not the knife. But a ballpoint pen. A thick one. Given to her at a museum party for her years of service.

As the killer began to bring the whip down, Lisa reached up with her hand. The pen caught him in the far-left side of his chest, near the third rib down. Fortunately for him, well below his eyes or neck. Still, when it pierced his clothing, and pricked his skin, it was stung, and it broke the motion of his arm. He lost his balance again, and fell down toward the desk, breaking his fall with his hands, his injured arm in much pain, and his right hand bruised from smacking against the table.

Momentarily freed, Lisa felt renewed strength from her counterblows. She stood up from her chair, her legs numb, and staggered away, toward the window, and toward the cannister on the ground. She tripped over herself, and crawled away on her knees and elbows.

Her attacker, enraged, pushed himself up from the desk. He turned toward Lisa. His eyes still stinging, he saw moving away. He was momentarily confused what to do. Which weapon should he use, he wondered. Or should he just strangle the wretched woman with bare hands?

He grabbed the dagger again, and took up the whip.

He saw her rise quickly, and turn toward him. Her face heaving with fear, her right hand gripping that damned cannister.

As she shot a blast of spray toward him, he lurched right, pressed against the desk, and avoided most of it. Still, the stench was horrendous, and his left eye teared up.

He began to fear for the first time that he, incredibly, might actually lose this fight. Defeated by this older woman, this wretch, little better than a librarian. And end up dead in her office. Such ignominy. For his righteous revenge to end in that way.

It was time, he realized, to 'go nuclear'. Despite the risk of alerting neighbors and the authorities. The blinds to the office were open. Someone outside might have noticed the commotion here, might have heard them. Might hear what was to come.

Meantime Lisa saw she had mostly missed with her second blast of spray. As she moved the can to her left, to point directly at her nemesis, her sweaty index finger slipped off the spray button.

The killer dropped his whip. Like an Old West gunslinger, he grabbed for the pistol on his belt. The infernal woman, he saw, was still holding the cannister.

He thought out his next moves furiously, in nanoseconds. It was probably too late before he got sprayed again. He might be blinded. If blinded, he figured out desperately, he would hold his breath and fire off a spread of bullets, waist high, from left to right.

And hope one or more would strike her. If that worked, he'd flee the building, hopefully before anyone alerted to the sounds could arrive. As he held the stubby FNX-45 gun out toward her, she seemed to hesitate. No spray came out of the can. Without hesitation, he fired off one round. The projectile struck her in the chest, smashing through her left, fourth rib, and lodging two inches from her heart. He feared the bullet might pass through her, and even through the wall of the house, alerting any passerby. That didn't happen.

The force of the slug's impact hurled Lisa against the wall. The cannister flew out her hand. For a moment she stood, her back to the wall, her arms and hands outstretched, as if she was about to walk zombie-like toward her tormentor.

But she couldn't move. She felt more weakened and disheartened than in pain. Beyond hope. Her right eye caught the gleam of the steak knife on the ground. She felt apathetic about getting to it.

Her back and rear slid down the wall. She collapsed, comatose, in a heap.

The fiend felt a great relief, to be spared a further death struggle. Then fear. Could the noise from their fracas have alerted a neighbor? He hoped not. The lights to the large, adjoining home, he recalled, had been out when he slithered up Oronoco St. to the museum. What about Washington St.? He went over to the window and peeked outside.

The mist had turned into a light rain, droplets glowing under the streetlights. The boulevard was empty of pedestrians. No cars passed along it. Far to the south the killer spotted a sedan and a truck, heading further away. He shut the window tight and closed the plastic slats.

His mission came back to him. Which was not so much to kill the woman, that was a given, but to send a message, his message, and to spread panic. He gauged he could spare a few more moments for that. He kicked the blasted cannister aside. He bent over the woman.

She was alive, he was surprised to find. Breathing shallowly. Unconscious. Her wound, though no doubt fatal, wasn't giving off much blood. A clean shot. Good. That would make his next act less messy.

He grabbed ahold of her armpits and pulled her up the wall, his own shoulder and arm aching. As expected, she was not too heavy, perhaps not even a hundred pounds. Blood was oozing from her nose, and spittle from her mouth.

He felt contempt for the woman. He considered her, in essence, a chronicler of evil.

Grunting, he lifted her off the ground, and hauled her back to the desk. He put her face down onto it, pushing her forward so her head hung off the far side, and her legs the near side.

He slapped her head: She was still unconscious. Maybe lapsing into a coma, no threat. He ripped off the shoulders of her dress, and pulled the fabric down to her waist. He savored a memory of his actions at the boxed tomb of the Unknown Soldier of the American Revolution.

He grasped his bull whip. He completely unwound it. He stood off to the side of the desk. And he began cracking his instrument.

One lash. Two. More.

Lacerations appeared on the soft white flesh of Lisa Bland.

With her face hanging down toward the floor, she became vaguely conscious of a pounding. No pain, but a sound. She idly thought it was the pounding of the Chesapeake shore.

She lost consciousness again. Permanently.

He kept wielding the lash, with growing excitement. Pleasureful. Almost an ecstasy, of control and command. The lacerations spread, turning the corpse's back into a bloody pulp.

When he had counted out exactly 39 cracks of the whip, he stopped. That was the normal number for a punishable offense. Though he had lashed harder than the norm. He checked her pulse, on both her wrists and neck to make doubly sure. No pulse. For her. His own heart was racing with excitement, an adrenaline thrill.

Filled with righteous triumph, he had one more action to perform. He wished he could take the whole thing, but it would be too heavy, too dangerous to take through the streets, unlike that night at Christ Church.

He took out a steel Medline scalpel. He pulled the woman's left arm up onto the desk, and began carving out letters on her still-warm flesh. He stopped, somewhat startled, when he heard the beep. It was her wristwatch, signaling the passage of every quarter hour. A time-obsessed archivist, he thought, consumed with petty things, while preserving evil things. The sound sparked a fear things were taking too long. Someone outside *might* have heard him. And a worker of hers might by chance come to the museum to put in some evening hours. Or perhaps a security guard might come by to check up on things.

He stopped carving; he wiped off the knife and placed it in a pocket of the daypack. From his pack he pulled out a compact hacksaw, and a trash bag. He had practiced for the next action in the cellar of his Old Town condo, two blocks from the old slave importation dock. Tried it out on a dog he'd grabbed near the Fort Lyon park.

He pulled her arm tighter across the desk, and got to work. It went easier than he expected. The tendons, the skin, the tissues and especially the bones. Not as much blood as one might have believed either. Though she had lost some from the whipping. Some of the red stuff did drip from her savaged back down to the floor.

He put the thing in the bag, bagged it, and put it in the daypack. He gathered the steak knife, the dagger, and the pen, and placed them in his pack with the whip. Messy—he might have to dispose of the things at his forested hideaway up from the Huntington metro.

He walked to the doorway. Though eager to make time, he paused in the threshold where she had first spotted him. He gazed at what was left of her, and took quiet satisfaction. He pushed a compress on the cuts in his arm and his chest. 'Nothing serious,' he told himself. 'That hag was feeble after all. How could I have panicked!?'

Then he panicked again. Surely bits of his blood and clothes were in the room after the struggle. 'I wish I had brought a bomb,' he regretted, 'to blow up the place, and the forensic evidence.'

Then he noticed a quartz paperweight on Bland's desk. And thought of something even better than a bomb. Within two minutes he had splashed the turpentine and other flammables from the room under renovation onto her walls, floor, and desk. Not the body so much. 'Let's give her *some* respect,' he thought, sardonically. He believed striking the hard rock with his steel blade would throw off sparks. It did. And with matter that combustible, he was nearly scorched by the time he ran out of the office. He strode rapidly down the stairs, which creaked like the sound of frogs croaking. But nobody to hear it now. Outside it was raining. No one was on the sidewalks of N. Washington. No flame had yet cracked the closed window of the office. He strode back up the cobblestoned street, past Lee's Boyhood Home, past the stump of the destroyed sign. He was unseen, again undetected, like a ghost from the past that strikes the present, then returns to its grave, to the past, to remain for a time. For a time.

He kept to very quiet residential streets, down Oronoco, then onto Queen. This reminded him of his silent, unseen walk away from the Freedmen's Cemetery on that eventful night. When he had sent another message, another warning to a hate-filled world. He examined the cuts on his left arm and chest; they were no longer bleeding. He'd tend to them later. Now down further along Queen, and only turning onto the normally busier N. Royal for the final short block. He knew the streets well, having worked near them for so long. Almost no lights were on among the large townhouses of the old gentry and the modest wood frame homes of the working men of yore. He saw no one; no one saw him. He was like a haunted soul from Alexandria's past, dredged up as a monster for its troubled present.

He turned to see a faint red glow in the block he'd left behind him. He heard sirens. That remarkable fire company on Prince St. was reacting remarkably fast again. It would put out the blaze before most of the museum was burned. But not before the room of Lisa Bland, and much of her already desecrated corpse, was consumed in flame. Later that night, the blaze extinguished, the firefighters would discover the woman was missing a limb, and had discernible laceration marks, and would deduce those ravages weren't from the fire.

The killer slowed his pace on Royal, knowing potential danger lurked. Latrobe's City Hall spire towered to the left, with Market Square just beyond. Police might be near. It was a risk, but the thrill of another victory outweighed any dread of being caught. He was still ecstatic from the noble butchery at Lee-Fendall. He was taking more chances. He craved another rush of joy.

At Royal and Cameron he stopped, careful to stay away from a streetlamp's illumination. He looked a block down Cameron to the corner where the lynching of 1897 occurred, where young Joe McCoy was strung up. "Revenge is so sweet," he breathed.

The lights of City Hall were subdued. Across Cameron was Gadsby's Tavern, closed from the pandemic, no lights on at all. Excellent. His next labor would be blanketed by darkness.

He slipped across the street to the hatch. The cover hadn't been opened for several years, however, so he could only lift it after three tries and considerable effort and a sharp pain in his injured arm. With a dull, scraping sound, it did come loose, tossing dust and rust into the wet night air.

He kneeled down, and his flashlight stabbed the dark expanse. The 11-foot-deep cavern flickered below. Seventeen feet across, with solid stone foundations to protect it from the ravages of the original Potomac River shore. At the bottom were scatterings of straw, as if it was still 1848. He hoped the straw wouldn't soak up too much blood. He wanted the thing to look as gruesome as could be. He'd aim for a corner where there was only bare soil and rock.

Then he heard the pattering. A stray, a mutt, a mix of huskie and pit bull, scampered up in the dark to his daypack. It stuck it its snout through an unzipped pouch. Its mouth frothed with excitement from the scent; its huff and puff were loud. Someone down the street might hear it.

Favoring his aching left arm, he knocked the dog hard on its rib cage with the side of his right fist. Its body was pushed back an inch, then was instantly was back in place. It ignored the blow, focused on the delectable, raw-red flesh inside. It was stubborn and intent. Most of its head slipped into the pouch.

He had no time for this interruption, this risk. He drew out the dagger. The mutt never knew. The blade plunged into its neck, severing the carotid artery. Without a whimper, it died immediately. Its blood spilled onto the brick sidewalk, began to drip down into the hole below. Pushing the animal aside, he opened the backpack and took out the plastic bag. He flashed the light down into the cavern again.

It was an oddity from the past which the city had renovated almost a half century prior. In the days before refrigeration, before electricity, a busy tavern and lodging like Gadsby's needed ice, to store its perishable foods and cool its hearty ales. Ice was hacked out of the frozen Potomac or at Hoofs Run in winter, then hauled or carted by the enslaved or the indentured or the free to this locale.

He chose a spot free of straw, the straw that old Gadsby, that slaveholder, had used to preserve the ice, if the weather obliged, through the spring and summer months, until a late-season freeze allowed the ice well to be filled again.

It wasn't an easy toss, as his arm muscles were stiff, his left arm sore from its wound, his shoulders sore from the whipping. But after its release, the bloodied arm thumped near hard-packed dirt by the circular wall—and plopped up against it.

He laughed at the sight. It looked as though a corpse had pushed an arm up from up out of the earth.

He got to his feet. The dog's body seemed to be stiffening already. What to do with it? 'Well, why not?' He picked it up, and tossed it down to the straw in the center of the well.

He snorted, and thought: 'That should give the local cops and the clueless FBI even more to chew on.'

He gazed cautiously up and down Cameron, and saw no one, not even a ghost. He crossed over to Royal, and like an avenging specter disappeared again into the night of the desolate city.

"I am Death, I am Invincible," he muttered. "No one can put a stop to Death." He was getting cockier, less cautious. He reflected fondly on his second secret lair, a perfect spot, much closer to his killing grounds. He would return there soon.

Chapter 53 – The Well from Hell

Very early in the morning, Ted lay in the wrinkled sheets of his bed, unable to fully puzzle out the mystery. His head was aching, his brain befogged, partly from the drizzle falling outside the windows.

Exercise, as ever, might help clear his mind and revive his body.

He was about to get up for his daily round of sit-ups and stretches when his cell buzzed loudly. He wondered what Harmony had to say. But it was Greco. Calling him directly.

The detective was himself baffled. And deeply upset. "Have you heard?!" He wanted Ted to come over fast. To Gadsby's Tavern, of all places. He didn't say why over the phone. "Just come," he said. Ted was immediately wide awake.

Halfway through his 15-minute bike ride over to the restaurant, he heard and felt a buzz in the back pocket of his shirt. He got off his race bike on an access road overlooking a swollen Cameron Run. It was a text from Harmony. She had seen the news on her feed; her text explained what was awaiting him. Back on the bike, his head swirled with grim possibilities.

He had known Lisa Jennings Bland. She was a good source of info on Lee-Fendall, on the Lees, and on Alexandria generally.

'Another link to Lee, to slavery, and the Antebellum,' Ted told himself, his heart pounding, as he rolled along, now more convinced than ever of his theory.

When he arrived in the dim, early morning light at Cameron and N. Royal, he found Harmony standing near Greco and a coterie of cops and EMS professionals. She was scanning through the latest news

567

about Bland's murder and the museum fire. Across Royal, Latrobe's spire hung from the morning overcast like Damocles' blade.

As he had been for weeks, Greco was grim. Yet this time his face, spotlighted by a streetlamp, had an ashen pallor. He nervously fingered the Orthodox cross hanging from his neck. The gold-plated icon seemed to have lost some of its luster.

Fueled by discussions with Ted, he had had his own doubts about McVeigh being the murderer. Those doubts now seemed confirmed. "Maybe we have a set of killers," he told the historian, while shrugging the concrete blocks of his shoulders. "Maybe several men, working at cross purposes." He ran a hand through his graying hair. "Or working together." The detective felt another headache coming on; he hoped it wasn't migraines. His wife had been telling him to quit the police force, and find work as a private security expert. Maybe she was right; she usually was. But not yet. Not during this crisis.

Greco turned to Harmony and confessed, "I wish and I pray, harder than ever, that I could solve this damnable case." He told Ted, "Maybe you two can help. Come with me." Their group stepped past a forensics specialist examining red specks on the ground near the ice well. It wasn't Paula Leeds, and Ted idly wondered why she wasn't there. "It is," Greco said to him and Harmony, "the blood of a dog." He stopped for a moment, as if to brace the duo for what they were about to see. He said, "But down below, there's something else, and definitely not an animal."

He led Ted and his lady friend past a phalanx of cops keeping back a small, masked crowd of the early-rising curious. Harmony reflected ruefully that, during the pandemic, only murders and press conferences seemed to attract an Old Town gathering. Behind the crowd, and standing up against the wall near Gadsby's front entrance, was the

Mysterious Stranger. Her arm damaged in the Wilkes St. encounter was in a white cloth sling. Otherwise, as ever, she was outfitted in tasteful, darkly colored clothes. Her eyes were sad, dreamlike, her face wan and drained of color. As if she were impersonating the ghost of Theodosia Burr in Room 8 of the Tavern behind her. Harmony briefly wondered if the woman had anything to do with what they were about to see, then banished the thought. The product, she judged, of jealousy, given Ted's admiration for the woman's beauty and mystique.

The two amateur sleuths and the detective went down a few grey steps to the plexiglass windows on the top sides of the ice well. In normal times, it permitted passersby a peek down into Alexandria's past. Firemen had taken off several of the panes, and had slid a ladder down to the bottom of the well. Police had set up electric lights; luminous shafts of light poured through the intact windows.

They took turns hauling themselves down. Greco's square bulk shook the ladder. Harmony gracefully slid down along the scale. Ted's left knee creaked with each step. Though the temperature on the street was mild, the cops and EMS in the well were shivering. Partly from the damp coolness, partly from something else.

Greco led them to the far side of the clammy chamber. They glanced at the bizarre sight of a dog, with a dark coat and a bloodied neck, lying stiff and dead on top of straw in the center of the well. But their attention riveted to the surreal sight of a disembodied limb leaning against a cold stone wall. Ted and Harmony would have been even more horrified if the sight hadn't seemed so unreal. The dried blood on the limb confirmed it was real.

"We did a quick DNA test," said Greco in an even yet sad voice, "and it matches, 95 percent." His words echoed against the cold dark walls. "The biochemist said it was something like the quick test for the virus, but more reliable. Leeds will check it out too, when we get ahold of her," he said, with a distant tone in his voice. "She'll do another, more accurate test.

"But it's hers—her. The lady murd—slaughtered—last night." Greco tilted his head down, as if mouthing a prayer. "Lisa Jennings Bland."

"So the fire didn't kill her," said Ted, almost matter-of-factly.

Greco almost imperceptibly shook his head. "Coroner makes it clear she was shot, stabbed—whipped—to death. The blaze was extra. Maybe the whipping too." Greco paused, almost disbelieving what he was saying. "Maybe the whipping came after the time of death. More tests will show…" His voice trailed off. Ted wasn't surprised at his surmise. An "accidental" fire was far too much a coincidence.

The thing by the wall was stiff. It looked frozen, as if it had spent weeks, not hours, in an ice well. Through Ted's flashed a strange memory—of shaking the hand of the arm, Bland's arm, when she was alive, the disembodied arm now propped up before him. As Harmony looked at it, her eyes swelled with tears.

Greco gazed at Ted, but seemed to look past him this time, instead of staring directly into his eyes. Normally he seemed to peer inside someone's soul. That morning, disconsolate, he seemed to be searching for consolation.

"By the way," the detective told him, his voice sounding faraway, "that woman from the Wilkes Cemetery, Miss Benedita, was already here when the police arrived. We don't really suspect her, but she said without prompting she has an alibi for last night. We're checking it out. She was also near the scene of the Old Presbyterian murder, supposedly." Ted recalled her being near Tony's killing too, but said nothing.

The detective bent down on his haunches next to the arm, and motioned the other two over. He swallowed hard. "Now take a look at this. Tell me if it means anything to you."

Ted moved in front of Greco, and stared where he was pointing. Above the wrist of the arm were letters. Reddish letters.

Carved into the flesh.

"We're not sure yet," Greco's voice resonated behind Ted, "but forensics thinks they were carved after her death."

Ted had to remind himself he was not in a nightmare, but the real world. The letters, each about half an inch in height, read:

"C H A R..."

Greco, normally steely and self-controlled, seemed close to despair. "What is it?! Because he was thinking of burning her too? 'Charring' her? After knifing and shooting her, and whipping her to a pulp!?" The veteran officer, who thought he'd seen it all, felt dizzy. The circular walls of the well seemed to slowly revolve around him.

For an instant, Ted felt his own head spin, as he imagined the letters spitting out, "CHARnel house". Then he got ahold of himself, his normal calm during tense moments returning.

'Think it through,' he told himself. He knew the Old Town of yore had been notorious for the deadly fires that swept through it. But he couldn't think of any connection between those conflagrations, the Lee-Fendall House, and Lisa Bland. What else could the letters mean?

Harmony was looking over his right shoulder, her sharp eyes studying the script on the arm. She asked a fireman for his large flashlight, and shone it on the scarred flesh. After a few moments, she asked Greco, "What is the fifth character?"

"What are you talking about?" he responded gruffly. But even as he said it, he grabbed the flashlight and shone it to the right of the "R".

Ted followed the beam: It seemed to be tearing into the flesh like a laser. There did seem to be a flap of skin near the "R". Greco took a pen knife from a pocket, inhaled deeply, and poked at the flap. It pulled out. On it was a letter:

"L".

The lettering was now:

"C H A R L..."

Greco moved the beam ever so slightly to the right of the L. Hoping to find another flap, another letter or letters. "E S", or "I E". But the hellish script ended at its fifth character.

Greco turned to Ted. "Can you tell me the significance? Who is Charles?"

Ted thought out loud. "Charles, CHARLotte, North Carolina? Charles, Carlos—Carlos Cordero, the first person murdered?

"Was the murderer thinking of his first kill during this kill?"

"It's possible," said Greco. "Someone this deranged might think back to another slaying. Mass murderers follow a pattern, a repeating pattern. They pride themselves they can keep killing, and never be caught. Yeah, they sometimes recall prior killings, even celebrate them somehow."

Ted had another suspicion. But he was hesitant to state an unproven opinion. He answered, "I'm not certain what to say. I need to think this over."

"Well, you think about it," said Greco. "Think about the possible history behind it. I'll tend to the contemporary angle." And he turned to Bradenson, telling him to run a crosscheck on anything between Lisa Bland and a man named Charles or Charlie.

"She's, she was single," noted Greco. "Maybe it's a boyfriend, a relative."

Ted interjected, "Make sure you check the full name,
Lisa *Jennings* Bland." He saw Bradenson look questioningly at his
superior. Ted stated, "For the *historical* angle. Jennings was a noted
family of planters, plantation owners, and also statesmen. Even slaves
took their names from them. Like Paul Jennings, the valet for President
Madison and his wife Dolley Madison." Even in a moment like this,
Ted couldn't resist going on a brief history tangent. "And," he added,
"the Blands were related to the Lees." Harmony, who was living in the
former home of Richard Bland Lee, nodded grimly.

Bradenson looked open-eyed and dubious at Greco. The latter said,
"Check it all out."

Standing by the grotesque limb, the detective rubbed his forehead in
distress. "CHAR, CHARLIE—Do we have a fiend who's now
autographing his victims?!"

Greco asked Ted if the ice well, or Gadsby's, might have any history
relating to the case.

Ted replied slowly. "The well, not sure. But Gadsby's has huge
historical significance. Why, the first six Presidents had inaugural
parties here. Gadsby owned slaves, who worked in the tavern." Ted's
earnest face had an intense, focused look. "Let's see. He also owned
hotels in downtown D.C. In one of them, the man in *Thirteen Years a
Slave* was kidnapped. And Gadsby bought what became Gadsby's from
a friend of George Washington. Some say Aaron Burr's daughter died
there. There's much, much else about Gadsby's.

"I have a lot to chew over. I'll get back to you on this, as quick as I
can."

"OK," said, Greco, who motioned the duo back to the ladder.

573

"And the nerve," he lamented, "the nerve of this guy. Or woman: It must be a man. To bring the arm, after committing the atrocity, to bring it here. Right in the shadow of City Hall.

"Like sticking a thumb in the eye of the city magistrates."

'The magistrates,' thought Ted. And he had a distant memory of a tour, given years before. There had been a large group of guests. But it was long ago, and he couldn't put names to any faces. Then the image of that terrible event from years before, the image that had flashed in his mind at the Freedmen's site again entered his brain, flushing away anything else. The image of a lynching, of a youth terribly mangled, and mutilated. Then the image faded away, like smoke from a funeral pyre.

After the clamminess of the well, they breathed in the street air as if it were pure oxygen. Ted told Greco, "Speaking of history, I think I've nailed down definitely the M.O. of the killing, the mutilation, at the Old Presbyterian's Tomb of the Unknown. The mutilation of the throat, and the limbs, and the anal, the anus, wasn't a coincidence, I'm convinced. It has to do with a famous death, of someone who many in the graveyard of Old Presbyterian knew well." He had the detective's full attention.

"Of none other than George Washington. He died a terrible death, of mistreatment by his doctors. Who gave him an enema, of toxic compounds. Who had him gargle various substances, and who thought of giving him a tracheotomy, cutting a hole in his throat. And who bled him, of at least 32 ounces of blood.

"It wasn't deliberate malpractice: These were common 'remedies' of the time. But they killed Washington. And this killer, unhinged as he is, he reenacted the means of Washington's death at Old Presbyterian. It explains the slash marks on Lily Harper's neck, the dirt pushed down her throat, the desecration of the anal canal."

As Harmony listened in, Ted went on explaining his insight into that murder. The historian concluded, emotionally: "I think we agree, Detective Greco that, whoever this crazed killer is, he's getting crazier. More extreme. More unpredictable.

"I fear he'll quicken the pace of his killings. And I think he may take out a bunch of people next time, not just one person."

Chapter 54 – Suspect Eliminated

Late that afternoon, a respite of glorious sun broke through the clouds. However, the streets and running paths were still too wet for a bike workout. So Ted took his RAV4 into town, parking it in front of St. Mary's Basilica and its adjoining Old Presbyterian Meeting House. His talk with Greco at the ice well on his mind, he took a walk over to Market Square and the waterfront.

Both of his knees were bothering him again, and not just the bad left knee which had long before been dislocated in a basketball game. That day his right knee was stiff and achy too. He paused, and bent his right foot behind his butt, holding the stretch for 30 seconds.

He paced through the mostly silent streets, past the towering heights of the Bland/Lee mansion, with the lights out in Harmony's apartment, and past the Montgomery Dent Corse mansion. Past Martha Washington's "tenement house", an investment property acquired by George for his spouse. When Ted pointed it out to Harmony once, she'd joked, "Does this mean Washington was a slum lord?"

The meticulously kept townhome from 1797 certainly didn't look like a slum. It sparkled with a new coat of white and gold paint fit for a king, or a President. It proudly displayed a Revolutionary Era "Join or Die" flag, which represented the newly independent states as allied segments of a dangerous snake, from its northern head of "VT", Vermont, to its southern tip of "GA", Georgia. The home's façade had a brightly colored wood medallion, in the guise of an official United States seal, announcing it as the first First Lady's property.

"It's no flop house," Ted had told Harmony. "As we know from the
grand townhomes around here, like the one you live in, this was, and is,
the classy part of town. George bought it as an investment property,
and Martha inherited it on his death."

Ted actually knew one of the owners, a fellow history buff who had
expensively restored and enhanced the property. The co-owner learned
his new abode had been the residence, incredibly, of Maria Reynolds.
She was the blonde bombshell who'd seduced Treasury Secretary
Hamilton, and then blackmailed him along with the aid of her ex-
husband as well as her new spouse, a professional grifter named, aptly,
Mr. "Clingman".

Sifter walked down from the tenement home to the corner of King St.
and the Marshall House site, the scene of the Civil War's opening
fatalities. He noticed anew the plaque, now scarred from acid,
commemorating those deaths from a Southern point of view.

At Market Square, Ted eyed the plaza around the fountain. The open
space was filled with media equipment—camera stands, portable lights,
and cables snaking along the ground, as well as network vans parked
along the curbs. Ted knew the latest press conference on the progress,
or lack of progress, of the murder investigations had been scheduled for
that time. Yet the Square was bereft of reporters and city officials.

A text from Harmony with a news link gave the reason. Test results had
come back from the FBI and city and state labs on the small amount
of McVeigh's DNA found at his coal plant "office". It had been
crosschecked with the few DNA samples gleaned from the Freedmen's,
Christ Church, or Old Presbyterian murder sites. There were no
matches with McVeigh. Samples of McVie's blood on the motorboat
he had stolen were still being analyzed. As of yet, analysts had found
no matches in the genetic databases, including for persons with violent

criminal records and with motives for committing the recent atrocities. Either McVeigh had left samples of someone else's DNA at the murder sites or, more likely, some other person, or persons, had committed the outrages. The killer of Lisa Bland, whoever that might be, was the most likely suspect.

Comitas and city officials, and the local police chief, had hoped to announce positive results at the press assemblage. And perhaps tag Bland's slayer as a copycat killer, but not the culprit in the other murders. But when the results turned out negative, Harmony explained, the law authorities cancelled the conference, and put out a simple press statement with the disappointing news. Ted could imagine Comitas' fear of public humiliation at such a gathering, as well as Greco's displeasure about being a bearer of grim news.

Indeed, City Hall and the City Council had publicly and angrily reacted to the latest revelations. From her office at Amazon, Harmony called Ted to give him more of the details. She told him the city website had posted a statement expressing "severe disappointment" with the law enforcers on the "tardy progress of their inquiries," "their mistaken assumptions and dead ends," and the "grave danger" in which they had put the "innocent residents of Old Town." In the same post, she went on quoting, the Mayor and City Council jointly announced they would hold a highly unusual press conference in Market Square "in the near future." They also demanded the heads of the local police and the FBI investigations "appear with them at that time."

Ted thought for a moment, and replied, "It may be that Comitas, and perhaps Greco, are refusing to appear. Hard to blame them: They'd just be whipping boys."

"I bet," answered Harmony, "the city authorities fire Comitas and Greco on the spot!"

Ted felt bad for Greco, and felt worse he hadn't been able to unlock the mystery for the detective. He felt less sympathy for the FBI man. Adding to the dismay and confusion, Harmony reported, was a bombshell, but short-lived, report. Strands of blonde hair identified as those of City Council Coordinator Forstandt had been found in the hallway down from the office of Lisa Bland. After initially denying she had ever been in Bland's office, the Councilwoman admitted she had met the museum curator over the name change issue, but claimed it was "days before her murder." And after initially failing to give an alibi for her whereabouts on the night of the killing, Forstandt tried to come clean to save her skin.

Far late into that night, Harmony continued breathlessly, "she confessed to partying with staff members, at the back room of a wine bar tasting room on King Street!" It seems she had left the party for several hours, but returned later. It was unclear, Harmony went on, if the politician was absent at the time of Bland's murder. At 3:20 a.m., she did leave the bar in an Uber, the company's records showed, "and headed back to her Robinson Condos townhouse."

Video and selfies of the hours-long party had leaked. Despite Forstandt's strident, prior demands that all Alexandrians mask themselves in public, she and the other partyers "drank and ate for hours, without masks, at a crowded table!" related Harmony. The damning video and photos were going viral, and Forstandt would at a minimum take a public drubbing for her hypocrisy.

In closing, Harmony mentioned that after wrapping things up at work she was going food shopping, at the Trader Joe's in North Old Town. Ted knew the boutique grocery: It was close by the Portner Brewery condos and the Old Cotton Mill where he had started his Civil War tour. They agreed to meet up that evening at her apartment, to devour whatever tasty items she brought back from the store.

Chapter 55 – Morbid Musings

As dusk approached, the setting sun was fighting off the horizon's storm clouds, at least for a while. Ted crossed from King St. onto S. Fairfax, and walked past the Stabler-Leadbetter drugstore museum. The old pharmacy and general store where Martha Washington had shopped for Mt. Vernon, and Robert E. Lee for Arlington House, when it was soon to be transformed by war into Arlington National Cemetery. Right across Fairfax was the Burke & Herbert headquarters where banker Harrison had his run-in with Anthony Lercino. A judge had indicted the cat burglar for break-ins, grand larceny, and the assault on Mr. Lowell, while investigators were still looking into the watchwoman's death at the Athenaeum.

Absorbed in thought, Ted went from King into the cobblestoned path, Swift's Alley, the lane of the merchant pirate. He reached the narrow walkway between the bank and the adjoining restaurant. Lercino had confessed he'd climbed to the restaurant's roof, then jumped to the top of the bank, from where he made his way into the attic storage rooms. Ted's knees ached from the uneven stones; he stepped over to the smooth bricks that had been laid in the center of the path, to ease the way for oxen drivers walking behind their beasts. He wondered if all the rain had made his balky joints more sensitive.

And, for the hundredth time, Ted ran through the murders. Lee-Fendall and Gadsby's, Old Presbyterian, Light-Horse Lee and the Confederate mound, the initial horror at Freedmen's. At least he'd been able to drop the Athenaeum death, the Prince St. break-in, and the waterfront watchman's assault off a long-enough list. The attack in the Wilkes Cemetery was in a gray area. He leaned to trusting Harmony's fervent belief the attacker was a foreigner, perhaps the escaped terrorist, and perhaps unrelated to the murders. He also recalled the shooting death in the housing project. The media and the public, except some in the African-American and law enforcement communities, had completely forgotten about that atrocity. But might it be related to the others? Again and again, his head aching about it, he pondered the possible meaning of "C H A R L". 'CHARLES? Charleston, South Carolina?' he asked himself. 'Chuck, Carl? CHARLENE?' He ran through the possibilities. He couldn't think of an abbreviation that fit such letters. Then there was 'CHAR': They had discarded that, yet the villain had shown himself capable of burning, as well as stabbing, a person. He drew on his encyclopedic grasp of Alexandria history, and couldn't think of an infamous crime where a fiend had deliberately burned someone. There was the woman who died from a fire on her wedding day, but that was an accident, not murder, and a personal, not a societally related, tragedy.

True, the city was noted for the many fires that swept through the waterfront's commercial districts over a century ago. The 1855 one in William Ramsey's store that had killed the fire fighters buried at Ivy Hill Cemetery. The 1871 one that extended from City Hall down King St. to the river warehouses. And it was possible the killer might turn to another means of mayhem. 'The City Hall,' mused Ted. 'That would make a fitting target for an arsonist.' He cringed at the number of city employees who might be caught inside such an inferno. When police discovered McVeigh's van, they found, along with the bomb materials, a sketch of City Hall, and the King St. courthouse and its garage. Several news sites had mentioned this. Might the fiend who was still at large be inspired to go after the same buildings, after reading about them? It was possible. Also, early in the city's history, Market Square had a slave auction site. The killer, who seemed obsessed with such things, might be enraged at that. Ted was ever more convinced the villain was spiraling out of control, and would attempt a spectacular crime that might kill many.

Fires, knives, pyromaniacs, bombs. CHAR. CHARL. The term 'Charing Cross', a clue in a Sherlock Holmes mystery, flashed through Ted's mind. Stepping along the alley's bricks, he gazed up to his right, at the twin, mammoth Jonathan Swift mansions. Where Harmony and he had stumbled upon one of Lercino's digs. 'Was Swift's treasure still hidden somewhere in Old Town?,' he wondered. 'Lercino made a pretty good reconnaissance, but he didn't get to, couldn't get to, every possible site. Perhaps,' he thought, smiling wanly, 'Harmony and I can continue the search—it could make us rich.' He recalled their first encounter with the crazy spate of crimes: the assault on the watchman at the excavated ship. Then he again turned his attention to the murders.

One thread in the mystery may have resolved itself, he estimated. The Lees, the Confederate mound, Old Presbyterian, Freedmen's, and Gadsby's all had a connection, directly or indirectly, to slavery. Lee because of his fighting for the Confederacy. The Freedmen's Cemetery, where former slaves reposed, and the Christ Church burial mound of Confederate fighters, those were obvious enough. Old Presbyterian, many of whose founding members were Scottish merchants, like John Carlyle, who owned sales. Thus the Carlyle House too, where Lercino was attacked. And John Gadsby had slaves working at his tavern.

Also, as Ted knew from research for his D.C. tours, Gadsby had enslaved workers at his old National Hotel on Pennsylvania Avenue, at a locale midway between the White House and the Capitol Building.

Indeed, in antebellum days it was dubbed the "Hotel of the Southland". Speaker of the House Henry Clay of Kentucky, who went back and forth on the issue of slavery, had resided there. And pro-Southern President James Buchanan was the possible target of a poison plot there by Northern advocates. John Wilkes Booth had even stayed at the Hotel while scheming to kidnap or kill Lincoln.

Ted thought of Gadsby's family crypt at Congressional Cemetery, two miles east of the Capitol. In its small, stifling chamber the corpse of the impoverished, former First Lady, Dolley Madison, had been kept for an incredible eight years, before funds could be scraped together for her final burial at the Madisons' Montpelier, Virginia estate.

The wide-ranging Gadsby had also owned the Decatur House in Lafayette Square, where he kept domestic slaves in its annex and courtyard. Kept behind closed doors to avert prying eyes, and possible escapes. The low-slung annex is still there, adjacent to the Decatur mansion, one block from the White House. Henry Clay had also resided in the mansion in the late 1820s, when he was Secretary of State.

'Henry Clay', thought Ted, 'Henry Clay.' And he turned over in his mind the many surviving images of the Speaker of the House, Secretary of State, and perennial candidate for President. From the paintings of the Kentuckian as a young frontier lawyer, and friend of Aaron Burr, to the daguerreotype of the aged statesman before his 1852 death. His hair whitened, cheeks sunken, eyes protruding, he rather resembled Lon Chaney, Sr. in the silent movie version of *The Phantom of the Opera*. Ted stopped, and he tapped his right foot on a worn-smooth cobblestone. There was something about Clay and the Decatur House that was linked, perhaps, to Old Town's recent acts of violence.

'Think harder!' he told himself. It was something relating to Clay and Gadsby. 'What was it?!' Then he figured that, as with most items history-related, the thing he was trying to remember would come back to him if he just let it rest for a minute or so. But it didn't. 'What is wrong with my vaunted memory?!' And he continued walking along the narrow brick way.

Chapter 56 –A Jihadi's Surprise

Abdullah Hamaas was impressed by the strong, full-bearded men of his newfound terror cell. Their choice of locale for this critical meeting underscored his admiration. It was a touch of genius to hold the council of war in the backroom of a kosher deli. Who would ever suspect them of meeting in such a place? And there were so many of the Jewish restaurants in Manhattan: Their own would just blend in with the others.

It was a facade, of course. It was owned by a Muslim man of mixed Syrian and American parentage, who had grown up in the Zionists' so-called West Bank, in the occupied territories of Palestine. When his brother was killed in a clash with Israeli police, Hezbollah had recruited him and, recognizing his multilingual skills, trained him for a special mission. To travel to New York and impersonate an Orthodox Jewish merchant and restaurant owner. His deli was just three blocks from the Freedom Tower itself.

Abdullah was thrilled, though a little worried, which was natural, that the plot was moving so fast. Yet the plan was genius. When the World Trade Centers were originally bombed in 1993, the bombers worked from the outside. They had to drive their Ford Econoline into the bottom garage of the North Tower, and then detonate the hydrogen nitrate explosives. The explosives went off, but the Tower still stood. The 2001 attack did work, but ever since airline security had been much tighter. It was time to go back to the original plan, but better. These days, the terror cell had numerous people working at the Tower. Working in the garage, and in building maintenance. They'd be part of a true inside job, the best and safest kind. For months these men and women had been bringing to work small amounts of explosive. Which were stored in a utility room. The small amounts were now a large amount, large enough to wreck the bottom of the Freedom Tower and, it was hoped, cause the whole structure to topple.

In his dreams, Abdullah imaged the 1,776-foot-high building and antenna breaking up, the antenna flung like a giant spear into Battery Park, while the skyscraper proper sheared off near its bottom, tumbling into the Hudson River, generating giant waves to inundate the shoreline, drowning hundreds. Or falling toward the site of the original Towers, and the desecrated soil of Trinity Church. Anywhere it fell, the symbolism would be startling. And the number of infidel deaths, and some regrettable Muslim ones, immense.

He and his nine brethren-in-arms sat at a long table in the basement floor of the deli's largest dining room. The whole space had been reserved for their meeting. The head of security had swept the room for listening devices before they assembled.

Mehmed, their thin-as-rails leader, ran this latest council of war. He sat at the head of the table, his back to an entranceway. Abdullah sat halfway down the table to his left, a closed basement window behind him. He smiled in recalling how Mehmed had urged mercy from his Alexandria imam, after the near-disaster of his Wilkes St. cemetery escapade, so much did he want the daring fighter to join his terrorist team.

The leader went over the plot, confiding more details than previously. There were to be four SUVs, not three, one for each corner of the Tower. They were all owned by building employees who were part of the conspiracy. At 10 a.m. of the appointed day, they were to drive to the utility room two floors up from the bottom of the Tower. The

587

supervisor of it was a confidante of Mehmed's. At 15-minute intervals, they would load their SUVs with the explosives stored there.

The terror leader paused, and said he would put in the order for their supper now. They would eat vegetarian dishes that conformed to both halal and kosher rules. Few at the assemblage felt any hunger; they were too nervous, too expectant. They were appreciative, however, at how Mehmed looked out for all their needs. And they admired his *sang-froid*: How he paused to order food during a meeting on killing a great mass of people. That was somewhat amusing, Abdullah thought. Instead of having a waiter come down, Mehmed simply called the order in from his cell.

"All right," he smiled grimly, "now the real business. All of you know the basic plan. Some of you will be in the SUVs, and some of you will be providing security, both inside the building," and at this he glanced at Abdullah, "and outside. As you know, due to our strict timeline, the drivers will not be able to leave the Tower after parking their vehicles in their appointed spots. Therefore, naturally, they will sacrifice their lives. For their final moments in this life, they will pray while waiting patiently in their cars for the detonations." A look of stern pride crossed Mehmed's countenance. "The wait will be short; they shall not feel any pain at all at the moment of the synchronized detonations. And their rewards will be eternal, and very sweet."

His listeners, though nervous, bowed their heads as in prayer.

Mehmed grew more solemn. "Let me formally recognize those who have been chosen for the honor of giving up their earthly lives on that sacred day." He nodded to men on either side of him, then to a man on Abdullah's right, and finally to a man at the opposite end of the table. He nodded again, and all four stood up, as hearty applause broke out from the five not accorded the honor.

"The rest of us, Allah willing, may survive that noble day. And for the rest of our mortal days, we'll pay tribute to the memory of those who exhibited such courage and faith." Their leader nodded again, and the four, faces flushed with pride, and some fear, sat down.

A knock came from the door. "It is time," said Mehmed, "for a respite, before we finish some details of the final plan." At that moment, a noise came from the basement window.

The room door opened, and a waiter entered with a tray.

He stepped quickly aside to his right. A loud scraping was heard from the basement window, as its shutter was opened from the outside.

In the doorway's threshold, four heavily armed men in black appeared, wearing flak jackets and grasping submachineguns. They rushed toward the table. Eight more members of the SWAT team followed. From the basement window, two more NYPD special operatives, automatic pistols in hand, jumped down into the room. Mehmed, Abdullah, and their fellow terrorists were stunned into stillness. The leader seemed to shrink into his chair.

From the table, two men, including two of the anointed suicide bombers, stepped away. And, as undercover agents, they joined the takedown by their comrades in the New York Police Department, Special Counter-Terrorism Unit, the world's most renowned squad of its kind.

They had been secretly recording the meetings, and fully informing the NYPD leadership. As Mehmed's plot came close to fruition, the Unit's chief, Lt. Patrick J. Maloney, decided it was the time to terminate the conspiracy.

As he was led away in handcuffs with the others, Abdullah's main sentiment was sadness, of having to endure many more years in prison. With not even a graveyard to walk through in a search of a victim.

Under interrogation that night, Abdullah Hamaas was gripped by the wanderlust that had seized him in Alexandria. In hopes of cutting a deal, and a shorter prison term, he quickly broke under harsh interrogation. He gave his questioners the details of his escape from jail, of the Wahabi terror mosque, and of his attack on the woman at the Wilkes St. cemetery. Learning this, Maloney immediately informed an old police friend of his, a Detective John Greco.

As with Lercino and McVeigh, another piece in a complex series of multiple crimes and multiple criminals in Old Town had been solved. But another piece remained.

Chapter 57 – A Walk in a Wicked Park

Leaving J. Swift's mansions behind, Ted neared the end of Swift's Alley. It was the most colonial portion of the Colonial Era town. He came up to the worn townhouse of the elder Washington brother, Lawrence. Its sagging walls, dating from the 1750s, were still blackened from one of the waterfront conflagrations of over a century before. Yet it was now a prized property, and none other than TV personality Katie Couric had resided a few doors away. Though best known for its distant past, Alexandria had for the last generation or two engendered nationally known media and entertainment figures. Namely Couric, and her fellow broadcast network colleague, weatherman Willard Scott.

Ted examined the exterior of the Lawrence Washington property, then turned his sights across the alley to the rear windows of an immaculately maintained art gallery, a target of the recent riot. The former Gilpin House art emporium had been named for Colonel George Gilpin, a relative of the widow Martha Custis who had introduced her to George Washington. Ted looked through a window at the fine, neo-traditionalist paintings within. He knew the arthouse had a sister gallery in another venerable port city: Charleston, South Carolina.

'Beautiful Charleston,' thought Ted. 'And, home to John C. Calhoun.' Whenever that name came up, Ted's mind turned to The War Between the States, or TWBTS, as some of the older history buffs and old-time Southerners in Old Town still dubbed it. 'Calhoun, apostle of nullification, the voiding of federal laws, the defender of slavery, the Philosopher and Prophet of Secession.' Ted had nicknamed him, 'The

Godfather of the Civil War'. Calhoun, he recalled, was the rival, during the U.S. Senate's so-called "golden age", of fellow lawmakers Daniel Webster and Henry Clay.

Calhoun and Clay. Rivals, but 'didn't they have something in common too?,' he pondered. Ted stepped to the end of the alley, and reached a barn dating from before the Revolution. Perhaps Lawrence Washington, and his younger brother, had kept horses there. Leaning against the barn's pitted bricks, he stretched his left knee behind his lower back again.

He turned around to gaze back up Swift's Alley. The path was alluring, evocative. In this nook of Old Town, you didn't even have to block out the automobiles, and the roar of the jet planes out of National Airport, to imagine you were back in 1776. Or 1861. The passageway had no lights, and was too narrow for cars. Even boys on scooters and men on motorcycles seemed to acknowledge an unspoken taboo against desecrating the place with the mechanisms of modernity.

Though now low on the horizon, the sun was still out, which kept the early evening pleasantly warm. Ted strode down the deserted stores of King St., made a quick turn onto N. Union, and another quick turn into Wales Alley, a little byway facing the Virtue Feed and Grain restaurant. It was ensconced, as its name signaled, in a former storehouse for animal feed, and as well wheat and corn for human consumption. In a superb, historical touch, its riverside wall retained the fading paint of advertisements for cereals sold there generations before. The passageway, despite the Wales moniker, was most associated with an Irishman, not a Welshman, namely Colonel John Fitzgerald. The aide and friend of Washington who owned the giant tobacco warehouse next door, now an Asian eatery, and the coffeehouse where the final act of the Old Town riot had occurred.

Its employees had propped sandbags along the thick foundation stones of the building, in hopes of keeping out further seepage from the Potomac's high waters. The cellar floorboards still had water stains from 2005's Hurricane Ophelia, whose mighty power had pushed the waters of the Chesapeake itself into the riverine towns of Georgetown, Alexandria, and Annapolis.

As with the nearby Indigo Hotel down Union St., Ted's feelings were mixed about the relatively new restaurant. In normal times, it was a fine and bustling place. It was said Virtue and Grain was operated by some of the same entrepreneurs who ran a highly regarded restaurant, The Majestic, on central King St. Its owners may have saved the historic waterfront property, in restoring it to something like its original appearance. But before its conversion to a trendy bistro, it had been Olsson's, the only large book and music store in Old Town, a town that may have the greatest proportion of writers of any place in America. People like Ted. But Amazon Books, of Arlandria's most influential contemporary firm, had helped pushed it out of business. 'Oh well,' Ted figured, 'better than converting it to another condo, or having it face the wrecking ball.'

Moving on, he was surprised to find people sitting at the tables outside. Had the restaurant opened up again? He looked through the tinted windows to the inside, and the lights were off. Perhaps folks were just taking advantage of the unusual break in the clouds, to lounge in the evening air, scented fresh from the earlier downpours.

At the end of Wales Alley, Ted found that the street paralleling the river was flooding. He stepped aside a deep puddle to enter the new Waterfront Park, or Fitzgerald Square, as some still called it. Although this term was frowned upon by some town officials because Fitzgerald, despite his service in the Revolution and his staunch support of religious freedom, had owned slaves. In fact, the city had brought in an artist to craft an unusual, temporary display of public art in the park. These were striking, larger-than-life, three-dimensional paintings of Africans facing the riverfront, near where they had been brought in as slaves during colonial times. The setting sun glimmered off the muscular backs of those depicted.

Ted strolled into the public space, and its small, artificial-grass playground on the river edge, and the larger, natural-grass lawn just to its south. This open area had an unusually large number of visitors. It had been mostly deserted since the pandemic and the wave of murders. But as the sun threw up a glorious, if blood-red, sunset on the park and up the narrow strip of King St., a crowd of mothers, dads, and children had taken advantage of the rare good weather to enjoy the riverine setting.

The number of people outside, about 75 of them, was the largest group he'd seen for many weeks in Old Town, apart from the riots and the Market Square press conferences. People of all ages and ancestries milled about, as Northern Virginia is an immigrant-heavy region with residents from 140 different countries. And Old Town attracts tourists from throughout the world seeking an easy day trip near the capital city.

Ted cut across the wide lawn, the thick grass cushioning the slight ache in his knees. He stepped up to the life-size statue of a sailor honoring the countless mariners that historic Alexandria sent off down the Potomac and beyond the Chesapeake, off to Europe or the Caribbean shores or as far away as China. Inevitably, he thought of two waterborne tragedies that had occurred near this very spot in the 19th century, and just four years apart.

One was the ill-fated voyage of the *Pearl*. In 1848, that schooner quietly passed by Old Town's busy docks while carrying 77 souls carefully concealed below deck. The passengers were hiding for a reason: They were on the run. They made up the largest slave escape in American history.

The *Pearl*'s return voyage, upriver past Old Town, was less quiet. A posse out of Georgetown had been formed. Men armed with rifles and a cannon and led by a big-time tobacco merchant had taken a steam-powered launch down the Potomac, and had intercepted the *Pearl* where the Potomac swells into the Chesapeake. As the posse's ship towed the *Pearl* and its captives back to Washington and prison, it passed the Alexandria wharves. Put on display, to the jeers of observers on shore, were the *Pearl*'s co-captains, two white abolitionists.

It was near this same site that many slaves were loaded onboard vessels for transit south, "sold down the river", to the major slave market of New Orleans. The *Pearl* Incident, among other events, such as the Washington Riot that ensued, nearly triggered civil war 13 years before the Civil War came.

To forestall that, Henry Clay stepped in, in old age, to forge his congressional Compromise of 1850. It brought California, one year after the '49ers, into the Union as a free state, but much strengthened the Fugitive Slave Act. It empowered posses and federal lawmen to track down and forcibly return escapees like those who'd boarded the *Pearl*.

'That Henry Clay,' thought Ted. 'He seemed to be everywhere, in the first half of the 1800s.' He looked out at the roiled river where the *Pearl* had sailed on its outgoing, and return, journeys, then turned his gaze back to the attractive new park. He had seen photographs of the decrepit, now-disappeared structures of the early-20th-century waterfront. Gone were the surplus stores, gravel storage pits, and warehouses leading down to the Robinson condo complex, itself a replacement for the vanished Robinson storehouses and factories.

An abrupt shift in the weather brought him out of his reverie. Clouds obscured the sun, suddenly turning the waterfront darker, and noticeably colder, as an offshore breeze kicked in. Moms and dads and their relations checked the sky and their watches and pulled on sweaters or raincoats.

As the river, so brightly illuminated minutes before, grew brownish in tinge, Ted's attention fell upon the ancient bronze cannon from the colonial wars. It had been a fixture on the waterfront for decades. A young boy with parents from El Salvador was sitting on the middle of the turret, while twin girls from Rajasthan were leaning against the cement block on which the gun was mounted. About a dozen adults and kids, mostly from Maryland, sat just yards away at picnic tables and plastic chairs. Even as they put on coats against the chill and the threat of rain, they wanted to linger: they wished the rare spate of warmth and sun would stay, and a semblance of normalcy remain in the town.

The sight of the artillery piece made Ted think of the second tale he often related here. Concerning the *U.S.S. Princeton* disaster of 1844. At that time, war threatened with the world's great navy power, Britain, over possession of the Pacific Northwest, including the future states of Oregon and Washington. To stymie the Royal Navy, America built the fastest warship on Earth, the *Princeton*, and equipped it with the world's most powerful guns, a pair of 14-inch cannons, one of which was christened, with irony, as the *Peacemaker*.

Its official maiden voyage out of Old Town was the military, and social, event of the year. On board was the President of the United States, John Tyler, as well as the Secretary of State, the Secretary of the

Navy, and Tyler's fiancé, the beguiling Julia Gardiner, along with Miss Gardiner's father. Also on hand were former First Lady Dolley Madison and a host of other luminaries.

The ship's unmatched speed derived from steam engines driving the world's first screw propeller, invented by naval engineering genius John Ericsson, later the Civil War designer of the Union Navy ironclad the *USS Monitor*. His warning the ship's cannons were insufficiently tested went unheeded. In fact, the ship's commander, Robert Stockton, of Princeton, New Jersey, had rushed the vessel into being, and financed it out of his own deep pockets when congressional appropriations came up short. The ship's financier got to name the ship after his hometown.

Not long out of Old Town harbor, the call went out to test fire the Peacemaker. Captain Stockton bent over the breech, lit the fuse—and the gun hurled a 228-pound cannon ball a full two miles down the Potomac. At which point the projectile skipped downriver—like a flat stone tossed along the surface of a pond—for another mile, before finally sinking below the waves. A huge cheer erupted from the throng on board. The U.S. now had mightiest warship of all!

As the *Princeton* powered downriver, its full-sail rigging augmenting the peerless pace of its steam propulsion, the call went out for a second test firing. Captain Stockton again bent over the breech, lit the fuse— and the gun again hurled a cannon ball two miles down the river. And again it skipped on the water's surface another long distance, before sinking into the Potomac. Deafening shouts of "Hurrah!" were heard once more.

Then came party time. Loitering off Mt. Vernon, eight miles south of Old Town, servants brought out all the fixings of a grand banquet. Toasts were raised to the mighty *Princeton*.

At length, the time came to return to Alexandria from Washington's mansion. In the noisy conviviality of the main deck, the Navy Secretary stated, 'Wouldn't it be grand if we fired off a third shot here, to honor the nation's first Commander-in-Chief?' Captain Stockton, standing at the Peacemaker, misinterpreted this suggestion as an order, and from the head of the Navy. Three times a charm, or sometimes, a harm.

Below deck, President Tyler was mounting the stairs to come above. He happened to pause for a moment when a nephew of his started singing a charming ditty. The President, who loved children and who had sired eight of his own with his late wife Letitia, stopped to listen. He cocked his ear—and heard a shattering boom from above!

When President Tyler reached the deck, he was met with a vision from Dante. Billowing, acrid smoke obscured his vision. Parts of the sails were on fire. And up among the torn canvas were disembodied arms, legs—and heads! In the rear of the deck, female passengers were weeping uncontrollably from the gruesome sights.

Among those blown to bits were the Secretary of the Navy, and the Secretary of State, and Julia Gardner's father. Six dead in all, including the Tyler's manservant, and over 15 people maimed and wounded.

The President came upon the remnants of the Peacemaker. Its breech had exploded, spewing white-hot metal onto the crowded deck and up into the rigging. Lying face up next to the great gun was Captain Stockton, motionless. And naked. And though a bearded man, he no longer had a beard, indeed not a hair on his head. The force of the explosion had blown away his clothes and body hair.

President Tyler was stunned when the captain opened his eyes. He wasn't dead as feared. He had been so close to the cannon he'd stood in a kind of vacuum, that ripped off his clothes and hair, but spared his life. He had been knocked unconscious and had facial burns, but was alive.

Stockton looked past the President, and up at the rigging and sails. And at the blood, guts, and severed limbs and heads staring down at him. He cried out, "My God! Would that I were dead too!"

It was the worst peacetime accident in U.S. Navy history. In fact, it was the worst day in Presidential Cabinet history. On that day, two Cabinet officers died.

With the ship damaged, and many passengers wounded, the crew took the *Princeton* back to Alexandria fast. At the Old Town wharf, sailors employed a broad "hurricane deck", used during emergencies for fast egress. The surviving passengers rushed out. Including Julia Gardiner, the President's young fiancé. But, distraught by the horrific death of her father, she fainted on alighting, and fell between the wharf and the onrushing ship, just before it slammed into the dock. She was about to be crushed to death! Then she felt two strong arms pull her to safety. She looked up and saw her rescuer—President Tyler. Four months later, they wed. They would have seven children. It was the silver lining to the debacle.

The Revolution, the Civil War, the world wars, armed competition with foreign powers: So much of Old Town's history, Ted soberly reflected, revolved around violence.

There was even the French and Indian War, which erupted soon after the town's founding. Whenever Ted, with his fascination for military history, came to this spot in the park, he looked over the cannon from colonial times. For years, he'd wondered whether the artillery piece was from the French and Indian War, or perhaps a little later, from the Revolution. And whether it was of British make, or a French gun captured by the British and their colonial allies like the young

Washington. Toward the breech end of the long barrel was a royal emblem and an insignia in Latin. But Ted couldn't tell if the logo represented the French or the British king, a Louis or a George. As he had done many times before, he leaned over the gun to examine it, and ponder its origin. Behind him was the delightful, high-pitched sound of scampering children at play.

Ted placed his left hand on the emblem, its metal a dull green from oxidation.

The metal cover moved.

That was odd. It had been fixed in place for years, if not centuries, by grit and accumulated dust and by chemical changes to the bronze and the cast iron.

Curious, Ted pushed a bit harder at the metal plate.

It moved freely aside.

He expected to see only the long, tapered cylinder of metal within.

Instead, there was a container, of modern material, of sturdy plastic. About 17 inches long and six inches deep.

The depression was filled with a substance. Of a slightly yellowish color.

Ted touched the material. It was sticky. It reminded him of modeling clay. He licked his index finger and touched it, then tasted it. It had no taste.

In the wake of the Aryan Bomber, as the media had taken to calling McVeigh, Ted, along with just about everyone in town, had read up on explosives. He felt a 'thrill of fear', a sickly feeling in his stomach, as he realized the material matched the characteristics of something called Semtex.

Better known as C4.

And on the breech cover, he saw, were bits of paraffin. And on the soil directly below it was a noticeable chunk of wax. That stuff again, that Harmony had found on Lercino. But the burglar was now in custody. Ted took a step back; his pounding heart had taken off like a SpaceX rocket. He heard the shrill shouts of children playing a game of tag around him. A young girl sat on the muzzle of the gun, her bandy legs hanging from either side of the barrel.

He took a breath, and another, calming himself some, and stepped back to the breech. He pressed his right hand on the material, moving it around. On the right side of the container a rectangular chunk of hard plastic was visible. It also was not centuries-old, but new.

It looked like one of the detonators he'd come across in his reading about bombs. Of the type that could be touched off, at any time, from afar. Or set to go off at a certain time.

He took three steps back from the cannon. He leaned over and stared below it. He saw a light-colored package barely visible at the end of the gun's concrete block. A person not looking for something would have never noticed it. He stepped forward, bent down, and examined its light-brown wrapping paper. The upper-left corner was torn. Inside he felt a malleable, light-yellowish substance.

More C4.

Ted stepped away from the ancient gun. He opened his mouth to scream, to yell out a warning. He stopped, lips parted, baring his teeth. What if his assumption was wrong? He'd scare these kids and their parents to death. And probably be arrested, by Greco, or Comitas, for disturbing the peace. Or for reckless endangerment. End up in the Alexandria Detention Center.

But his eyes and his gut told him otherwise. He stepped away from the breech and over to the muzzle of the cannon. He felt an impulse to look inside. He did so.

Even with the growing darkness, he could see within that the muzzle was smooth as always, and empty near the top. But there was a substance in it, starting five inches from the opening and extending some distance within. He shone the light of his cell into the cylinder. He reached his left hand inside, and felt around. The material felt like the stuff in the breech.

Someone had really gone to town with the cannon. It had three packs of explosives.

He straightened up, stunned, breaking out in an icy-cold sweat. He imagined himself blown to bits like a sailor on the *Princeton*. He imagined the playing children horribly maimed.

His clear blue eyes happened to turn toward the Torpedo Factory, 75 yards away across the playground. A warning shout was starting to leave his mouth, when his jaw suddenly froze.

At the corner of the Factory, he spied a man.

A tall man. An old man, with white hair. And a white beard. No, a fake beard, which was pulled askew. Revealing a much younger man.

A man that Ted recognized.

As Lisa Bland had before her death.

A man Ted had spied at the Old Town riot, from the rear, and couldn't place him, but now he could.

'CHARL', Ted thought. He was surprised, but surprisingly, not shocked. CHARLOTTE.

The man's name jumped into his head. And then that of Henry Clay. 'Henry Clay', he thought. 'DUPUY.

'CHARLOTTE Dupuy.' The slave who had sued Clay for her freedom.

The man had a backpack. Big enough to carry around explosives.

The sight of him ended any hesitation Ted had.

As the man pulled the white wig off his head, Ted screamed, straining his lungs with the shout:

"A BOMB!

"There's a *bomb here*! Everyone out!!

"Leave this park! Out! Everyone go! RUN!"

His screeching yelp must have hit 120 decibels. The children around him stopped cold, shocked, and stared at him. The adults looked at him with annoyance, which quickly turned to concern.

"This is not a *joke*!" he shouted. "There are BOMBS here!" He pointed at the cannon, his arm stiff. "Everyone leave—NOW!"

Anxious parents began to gather their children. Slowly at first, then faster, and faster. Kids began to cry as dads and aunts and cousins whisked them up.

At the Torpedo Factory, the man, alerted by the screaming, had fixed his gaze toward the cannon, and Ted. His face had a look that made it clear he recognized Ted. Ted surely recognized him. The man nimbly scampered over to a side door of the Factory, and disappeared within.

Chapter 58 – From Ploughshares into Swords

Ted started running towards him. As he did, he pulled out his cell to call 911. He got a busy signal. "Unbelievable!" he swore. He stopped, and yelled at more stunned tourists and locals to get away from the cannon. He sprinted about halfway to the Torpedo Factory, and stopped again, and dialed Harmony. He got her.

"Hello—"

"—Call the police! Just listen, and do it," Ted spoke loudly, in rapid-fire bursts. "Call the police, and tell them, there are bombs, bombs in the cannon—at Waterfront Park, the old cannon, you know, the French and Indian one!" Ted knew she knew of it.

"OK, I will," she replied, her voice high-strung with alarm. She paused, then said rapidly, "I'm at the Cotton Mill, I passed by it and went to its rear—"

"—Call them!" Ted yelled into the cell, his eyes fixed on the door through which the man, the killer, had disappeared.

Above, the sky had darkened to black from the sunset and the encroaching rain clouds. Ted started running again, the ache in his knees temporarily gone, masked by adrenalin and endorphins. 'Where was it Harmony said she was?' he asked himself absently, intent on catching the man. He looked to his left at King and Union Streets, and the masonry walls of Col. Fitzgerald's tobacco warehouse rising up to, and fading into, the gloom. Often local police were stationed there. But not that evening.

Wait! There was an Alexandria cop car at the corner, in a vehicle facing south on Union, next to the restaurant that had stayed open at the start of the pandemic. Ted stopped to yell at it. But the car was pulling away. Its windows were shut; the officer within hadn't heard the noise of the crowd fleeing from the park! Usually a driver would pass very slowly from this normally busy intersection. But not with the relative lack of traffic from the virus. The cop car sped away rapidly, and out of sight.

Cursing, Ted ran up to the converted armaments factory. High stories of brick, concrete, and steel stretched north and west for several blocks. Its artist studios had been shut down since the plague, but the killer—he had to be the killer!—had pried a door open. Ted wondered if, like McVeigh, he might be keeping a lair inside the now-deserted place. In front of the Factory, the riverside piers with their docked pleasure ships were empty of boaters, as were the tables for the normally packed restaurant overlooking the boats. The people he had chased away from the cannon were vanishing deep into Old Town.

Suddenly, Ted felt very alone. He pushed, then pulled, at the heavy door. It opened. The killer didn't, or couldn't, lock it behind him. Ted thought of going back to get the police, then impulsively stepped inside.

Ted was surprised at discovering the man's identity, but not shocked. 'Clay, and Charl'. Of course.'

The man had, like Ted, an intimate knowledge of the town's history. He was the man the historian had tried to remember r, from a tour near the Lee-Fendall House some years before. The man who had taken such an interest in the Charlotte Dupuy tale. At the time, he wasn't as well known in the area, and Ted had forgotten about it.

What a monster he was, to go from individual slayings to the bombing of a play area! Ted only could pray and hope that all the kids and parents would get away before the device went off, or that a bomb squad would arrive to defuse it.

The historian-sleuth entered a darkened vestibule, and pushed through a swinging door into the cavernous, century-old, first floor of the Factory.

He was familiar with the complex. At the start of his waterfront tours, he'd frequently take the guests into the unusual place, explaining its world-wars role as an armaments plant, and then its function, during Old Town's recovery from its mid-20th century decline, as an artists colony. He'd long admired the work of several of its painters and sculptors who kept studios on the second and third floors.

That evening, however, the Torpedo Factory had a desolate air. Since its closure, only some infrared lights were kept on. The ground floor stretched out eerily for 90 yards in a dull red glow. This floor had a few historical exhibits and some studios, while the floors above were packed with small office studios every 15 yards or so. Up above, he could barely make out the outlines of the paintings and craftwork that artists had placed inside the glass walls of their studios.

The killer was not in sight. Ted realized he may have already escaped through the waterfront exit 50 yards to his right, or the Union St. exit on the other side of the atrium to his left. 'Were those exits locked?' he wondered. 'Had they been jimmied open?' He paused, and listened hard, cupping his hands around his ears. He heard the loud pulse of the electrical cables running along the ceiling. He heard a faint sound of fire engines, an hoped that firemen were racing to the cannon to shoo away visitors from the park.

He took a few paces forward, his steps echoing on the formica floor. Then he saw a blur, a moving figure, on the second floor, up to his right. And heard the quick patter of steps. It was him!

The historian sprinted forward. Soon he was at the reception desk in the heart of the ground floor. He rushed up stairs to the second landing. He was very nervous, but he also thought, absurdly, 'My knees are much better going up than going down.' Then in the dim light he misjudged a step, and stumbled, almost falling on his face. He got up, breathing hard, and scampered to the top of the stairs.

In front of the landing was a short walkway between a large, windowed artist's office and an iron railing that ran the length of the second floor. It went along a corridor of studios where he'd seen the man running. He rushed to the corridor, and looked down both sides of it: No one was there. However, one of the studios was faintly lit. And its door was open.

He approached it, slowly, almost on tiptoe. He paused, pulled out his cell, and dialed 911. The phone flashed the words, "No Signal". He cursed wordlessly, his breath coming out like a low hiss. There was no reception inside the concrete-and metal-lined place.

Ted thought of going for help; he crept toward the office instead. He actually knew this studio, and its artist. She specialized in surreal, disturbing paintings and photographs, in the style of Diane Arbus. The kind of subjects one might have found in a traveling circus of old—sword swallowers, midgets, depressed clowns, two-headed twins, and Fat Ladies—but with their weird features exaggerated even more. Her illustrations had a sort of strange beauty to them. Several illustrations were propped up behind the office window.

He crept to the side of the window glass, and peeked into the office. Traces of light flickered on some on the grotesque creations—a severed arm growing in a garden, and a Crown of Thorns wrapped around a child's neck—others were lost in spooky shadow.

'Our town is in a real-life house of horror,' Ted told himself. He knew he himself was facing possible, sudden death. He took two cautious steps up to the open door, then one tentative step inside.

Then he heard steps. From where? He stood, sweating, heart racing, trying to control his breathing as he did during difficult races. He listened. The sound, he realized, was coming from the other side of the floor. But how? How had the man gotten there? He turned and rushed back down the short walkway, the large office on his left, its space dimly illuminated from an overhead fluorescent. He perceived an open door on its far side. Had the killer fled through the office?

He heard footsteps again. And saw a blurred shape run down the stairs back down to the first floor. Despite the weak light, Ted could see he had put his wig and beard back on. The historian ran down the walkway, and twisted his left knee on the sharp turn toward the stairs. Unable to run, he limped down them as fast as he could.

At the bottom, he didn't see anyone. He heard distant footsteps, echoing dully off the high ceilings. He couldn't determine their direction. He stopped, listened, and the foot sounds faded away. The man might have left from any of three exits. Ted gambled on the Union St. one.

Outside, he swept his eyes up and down the street, rain clouds puffed out from the dark sky. He spied a few people still scrambling away from the park. But he didn't see the suspect.

Had the man run into the old Torpedo Factory offices across the way, near Sharp's Alley? Or had he fled north toward Founders Park? Somewhere else? Likely as not he had left through another exit. Ted stood paralyzed, wavering. Which way?

He looked down to the corner with King St. There was a bustle of action there. A long hook-and-ladder fire truck, two fire engines, and four police cars, all with their red lights blinking, sirens sounding. A small crowd had gathered near the vehicles. People were talking excitedly to one another, and gazing into the park toward the cannon. Ted went down Union to the women's clothing shop, in the old William Ramsey general store diagonally across from the park, the one pilfered during the riot, to get a glimpse of the cannon. No signs of an explosion. Not yet. And, except for some firemen in yellow rain jackets and a knot of cops shooing people away, the park was empty. That was good at least.

The he heard the rumble of tires and the blast of an engine, and a police truck flew past him from N. Union St. It turned sharply left into the end of King St., then veered right onto the Strand, a narrow access street between the park and the Fitzgerald warehouse. The street was still flooded, so the truck threw up plumes of filthy water, before stopping outside Virtue Feed and Grain.

The policemen who emerged looked like astronauts, or soldiers from the film *The Hurt Locker*. Their heads encased in helmets, their bodies in thick, bomb-resistant suits. They lumbered over toward the cannon, several of them carrying heavy metal plates in front of their bodies, like knights holding up shields against an angry dragon. Ted wished to God the bombs wouldn't go off while they inspected them.

He'd given up spotting the killer. He looked around for Greco, but didn't see him. He should tell him of the man he'd seen. He was surprised no cop had come up to question him about his warning about the bomb. Shouldn't some among those who fled have told the cops about him? But the police were preoccupied.

'I'll call Greco,' he thought. But then the excitement and danger of the bombs and the chase overcame him. Dizzy, dazed, he stumbled down Union back toward the Torpedo Factory entrance. He breathed in and out slowly in an attempt to steady himself. He rested for a few minutes.

He looked around. Leaning against the Factory entrance steps were rent-a-bikes and electric scooters. And a motorcycle, its engine on, the key in the ignition. Its rider had rushed over to Fitzgerald Square to check out the commotion.

Chapter 59 – Chasing Demons

Thoughts flashed through Ted's troubled mind. 'The killer. The clumps of wax. Harmony. My tours. The Cotton Mill. Lee-Fendall. Henry Clay. Harmony and the Mill. Wax, wax, Lee, Clay…'

It hit him. 'Could it be!?' Or was his wild imagination out of control? Could the killer be that depraved? Yes, he could.

He thought back to his brief, frantic call with Harmony. Did she say she was at the Old Cotton Mill?

'No, no, don't let it be!' It couldn't be.

He called her. No answer. He called again. A connection, but no voice. He heard a sound come out of the phone. Like a shout.

Or a muffled scream.

His heart began pounding again. He should get the police. But the ones he could see were preoccupied, rushing to or from the park. And what would he tell them?

About one of his hunches? It would take time before he convinced someone.

His natural impatience, and protective instinct, took over. He had to do something, and now!

Without thinking, he found himself on the motorbike.

He would return it when he was done, he told himself absently, his mind focused on Harmony, on the killer, on the clues he had missed, and was finally unraveling.

He began racing down Union St. as rain, after the brief respite, started up again. He told himself he would call the police on route. He heard a man yell behind him, probably the motorbike owner. He ignored him.

Frantic, Ted flew up Union and, barely pausing at the intersection,

swung a hard left onto Cameron, skidding on the wet pavement. He'd
only ridden a motorbike a few times, trying them out for possible
purchase. Ignoring the danger, he sped on, figuring it would take him
just three or four minutes to get to the Mill.

Gambling there'd be little traffic, he barely paused at the Lee St. stop
sign, the site of the 1898 lynching, or at Fairfax, down from where he
and Harmony had found Lercino entombed. All about him were ghosts
from the past, merging into a bloody present.

Just before Royal St., and Gadsby's Tavern and the room of the Female
Stranger, he wagered no cars were coming from either direction. He
blew through the intersection; luckily, the streets were empty.

He rolled through Pitt St., and past George Washington's townhouse
across from the domicile of the enslaved Ball brothers, who'd escaped
North along the Underground Railroad. At the St. Asaph turn he
swerved to a stop, in the middle of the intersection, to call Greco. As he
clicked the detective's number, he glanced past the grand William
Fairfax mansion toward the house next to Light-Horse Harry Lee's,
where Tony Hill had met his horrific end. Murdered by the man he'd
now identified.

He listened hard: No answer! Maybe Greco was at the bomb scene by
now, preoccupied. He started to dial 911 but impatience and dread
consumed him. He roared north up the slick pavement without dialing,
the phone in his left hand, steering with his right, skidding crazily
along.

At Queen St., he stopped suddenly after almost crashing into a Hyundai
Elantra, driven by the owner of the "Spite House" there. The former
narrow alley turned in 1830 into "America's Smallest House". Ignoring
curses from the driver, Ted seized advantage of the unwanted stop to
call Greco again—and got him!

"Greco, it's Ted," he stated rapidly, his voice high-strung. "I know you're super busy right now, with the bomb——"

"But how'd you know?"

"Send anyone you can spare to the Old Cotton Mill!" He added, "Harmony's in danger there, I think.

"And I'm sure I know the murderer!"

All Greco could say was, "Cotton Mill on North Washington, right?" and Ted slammed the phone into a pocket, and skidded off, leaving the Spite House owner spiteful indeed.

Gripping the controls with both hands now, he careened into Princess St., and exploded out of the intersection, alongside a renovated condo, the old city jail before the building of the new prison where Abdullah made his escape.

His stomach almost retched from the stop and starts and skids, but he closed on his destination. Swooshing by on his left was Oronoco's short, cobblestoned street, then Lee's Boyhood Home, and up from it the Lee-Fendall site of the Lisa Jennings Bland massacre, across Washington St. from the home of Edmund Jennings Lee.

'Have I guessed right?' he thought, as the back wheel sent gravel flying up behind him. 'The Lee properties are so close to it!' He nearly cried tears in frustration. 'This is the old Lee Neighborhood. An obvious target for the killer. The Lee-Fendall murder. The Light-Horse Lee house. How could I not have thought of it before!?'

The smell of rubber mixing with moist air, Ted screeched to a stop outside the Old Cotton Mill's construction site. He snapped off the ignition, and lay the motorbike roughly down on the asphalt.

In the damp night glow of streetlights stretched the renovations in the rear of the Cotton Mill. About a half a city block in size, it was a rough, uninviting jumble of things. Mounds of gravel, broken-up concrete, thick metal wiring with sharp edges, stacks of wooden flooring, insulation materials, and Komatsu and John Deere excavators. Behind it loomed the Mill, four brick stories high, its white paint glowing faintly, and topped by its graceful cupola, which seemed to float up to and disappear in the dampened sky.

The black outline of the "Ghost of the Old Cotton Mill" was visible from one of the rear windows of the cupola, which was faintly lit. Which was doubly odd. The wax replica of the security guard slain at the Mill in 1854 had been placed for many years on the cupola's southeast side. Making it visible from the northwest side of Washington St. Ted had been right, during his Civil War tour, when he couldn't see the ghostly waxen figure from the boulevard, and deduced it had been moved.

Even though he thought the renovations hadn't yet touched the top floor of the building. Which had remained cloaked in darkness, its lights turned off.

But not this night, as a faint glow was discernible behind its panes. The construction site was surrounded by a seven-foot-high, wire-mesh fence, with spikes and barbed wire on top. Ted frenetically looked about for an opening. If he couldn't find one, he'd ride the motorbike around the block to the front entrance. But that was probably locked. Again he tried Harmony's phone. Again he only got muffled noises, a kind of shout, or shouts. The noises weren't pleasant.

Chapter 60 – Curiosity Gets the Better

Not long before, Harmony Jain did her planned food shopping at the Trader Joe's just up St. Asaph St. from the Old Cotton Mill. The store was open under limited hours, with a cap on the number of shoppers. The restrictions were hardly needed, as there were only a handful of customers. Harmony asked a produce manager how people were managing to eat during the virus. He replied that many were getting their food delivered, or were picking up orders to go. She arranged to have her own items sent to her apartment. That way she could get some exercise by walking the mile and a half back home.

Harmony left the well-regarded boutique grocery and passed the former Portner Brewery, now a distinctive-looking condominium with a modern top floor built over the original construction. Across Pendleton St. to her right was the big dark rectangle of the Cotton Mill. Harmony knew it was just two short blocks from Lee-Fendall, the scene of Bland's horrific murder and amputation. Suddenly wary, she looked up and down Pendleton, but saw only a lone pedestrian, an elderly woman adjusting the collar of a rain jacket with one hand as she walked a dog down toward the river.

She began to turn up Pendleton, at the corner of the Mill's construction site. Harmony intended to walk back via S. Washington, which was well lighted and safer. Then she got the frenetic call from Ted. Alarmed, she punched in 911, and relayed Ted's message to the dispatcher. She checked her news feed. Just one local blog had a sketchy blurb on a report of a bomb at the waterfront.

Somewhat reassured, Harmony happened to look toward the Mill's backyard. She scanned its high fence and barbed-wire enclosures. Her alert eyes noticed a gap where parts of the fence had been loosely locked together. 'It kind of seems like the gate on the north side of the coal plant,' she told herself. 'But nothing to fear from 'The Joker' now—that killer drowned in the Potomac.'

Yet she spotted something odd at the southeast portion of the site, not far behind the fence. The soil there was mostly smooth, the remnant of a park for the Mill's previous owner, an international association of police. She remembered Ted taking her there and telling her about the cops' association. But a portion of the ground looked odd. She peered closer at the clay soil; it had been disturbed. Not by excavators or bulldozers, it seemed, but by some person's or persons' feet. As if the ground had been stomped on. She touched her iPhone SE camera into zoom mode, and night mode, and zeroed in on the area. The clay had definitely been churned up. Not by footsteps, but by the stamping of feet. As if there had been a struggle there.

With the aid of the magnification, her keen eyes noticed discoloration in the tossed-up soil. Not the dully red Virginia clay, but a brighter shade of scarlet. Like the flecks of red she'd spotted on the grounds of the Carlyle mansion.

Flecks of blood.

She felt a chill, soon overcome by excitement.

Her assumption could be wrong, she told herself. She was likely jumping to conclusions. But her adventurous spirit pushed her to find out. The gap in the fence was narrow, but not too small for her slender physique. She slipped through, and examined the moist, disrupted ground. The soil reminded her of her days playing JV soccer, when the turf was all kicked up on a rainy field. She got on her hands and knees. She sniffed and stared at the scarlet specks. A passerby might have mistaken her for a dog inspecting a gopher hole.

She confirmed her suspicion about the red matter. It was blood.

She thought she'd call Ted, while noticing the specks led toward the Cotton Mill. Bent over, a bit scared, but intrigued even more, she followed the droplets. They weaved around a John Deere tractor, and a pile of discarded boards. About two thirds of the way to the Mill, the flecks stopped. But their direction was clear. They made up a trail pointing directly to a rear entrance.

Halfway to it, Harmony came upon a patch of smooth ground. This soil wasn't disrupted. But footprints could be made out. One set of footprints, clearly defined. The boot prints of a sizeable person. Along it was two parallel grooves set close together. As if someone was being dragged along, with the heels digging out the shallow tracks.

She came up to the Cotton Mill's back door. It was weather-beaten, fashioned from before the time of the police association, maybe even from antebellum days. It was shut. However, when she pulled on the rusted door knob, it pulled open, the hinge creaking.

The ground floor ahead was cavernous and dark. Harmony was able to make out a pile of discarded office furniture, which blocked the view directly in front of her. But she recalled the time she had gone there with Ted, when they had slipped into the place trespassing, with Ted's cover story of 'a historian inspecting a historic locale'. She remembered the staircase was in the front part of the Mill, near the windows facing Washington St. In the gloom, cell flashlight glowing, she stepped carefully, but nimbly, around discarded desktops, computers, and shelving.

Her heart was thumping; she felt the blood roaring through her neck. 'Maybe I should call Ted,' she told herself. She took out her cell and, while picking her way forward, phoned him. As she did, she remembered the blood on the ground outside. 'Perhaps yet another person is in mortal peril!' she thought, suddenly becoming alarmed. 'Every second might count!' Without thinking, she slipped the phone back into a pocket, and moved ahead.

She reached the other side of the ground floor. The view into Washington St. from the windows was blocked by moldy old drapes. She began to mount the wooden staircase up to the cupola. She tried to step lightly, as the ancient stairs creaked under her tread.

Harmony stepped carefully yet quickly up the stairs. One step creaked loudly, making her wonder if the ancient stairway was safe. Impelled by fear another's life was in danger, she kept ascending.

At the top of the stairs was a small landing before a battered door with rusty hinges. She took a penlight from her pocketbook and shone onto the floor. It was covered with dust; some of the floorboards were warped with age and sticking upward. She peered at the wood in front of the door, and perceived the faint outline of a muddy boot print. "Does it match the print I saw in the work yard outside?' she wondered. 'It seems to.' Harmony had taken out her cell again when she heard a noise from behind the door. A muffled sound. A scream? A cry for help?

As with Ted, sudden impulses sometimes overcame Harmony's better judgment. Casting aside caution, she strode to the door and turned the green-mottled knob. The door opened easily. She stepped within. For a moment she was reassured.

Before her was the cupola room: a high, domed ceiling, and rectangular windows with dirty slats and curtains. And no one there. She thought. For an instant.

Then, as she took another step forward there appeared the grotesque sight of something in a vat, with steam rising from it.

It was a man, a fat man, mostly naked, his body half in the barrel, and half suspended over it!

Before she could react she felt a sting, and a pain that penetrated to the marrow. It dulled her nerves, and sent a searing pain down her left side. For an instant she thought a lightning bolt, on that rainy right, had struck the summit of the Old Cotton Mill.

She turned reflexively, but very slowly, painfully, to her left, wondering groggily if the lightning rod for the ancient building had been removed.

Harmony saw another man, a large man, crouching, with a gun of some kind in his right hand. 'No,' she saw, 'a Taser!'

He was double-masked. She got the impression of someone who was robust, energetic. In fact, he seemed to quiver with excitement. Like a hunter at the climax of a hunt.

Despite the fog in her mind, Harmony knew she was in mortal danger. As the man fiddled with the Taser, she tried to move backward, but her left leg felt as heavy as a concrete block. She slowly crouched downward in a defensive posture.

The man took three quick steps toward her, and stopped, right knee bent, the Taser pointed two feet from her chest. 'Was this the killer?' she wondered. She felt horror. Yet also determination.

She sensed some feeling in her left leg, and her right leg felt strong. She remembered her massacred friend Tony. She grew angry. Pivoting on her left leg, Harmony swung her right leg up fast. Her running shoe hit the man in his left ear, as her thigh caught him in his neck.

He grunted in surprise, and fell onto her chest, sending her tumbling backwards onto the floorboards, his weight crashing down on her. She landed on her upper back and head, the breath got knocked out of her.

Harmony felt a spreading pain in the bones of her skull. She swiveled her neck, and glimpsed the man in agony over a steaming vat. Then she blacked out.

Chapter 61 – View from a Killer

'Perhaps I am overdoing it,' he thought, breathing hard from the exertion. 'But no,' he corrected himself, 'it will be a high point of my mission.' He expected the explosion at Fitzgerald's park to occur at any second. If it hadn't happened already. He wondered if he could hear, from this distance of about two miles, the sound of a loud explosion. The remote detonator hadn't worked from inside the Torpedo Factory. Or later, from outside it. Perhaps it had malfunctioned, perhaps he had been too far away. Then there was his haste to leave the Factory, and to drive back here, to his 'secure location'. Still, he had put timers in the bombs at the cannon as backups. They were due to go about now.

He realized it had been stupid, after Sifter recognized him, to try to hide in the Torpedo Factory. He should have run directly to his car parked on Cameron St., just off Union, which he did do after fleeing the Factory. Then he had driven at high speed to the Old Cotton Mill, taking just a few minutes. Parking on Washington St. near the front entrance, then heading inside using the duplicate key he had made. Though he didn't know it at the time, he arrived just a minute before a certain nosey woman who was then inspecting the grounds at the rear of the Cotton Mill.

He would keep checking his cell for any news of an explosion, and deaths, at the waterfront. However, he was then very preoccupied. He stood with his back to the cupola's west window, one of the windows facing Washington St. He had rigged up some dirty curtains and blinds, which blocked the view from the street. A modicum of light from a single, naked light bulb glowed from the ceiling. He looked over to his left, just past the north window, and the large, wide barrel. It looked rather like the hogsheads of old, when jammed with the fragrant leaves of the region's cash crop, that slaves had rolled down Tobacco Quay to the riverside piers. He had found the vat at the Mill's construction site and had lugged it upstairs.

Instead of tobacco, the vat was filled with gobs of melting wax and gallons of water. A portable heater was below it. The heater was on; steam rose up from the big barrel. It made the air of the closed-in space on that warm, damp night very uncomfortable.

Occasionally he cracked open the south window to let in some of the evening air, to bring some relief from the humidity, and to hear, he hoped, the sound of a detonation. Over the last week, it had taken several trips to this hideaway to arrange things, but he knew now it was worth it.

A big-bodied African-American man was in the barrel. 39 years of age, he was shirtless, without trousers, wearing just his soaked underpants. He was up to his amply belly in the waxy water, which was steadily getting hotter, now at about 150 degrees, his tormentor figured. Still well below the boiling point, but above the point of pain. It was a nice touch to his continuing mayhem, a classical reference, so to speak, to another horrific crime from long ago.

The policeman, hanging from the hoist on the metal bar above, tried again to scream, out of agony or for help, or both, it wasn't known. But the gag stuffed between his lips was secure and made of a strong synthetic fiber, thwarting his desperate attempts to cry out, or to chew through it.

At times the cop's suspended body swiveled left, and he caught sight of the wax figure propped up against a wall, its distorted face seeming to leer at him. When he saw the figure's head, crumbling from over 150 years of heat and cold, his eyes seemed to pop from his own head, as if he was witnessing his own baleful fate. And in fact he was, for his tormentor intended to make waxed corpses of his next victims.

The captive's body swiveled back to his right, and he again saw the killer. That pitiless man seemed lost in thought. And he was thinking, of Freemen's Cemetery, of Tony Hill's home and adjoining property, of the Meeting House tomb, of Lisa's Bland's museum and Gadsby's ice house. He savored going over his "achievements". And now this, the Cotton Mill, the very symbol of the slave economy. Two more notches on his belt of revenge.

When he was done, he figured, he'd hang one of the waxed corpses from the southwest corner of the cupola. For a while at least. And no one gazing up from Washington St. would notice the difference with the original wax dummy. From the street, it was too far away to tell. He laughed. 'What a wonderful trick,' he reflected, 'to play on the clueless people of this hateful town!'

He knew this hiding place wouldn't last forever. The reconstruction of the cupola was due to start in six weeks. But it had been his special place for a time. An historic place to revel in, during this great period of his life.

He looked over to his right, to the rear of the cupola, and to his latest victim. She lay on the floor, gagged, breathing convulsively, hands bound behind, and a chain stretching from the belt on her waist to a wall manacle. The metal rings at the bottom of the wall, he thought, could have secured the shackles of a slave. They may have been attached to pulleys to haul up materials to the cupola during an earlier renovation. They proved useful in this situation.

The woman lay on the ground gasping and weeping, or crying for help, or moaning, again it was hard to tell due to the gag. His mind reached back to the murder in the house next to the Light-Horse Lee home. He had heard her coming down to its basement, just after he had finished the kill, and managed to slip through a basement window before her arrival. 'She is a nuisance, this Harmony Jain,' he said to himself. 'But now she is getting what she deserves.'

Another annoyance was her colleague, or boyfriend, whatever he was, that snoop, Ted Sifter. His feeling of triumph softened. Sifter had surely recognized him outside the Torpedo Factory, and had almost got to him inside the place.

It was possible Sifter was already trying to find Jain. That was a concern, but he had eliminated so many others he little feared the historian. More worrying, it was quite possible he had already contacted the police, and that imbecilic detective Greco. Yet it was his impression that he, and she, usually acted alone. She certainly had, and would pay a fatal price. If Sifter did convince Greco he was the killer, he might have to put the historian, and the detective, next on his target list. Sifter would be easy to murder at his duplex, he gathered. Greco might be harder to take down. If they were eliminated, no one would suspect him, just as no one had before. The identity of Old Town's serial killer would remain unknown, he estimated.

In any event, he expected to kill a great many other people that evening, if he hadn't already. 'Another triumph,' he reflected, 'then I'll move on to other slayings.' When he abandoned this refuge, he would simply continue to operate out of his Old Town home, with an occasional visit to the Fort Lyon site to dispose of messy evidence. He cracked open a window again, listening intently. 'It may be the detonator has malfunctioned,' he estimated. He heard nothing but the wind and the light rain spattering against the dormers of the roof. He closed the window, and returned his gaze to the steaming barrel.

The off-duty cop had come upon him at the Mill's construction site late that afternoon, after the site had been left unattended for weeks. He had been through tense situations at the murder sites, however, and knew enough to stay calm. As usual, he had the element of surprise, and a greater will, he believed, than the unsuspecting weaklings he put to death.

He had let the policeman, an immigrant from Jamaica, approach him on the grass, luring him over by playing dumb, not responding to the shouted warning that he was trespassing. The cop had pegged the man with the beard and ragged hair for a crazed, homeless man, and had walked up unsuspectingly.

Then from three feet away, he'd been zapped with a Taser Pulse gun. The cop was stunned and unable to defend himself, but not knocked unconscious. The killer had led him, stumbling and muttering helplessly, to the rear entrance. There the cop's head began to clear. He regained a little strength, and started to offer resistance. At which point putting a gun to the befuddled man's temple proved persuasive. The cop let himself be walked slowly up the stairwell to the cupola. Then a sharp blow to the side of the head had knocked him out.

Hauling him over the rim of the barrel had been difficult. Hoisting him upward was also hard. The killer's arm had ached from the wound he'd received during the fight with Lisa Bland. A pleasurable thing about it, though, was how it reminded him of hoisting Carl Cordero up onto the Freedmen's sculpture. His first great triumph. An unfortunate thing: The man in the vat was of African ancestry. Yet he reckoned, as with Cordero, that 'some persons of color must be sacrificed for the greater good.'

Moreover, the cop's surprise intervention had erased his problem of how to lure someone to the cupola for his waxed corpse scheme. 'This poor fellow will do just fine!' he enthused. And in rifling through his wallet, he found he also worked part-time as a watchman, at the Masonic Temple no less. The fact he was a sentinel, like the man murdered at the Mill back in 1854, made for a delicious parallel. 'Simply icing on the cake!' he told himself with glee.

The unfortunate fellow had awoken in Hell, when the heat burning into his genitals ended his slumber. His chest constricted by the hoist, his legs dangling, he'd looked down in horror at his imprisoner. Over and again he tried and failed to scream, blood from the gash on his head streaming down his cheek, then dripping into the steadily growing bubbles emanating from the vat.

The female interloper had been harder to subdue. When he heard the creak of her footsteps on the stairs, he chided himself for having not installed a sensor system in his temporary abode. But he'd reacted fast, positioning himself on the south side of the doorway, with a clear view of anyone entering. She'd foolishly resisted, but was now chained to a wall like a slave, like a latter-day Charlotte Dupuy, and faced a fate of watching, then experiencing herself, a slow and torturous death.

Chapter 62 – A Harrowing Ascent

After slipping through the gap in the fence where Harmony had entered the Mill's construction site, Ted had raced to the rear entrance. He pulled open the door and stepped inside. With the glow of his cell illuminating the way, he stepped to the Washington St. side of the Mill, and examined its staircase. He worried about a trap; he figured one awaited him. A student of military history, he knew whoever held the high ground had a great advantage, and the man in the cupola had it. But Ted, a student in particular of Stonewall Jackson's campaigns, reasoned the best way to assault a strong position was to go around it, and attack from the side. From his previous explorations of the Cotton Mill, he knew there was an old elevator shaft near the stairs that led up to the roof and the cupola.

The elevator itself had been removed years before, but there were two scaling ladders on its shaft's southern and northern walls. Peering up, holding aloft his cell, he saw to his dismay the north ladder ended 10 feet up the wall, its upper portions having broken apart. The south ladder was still intact. However, it was made of wood, and looked rickety. Ted realized if it fell apart on him, near the top, he'd plummet 35 feet down, and likely be maimed, or killed. But he was desperate. He thought of taking the stairs instead, the direct approach. On an impulse, he started climbing the shaft.

As he went up in the dark he found that, though some of the middle parts of the rungs were missing, the sides of most of them were stable. His left knee aching, he went from rung to rung, using his arms to help pull himself up, though his shoulder ached from its rotator cuff tear. To grip with both hands, he put his cell away, so the climb was mostly by feel in very dim light. Fortunately, the rungs were placed at equal, predictable intervals. They were clammy and slippery, however. Halfway up, drops of water began falling from above. The rungs got wetter. His hands were already moist from sweat, and Ted felt his left hand give way! He had the terrible sensation of vertigo, as his body swung sideways and his body dangled into space. But his righthand grip held, as did the rung on which he put back his feet. Sweating hard, breathing harder, he screamed to himself, 'I must make it! For Harmony's sake!'

He started going back up, his feet slipping at times on the wet rungs. His Capricorn sign, the image of a goat stubbornly stepping up a mountain, entered his mind, as it sometimes did when he biked or hiked up a steep hill. 'Never refuse a hill challenge,' he would tell himself. But he'd rarely had a challenge like this.

As he neared the top of the ladder, Ted prayed he'd be able to get through the elevator shaft's cover. He thought he remembered it, during his last visit there, as busted up, falling apart, but he wasn't certain. And it might have been repaired during an early stage of the renovations. It'd be logical for a construction firm to repair holes in a roof, to stop rainwater damage. He had no tools with him to get through the cover if it was intact. But drops of water, in greater volume it seemed, kept pouring down, filling him with hope the shaft was open to the air above, even as the raindrops made the rungs ever more slippery. Because of the darkness, fear, and uncertainty, the climb felt like two hours. In fact, it took the athletic historian just a few minutes, despite soreness in his arms and legs. At the top of the ladder, he peered upward, and was relieved to see large openings in the roof cover. He could now see better due to the ambient light streaming through. But his heart fell as he realized the covering was intact where the ladder ended just below the roof. He was blocked there. Why hadn't he taken the stairs?!

Above and over to his right, however, he saw that the wooden cover was broken in a few places. And further over, the openings were larger. He figured he'd be able to slip through or smash his way through the busted-up boards at that location. However, the openings were about five feet from him. To get there, he'd have to leap off the ladder into space. Whether he could cover that distance was unknown.

He moved his feet lightly over the rungs. The slats were rickety there. Would they hold together when he pushed off them? Even worse, after jumping he'd have to get a handhold on a narrow ledge under the cover. He stared at the ledge in the dim light. He couldn't tell if it was solid, or crumbling. Also, it was probably wet, and slippery. If his leap missed the ledge, or if he lost his grip, he'd plummet to the base of the shaft. At a minimum, broken bones, and possible paralysis. More likely, death.

Again, death. Omnipresent death. The thought of it almost overcame him. Would death's baleful presence ever leave Old Town? It seemed the place had become cursed.

Both his knees ached now. His rotator cuff throbbed with pain. he couldn't differentiate the loud beats of his pounding heart. He looked down into the blackness of the shaft. He could go back down the ladder, and mount the stairs, and try to get through the door of the cupola. That would take precious minutes. Harmony might be dead by then. She might be dead already—he pushed away the thought. But the thought came back.

And another thought emerged. A determination, a vow. If she had been killed, he would kill the killer.

He stared up at the openings. His eyes filled with tears from the sweat pouring into them. He thought again of Harmony, and the moans he'd heard from her cell phone. No more hesitation.

He coiled his body against the ladder. He bent his knees, prepped his legs. After the deepest of breaths, he leapt into the dark space of the lift. He ended up somewhat higher and further than he had calculated, as his hands and elbows smashed down onto the far, flat side of the ledge. However, he felt a splinter of wood enter the flesh of his left arm. And he had no firm grip!

His fingers clattered on the ledge, kicking up wet filth that flew into his face. And for a horrifying instant, Ted felt the weight of his body pulling him down into the shaft.

He flung out his hands further, and his fingers clawed onto a side of the ledge which had a metal strip between it and the roof. The tips of his fingers held to it, barely. His eyes burned; he sneezed hard after breathing in the dirt. Desperately, he tried willing his fingers forward. His left hand slipped back; the right hand reached further onto the strip. He forced his left hand forward, and both hands got a solid hold.

But his legs were suspended in space, his chest on the ledge's edge. Would the metal strip come loose, and with it his hold? The notion filled him with terror. He wasn't falling, yet, but he found it extremely hard to push and pull further forward.

Hanging over the abyss, he could make out sizeable openings two feet up and to the right, on the far side of the ledge. He squirmed and struggled in that direction, heaving his chest and belly almost up to his hands. His fingers were aching and numb, yet holding their grip. He balanced precariously on the ledge, dripping sweat, hands slick, breathing almost uncontrollably, his exhalations kicking up dust and dirt from the ledge that almost choked him. His rotator cuff felt like it was tearing again. He sneezed again through his clogged nose, spraying snot and dust all about.

He could go no further. At some point, he'd have to release his grip and try for the further part of the ledge. When he did, his body might lose its delicate balance, and slide down into the shaft.

He had come to another leap of faith, so to speak. There was no going back.

He pulled out his hands and thrust them forward.

Spasms of pain ran through his shoulder and upper back. He ignored them as his hands grabbed at air and wood. His body teetered; his legs hovered over the shaft of death. An awful fright raced through him as his belly started to slip backward. His left and right hands extended to their breaking point. Somehow he stopped the backward slip, and wiggled his stomach forward an inch.

Then, there it was! The fingers reached the openings past the far side of the ledge. The grip was tentative, but holding. With the spasms spreading to his middle back, he pulled his legs up to the ledge. His body was squished together, but safe, for the time being. He rested for a few seconds and, his back still aching, his shoulder feeling like it was broken, he pulled himself to the cover's apertures.

Ted could not quite squeeze through it, he judged. So, leaning on his left side, he punched back the boards with his right arm. The wood gave way. He'd make it through after all!

He exhaled the greatest sigh of relief. He had survived, barely. Then came another wave of fear: Had knocking out the boards alerted the fiend inside the cupola?

Ted stumbled onto the slanted roof, as rain splattered his filth-stained clothes. He leaned over to the angle of the slope, his knees buckling over the worn linoleum. He bent down lower, so that the remnants of the shaft's cover would block the view of him from the cupola. He pulled up the shirt sleeve which the splinter had pierced and, wincing, pulled it out. The cut bled for a few moments, then slowed to a trickle. It didn't hurt much. The ache in his shoulder had also dulled. The dank air outside was warmer than expected from the humidity.

He stepped cautiously to the side of the covering, ankles bent from the slant, and looked toward the cupola.

It was further away from the shaft than he remembered. About 25 feet. Good: Given the distance, and the rain, it was less likely the killer had heard him. Dark-gray curtains and blinds mostly covered the inside of the cupola windows facing him. Excellent. That would make him even harder to spot. But he also might have trouble seeing what was happening inside.

Ted got on his hands and knees, and crawled toward the southeast window. Puddles on the roof's graveled floor soaked the knees of his pants. He reached the far right of the window, and hid himself below its sill. The curtains and blinds didn't completely block his view there. The glass was spotted with raindrops, but he could see clearly enough through a portion of the pane.

Chapter 63 – Desperate Denouement

Very, very slowly, he lifted his head above the windowsill, ready to snap his head back if he saw the killer looking his way.

What he saw was horrific.

In the far corner was a wide barrel, its contents simmering. Ted could make out vapors rising from it, making the far wall seem to shimmer. In and above the vat was a figure in agony. A man hanging suspended, writhing, the lower part of his body immersed, his silent screams muffled by a gag. Ted felt a pain in his entrails from viewing the ghastly scene.

He shifted his gaze right, closer to the window—and flinched on seeing Harmony. She lay on her left side along the wall, between the entrance door and his window. A tether of some kind ran from her waist to a shackle in the wall. Her face was bleeding. It was hard to tell if her eyes were open a bit, or completely shut from swelling. Far worse, from his vantagepoint Ted couldn't tell whether she was breathing. A thin handkerchief was twisted around her neck. A gag. Evidently she had freed it from her mouth at some point.

Ted had to take action, to save her—if she were still alive. And to do something about the man being tormented in the vat.

But Ted didn't see the killer. Could he have left and gone down the stairs while he had come up the shaft? That would be a stroke of luck. He might be able to free the other two while the fiend was away. But Ted figured it more likely he was out of sight on the cupola's southwest side, to the left of the window.

The question was how and where to enter. He examined the window's exterior. As the various organizations that had occupied the old building had kept, as a kind of darkly humorous tradition, the wax figure in the cupola, the cupola itself had been renovated over the years. It thus had fairly new windows in decent condition. The one in front of Ted could be slid upward. While keeping alert for the appearance of the killer, Ted peered at the latch. It looked to be unlatched.

Ted ran through his options. He knew of no hatch in the cupola's ceiling, so no entry there. If he tried to enter through the other windows, the killer would likely have a better view of him entering, or spot him before he entered. Harmony could already be dead, or nearly so, and that seemed to be the case with the man in the barrel. He had to act, now.

Kneeling down, he reached both arms under the window's bottom frame, and pulled upward. The frame moved only slightly, though noiselessly. Was it stuck?

Sighing in frustration, he pulled up on it some more, harder.

The windowpane jumped up several inches, and made a low screech.

Ted silently swore. Had the killer heard it?

At least one person, an alert person, had.

Harmony's eyes opened wide at the sound. She tilted her head up a bit from the filthy floor, and looked in the direction of the noise.

Her eyes met Ted's. A burst of adrenalin, and hope, burst through her. A wave of joy burst through him.

She looked toward the part of the cupola hidden from Ted, then looked back. She gave a barely perceptible, knowing nod. Her eyes darted, twice, in the direction of the cupola hidden from Ted. Then she did it again, with her eyes opening wide each time.

It was a signal. A signal of someone, of danger, lurking where she had glanced.

A few moments passed. Ted readied himself to enter, and confront the still-unseen menace.

Then Harmony pulled herself up on her knees and, shimmying her broad hips, loudly rattled the chain. She looked to the hidden part of the cupola, and moaned, "Why me?! Let me out of here! Why are you doing this?!"

'Wonderful gal,' thought Ted. She was making a diversion. He cringed. 'But maybe with the price of her life!'

Stepping quickly into view was the killer. He was surprised by the woman's sudden motion and plea. He had taken one of his masks off, and now he ripped off the other.

The hateful visage of the Deputy Mayor appeared under the faint glow of the overhead bulb.

"Quiet, you witch!" shouted Sean Morenis. He stopped two feet from her, glowering over her prone figure.

He paused, and actually considered the question she'd posed.

"Isn't it obvious by now?" he answered loudly. "I've committed, not the perfect crime—but the perfect *crimes*. Murders, no, but sacrificial offerings—to avenge the great crimes of the past, and present.

"Perfectly calibrated, to instigate a race war today!"

He cackled, and turned his head up the ceiling. His face took on a truly maniacal look. "Vengeance is mine, saith the Lord!" he yelled sarcastically. "Actually, it's mine, saith Sean Morenis, Deputy Mayor. All mine!" And he spat at Harmony.

"You have to give me credit," he cried, suddenly eager to explain himself. "Killing a black at Freedmen's, then a white man near Christ Church, to throw everyone off the track. Then a descendent of a

635

Confederate general, A.P. Hill, near Light-Horse Harry's home. Then Old Presbyterian, to stupefy the stupid cops again.

"And my *piece de resistance*: Blowing up Washington's cannon on the waterfront, the greater slaver of Mt. Vernon, on the very spot where slaves were brought onto the docks of Alexandria!"

Looming over Harmony, Morenis seemed even taller than his six-feet-plus height. He took a deep breath, and continued. "But the sweetest was the slaying, and even more, the whipping, of Lisa Jennings Bland." His eyes gleamed, his whole being hyperexcited. "Just what a Lee descendant deserved! And horribly maimed, just like Anthony Hill and Lillian Harper!"

A shocked Harmony took all this in, and thought desperately, determinedly, for survival. 'Stall for time,' she told herself. 'Ted is here. Greco should be coming too. Keep asking questions.'

She threw out a speculation of Ted's, while posing it as a certainty. Maybe it would confuse the killer.

"Why did you lead that riot through Old Town?"

Morenis looked at her with surprise. "You knew that!? Sifter knew that?" The killer paused in surprise. "Yes, Avril Forstandt and I were among the leaders of, of the insurrection. But in disguise. At least I was carefully disguised. Unlike that reckless bitch."

He turned to the unfortunate man slowly roasting in the barrel. "But that was small change." He grinned like an apostle from Hell. "Now I conduct a grand commemoration, of Light-Horse Lee's maiming!

"His beating by the Baltimore mob. Their cutting up of his body. Their pouring of superheated wax, and of boiling oil, sacred, cleansing oil, onto his head. Blinding him, a fitting penalty for any Lee! But I'm going a step better—boiling wax, for the whole body!"

He pointed to the cop, then gestured toward the crumbling wax figure at the back of the cupola, the 'Ghost' of the Old Cotton Mill. Then gestured again at the terrified man over the barrel. "This fellow is a fine, fine choice to become the second waxed effigy of this place." He screamed at Harmony. "And you'll be the third!"

As he had in the elevator shaft, Ted bent his knees and coiled his legs, ready to explode forward.

The Deputy Mayor stopped, his face truly that of a madman, his features distorted from spite. He added, "But first, I may amputate a limb, like I did with Mary Bland after the fact! Your pretty little leg perhaps!" He then walked over to Harmony, and gave her a hard kick in the ribs.

The weeks of plotting and stabbing and shooting and whipping had unhinged Morenis. He was completely overcome by the emotions that had fueled his campaign of rage.

He pulled his **Springfield Hellcat** from a belt holster.

"Maybe I should just finish you off now! Instead of waiting, like I wanted, to boil you alive!"

At that, the cop uttered a stifled, yet still-discernible moan. The killer turned in his direction.

At that, Ted pulled the window pane up hard.

Morenis heard the window screech, and turned toward it.

Ted jumped onto the window ledge, crouching low, and leapt onto the floor of the cupola.

The Deputy Mayor was startled at Ted's appearance. Just 15 feet separated them. He hesitated. Ted didn't. In a mad bull rush, head down, shoulders square, he exploded toward him.

He was just three feet away when Morenis swung the gun toward Ted.

Harmony, at the same time, pivoted on her hips, and swung her right leg up at Morenis.

The killer's index finger was on the trigger. He moved the gun barrel toward Ted's skull.

At that instant, Harmony's leg caught him in the waist.

Morenis was pushed off balance as he fired. A .380 bullet whizzed by Ted's face. He actually sensed the wind from it. It smashed through the southwest window. Harmony's kick strained her thigh muscle; she grabbed it in pain.

Ted crashed into the side of Morenis' tall, well-conditioned frame. The pistol went scattering across the floorboards toward the steaming barrel. The killer staggered back a couple of yards. Ted regained his balance, pivoted, and rushed toward the boiling vat to get the pistol.

The cop moaned above him. Harmony struggled to get to her feet.

Seeing his way to the gun blocked, Morenis backed up to the cupola's other end, where he had his weapons stash. He reached for his Taser.

Ted looked over his shoulder, seeing the killer had grabbed the Taser. He reached down for the gun, and as he did, Morenis fired the Taser. Its dart flew past Ted's neck and smashed into a wall.

Ted picked up the gun. He stood up straight and pointed it at the killer. His heart was racing, but his hand was steady.

Morenis stood frozen. 'Has it come to this?' he reflected in agony. 'Will my great mission end this way?! At the hands of this, this *tour guide*!?" He dropped the Taser.

Ted knew enough about guns to aim for the broad torso, not a narrow limb of the target. He went for the middle of the chest. For a bizarre instant, flashing through his mind was a story of the first attempted presidential assassination, when the would-be killer had fired pointblank at Andrew Jackson.

Ted aimed. Morenis' abdomen was right in his sights. The killer stood stunned, motionless, the tables turned on him, watching Death in the face.

The man in the vat moaned, and Harmony, grunting in pain, staggered to her feet, the drama about to end.

Ted judged Morenis was about to dart aside. He squeezed the trigger. The gun misfired!

Morenis was startled for an instant. Then he grinned, and eyed a dagger on a table next to the west window.

Harmony steadied herself. 'Better to take on a knife attack standing up', she figured. 'As at the tomb of the Female Stranger.' As she did, she heard noises outside the cupola on the street below. Mechanical sounds.

Meantime Ted reacted with incredible speed. As Morenis reached for the knife, he broke like a sprinter from the starting blocks.

He raced forward, and smashed into Morenis. Both men tumbled over the table, and crashed into the window. They broke the glass, busted up the part of the frame, and fell into it. Momentarily, they found themselves stuck among the broken wood and shards of glass.

The two grappled briefly, then their momentum pushed them clear of the frame, and they tumbled onto the slanted roof.

It was raining hard now, but the sound of the downpour on the linoleum roofing was eclipsed by the screech of sirens.

'Greco finally got here!' thought Ted, as he scrambled to his feet, with small cuts to his arms from the window glass.

As he stood up straight, the blood rushed to his head, as he tried to gain his footing on the slant of the roof. His head spinning, he nearly fell over. He was an easy target for Morenis, who stood just a few feet from him. But the killer, while balancing uneasily himself, was looking past him to the roof edge, toward the sound of the police below.

Suddenly, the sharp retort of a pistol shot sounded from within the cupola. Ted turned toward the busted window to see, and Morenis took advantage by slamming into him. Ted was knocked down onto wet linoleum; the killer leapt on top of him. Morenis grabbed a fistful of gravel, and hurled it toward Ted's eyes. But Ted turned his head away in time and, after pushing away his attacker, rolled over and over down the slope of the roof.

Getting to his feet, Ted played for time. He knew the arrival of help was imminent; he needed to hold on. But Morenis, his rage and desperation growing, would have none of that.

He slid and slipped down the slope to Ted. He reached the historian, and grabbed him by the shoulder and neck. He screamed: "Bastard! Scum! Foiling my noble scheme, to right the wrongs of the past!"

Ted looked in horror at Morenis' face. The ambient light from the lampposts of Washington St. illuminated his visage. It was as white as a corpse, and twisted into a mask of inexecrable hate. The rain poured off his brow like a flood of pale blood. He was hate incarnate.

Morenis stared back. "You must die!" he cried. He fingered a dagger on his belt, the very knife that had slashed Tony Hill to death.

Ted twisted his chest and shoulders hard, breaking the grip, but falling down. He rolled away and down the slope, hitting the back of the dormer overlooking the street.

He sprung back up, his back to the dormer. Morenis was four feet away, dagger in hand, sizing up his prey. Ted sized him up. His foe was taller, possibly stronger, high on adrenalin and spite. 'Play for time!'

Like a boxer avoiding a jab, Ted swayed back and forth, a moving
target, the wet soles of his running shoes sliding on the slick slant of
the roof.

Beyond Morenis he heard, through the slashing rain, a dull pounding of
footsteps. He glimpsed the cupola's doorway through the smashed-up
window.

Greco and his men had arrived!

Morenis took a step toward Ted. It was unclear if he heard what Ted
had heard. Ted eyed him, searching for a weakness, an advantage. 'Will
he kill me just before salvation arrives?' he anguished. 'And how badly
is Harmony hurt?!'

Morenis took another step forward, flicking the knife, grinning, the
downpour gushing off his grotesque face.

'Can I kick gravel in his eyes?!' Ted thought furiously, pressing his
back and the palms of his hands against the dormer. The gravel would
likely hit his foe in the legs, not the eyes. Ted imagined Morenis' knife
piercing his chest, ripping his heart, ending his life.

His left hand felt the edge of the dormer. He sidestepped left, knowing
it was a few feet from the dormer to the low wall of the roof. Buying
him maybe another few seconds before the attacker struck.

He took a step back toward the wall, and Morenis took two short steps
forward, but cautiously, as he slipped on the wet slope.

The sounds of the cops' voices within the cupola grew louder. But the
killer was intent on his prey. Ted cursed. It didn't seem Morenis heard
the noises behind him, wasn't distracted by them.

He backed up against the short wall of the roof.

Morenis tracked him closely, stalking him, as he had stalked the others
in the previous weeks. He had in fact heard the voices within, and

guessed who was coming. He was now aware this would be his final kill, but oddly, he immediately came to terms with it.

He had accomplished much, he told himself as he handled the blade. He had brought Old Town, sinful Old Town, to its knees. He had brought Alexandria, and probably America, close to outright war. He had made some restitution for slavery and the other transgressions of the past, he believed. A second, cleansing Civil War might in the offing, and all due to him!

His attitude was rather like that of McVeigh, during his final, fatal race across the Potomac. He would die without regret, in his mind a warrior worthy.

No, he would not. Not in peace. The unhinged rage that had consumed him over the months and years came raging up to seize him again. He gazed with burning contempt at this historian, this falsifier of the past, he thought, this operator of "fun, informative" walks to locales of genocide and injustice, inequity and oppression.

He raised the blade higher, moving forward, a view to a kill.

'Whatever happens after this,' he thought, 'let me commit this righteous act, as a sacred way to leave this world, if that is my fate!'

Ted felt his haunches back up against the low wall. He had to be careful: The barrier was only three feet high. He knew he must not topple over it by mistake, which would send him crashing down into the Washington St. sidewalk.

Morenis sized him up. He had this despicable author cornered, this pest who'd unmasked him, he and his shrill, disgusting girlfriend. 'This bastard deserves to die!' he raged. Morenis licked twisted lips in triumph.

Over the fiend's shoulder, Ted saw Greco and his police moving quietly through the broken frame of the window.

'Play for time.'

Ted spread his arms apart. "See reason, Morenis! You, you and I have a lot in common."

The city official snarled. "We have nothing in common, in anything that counts."

"We have much in common," Ted countered, "like our, our love, our appreciation, of the history of this place…"

The transparent ploy didn't work. Morenis rushed forward, thrusting the knife at Ted. Ted sidestepped agilely to his right. The killer missed, and took a step back.

Ted shifted left, his shirt tearing on the bricks of the wall. He stole a look at Greco, who was now on the roof. The detective went into a crouch, gun at the ready.

A thought flashed in Ted's mind of his tours, when he'd reenact the end of a duel or assassination. Playing the losing party to the delight of the guests, he'd hurl himself to the ground.

He looked past Morenis at the detective again—and threw himself onto the gravel.

Greco had been waiting for something like that. He fired his Smith and Wesson twice at Morenis' upper back, and well above where Ted lay prostrate.

The shots found their target.

Greco prayed the bullets wouldn't ricochet downward. They didn't. Morenis whirled from the force of the shots, eyed Greco for an instant, continued to whirl violently, and flew past Ted.

The Old Town Horror toppled over the wall, and plunged toward Washington St. He landed hard on the roof of the Old Cotton Mill's columned portico, an imitation of those fronting the plantation houses of the Old South. He tumbled off the portico roof and down toward the sidewalk. His broken body crashed into a marker explaining the history of the Mill. Morenis cried out, his back in agony, and lost consciousness.

Chapter 64 – The Aftermath of Another Quest

Inside the cupola, Greco's squad discovered that Harmony had been busy before their arrival. The gunshot had been from her. After Morenis' pistol had scattered across the floor, she had stretched out to recover it, then shot out the chain attached to her waist. Freed, she rushed to the barrel and turned off the heater. A fireman medic that accompanied the police hoisted the tortured cop out of the water. The medic judged he had second- and third-degree burns on his legs, groin, and waist. It would be a tough recovery, but he would live.

On the street below, an EMS team, after staunching the wounds, placed a severely injured Morenis on a stretcher, and into an ambulance. The work of a surgical team at Alexandria Inova Hospital would determine whether the injuries proved fatal. Harmony and Ted had bruises, welts, and sore muscles, and Ted had splinter cuts in his arm, and a restrained rotator cuff. Yet neither was very seriously hurt. Far from being exhausted, both were on an adrenalin high. "An endorphin high!" said Harmony with glee. "Like after a swim." "An 'endolphin' high!" quipped Ted.

As the ambulance pulled up N. Washington St., Ted and Harmony watched from the rooftop wall. They were bloodied, but unbowed. Greco joined them.

Ted chuckled, and told Harmony, "Once you got the gun, you could have at least come out here to help me."

Harmony, looking luminous despite swelling around her eyes, smiled the smile of the saved. She nodded toward the detective. "I could have, but I figured I'd leave it to the police."

Greco, looking relieved, even relaxed, for the first time in weeks, pointed to the small knot of spectators on the sidewalk below. They were gawking up to the roof as they stood near police and FBI cars along the curb. Next to a government van was Comitas, who was speaking sternly into a cell.

"He's probably," said Greco, "taking credit for nailing the killer."

"Based on his performance," answered Ted, "he should be calling an employment agency."

Harmony hadn't heard him. She was staring at her text. She showed it to Ted.

Ted read it, and thought for a moment. Then he took her hand, nodded, and they began walking back to the cupola's busted window.

"Where are you two going?" asked a concerned Greco. "The hospital?"

"Our wounds are rather minor, and can wait," replied Ted, after pausing with his friend. He thought of Teddy Roosevelt, who'd been shot while giving a speech and then, judging the wound slight, had finished the speech.

"Going to look for buried treasure then?" laughed Greco. It was strange to see him smiling.

"We've got plenty of time for that," remarked Ted.

"We just got a text," explained Harmony. "About a murder in Georgetown. In a historic townhouse, near the Francis Scott Key bridge."

"A place," added Ted, "that's said to be haunted."

"We should get an Uber," Harmony told him, "to check it out."

Ted shook his head. "I already have transportation. Two wheels, with a motor." He looked at Greco. "You'll probably get a stolen vehicle report tonight. But don't worry. I'll return the motorcycle in the morning."

Greco shook his head and, grinning, turned his gaze back to Washington St., and toward the heart of the city he had sworn to protect. And had helped to protect. With the aid of his two fellow sleuths.

The ambulance was well up the boulevard now, fading away in the rain.

And taking the Old Town Horror with it.

The Old Town Horror

Made in the USA
Middletown, DE
16 October 2023